Books By Tilly Rose

Going To California: A Prayer For
Veterans From Every War

A SPIRIT

CALLED

ALCOHOL

BY TILLY ROSE

Front Cover: Sun Dance Arbor
After Ohiya's Last Heyoka Sun Dance
July 2009

DEDICATION

Thank you Infinite Creator for my very breath and heartbeat and all the love throughout the centuries. Thank you to the heavenly band of Angels who have come to set me free. I am most grateful for my deepening sobriety, abstinence and love.

Thank you to my true friends, the ones who sustained me when the money ran out, when the refrigerator was bare and the gas tank was on empty. For those people, I am most grateful. Thank you for your charity, for believing in me and for your unselfish demonstrations of love.

Thank you to my false friends, the ones who taught me discernment and deepened my heart through the pain of understanding.

Thank you to my enemies. You have taught me the most about myself. Sun Tzu said in the Art of War, "*If you know yourself and know the enemy, you need not fear the result of many battles. If you know yourself, but not the enemy, for each victory won, you will also suffer defeat. If you know not the enemy nor yourself, you will succumb in every battle...*"

It was through every battle, every bone crushing loss and glorious victory, where I learned about myself. It forced me to dig deep within to find my courage, to face my fears and know my strengths.

Thank you to every Sun Dancer who pours water in the Inipi. Thank you to everyone who dares to walk sober and carry the message of sobriety to another. Thank you to my mentors, who were willing to alligator wrestle with me and love me until I could love myself. To you, I am forever grateful.

Thank you to the men whose stories I promised to tell, sharing their life's struggle. We strolled a poignant stretch of highway together. God bless you Hal, Hank and Ohiya for your stories and your love. May you walk forever with Great Spirit. See you again on the great highway.

Thank you to my parents for giving me life. For the

sacrifices you made everyday, so that I may live on Mother Earth. May God bless you both, always. Thank you to my son. You are my heart, always. I love you.

TABLE OF CONTENTS

WARRIORS

A strong, warm breeze came from the south, blowing your long dark hair off your shoulders. My lips were parched as we rode down to the river. The blazing afternoon sun was directly overhead. I felt its warm rays on my face when we slid down off our paint ponies, letting them take a long cool drink. Staring off into the distance, you had a faraway look in your eye. I had seen it before.

You had battled other fierce warriors in the past. It became your mission to avenge any injustice. Often, you found yourself among other such men of mettle. Yet, it became a lonely practice. It didn't settle your soul. And the more you fought, the emptier you became. It no longer mattered if you lived or died. You would throw yourself into a battle with no thought of surviving. But somehow that gave you strength. It was the element of not fearing death, which gave you incredible power. Almost an insane look in your eyes would pierce your opponent's soul and he would find his fear of death, thus failing in his mission to win at battle.

I could sense a coldness come over you as you relived these moments with me in the meadow.

"Did you ever find the men who murdered your wife?" I finally asked.

You stopped. A look came over you. The sacred fire in your heart lay smoldering and a fury took its place. The pain of that memory was overwhelming. How could it not be?

CHAPTER ONE: GRANDPA'S STORIES

The warmth of the afternoon sun spilled through the large double doors as they wheeled the casket of his grandson John out of the gymnasium. An old poster hung near the gymnasium door. It caught the old man's eye as he followed his family behind the casket. It was titled "Success." As his eyes rested upon it, he remembered when the old coach, a white man, had hung it up there. It was written by someone named Ralph Waldo Emerson a very long time ago.

"Success"
"To laugh often and much,
to win the respect of intelligent people

and the affection of children;

to earn the appreciation

of honest critics

and endure the betrayal of false friends;

to appreciate beauty,

to find the best in others,

to leave the world a bit better,

whether by healthy child, a garden patch

or a redeemed social condition,

to know even one life

has breathed easier

because you have lived,

this is to have succeeded."

"It wasn't so many moons ago," the old man thought to

himself, *"when he listened to his grandfather's stories about the victories of a good buffalo hunt. It was always topped with a celebration and a grand feast. In the time before reservations, happiness was brought by the sound of a new born baby's cry or the war whoop after counting coup on your enemy."*

Nowadays, the dark spirit of misery, crime and selfishness were upon his people. Their prosperity was measured against a foreign nation's social-economic status. Yet, his people had walked Turtle Island for several lifetimes. How could a foreign nation measure their prosperity, when for centuries, Creator had provided all they needed? Especially since this foreign country was only a couple hundred years old.

These days, many living on the reservation were lost in a blur of alcoholism. The grip of poverty crushed their spirits. Without opportunity, even the brightest felt doomed to a life of unemployment and welfare. In their destructive bloodlust, white hunters nearly destroyed the buffalo nation a century ago. The aftermath of this selfish act, left the Indian nation on reservations, without. A good feast today consisted of macaroni and Velveeta cheese and a can of Mountain Dew.

No stranger to the firewater spirits, the old man watched helplessly as his grandson's life was taken by the demons in the bottle. This curse was given to his people by Blue Coats over a lifetime ago. It was a weakness they struggled to overcome. It destroyed their happiness. The demon spirits in the whiskey bottle brought them to their knees. It damned them to a life of slavery.

Mankind liked to exalt himself and boast as being the highest of Creator's Works. But his failures were worse than any living creature under the sun. How many households were filled with drunkenness and violence? How many were turned to beggars? How many wars were fought over conquest of land, when there was enough space on Mother Earth for everyone to live? How many soldiers killed innocent women and children? How many widows and orphans did this

3

senseless slaughter create? Did the cries of anguish stop these madmen from their destruction? No! They just burned down the village and destroyed all the crops. Mankind had fallen from grace, alright. For every wealthy person, there were thousands who lived in poverty. The greed of a few caused the suffering of many.

As he waited behind the casket, an angry fire burned down deep in the old man's soul. He realized this "chemical warfare" was the bitterest curse ever visited upon this once noble people. It weaken the fabric of their very being.

The heaviness of this deep ache settled over the prairie. It's weight bore down on everyone as they gathered around to watch the casket being wheeled out to the hearse. The wind sang a mournful song as she whistled through the sparse trees lining the parking lot.

Dressed in his funeral best, the old man walked out of the gymnasium. He wore black Levi's, a black button up shirt and a pair of old eel skin cowboy boots he'd bought at a rodeo years ago, when he used to ride horse. His black cowboy hat shielded his eyes from the sun as he walked out into the day. So heavy was his tattered heart, it even hurt to breathe. As the back doors of the hearse creaked open, the pall bearers slid the casket inside. These final moments brought a tear to the old man's eye.

As the hearse pulled away, Daniel wanted to escape. He'd been at the all night wake and took part in the funeral ceremony. Now he felt tired and overwhelmed. If he hadn't drank so much coffee, he'd just go to sleep. Looking at his family, he felt their deep grief and regret. Relatives and friends gathered round in small circles, consoling each other. Walking across the parking lot, Daniel opened the door of his truck. A cool breeze blew up from the Missouri as he started the engine. He knew a few others who wanted to go get food in town.

"Grandpa, come on! Get in the truck. We're going to town to get something to eat," hollered his oldest grandson Daniel. His one long braid went practically to his belt. It was tied with a leather cord. On his ball cap, it read "NATIVE PRIDE." He wore it backwards with an embroidered eagle feather above his forehead.

"You go. I don't want to. I got to go walk," called the old man as he started across the parking lot.

"Can I come walk, Grandpa?" asked Sam, his youngest grandson, tugging at the old man's belt. Sam was still pure of heart, not like the other boys who were already chasing trouble down.

"I'm just headed down to the river, boy. You sure you don't want to go eat at the buffet with all your cousins?" the old man asked.

"Naw, I see them everyday. I'd rather take a walk with you. OK, grandpa?" Sam's big brown eyes shone like great orbs of light reflecting the purity of his soul.

"Suit yourself," said the old man as they headed down in silence to walk the Missouri. Unlike the houses on television, the small villages which speckle Indian Country didn't have manicured lawns and flower gardens. Everywhere you looked, the tall buffalo grasses covered the land. Without any fences to corral them, the rez dogs freely roamed the streets. The old toothless growlers were the most ornery. They often barked at passersby, while the younger ones chased down cars.

The sound of their footfalls crunched along the gravel road as they walked passed the empty playground of the elementary school. Standing alone on a patch of overgrown grass, was a monument to the lost soldiers who'd gone to war from this small village. The names of old man's mother and father were inscribed there for their efforts during the war. As they headed to the river, beer bottles littered the side of the road. Some of the older boys parked there to get drunk.

Sneaking up on the old man, a great gust of wind came up and blew off his hat. Tah-tay teased him mercilessly. Her laughter swirled through the leaves of the cottonwood trees as he chased his hat before it tumbled into the water. Thankfully,

5

his hat got snagged on a log. Snatching it up, the old man hollered at the wind. "TAH-TAY!!! What did I tell you about blowing off my hat!"

"Grandpa?"

"What boy?"

"Why do you yell at the wind that way?" Sam asked.

"Oh, I know Tah-tay very well. She's my sister. She likes to taunt me when I get too serious." The old man smiled. Sam was quiet for a long moment.

"What are you thinking boy?"

"My dad said you were a medicine man. But you gave it up after grandma Elsie died," said Sam, looking at the ground.

"Oh yeah, what else did your dad say about me?" asked the old man.

"He said you could talk to spirits and see things that were going to happen. But after grandma died, you didn't want to see anymore. Is that true?"

"When your grandma died, she took my heart with her. She almost took my spirit too. But they, the Spirits," the old man pointed at the sky, "didn't want me yet." The old man laughed. "They told me I had to stay here. My work wasn't done. I told them, since they took my Elsie, I didn't want to do anything without her."

Glints of sun sparkled on the small waves as they lapped upon the river bank. Along the water's edge, cottonwood trees stood, swaying in the wind. Driftwood littered the shoreline. Knowing the old man so well, the wind whispered sweet nothings through the leaves of the trees as she followed them along.

"Then what did the Spirits say, grandpa?" Sam asked, looking up at the old man.

"They told me too bad. I hadn't finished what I signed up to do."

"What did you sign up to do, grandpa?"

"They didn't say." said the old man, bending down to pick up a stone.

"Why not? Why didn't they tell you what you had to do?" Sam asked.

"That's the great puzzle of life boy. You come here to do something great. But once you're born, you cross over the River of Forgetfulness. You forget who you really are and what you came here to do." The old man laughed at the irony of it all. "Do you understand what a great challenge that is boy, to figure out why you're here? You can spend your whole life wondering if you got close or not."

"How do you know if you finished? When are you done?" Sam looked at the old man intently.

"Only Great Spirit knows the answer to that question, boy. Great Spirit hides what you came here to do in your heart. When you follow the dreams of your heart, you'll be on the right track. If you learn to listen to Great Spirit, He'll guide you," the old man said lovingly as he tussled Sam's hair. "As long as I'm alive, I guess I'm not done."

"But what if you don't know what the right track is, grandpa? What do you do then?"

"Well, when your spirit comes to visit Mother Earth, there are only two paths you can go on. One road is very tough. It's the high road. It's where your heart leads the way and you spend most of your life serving Creator and other people. But then, there's another way. It's full of selfishness and fear. It's a road paved with good intentions and empty promises. My friend Hal called these people the carrot-danglers."

"What's that grandpa?"

"Well, if you want to get a mule to move, you dangle a carrot in front of him. But you never give it to him."

"That's plain mean, grandpa," remarked Sam. "Teasing

an animal like that."

"Well," started the old man. "There are plenty of tricksters around, Sam. They're busy sucking the goody out of life, until there's no goody left. They got no thought for anybody, but themselves. Oh sure, they make promises. But chances are, they'll never keep them. They'll trick you into doing the hard work, so they can sit back and relax. Some will try to get you to do all their work for them."

"Oh," said Sam as he started to comprehend. "I know kids like that. They want the answers to the test, but don't want to do the homework."

"Exactly," said the old man. "Now if you want to learn something about a man, don't listen to what he says, but watch what he does. That'll tell you more about him than anything else. If he sticks to his word and walks his talk, then you can trust him. But if he's just blowing hot air, run the other way."

"The other thing you got to know Sam," the old man continued. "Sometimes the easy road looks more exciting. But, excitement usually leads to disaster. All that hubbub will blow up in your face. When you come to Mother Earth, you decide what road you want to walk on. There are great lessons to be learned on both."

While Sam mulled everything over, a gentle breeze rustled through the cottonwood trees. The old man and Sam stopped for a while and sat on a fallen tree at the river's edge. Rubbing a stone he had in his hand, the old man felt peaceful as he looked over the water. Sunlight glistened like sparkling diamonds on the waves. As the river sang her water song, the stress of the day washed away.

"Do you know Sam, this is one of our oldest relatives," the old man paused as he held the stone in his hand. "This stone I'm holding in my hand, right here?" He peered at the young boy, waiting to see what he would say.

"What do you mean, grandpa?"

"Well, it was told to me like this, by my own grandpa," he paused. "You see, the Stone People, the Inyan Oyate, were here long before man ever came to Mother Earth. So they've seen everything that ever was. They have a Spirit, just like you and me. Even science will tell you that. But scientists call Spirit by another name. They call it energy," he laughed. "Sometimes I think scientists are allergic to spirits. They don't want to believe in them. So they call them by other names."

The old man got up and walked to the river's edge. "Want to see how the spirit of the stone flies across the water?" he asked smiling, with a glint in his eye.

"Sure grandpa," said the boy following the old man.

Crouching down slightly, the old man held the stone between his thumb and forefinger. The wind held her breath as he brought his arm back. Then, leaning forward onto his front leg, he hurled the stone across the river's plane. Flying across the water, the stone skipped again and again. It created small ripples, until it plunked down into the water.

Finding more stones, the old man skipped them across the water. He watched them bounce seven times before they disappeared. Soon the boy tried it too. But his stone just clunked down with a splash.

"You got to choose the right stone boy. The one you picked was too heavy to fly. It was fat like a bumble bee. Did you know it's a wonder a bumble bee can fly at all? With that fat body and small wings. We got to find you a good flier."

Shifting though the sand on the river's edge, the old man found a rounded flat stone. "See this one boy? You hold it like this, right between your thumb and forefinger. Then, send it flying over the river and let it skip on the water."

The boy held the stone in his hand. It was smooth and fit right in the crook of his forefinger. Sam handed it back to his grandpa and watched him send it flying across the river. It skipped several times before it disappeared beneath the glassy waters.

9

"Now you go find your own stones," said the old man as Sam bounded off.

Once the boy was out of earshot, the old man leaned down towards the water. "Hello my lady," he whispered to the river, touching the water. "I haven't been by in a while. My heart's grown weary since they took my Elsie away. Now I watch the boys drink themselves to death, like my grandson today. But these boys don't want to listen to the words of an old man. They don't see me anymore. My medicine has grown cold."

In a quiet moment, the tree branches swayed as the wind whistled her song through the cottonwood trees. Looking up, the old man cautioned the wind. "I wasn't talking to you Tah-tay. I was talking to my lady here, the River." The wind howled slightly.

"What, are you jealous?" laughed the old man while the waves splashed his boots, getting them wet. Jumping back, the old man laughed. "Oh! Now you're picking on me too!"

"GRANDPA! GRANDPA!" yelled Sam running like he struck gold. "Look at these stones, grandpa. Do you think I can get them to fly?"

"Let's see boy," said the old man as he examined the stones. "You got to hold the stone like this. And crouch down a little. You throw it from the side. Not like a baseball over the top, but from side, like this. You want it to fly."

Sam crouched down a little like his grandpa. He held the stone in the curve of his forefinger and thumb. As he started to hurl the stone from the side, his grandpa interrupted.

"FEEL it first, Sam. Feel your body move. Practice before you let go of the stone. Feel how the stone is part of your body. A part you're going to let fly out into the world."

The old man demonstrated the movement a few times. "Snap your wrist, like a baseball throw. But it's down on the side of your body, not over the top."

Sam followed his grandpa's movements, practicing a few times to see how it felt.

"Okay now, give it a go." said the old man.

Standing back, Sam looked at the water. He saw a place where the river was smooth as glass. As he focused, he felt the whole rhythm of his body flow into the stone and let it soar. The stone sailed across the water lightly touching down, bouncing as it skimmed across the top. It bounced, and bounced and bounced again...three times.

"I did it! Grandpa! I did it!"

"Yeah you did! Sonny boy, you sure did," said the old man as a tiredness overtook him. They were quiet for a while. The old man sat down on a fallen tree while Sam went off hunting for more stones. The sun glistened on the water, as it caught the sparkling rays of light. Caught off guard, the stillness pierced the old man's soul. He had seen so much in this life.

"Grandpa," said Sam as he joined the old man on the tree trunk.

"Yeah," was his reply.

"Why did Johnny have to die? Mom said he was a drunk." Sam kicked the dirt under his shoes.

"Yeah, what else did your mom say about Johnny?" the old man asked.

"She was talking to Aunt Nora on the phone, when she found out Johnny died in that car crash. She said he was hanging out with those Taylor boys from Wheeler Ridge. She said those boys were trouble, through and through. Johnny got himself mixed up with a bunch of rowdies." Sam kicked the dirt as he talked.

"I knew Grandpa Taylor from way back," started the old man. "He was a bootlegger. He made his living smuggling whiskey across the Canadian border and brought it to the rez, back when they had the Prohibition. White man's law wanted to stop people from making whiskey. So old man Taylor made his money selling liquor when it was outlawed. He was smart though, he never drank it. He told me whiskey was for selling not for drinking. I figured he knew something about whiskey that most folks didn't."

"You ever tried whiskey, grandpa?"

"Yeah, I did. But I wasn't very good at it," laughed the old man.

"Why not, it's just a drink, right?"

"Oh grandson," the old man said with all earnestness. "That firewater is a powerful medicine. And medicine can be used for good or not good. Like all things, firewater has a Spirit."

The old man took off his hat and ran his hand through his long hair. "Your grandma Elsie, she'd always braid my hair for me. That way it wouldn't get in the way of things. I cut it off when she died. My hair always grew fast, but now I got no one to braid it for me."

"I know you miss grandma," said Sam gently. "Want me to braid your hair?"

"Naw that's okay son. I don't got nothing to tie it with," smiled the old man.

"When did you drink whiskey grandpa?" Sam's big brown eyes wanted to know things.

"When I was a young man. My elders told me I had to become a warrior. It was tradition for men of our clan to be great warriors. So they told me to sign up with the Army and learn from the best. But I always wanted to be in the Marines. They were the fiercest warriors. So that's what I did. And I was good at it, grandson. I could shoot their rifles. And I was fast. I ran like the wind. So they put me in special training and I became a fierce warrior. In the military, I had my first drink."

"What's it taste like?"

"Oh, that firewater burns hot when it goes down your throat," the old man started. "It's a powerful medicine, Sam. After my first drink, I didn't feel anything. So I ordered another drink and then another. I sat down at a bar, drinking shots. One after another. But then, that firewater hit me like a lightning bolt. It threw me off my chair. My buddies didn't know that I'd never drank before. So here was this Indian, a great warrior, falling down in the gutter. My legs were like Jell-O and I couldn't walk. My head got all wobbly. My eyes spun round and round. But for a minute, it made me feel good. So guess what? I did it again and again and again."

"Why did it make you fall down, Grandpa?"

"Well you see, the spirit called alcohol has two sides. One is for healing, like when you get a scrape on your knee. Your mom can put some rubbing alcohol on it. It'll clean out the wound and start the healing."

"Yeah, I had some good scrapes and mom poured it on my knees. It burned so bad I screamed."

"Well, there's an unfriendly side to the firewater spirits. It's a trickster. It feeds you lies, telling you this and that. But none of it's true. That's what happened to me. And that's what happened to Johnny. When people feel low, they look for something to make them feel better. You ever do that, Sam, look for something to make you feel better when you had a bad day?"

Sam thought for a minute. "I like to play video games."

"Yup, that'll put you in another world," the old man agreed. "Well, firewater puts grown-ups in another world too. When they feel bad, they call on the spirits in the bottle to make them feel better. Now that firewater spirit says "Sure, I'll make you feel better, but there'll come a day, when you'll have to pay up."

"Like what grandpa? What do you have to pay?"

"Oh, first those spirits make you do crazy things. Things

you'd never do sober. When you pour whiskey down your throat, its fire burns all the way down. Then, the whiskey spirit wiggles into your body and takes over your mind. You feel it swimming around in your head. It makes you feel dizzy. When it has you under its spell, you do whatever it tells you to do. It has the power to make you forget everything, sometimes for days at a time. It's power can numb the hurt for a while."

Images of ghostly spirits in whiskey bottles whirled around the young boy's head. It wasn't uncommon to see a drunk staggering through the streets of the reservation. Most stumbled around and fell down. "What did you have to pay grandpa? What did it make you do?"

"Oh grandson, those spirits are very cunning. They tell you lies about yourself. When they wiggle into your body, you feel different, happy, silly. They whisper in your ear, telling you that you're strong and handsome. Or maybe that you're invincible like Superman. And you believe it. You believe you can do anything. Oh I've seen drunken men, puffed up like proud roosters, crowing about how great they are. Truth is, they ain't shit and it's all lies."

"Them roosters make a lot of noise, grandpa and not just in the morning," Sam said.

"Ah, but then comes the humbling," the old man shook his head, "when you fall down and act stupid. Sometimes you end up in jail. Or worse, you kill someone and don't remember. When I drank, sometimes I'd black out for days. I couldn't remember where I was or what I did. Those spirits took me for a wild ride and I did whatever they wanted me to do."

The old man paused. He wondered how much he should tell his young grandson. Would his grandson understand? He'd just have to see.

"One night, I had too many shots of whiskey. I stumbled out of the bar. My head was spinning and I couldn't stop throwing up. I was very sick. My body was covered in sweat.

It was trying to drive this demon out. But it had me in its grip. I found someone's front lawn and lay down in the grass. It was cool against my burning head. Then, I closed my eyes and I was taken to this place. There was a ceremonial fire burning and my ancestors were there. My grandpa stepped out of the crowd and walked over to me. He brought me to a council where the Elders spoke to me."

"What did they say, grandpa? Do you remember the ancestors who were there?" Sam was paying attention to every word.

The old man got up from the log to stretch his legs. "Let's walk," he said. "I will tell you what happened to me. But you must listen. Don't interrupt and keep this between you and me. Can you do that boy?"

Sam got up and followed his grandpa down river. "Yes, grandpa."

"When I sat with the Elders, my grandpa told me 'Great Spirit cannot protect you if you keep drinking the white man's whiskey. You have called a great darkness upon yourself. The spirits of darkness have come to claim you as their own.' All the Elders nodded when he said that," the old man paused to gather his thoughts. Sam waited, not saying a word. Finally the old man continued.

"My grandpa showed me the dark spirits I had drawn to myself. They were the firewater spirits and all their relations. I recognized them all. They were the spirits of anger, lust, greed, pride and envy. They lived in the shadow land with doubt and fear. He showed me how as a child, my spirit was strong, innocent and pure. But, since I surrounded myself with the firewater spirits, my mind had become soft and weak. Soon, my grandfather said, I'd lose this battle. Those dark spirits would claim me for their own." The old man paused. He could still see the sparkle in his grandfather's eyes as they sat around the council fire.

Sam tried to be patient as he waited through the long

silence. "Then what happened grandpa?"

"Oh," said the old man. "I guess I drifted off. Well, after that, I was shown two paths. One path was serving myself and the other path was serving Creator. The path I was on would lead to my ruin."

"When I asked my grandfather why this was so. He told me that firewater is a spirit. That being so, it'd claim my spirit because we struck a deal. I had to make good on the deal. Does that make sense boy? The firewater spirit would take my spirit to make good on the deal. That's how Johnny died. The firewater spirit took Johnny's spirit because he had to make good on the deal. The firewater gave its spirit for Johnny to have a good time and then the firewater spirit came to collect its due. It wanted spirit for spirit. "

The old man stopped and sat down on shore of the Missouri, leaning on a tree stump. Sam sat down next to him and they were quiet for a while. Listening to the waves washing up on the shore, soothed the old man's soul. His bones were weary. He was ready to be with his Elsie. As he looked at this young boy, his grandson, he wondered. Is there anything he could say which would make a difference?

"Boy, does this make sense to you?" The old man looked into Sam's young eyes. He saw the Spirit of the Universe inside them.

"Yes, grandpa. I understand. But how did you get free? Why didn't the firewater spirit take you?"

"That's a good question boy," said the old man gathering his thoughts. "The Elders told me that only I could change the deal I made with the firewater spirit. I was responsible for my choices and I had to choose another path. Once I chose the higher path, then Creator, all my ancestors and the Spirit-helpers could help me. But first it was up to me. There are two paths in life. The lower path is marked with pure selfishness. All you think about is, 'what's in it for me?' The higher path is being in service to All Life."

"After that, my grandfather told me the council meeting was over. As we walked away from the council fire, my grandfather looked me in the eye with great compassion. He said it wasn't my time. But I could stay with them if I wanted. Then he showed me what I came here to do. My learning on Turtle Island was not finished. He said it was best if I went back. As I turned around to face the Earth, I felt the cold-hearted fear and all it's pain. My spirit fell back down to Earth. It crossed over the River of Forgetfulness and slipped back into my body."

"That morning, I woke up in the hospital. Those white coats told me I'd died that night. I almost lost my life to alcohol poisoning. I was dehydrated and my whole body ached."

"What did you do, grandpa? What did you tell the firewater spirit?"

"Oh, I wish I could say I was smart and did the right thing, Sam. But, when I got out of the hospital, I figured I'd beat this thing on my own. It wasn't long after I got out of the hospital, that I ended up in a bar again. But this time, I went to jail. I drank the white man's whiskey and went to jail."

When Sam heard that, he couldn't believe his ears. He shook his head in disbelief. The old man sensed Sam's disappointment.

"Lots of Indians go to jail for drinking the white man's whiskey," the old man said as he shook his head. "Those whiskey spirits didn't want to let me go. They claimed me for their own. Just like my grandfather said. And now I had no protection from Great Spirit, because I had chosen the wrong path."

"But something good happened to me on the Other Side. I could see things I couldn't see before. Back then, Sam I was such a hard head. I was too proud to ask for help. So I did it my way. I heard a saying once and it stuck with me. IF YOU ALWAYS DO, WHAT YOU ALWAYS DONE, YOU'LL ALWAYS

17

GET, WHAT YOU ALWAYS GOT. And that's how it went for a long while." The old man paused for a while. "Do you really want to hear this whole story, grandson?"

Sam looked up at the old man. "You tell good stories, grandpa. You can't stop now. Because I don't know what happened next."

"Alright then, you sure you don't want to be running around with those other boys? I don't want to hold up your whole day."

"Naw grandpa, I see them every day. Finish the story grandpa!"

"OK then," said the old man. "After I spent the night in the drunk tank, I was real hungry. I don't know how the cooks in jail can make the food taste so bad, but you never want to eat there. When I got out, I hitched a ride to a tavern to get a sandwich. The place was called "McCluskey's" and it had a bright neon sign on the roof. The sign said "SPIRITS." It was a little restaurant with a bar in the back. I walked up to the counter and ordered a sandwich. But something pulled me towards the bar."

"Now before I walked in there, I'd made up my mind. I wasn't going to drink. But, I poked my head in the bar. Something drew me in there. Down at the end of the bar, I see this man. He's sitting by himself. He wearing a camouflage jacket with VIET NAM written on it. There were all kinds of spirits milling around him. I could see them. Just like I see you. But these spirits were angry. I don't know what made me do it, but I went in the bar and sat down next to him."

"Were you scared grandpa, with all those angry spirits?" Sam was leaning forward, hanging on to every word.

"No, I wasn't scared. Those spirits weren't angry at me. When I sat down, he barely looked up. He had a bottle of whiskey in front of him."

"What did you say grandpa when you sat down next to

18

him?" The boy asked. No one else ever heard these stories before.

"Well, maybe I was crazy for sitting down next to him. He was gnashing his teeth, muttering to himself. He was a real crazy man. I figured he drank to drowned out the hungry ghosts who wouldn't leave him alone. So I ordered a shot of whiskey and a coke."

"That's crazy grandpa, after going to jail and almost dying. I can't believe you ordered another whiskey." His grandson shook his head.

"Well, Sam, if you're lost, stuck down deep in a pit. Someone's got to go down into the pit to get you out. The way I saw it was, maybe we'd get out together. When you're lost, you need someone who knows the way out."

"Did you know the way out?" His grandson asked.

"All I knew was, I had to go where he was, so I ordered a drink."

"What did you say to him, when you sat down?"

"I said, 'Hey, did you know you got a lot of angry spirits around you?' He turned his head sideways and gave me a mean look, like I was crazy. Then he asked me, "What did you say? Something about spirits?"

"Yeah, you got a lot of angry slant-eyed spirits around you."

"I thought that's what you said," he looked at me sideways. Then he took another drink and was quiet for a while. I was getting up to leave, when he looked at me and asked, "What do they want? The spirits, I mean, what do they want?"

"So I told him, 'They're angry cuz you killed them. Now they're tied to you.'

"Then in a gruff whiskey voice, he said his name was Hank. After a while, he said he had over 100 confirmed kills to his name. I asked him if he was proud of that."

In his mind's eye, the old man flashed back to the bar. He saw the whole scene as he relayed it to his grandson.

"Well," Hank said, 'That's what they trained me to do. I am a killing machine. They ain't got no use for me here, in the country where I was born. I don't have much of a resume, if you know what I mean."

"Yeah, I don't either," I said, watching those hungry ghosts milling around him. "Do the spirits still come into your dream time?"

"Well, funny you should mention that," he said. "There is this Cambodian I've dreamt about every night for almost 30 years. Every night, drunk or sober, after I drift off to sleep, this Cambodian comes out of the bush. He fires a French RPG missile right passed my head." As Hank mentioned the Cambodian, his spirit stepped out of the crowd. The Cambodian was ranting and raving how Hank hurt him many times."

"Yeah, the Cambodian is here alright," I tell him.

"What does he want?" Hank asks me. I tell him the Cambodian was screaming how Hank hurt him many times. Hank throws his head back and gets the most evil laugh."

"Yeah, that motherfucker tried to kill me. He shot French RPG missile right passed my head. It missed me by that much." Hank held up his fingers about an inch apart. "After that rocket blasted passed my ear, I was wide awake. I ran after that sucker. I pulled out every pistol I had and started shooting. I shot him in the back and watched him fall face down. Then I ran up to him. I rolled him over with my boot and looked at him square in the eye. And that's when I shot him here and here and here and here." Hank was pointing to the Cambodian's elbows, his knee caps, then his groin, then his shoulders. "Yeah, I guess I hurt him many times. But he missed, that son of a bitch. Then I watched him die. It took him a long time, like 20 minutes." As Hank told his story, the

Cambodian glared at him. There would be no peace between them."

"So what did you do then, grandpa?" asked Sam. This story was getting better all the time.

"I ordered another whiskey. This time no coke."

"But what happened to Hank and the Cambodian and all those spirits?" Sam was desperate to know.

The wind was picking up. Across the river, the Thunder Beings were gathering out in the west. After walking for almost an hour, they were close to the old man's cabin. It was an old run down shack with a tin roof, creaking wood floors and a broken window. The old man was quiet for a while.

"You see those Thunder Beings over there," said the old man pointing towards the west. "I think we'd better get in before it starts raining. You hungry, boy? Because I don't have much to eat. But we could sit on the front porch and listen to the rain beat down on the tin roof for a while."

"Sure grandpa. Will you finish your story?" asked Sam, not wanting to let this one drop.

"Yeah, let's make some coffee and see what I got in the fridge. Or we can go to Kelly's. I got enough coins in my pocket for a burger and fries." The old man smiled. His weathered face showed the story of his life. Since his Elsie died, he spent most of his time alone. It felt good to have some company.

The wind started howling as they ran up to the old man's cabin. Thunder claps jolted through the heavens in the distance as turbulent clouds swirled in the sky. Lightning bolts flashed and crackled, lighting up the sky as the storm slowly marched overhead.

Inside the cabin was a pot belly stove, an old coffee pot and some old dishes were in the sink. The small wooden table was pushed up close to the window. It had two chairs on either side. A single bare light bulb hung from a cord over the table.

21

Over in the corner was a full size mattress. It was so old, it had a dent in the middle from sleeping on it so long. A beautiful star quilt covered the bed. It was made by grandma Elsie before she died.

As soon as they got the fire lit, they heard a truck pull up in front of the cabin. The old man went to the window. He saw his grandson, Daniel, running for the door. He hurried in to get out of the rain.

"Daniel's here," the old man said as they heard the truck door slam and Daniel's boots stomp across the front porch. Daniel walked in the front door. "Hey, grandpa, Sam. Ma wants to know if you're coming to dinner? There's a great feast, lots of good eaten."

Sam looked at grandpa, to see what he'd say. Grandpa was silent for a long second. "I was going to see what I got in the fridge or maybe go to Kelly's and get us a burger and fries."

Sam chimed in, "Grandpa's telling me stories."

"Oh, so grandpa's telling you stories, huh?" Daniel tussled Sam's hair. "Yeah, I loved listening to grandpa's stories when I was a kid."

The old man opened the fridge, but it was bare. There was just some milk for his coffee and a couple of potatoes. "Not much in the fridge, Sam. Do you want to go to the feast? It's up to you."

"I'd rather hear about what happened to Hank and all them spirits," said Sam.

"I'll give you a ride to Kelly's, if you want," said Daniel.

Grandpa opened the cupboard to get the sugar jar, where he kept a few dollars. He found his coat and hat. "Let's go."

They drove in silence while the rain and some hail pelted the truck. The windshield wipers slapped back and forth, as the rain gushed down. Daniel pulled in front of Kelly's. Splashing through a big mud puddle filled with water, Sam and the old man got out of the truck and bolted for the door. Rolling down the window, Daniel yelled. "You want me to come get you in a little while?"

"In a couple hours or so," the old man hollered back. He never liked being rushed around on anyone's time schedule.

"OK," said Daniel as he drove off.

Kelly's Tavern was nothing special. It was down at the end of the River Road overlooking the Missouri. Though he was an old man now, Kelly had collected many Indian artifacts over his life time. The walls were cluttered with arrowheads and tomahawks, old Indian photographs and multicolored woven rugs. It was nice enough on the inside. The fire place was lit. It gave the tavern a cozy feeling. Walking past the swinging doors to the bar, the old man and Sam found an empty table near the back so they could speak in private.

From their table, the old man could see into the bar. Saddled up next to the drinkers, were the ghosts of old drunks. While these gruesome spirits leaned into the drinker, they whispered their shallow pleasures into the thoughts of weak men. The drinkers poured whiskey down their throats. The hungry ghosts put their ghastly arms around them. Leaning in real close, they breathed in the whiskey vapors again.

Standing against the counter, the waitress watched as the old man and Sam took a table. It was a slow afternoon, with the storm brewing outside. As she sauntered over, she brought a couple menus and plopped them on the table.

"How y'all doing today? Can I get you two something to drink?" she said as she smacked her gum.

"We don't need these," said the old man handing the menus back. "Just bring us two cheese burgers with fries and 2 cokes." After the waitress wrote down the order, she walked away.

As soon as they shed their coats, Sam noticed how something captured his grandpa's attention. His eyes were fixed intently on the bar. "What is it grandpa?"

"Oh nothing boy," the old man fibbed. He didn't want to scare the boy.

"Are there spirits in the bar, like you said before?" asked Sam, not wanting to be shut down.

"You tell me," tested the old man with his eyebrows raised. "Look in there and tell me what you see."

Sam let his eyes go soft. He focused his vision into the dimly lit bar. As his vision softened, he saw the ghosts milling around. "There is a man, down at the end of the bar, sitting by himself," Sam started.

"What about him?" the old man asked, not feeding him anything.

"I don't think he's alone. There is something around him," Sam said.

"Is it more than one?" the old man asked.

"I think so," Sam said.

"You're more sensitive than I thought." His voice trailed off as he drifted deep into thought. While the old man got quiet, the waitress brought over two cokes. Sam and grandpa sipped their cokes in silence for a moment.

"Where did I leave off?" the old man said after a time.

"Hank and the Cambodian," said Sam, thinking his grandpa almost forgot.

The old man had a faraway look in his eye as he remembered back all those years ago. "Yeah, that night we sat down at the bar and Hank told me all his stories. Hank's grandpa had a family farm and promised to give to Hank in his will. But before he died, his grandpa sold it off. The old buzzard left Hank with nothing. Hank was so angry at his grandpa, he joined the Marine Corp at 17 years old to get away."

24

"When he was in boot camp, they figured out he was a smart country boy. He was good with a rifle and got sent to Special Forces, out there in Virginia. That's how he became a killing machine."

The waitress brought over the burgers and fries and put the plates on the table. "Anything else I can bring you two?"

"Maybe another coke for me and my grandson," the old man smiled.

"See grandson," started the old man, gathering his thoughts. "During Hank's tour of duty, there was an opium war going on in South East Asia. Opium is a strong medicine when it's used in a good way. But if you make the wrong deal with sister opium, she can be a deadly dragon. Hank and a lot of young men were sent there to destroy the opium trade. He didn't know much about sister opium before he got over there. But one day, in this small village, a lady called him over, saying 'Hey daddy come here.' She told him to pull down his pants and when he did, she put a ball of opium up his rear end. Hank told me it was the best high he'd ever had. After that, he was hooked. He'd been chasing the dragon ever since."

"What dragon is that?" asked Sam.

"The dragon of death and broken promises," said the old man intently. "It lies to you. It tells you if you do it again, you'll get that good feeling. But it's a lie."

Munching on his French fries, Sam listened to every word.

Pondering how much of the gruesome truth he should reveal, the old man paused to eat his burger. Most of the soldiers who served in Southeast Asia during the opium war, never were recognized for their military efforts. Viet Nam vets were scorned because Americans did not support the military action. Many of these vets were addicted to heroin and homeless.

"Now Sam, when Hank and his men were in the jungle,

they had a scout. It was the scout's job was to spot the opium truck. After he spotted it, the scout would radio Hank and tell him the truck was coming. Hank's job was to destroy the opium. So while the truck drove down the road, Hank, this big white country boy, stood in the middle of the road, waiting. He waved the truck down."

While his grandpa told his stories, Sam pictured the whole scene in his mind. He'd seen pictures of the jungle and knew what Asian people looked like.

"Now these Asians never saw a big white man before. When the driver stopped, Hank smiled and handed him a bomb. Hank said the driver was polite and even nodded with a smile. Then Hank ran. He took cover and watched the truck blow up. After it exploded, there was opium raining down from the sky. The bomb blew the top of the cab clean off. In the truck, all that was left of the men were their legs. They were sitting on the bench seat with their bodies blown clean off."

It was a good thing Sam already finished his burger, because listening to this, he lost his appetite. He was no stranger to war movies, but never heard of something so horrible. They ate their burgers in silence for a while.

"Hank sounded like a bad man, grandpa. I don't think I like him," Sam said after a while.

"Grandson, when you go to war, they convince you that you're killing the enemy. Now, enemies have all kinds of names. Back then, they called the Asians 'gooks.' This way you forget they're human. You forget they have mothers and fathers, brothers and sisters. But they bleed red, just like you and me. Nobody knows that better than Indians. The Christians called us savages. It was the Spanish pope who sent his conquistadors, the Christian soldiers to take over our land. They slaughtered our people and made us less than human for a long time. Are you sure you want to hear these stories? I'll stop if you're uncomfortable."

Giving it some thought, Sam was silent for a moment. In

his mind's eye, Sam saw everything his grandpa told him. The scenes played out like a movie. "It's okay grandpa, I want to hear the stories. I want to know what you did.'"

"Now you remember how I told you about sister opium?" asked the old man before he continued.

"Yeah," said Sam.

"Now if you use sister opium in a selfish way, she's a heartless killer. When her spirit takes over your body, she'll bleed it dry. After a while, I asked Hank if he killed anyone he regretted. His steely blue eyes were cold, like black ice. The ache in his frozen heart was deep. He didn't answer me right away. But when his mouth opened, it all spilled out."

"One day, his team was moving through the jungle. They were high on opium. They spotted two small boys rolling a metal wheel down a dirt road with a stick. One of his buddies bet Hank ten bucks that he couldn't shoot the boy's heads off. Well, Hank was a sniper. He aimed his rifle and got a clean shot. When the mother heard the gun fire, she came running out of a hut with another woman and a man. Hank killed all of them."

"After Hank told me this story, the children and their family stood in front of us. I watched them as they waited. Something touched Hank deep in his heart. I saw small tears in the corner of his eyes. Then, he confessed he felt bad about killing them every day of his life. If he could, he'd take it all back. When he said this, the spirit of the children climbed on Hank's lap and kissed his face."

"When these two boys kiss Hank's face, it touched my heart. I said, "Why don't you tell them. They're right here.""

"In his whiskey voice, Hank muttered an apology for taking their lives without permission. Then something happened. The spirits of the family turned around and faded away."

"When I told him the family went home to Creator,

Hank smiled for the first time. The Spirit of Forgiveness had blessed him. We spent all night talking about everyone he killed. Hank made amends to every spirit for taking their lives. The only one left was the angry Cambodian."

"What happened with the Cambodian, grandpa?"

"Oh, he wanted his pound of flesh. He had a bone to pick with Hank and wasn't going to let Hank off easy. So, the three of us sat there in the bar almost till daybreak. Finally, Hank asked the Cambodian what his name was."

"What did he say, grandpa?" Sam was leaning forward to hear every word.

"Chu, he said his name was Chu. He grew up in a small village. He was a soldier and had a family. Hank's dog, Nifka, was laying down by his feet. At one point, Chu looked at the dog and said "We eat dog.""

"Well, Hank got all bent out of shape, when he heard Chu say that. He said "You ain't eating this dog motherfucker!!!" Oh, they went at it for a while. But at the end, Hank realized that Chu was a man, just like him. And then Hank made the sincerest apology I had ever heard. Spirits can tell if you are not being honest. After that, Chu turned around and faded away. Finally, the bar was empty of spirits and Hank had some peace. When they closed the bar, the sun was just creeping over the east. The last thing Hank said to me was that he was going to quit drinking. I never saw Hank again. But he was free."

"You know what grandpa, the Christian preacher said the spirits of our loved ones go to heaven. But from the looks of it, there are a lot of spirits still here."

"Some of them go to heaven, Sam. You see, on the other side of the West Gate, there's a woman with a scale. After you cross over, she puts an eagle feather on one side of the scale and your heart on the other. If your heart is as light as the eagle feather, you go up. But if your heart is heavy, full of woe for the hurt you done to others, then you come back down here to clean up your mess. Some spirits are afraid of the Light because they lived selfish, miserable lives. So they stay stuck in the In-between. Then there are those, like Chu, who have an ax to grind. They want revenge and become evil. They'll haunt those who harmed them."

"I hope my heart is light as a feather," Sam said.

"Just don't kill anybody," smiled the old man.

"I WON'T!!!"

There were just a few French fries left on the plate, when Sam looked at his grandpa intently and asked "So where did you go when the bar finally closed?"

"Well, that was the beginning of the end. I had to go back to the military base. So I hitched a ride and just settled into my bunk to sleep, when the Military Police rousted me out of bed. They dragged me down to see the sergeant. He didn't have any good words to say to me for skipping out on my duties. So, they put me in the stockade for a few days. I was on shaky ground in the stockade. I got so sick, they sent me down to the hospital. I had what they call the DT's, Delirium Tremens. That's when your body needs alcohol to stop from shaking."

"Once I got detoxed, they set me up with the talking doctor and he kept me locked up. That old grizzly buzzard with his white coat and shiny black shoes, told me I was a hopeless alcoholic and I believed him."

"Then what happened grandpa?"

"Well, that old buzzard couldn't rehabilitate me in the military hospital, so he locked me up in a psych ward. See back then, there was no treatment for a man like me, an alcoholic. Most alkies die drunk or end up in jail. One time they stuck me in a rubber room, so I couldn't hurt myself. I knew my spirit was shot full of holes. When I looked in the mirror, all I saw staring back at me, was a dead man. I was lost, deep in the hole."

"Then one day, this big Indian from Canada comes into the psych ward to give a talk. His name was Hal and he found me. When he said he hadn't had a drink in a year, I knew he was lying. But he said he needed to talk to alcoholics, so I let him talk. Looking back, his words of truth and love were strong medicine. Before he left, he gave me a Big Book to read. It had stories about other alcoholics in it who got sober. Through their stories, he said, I'd find my way back to Great Spirit. Hal had powerful words that I'll never forget. He said the root of all suffering is selfishness. That alcoholics are selfish, self absorbed people. They don't see the pain they cause others. They only see their own suffering. By then I was ready to listen. I felt the medicine in his words. He walked his talk."

"Dad said you were in A.A. when you were in the military." Sam smiled.

"Oh yeah, what else did your dad say about me?"

"He said that's when you became a great medicine man."

"That was many moons ago," said the old man.

"But why did you give up grandpa?" Sam said with his eyes pleading.

"Who said I gave up?" the old man was indignant. "Do I look like I am dead?"

"No, grandpa, but Johnny is."

"Johnny's dead because he made a bad contract with the demons in the bottle. When you make a deal with the firewater spirit, it comes along to collect its due for giving you a good time. When it does, it takes spirit for spirit. Because it is a spirit, it demands your spirit in return. That's the deal. Many of our people have sacrificed their lives to know the magic of firewater," the old man said sadly. "The problem is, that magic is black."

"So what's the answer grandpa?" asked Sam.

"Sonny boy, only the Great Mystery knows the answer.

Every man has to make the journey back to Creator in his own way. No one can force that upon him. But if you stick close to Creator and do His work well, He'll give you life."

The waitress came by to collect their plates. "Can I get you two any dessert?" she asked.

The old man's eyes twinkled as he looked at his grandson. "You want some dessert Sam?"

Sam nodded his head yes.

"Sure," said the old man. "Give us a slice of apple pie, hotted up with a scoop of vanilla ice cream." Just about that time, Daniel walked in through the front door.

"You two about ready for a ride home?" Daniel asked. "The rain let up a little while ago."

"We're gonna have some apple pie with vanilla ice cream," Sam smiled.

"Well, you both are sure living it up tonight," Daniel laughed as he took off his coat and sat in the empty chair. "So what kind of stories has grandpa been telling you?"

"Well all kinds," said Sam. "Mostly about the war, drinking and talking doctors. Right grandpa?" Sam winked at the old man, not letting on what kind of stories grandpa told.

"Yeah, I bet. They must be pretty interesting. You've been here for hours. I almost forgot to come get you. Except mom asked me where you were and told me to come fetch you." Daniel yawned. He had classes over at the Indian College in the morning. He was studying agriculture and Native American Studies.

The waitress came over with a slice of hot apple pie a' la mode. "Bring me some decaf," said the old man. "You want some coffee Daniel?"

"Naw, I'm good. I got to get up early. But I'll have a few bites of pie though," Daniel said. After they enjoyed the pie, they piled into the truck and drove the old man home.

"Now listen up Sam, if you want to hear some more stories, you come by again, okay," said the old man as they dropped him off.

"OK grandpa, thanks for the burger and pie." Sam waved out the window as they drove off.

It was chilly inside his cabin as the old man turned on the light. There was a bucket in the corner with some chopped wood. He placed a few logs inside the pot belly stove, along with some kindling and struck a match. Soon the fire would make the room warm.

Sam struck the old man as a curious boy. He was much different from the rest of them. For ages, he'd looked for a student, someone to share these Old Medicine Ways with. But most were distracted by the white man's toys. He'd wait and see if Sam was the one he'd been waiting for.

As the fire started to crackle, he stood by the stove and rubbed his hands together. Grandma Moon rose in the east. Only the wind was heard whispering through the buffalo grasses. It seemed she kept him company most nights now.

A few months later, just before dusk, a white woman drove her car in a drunken blackout. Careening down the River Road, her big Cadillac veered around a bend at full speed. In the twilight, she ran over and killed two of the old man's grandsons. Blurry eyed, she didn't even see them as the car hit the men dead on. They were having an argument in middle of the road after getting a flat tire. Donald's body flew about 20 feet into the corn field. While Darrel got dragged under the car almost a half mile.

It wasn't until she heard a terrible clunking noise, that the woman finally stopped. Sitting in a parked car, by the side of the road, Donald's sisters watched in horror as the terrible accident happened. An ambulance came to take the bodies of the two men away. They were pronounced dead at the scene. The firewater spirits claimed two more souls. Being the daughter of a wealthy white lawyer, no charges were ever filed against Annie Mae for the deaths of Donald and Darrel. Nothing was ever done to make it right.

The morning after the accident happened, killing his two cousins, Sam got out of bed. He heard his Auntie Lynn crying and yelling. Both of her sons were dead.

"You know, they tell you to watch out when you go off the rez. Those white people will shoot you as soon as look at you. But my boys got killed right here. Right on the River Road, by that drunken Annie Mae. And the sheriff ain't done nothing to make it right." Auntie Lynn was inconsolable.

"That sheriff's got no power. He's not going to do anything," said Tess holding her sister Lynn. "He knows where his bread is buttered. It's always been that way. As far as they're concerned, the only good Indian is a dead Indian. Those whites have been killing us off for centuries." Sam's mother Tess tried to console her sister. The heartache on the reservation went deep.

"You know Tess, I got a mind to go over to that man, the one who lives down in the hollows," Auntie Lynn said with a dangerous, crazy fire in her eyes.

"Lynn, don't you dare. All that dark magic will come back to haunt you, not him, when it circles back around. It never makes it right. That white woman ain't worth the trouble. Emma called me this morning after she got to work down at the white doctor's office in town. Annie Mae was in there first thing this morning. She's feeling so bad, she can barely walk. She was complaining she can't sleep a wink. She keeps dreaming about the accident, seeing the faces of your boys. Don't you see she's haunted already."

Sam stood in the kitchen doorway listening. His young mind was getting a keen understanding of the nature of the demons in the bottle. Like his grandpa said, those dark spirits don't just kill the drinker, but anyone who got in the way. By now, the whole town heard the news about Donald and Darrel. The phone was ringing off the hook. His stomach was growling as he slipped into the kitchen to get something to eat. After he got dressed, he was about to bolt out the front door when his mother saw him.

"Where you going?" Tess asked her son.

"Grandpa's," said Sam before the screen door slammed.

"Where's he going?" asked Lynn, drying her eyes.

"Oh, he's going down to see grandpa. Papa's been telling him stories. It's good, it's good. He's kept too much to himself since ma died."

"Don't they got that alcohol meeting tonight? The one dad goes to," Lynn asked as something turned in her mind.

"Well, it's Thursday. Yeah, they have it down at the community room at 6 o'clock. Why?" Tess could see the wheels turning in her sister's mind.

"Well, I think I'm going to go there tonight," said Lynn wiping the tears off her cheeks. "Maybe they got some answers."

"Lynn, what are you thinking? They're just a few old men who don't drink anymore. What could they have to tell you?"

"I don't know, but I am going there tonight. Something's got to make this heart of mine feel better. There's got to be some sense to all of this craziness."

"I know you," Tess warned. "When you got something on your mind, there's no stopping you. If you want, I'll go with you and listen to those old men." Tess didn't know what she'd be signing up for. But, she knew one thing. Grief is a purifier and it causes people to do unusual things.

"Thank you," Lynn said as she hugged her sister. Then, she grabbed her car keys and a paper towel to wipe her eyes and blow her nose. "I'll call you when I'm leaving the house. Be ready, okay. Don't take forever. It's not a date!"

"Oh shut up!!" Tess smiled as she walked her sister to

the door. Her sister hadn't completely lost her sense of humor.

Running faster than greased lightning, Sam's feet barely touched the ground as he took off for his grandpa's house. Chasing the wind, it wouldn't be long before he got there. All he wanted to do was to listen to his grandpa's stories before the sadness put a death grip on him.

Warming his hands with his coffee cup, the old man stood on his front porch listening to the wind. Tah-tay knew him best. That morning about 3 am, he was shook out of his sleep. Standing at the foot of his bed were the spirits of his two grandsons. They were furious. A wild lightning storm came from their eyes. At first, the old man felt frightened, not knowing who was visiting him. Spirits communicated with emotion and thought.

After the accident, Darrell and Donald's spirits were jolted out of their bodies. Neither one was ready to die. No one could see them. No one could hear them. As they watched along the roadside, the ambulance came. Their lives were robbed from them at such an early age. Both were in their twenties. Darrel worked up north on an oil field and Donald had just finished his first year at the college. Only one year apart, they were complete opposites and always competing in something.

"What do you want me to do Tah-tay?" the old man whispered to the wind. A heavy coat of hopelessness and grief blanketed the land. "No one understands how deep the pain is here. No one understands how deep our souls are wounded."

The wind gently brushed his cheek with her silky touch. Setting his coffee cup down on the porch, the old man picked up his hand drum. It was an old drum he made long ago, back when he first kept fire for ceremony.

In a sorrowful way, he sat down on the porch steps and started drumming. His heartache eased as he sang Inipi medicine songs. These songs were passed down through generations of old holy men. Song after song poured forth from his heart. He sang to the wind, sang to Creator, sang to the spirits of the land and the spirits of his grandsons who just passed on. While his heart poured into the songs, the wind carried his voice over the prairie, through the village and into the Great Beyond.

His young feet flew across the earth as Sam heard his grandpa's drumming. Enjoying the chase, the wind swept up behind Sam, lifting him up so he could fly. As he rounded the corner to his grandpa's house, Sam saw him sitting on the porch.

"ATE WAKAN TANKA WEY OH WAY OH HEY! ATE WAKAN TANKA WEY OH WAY OH HEY!" Carrying his songs across the prairie, the wind lifted his prayers to the Great Mystery. The more he sang, the lighter his heart became. Coming to a stop, Sam quietly stood before his grandpa, but the old man had his eyes closed. In the cool of the morning, Sam sat down beside him, but the old man kept singing.

So Sam sang along. Together, their voices carried across the prairie. They sang every Sun Dance Song, every Inipi song, every song the old man knew and some of them twice. Finally the drum stopped beating and the old man looked at his grandson.

"You hungry Sam?" It was still morning and the old man hadn't had his breakfast.

"I can always eat, grandpa," smiled Sam.

"Oh I bet you can!" laughed the old man. "You're still growing. I was going to Kelly's to get some chicken fried steak, eggs and pancakes. I'll never finish it. So you want to split it with me?" One thing he never got used to, was not having Elsie's cooking.

"Yeah, sure," replied Sam. The old man went into the house and put his drum on the table and closed the door. It was quiet between them for a time. Then Sam broke the silence. "Did you hear about Donald and Darrel, grandpa?

"Yeah, I did." Then more silence.

Kelly's Tavern was almost empty this morning. They took a table in the back so they could talk privately. The waitress came over and brought the menus. The old man handed them back to her.

"I know what we want," the old man said. "Just bring me a cup of decaf and my grandson some orange juice. I'll take the chicken fried steak, eggs over easy and a side of pancakes. Bring an extra plate, so the boy can have some too."

"You want me to have the cook just split it down the middle?" She wasn't the pretty waitress who worked at night. This was the mean one who worked breakfast. She didn't smile much and wasn't any good at small talk.

"Naw, that's alright, we'll do it here. Just bring an extra plate and silverware." Grandpa had known this waitress for a long time, but there was no pleasantries exchanged between them.

"Suit yourself," said the waitress as she walked off. She came back shortly with decaf and orange juice. The maple syrup and ketchup were already on the table.

After he fixed his coffee, the old man stared off into nowhere. Sam knew his grandpa to be silent for long periods of time. It seemed his grandpa was having a conversation with someone in his mind.

Then, the old man turned to Sam. "Donald and Darrel spirits came by early this morning and woke me up. They were mighty angry. At first I thought it was a couple of evil spirits, they were so fired up. They told me this drunk white woman had run them over. She came barreling around the corner, swerving all over the place and plowed right over them. Donald said she hit his body so hard, that his spirit flew right out of it. Darrel's spirit tried to hang on. But he was being dragged so far under the car, that he just couldn't. His spirit just had enough." The old man's eyes got misty.

37

"After they told me what happened," the old man continued. "I looked at them and said 'What the hell were you doing in the middle of the road?' I couldn't believe what I was hearing. I got mad because they put themselves in harm's way. When they were young, I couldn't get a word in edgewise with them boys. They were so headstrong. They told me they were right sorry that it happened. But they saw my Elsie and she told them it was going to be alright."

"Did mom or Auntie Lynn tell you?" Sam asked.

"Naw, they didn't have too. The boys came by in spirit and told me all I needed to know. That white woman, she won't last long if she keeps driving like that. She's bound to run herself into a ditch." He took a long sip of coffee. "You see grandson, we're here for a short journey. You must be mindful of putting yourself in harm's way. Creator can't protect you if you contract with the Darkness."

"But grandpa, how did Donald and Darrel contract with the Darkness?" Sam felt confused.

"I didn't say they did. But, they stood out in the middle of the road yelling at each other. They weren't paying attention to that idiot woman driver. I don't fault them none. I just see how it all played out. That drunk woman has a lotta making up to do. Points in the negative stack up. It'll wear out her body, then her mind. If you saw how the Darkness lays in wait for you to mess up, you'd be so careful."

"How do you know that grandpa?"

"Because the Darkness lay in wait for me, grandson. And I was ripe for the picking. There was a time when ice water flowed through my veins. My heart was hard because I lacked respect for myself and Mother Earth. Back then, I turned away from Creator and the truth. And I was ashamed of my heritage. Once I even told a woman I was half Italian, so she wouldn't know I was Indian," said the old man as he took a sip of coffee.

"Did she believe you, grandpa?" asked Sam.

"Oh, it didn't matter Sam. See, I was poisoned against my own people and our traditions. I believed the white man when he said we were less than human. He called us brutal savages with barbaric ways. After that, I snubbed my family. I forgot what was honorable in life and looked for happiness in shallow pleasures. Soon, everything I touched got destroyed. The more angry I got, the more I thought life owed me something and that it was unfair."

"It sounds terrible, grandpa," said Sam.

"That it was, my boy. You see, son, in life, there are no answers. There are only choices and consequences for the choices we make. After I met with my grandpa and the council Elders on the Other Side, I didn't stop drinking. I didn't heed their warning. I got worse. After that, I lost the power to choose. That's when I gave those demons control. I got mixed up with a fella with a nasty drug habit. One night after I smoked an unholy pipe, my spirit left my body. But I wasn't dead. I was taken down to the bowels of the Earth. Those ghouls pulled me down to show me the world they'd made. I went there because I drank and used mean-spirited drugs." His voice got serious.

"What was it like?" Sam asked not wanting to miss anything.

"You ever been in a place so hot that you couldn't catch your breath?" The old man's eyes bore into his grandson.

With big eyes, the boy shook his head. "Nah uh."

"Well, this place was so hot, I was suffocating. The heat came from all directions. The fields were ablaze with flames and the mountains were made out of red hot iron. The rivers flowed with bubbling hot molten lava. The skies rained down with sparks of fire. I wanted to run, but all pathways were made of burning metals. If I stayed where I was, I'd be turned into charcoal. But if I ran, I'd surely burn to death. The walls were made out of big stones. It was hot, cramped and tight. There was no place to move. Then I heard his voice, the voice

39

of the Darkness."

"What did he say, grandpa?"

"His deep voice growled, 'THIS IS THE WORLD THAT WE HAVE MADE!!!' His words thundered through my being. I heard them echo across that molten valley. I couldn't shake it off. They came into my dream time and dragged me down to the Underworld, where the sun never shines and your thirst is never quenched."

"When did this happen to you, grandpa?"

"It was before I went in the talking doctor's hospital. I knew I was losing my mind. I wanted to die, but I was afraid I'd go into the Darkness."

"How did you get away, grandpa?"

"Ceremony and AA, grandson, ceremony and AA. Remember Hal, the Indian from Canada who I told you about?"

"The tall man," said Sam. "Who came to the hospital and gave you the Big Book."

"Oh, you do have a good memory," said the old man. "You see, his relations were part of our people before the imaginary border between Canada and the US. There was a time when we were a great nation of people. Some of Sitting Bull's relations still live in Canada. One day, Hal came to the hospital with a fella named Wyatt. They ran a sweat lodge, an Inipi ceremony. They had just come from Sun Dance. Wyatt was a Sun Dancer and sober quite a few years. His Sun Dance Chief said he was ready to pour sweat lodges. Hal wanted to do it for Native veterans. So that's how they came to find me. The funny thing is, Wyatt was white and he brought Hal to his first sweat lodge after they met in AA."

"How did a white man get to be a Sun Dancer?" asked Sam, curious about Native ceremonies.

"Funny things happen out West, sonny boy. I heard there are lots of people in Europe who want to be Indians too," said the old man with a chuckle.

40

"You think they want to live on the reservation?" asked Sam.

"Naw, they just wanna run around in a loin clothe and wear an Indian war bonnet with all the eagle feathers," chuckled the old man.

"Finish your story grandpa," said Sam.

"Where was I," pondered the old man. "Oh yeah, the Inipi. Well, from my eyes, Hal could tell I'd been in the great abyss. Most people just get to the edge of that dark hole before they lose their ground. But he knew, I'd been inside it."

"What did he see in your eyes, grandpa?"

"Hal told me I had crazy eyes. For a big man, he was sure gentle. We sat by the fire and he told me about the firewater spirit and all its relations. Being that we had free will, Creator allowed us to choose which master we'd serve. Because in the end, we always came home. If I wanted sobriety, Hal would help me do a ceremony to break the contract I made with the firewater spirit. Then, I could come back to the world of the rising sun. I told him I was scared. I knew I was going insane. I was ready to die."

"What did he say to that, grandpa?"

"He laughed. He said that's the drama of the alcoholic mind. The Spirit of Darkness didn't really want me. Because it couldn't have what it didn't own. I was created by Creator and to Creator I'd return. But, Hal said, I was free to journey through the Valley of the Shadow of Death. It was a good creep show, but nothing more. To get rid of the dark, all he'd have to do is light a match, pray and the darkness would go away. You see, grandson, Light is stronger than the dark. Out in the yard of the Army hospital, we sat outside and watched the sun travel across the sky. Hal pointed out how it lit up the shadows and cast them aside. That's how the Light of Creator works. It casts out the shadows."

Finally the food came. The waitress set down a plate

with the chicken fried steak, eggs over easy, fried potatoes, toast and another plate with a side of pancakes. She set down an empty plate in front of the boy.

"You want anything else?" the waitress asked grandpa.

"Just a bit more decaf," grandpa said. Then he poked some fun at her. "Did you get these eggs fresh from the chickens this morning?"

As the waitress turned her back, Sam heard her mutter "smart ass" under her breath. She brought back the decaf pot and dropped the check off on the edge of the table. "You let me know if you need something else."

"You want some of these eggs," said grandpa as he cut everything up.

It smelled good. Sam said, "Sure."

While they ate in silence, Sam had the feeling that his grandpa was having a conversation with someone in his thoughts. After a while, grandpa put his fork down and stirred his coffee. "You get enough to eat, boy?"

With his mouth full of pancakes, Sam nodded his head.

"Good," said grandpa. "You know, it was pretty tricky when they locked me up in the talking doctor's hospital. If you're not careful, they'll keep you locked up for a long time. Especially, if they find out you can talk to spirits. They have a special name for that."

"What did they call it?" Sam asked between mouthfuls.

"Well, let me think a minute. I know it wasn't good. It starts with an "S"... Schizo...phrenia. In our culture, you'd be called a holy man, Wicasa Wakan. But," the old man shook his fork at Sam, "Watch out in the white culture, if you have a vision or talk to spirits. Those talking doctors like to experiment on people. Hal warned me not to tell them I had visions or was gifted with eyes to see."

"What would happen to you grandpa?"

"I'm not really sure, but I know they hooked one guy up to this electric machine and shocked his whole body. I think his spirit left his body that day. He walked around like a dead man. His spirit had left his eyes. So I never said anything."

"I am glad you didn't, grandpa. But what did the talking doctor do to you?"

"Well, we'd sit around in this circle in the day room. They'd ask us questions and tried to get us to talk," said the old man between mouthfuls.

"But I never said anything to them, unless they asked me directly. I didn't want to make any mistakes. I knew I didn't belong there. Those talking doctors were very interested in my thoughts. They said my thoughts made me do things. They wanted to change my thoughts."

"Did it work, grandpa?"

"Well Sam, our thoughts are powerful. That's how we talk to Creator. Our words are powerful because they come from the heart. You can always tell a person's heart by what they speak," said the old man.

"How's that, grandpa?"

"Well, it's simple really," said the old man. "Your heart is the motor. If your heart is pure, so are your words. The mind is the steering wheel. If your heart is broke and angry, your mind will steer you the wrong way. If you think bad thoughts, it's like a magnet and bad things will come to you. But if you stay close to Creator, even when bad things happen, you'll get through them."

"So how'd you finally stop drinking grandpa?"

"I'd be lying if I said I did it on my own," the old man admitted. "When Hal and Wyatt ran the sweat lodge down in the yard at the VA, something happened. I didn't notice it at first. But once a week, Hal kept fire while Wyatt poured the lodge. Hal told me about his sobriety, how he stopped drinking with Creator's help. We had lots of ceremony. Then one day,

43

Hal came by to see if he could take me to a meeting for alcoholics. The talking doctors trusted him, so they let me go. I got sober shortly after that."

"Now, Hal was the only drunk who liked tequila so much, he'd pour it on his pancakes. One night, Hal went to jail for being drunk and the spirit of tequila came to visit him. Its spirit crawled right out of the wall. Hal said it looked like a turtle in the shape of a tequila bottle. He watched that turtle crawl under his bunk, up the wall and disappear into a vent on the ceiling."

"The spirit of tequila sounds like cartoon character," Sam laughed. "You still go to those meetings grandpa?"

"Yes son, I do. Those fellas in AA told me I only had a daily reprieve. I'd better be mindful because the firewater spirits were always waiting around the corner. So, I'd better keep my spirit fit. If I wandered off the path, they'd catch me."

"It must be a very lonely spirit, if it keeps waiting around for people," Sam said.

"Well, I don't know if it is lonely. It's surrounded by other spirits. The spirit of suicide, lust and greed are around it all the time," grandpa said.

"But they don't sound like much fun, grandpa."

"Well, the spirit of greed takes the fat. It's a wasicu. It always takes the best for itself. It don't share with anybody," the old man started. "You look around on the TV. It shows empty-hearted people filling themselves up with junk."

"It's the commercials," said Sam having a realization of how people are manipulated by moving pictures.

"Ah, that's only part of it," the old man shook his head. "Only a fool feeds on trash, trying to fill up his emptiness. But, it never works," the old man shook his fork at Sam. "That hole only gets bigger. You can't fix what's broke inside with junk from the outside."

"Their spirit must be as empty as a hollow log,

grandpa." Sam was getting an earful this morning.

"I think you're right. They're like gamblers, who take the grocery money and spend it all down at the casino. After they lose their money, they come begging because they got no milk for the kids." The old man didn't have much use for the casino, because it made money on people's weaknesses.

"You know what grandpa, that happened last week. Billy's grandma asked mom for money. But, mom gave her eggs and bread instead. No money, because she'd blow it at the casino." It all started to make sense to Sam now.

"You just made me remember something boy. Your grandma Elsie loved to read. One night, she read me a story about Ebenezer Scrooge. He lived across the big water in England. They got a big clock there, named after me. Well, ol' Scrooge had so much money. But, he was a stingy man. His heart was pinched and cold. It was black as coal. He'd just as soon let a homeless child starve. Well, one night Great Spirit got sick of Ebenezer's stinginess. So, He sent Scrooge four spirits."

"All in one night?" asked Sam.

"Yup," the old man's eyes twinkled. "They came to visit him when he was sleeping. But, old Scrooge didn't want to go with those spirits. Oh no! He fought tooth and nail and begged not to go. But those spirits took him anyway. They showed him all the choices he'd made in life. Even how he let his heart go sour to the goodness of life because a woman broke his heart. Some men never get over their broken hearts, grandson." The old man paused for a second. Then, his grandson asked a telling question.

"Are you ever going to get over your broken heart grandpa? Grandma wouldn't want you to be sad forever."

"You're right, she wouldn't. She'd be the first one to tell me, I was being plain selfish, sitting around, wallowing in my loneliness," sighed the old man. "But I've enjoyed telling my stories to you. I don't feel so lonesome now."

"I like listening to your stories grandpa. So what happened to old Scrooge?"

"Well, those spirits took him all around. They showed him how his selfishness had hurt people. Then came the moment that shook him up but good," the old man's eyes twinkled.

"What was that grandpa?"

"They showed him how he died and no one came to his funeral. His cold, prickly heart bought him a lonely death," said the old man with conviction.

"That's sad, grandpa," said Sam.

"But the spirits also showed him another way. If he had a change of heart, he could help a lot of people. The spirits got it all done in one night. The next morning was Christmas. He was so grateful to be alive, he bought food for others and even saved a little boy's life. But it took the spirits to show him all these things. That's a lucky man. I heard it said, 'to whom much is given, much is expected.'"

There was a long silence while the old man remembered his growing up. As a young boy, his father was a proud man, who provided for his family. But then, the firewater spirits had their way. His dad became a raging drunk, who died dirty and homeless. It left deep scars on the old man's heart. The shame he felt as a boy was still with him.

"You know, grandson, my heart didn't break when your grandma Elsie died," the old man sighed. "It broke long ago, watching my dad die his alcoholic death. Back then, I didn't know how to talk about the pain. My older sister remembered him for me. He was a proud man. But that was before that wily, no good shopkeeper traded him whiskey for furs. My dad built things and showed my sister how to trap. He built a log cabin out in the woods. She remembered him for me. He was a proud man, a strong man, who loved his children. I came late. I was the youngest. My sister told me he was proud to finally have a son and how much he loved me. He'd hold me up in his

46

big arms, with a smile from ear to ear. But I never knew him that way. After he started drinking, that spirit of whiskey got a hold of him and my dad never came back."

"I'm sorry grandpa, that your daddy died that way."

"He didn't know he had a choice. Heck, neither did I until Hal came along. Those talking doctors said there was no cure for alcoholism. All I got is a daily reprieve, providing I keep close to Creator and do His Work well."

"I never knew one spirit could cause so much pain," the young boy said.

"Well, that crafty, no good, son of a ....whatever he is, " the old man started. "He's got a lot of bad company. Take for instance, the spirit of suicide. Nothing is more deadly and cunning. When you're feeling down and worthless, it whispers in your ear."

"What's it say, grandpa?"

"Oh, things like, the world will be a better place when your dead! Go ahead, pull the trigger! You're useless, so you might as well die."

"Sounds terrible," remarked Sam.

"Oh, it is. Hal said this was the most selfish spirit of all. He had no use for people who wallowed like hogs in self pity. He'd tell them to pull their heads out of their ass and wipe the shit out of their eyes. After all, Creator gave them brains to use. I made sure to never feel sorry for myself in front of Hal." The old man laughed.

"I wouldn't either, grandpa," Sam laughed too. "What other spirits keep company with the firewater spirit?"

"The worst spirits are the twins, Doubt and Fear. If you listen to them, they'll cripple your mind. They're like little worms chewing away your confidence. Once they get a hold of your thoughts, you'll never make it in the world. See, the spirit of doubt is a trickster. It throws a wet blanket over the Sacred Fire of your dreams. People haunted by the spirit of doubt give up on everything. They got no elbow grease." He took a few more bites of his breakfast before it got cold. He enjoyed telling his stories.

"What about fear, grandpa?" Sam asked, keeping his grandpa on track.

"I was just getting to that one," the old man said chewing his last bit of chicken fried steak. "You see, when you're hunted down by fear, your problems seem bigger than Creator. But Creator always plants the mugwort next to the poison oak."

"What does that mean?" asked Sam.

"Well, for every problem, there's a solution," the old man said. "See, the spirit of fear is a whisperer. It sits on your shoulder and whispers that you'll lose all you got or not get what you want. That's why people build fences and keep to themselves. With fear, there's never enough. Fear and anger are close relations. When people are afraid, they get mighty angry."

"Grandpa, I was afraid of this bully once. He was older and pushed me to the ground in front of everybody. One day, he wanted my lunch. So, he knocked me down and ate my sandwich right in front of me. I was so hungry. But, who could I tell? Everyone else was afraid of him too. I figured I'd have to kill him or else he'd never leave me alone. Then one day, I heard by the water fountain, how his mom died. And nobody wanted to take care of him, not even his grandma."

"I know the boy you're talking about, son. He's had a hard life. His daddy got stabbed in a bar fight and never found work. His mama, well she was a drug addict and overdosed. That poor boy was left alone. Of course, he was angry inside. He had to take it out on someone. I guess that someone was you."

"I felt bad after I found out his grandma didn't want him," Sam said quietly. "The next day, I had mom pack me a second sandwich and I gave it to him. I gave him my chips too."

48

"Oh Sam, we'd live in a different world if more people were like you. So what spirits do you think were living in his house?" asked the old man to see if his grandson was paying attention.

"Mostly dark ones, grandpa."

"Yeah, but which ones? Think about it a minute. You know his dad almost died in a bar fight. His mama died of an overdose and his grandma didn't want him. He was an angry boy."

"Okay, definitely the firewater spirit and anger were around his dad. His mom was probably feeling sorry for herself, so the spirit of suicide made her overdose and die," said Sam confidently and then he got quiet for a moment. "But Grandpa, I don't know what would make a grandma not want her grandchild."

"I knew Nelda, his grandmother, when she was a little girl. She didn't have it easy. When her mom got pregnant, she wasn't married. And Nelda's father was a no good drunk. He said the baby wasn't his. When Nelda was born, she wasn't wanted. She got passed around from one aunt to another. Maybe Nelda was too broken herself to handle a boy so angry. Maybe she didn't have enough to give him. Not even enough love. What spirit did the boy have around him?"

"He was angry, mean and liked to hurt people. So the spirit of anger, for sure," Sam said confidently.

"Boy, I believe you are right." The old man smiled. It'd been a long time since he shared his knowing with anyone. "You revealed a side of the firewater spirits, most never talk about. This boy is a good example. When dark spirits take over a family, the little ones get neglected and abused. Some get beat up. Many don't have food or clothes or even socks."

"It's sad, grandpa," sighed Sam.

"Yeah, it seems so. Those spirits are hard lesson givers. They teach us how not to be," the old man sighed. Sam

49

cogitated on what his grandpa said.

"Sam, did you know, each one of us is a spirit pretending to be human walking around on Mother Earth?" asked the old man with a twinkle in his eye.

"Really grandpa?" Sam asked as he mulled it over.

"Yup, that's why most of us are so tenderhearted. Our spirit remembers the pure love that we were created with. It's hard for us to live on a planet calloused with so much hate and selfishness," said the old man.

"Why is love so hard to have here, grandpa?" asked Sam, wanting to understand.

"This is the way I heard it told by an old black man out west. He said:

> 'True love cannot exist except between equals. Jealousy is the poison ivy that grows around the Tree of Love. It chokes its branches and withers its roots. So if love cannot exist except between equals, then jealousy is when love is not equal."

"I never knew it was so complicated," said Sam with his head in his hands.

"True happiness comes from the heart, Sam. It ain't about chasing after the things you see on TV. It not about things at all," said the old man pointing to Sam's heart. "Happiness is an inside job, plain and simple. Do you remember how the spirits told me, I couldn't go home because I wasn't done yet?"

"I do, grandpa."

"Well, before we were born, we lived in the Spirit World. That's our true home. Mother Earth is our classroom," the old man started to explain.

"How so grandpa?"

"Well, each of us has a gift, Sam. We brought it here to share with others. Before we were born, we met with the

Council of Elders. We told them what we wanted to create and made a soul contract. Some things we came here to learn and some to teach. But in any great game, there is always an enemy. It's only when you go up against a rival, that you see who you are. The challenge reveals your strengths and weaknesses. Did you know, your enemies are your greatest teachers?"

"Really, grandpa. Like that bully I gave the sandwich too."

"Exactly, I bet he never picked on you again after that."

"He was still mean," Sam gathered. "After that, mom packed an extra sandwich and I gave it to him. I think he was just hungry. Dad gets mean when he's hungry."

"Yeah, your daddy does, even when he was a boy," the old man laughed. "That is one of the faults in men folk. We're ornery when our stomachs are empty."

The waitress came by to fill up the old man's decaf. "You two want anything else?"

"I can't think of anything right now," the old man said. Looking at his grandson, he admired how wise he was for such a young man. "Sam, you had enough of my stories for today?"

"Grandpa, I can listen to your stories all the time. But I understand if you talked enough for one day."

"Well let's pay our check and you can walk with me to the house. I got to get my things together for the meeting tonight."

"Is that the AA meeting, grandpa?"

"Yup," said the old man as he paid the bill and left a few dollars on the table. "Let's go."

Opening the door, the bright sunlight felt warm on the old man's face. Blowing from the west, a cool breeze swept up behind them. In no hurry, they ambled past one of the dozen churches. Sam noticed an abandoned, broken down red car in

51

the driveway.

The church grounds were overgrown with tall buffalo grass. The white paint was chipped and peeling on the church's plank wood walls. At the top of the highest tree branches cawed several crows, sending their voice. Towering overhead, the steeple had a crucifix at the very top.

"Grandpa, do you know who Jesus Christ is?"

The old man smiled. His grandson was full of questions today. "What makes you ask about Jesus Christ?"

"Well, that's the Christian Church. Down the road is a Baptist Church. Way down by the river is the Catholic Church. The other day, mom and I were at the mall. There were women sitting at a table. They asked mom if she'd been saved by the Lord Jesus Christ?"

"Did they tell your mom what she needed to get saved from?" the old man queried.

"I don't know. They didn't say. But, they were pretty scared for mom. They told her if she didn't get saved, bad things could happen." Sam was concerned.

"Ah, the old fear tactic," the old man chuckled. "They use that one a lot. Once they get people riled up, it's easy to persuade them. Especially, if they make them believe something bad will happen. Did they ask your mom to buy something or ask her for money?"

"I don't remember, grandpa. They kept telling her she needed to get saved."

"Well, you asked me a question and it deserves an answer. But you got to understand, there is a big difference between the man, Jesus the Christ and the people who call themselves Christians," the old man looked at his grandson to see if he followed his train of thought.

"What's the difference?" Sam asked.

"Now that's the question, right there," the old man

began. "Well, the way I understand it, Jesus the Christ was a great medicine man. He was a way shower, because he was close to Great Spirit. For all I know, He might have been one of the first Sun Dancers."

"How's that grandpa?" asked Sam knowing that Sun Dance was an Indian ceremony.

"Well, He was pierced to a tree for four days," started the old man. "When he went up on the hill, His vision quest lasted 40 days and nights. Which is the longest I've ever heard of. When Jesus was out on a boat and a storm came up, he talked to the wind and told her to calm down. It seems the old girl listened much better to him, than to me." As he finished his sentence, the wind came up behind the old man and blew his hat clean off his head. It rolled down the dirt road ahead of them.

"Hurry up, Sam! Get my hat before that old wind blows it down to the river!"

Sam raced off after the hat and snatched it up. "Got it grandpa!"

The old man took back his hat and dusted it off. Then, looking skyward, he shook it at the wind. "TAH-TAY!!!" the old man hollered. "What did I tell you about messing with my hat?!"

"Grandpa, maybe you shouldn't holler at the wind."

"Oh don't worry yourself about it. The wind and me, we understand each other just fine. If she wasn't teasing me all the time, I think there'd be something wrong." The old man tussled his grandson's hair. "Now where were we? Oh, Jesus the Christ..." the old man paused for a while to collect his thoughts. "Now Jesus was a mighty powerful healer. In a blink of an eye, He'd cast out spirits from a man's body. Then there was the time, He smeared mud on a blind man's eyes and made him see. He even told a dead man to get up and walk."

"Did the dead man get up and walk, grandpa?"

"Oh, he did," said the old man with a gleam in his eye. "It's not hard when you understand how it happened. See, when a man dies, his spirit leaves his body. But it doesn't go far away, at least not for the first few days. Knowing this, Jesus walked up to old Lazarus and said 'Get up and walk!' He told his spirit to get back in his body. Jesus understood the matters of Spirit. The people thought it was a miracle."

"What other kinds of miracles did he do, grandpa?"

"Well, one time they were at a wedding and the host ran out of wine. So his mother asked Jesus to turn the water in the jugs into wine. But from my recollection, Jesus never drank the wine. So he must of known something about the firewater spirits too."

"He sounds like a Holy Man, grandpa."

"Well, I believe he was, Sam. He talked to spirits all the time. When he was on his vision quest, the Tempter, that old Spirit of Darkness paid him a visit and made him an offer."

"What was the offer, grandpa?" Sam's curiosity was peaked.

"Well, that old conniver told Jesus, if he came over to his side, Jesus could have the whole world."

"What did Jesus say?"

"Well, Jesus turned him down flat. Why would he want the whole world if he'd have to give up his soul?"

"That's a good point, grandpa. Jesus must be pretty smart."

"That he was, grandson. But more than that, he was pure of heart and didn't have blood on his hands. Which makes a big difference in the Spirit World. Once you kill someone or do them great injury, you've got to clean it up. Otherwise those gifts can't come to you."

"What do you mean, grandpa? What gifts can't come to you?"

"Well, Jesus had a group of fellas following him. He taught them to do all the miracles he did, as far as calming the wind, healing the sick and raising the dead. That is the work of Great Spirit and all of us can do that work. But first, we must be pure of heart."

When they got to the old man's cabin and opened the door, it was dark and cool inside. "You see, grandson, our spirits came from the Star Nation. Each one of us is a bright shining starlight in Heaven. The purer your heart is, the brighter your light shines. Now, that doesn't mean you won't get challenged by the Lords of Darkness. Oh, most times they're lurking around the bend. They'll try to snag you to their side in a weak moment. But, we came to Earth to do great work, Sam. And that's the greatest message I ever got from Jesus the Christ. The one thing I want you to understand, more than anything is; there were many great teachers who came to Mother Earth. But the greatest of all of them is Great Spirit, the Infinite Creator. He is the Father of us all."

"Even all the bad people, grandpa?" asked Sam.

"Yes, sonny boy, even all the bad people. Even old Zelda over at the post office is a child of Great Spirit. She just don't act like it," smiled the old man. "Everything we see and don't see comes from Great Spirit; the good, the bad and even the ugly ones."

"But why would Creator make ugly ones, grandpa?"

"Well, I suspect there is a great soul learning that comes from living that life," suggested the old man. "And that's what our souls came here to do, Sam. We came here to learn."

Sam thought on this for a moment. "What did we come here to learn, grandpa?"

"Well son, those lessons are deep inside your heart," started the old man. "Creator hid them there. He knows the most obvious place to hide something, is the last place people look. They'll go looking everywhere outside themselves, when it was hidden in their heart the whole time."

"It sounds like a game of 'hide and go seek," said Sam.

"Well, that it is," said the old man. "You see, you were created out of love, the greatest kind of love there is. And that's what you're here to find. Now, it's not the kind of love you see on T.V. where the boy meets girl. It's even deeper than that. It's when you can see Creator's thumb print on everything and everyone you meet, including yourself."

"How do you see that?" asked Sam.

"That is the game, Sam. That is the game. Look around you. Can you see the spark of Creator in all life?" asked the old man.

"You mean, even the bugs or rocks on the road?"

"Yup, even those."

"What about mean people?" asked Sam.

"Yup, that's when the game gets interesting. Try seeing Creator in things you don't like. That's the greatest test of all," said the old man. "Do you love me, even when I'm grouchy?"

"Oh grandpa," smiled Sam. "What kind of question is that?"

CHAPTER TWO: OLD FRIENDS

The spirit of a woman stands straight and tall
Unwavering, as others around her fall
Bending only to the heart that is true
No matter the toil, the struggle she knew
Praying to the Heavens at morning Light
Knowing in her heart, They'll make it right

Lynn's phone hadn't stopped ringing since she got home from her sister Tess' house. Almost the whole town called since her two sons were killed on the River Road the night before.

"I don't know what I am going to do about that white woman," said Lynn talking to her friend Patty on the phone. "She was drunk driving when she killed my boys. I got half a mind to visit that man down in the hollows, but Tess won't hear none of it. But I'm going to that alcoholic meeting tonight. I want to see if those old men have any answers to what's going on, here on this reservation."

"What kind of answers do you think those old men would have, Lynn?" asked Patty.

"I don't know, but I am going down there. Those old men must know something. Tess said she'd come with me. My dad goes there. He always said we were welcome. I want to see what they know."

"Well, if you think it would help, I'll come with you."

"Patty, all we got is each other. Thank you my friend. I got to go get dinner started, but I am going to leave about quarter to six. I'll see you then." Lynn hung up the phone.

Back at the cabin, the old man arranged his eagle fan

with some smudge, along with an old copy of the AA Big Book into the small suitcase. He kept his Sacreds in a cedar box at the foot of his bed. All his Sun Dance Regalia, his worn moccasins which Elsie beaded herself, were down at the bottom of the box. After Elsie died, he lost interest in the ceremonies which had sustained him most of his life. Holding those things in his hand for a moment, the memories of their life together flooded back into his mind.

For a brief second, in the stillness, he found himself catapulted back into the Sun Dance Arbor. The Love of Creation flowed into the Sacred Circle as the smell the cedar smoke wafted through the air. He heard the eagle bone whistles blowing, as the Tree of Life swayed in the wind. The big drum beat in time with the heartbeat of Mother Earth, as his moccasin-ed feet danced across the Arbor. Harbored in the memories of his heart, were the things he still held dear.

Generally before the AA meeting started, he'd smudge off the community room while singing a few medicine songs. This way, he invited Great Spirit and the Higher Powers into the AA meeting. When people showed up, he smudged them off at the door while he greeted them. Most times, he got to the community room early to start the coffee and put the chairs in a circle. Sometimes as many as 5 people showed up. He didn't expect tonight would be any different.

The old man put on his hat, which hung on a nail by the door. Old habits, familiar things, were all he had left. Sometimes the quiet took him by surprise. As he closed the front door behind him, he knew when he got home tonight, everything would be like he left it. The dishes would still be in the sink. The coffee cup would still be on the table. Elsie wasn't around anymore to clean up after him. Not that he ever felt it was her job to do so, but she did. It's not that he was lonesome, but he definitely knew he was alone. Having Sam around brought a spark to his heart he hadn't felt in a long time.

There was a slight breeze coming up from the Missouri

as he walked the short mile to the community center. Actually it was just a small room attached to the gymnasium next to the post office. Walking passed three churches, he realized those bible toting Christians left an indelible mark on the Spirit of the Red Man.

When he was about 7 years old, he was forced to go to a Catholic boarding school. A nun there told him the best he'd ever to do was end up in purgatory. He didn't know what purgatory was, but it didn't sound like a good place. Like he told his grandson, it wasn't Christ he had a problem with. It was the ignorant bible thumpers who proclaimed the Word of God while they instilled fear in everyone. This thought made the old man cringe. Great Spirit wasn't trapped in a book. He was the Breath of Life in every dew drop, every breeze and every star filled night.

There were no cars in the parking lot when the old man got to the community room. Pulling the key from his pocket, he unlocked the door. As it swung open wide, the old man kicked a brick against the door to hold it open. The florescent lights buzzed on as he flipped the switch and he opened a window to let in some air.

In a cabinet drawer were some signs he set up, letting people know they were in an AA meeting. Afterward, he got busy making the coffee and setting up the room. All the while, he sang a spirit calling song. He opened up his suitcase and put the AA Big Book up on the table in the front of the room. Putting a match to the sage in an abalone shell, he fanned the smoke as it billowed through the room with his eagle fan. He walked clockwise around the room, singing his medicine songs.

A little after 5:00 o'clock, he heard the first truck pull into the parking lot. Usually it was old Max coming from the next town over. But, it was a little early yet even for Max. Walking over to the door to see who it was, the old man didn't recognize the beat up, blue pick up truck with California plates. The whole tailgate was covered in bumper stickers. Whoever it was, they took a long time to come in. The old man just kept smudging.

As the smoke from the sage billowed out of the door, a long, tall shadow of a man cast itself across the floor. Standing in the doorway, the sunlight streamed in behind his large frame. Turning around, the rays of sunlight blinded the old man, making it hard for him to tell who it was.

"Are you sending up smoke signals up for the AA meeting tonight?" the tall shadow asked. The voice sounded distantly familiar, but it wasn't one of the regulars.

"Well I haven't set off any smoke alarms yet, but the meeting starts at six. Who is that?" asked the old man squinting as he shaded his eyes. "I can't see you with the sun in my eyes."

"Ben? Is that you?" the shadow said.

"Well, of course it's me," answered the old man sarcastically.

"Ben, it's Hal," said the tall shadow as he stepped into the room.

"Hal..."

Moving closer to the door, the old man stopped smudging. And there he was, tall and lanky, just the way Ben remembered him. From the looks of it, Hal wasn't worse for wear. But the crows had sure danced around his eyes some, leaving their familiar footprints. Hal's smile was still missing the same front tooth like it was back in the day.

"Well, I'll be... what brings you way out here?" Ben asked, as he walked up and shook Hal's hand.

"Well old buddy, I was down in Colorado working a rodeo and thought I'd take the long way home. I hadn't been to a meeting in two weeks and was getting mighty thirsty. That's when I remembered you lived out this way." Hal slapped Ben on the back.

"You know I was just telling my grandson about you,"

Ben said.

"Maybe that's why my ears were ringing," Hal laughed.

"Well, where are you staying tonight?"

"I've been sleeping in my truck mostly. I got it all rigged for traveling. The truck stops got showers, so I got cleaned up before I come."

"Well, I got an old pull out couch. I don't know how comfortable it is, but you're welcome to it." Ben smiled. "And why don't you lead the meeting tonight. I get plenty tired hearing the same old complaints every week. It'd be good to have some fresh blood."

"I'd be honored Ben," Hal said humbly.

Ben heard another truck pulling into the parking lot. "That'd be old Max. He just turned 87 years old and has 5 years sober. Can you believe it? Got sober in the nick of time, he did."

"Goes to show you, you're never too late to greet Creator with clean hands and straight eyes," Hal said.

Walking with a cane, Max came in through the door. His long white braids were nearly down to his waist. His bright smile radiated sobriety. Max had spent most of his life drunk. When the AA meeting started at the community center, Max was dumped off at the door. Of course he was drunk at the time. But 3 men in the meeting kept giving him hot coffee and something to eat. Usually one of the wives made some food for the men. Being soul sick and hungry, old Max brought his feeble body back every week for the hot coffee and something to eat. Then one day, the Spirit of Sobriety wrapped its warm blanket around Max. After being chilled to the bone for so long, old Max was nestled in a blessing. He never shivered in the cold again and celebrated his years of sobriety with the group.

"Hey Max, welcome," said Ben shaking Max's hand. "This is Hal, come all the way from Colorado. He's going to be leading the meeting tonight."

"Oh, good to meet you Hal. Listen Ben, there's some beef stew my daughter made in the cab of my truck. She put some plastic bowls in there and some spoons for us. Can you go get it out of the truck for me? I got this cane, which makes it hard to carry."

"Sure Max, no problem. We got a hot plate or we can heat it on the stove in the kitchen," Ben said as he smudged Max off.

"It's good that you do that smudging, Ben. Gets rid of all the unwanted ones." Max smiled.

Soon Ed and Marcus showed up. Ed was on the revolving door plan. Since he wouldn't admit he had a problem with alcohol, he kept going in and out. His last bout with firewater ended him up in the county jail for 6 months. Now, he had to get a court card signed to prove he attended AA meetings. Faring a little better, Marcus just took a 6 month chip. His mind was getting clear.

"Hey Ed, hey Marcus. Good to see you both," said Ben as he shook their hands. Turning back, Ben hollered, "Hal, would you smudge these two off? I'm going to get the stew."

"Sure thing," Hal answered. "Evening gentlemen, I'm Hal," he said as he smudged the young men off from head to toe.

"Thanks, Hal. You're not from around here are you?"

"No, I was just coming through from Colorado. I did some rodeo work down there."

Finding the hot plate, Ben set the stew on the counter in the back of the room. The stew's deep aroma filled the room as Ben stirred it with the ladle. It was still pretty warm. His stomach growled as Hal got a whiff of stew from across the room.

"Boy that smells good," said Hal walking over. "I've been hankering for a home cooked meal for a long time."

"Well go ahead, if you want some. Since you're leading, the rest of the room will get it before you do. Some of them come in pretty hungry, so you better have some now," said Ben.

"Don't mind if I do," said Hal grabbing a bowl and filling it with stew. "Out West, during the summer, we had a pot luck meeting every Thursday night. For a buck, you could get dinner." The stew was chocked full of potatoes, carrots, celery and chunks of beef. "You know, I got some bread out in the truck. Mind my bowl and I'll go get the bread. I may even have a chunk of butter."

"Will do," said Ben as he heard another truck pull up. With smudge in hand, Ben greeted Frank and Ernie and welcomed them in.

"Hal, meet Frank and Ernie," said Ben. "Hal's speaking tonight. We met before I got sober. He brought me to my first AA meeting."

"Oh, well that's a while ago," said Frank shaking Hal's hand.

"Sure is. I'd like to say I haven't changed much since then, but I'd be lying." Hal laughed.

A few more people trickled in, the closer it got to meeting time. The room felt good as Ben greeted everyone and smudged them off. Hal settled in to his seat and opened notebook with the necessary AA readings, so he'd get familiar with the format of the meeting.

"You're going to share for about 25-30 minutes, then we have open sharing. We usually only get about 5 or 6 people in here, so it won't be too long. Every now and then we get a new comer. If that happens we give them time towards the end to ask questions. It's not too complicated," said Ben.

"Sounds simple enough to me," said Hal as he read over everything.

With most of the regulars already in the room, Ben was surprised when more cars pulled in the parking lot. Curious,

63

he went outside to see who else was coming. He spotted his daughter Lynn's car. Tess was with her. Lynn was carrying a pie and Tess had a plate of sandwiches. A few people were friends of Donald and Darrel. Grief brought people together.

"Hey Frank, Ernie, looks like we got more people coming. Can you get some more chairs out? Maybe about 10?" hollered Ben as he greeted everyone.

"Sure thing."

Standing in the doorway with the sage, Ben saw the pained expression on Lynn's face. She was tough, much tougher than him. Tess, on the other hand, was the soft one, the reasonable one. Lynn was the bulldozer, relentless when she wanted to get something done.

"Hello my sweethearts," Ben said as he embraced his daughters.

"You heard about Darrel and Donald?" Lynn said scowling. The old man felt the anger and hurt in her restrained voice.

"Yeah, I did...," he paused not knowing what more to say, while they were standing at the door. "We'll talk about it after the meeting," he said squeezing her hand. "Go find your seat now. You're staying for the meeting, right?"

"Yeah, we're going to stay," said Lynn easing up a little.

"Hi pop," said Tess as she gave the old man a peck on the cheek.

Radiant colors splashed across the Great Blue Yonder as Ben glanced to the west. Angels of the clouds danced through the firmament with their paint brushes in hand. While the sun began to sink low in the west, blazing neon colors swirled through the vast blue sky. Fanning the clouds, the wind made them ready for a brilliant sunset.

More cars pulled into the parking lot. The old man recognized most of them. Watching the wind dancing with a pile of leaves, he felt something brewing. The sage kept burning, as he greeted everyone at the door.

Just before meeting time, there were more than 25 people in the room. As everyone milled around, Ben overheard snippets of conversation about his grandson's untimely death. People offered their condolences. Ben looked at Hal and said, "This hasn't happened in a long time. Usually there are only 5, sometimes 8 people here."

"No worries, Ben. Great Spirit is in charge. As trusted servants, we just carry the message," said Hal. In the moments before the clock struck six, Hal prayed to Creator. He asked Creator to speak through him and find the one person in the room who needed to hear the message.

The smell of fresh coffee brewing and beef stew wafted through the air as small huddles of people chattered away. It was close to meeting time. Ben wondered how to get everyone to take their seats. He remembered the conch shell he had in his suitcase. It was a gift from an Indian medicine man from the southern tribes, where it is used to call on the four directions. He'd never used it here before. But tonight was a different story.

Holding the conch shell in his hands, Ben stood facing East and blew into the shell. Immediately, all the talking stopped as the sound of the conch called the meeting to order. Echoing through the room, the trumpet of the ocean penetrated into everyone's heart. While Ben honored the four directions, peace and order came to the meeting.

Placing his conch shell back into the suitcase, Ben stood in front of the room. "Welcome everyone, please take your seats so we can bring this meeting to order." While people took their seats, Ben passed out the readings, such as the AA Preamble, How It Works, More About Alcoholism, the Twelve Traditions and the Promises. It was good to see so many people here tonight.

"Welcome to the Thursday night meeting of Alcoholics Anonymous. My name is Ben and I am grateful to Great Spirit and AA for my sobriety today. I am your secretary and all are welcome. Will you please join me in our opening prayer. For those who don't know it, it's hanging on the wall."

O, Great Spirit
Whose voice I hear in the winds,
And whose breath
gives life to all the world,
Hear me, I come to You
as one of your many children
I am small and weak.
I need your strength and wisdom.
Let me walk in beauty,
and make my eyes ever behold
the red and purple sunset.
Make my hands respect the things
You have made
and my ears sharp to hear Your Voice.
Make me wise so that I may understand
the things you have taught my people.
Let me learn the lessons you have hidden
in every leaf and rock.
I seek strength,
not to be greater than my brother,
but to fight my greatest enemy, myself.
Make me always ready to come to You
with clean hands and straight eyes.

So when life fades, as the fading sunset,

my Spirit may come to You

without shame.

As they invited Creator into the meeting, a peaceful calm washed over the room. Ben followed the meeting format. "I have asked Max to read the Preamble of Alcoholics Anonymous." Ben took his seat next to Hal. Listening to Max read the preamble, everyone settled in. Ernie read How It Works. Frank read More About Alcoholism. Ed read the Twelve Traditions. Having heard these words read over again for years, they had the same calming effect every time.

"Thank you everyone," said Ben. "I have a few announcements before we get started. If you brought food, go ahead and put it on the counter. If you're hungry, quietly help yourself, so not to disturb the person speaking. If you need to talk to someone privately, go outside away from the door. I got a real surprise tonight when I was setting up and an unfamiliar truck parked out front. This tall Indian gets out. And it turns out, Hal, who is our speaker tonight, took me to my first AA meeting many years ago. He brought our ancient ceremony to the VA hospital I was in and brought me back to our Old Ways of life. So tonight, please welcome Hal."

"Good evening Ladies and Gentlemen." Hal's voice boomed across the room. Taking a deep breath, he rarely spoke in front of this many people anymore. "My name is Hal and I am, thanks to Creator and AA, a sober member of Alcoholics Anonymous today."

"HI HAL!!!" responded the room.

"When I got here tonight, I didn't know what to expect. Except, this is an AA meeting and we'd be talking about firewater, alcohol or booze. You can name your own poison. Now before I get started, I want to thank the men who read tonight, Max, Ernie, Ed and Frank. For those of you who

67

nodded off during the readings, I want you to know, the readings are meant to have a calming effect. They let you shake the trail dust off your boots and settle into your seat. But, more importantly, they're meant to inform you as to why we're here. I'm reminded of this, because Ben said this is a bigger group than his normal 5 to 8 people."

"But, also because there might be someone in this room tonight, who's really asking themselves, if they got this thing, this terrible disease called alcoholism. For that person, or maybe persons, if there be more than one. I want you to know, tonight you're SAFE. And from here on out, you don't ever have to drink again, even if you want to."

"You see, when Ed read the Twelve Traditions, he read Tradition 3, which states the ONLY REQUIREMENT for AA membership is a desire to stop drinking. That's it! The only thing you need for membership to this simple program is to have a desire not to drink again. So if you're that person or persons here tonight and you're wondering if you belong here, I want to welcome you."

"Now you may be wondering if you're a real alcoholic. That's what Frank read about in More About Alcoholism. I'm going to tell you tonight, there is a test to know if you're a real alcoholic. And it's pretty simple. You see, if you honestly tried to quit drinking, but couldn't. Or when you drink, you can't control how much you drink, then you are probably alcoholic."

"Now, all the times I tried to quit, I couldn't stay stopped. And for me, when I drank, I wanted to get drunk. The quicker the better. That alcoholic oblivion let me forget the horrors of life which haunted me. I wasn't interested in controlling my drinking, ladies and gentlemen. I was only interested in the effect, because I wanted out. I wanted out of wherever I was and I counted on alcohol to get me there. But here's the tricky part about alcohol. It's **only** a symptom of the problem. The real problems are buried down deep. You must get to the heart of the matter to solve the problem. And the solution, ladies and gentlemen, lies in thoroughly working the

12 Steps of Alcoholics Anonymous."

"Now out West, there was a group of yahoos. I call them the Big and Brawnies. They were a bunch of gorilla chested, muscle pumpers strutting around with their sleeves ripped off their t-shirts. These fellas were constantly boasting about how they were real alcoholics."

"Now I've seen enough boozers and losers, before and since I came into these healing halls of AA. Quite frankly, I am not interested, as to whether or not, you are a real alcoholic. For all I know, you may be a potential alcoholic. But the hair of the dog has ripped a hole in your shorts, just big enough to get your attention."

"You see, what interests me more, is whether you become a real man or woman, as the case may be, by working the 12 Steps as outlined in the Big Book of Alcoholics Anonymous. Because you see, a real man, ladies and gentlemen, is not the one strutting around, showing off his puffed up biceps. No, a real man is the one who tucks his children in at night. A real man is the one who is faithful to his wife. A real man has the courage to admit when he's wrong and clean up his side of the street. A real man, ladies and gentlemen, is honest and kind because he walks with Creator in the Sunlight of the Spirit."

"Now you don't have to be a gorilla chested Brutus or a tattooed Calamity Jane to be a real alcoholic, no sir. Out West, I met many lonely, well-to-do housewives. These women drove their kids home drunk from school, after they sipped too much wine at their ladies luncheon. My heart went out to a young mother, who left her small babies strapped in their car seats for hours in the hot desert sun. They died from the heat because she was passed out drunk in the house. The demons in the bottle made her forget she was a mother and she lost her freedom and her children in one afternoon. Her guilt and heartbreak alone, would have killed a horse."

"I've met a pickled priest and intoxicated musician. And what they all had in common was, they lost the power of choice, when it came to the drink. I've met a few Christian alcoholics. And the only difference with them was, they were FORGIVEN."

The deep timber in Hal's voice nestled into the crannies of the minds of those who were paying attention. There was a gentleness in his speak which calmed even the most angry drunk sitting in the room.

"The only difference between a real alcoholic and common drinker is, the real alcoholic can't quit drinking, even when they truly want to. And most can't control their drinking once they get started. We alcoholics are defenseless against the first drink. Where one drink is too many and a 1000 is never enough. Why you can't even get a good buzz on with just one drink. So what's the point of that? What I have is, the disease of I, ME, MINE, MORE, NOW, I'M SORRY AND NEVER AGAIN!"

"Now, people often confuse sobriety with merely being dry, abstaining from alcohol. But there is a big difference, I assure you. Any drunk can get dry for a while. But in the back of his mind, there is always a reservation. There's always some good reason to go out and tie one on again."

"White knuckle abstinence, ladies and gentlemen, is pure hell. There is nothing more pitiful than a self-depriving drunk on the water wagon. Because they're in pure agony. They're still arm wrestling with the demons in the bottle because they have not yet surrendered. They have not conceded to their inner most selves, that to drink is to die. When you see these fellows in meetings, they rarely smile. They are very somber and often grouchy. Because they are practicing a form of self-restraint. They're still in self will and refuse to admit defeat. And they will often allude to the fact, the program isn't working for them."

"For a drunk to walk sober, is truly a miracle, ladies and gentlemen. Because sobriety comes from a change of the heart. You see, when a drunk finally hits bottom, he admits and accepts that he's been defeated by the demons in the bottle. Only then can he surrender and come over to the winning side, to walk with the Spirit of Sobriety."

"Only then, will he be empowered with the muscle, brawn, grit and courage of Creator. This humility makes him capable of fulfilling the conditions to maintain his sobriety. It's only when a man has trudged through the darkest valleys, that he can fully appreciate the view from the summit of towering mountain peaks."

"Sobriety isn't just about abstinence from alcohol, it's about becoming all we were created to be. And to do that, we work a program of action, as demonstrated in the 12 Steps of Alcoholics Anonymous. This is where the rubber meets the road. This is how a drunk stands sober."

"Now tonight, I realize I'm speaking on an Indian Reservation. I grew up on a reservation north of the Canadian border, when I was a boy. I left there before I became a young man. You see, I enlisted in the military to become a warrior. This is part of our culture. But more than that, I left to escape a darkness which was choking me. In my home town, I witnessed drunkenness every day. Most of the alcoholics there died. Some drunks froze to death sitting up against a building in the frigid winter snow, after they passed out. No one was waiting for them at home, because they didn't have a home to go to."

"I have been to many funerals and witnessed much sadness. Our people have only been drinking for a few hundred years and we don't do it very well. We haven't had the centuries of practice afforded the white man."

"But in our hearts, we carry a deep sadness. It hardly ever goes away and many of us drink to escape our misery. Now taking a drink to escape from sadness works as well as peeing your pants in the middle of a frosty blizzard. You'll feel warm...," Hal paused, sipping his coffee. "For a minute." A few soft chuckles came from the audience.

"Now those demons in the bottle, made me feel warm for a minute. Hell maybe even 15 minutes. But no sooner was I feeling comfortable when those bastards unleashed a hell which scarred me for a lifetime. What troubles me most, are the families and the children. They're the true casualties of the disease of alcoholism."

"In my hometown, every day some drunk passed out and left half empty liquor bottles laying around. Of course, with nobody watching, little Sally found that booze and drank it down. That booze made her very sick. Her little body couldn't handle the alcohol. Fortunately, grandma walked in. Otherwise little Sally might have died from alcohol poisoning. After that, she went to live with Grandma, because at Grandma's it was safe."

A slight breeze came through the door as Hal stopped for a moment and sipped his lukewarm coffee. His eyes were drawn towards the window, just in time to see the brilliant colors of the fading sunset. It had been a long time since he told his story. It felt good to be here, sitting next to Ben so many years later. Ben motioned to Hal, asking if he wanted a fresh cup of coffee.

"Yeah, thanks," said Hal as Ben got two more cups of coffee.

"Now, with that being said, all of us are entitled to the dignity of our own lumps. When I was a little tike, I never got in trouble. My older siblings always ran interference and covered for me. Later on, they weren't there and I had to face my lumps on my own. I can't tell you how many times I made bad choices that put me in a position to be hurt. Being a hard-head, it took me a while to figure out that learning the hard way was the only way I paid attention."

"Before the meeting, I was telling Ben here, how I'd been traveling with the rodeo circuit. And those cowboys do like to drink. Watching them get stupid on booze, reminds me of why I don't drink."

"When I saw Ben making the coffee and setting up the room, it did my heart good. You know, when we first met in the Army hospital psyche ward, he wasn't doing so good. And I was just shy of a year sober. The guys at my meeting said that I needed to be of service. They pretty well ordered me to find one drunk who was worse off than me and help him out. That's when I found Ben. And he was locked up. So, he was worse off than me."

"See, my basic problem was, I was selfish to the core, full of fear and self pity. Not an attractive combination, if you ask me. Now its true, I'd felt second class most of my life. And I never thought I'd amount to anything. But in my home town, none of my people were sober. Drunks died alone every month. Most were homeless, uneducated and unteachable."

"Well, Harry, one of the guys from my meeting, got plum pissed off about how I carried on. I'll never forget, how his freckled face turned beet red. It was almost the color of his hair. He stood up and slammed his fist on the table. "Hal," he said with his fist in my face, "If you got a poor mouth, you're gonna have a poor life!"

"Then he told me to get my head out of my ass and wipe the shit out of my eyes. That way, I'd have a better view! He said I'd always be a miserable SOB if I compared myself to others and wanted what they had. Then he hit me with the spiritual two by four, saying, 'Happiness is not getting what you want, it's wanting what you have.'"

"What did I know about happiness? NOT MUCH!"

"Oh he grilled me up and down, asking me, "You got two hands?" I said "Yeah." "You got two legs?" I said, "Yeah." "Does your mind work, can you think?" I said "Yeah." After his Spanish Inquisition, he says, "So you admit Creator gave you the basics to get around in life, just like everyone else."

"That's when he demanded that I find a drunk worse off than me and help them. Ben was the first drunk I found. I had to give Ben the best I had. Because if I gave him second best or less, he could die. People die from alcoholism, so I had to give Ben my best or he might die."

73

"When me and Wyatt first visited the drunk ward at the army hospital, I didn't know what to expect. Here was this sorry Indian drinking Acme beer, poor and pathetic. He was bit by the hair of the dog pretty good. I knew Creator sent me there to talk to Ben. So I visited Ben a couple times a week."

"After a while, I got permission to pour a sweat lodge with Wyatt in the yard at the Army hospital. Then the doctors let me take Ben off site to an AA meeting. The only way I can keep my sobriety is by giving it away. Having the willingness to follow a few simple spiritual principles, I now have freedom."

"Now Ben didn't know I needed him, more than he needed me. But doing Creator's work, I stopped feeling sorry for myself. I was useful to someone else, without a motive or any self interest. Now that's important, because I always wanted to know what's in it for me? Sobriety gave me a purpose and I finally had something worthwhile to give."

"The only purpose drinking ever gave me was cleaning my boots. Not so much because I wanted to. But because I puked all over them and the stench made my stomach churn. You can well imagine what I must of smelled like before I got sober. I was mucking out stalls all day, covered in horse shit, with puke stained boots. Yeah, boy was I a pretty sight." Hal laughed, remembering his life back then. "Sobriety made me smell better, that's for sure. But there are other smells that I appreciate about sobriety, like good perfume, shoe polish, good coffee and aftershave."

Taking a deep breath, he felt his heart pounding as he looked into the sea of faces. There was a sense of urgency. Did he have what they needed tonight? He trusted Creator did, what ever it was.

"I was introduced to firewater when I was fourteen. I was cutting up a silly crawdad with Hazel in our biology class when she whispered in my ear. In one sentence, she changed my whole life. She said the night before she'd gone out with the guys and they drank wine and had fun. It sounded good to me. So that night, I had a dollar in my pocket. I found an older guy

74

to buy a couple quarts of wine."

"Now it didn't occur to me that it wasn't legal for me to drink wine. All I could think about was having fun. The wine made me feel alright. It made it okay to be second class. It was the first time I got sick and puked all over my shoes. But it wasn't the last."

"I found out too late, drinking don't make you get smarter in life. Neither did it make my drinking buddies any smarter. In fact, I'd say the more I drank, the more stupid I got. By the time I got to high school, I was well acquainted with the bootleggers on our reservation. One of them made a moonshine he called 'white lightning.' After a couple swigs of that, by gawd, you were seeing stars."

"One night, I got laid out flat drinking moonshine. It took me where I wanted to go, which was out. After that, I kept a bottle of it with me wherever I went. Not so much because I liked the taste. That rock gut was plum awful. No, I kept it with me because it got the job done."

"High school was pretty much a blur. Me and my buddy Buck kept a pint of whiskey in the glove box of his dad's old pick up. That way, if it got too tough in class, we'd go out to the parking lot and have a nip to take the edge off. By 17, I was a troubled drunk. By then, everything I did had alcohol around it."

"Now, Hazel's life didn't turn out so good. By the end of high school, she was pregnant, but was too drunk to be a mother. So they set her baby boy up for adoption. Then Hazel got mixed up with a bunch of rowdies. Her shame became too great. One day, they found her body hanging from a rope. She had been repeatedly raped and beaten. But no one was ever charged."

"But that wasn't enough to convince me that drinking was no good. Then, there was my buddy Buck. He had a mouth on him. After a couple shots, he was mean drunk. I knew we were headed for trouble, the minute he pulled the cork

75

and his mouth started running."

"Now, I'm a big guy. I can hold my own, but not Buck. One night, it got ugly. Buck had made a few enemies shooting his mouth off. He got into a bar fight and the other guy had a knife. Buck got stabbed. He survived but he was never the same. Shortly after that, I enlisted in the Army. I knew if I stayed there any longer, I'd be dead too."

"By 19 years old, I barely took a sober breath and went to jail for the first time. There were other times after that. That first night, trapped in those stone walls, I stared at the ceiling. Out of nowhere comes this turtle shaped like a tequila bottle. It came right out of the wall. I couldn't take my eyes of it. It crawled up and down and finally disappeared back into the wall."

"At the time, it didn't occurred to me that alcohol was my problem. After that, they rotated me between the drunk tank, the stockade and psych ward. Finally, they put me in a rubber room. I thought it was just dumb luck. Back then the doctors had a name for my condition. They called it dipsomania, which is a fancy name for a drunk."

"By 30, my life was completely out of control. And I was dying in a chicken coop over in National City. There weren't no chickens left, just feathers. See, when I got to California, as an enlisted man, I was introduced to tequila and margaritas. Now I loved tequila so much, I put it on my pancakes. I never met anyone else who put tequila on their pancakes."

"Let me back track for a moment. When I was 26, I did quit drinking for about 2 years. I was working at a good job. Drinking was getting in the way, so I put it down. A guy at work named Jim came up to me one day, and said "Hal, you used to drink didn't you?" I said "Yes, but I quit." Then Jim asked if I went AA? I said 'No, I don't drink.' Then Jim said "You will." I didn't know it then, but Jim planted a seed, the seed of AA."

"Now of course, he was right. I did drink again. I was

bone dry and pretty lonely. But, I did some finagling and I got this pretty girl to go out with me. Of course, she suggested we go over to this bar. Well, I don't have to tell you much more. But in a hot minute, when that tequila hit my lips, my two years of not drinking, was over in a snap. Within seconds, I lost my job, lost the girl and lost my self respect. And that's how I ended up living in a chicken coop."

"By now, desperation was a familiar companion. It sets deep into the being of every alcoholic. It's the moment when you know you can't handle the next step down. When I finally hit the moment of total desperation, I was scared. Because this demon had me in its grip and I didn't know how to get out. The power of my intellect and self will didn't work against it anymore."

"It's no mistake I stumbled into AA. I had many qualities which set me up to be a promising candidate. First, I am maladaptive. Basically, I don't fit anywhere. I'm selfish, self centered and emotionally immature. I can't seem to handle the fact that life's going to give me exactly what I give to life. I have a lingering sense of inadequacy in every area of my life. I'm not any good at relationships, but I can't stand my own company. Idleness is mighty boring, but getting a job is a bum rap. And most of all I have a body that can't drink and a brain that says I have to."

"At that moment, I was at the crossroads. Either get help or die an alcoholic death. And I was no stranger to the ugliness of dying drunk. I already witnessed my relatives dying in gutters, drinking themselves to death. Back home on the rez, we had more funerals than weddings. In most of the funerals, alcohol played a part."

"And there I was, dying in a chicken coop in National City. But then I remembered something. Something Jim said about AA. How he said I'd drink again. While this thought rattled around in my brain, I stumbled over to the corner gas station. There was a phone booth. You don't see those much anymore. But that day, it was there. I dialed zero and got an operator. I asked her to connect me to Alcoholics Anonymous."

"I remember every detail of that day. I can still see where the sun was in the sky, the smell of the wind. I even remember the red Chevy filling up at the station. The operator came back with the phone number and connected me. The phone rang three times. I hesitated and almost hung up. But then, there was a voice at the other end of the phone. 'Alcoholics Anonymous. This is Howard. How can I help you?'

"For the first time I was honest. I told Howard I wanted to stop drinking. And he seemed to care. I asked him how much it would cost. Because, you see, if it cost 50 cents, I couldn't go."

"Howard said just as I was a drunk, I had earned a seat. I had paid my price. But I was going to have to bring my hurt, my humiliation, an open mind and a trusting heart. Now I didn't know what that meant. But he told me AA had no dues or fees. Just come as I am. Then he asked me if I needed a ride. Because he could send someone to fetch me. I told him no. I'd make it there. Truth be told, I didn't want anyone to see me, the way I looked. But he gave me the address of a meeting hall in town."

"Now when I got to the meeting hall, I was alone. I don't recommend anyone go to their first meeting alone. But that's how it happened for me. I stood in front of those double doors, walking back and forth for what seemed to be an eternity. Then the fear of what was inside those doors was less terrifying than what I knew to be outside and I opened them up. I will never forget what I saw."

"Inside the door was this ruddy little Indian, probably from the southern tribes. He had a big smile on his face and his hand out. "HI! I'M JIM!!" he said and he welcomed me in, no questions asked. I was accepted just as I was. Jim showed me where to get a cup of coffee and they had a tray full of donuts."

"Now, I must tell you, before the meeting, I scraped

together every last penny and bought two shots of tequila. I needed liquid courage to open those doors. I don't recommend anyone do it that way, but that's the way it happened for me. Then at the end of the meeting, they said "KEEP COMING BACK!!"

"Week after week, month after month, I sat in that meeting with those crummy people in that crummy little building and their crummy chairs. I listened to their stories and one day it struck me. They were laughing. And they had peace. And no matter how terrible their life was, they didn't drink."

"After a while, they started to talk to me. They told me how they stayed sober. And if I wanted what they had, I had to do what they did. Which was work the 12 Steps and adopt a set of spiritual principles so I could live. If I was going to stay sober, I had to be willing to give up drinking. Now I had quit drinking before, but I never surrendered. And in order to recover, I had to change."

"Change what?" I asked them. And they said, 'beats the hell out of us.' They didn't give me the answers. They said I'd have to change enough in order to recover from alcoholism. I had to admit nothing I'd tried worked for long. On my own power, I might get a day, a week, even a year. But I went back to the bottle every time. I had to become willing to change everything in order to recover. That was the price of recovery. If I wanted to live happy, I had to be willing to live a life based on spiritual principles. I had to get spiritual enough, because anything less and I could die."

Hal grabbed the AA Big Book which was sitting on the table and held it up. "They told me, READ THE BOOK, WORK THE STEPS AND CARRY THE MESSAGE! It sounded simple enough. Everything I had to do was outlined in the first 164 pages. Those weren't unreasonable demands to walk with the Spirit of Sobriety and be filled with peace."

"See the spirits in the tequila bottle couldn't give me peace. But, working the 12 Steps and being of service to others did. When I had true inner peace, it didn't matter to me what I had or didn't have. But without peace, all my chattel was meaningless."

"Now, I was un-drunk about nine months when I met Arlene. I like the word un-drunk, because even though I hadn't drank in 9 months, nothing inside me had changed. And I need to tell you this, before I go on with my story. I wasn't drinking, but something inside me was missing. I was unfulfilled. I knew I didn't want to go back to my old life with the chicken coop and the feathers. But I was still looking outside myself to find something to make me happy. Trouble was, even when I got what I wanted, I didn't have inner happiness."

"Then came Arlene and she took my breath away like nothing else. I got lost in her smile, the smell of her hair, her sweet perfume. And those were only a few of her many fine qualities. She was also 5 years sober, her car was running and she had a good job. Her apartment was clean and she could cook. Oh, nothing soothed my wounded beat up soul, like the smell of her cooking and her smile. A few months later, we were married. We were very active in AA. Boy, we did everything they told us to do. But there came a day, that fateful day, when the spirits in the bottle came calling to collect their due. And I was vulnerable because I was un-drunk and nothing inside me had changed."

"Back then, I was pretty cocky. I was sure me and Arlene had this alcohol problem licked. From my perspective it was pretty well snuffed out. But I failed to fulfill the requirements to maintain my sobriety. And the spirit of tequila called to me again. This time, I took Arlene with me."

"See, I got too busy with work to go to meetings, too busy with life to be of service to my fellows. I had 5 years without booze, but I forgot what puke tasted like. I forgot about the feathers in the chicken coop. I forgot about Hazel and Buck. I forgot about jail and the insanity of the drink."

"But most of all, I failed to fulfill the requirements to

maintain my sobriety. I quit going to meetings. I quit being of service and I stopped working with other alcoholics. Nothing inside me had changed, because I hadn't thoroughly worked the Steps. I was bedeviled with resentments and ran amok with character defects. I never made right the wrongs I had done to others. And I only prayed when I needed something. Nothing inside me had changed. The worst of it was, it was hard to trust in a God who'd let me down my whole life."

"Oh I talked a good game. But in my laziness and arrogance, I convinced myself, that I was different from the crazies in AA, who needed to work the program. Without doing the work, I couldn't fight off my greatest enemy, myself. So I drank again. And this time I brought my lovely Arlene with me. Within a year, our drinking took us to new lows. She started mixing sleeping pills with booze. Then one chilly December morning Arlene didn't wake up. She just lay there, not breathing and cold. It was a chilly December morning and she just lay there not breathing and cold."

"You see, nothing inside me had changed. It wasn't the program that failed. It was me. So many times, I hear people say, oh the program doesn't work for me. But it was me who failed to meet the requirements necessary to maintain my sobriety. I failed to do the Steps. I gave lip service to the program when it required elbow grease. And I lost Arlene to booze and sleeping pills. I finally reached the end of the line. This time, I would suffer it out. I drank again and walked with the demons because I failed. Wine and pills kills drunks. She drank again and died. And I was alone."

Hal's lip quivered and he fought back the tears of that awful memory. You could hear a pin drop in the room. Looking into the eyes of the people, Hal sensed they all knew the feeling of being alone. It clawed at the very fabric of their being. He cleared his voice and took a drink of water.

"Now it took a couple years before I came crawling back into the Healing Halls of Alcoholics Anonymous. I spent two years walking with the demons. I wandered the lonely path, which only an alcoholic knows. Then one morning, I passed out under the pier. The ocean waves just a few feet away. Who knows where I'd been the night before. Sometimes I'd black out for days. But I came to under the pier and I heard their voices. Someone was reading 'How It Works' and there was a table with coffee and goodies on it. Well, my stomach rumbled and I got brave enough to sneak over to the table and get something to eat."

"As I'm stuffing my pockets with cookies, this old black man named Lenny comes up to me. He looks me dead in the eye and says, "You never have to feel this way again." And then he winked at me. I mumbled something to him. But I was quick to grab my goodies and leave."

"Once again the seed was planted and the Spirit of Sobriety started singing in my ear. It called to me on the wind. This time when I walked back into those rooms, I was ready to change everything to stay there. I gave it all I had, and then a little bit more. I was finally willing to bring my hurt, my humiliation, an open mind and a trusting heart."

"Well, old Lenny became my friend and mentor in AA. We had things in common. We both knew prejudice and hate because of the color of our skin. We understood being forced to assimilate into a world we knew nothing about. We weren't like the dominant culture. Our different tribes, his people and mine, knew the ravages of alcohol. We knew what the injustices of the white man could do. But through our common pitiful and incomprehensible demoralization, we could heal. We paid the price and we could heal. In the fellowship of AA, I found the acceptance I had craved my whole life."

"This time, when those old fossils of AA, with their bald heads and fake teeth, snarled at me to sit down, shut up and listen, to take the cotton out of my ears and shove it in my mouth, I humbly took direction. They told me DON'T DRINK, NO MATTER WHAT! Even if my ass was falling off, I could put it in a bag and bring it to a meeting."

"This time, I had no reservations. When I bowed to

Creator, I turned my will and my life over to His care. I worked the Steps and worked with others. I felt a powerful love weave itself into the blanket of my sobriety."

"When a drunk stands alone in the freezing cold, with his candle facing the howling winds, he is lost and powerless. But once he surrenders to the dictates of a Higher Power, a band of heavenly Angels comes to set him free. You see, ladies and gentlemen, I only had two choices, if I was to live. Either I found Creator and did His Work. Or I'd take up with those demons in the bottle and they would kill me. To live by spiritual principles or die an alcoholic death were the only two choices I had left."

"The Big Book tells me to trust God and clean house. The price of recovery is trust and willingness. The Steps demand certain things of a man, such as conduct of a decent human being. You have to be exactly who you claim to be or you can't stay. My life's not perfect. I am an orphan. I have no parents, no wife and no babies."

"About that time, I'm working my Steps with Lenny. He suggested I stay away from women my first year sober. I was willing to go to any lengths after Arlene died. In my gut, I had a guilt that burned deep in my soul. I never thought anything would take that away. There wasn't enough booze to drown out the guilt I carried for bringing those mean-spirited drugs and firewater back into our lives."

"Now, the 12 Steps and ceremony were my saving grace. We had a men's AA group, where I met Wyatt. He's a white boy and I'm a full blood. But Wyatt took me to my first Inipi, my first Native ceremony. What's more ironic is, Wyatt is a Sun Dancer. He honored the ways of my people by learning the sacred songs and respecting our traditions. Creator brought me back to our traditional healing ways through a white man. It wasn't long after when I became a fire keeper. And after four years of keeping fire, I sun danced myself."

"Much of my recovery I owe to a medicine man. Most of what he said could come straight out of the Big Book. But he put it in a way I understood. He talked about becoming a hollow bone. For Creator and the Higher Powers to work through us, we had clear away the wreckage from our past. Mainly our doubts, fears, reluctance and resentments. And most important, I had to make right the wrongs I committed against others. It wasn't enough to say I was sorry. I had to walk my talk and show people my change of heart."

"This happens naturally when I think good thoughts and do estimable acts. When I'm clean like a hollow bone, Creator fills me with indestructible faith, untold possibilities and the power which comes from living in spirit."

"Our medicine man was humble with a pure heart. He showed me how to have the right relationship with Creator. When he performed a healing, the power of Creator worked through him. Since he was a hollow bone, the power flowed through him. He took no credit for his healing. For if he did, the power would dry up and be no more. All I had to do was live the way he lived and do what he had did and the power of Creator would work through me as well. He'd lived on the reservation his whole life, but never drank alcohol. I was blessed to sit with such a powerful man."

"My Sun Dance Chief, Ohiya told me we are all pipe carriers, because we are children of Creator. But few choose to heed the calling. A pipe carrier is a person who walks with the power of Creator. When I worked Steps four through nine, I learned to be kind instead of jealous. When I went on my first vision quest, I learned to be quiet. I sat for four days up on the hill, fasting and praying without food or water. What I learned from that experience was how to live in truth and sacrifice. There was a moment, up there on the hill, when I felt at one with all life. I was one drop of water in the great ocean of Life."

"Gaining wisdom is a lonely practice, because it takes solitude to get to know yourself. Up on the hill, I could see for the first time that as I gave to others, I gave to myself. Because, you see, we are all ONE. If I hated others, I hated myself. I didn't escape how I felt about someone else, because that feeling was in me first. If I felt hatred for somebody else, I really felt hatred for Creator, because we are all His Children."

"The other thing that I learned is I don't own anything but my name. When I leave this blessed Mother Earth, I don't take my body with me. As an ex-drunk, I chose to live that way and follow the dictates of a Higher Power. Because anything less is to die."

"There is a law which is greater than any man-made laws. I learned that law through working the Twelve Steps and ceremony. It's Creator's Law of Love. When I live by this law, ladies and gentlemen, my life is in harmony with all life."

"On page 63 of the Big Book, it says that we had a new employer, being all powerful, He provided what we needed, IF we kept close to Him and performed His Work well. And that word 'if' is a big word, ladies and gentlemen because my whole life hinges on it. You see, this is a partnership and I have to do my part. Between AA and ceremony, I have a good life."

"You see, I got lucky. I found out I'm not so tough. The tough guys go out there and die drunk. I also found out it's not about winning, but about playing it right. Drunkenness is not a moral issue, but sobriety is. So what is moral, you ask yourself. Moral is so you feel good about yourself. That you can walk down the street without looking over your shoulder. That if you had but a short time to live, you wouldn't change anything."

"Tonight I am wearing shoes that ain't been puked on or pants that ain't been peed in. I can still remember the taste of vomit. I can say that I am exactly who I say I am. I am a child of a living Creator and a sober member of Alcoholics Anonymous. When I came to AA, I was lost and dying in a chicken coop. Those fine people gave me all they had. They loved me until I could love myself. Now, I give away all I have. The same way it was given to me. I thank you for listening to me and I will now open the meeting to all who care to share. Who would like to go first?"

As people in the meeting gave Hal a round of applause, Max stood up and placed both hands on his cane as he looked around the room.

"My name is Max and I have a disease called alcoholism."

"HI MAX!" said the people in the room.

"It feels good that people know my name," said Max. "Before I got sober, people called me all kinds of bad names. I like the sound of my name now. Sometimes my wife even calls me honey. She didn't call me that for many years. I didn't deserve being called nice things, because I wasn't a good man. All I knew was the bottle. And the bottle took me to places, I'd never want to go. But I went, because I was a slave to the bottle. I did whatever it wanted me to do."

"Now, when you're an old booze-hound like me, you're always looking for your own kind. Trouble is, my kind lived in the shadows. My heartache never went away. Everyday was filled with bad news. So I drank hoping it would go away. But things only got worse. The more I drank, the worse things got."

"One day it got so bad, I pulled my old shot gun out, loaded it full of ammo and put it in my mouth. It was pretty late and nobody was around. Seems my darkest hours were always late at night. Years ago, I was court ordered to go to AA. But I never took it serious. I showed up late and got my court card signed. But I never stuck around. It wasn't for me. But there I was, drunk with a gun in my mouth." Max paused for a moment, a small tear formed in the corner of his eye.

"Then, out of the blue, the phone rang. I sat there, staring at it. It rang and rang and rang. Then it stopped ringing. But then it started ringing again. I sat there, dumbstruck, thinking who in the hell would call me now? It stopped ringing again. But this time, when it started ringing again, I put the gun down. Then I answered it. "HELLO!" I said. This voice says "Max, it's me. What are you doing?" I was too drunk to lie about it, so I told the voice on the other end of the phone, "Well, I was just sitting here with my shot gun in my mouth, thinking about pulling the trigger." Then the voice said "I'll be right over."

"I didn't even know who the guy was. But in 5 minutes, there were three guys pounding on my door. I'd met them at an AA meeting a while back. I had forgotten all about them. But they hadn't forgotten about me. Well, they took my sorry ass and threw it in the back of the truck. Two of the guys were on each side of me so I wouldn't jump out. I still remember the cool wind on my face."

"Well, the voice on the other end of the phone was William Broken Arrow. And for the next two years he shared his wisdom with me and how he lived sober come what may. It took me about a year to ask him why he called me that night. He told me he didn't really know why, he just dialed my number. HE JUST DIALED MY NUMBER!"

"That boggled my mind. When William died, we had an AA memorial for him. So many people showed up. He touched many lives. Some of them were sober, some not. But William walked with the Spirit of Sobriety, through the best and worst times."

"William lost a daughter to this disease. One night, she drank too much and didn't wake up. Not long after she died, her son was lying on the couch. He was just ten years old, missing his mom. All of sudden, her spirit is standing in front of the frig. That boy saw his mom's spirit open the refrigerator door. Then, she looked his way and said "Hey, where's the bologna?" He ran in to tell his grandma and they fixed his mom a spirit plate with all her favorite foods. That afternoon, he took the plate outside and prayed with it for two hours. He brought his mom a bologna sandwich in the spirit world," Max exclaimed.

"I watched how William walked through heartache. It wasn't always pretty, but he did it sober. Now, my life ain't perfect. But whatever I face, Great Spirit and the Spirit of

Sobriety walk beside me. I am grateful for that. I never had to put a shot gun in my mouth again. That's enough out of me. Thank you for listening."

Max sat down, while the room applauded.

"Whose next?" asked Hal.

Lynn stood up. Tess sat right next to her. "My name is Lynn. Ben is my father, our father. This is my sister Tess. Two nights ago, my son's were killed by a drunk driver, a white woman who lives down the River Road. She ran my boys down. One of them flew off into the corn field and she dragged the other one under her car. They both died right there. They were only in their 20's." Lynn's eyes filled with tears, but she held her chin strong, unwilling to give in.

"What are we going to do? We buried our nephew Johnny barely a month ago. He drank himself to death. What are we going to do?" Tears were rolling down her face. But she stood there. Her strength and will demanded an answer. The room grew painfully silent, but Lynn didn't sit down.

Feeling put on the spot, Hal looked at the Big Book. There must be an answer in there somewhere. "I don't know why your sons were called home to Creator. I only know what I was taught." Hal paused as he felt the anticipation of the whole room.

"There is a solution," he said feeling uncomfortable in the light of such great sorrow. "I never liked it when I heard it, but it's the only thing that ever worked for me. Whenever I confronted Lenny with a big problem, he'd tell me to pray about it, whatever it was."

"PRAY ABOUT IT!!!" Lynn's voice grew shrill. "YOU WANT ME TO PRAY ABOUT IT!!! What are we..." the words choked out between gasps. "What are we doing here, in this life? Who is this Creator... you pray to... who took away my sons? Whoever He is, I think He's forgotten about us!!!" Tess stood up and put her arm around her sister as Lynn broke into uncontrolled sobs.

An uncomfortable stillness enveloped the room as Hal waited for someone to speak. But no one stirred. After a few moments, Lynn's sobs began to quiet down. The long suffering were prone to silence. As the clock ticked off seconds on the wall, Hal felt compelled to talk.

"A couple years ago, just before Christmas, my Sun dance Chief, Ohiya, was murdered in the county jail, up there in North Dakota. When he got off the train in the middle of the night, three cops were waiting for him. They arrested him because the medicine he carried was not legal in North Dakota. Two hours after they arrested him, Ohiya was dead. The sheriff told his woman the next morning that Ohiya had hung himself with a sheet. But, she didn't believe him."

"Now anyone who knew Ohiya, knew he'd never take his own life. Ohiya was a Sun Dance Chief. He sun danced more than 35 years. He had seven children and was a decorated veteran. He was no stranger to pain."

"You can just imagine the grief. Ohiya knew people all over the world. After his death, quite a few people sought council from channelers, readers and Yuwipi men all over the country. We needed to know what happened to him from those gifted with eyes to see."

"Now, this is where it all gets a little sticky. See, it didn't matter if the reading was done in Montana, Idaho, California, Florida or North Dakota. EVERY READING CAME BACK THE SAME!!! Not only did Ohiya not take his own life. Every reading said two men killed him in the county jail and made it look like suicide."

"Now, Ohiya's woman went to a sweat lodge after he died and told his story. While listening to her words, the sweat leader heard her pain. After she finished talking, the leader didn't speak for a long time. When he finally spoke, he told her to pray for the healing of the men who did this to her man. Because, now listen to this. Healing could only happen if the truth came out."

"Well, Ohiya's woman reacted just like you. She didn't want to pray for the bastards who took her man's life. But she did it anyway. Over and over she prayed for the purification of that hardhearted town and its people. She told Creator to flood those people with avalanches of Light. That way, the evil would be annihilated and the truth could be revealed. In ceremony after ceremony, she prayed for purification of those involved in Ohiya's death."

"Now the other thing you need to know about Ohiya is, he was Heyoka. He worked directly with the Thunder Beings. So his medicine was in every drop of rain and every snow flake. The first year after Ohiya died, he was honored in ceremonies all over the country. His picture stood in an empty chair at the west gate at Sun Dances from New York to Oregon."

"Now Ohiya's woman is like a pit bull, once she gets her jaw set on something. She was determined to find JUSTICE for Ohiya through the white man's courts and attorneys. But all those roads seemed blocked. One attorney told her, they didn't have police brutality in North Dakota because there weren't enough police."

"In a moment of madness, she wrote to the President of the United States and told him how Ohiya was murdered in the county jail. She left no stone unturned. More people wrote the White House demanding justice. But, the White House closed their eyes."

"A year after Ohiya died, the North was hit with a brutal winter. It was one of the worst winters the North had ever seen. Temperatures in North Dakota dropped to minus 53 degrees. The Midwest was battered by blizzard after blizzard. The ice in men's hearts mirrored the cold winter days."

"After working for over a year, Ohiya's woman didn't find anyone to help. She almost lost hope. Then, one evening in late spring, the news came. The town where Ohiya was murdered was under 15 feet of water. And it was still rising."

"Turns out, that spring, it rained and rained and rained.

Now, couple that with the melting Canadian snow, the raging rivers in North Dakota flooded their banks. I'm sure more than one person thought about old Noah and building an Ark that day," Hal paused as he remembered seeing the flood on television.

"But, try as they might, there weren't enough sand bags to hold the waters back. The levee's broke and that raging water washed out the bridges. More than 4000 houses were under water. On the television, all you could see were their roof tops. Thousands of people were evacuated. Them big cowboy, half-ton trucks were swept down river. And the waters kept coming. Mother Earth unleashed her fury and nothing could hold the waters back. The National Guard was called to rescue people. But understand this now. There were greater Powers at work here. Great Spirit and the Thunder Beings had their way and purified that North Dakota town."

Hal paused for a moment and looked directly at Lynn. "Now do you understand the power of prayer?" Meeting Hal's eyes, Lynn nodded yes.

"All righty then, who's next?" Hal asked the room.

Another brave soul stood up. Draped in a baggy sweatshirt, she was a big girl, almost 300 pounds. The deep creases in her forehead revealed her anger. Her long dark hair was piled in a bun.

"My name is Jeannie. I drink a lot," she started. Her hands were shoved down in her pockets while her eyes stared down at the floor. "It helps me forget the bad things that happened to me when I was a kid."

"I liked your story," she said as she glanced up and met Hal's eyes. "My heart hurts all the time too. It started when I was little. I watched my parents get drunk every night. That bottle was more important to them than us kids. When I was growing up, I was invisible. Bad things happened to me and there were lots of fights in my family. It was hard to sleep with all the screaming and yelling."

91

There was an edge in her voice. Hal sensed that if she ever blew up, she'd be a volcano.

"When I was ten, I went to live with my grandma because my mom was always intoxicated. She worked in a bar and drove home drunk all the time. In junior high, I started to hurt myself. I took a razor blade and cut my arms. I couldn't feel anything, except the pain when the razor cut my arm. One night, it got bad and I cut myself almost to the bone. I had to go to the hospital to get stitches. They wanted me to see a therapist, but his office was far away and I didn't have a way to get there."

"All I remember was the night the bad things started. My mom couldn't get a sitter. So, my parents took me and my little sister over to their friend's house, so we wouldn't be alone. Their son, Jason was supposed to watch us while our parents were drinking in the kitchen. He was about 15 and I was 7, my little sister was 3. We were playing in his room, making paper boxes when Jason asks me, "Do you want to do something that mommies and daddies do?" I said yes. I followed him into his parent's bathroom. That's where he raped me. He told me not to tell anyone, because it was our secret. I was 7 years old and it changed me forever. I never felt good about myself after that. I had no one to talk to. No one understood. I know if I told my dad, he'd kill Jason. So I kept quiet. For a long time, I felt guilty because I said yes to him. But I didn't know what he was going to do. I was only 7 years old. How could I know what was going to happen?"

"After that, I started drinking. I was about 8 or 9 years old. I finished all the drinks my parents left sitting around. It made the hurt go away for a while. When I got older, I'd see Jason at parties. His smile made me sick to my stomach. I knew what he was thinking. When I saw him in town, I'd walk the other way. I hated him for what he did to me. I was never a little girl after that. I could never be a child again. The drinking helps me forget, but only for a little while. The heartache never goes away." Jeannie sat down.

Kyle heart burned with fury as he listened to Jeanie share. Like her, he hadn't taken a sober breath most of his life. His father, Jed, sat next to him. Jed was barely sober two months now. He brought Kyle to AA meetings, hoping the Old Ones might share some wisdom.

With his dark hair cropped short, Kyle wore a baggy t-shirt and khaki colored baggy pants which hung half way down his butt. His navy blue boxer shorts were hard to miss. Staring at the floor, Kyle glanced at Jeannie when she talked about of Jason. When she finished, something compelled him stand up.

"My name is Kyle. My dad brought me here. He's got two months sober. He thinks if I come here, I'll catch what he's got. Like sobriety is contagious," Kyle chuckled nervously. "The reason I stood up, was because I know that dude Jason. He used to hang out with my older brothers. One day Jason came over when my brothers were gone. I was alone in my room. No one was home. Jason did the same thing to me, that he did to Jeannie. I never told anyone. He said it was our secret."

"But he drown in the Missouri last year and I don't want to carry his secret anymore. I was 8 when he got me drunk. He said we were going to play a game, a secret game. He took me to a trailer and showed me these pictures of naked girls. I didn't know what he was going to do, but he got me drunk. And then he DID IT." Kyle looked down at the floor. His fists were clenched and his jaw was set tight. Anger masked the hurt down in his heart.

"I don't want to carry that secret anymore. I have the pain you talked about which doesn't go away. After Jason hurt me, I never fit in anywhere. I tried committing suicide last year. But I couldn't do that to my mom. I didn't want her to come to my grave site and cry over her son. She already cried too much over my dad. I didn't want to break her heart."

Facing Jeannie, Kyle addressed her directly. "That was brave, Jeannie to stand up and say what you did. I never would have told anyone if you didn't stand up. I can't believe I'm saying it now, but I'm still buzzed from the whiskey I drank. I admit it, I drink every day. Nothing stops me. I get up and I drink. It's the only thing that works. Nobody talks about this sick shit! Nobody talks about little kids getting molested and raped by drunken assholes! NOBODY! There are times I wished I drowned in that river, so I wouldn't feel this way anymore. So I couldn't remember what Jason did to me. At night, when I try to sleep, I still see his face, his sick, twisted smile. Oh sure, I try to drown out the pain, but it doesn't go away. IT DOESN'T GO AWAY!" Hesitating for a moment, Kyle thought he had something else to say. But then he sat down.

Stirred by the honest sharing, Ben stood up. "Hi my name is Ben. I am a grateful sober member of AA. This sharing moved me. It's from the heart. It takes brave people to share from the heart; to open themselves up and reveal their pain. The Spirit of Sobriety has been missing from our people for centuries now. It's not our way to crush grapes and make wine. We didn't grow grain to make whiskey and we didn't let our berries sour so they'd ferment. Alcohol isn't our medicine. But it's destroyed the soul of our people for hundreds of years."

"I was told that I can't save anybody. All I can do is be an example of sobriety. I know the shame and heartache that we talked about tonight. From what I know, every alcoholic does. No one comes through these doors for the heck of it. We come to AA when we're bottomed out. The pain makes us willing to do what it takes to recover. When I worked the 12 Steps, my spirit was brought back to life and made whole. Today, I walk a free man. I'm not a slave to the spirits in a whiskey bottle. What happened for me, can happen for anyone who does this work."

"As of late, I lost 3 grandchildren, countless relatives and some close friends to the spirits in the bottle. The grief would break me in half, if I knew there wasn't a solution. But, there is a solution. And it is here, in these rooms and in this book. There is nothing that can't be healed, when it is laid at Creator's feet. And this is where we bring our hurt, our wounded soul and allow the Great Mystery to heal our tender hearts and mend our spirits."

"Some may not agree with me. Probably because they're still dancing with the firewater spirits and are seduced by its effect. I believe the only thing that will save our people is to give the white man back his medicine. Give him back his alcohol. Give him back the jealousy and rage which live inside the demons in the bottle. Give him back the disease, the anger and the hopelessness of a drunken way of life. Because it was never our way, until the white man arrived."

"Whoever gave our people guns and whiskey knew it wouldn't take long before we destroyed ourselves. Guns and whiskey are a deadly mix."

"How can anyone walk in the Sunlight of the Spirit when they're being strangled by the dark night of the soul? Yet the light of Creator is always there. He is only as far away as our next breath. He exists in every heartbeat of Creation. But, we must be willing to meet Him and change our ways, so we can heal."

"I know the demon in the bottle well. He spoke to me and call my name. Thanks to Hal, Creator and the 12 Steps, I don't live that way anymore. Hal was desperate to stay sober when he found me in the Army hospital. The doctors told me I was a hopeless alcoholic. He brought me to my first AA meeting and then to ceremony. Now I have peace. I am grateful to Creator and AA for my sobriety today." Ben sat down next to Hal.

That night twenty five people shared their tragic heartfelt stories. The meeting which usually lasted only an hour tops, went late into the evening. Husbands came to find their wives and grabbed a chair. They stayed to hear the music of sobriety and the hope of a new day. The Spirit of Sobriety wove its loving blanket around each one. It enveloped them in the warmth of a shared faith. A God of Evidence allowed men to walk sober, who once were drunk and hopeless.

When the last chair was put away, Ben walked around

and blew out all the candles. He put his Sacreds in his suitcase. The women cleaned up the food and wiped down the counters. A small group of people were still outside, when Ben locked the door. Hal was over by his truck talking to Kyle and his dad. There was something familiar which they all understood. It was the language of the heart.

Ben walked over to Hal's truck. "Hey, you still staying over?"

"Yeah sure, let me finish up here," Hal said.

"Hey, can we get together tomorrow?" asked Kyle. "If you're still here."

"Kyle, like I said, I'm an orphan. Nobody's waiting for me back home, so I am not in any hurry. If you want to talk some more, I'll be at Ben's in the morning."

When Kyle's dad, Jed, heard this, he wrapped his arm around Kyle's shoulders. That was the best news he'd heard in a long time.

"Why don't you come over and we'll have some coffee," said Ben putting his suitcase in the back of Hal's truck. "How about 9:30 or 10 in the morning?"

"That's pretty early for this boy," laughed Jed.

"Yeah, I'll be there," said Kyle. "Good night Hal. Thanks Ben. It was a good meeting."

"We'll see you in the morning," said Hal.

Looking forward to a good nights sleep, Ben got in the truck. It'd been a long day. Hal got behind the wheel. "Man that was one of the longest meetings I've ever been in. Out West, meetings run an hour tops. If you talk longer than 3 minutes, those old buzzards got a timer on you! They'll tell you when to quit talking."

Ben sighed. "I don't know anything about that. Sometimes people got to puke the junk out of their soul. How do you tell someone when to stop puking? It was rough when my Lynn got up. I know she came tonight looking for something."

"Hope she found it," said Hal starting the truck. "I'm sorry to hear about your grandsons. What's going on? Why are you burying so many of your young ones?"

"Go right out of the parking lot. And turn left on River Road. I'm just down by Kelly's Tavern," Ben sighed as he gave Hal directions. "I don't know what to make of our young ones. Except they drink and die here. Some will stumble around for a while. But unless some miracle happens, they die drunk. Life expectancy for a man on the rez is about 40 years old, unless you get sober or move away to the city. You haven't lived on the rez in a long time, have you?"

"Naw, I'm a nomad," said Hal thinking about his life. "I been doing rodeo work for a while. I lived out in California, but it got pretty expensive to live there. After Arlene died, well, I never did get to settling down."

"I know what you mean. I miss Elsie, the sound of her voice and her cooking. Seems like I eat at Kelly's more than anywhere else. You're not still bustin' broncs are you?"

"No, I retired from that a while ago. Broke too many bones. Most of the time, I get dressed up like a fool and go save the bull riders from getting gored to death after they fall off. Rodeo Clown, that's my official title. But I don't even do much of that anymore."

"So where's home for you?"

"Well, this old truck takes me from one place to another, so I guess this is it."

"Don't you get a little lonesome sometimes?"

"Alone doesn't mean lonely, Ben. When I've got a sky full of stars and a cool breeze comes up, I drink my cowboy coffee and breath it all in. I never bought in to the American Dream. It seems like more of a prison than a dream. All those people scrambling to pay their mortgage. They're constantly waging war between buying groceries, filling their gas tank and saving money for college. The loneliest women I ever met were in California. Sure, they lived in fancy homes. But, their husbands were chasing after the mighty dollar. What a waste of life chasing after a piece of paper, when this Great Mother provides everything we need. I never saw that dream for myself after Arlene died."

"I'm right over there," said Ben. "Down the road from Kelly's." Hal pulled his truck up in front of the small cabin. "On a quiet night, you can hear the river flowing, if I got the window open." Ben chuckled. It was always quiet out on the prairie. The nearest city was about an hour away.

"Well Ben, this is the first night I've spent under a roof in a while. Thanks for the hospitality."

"Don't mention it," said Ben. "You saved my life a long time I ago. It's the least I could do."

"That was one desperate drunk trying to help another, Ben. That's what we do. People like us trusting our lives into the hands of people like us. I didn't come up with the idea. The men in my home group took being of service very seriously. If I didn't carry the message, someone might die. That someone might be me, if I wasn't careful. I was grateful that you were willing to listened to me, if you want to know the truth," said Hal as he pulled the truck up in front of the house. It was still a warm night out on the prairie. Opening the front door of the cabin, Ben turned on the light. Everything was just like he left it. Living alone took some getting used to.

"That's the pull out couch over there. See if that's okay," said Ben.

Hal went over and pulled the couch apart and laid down on it. It sagged in the middle, since the springs were worn out. "Do you mind if I put the mattress over here on the floor? With my back, I need to sleep on a hard surface."

"Sure, suit yourself," said Ben glad for the company. "I'll get you some sheets. Do you need a pillow?"

"I got my stuff out in the truck. I'll get it in a minute," said Hal dragging the mattress in the corner. He put the couch back together, so there'd be a place to sit.

As the two men settled in, the prairie was peaceful. The sounds of barking dogs and the river flowing came though the open window. After all the bustle and commotion of a full day, sleep came easy.

CHAPTER THREE: GHOST BUSTERS

"It's not tragic," said the owl to the moon
"For morning will be here soon
And the sun will guide us through the day
So we will readily find our way
So let us enjoy the night
And dance in the twilight
For morning will be here soon"
Said the owl to the moon

A deep mist blanketed the Missouri River while a sliver moon hung low in the western sky. Jason waited for Kyle on the river bank, sitting on a fallen tree facing the water. He heard Kyle heavy foot steps coming up behind him. As Kyle approached, Jason turned around.

"I've been waiting for you," Jason said.

"WHAT THE FUCK ARE YOU DOING HERE!? What do you want from me? Didn't you FUCK ME UP ENOUGH?" hollered Kyle as he lashed out in anger.

"I heard what you said about me in the AA meeting. I know I hurt you pretty bad. You were just a kid. But you got to understand. It wasn't really my fault..." Jason stammered.

"What do you mean it wasn't your fault? I was a little kid. YOU GOT ME DRUNK AND RAPED ME!!! WHO'S FAULT COULD IT BE!!!?" Kyle screamed.

With his heart pounding through his chest, Kyle woke up in a full sweat. Jason's face faded into the shadows. The dream hung heavy all around him.

"That mother fucker!!!" Kyle muttered under his breath as he looked at his clock. It was 3 am. His mouth was parched. He wanted a drink NOW! He opened his dresser draw to find a half empty bottle of bourbon. Cracking the bottle open, he stopped short. He remembered that he was meeting Hal and Ben for coffee in the morning. He didn't want to mess that up.

Getting out of bed, Kyle paced back and forth. He hated these nights. The nightmares gave him no peace. He woke up fully sweated with his heart racing. On the top of his dresser, was some sweet grass. His aunt brought it back from Sun Dance last year. She told him if he felt bad, he should burn some. The sweet grass got rid of dark spirits. With his lighter, he lit the sweet grass on fire and swept it through his room. It burned out fast, but the sweet smoke lingered.

Lying back down on his bed, Kyle's breathing calmed down. His mind whirled. He thought about Jason's comment. *"What did Jason mean, it wasn't his fault?"* Since his death, Jason's spirit had come into Kyle's dream time a few times.

Now Kyle was wide awake. He stared at the ceiling, unable to fall back asleep. His stomach growled. Careful not to wake his mom, he tiptoed into the kitchen to make some coffee. There was a box of pastry next to the toaster. Quietly, he took a couple slices and put them in the toaster.

Looking out the kitchen window, the faint moonlight cast eerie shadows across the prairie. Watching the Coffee Mate swirled around his mug, he couldn't stand being in his own skin. A desperate feeling pressed on his chest. He felt the four walls closing in on him.

His hands shook slightly as he sipped the coffee. Nothing eased his mind. The bourbon started calling his name. One good swig and it'd all disappear. Oblivion would drowned out the faces of the past.

Kyle felt jittery. He knew he needed to get out of the house before he gave in and had a drink. Moving fast, Kyle got dressed. He found his shoes and put them on. Quietly, he opened the front door. The brisk morning air hit his face. As he walked, the steam from his breath hung in the air, creating small clouds. He shoved his hands down into his pockets to keep them warm. Bright morning stars glittered through the predawn sky. The gravel crunched under his feet as he walked down the driveway. Nothing stirred, save a few crows cawing in a grove of trees.

A soft morning glow rose in the east as the first rays of light illuminated the sky. The brisk walk did him good. His mind started to clear. There were no fences separating one house from another. Without boundaries, the dogs roamed freely. Not all of them were friendly. They hung out in packs and chased cars down the street. Nothing went unnoticed as they barked in protective alarm.

This morning wasn't any different. One of the rez dogs came up to sniff Kyle and growled. As he walked to the outskirts of town, there was nothing but the rolling waves of buffalo grass. Small farms speckled the countryside as he walked passed the acres of cornfields. White farmers leased the farms from Indian families for mere pennies. On the sloping hillsides, were small herds of grazing cattle. Barking ranch dogs chased them all over the pasture.

Trudging the couple miles down the River Road, Kyle spotted Ben's rustic little cabin. Curling smoke rose from the old stove pipe on the roof. It was barely dawn when Kyle heard the truck door slam shut. Hal was walking towards the front door. The hair on Hal's neck stood up as he felt someone's eyes upon him. He stopped and turned to see who was coming down the street.

"Hey, what are you doing up this early?" Hal called out to Kyle.

"I had one of those dreams. It woke me up and I couldn't go back to sleep. I've been up since 3 am," Kyle said.

"OH the witching hour! Must have been a powerful

dream if it kept you awake," said Hal. He noticed Kyle's pants hanging way below his boxer shorts, with his rear end hanging out. "Can I ask you something?" asked Hal.

"Yeah, what?" said Kyle folding his arms across his chest.

"Where'd you learn to dress like that, with your butt hanging out?"

"I don't know. All the guys are doing it," Kyle shrugged.

"Well, not to tell you what to do. But when I was in the joint, the guys who dressed like that were advertising. You know, 'easy access'," said Hal as he put his thumb in his mouth. "That's how they let you know they're willing to take it up the ass. They wear their pants down low, like that, to let the other inmates know. If you catch my drift. I called them the Butt Boys."

"No way!" said Kyle shaking his head.

"Yeah way!" said Hal in a half serious tone. "So are you advertising? Because some jail bird might think you want it up the rear. I just thought I'd let you know."

"That's gross!" said Kyle as he adjusted his pants to cover his butt.

Hal chuckled a little and slapped Kyle on the back. "That's better. Now you look like one of the guys. Well, come on in. The coffee's brewing. Looks like it's going to be a fine day."

Kyle looked around. The dawn's early light edged over the hillsides. Kyle stepped up on the porch and admitted, "I'm never up this early."

Hearing voices on the porch, Ben opened the front door.

"Look who I found walking down the street," said Hal.

"Hey Ben," said Kyle. "I'm not sure, but I had a feeling you could help me."

"Kyle had himself a dream. It woke him up at 3 am," said Hal with his eyebrows raised.

"Well, come in," said Ben. "Tell me about your dream."

"I got to warn you, Kyle," said Hal laughing. "Ben makes coffee so strong, it'll put hair on your chest. And Indians don't have hair on their chest."

"Now, you listen here Hal! Elsie always made the coffee around here. It was her kitchen and she never told me how much to put in. So I've been winging it for a while. But, I got enough sugar to calm it down."

Getting a coffee mug out of the cabinet, Ben filled it up with coffee for Kyle. "You want some milk and sugar?"

"Naw, I'll just drink it black."

"Trust me son," chuckled Hal. "You'll want milk and sugar in this coffee!"

"Well, let me try it," said Kyle as Ben handed him the coffee mug.

Taking a sip, Kyle sputtered, shaking his head. "Whoa! Is this diesel fuel? It must be industrial strength! Where's the sugar?"

"Don't be surprised if you got chest hair by tomorrow," laughed Hal.

"OH! Shut up Hal! A man can't be blamed for things he was never taught." Ben went to the cupboard to get the sugar.

"Oh, I'm just funning with you."

"Kyle, get one of them chairs off the front porch and bring it in here," said Ben as he felt his spine tingle. It signaled to him that something was up.

While Kyle went out to get a chair, Ben found his sage. He lit the candle on the counter and they settled around the table.

"So tell me about your dream," said Ben gently.

"Well, I was walking through a deep fog down by the river, when I see Jason sitting on a fallen tree. He's looking at the river when I come up behind him. Then he turns around and says he'd been waiting for me. I get pissed off and tell him that he ruined my life. He starts to say it wasn't his fault, but I cut him of and tell him he's full of shit. Then, I woke up and saw him fade away. I couldn't shake it off, it felt so real." Kyle took a sip of his coffee. "Man this is some strong stuff."

Taking it all in, Ben sat silent for a moment. He wasn't sure if Kyle could hear what he was going to say. Jason's spirit was standing right next to Kyle. "Well Kyle, the coffee will keep you awake for what I got to tell you. That was a medicine dream. Which isn't a dream at all. When your body sleeps, your soul does work in the Spirit World. Jason's spirit is here right now. He's standing right next to you."

Hearing that, Kyle jumped out of the chair. "What does that asshole want from me?!!"

"Calm down, Kyle. He can't hurt you," said Ben gently. "We'll find out what he wants." Turning to Jason, Ben addressed him with his thought and asked him what he wanted.

"When Kyle was a little kid, I did bad things to him," admitted Jason remorsefully. "I need to make amends for the hurt I caused. I tried to tell him that it wasn't my fault. But Kyle wouldn't let me finish. My uncle Jeff molested me for years when I was little. It was sick. But, I didn't know any different. It wasn't until after I died that I realized all the hurt I caused. I heard Kyle talking about me at the AA meeting and Jeannie too."

At the mention of his name, Jeff's spirit appeared next to Jason. Ben knew Jeff since he was a little boy. At an early age, Jeff was removed from his family and put into a Catholic boarding school like so many Indian children were forced to do. Getting crowded, the little kitchen was consumed with heaviness. Ben realized there was a mountain of hurt here. It needed to be crumbled to ash, if Kyle was going to survive this life.

Feeling anxious, Kyle got up out his chair and started pacing. "What's Jason saying? Are you talking to him?"

Knowing what was before him, Ben took a deep breath. Spirit work was hard sometimes. "Jason wants to make amends to you. The reason he said it wasn't his fault was, because Jason's uncle molested him when he was a little boy. Jason didn't know any different," said Ben with a heavy sigh.

"THAT'S TOTAL BULLSHIT!!!" Kyle raged through the kitchen. "That asshole didn't know raping little boys was wrong!!! I can't believe that crap! I don't know if I am gay or straight."

"OH KYLE, don't worry! You're not Winkte. You weren't born with Twin Spirits. Twin spirits are when a female soul is born into a male body. The Winkte carries both male and female spirits in one body. That is not you. You're confused because Jason wounded your soul and he is here, trying to make it right," Ben said. "Jason's uncle, Jeff, is here too. He wants to tell me something."

Thunderstruck, Kyle stopped raging and leaned against the kitchen counter. Nothing prepared him for this.

Hovering in the corner, Jeff's spirit spoke to Ben. "I was almost 7 when the white woman came for me," he started to say. It was obvious to Ben that this was a painful moment for Jeff. "She took me to the Indian boarding school. I lived there until I was fourteen years old. They cut off my braids and put me in a uniform. If I spoke our language, they'd beat with a leather strap. But, the worst of it came at night, when they'd visit my room. They did things I didn't understand. They put their hands on me and made me touch them. Three priests molested me over the years I was there. When I was older, I touched other kids the way the priests had touched me. I learned this shame from the priests."

Listening to Jeff speak, Ben's rage lay just beneath the surface. He'd heard stories about the horrible treatment Indian children received in the boarding schools. But, now he was hearing it from a tortured soul who was stuck in the In-between. Jeff paused for a moment, but Ben urged him to go on.

"When I finally got home, I was a stranger to my family. I didn't understand our language anymore. I lost myself and my family. I was ashamed of them even though they were good to me. That school made me believe our sacred ways were bad and I was ashamed of our people. So, I hid behind the bottle and tried to hide what they did to me. When Jason was little, maybe four or five, I'd watch him. The sickness came over me. But, drinking made the sickness okay. It became okay to touch him in shameful ways when he was little. It's my fault that Kyle hurts so much. I brought this sickness to our people and infected my family with it."

While Jeff confessed all this to Ben, three priests appeared behind him. Their guilt and shame seeped through their black robes. Unexpectedly, these men confessed also to being molested as young boys. They carried the guilt and shame of these unholy acts which they committed against helpless children left in their care.

Having heard enough, Ben pushed his chair away from the table with a heavy sigh. He was silent for a long while. It was plain to him how deep this pain went. These souls were trapped in the In-between because of the terrible debt they owed.

"Kyle," Ben started after a while. "This hurt infecting your soul goes back many generations. Not only did Jason get wounded by his uncle. But his uncle was molested by priests at the Indian boarding school. And the priests...," Ben shook his head in disgust. "Were also molested as young boys. There is no telling how many generations were infected by this sickness. The Catholic Church is taking a beating for letting this happen to children all over the world."

Silently watching this whole thing, Hal finally dared to interrupt. "You mean there are 5 spirits in this room right now?"

"Yup. Sometimes more, if I go to Kelly's. When those spirits get wind I can see them and talk to them. Oh, they'll wake me up in the middle of the night, telling me their woes if I don't chase them out." said Ben somewhat exasperated. "Making peace between the living and the dead isn't easy."

"You mean there are spirits at Kelly's Tavern?" asked Kyle a little spooked. "I'm never going there again."

"OH what, Kyle. You think you're alone when you twist off the screw top from that cheap bottle of wine? You really think you're alone?" Ben had the patience of a saint when he was doing this work, but had no time for ignorance.

Not knowing what to say, Kyle stood there dumbstruck by what Ben was implying. "I don't know. What do you mean?"

"Oh Kyle, spirits are everywhere. When you walk across a battle field, the spirits of the soldiers who died there, are still walking around. They're stuck in the In-between, especially if someone killed them," said Ben as he got up to refill his coffee. "Soldiers are the most haunted and hunted people on the planet."

Confused, Kyle stammered, "I thought they all go to heaven."

"Oh, is that what they taught you in the Christian church your mom goes to?" Ben smiled understanding Kyle's confusion.

"Well... yeah," said Kyle. "If you believe in Jesus Christ, all you have to do is call him and he'll take you to heaven."

"Well, that's true, if you believe in Jesus Christ," said Ben in a gentle voice. "He'll come if you prayed to him. Don't get me wrong, there is a moment when a spirit can cross over. But many don't. Some spirits are afraid because they lead impure lives here on Mother Earth." Ben paused to take a sip of coffee.

"When I was in the Army hospital, there were lots of earthbound spirits. If you've got blood on your hands, chances are you'll be haunted by those you killed. And spirits who got murdered, like the warriors who died on the battle field, are relentless. Most of the time, they don't know they're dead and keep fighting, tooth and nail. They get pretty crafty too. During the day, they'll dog your every step. But the worst of it comes at night. Then, they'll come into your dream time the moment you close your eyes and thrash out the whole battle all over again."

"I feel bad for those poor soldiers coming home from the war," Ben went on. "They try to drink their way out of being hunted down by the spirit of their enemies. But it don't work. No amount of alcohol or drugs will drown out the voices of the dead. I bet you didn't know this, but most, long term mental illness is brought on by disgruntled spirits haunting the living daylights out of people?"

"No, I didn't know that. So what do you do?" asked Kyle beginning to understand.

"There's really only one way that I know of," said Ben, looking around the kitchen at all these lost souls. "There's an amends that needs to be made."

"What does that mean?" Kyle asked indignantly.

"Well, in that holy book those Christians carry around, Creator gave a command," Ben started. "When He said 'Thou shalt not kill,' He meant it. When we kill our brothers on the battle field, we are killing His children. That's not right. So, we got to make amends. Jason's sickness deadened your spirit. Your body wasn't dead, but it may as well be."

Kyle looked confused. The whole concept of amends beyond the grave didn't make sense to him. "What are you saying?"

"It's pretty simple really," said Ben. "See, the pain of his wrongdoing binds you together. Right now, there's a dark cord tying you to Jason. Sometimes these dark cords carry over

109

from lifetime to lifetime. To be free, you got to clean up the mess and cut the cord. The only way to do that is to forgive him of his wrongdoing and let him be on his way. It's the only way. Unless you let Jason clean up his mess and forgive him, you'll be tied to him through all eternity."

"That's crazy Ben. Are you telling me I got to let Jason off the hook, by forgiving him? Are you kidding me? These guys should rot in hell for what they did to children, to me, to Jeannie. I don't want to forgive them!" Kyle's anger escalated.

"Whoa, take a deep breath there, cowboy," said Hal. "This ain't our first rodeo. We've all had bad things happen to us. I haven't had an easy life, but Creator never promised me that. I had to make amends to the people I'd hurt or I couldn't live sober. Ben's right, you can't be free if you don't forgive. You'll carry the pain with you the rest of your life. Then, Jason will meet you in the afterlife and you'll duke it out there. This is a good opportunity for you, if you take it. It'll let you start a new life, free of Jason, free of all this shame."

A long silence fell over the kitchen as Kyle crossed his arms in front of his chest. The walls of distrust and fury blocked all communication.

Rays of sunlight burst over the rolling hillsides. The early morning light streamed into the kitchen window. Ben wasn't going to sit by and watch this spiritual standoff happen in his kitchen. He saw what he had to do and walked out the front door. Around the back of the house, was an old clothes line where Elsie used to hang laundry. Taking the rope off the poles, Ben rolled it up and carried it back in the house.

In a kitchen drawer, he found his buck knife. Then, he gathered a box of matches, the rope, some sage, his sacred pipe and buck knife and put them into a small bag. Finding his eagle fan, he put it in the small of his back, held in by his belt. Without a word, Hal and Kyle watched as Ben gathered these things.

"Come on, we're going for a walk," said Ben as he went

out the front door. Hal grabbed his hat and they headed towards the river. Focused on what he had to do, Ben didn't say a word. The small parade of spirits followed close behind. While the sun move across the Heavens, it cast off the shadows of the morning.

The earth was still moist from the morning dew when they got down to the Missouri. As it was in Kyle's dream, a heavy mist covered the river. Stopping at the river bank, Ben took out his buck knife and the rope and cut it into 5 equal pieces.

"Hal, I need 5 good logs, pretty heavy, brought over here," said Ben.

"Okay, Kyle. You heard the man, let's get him 5 good logs," said Hal.

"No, let the boy be. You and I are going to do this," said Ben. "Kyle, you go sit over there," said Ben pointing to a fallen tree. As Kyle sat down, he remembered hearing stories about the old man, but never knew them to be true. Until now.

Finding some heavy logs, Hal dragged them over to where Ben was standing. Ben inspected each log and tried to pick them up. "Kyle come see if you can pick up these logs."

Confused, but willing, Kyle followed directions. "Yeah, I can."

"Good," said Ben. "Hal, tie the ends of these ropes to each log. Make sure they can't slip out. You can cut a notch in the log if it holds the rope better."

"OK," said Hal and started to work on the logs.

Taking the other ends, Ben tied a rope to Kyle's legs, arms and torso, with the log attached at the other end. At this point, Kyle thought the old man must have lost his mind.

"Okay now, Kyle," said Ben looking the whole situation over. "I want you to walk. We're going to walk the river. You'll walk with these logs tied to your body."

"What is this, some kind of warrior training?" Kyle asked looking at the ropes and logs tied to his body.

"No, but you could use some," said Ben with a note of sarcasm. "Come on now, walk. Show me what you got."

Kyle was no small boy. He weighed somewhere between 250 to 280 pounds depending on how many burgers, fries and chocolate shakes he put away. But he wasn't no dough boy either. He could practically bench press his own weight. He was one solid hunk of muscle.

As Ben and Hal started walking down river, Ben turned around to see Kyle staring at the logs. "That boy thinks I'm crazy," Ben whispered to Hal.

"Well, you do have him tied to logs, down by the river," Hal chuckled.

"Let him figure it out. Let's see what he's got," said Ben turning around.

Up for the challenge, Kyle walked. He wasn't going to let himself be bested by two old men. With a little slack in the rope, it was easy to move. But once the rope got taut, he had to pull hard with his hands and legs. He eventually made some progress, but it was hard work.

Turning around, Kyle surveyed the situation. He figured he could carry three of the logs. As he lifted them up, he felt as strong as a behemoth.

Kyle picked up three logs and dragged the other two behind him with his legs. With each stride, the logs bounced along behind him. But then they got caught on dead wood and stones strewn along the river bank. Sweat poured down Kyle's face. He set the logs down and untangle the rope where the two logs were caught. It didn't take Kyle long before he sat down, completely frustrated.

"What's the matter? Why'd you stop?" hollered Ben back to Kyle.

"What kind of STUPID, CRAZY TEST is this, dragging

all these DAMN LOGS AROUND?!" Kyle hollered completely exasperated.

Turning around, Ben walked right up to Kyle and got in his face. "This isn't a damn test Kyle! This is your life! You're dragging all that hatred and anger at five dead men around behind you. They are the dead wood of your life. Everything you do, everywhere you go, you drag that crap with you. This is your life, Kyle! Does it make sense NOW, why you can't get anything done?! Why you don't have a girlfriend! And why you NEED to drink? This is your life! But no one ever showed it to you this way!" roared Ben. "CAN YOU SEE IT NOW, KYLE?! CAN YOU SEE IT NOW?!!"

Glaring at the old man, all the venom, poison and disease welled up in his throat. "Who told you I don't have a girlfriend? How do you know what I get done?"

"Well do you?" asked Ben stepping back. "Who else besides your mother puts up with your crap? Do you have a woman in your life? Or a boss or even a teacher for that matter? I've seen you skulking around town, bumming money for booze. Do you think I haven't noticed? I see everything that happens in this town. I knew Jason and his uncle, too. Do you think I don't hear the talk? Kyle, do you have anything in your sorry life, besides hatred and a need to drink?"

Looking down, Kyle kicked the dirt and said nothing.

"I didn't think so!" shouted Ben as he threw up his hands and walked away. But, something tugged at his heart. Turning to face Kyle again, his voice was softer and more gentle. "Kyle, no one can heal the unwilling. No one. Willingness is the one thing I can't give you. I can't make you want to heal. I can't do the work for you. To heal, you have to be willing to do whatever it takes. I can guide you. But you and Creator have to do the work. Great Spirit is the Healer, not me. I am just a conductor on this train. Do you understand?"

Struck by lightning, Kyle was furious. He threw down the logs he was carrying. "Creator?!! You want to talk to me about Creator? Why did He let this happen in the first place? Why does He allow bad things to happen to children? Why would He let the white man to shove us onto a reservation? Look at our people. I heard stories about how great we were! But look at us now. My mother is afraid to go off the reservation. Why would Creator let this to happen?"

Thunder and Lightning stirred in the Heavens as these two bulls faced off against each other. Fury and passion fueled the fires deep within their wounded hearts. Neither one would back down now.

"FREE WILL AND CHOICE!!!" Ben roared as passion moved through him like a thunderbolt. "AS CHILDREN OF CREATOR, WE HAVE FREE WILL AND CHOICE!! One way or another, Kyle, you invited this crap in or allowed it to happen."

"WHAT?!!!" Kyle bellowed. "WHAT DO YOU MEAN I INVITED THIS CRAP IN?"

"WELL," Ben started. "Did you drink the poison Jason offered you?"

"I WAS A KID!!! How the hell would I know what he was giving me?" Kyle retorted.

"Evil preys on the weak and ignorant," Ben started. "It don't matter how old you are. The dark is looking to steer you the wrong way. If it gets you when you're a kid, so much the better for them. Why do you think gangsters groom their little ones to do things for them?"

Kyle was silent as he stared at the ground fuming.

"Look, you only got two choices in life," Ben explained. "Either you'll serve yourself or help others. Light or dark, that's it. Those are the two paths. You'll decide which master you'll serve. Either you'll create or destroy. But make no mistake, Kyle. You'll get what you give, sometimes many fold. The Power of the Wakan is constructive. The forces of Darkness are destructive. Choose one or the other, but you can't serve both.

On this planet, what happens to one, happens to all. There is no free ride!"

Pandora's box flung open wide and Ben was on a roll. There was no stopping him now. "You take the black man. They put him in chains and enslaved him to pick cotton on some white man's plantation. Some of those African men were great chiefs, great warriors. But, they got shackled and taken away on slave trading ships. Do you know how they got there, Kyle?"

"No," Kyle said staring at the ground.

"They lost the war and their enemy sold them to Portuguese slave traders. Then Portuguese slave ships took the African people across the big waters and sold them to plantation owners. The white man beat them with bull whips, raped their women and sold off their children. That's how the white plantation owners controlled their slaves. These once great people of Africa lost the war to their enemies and were sold into slavery." Ben paused a second to see if any of this was hitting home with Kyle. "Are you following me so far?"

Kyle nodded.

"Now understand, Creator didn't do this to them. Men did. Men who lusted after power. They wanted someone to control. They wanted someone to cook their food, pick their cotton and pick up their dirty laundry. So they beat the black man down and turned him into a slave."

Hal sat on the sidelines watching this ruckus. He'd studied about the slave trade. He knew it wasn't just the Portuguese, who had slave ships. The British and the Dutch were slave traders too. Not only that, but when the Spaniards came to West Coast, their very own padre, Father Serra rode his donkey through California, founding missions. Then he and the Spaniards turned the Native people into slaves to work the missions. Nowadays, the Chumash tribe didn't have their own language. They spoke Spanish. Even though the United States Constitution declared all men to be equal, Hal had a sneaking suspicion it only meant elite white men.

"So they lost the war too, just like us." Kyle looked up.

"Yes, Kyle, they lost the war. Just like us," Ben nodded in understanding. "We don't have it so different from them. The government made them second class citizens. Even after Lincoln freed the slaves, the Klu Klux Klan did their best to keep the black man down. The black man had his struggles, make no mistake about it. But, Creator didn't do this to anyone. Men made war against each other."

As Ben wheeled around, he saw the five spirits, Jason, his uncle Jeff and the three priests sit down on the logs Kyle was dragging. "Oh, now that's great!" said Ben sarcastically.

"WHAT!!! What's great?" snarled Kyle.

"Well, you won't like this at all," said Ben. "But Jason's spirit is sitting on that log. Jeff is on that one and the three priests are on those logs. It's perfect. All your anger, fury and pain has you chained to them. Which makes it impossible for you to have a life." Looking at the situation, Ben was unable to change it. "Don't you see, boy? Your hatred ties you to them. Until you let go and forgive, that's how it'll be."

"YOU GOT A KNIFE!!! CUT ME LOOSE!!!" screamed Kyle tugging at the ropes trying to get them off.

"It won't matter if I cut you loose," said Ben. "Those ropes don't tie you to them. Your hatred does. They suffered, just like you. Why you had this lesson, I don't know. But it's a festering wound. It needs to be cleaned out and healed before it'll go away."

While Kyle brooded in silence, the sun tried hard to break through the dense fog. The glowing orb tried to shine its light though in small patches.

"You see how hard the sun is trying to burn through this fog, Kyle?" asked Ben breaking the silence.

Looking up, Kyle noticed the glowing orb burning its way through the murky fog. "Yeah, I see it."

"Well, that's how hard the love of Creator is working to burn away the hatred in your heart. And burn away your ignorance. It keeps you locked in your misery," said Ben gently. "And away from who you really are."

"So what do I do?" asked Kyle after a long moment of silence.

"First you have to understand something. None of them got away with it. They all felt the same shame you did. Not only that, they carried it with them right into the grave," Ben explained. "What are you willing to do? Jason is here to make amends. Can you forgive him?"

"I can try," said Kyle honestly.

"Well that's a start," said Ben as he turned to Hal. "We need to make a fire. Can you help me get a fire going?"

"Sure thing," said Hal as he got up to look for kindling.

"Kyle," said Ben, a little more hopeful. "Sit here and think about what you need to say to Jason and the other spirits. Tell them the truth. But don't start talking to them until we get the fire going."

"Okay," said Kyle.

As they went in search of dry wood, Hal fixed his gaze on Ben as soon as they were out of ear shot of Kyle.

"WHAT?" asked Ben feeling Hal's eyes bore into his being. "I can feel you looking at me."

"How long you been doing this?" Hal asked.

"Doing what?" Ben replied.

"Talking to spirits."

"Most of my life," said Ben. He recalled back to when the first spirit came to talk to him. "When I was four, I didn't know other people couldn't see them. My dad told me to stop talking to spirits in front of people. They might think I'm crazy."

"What happened when you were four?" Hal asked.

"I was sitting on the roof at my grandma's house. Her cabin was built into the side of the mountain. This spirit came and called my name. He told me to come with him. So I got down off the roof and I followed him. It wasn't until I waved good bye to my grandma, that she knew what was happening. Oh, she made quite a fuss. She yelled at the spirit. She told him to get on his way, being that I was a little boy. I guess she saw them too, but never let on. She knew about herbs and healing."

While Hal thought on this, they came upon a dead cottonwood tree. All its broken branches were lying on the ground. "How much wood do you want?"

"It depends on the boy, how fast he can let go."

"This could be a long ceremony," said Hal.

"Maybe, maybe not."

As they walked back with an armful of wood, Hal spotted a large orange butterfly. It was caught in an enormous spider web. Its wings were fluttering furiously trying to get out.

"Well, will you look at that," said Hal. Both Ben and Kyle came over to see what Hal was pointing to. Across the web, was an enormous spider. It was about the size of a half dollar.

"This old silk weaver got a neon yellow back and long black legs. It's just waiting to deliver its death blow to the butterfly and devour it. I don't know if its wing is broke," started Hal as he set the wood down. The butterfly struggled with all its might to get free, but the spider web had it stuck tight.

"Look at the size of that spider," said Kyle. "I've never seen one like that with a yellow hairy back. It looks like it came out of a horror movie."

A compassion came over Hal as he watched this beautiful butterfly struggle to get free. He pulled on a piece of tall grass and tried to break the silky web apart. As he poked at it, the sticky spider silk stuck to the straw. "This is a strong web," said Hal. "It's got that butterfly in tight. Nobody should have to die this way."

Kyle tugged on his ropes and pulled himself closer to the web. The gargantuan black and yellow spider loomed about two inches above the butterfly's head. Kyle found a small twig and worked on the web. Between the two of them, it didn't take long to cut the web.

Ben silently watched as Hal and Kyle cut the web and freed the butterfly. Once it was free, it fluttered to the ground, beating its wings trying to fly. It managed to get a few feet up the riverbank away from the spider.

"Well, that was a close call for that butterfly," Hal said as he watched it fly off. "I sure as shit wouldn't want to get devoured by a monster spider like that! It gives me the willies just thinking about it."

After they watched to butterfly escape to safety, Hal gathered up the wood.

Kyle already dug out a hole in the sand. "I figured you might want a fire pit."

"That looks good Kyle," said Hal approvingly. "I'll start stacking this wood and we'll get this ceremonial fire going." Having kept fire for many ceremonies, Hal built it with a prayer in his heart. He found some kindling wood and put it inside the stacked wood. With a pinch of tobacco, Hal made a prayer of gratitude. He struck the match and watched the kindling start to burn. Then, Hal went back for another armful of wood, in case Kyle's ceremony needed it.

While Hal was busy lighting the fire, Ben opened his bag and took out his Cannupa, his sacred pipe. While he sang medicine songs, Ben loaded the Cannupa with Chan-shasha, a red willow bark mixture. As he held the pipe smoke over his head, he called on the ancestors of the four directions, Mother Earth, Father Sky and the sacred space within, the Wakan. He called to the Spirit of Forgiveness to release Kyle and the other spirits from the cords of hatred. Once the sacred pipe was loaded, he leaned it on a stump next to the fire. "You know, Kyle, nature gave you a powerful example of the dilemma you're in," Ben started.

"What do you mean?" asked Kyle.

"Well, the way I see it, your life ain't so different from the butterfly you and Hal just cut loose. Except your web is made out of cords of hatred and without help, you're going to die in it."

Kyle looked over at the gargantuan yellow and black spider. He witnessed how desperately the butterfly beat its wings to get out of the web. But, without help, that butterfly would have been dead and eaten. The realization that his life was no different sunk in deep.

"Are you ready to cut the cords of your past, Kyle? Can you let this go?" queried Ben.

"Yeah, I think so. I don't want to drag this behind me my whole life," Kyle said looking at the ropes and deadwood he'd been dragging.

Finding his cedar bag, Ben sprinkled cedar on the glowing coals. "That's what most people do. When something bad happens, they cling to it. It poisons their lives until they get bitter. Then, they nurse that bitterness until they see nothing else. That bitterness eats them alive, from the inside out. At least when this work is done, if those spirits cross over, you won't have to deal with them anymore."

"Why do you say if?" asked Kyle with his eyebrows raised.

"Well, it's tricky with spirits. They're not so different from when they were human. If they were earthbound for a long time, like those priests, they might be afraid to cross over. No one wants to meet their Maker with dirty hands. Especially a priest who hurt little children," said Ben.

"So they could get stuck here forever?" asked Kyle.

"I don't know. After they died, they had a chance to cross over. But instead, they stayed in the In-between. Most likely because of the unfinished business they had with the living. What I'm trying to do is clear up your unfinished business with them. Then, you'll be free."

"I get it," said Kyle. "If I keep hating them, they'll never go away."

"Exactly," said Ben hitting pay dirt. "What they did was wrong. There's no denying that. Most evil people never get prayed for. They're just damned to hell. When our ancestors did ceremonies for the dead, it was to honor them by keeping their spirit close by. Then, after a year or more, the spirit was released back to Creator. That's when we dried our tears and let them go."

"Without a prayer, the evil ones get stuck and cause chaos for the living. Most of those are good candidates for the man who lives down in the hollows, doing his black magic." What Ben knew most of his life, was if he didn't align himself with the Higher Powers, he'd be preyed upon by the dark. Without protection from on High, he could succumb to it. There was a time, when the man who lived down in the hollows challenged Ben to a spiritual dual. If he didn't have strong, loving spirits around him, Ben knew he wouldn't have survived.

"I heard stories about that dude, but I never thought they were true," said Kyle intrigued. "How does it work? Does he make those spirits do things?"

"Oh, we'll save that talk for another time. Hal's getting the fire lit and we'll get a parade of spirits over here if I'm not careful. Fire attracts spirits to it, but the cedar will weed them out. Come by the house one day and I'll explain it to you, okay?"

"Yeah, sure," said Kyle as he wondered how his life was affected by spirits.

As the fire began to blaze, it popped and crackled from the dampness of the wood. Ben stood tall with his hands raised to the heavens. He called on the Higher Powers with his medicine songs. Standing close to the flames, the warmth of the fire felt good. They listened to its crackling melody. Once Ben finished his songs, he turned to the five spirits who sat on their logs.

"Okay, Kyle, this is where you come in. You and Creator are doing this work together. Sitting on the first two logs are Jason and his uncle Jeff. The last 3 logs are the priests. Before you start, ask Creator to help you. Call on the Spirit of Forgiveness to light the way and bring healing. Then, you'll say your peace to all of them. If they have something to say to you, I'll tell you what it is. After you finish talking, cut the cord from each one and throw it in the fire. That way we'll burn the cords binding you together. The fire will purify the anger and hatred you harbored in your heart. When this work is done, compassion will replace the hate and peace will replace resentment. Do you understand the instructions?"

"I think so," said Kyle feeling a little awkward and self conscious.

Reaching into his cedar bag, Ben threw some on the coals of the fire. As the cedar smoke curled above the fire, Ben smudged off the area with his eagle fan. "Go ahead, boy. Talk to Jason first. He's at the first log."

Not wanting to look like an idiot talking to a log, Kyle's words got stuck in his throat. His eyes glanced towards the heavens as he muttered "Please help me."

After that, the log jam behind his Adam's apple moved out. "Jason, when you came into my dream time this morning, I was pissed. I thought you were trying to get off the hook. But, now I see you went through the same thing with your uncle, who hurt you. What you did to me, changed me forever. I can't erase it. It doesn't go away. Living with that secret, almost destroyed me. I was afraid of anyone finding out, because I knew my life would be over. But then at the AA meeting, Jeannie said you molested her too. I couldn't hold it back any longer. I hated you. If I could, I'd kill you all over again." As the anger and hurt flowed out of his mouth, Kyle's heart felt lighter. Small tears gathered in the corner of his eyes.

"I'm not letting what you did, destroy my life. Dragging these silly ass logs around, I saw how the sickness infected everything. I'm sorry your uncle hurt you. I forgive you for what you did to me. I know you were sick. You were infected by some kind of perverted disease. I pray you get well and don't have to live another life of sickness. I forgive you and let go of what happened between us. Good bye, Jason." Kyle looked at Ben. "Now what do I do?"

Standing close by, Ben saw how Kyle's words eased the tension. "While you cut the cord, say a prayer for compassion for Jason. Ask Creator to take away the hurt, anger and hatred that tied you to him. Once you're cleaned out, ask Creator to fill you with compassion for all your relatives. Then, put the log in the fire with the rope. Let it purify the hurt binding you and Jason together. You've dragged this dead wood around long enough. It's time to let go."

Following instructions, Kyle felt his gut release a mountain of hurt as he cut the cord. "Can I have a pinch of tobacco, Hal?" Kyle asked.

"Sure, here you go," said Hal pulling the pouch of tobacco out of his pocket.

Standing in front of the fire, Kyle held the tobacco above his head. He offered it to Creator. Overcome with emotion, he prayed for his hurt and hatred to be removed. He asked for healing and compassion for those who harmed him. When he finished his prayer, he threw the tobacco in the fire. Kyle tossed the rope and log into the fire and watched the flames engulf them.

With the cords of hatred cut and burning, Jason fixed his spirit eyes on Ben.

"What do you want to say, Jason?" asked Ben in his

thoughts.

"Tell Kyle thanks for hearing me out and his prayers of forgiveness. I never meant to hurt anyone. I know what I did was wrong. For that, I'm truly sorry."

"I'll tell him," said Ben.

"Tell me what?" asked Kyle overhearing.

"Kyle, Jason apologized for hurting you. He knows what he did was wrong. He is thankful for your forgiveness and letting him tell his side of the story. I think he can go in peace." As Ben said those words, the sun broke through a hole in the deep mist. Hearing the voices of his ancestors, Jason turned around and walked through the mist into the light.

"He's gone," said Ben as he threw more cedar on the fire. "Now do the same with his uncle Jeff and the 3 priests."

"I don't really know them," Kyle hesitated.

"No matter. Just tell them how you feel about what they did."

Turning to the next log, Kyle faced Jeff, Jason's uncle. Inside him, Kyle felt the heartbreaking pain Jeff had carried. He'd heard stories of children being dragged off to boarding school and getting molested there.

"Jeff, we never met, but I'm sorry about what happened to you at boarding school. Those sick priests infected you. And who knows how many generations it went back. What you did to Jason was wrong. He drank himself to death and drowned. He was in a lot of pain, like me. He was a little boy when you molested him. But, you were little when the priests did it to you. I forgive you for what you did to Jason. Go in peace."

His heart felt lighter as Kyle cut the rope and threw it in the fire. All the while, he prayed to Creator to forgive Jeff, so he'd find compassion on the Other Side. After he threw the tobacco in the fire, Kyle tossed the rope and log in the fiery blaze.

Jeff's spirit leaned towards Ben. "Tell Kyle, he's awfully brave for doing this, for not letting the sickness destroy him."

"I will," said Ben.

"What did Jeff say?" asked Kyle.

"He thought you were brave for doing this, for not letting hatred and pain destroy you." Burning a greater hole into the mist, the sun shone directly on the fire. The light enveloped Jeff's spirit as he walked into the glowing sunlight.

"He's gone," said Ben as Kyle turned towards the priests. This time Kyle didn't hesitate. He addressed them all together. Many children were molested in Catholic boarding schools. The church turned a blind eye to this horror and shuffled the molesting priests from one parish to another. The pain suffered by these young ones was unbearable. As adults, these brave children came forward. One by one, their voices were heard. Together, they were no longer silent. The scandal forced the Catholic church to pay millions of dollars to people molested as children. Many priests were jailed.

"I don't know why the Catholic church protected you. It was supposed to protect the children. So many Indian children were damaged. They were forced to leave their homes and abused by people hired to take care of them. I get you were molested as children. That sickness must be deep within your church and your souls. I pray for the children you abused. I pray for their healing and yours. I pray the truth comes out everywhere and no one ever harms children again. I forgive you. I don't want to carry this shame with me anymore. Go in peace."

After he tossed the tobacco in the fire, Kyle cut the rope from his legs and his torso. He jerked the dead wood with such force, it almost knocked him down. Close to the finish line, he watched the rope and wood go up in flames. Kyle grabbed another pinch of tobacco and held it above his head in offering. With a powerful voice, he began. "Creator, forgive these men who hurt the small children in their care. Forgive those who infected these priests with this sickness. Clear it out of my heart and out of the hearts of all children. Please remove the hate from my heart, so I am free. Fill my heart with compassion, so I walk a free man. Creator, let me walk in gratitude for everything I've learned. Bless my uncles here, Ben and Hal, who stand with me as a witness to this prayer. Thank you, Creator. Aho Mitakuye Oyasin." With that, Kyle threw the tobacco in the fire.

Deeply touched by Kyle's prayer, Hal's eyes welled up with tears. Grateful it was done, Kyle watched as the rope blazed away in the fire. The sun burned through the mist. Its glowing light embraced spirits and humans alike. With gratitude, the priests nodded at Ben, Kyle and Hal as they vanished into the golden rays of sunlight.

"They're gone," said Ben feeling empowered as he picked up his drum to sing his medicine songs.

A blazing heat radiated as the fire danced, crackled and swirled around the dead wood. Curls of smoke drifted into the heavens and carried the prayers up. Watching the fire, Ben was grateful to the Higher Powers for their blessings today.

Ben reached for his cedar bag. He tossed a handful of cedar onto the burning coals. Afterward, Ben motioned to Kyle to stand by the fire. The cedar crackled and popped while the smoke filled the air. In a sweeping motion, Ben brushed Kyle off with his eagle wing fan. The fire spirits burned away the dark residue left on Kyle's being. "By the Power of Great Spirit and this sacred fire, you are cleansed and made free," said Ben. "Aho Mitakuye Oyasin."

Getting off the stump, Hal moseyed to where Ben was smudging. "I think I want some of that."

"I thought you'd never ask," smiled Ben tossing more cedar on the embers.

"What's that supposed to mean?" Hal asked as the cedar smoke curled around his legs.

"You'll figure it out," Ben teased as he cleaned Hal off with his eagle fan. As the logs burned down, Ben lit his sacred pipe. First, he blew the pipe smoke on the pipe stone bowl and then on the stem. Next, he blew some smoke toward Hal and Kyle. After he took a few strong pulls, Ben passed the Cannupa clockwise to Hal. Hal gingerly took a few good puffs. He blew the pipe smoke at the earth, the sky, Kyle and Ben. Then Hal passed the Cannupa to Kyle.

"Go ahead, Kyle," Ben instructed. "Hold the bowl in your left hand and the stem in your right. Give it a good few puffs. It's pure pipe smoke, no funny tobacco."

As Kyle drew the pipe smoke into his mouth, a peace came over him. He felt a gentle knowing that the Spirit of the Divine was with them. While Kyle smoked the Cannupa, the dense fog began to lift over the Missouri. The sunlight revealed a beautiful morning. Drawn into an ancient, sacred fellowship, Kyle passed the Cannupa back to Ben, who finished off the smoke.

While the logs were slowly reduced to ash, the wind came up and blew away the receding mist from the Missouri. The sun shown brightly across the heavens, as a great weight lifted off Kyle. His heart was free and ready to burst open.

"I feel different," he noticed turning to Ben and Hal. "The heaviness is gone and I feel free."

"I can see it in your smile," Hal agreed. "You look like a man who just got out of prison."

"Are they all gone, Ben?" Kyle asked as he looked around the fire place. "Are those spirits gone?"

"Well, from where I am standing, I don't see them anymore." Ben stood up and looked around. "But don't go calling them back just to see if they'd show up. You did some big work here today. There's no sense in undoing it. Don't cross your prayers, if you know what I mean."

"Oh no, I won't," said Kyle relieved.

Moving the ashes around, Hal had to admit, he'd rarely seen such courage. Most folks guffawed at spiritual matters, but Kyle took the bull by the horns. "You got some true grit, boy. It was right brave of you to trust me and old Ben to do the work we did today. Are you coming back to the meeting next week?" Hal asked intently.

"You gonna be there?" Kyle asked back.

"Could be, could be," said Hal looking up at Ben.

"Of course Hal's going to be there! He's an orphan! He's got no where to go. Maybe he'll take you through AA's 12 Steps and get you all figured out with Creator," said Ben encouragingly.

Mulling it over, Kyle replied, "That'd work."

"Yeah, you hard-head! You think you're ready to get humble and work the Steps?" asked Hal.

"It couldn't be any harder than what we did today," said Kyle.

"No, we did a fine piece of work here today, Kyle. I can't expect the rest of the Steps would be harder," said Ben. The fire burnt down to embers when Ben threw his last cedar down and looked up at the heavens. He gave thanks for this healing and for another day of living.

"Well, I don't know about you, but I'm hungry," said Ben as his stomach growled.

"Oh man, me too," said Hal. "Kyle, you want to get some hotcakes at Kelly's? My treat."

"I thought you said there were ghosts over there," said Kyle looking at Ben.

"There are spirits everywhere, Kyle. It never stopped me from eating though," laughed Ben.

"Yeah, I guess not. Sure, I'll eat some hotcakes."

Kicking dirt over the remaining embers with his boots,

Hal and Kyle smothered the fire with sand from the river bank. Ben found an old cup at the water's edge and filled it with water. As he poured the water on the embers, the steam spit and sputtered. A feeling of great accomplishment swept through them as they covered the fire pit. It was a brand new day.

"Let's get a move on," said Ben as he packed up his bag. "My belly's rumbling."

"You ever been to a sweat, Kyle?" Hal asked as they walked to Kelly's.

"Naw, I was too drunk for anyone to ask me to go," Kyle said.

"Yeah, that'd stop me from asking. Ben do you got an Inipi around here?"

"Use to. It's down by the river, right on my land," Ben said.

"What happened to it?"

"Too many Christians," Ben gathered. "There weren't enough people around who remembered the Old Ways."

"Yeah, I did notice a lot of churches in this small town," said Hal.

"Yeah, we got 14 churches and about 105 houses. I've got nothing against Christ, but I ain't met a Christian yet who could do what He did," said Ben.

"What do you mean?" asked Kyle intrigued, since he was raised Christian.

"Well, when Christ came to Mother Earth, he wasn't fooling around. He got busy raising the dead, healing the sick and casting out demons. Then, he taught others how to do the same. Christ even said in their holy book, 'All these things shall yea do and even greater things shall yea do.' But I ain't seen one Christian minister do Christ's work," said Ben getting his dander up. "Oh sure, they can quote the Bible backwards and

129

forwards. And they got their collection basket out, preaching about what the church needs. But get them to do what Christ did," Ben paused, shaking his head. "Not likely. They talk the talk, but don't walk the walk."

By the time they walked to Kelly's, it was getting pretty warm. The sun was bright and high in the sky, while a cool breeze came up from the river. They found a table near the back. Hal noticed the heaviness was gone.

Whispering, Kyle turned to Ben. "So are there spirits in here now?"

"Why, you worried you might pick up some strays?" Ben laughed poking fun at Kyle. "There was a ride at Disneyland, can't remember what it was called. But it was a big house full of spooks. Do you remember that ride Hal? I think I was there with you."

"Yeah, I remember. It was called the Haunted Mansion," said Hal recollecting. "You got out on a 5 day pass and we headed up to Los Angeles. We got lost in Hollywood, hoping to catch a falling star."

"That's it. Remember how at the end, they said "BEWARE OF HITCH HIKING GHOSTS!!" Ben started laughing. "And they showed a ghost sitting in the car with us in the mirror!"

"Yeah, I remember that," said Hal. "Kyle, are you afraid you'll pick up spirits again?"

"Not really," Kyle lied as he looked down. "BUT how do you know when they're here?"

"Ah Kyle, don't worry. It's too early. There ain't any drinkers here yet. Those hitchhiking ghosts only come around when the drinkers get here. They want a whiff of whiskey. You're safe for now," Ben chuckled.

The waitress came and put menus down. "Y'all want some coffee?"

"Yeah, love some," said Hal. "It's got to be better than

the mud Ben's got at his place."

"Don't be so sure," said Ben. "I'll take a cup.

"I'll take one too," said Kyle. "And a glass of water."

"Bring us 3 plates of hotcakes, please," said Hal. "Do you want bacon?"

"Yeah, sounds good," said Ben.

"Bring us a couple sides of bacon. That'll do it for now," said Hal.

After the waitress brought the coffee, the men silently pondered everything that took place that morning.

"That was some powerful work we did today," said Hal.

"You'll be doing the real work when you take Kyle through the Steps," said Ben. "After you clear out the wreckage of your life, Kyle, you'll become a messenger for Great Spirit. Then, He'll work His power through you to help others."

Thinking it over, Hal looked at Kyle, like he was looking through a window. "ARE you done, Kyle? Are you done drinking? Because if you still have some experimenting to do, it's pointless to begin the work. It'll will slide off you like a non-stick coating. Search yourself and figure out if you are done."

Kyle didn't answer for a while. How does anybody know if they're done? "Hal, all I know is, when I woke up from dreaming about Jason, I wanted to drink. But you and Ben crossed my mind. I didn't want to blow you off, like I do everything else. So I sat down on my bed, until I couldn't stand it anymore. Then I decided to take a walk. So something in me changed. At least for right now."

"Well that's good enough for me," said Hal. "All we got is today. I got a Big Book in my truck. We'll make good use of that. When do you want to start, Kyle?"

"I thought we started already," Kyle said.

131

"By gosh you're right. Well then, we'll start on the Big Book. You busy tomorrow morning?" asked Hal.

"Tomorrow's good for me."

"Good, works for me too." Hal smiled.

While the two of them talked about making plans, Ben's mind wandered back to a boy he'd adopted years ago. *Many Lights* is what Ben named him, but the boy's given name was Tyler. Tyler was a true Winkte, true Twin Spirits. One of the few Ben had ever met. Gazing out the window, Ben had a far away look in his eyes. Back then, his life was busy with their first grandchild.

Little Tyler kept Elsie pretty occupied. As he called her to mind, Elsie's radiant smile soothed his tattered soul. Her spirit was drawn to him by his thought. *"Oh Elsie,"* he thought to himself. *"I miss you, woman. I miss the life we had together."*

As the waitress plopped the heavy plates of hotcakes and bacon on the table, the smells of breakfast jarred Ben from the whispers of the past.

"Here you go, gentlemen," said the waitress. "Do you want some more coffee?"

"Yeah, that's great," said Hal. "You okay Ben?"

"Yeah," he sighed wistfully. "I was remembering another time. Back with my first grandson, who Elsie and I adopted as our own. I named him "Many Lights" because his eyes were so bright."

"I don't think I ever heard you talk about him," said Hal.

"Yeah, he and his mother moved away. I haven't seen them in a while. But as a little boy, he was the apple of my eye," the old man sighed.

"Where did he go?" asked Kyle. "What happened to him?"

"Well, you got time for a story?" Ben paused.

Hal looked at his left arm, where his watch used to be. "According to my time piece, which I don't wear anymore, I got time. You got time, Kyle?"

"Yeah, I can hang out."

"Well after the kids moved out, the house was finally quiet. I liked the peace. But Elsie hated it. That empty house drove her nuts. She felt lonely if there wasn't a racket going on. Then came Cedar. I'd known her daddy since she was a young girl. But he was a drinking man and it did him in. It didn't take long before Cedar started in, just like her old man, drinking and drugging. One day, she asked why I didn't drink like everybody else? So I told her how I got sober."

"Well, with drinking, she got into a bad way. One day she's on my front porch crying. She was with a man who beat her. He was a real macho man with big muscles and a big truck, but he liked to beat up on women. This time she had a black eye and bruises all over her body. Elsie cried. Then Cedar let the bomb drop. She was pregnant."

"Now Elsie wasn't going to let Cedar go back to that idiot. But I knew she'd have to choose. So we sat down and I told her straight. If he beat her up again, she could lose the baby and he'd go to jail for murder. But, it was her choice. If she was willing to get sober, I'd help her all I could. But if she kept drinking and destroyed the baby, I wouldn't stand by and watch."

"She said that was fair and it was decided. So we made her up a bed and Elsie had someone to take care of again."

"Well those women spent their time making plans for this baby. Elsie pulled out her old sewing machine. They made star quilts and whatever else was needed to bring this child into the world proper. But in my gut, I felt the storm clouds coming. Something wasn't right. Then sure enough, I'm walking home one morning and Mister Macho and his big truck are in front of the house. Cedar and Elsie are on the porch and there's a lot of yelling going on. Then, Mister Macho grabs

133

Cedar by the hair and drags her swollen body into the truck, kicking and screaming. I start running when Elsie gets up in his face and he pushes her on the ground. After I picked Elsie off the ground, Mister Macho shoves Cedar in the truck."

"Now, Cedar is like a daughter to me. But, she had no sense when it came to men. If you lined up a hundred men, she'd fall for the one psychopath in the bunch. Well, it don't take a second before I got Mister Macho on the ground. I got my boot on his chest and my buck knife at his throat. His eyes bugged out so far, I almost started laughing. There was a little trickle of blood coming from his Adam's apple where the blade cut him after he swallowed."

"Now Elsie never saw this side of me before and she begs me not to kill him. But I got no use for wife beaters, especially the alcoholic ones."

"I would have cut his throat right then," said Kyle. "If someone did that to my sister or my mom. Oh, he'd pay alright."

"Yeah, I'd say I had Mister Macho's full attention. I can still see his bloodshot, black eyes staring back at me, wondering if this was it. So I asked him, "You want this to be your last breath, boy? Because all I got to do is shove this buck knife in your Adam's apple and it will be." Ben paused for a moment, sipping his coffee.

Hanging on to every word, Kyle couldn't stand the suspense anymore. "So WHAT DID YOU DO?!"

"You mean did I kill him?" The question hung heavy in the air as Ben took a deep breath. "It's a powerful moment when you've got a man's life in your hands. I was grateful to be sober then. Otherwise it would have gone much differently. My eyes never left his gaze, but I told Elsie to call the sheriff. I held the buck knife to Mister Macho's throat until they got there. Now by that time, the neighbors had come out of their house when they heard all the yelling."

"Once the sheriff got there, they found drugs in the

truck. Turns out Mr. Macho was from a drug cartel, south of the border and was peddling meth on the rez. He convinced poor Cedar that he wanted to marry her. But like a snake, his real motive was getting free federal benefits from marrying an Indian girl, like those squaw men back in the day. He thought he had it all figured out. He was ready to set up shop and deal his drugs. So off to jail he went. That ended it for a while."

"That's how the bootleggers used to do it, bringing the liquor on to the rez," said Hal. "Money and booze is a bad combination. But why do you say for a while?"

"Well, he got out eventually. In prison, groups come in from AA. Well, mister Macho gets sober in the big house. If you can imagine that. Usually there's more drugs in there, than there are on the outside."

"I heard that too," agreed Kyle.

"Well, Cedar, she get's sober and this time it's for keeps. Watching her work the program, she gets a rosy glow, the way most newcomers do. Her life starts improving. With Creator's help, she finds work and wants to go back to school. As her belly grows, she's glowing with the spirit of a new life inside her."

"Now Elsie's in heaven, because we adopt Cedar and the new baby into our family. We're going to be grandma and grandpa. Then, the day comes. Creator blesses us with this baby boy."

"Cedar names him Tyler. His eyes were a deep slate blue, like the midnight sky. His face is handsome like a chiseled china doll. I'm holding him in my arms and something tells me, he's not going to be like other children."

"By that time, the house is turned upside down and inside out with baby fixings. With Elsie's help, Cedar becomes a good mother. Women have an huge gift for giving and loving. The boy grows up healthy and happy. But he's different. He's always playing with girls. Tyler's not a rough and tumble kid, like the other boys. At first, I thought the women babied him too much, like mother hens. So I took it upon myself to man him up, by having him go out with me. Then one day, we're walking down by the river. He's two years old, almost three, when he looks up at me and says "Grandpa." I say, "What son?" He says, "Grandpa, outside I'm a boy, but inside I'm a girl."

"Whoa," said Hal. "He's a Winkte boy, Twin Spirits."

"Yeah, but that's just the half of it. The Christmas before, Cedar's father, Dave passed away. Tyler just met Dave that spring for a couple weeks. Then, almost at the moment of his death, Tyler says, "Grandpa." I say, "What?" Tyler says, "Grandpa, Dave's gone. Dave's up there." And he points to the sky."

"Whoa..." said Hal munching on some bacon. "So what do you do with a Winkte boy with spirit eyes?"

"Good question," Ben sighed. "I wish I'd been better educated on that. When he was a young boy, we'd feed the chickens and collect the eggs. He'd chase them all over the yard, laughing and screaming. I laughed so much, my sides ached."

"Well, one morning, I killed a chicken for dinner. Tyler wasn't around. Later on, when Elsie put the bird on the table, I told him it was a chicken. He caused the biggest fuss. I went to carve it up with a knife and he screamed at me. "NO! Grandpa, NO!"

"There was no peace until I put the bird back together. We didn't eat chicken that night," Ben shook his head. "When he got older, he saw spirits come into the lodge. He told me how the spirits went to each person. It was an amazing thing."

"Sounds challenging. How did it all work out?" asked Hal.

"Not so good at first. All hell broke loose by the time Tyler was in fourth grade. The kids picked on him at school. They called him names like "Girly boy" and "faggot." He was so tenderhearted, it really tore him up."

"One afternoon he couldn't take it anymore and he pulled out a big carving knife. He tells me he's going to kill himself. He's only ten and he's dead serious. I'm the only one home. I know he's Winkte, but the rest of the world don't accept him. He gets bullied all the time. I try to tell him I know he's Winkte, but he won't admit it. In fact, he tells me he's not."

"Wow," says Kyle. "I know that pain. It tortured me wondering if I was gay or straight. What Jason did, messed up my head. Kids in school are brutal."

"No doubt they are. Their viciousness almost destroyed his life. By junior high, he dressed all in black. He even had black finger nails. That when the drugs came in. One night, at a party, someone stole some jewelry. Tyler got accused and they told him he was going to jail. He couldn't handle it, so he downed a bottle of pills. That viciousness pushed him right over the edge. By the time he got to the hospital, he's in a coma."

"I'm so sorry," said Hal, shaking his head. "I've been there. After Arlene overdosed on sleeping pills and booze, she never came back."

"It's tough," Ben agreed. "There I am, watching Cedar lose her mind in the ICU while the boy's almost lifeless body is crumpled in a hospital bed. His blood pressure was 49/19 and he's pretty much in the Spirit World. All I can do is sit on the edge of his bed praying. I begged Creator not to take our boy from us."

"Well, hours go by with no change. Tyler just lays there like a lump. I'm staring at the wall. It's got a wall painting with mountains and tall pine trees around a lake. Suddenly Tyler sits straight up with his mouth wide open, pointing to the wallpaper. He yells, "Grandpa! Do you see the deer?"

"And sure enough a deer spirit came right out of the wall paper. It crosses the room and goes into the ICU. Tyler's

137

pointing his finger at it the whole way. Then, he passed out for 6 more hours. Right then, I knew Creator answered my prayers. He gave me a sign. The deer spirit brought back Tyler's life."

"Wow," said Kyle with his head cupped in his hands. "That's a hell of a story. Where's Tyler now?"

"Oh he moved to the big city and went to a fancy hairdresser school. He wanted to do hair and make up for the movies. When he was little, he'd brush Elsie's hair for hours. He was born with a hairbrush in his hand."

"You know, Ben," said Hal. "Your story reminds me of a sassy little red head I met out West. Her story was the worst I'd heard. We called her Calamity Jane. She tended bar at a little cantina. We'd go there after working with horses all day. Her long red hair was pulled back in a ponytail and she'd look at you with her fiery green eyes, asking, "What'll it be, boys?""

"Was this before or after you got sober?" asked Ben.

"Oh, it was after I got sober the second time, maybe 2 years after Arlene died," said Hal. "Why?"

"Well, I'm not interested in hearing about some coyote ugly morning with some fiery red head. Kyle don't need any new ideas, either," said Ben.

"Oh, naw. It was nothing like that. We never... well you know."

"Didn't it bother you to go into a bar?" asked Kyle.

"No, by then the obsession to drink was removed. I never wanted to drink again. But, I liked good music and this cantina had some fine musicians. All I ordered was ginger ale. Nobody ever questioned me about it. I told them, Indians can't drink and they left it alone," said Hal.

"So what was it about this calamity girl that makes you remember her now?" asked Ben.

"Well, like Cedar, Calamity always found the one

138

psychopath in the bunch. One night, it was slow at the cantina and we got to talking. Now she's a hard drinker and that night was no exception. Somehow, she'd manage keep her head on straight if she was busy. But, the minute it got slow or close to quittin' time, she'd tie one on. And she liked my brand of poison, tequila," said Hal.

"Aw, that's dangerous," said Ben.

"Oh you bet. In the two years I knew her, I fished her out of jail a couple times. I tried bringing her to AA, when she got real bad. But with this one, AA didn't stick. At least not in the time I knew her."

"Doesn't work for all people. They got to want to stop drinking," said Ben. "Just like it says in the book, 'If you want what we have and are willing to go to any length to get it, THEN you're ready to take the Steps."

"I know that, but something made me keep trying to help her," said Hal.

"Did you love her?" asked Kyle.

"Not in the way you're thinking boy. She was married to a mean drunk. One day, she came to work with stitches on her forehead. She told me a horse kicked her. I said, that's a lie. I know what a hoof print looks like. Well, then the damn burst. She started crying and told me her husband got jealous and shoved her head into a door jam. She couldn't tell anybody."

"My blood damn near boiled over. I wanted to kill that son of a bitch. She said the bastard moved out, but she was afraid to go home. So like an idiot, I took her home to check things out and see if it was safe. That's when I got reeled in." Hal shook his head.

"Oh," said Ben knowing that dilemma well. "That's a dangerous spot, you were in. Reminds me of them Sirens, who bewitched sailors with their singsong 'til the sailors were so dizzy, they crashed their ships into the rocks."

"Yeah, well that night we talked almost 'til sun up. The

more she told me about her life, the more my heart broke. When Calamity was six, her mama died when their tinderbox house caught fire. They lived in the back woods of Colorado. The poor woman drank herself into a stupor and fell asleep smoking a cigarette."

"That little girl was coming back from the neighbors, when she saw the house burst into flames, with her mama inside. She was running barefoot because she forgot her red tennis shoes in the house. That poor child stood outside, helpless and watched her house burn down. She was heart broke after that."

"Then, her daddy married some pregnant woman carrying another man's kid. That drunken son of a bitch was a piece of work. He started molesting Calamity when she was eight years old." Hal was shaking his head.

"You felt sorry for her," said Ben knowingly. "And that hook reeled you in. I bet she made you feel like a hero."

"How could you not feel sorry for a woman who went through hell as a child? You'd have to have ice water running through your veins." Hal got defensive. "But you may be right, Ben. I had strong feelings about protecting her, like a little sister."

"Protecting women and children is what men do, Hal. Those are a man's normal feelings," said Ben.

"I reckon so, Ben. Funny thing is, one morning I'm getting dressed and this Voice says "Go to Calamity's house right now!" But I'm getting ready for work, so I tell the Voice I'll see her later at the cantina. But, this Voice demands that I get a move on and get in my truck. I'm already late for work, so I shrug it off . But then, something shoves me in the shoulder and I hear this Voice say 'RIGHT NOW!' Well, that gets my attention. So I say OKAY and I drive out to her house in the canyon."

"As I'm walking up to the front door, I get this feeling something's not right. The front door's open, but no one's around. I start hollering her name. But, there's no answer. I push the door open and the house is totally trashed. The tables are knocked over. There's glass all over the floor. There's a hole punched in the wall. Now, I'm yelling her name, but no one answers. Then I push open her bedroom door and she's laying on the floor, shaking and talking out loud. Her eyes are fluttering, like she's dreaming. But I know she's not."

"I try waking her up, but nothing works. And that's when I see these empty pill boxes everywhere. All this over the counter crap. She's got bruises all over her body and her head keeps rolling side to side. Then, in this little girl voice, she's talking about her red tennis shoes and my eyes tear up. Her mind is back at her mama's house. She's going after her red tennis shoes." Hal got quiet.

"What happened then," asked Kyle.

"I called 911 and the fire truck came. They got her to the hospital. The nurse told me Calamity was in a psychotic coma. She took an over dose of pills. If I hadn't of gotten there when I did, the pills would have destroyed her liver and she'd have bled to death inside."

"So you did save her life," said Ben gently. "Maybe you are a hero, Hal. Spirit trusted you. It told you what you needed to do. She didn't die. Just think, if you didn't listen to Spirit, she'd be dead."

"Yeah, I don't know about that," said Hal visibly annoyed. "After she came out her coma, I went to visit her in the psych ward. She told me the bastard came home all coked up and beat the shit out of her. That's when she tried to kill herself. Then while she's in the psych ward, that jerk shows up with a dozen roses. That son of a bitch says how sorry he was for what he did, and she went home with him. Go figure that out."

"Oh my brother," said Ben in the most tender voice. "This woman was damaged, like a dented can. No telling how many times she got beat after that. We can't save anybody.

141

Even the Big Book says no human power can relieve alcoholism. They have to want to get sober, more than they want to drink. All we can do is carry the message and be a good example of the Big Book. Creator is the only one who can save anyone, but they got to want it!"

"It's frustrating," sighed Hal. "Years ago, back on the rez, one of my dad's buddies, Harry, tried to stay on the water wagon. But he had a devil of a time quitting drinking. One night, his wife goes to her sister's and leaves Harry alone with their six kids. After his wife is out of sight, his buddy, Cal comes sneaking around the corner with a bottle. Cal's a bad drunk and Harry's wife don't tolerate drinking. Everybody knows it. Harry tries to beg off, telling Cal no thanks, he's not drinking. And swears this time he's quit for good. But Cal don't want to drink alone and pesters Harry to take a nip. Harry gets weak in the knees. They get so drunk they pass out in the truck. That night, I guess his oldest boy built a fire in the wood stove to keep warm. But some embers pushed out and the house caught fire. All six kids died. I never saw a man so broken as poor Harry. But, by his own power, he couldn't resist the temptation."

"That's a hell of a price to pay for any man," said Ben sensing Hal's heartache. "But no drunk has the power to resist temptation on his own. Only Great Spirit gives us that. We have to be Higher Powered, because that firewater spirit is a trickster."

"What do you mean by that?" asked Kyle. "What is Higher Powered?"

Looking at Hal, Ben gave him the floor. He'd done enough talking.

"Well," started Hal. "You see Kyle, it's like this. Take a gander at those bottles behind the bar over there and tell me what you see."

As Kyle scanned the dimly lit bar, he noticed bottles of every kind of alcohol. "Bottles of booze. It's the same in any bar. What about them?"

"Well, inside those bottles are spirits. The lowest, meanest scoundrels you'll ever meet. They're nothing but trouble. When they come calling and whisper in your ear, that temptation sets in and it's hard to resist. So you take a drink. But, that's when they take over your body and drag your ass through the mud. Maybe you end up in jail or better yet, the nut ward."

"By then, you'll want to quit. But you can't. Those demons got their hands wrapped around your neck and are squeezing the life out of you. That's when you're finally sick and tired of being sick and tired. You're on your knees, in a heap of trouble, begging Creator to bale you out. If you're lucky, like I was, you'll do a ceremony and let the scoundrels go, by trading up for a relationship with a Higher Power, the Creator," explained Hal, sounding educated.

"AHH!! Listen up, boy!" Ben chimed in. "The spirit of Freddy Krueger lives in those bottles behind the bar!!! See... and when you drink that liquid lightning down, the spirit of Freddy Krueger takes over your body. Then, he does whatever he wants! Causing all kinds of mayhem and hurting countless people! When he's done with you, he leaves your body laying in a ditch by the side of the road! After you come to, you're face down in your own vomit, sick and out of your mind, feeling like shit!"

"Well, that pretty much explains it! I thought I had this one!" said Hal.

"AHH! You got to explain it simple. Don't bring out the holy book, just tell him straight," said Ben impassioned. Leaning across the table, with a intense look in his eyes, Ben fixed his gaze on Kyle. "You know who Freddy Krueger is, don't you Kyle?"

"Course I do," said Kyle.

"Well," started Ben. "Once the spirit of Freddy Krueger has his eye on you, you'll barely have a moment to escape before he comes calling again. And he will come calling again! Because see..., he needs your body to commit his mayhem. So he calls you and calls you and calls you, saying 'come have a drink, you'll feel better.' But that's a lie. That's what the white men who wrote the AA Big Book call an allergy of the body and an obsession of the mind."

"So how do you escape?" asked Kyle intrigued.

"Well, like I said, you'll only have a moment to escape once the spirit of Freddy Krueger comes calling. But IF, in that very moment, you call upon Creator for help, well...ol' Freddy Krueger has got to back off. Because you've called on a Higher Power for help. Now, Freddy doesn't stand a chance against the Higher Powers. The shadows fear the Light. That's why they keep saloons so dark, because those black-hearted demons living in those bottles can't stand the Light!" said Ben. "And that's how it's done!"

"Well...," said Hal turning to Kyle. "Does that make sense to you?"

"Well, if you put it that way. It sounds like a spiritual tug-o-war to me. But I still don't get what it means to be Higher Powered," said Kyle.

"AHH! It's when you tell Freddy you ain't interested in his business anymore. And you're only doing business with Creator," exclaimed Ben. "But, if you get cocky, and think you got this one licked, you might be headed for trouble. Because, I tell you what, Freddy and those devil spirits don't give up their drunks easy. They'll always take you back, just long enough to get you unhinged. They're always waiting around the corner."

The waitress brought over the check and set it down on the table. "You gentlemen want anything else?"

"Naw, we're good," said Hal, reaching for his wallet. After he pulled some money out, Hal leaned across the table. In a low voice Hal whispered, "PSST! Listen up Kyle, do you know what you get when you don't pay your exorcist?"

"No, not really," Kyle said, feeling on the spot.

"You get repossessed," said Hal as he leaned back and laughed.

Ben pushed his chair back and looked at the both of them. "You two ready to go or are you fixing to perform an exorcism on this roadhouse?"

Raising her eyebrows, the waitress shot Ben a look like he was crazy.

"Aw, don't mind him," said Hal to the waitress. "He's been watching too many horror movies. Let's get out of here. I done sat for too long already."

After Hal paid the bill, he walked back to the table and left the waitress a few dollars. As much as he traveled the open road, he appreciated a good waitress. She made all the difference in a lonely day.

Walking out into the daylight, the rays of the sun felt warm on their back. They strolled down the road, laughing and joking. A huge weight was lifted off him. Kyle felt lighter than he had in a long time.

When they got to the house, Ben went inside to put his Sacreds back in his cedar box. Hal headed towards his truck and opened the tailgate to sit down to finish talking to Kyle, before he went home. "So it looks like I'll be staying on a few days, give or take," said Hal.

"Thanks for your help today, you and Ben," said Kyle.

"Well, are you interested in working the 12 Steps the way I was taught?" asked Hal, not sure if Kyle knew what he wanted to do next.

"Yeah, maybe tomorrow, sometime after breakfast?" asked Kyle, as he turned to walk home.

"That works for me. Come by and we'll get started," said Hal as he got out his fishing pole and his waders. Hal was accustomed to catching his dinner. The glistening waters of the

Missouri beckoned him to go catch some fish. Fried up with some butter, the fish would go well with the potatoes and green beans he had in the truck. Hal walked back into the house with his fishing pole, to let Ben know. "Hey, how do you feel about a fish fry later? I'm headed back down to the river to see what I can catch. You wanna come?"

"Naw, that's okay, you go. I'm plum wore out. There's bass in the ol' Missouri, maybe even some pike."

"Yeah, I figured you'd want some down time after this morning. That was some good work, though. I think Kyle wants help," said Hal.

"Seems so," said Ben taking his boots off and reclining on the bed. "That boy got himself mixed with a bunch of rowdies, so I'm not sure how long it will last. Somewhere in the last few years, these gangs have crept onto the rez and took over. Be mindful of them."

"I'm pretty familiar with gangs. They're all over out West. Down every alley, they'd mark their territory. Most sold drugs and caused trouble. In some parts of town, if you backed into the wrong ally, you'd never make it out alive," said Hal.

"Can't say it's much different here. Things happen so fast now. Things I never knew growing up. When they built that Indian casino, it cast a shadow over our land. It attracted dark elements from all over. Now, everyone wants a cut of Indian money. Oh, the promises they made when they built the casino were too good to be true. The rez would be rich. Seems to me, only a few people got in on that cash cow," said Ben.

"Yeah, mixing booze together with the lure of easy money, is a powerful force. It corrupts most people. But, I'm burning daylight. I got to go if I'm gonna catch anything," said Hal as he grabbed his fishing gear and headed out the door.

"Hey, Hal?"

"Yeah," said Hal, as he stood in the doorway, about to leave.

146

"It's good to have you around," said Ben.

"Thanks Ben, It's good to be here," said Hal as he closed the front door. He started whistling a catchy tune as he walked down towards the river.

When Kyle got home, he flopped down on the couch and zoned out in front of the television. His younger sister was watching the movie 'Ghost-busters.' The scene opened to where the Ghost-busters were rushing in to save a baby. They were dousing the evil man with slime. "Is he dead," asked the mother of the baby. "Na ah," answered the Ghost buster. "This slime is positively charged. He's going to wake up feeling like a million bucks."

Hearing that, Kyle was struck with the thought he'd spent the morning with true ghost busters. As his eyes grew heavy with sleep, he got up off the couch and went into his room. Laying down on the bed, Kyle fell into a deep restful sleep, one he hadn't had in a long time.

CHAPTER FOUR: CAMP SOBRIETY

There's a place where
The grass grows tall
A place that echoes
When little pebbles fall
There's a place down deep
Where my spirit dwells
It holds all the memories
And stories to tell

I ask you now
To hear my tale
Stay with me until
The morning light pierces my veil
Know me down, way down deep
In the places far away where I keep
Near the hollow of my aching soul
The stories of mine yet never told

As we traverse this lone mile together
With some burning sage and an eagle feather
Our hearts come together as one
As we dance again, under the Sun
Breaking free from ties holding us to the past
Our hearts and souls together, are free at last

Unfettered from the chains,

We longed to be

Yearning for our souls

Like eagles, to now fly free

Washing our blood stained hands

With Great Spirit's Power

Knowing His Love is in

The Great Thunder's shower

At last, with clear eyes, our hearts finally see

How our Creator meant us to be

It was well before the crack of dawn when the whippoorwill sang its morning song. It sat on a limb outside Kyle's window, greeting the brand new day. As he lay awake in bed, Kyle realized it was the first time he didn't pull the pillow over his head and curse the song of the morning birds. He wasn't hung over and he didn't have to run to the bathroom to puke his guts out.

Hearing the birds chirping and the barking dogs as they chased a car down the street, Kyle rolled over to catch some more shut eye. Down the hall, he heard his mom's bedroom door open and her foot steps go into the kitchen. The cupboard doors creaked open when she got her coffee cup. After she filled the coffee maker with water, he heard it brewing. His stomach rumbled as the scent of fresh brewed coffee wafted through the air. Willing himself out of bed, he toddled into the kitchen where his mom sat at the breakfast table, drinking her coffee.

"Hey, what are you doing up so early? Can't sleep?" said Vera, Kyle's mom.

"Naw, I slept great," Kyle yawned and stretched his arms. "But I'm really hungry. What do we got for breakfast?"

That request hadn't come out of her son's mouth in a long time. As she got up from the table and walked towards her son, she stifled her surprise when she couldn't smell the alcohol fumes coming from his breath.

"You're not hung over?" she asked tentatively, knowing from past experience, her prying questions often lead to a horrible fight. Especially, if he was hung over and she said the wrong thing.

"No mom, I'm not hung over," Kyle chided. "In fact, I haven't had a drink since the day before yesterday."

"Well, go get something on your feet and I'll make you some eggs and toast," she said.

"Oh mom," Kyle groaned. "When are you gonna stop treating me like a kid?"

"Go on now, no arguing," said Vera shoeing him out of the kitchen. "We don't need to be catching no colds in this house. Them doctors are pushing everybody to get flu shots down at the clinic." Working as a receptionist down at the Health Clinic, Vera knew everything that happened on the rez.

Back in his room, Kyle rummaged through his room and found some old socks strewn on the floor. After he put them on, he noticed how things felt different this morning. Being hungry was different. When he was hung over, the last thing he wanted was food.

Warming up the griddle, Vera hummed one of her favorite songs. She greased it up with some margarine. Then, she hollowed out the middle of two pieces of bread and put them on the griddle to brown. Afterward she went to the fridge to get the eggs. Once the toast was brown on one side, she flipped them over and cracked the egg in the hollow part. The egg yolk sat in the middle of the toast like the sun on a cloudy day. She sprinkled a little salt and pepper on the eggs and put a big lid on the griddle to cover them up. Now, they would cook.

As Kyle walked to the kitchen, the aroma of fresh brewed coffee and breakfast cooking awakened a sleeping joy in him. Seeing his mom cooking and humming, like she used to, made him realize how long it had been.

"You want some coffee?" Vera asked her son.

"Yeah, that sounds good," said Kyle as he got a coffee mug from the cupboard and poured his first cup. The strong smell of coffee revived his senses.

"You were gone yesterday morning, pretty early," said Vera curious about her son's new sobriety.

"Yeah, I went to old man Ben's house. He's got a buddy from Colorado staying with him. Me and dad met him at the AA meeting."

"Oh," she said nodding her head. "Tell me more, tell me more."

"Well, dad's been sober for about 2 months now," said Kyle fixing his eyes on his mother, as he leaned against the kitchen counter.

"Well, that's good to know. I'm glad he's trying," said Vera guardedly.

"And dad's been trying to get me to go to those AA meetings with him. He thinks it'll rub off somehow." Kyle knew talking about his dad was still a touchy subject for his mom.

Kyle sat down at the kitchen table. He gazed out the window to watch the sun's early light creep slowly over the rolling hillsides in the east. After Vera finished cooking the eggs and toast, she put them on a plate and placed them in front of Kyle.

"Well, the good Lord must be hearing my prayers. Not a day goes by when I don't pray for your dad, Kyle. Now, eat up before it gets cold," she said.

The lingering heartache over her husband got caught in her throat. Vera never had a drink in her life. As a child, she watched helplessly as her father drank himself to death. At his funeral, she vowed never to drink. Hard times fell on her mother after he died and she couldn't afford to take care of all the children. A white Christian woman convinced her mom that Vera would be better off at boarding school where she could learn about Jesus Christ.

Taking a whiff, Kyle changed the subject. "Thanks mom, this smells good."

"So what were you doing over at Ben's house so early?" Vera inquired, still curious about the change in her son.

"Well Hal, Ben's friend from Colorado, invited me over for coffee. I couldn't sleep, so I got up early and went over there," Kyle said as he wolfed down the eggs and toast in a hurry. "You ever meet someone who feels familiar? Something Hal said at the meeting just clicked with me. It felt like I knew him already. Everything he said made sense."

As Vera watched her son chow down his breakfast, she went to the freezer. "You must be pretty hungry. You want me to make some tater tots?"

"Yeah, would you?" said Kyle.

"Sure," said Vera getting the tater tots out of the freezer. "You want another piece of toast?"

"Yeah, maybe two," said Kyle.

After putting two more pieces of white bread in the toaster, Vera poured oil in the skillet and turned on the burner. When the oil heated up, she put the tater tots onto the skillet. The grease splattered as the frozen potatoes hit the pan.

Commander of the kitchen, Vera grabbed the toast as it popped up from the toaster. She smeared it with some margarine and jam before she put it in front of her son. Then, she went back to mind the potatoes. "So what did you guys do yesterday morning?"

Knowing his mother's prying nature, Kyle kept it light, fearing she'd never understand the real work they did yesterday morning. "Oh, those guys tell the best stories. Hal met Ben when he was locked up in the Army psyche ward and took him to his first AA meeting. Can you believe that?"

"That must have been a long time ago," Vera commented.

"Well, the other night, Hal showed up at the AA meeting and Ben asked him to speak. It's amazing what they know. I'm starting the Steps with Hal. I'm going over there in a little while."

"Oh," said Vera watching the potatoes brown.

"Poor Ben, though," said Kyle. "He really misses his wife."

"Yeah, I think Elsie's been gone a little over a year. What makes you say that?" asked Vera as she placed the potatoes on the table.

"Oh mom, his coffee sucks. It's the worst coffee I ever tasted," Kyle chuckled as he remembered the ribbing Hal gave Ben over his coffee. "He said his wife made the coffee and he never learned. You need a pound of sugar to make it worth drinking."

"Oh, the poor man," said Vera compassionately. "Hey, you know what, I got a coffee maker from the church Christmas raffle I never used down in the basement. I don't need it. Why don't you take it and give it to Ben? They're easy to use. I've got some filters to give him too."

"That'd be great mom," said Kyle as he finished of his tater tots. After breakfast, Kyle fished around in his closet for a pair jeans that covered his butt. Underneath his clothes, he found a half empty wine bottle. The spirit of Freddy Kruger flashed across his mind, as Kyle took it to the bathroom. With sweaty palms and a racing heart, he poured the wine down the toilet.

Anxiety gripped him because he didn't know how many bottles he'd hid throughout the house. A disgust grew in him when he realized the wine bottle wasn't the last one. Grabbing a broom, he found more bottles under his bed and he poured them out. For the first time, Kyle felt empowered. If he didn't drink, he had a chance.

"That was a close call," he thought to himself. How differently the day would have gone, if he didn't commit to meeting Hal this morning. Slightly shaken, Kyle closed his bedroom door and headed toward the front door.

Hearing Kyle's footsteps walking across the linoleum, Vera hollered from her bedroom. "Kyle, don't forget the coffee maker."

"Oh, yeah. Thanks mom!" Kyle grabbed the coffee maker from the kitchen table, tucked it under his arm and went out the front door. The morning air was brisk and cool. A slight breeze came up from the river. He hadn't given into the drink for the second morning in a row. Kyle was grateful to not be hung over. Bringing Ben the coffee maker for the work they did yesterday felt good.

Hearing the old roosters crow, Ben had been up since before dawn. Hal snored away, sleeping on the mattress in the corner. Not wanting to wake Hal up, Ben crept quietly around the room to get his sacred pipe and drum from the cedar box. His old Indian blanket lay over the chair. He wrapped it around his shoulders, before he walked out the door.

Every morning he climbed the small hill behind his house, to greet the new day and pray. Dew sparkled on the ground as he walked up the small trail to the top of the knoll. With a chill in the air, his breath turned to steam. At the top, Ben faced east watching the dawn's early light cast a glow behind the low sloping hills. He placed his old Indian blanket on the ground. With reverence, Ben laid out his Cannupa, the Chan-shasha and sang his medicine songs to the morning. His old friend, the wind, swept up behind him and carried his voice to the Great Beyond. Joy touched his heart as his songs commingled with the early morning sounds.

Behind him to the west, lay the Missouri river. It was blanketed in fog, as it had been the day before. The melting snow coming from down from Canada made the Missouri particularly wide this year. The wind whispered softly in his ear.

"Good morning, Tah-tey," he whispered to the wind. "I thought you were flirting with someone else this morning." Ben joked as he knelt down on his blanket, facing rising sun. The first rays of sunlight illuminated his face.

Gingerly, he took his Cannupa out his pipe bag. In an abalone shell, he took a little sage and lit it on fire. After he blew out the flame, he smudged off the pipe stone bowl he'd carved years ago, with the sage smoke. Then, he smudged the pipe stem he made from a sapling cottonwood tree. Connecting the two pieces, he offered his sacred pipe to all the directions. He gave thanks for another day. While he prayed, Ben loaded his Cannupa with Chan-shasha, a red willow bark mixture. He reflected on the last couple days since Hal had stayed with him. It was good to have someone to be honest with. It brought him great comfort.

"Thank you Grandpa, for bringing Hal back into my life. I've long missed having a friend, a true Kola. Bless Hal and his relations with every good thing, now and forever. Thank you for all my blessings, my sobriety and my life. Aho Mitakuye Oyasin."

Striking a match, Ben lit his Cannupa and blessed off the pipe bowl with smoke. Then he blessed off the wooden pipe stem. Afterward, he blessed off himself and the Earth and blew out smoke for everyone. A gentle peace settled over the land as he puffed away on the last bit of holy smoke. Once his sacred pipe was fully smoked, he blew out the ash in a hole in the dirt. He made sure no glowing embers were left. He offered his Cannupa to the Heavens, to the Higher Powers who made it possible to live in near impossible conditions.

155

Sitting in the silence of the new day, Ben pondered his life. The sun crept slowly up over the hillsides of the east. A quiet tranquility filled his heart. Having survived so much over the span of his life, Ben remembered the wisdom and stories of the Old Ones. For many lifetimes, they lived free to roam the Great Plains, with Great Spirit providing all they needed.

Looking back, his people barely survived the endless bloodshed during the great transition. After the Nina, Pinta and Santa Maria landed on the East Coast, a sickness crossed Turtle Island. It poisoned everything it touched. Now, they were imprisoned into a communist state on the reservation. The silent heartache of that time still remained on the land.

But the story wasn't finished yet. Try as they might, his people wouldn't be extinguished. He couldn't blame them for losing faith in Creator at times. But, they were still here and their stories must be known.

Down at the house, the front door slammed as Hal stomped down the front porch step and headed towards his truck.

"Hey, I'm up here," hollered Ben down to Hal, who shielded his eyes from the bright sunlight. Hal saw Ben sitting at the top of the knoll and waved back.

"Come on up and greet the morning," hollered Ben.

Covered in morning dew and the mist from the river, the slippery wet prairie grass made it tough going in his leather soled cowboy boots. Slipping and sliding, Hal hiked to the top of the knoll. But he made it up just the same.

"Morning Koda. So this is where you come sit in the morning," said Hal. "I heard you get up yesterday, but I didn't ask."

"I knew there was something different about you," Ben said with his eyebrows raised and a wry smile. "We say 'Kola' around here. Come, sit down," said Ben as he made some room on his blanket. "You know, we all got the same 24 hours, but

156

few remember to give thanks for a new day of living."

"Where I come from, the scattered few left of Sitting Bull's people, we are Dakota. You're the ones who are different," laughed Hal. "But you're right about the 24 hours, old buddy," said Hal looking across the landscape. "Heck, I'd bet my bottom dollar there's a few out there puking their guts up right now after a good night of drinking."

"Yeah," sighed Ben in agreement. "That's the sad truth of it. I'd be one of them, if you hadn't of showed up at the Army nuthouse, all those years ago."

"Aw, you'd have been dead already," Hal laughed sitting down on the blanket, enjoying the view. "No Indian ever gets qualified as a hopeless drunk in the Army's cuckoo's nest and lives to tell about it."

"You remember that," Ben laughed. "You're spot on, there. You know, after I got sober, I had a good life. Once I met Elsie, we had a good family. It's been pretty rough lately, with the boys dying. It breaks my heart. It'd damn near destroy me if I let it. But I can't do anything but pray for them. They won't listen to an old man, anyway. It's not like when I was a kid. I'd never disrespect my grandparents the way most do now." The two men sat in silence for a while, listening to the sounds of the morning.

"So where'd you meet Elsie, anyway?" asked Hal.

"Oh, at a Powwow," said Ben as his eyes lit up. "She was selling her bead work at a table. That girl made some beautiful bead work. There were a pair of moccasins which caught my eye, but she didn't have my size. My heart moved, the first time I looked her in the eye. I saw the whole universe in her eyes. Her smile could melt butter in a snow storm," said Ben reminiscing. "You probably don't know this, but I was kind of a big deal back then."

"Oh, you don't say," laughed Hal.

"Oh yeah," said Ben. "I won a quite a few competitions

as a Fancy Dancer. We traveled all over the Midwest in my beat up old Buick. They don't make rez cars like that anymore. We ran that car right into the ground, drove it till it the bumpers fell off."

"Yup. Sounds like you made the BIG TIME, all right," laughed Hal.

"Oh sure, go ahead and laugh, Mr. Rodeo Clown," chided Ben. "After Elsie beaded me my own special moccasins, my feet moved like greased lightning. You know, the moment I saw her, I didn't think she even noticed me. She was busy with other people looking over her wares. But then she came to the next powwow and pulled out these beautiful beaded moccasins. She told me she'd made them for me."

"When I put them on, before my next competition, I danced like I was walking on clouds. I don't think my feet ever touched the ground."

"There must be some pretty powerful prayers in her bead work," chuckled Hal. "You were twitterpated, old buddy. Do you still have them, the moccasins?"

"Oh yeah, I'd never throw them away. I wore them out pretty good. But Elsie would put a new sole on them and I'd wear them another season."

"You were a lucky man, Ben," said Hal genuinely. "To get sober and have a good woman. Doesn't get any better than that."

"I have to agree with you there," said Ben grateful for the good life he'd lead. Looking north, Ben spied Kyle walking down the River Road towards his house.

"Here comes your boy, Hal. Looks like he's got something under his arm, but I can't make it out. Can you?"

"No, I can't tell either. But, I'll go down now and see," said Hal as he got up and groaned, clutching his back. "Oh, this body..."

"I got some good ointment for that," said Ben as he

158

packed up his Sacreds and rolled up his blanket. "I'm right behind you."

Ambling down the hill, Hal came up behind Kyle as he was knocking on the door. "Well, you're up early," said Hal.

"Yeah, I conked out yesterday afternoon and woke up with the birds chirping. Check this out! Mom gave me a coffee maker for Ben. I told her about the crude oil he was making..." said Kyle before he saw Ben come down the hill.

"I heard that!" said Ben, a little gruff as he stepped off the trail. "What about my coffee now?"

"Well... no disrespect, but that ain't coffee you're brewing. It's more like crude oil," started Kyle

"CRUDE OIL!!!" Ben grumbled. "Well, maybe that's why my joints don't creak, like old Hal over here."

"Oh, I see where this is going," Hal chuckled. "Starting to take pot shots at me already, are ya?"

"OKAY, well...." started Kyle not sure what he was walking into. "My mom got this extra coffee maker at a church raffle and she wanted me to give it to you."

"Ah, how nice," said Ben eyeballing the packaging. "Bringing me one of them fancy white man contraptions."

"Yeah, you just plug it in..." started Kyle.

"I can read!" said Ben feeling somewhat cantankerous.

"Here, I've got some coffee filters and a pound of her good coffee too," said Kyle handing it all to Ben.

"Well, let's give it a whirl and see how this machine works," said Ben to Hal with a sly smile and a wink. Ben was in a rather wily mood this morning.

Ben pulled the coffee maker out of the box. "Oh would you look at that. It says MR. COFFEE. And it has marks right on the coffee pot so you know how many cups you're making. This is a darn right, smart machine, Kyle. Make sure you tell your mother thank you for her thoughtfulness."

"Oh shut up, you old smart ass!" said Hal as he walked over to the counter and started putting the coffee maker together.

"I wasn't being a smart ass," Ben cloyed. "This is one of the nicest gifts anyone's given me in a while."

Ben opened up the can of coffee. He found a green scoop inside. "Oh, would you look at that. This little green scoop measures exactly how much coffee to use for a cup. I can't go wrong there."

Ben's sarcasm agitated Hal like fingernails running across a chalkboard. Hal growled as he snatched the green scoop and coffee out of Ben's hands. "GIVE ME THAT! And go sit down Ben. I got this!" Hal put the paper filter in the coffee maker and measured out enough coffee for everybody to have 2 cups, plus an extra scoop to make it a little stronger.

"You got any cinnamon, Ben?" asked Hal.

"What do you need cinnamon for?" Ben asked with his eye brows raised.

"You add it to the coffee and it tastes good," said Hal wondering if Ben had ever been to a coffee house. "They drink it that way out West."

"Oh, do they now," said Ben pulling Hal's chain. "I don't believe I ever had cinnamon in my coffee before. But, I'll give it a whirl. You'll find it in the cupboard over the stove, next to the salt and pepper."

Looking in the cupboard, Hal found the cinnamon and sprinkled a little right on the coffee. Not sure what was going on, Kyle laid low while the banter went back and forth between the two of them.

After Hal put the water in the coffee maker, he turned on the power button and he looked over at Kyle. "You got pretty quiet Kyle. Cat got your tongue?"

"Not really, I'm just sitting over here dodging bullets," said Kyle.

Ben burst out laughing, slapping his knee. "These ain't bullets Kyle, they're slings and arrows. I ain't even pulled out my tomahawk yet."

"Oh, I'll be waiting around for that," Hal chuckled. "You and your cockamamie coffee maker!"

"You guys remind me of my grandma and Aunt May," said Kyle. "Bickering in the kitchen about who made the better mash potatoes. They'd go at it for hours, till you were afraid to go in there."

"Aw, we're just having some fun, right Ben?" said Hal.

"Speak for yourself, I'm just warming up for the second inning," Ben snickered as he pretended to take a swing.

"Well hang on, let me go get my bat and ball," said Hal.

"You know, that reminds me of the first time my dad took me into town. There was a black and white television in this mercantile window with two teams playing baseball. Me and my dad stood outside the window watching the game for the longest time. Then, my dad says to me real serious, 'Wonder why they're wearing their pajamas?' We burst out laughing."

As the coffee maker started brewing, the smell of fresh roasted coffee filled the room. They waited in expectation for this contraption to finish making their morning brew. Hal got out 3 coffee mugs, cream and sugar and put them on the table. As the last few gurgles of steam signaled the water had all boiled out, Hal poured each of them a cup. No one spoke as they fixed their cups of precious brew. Kyle waited for Ben to take his first sip. The silence was deafening. Kyle waited to hear what Ben was going to say.

"What do you think, old man?" asked Hal breaking the silence.

"Not bad, not bad at all," said Ben. "I like the hint of

cinnamon. It gives it a little kick. You learned that out West now, did ya?"

"Yes sir, I did. They got some fancy coffee houses out there. They put all kinds of ingredients in their coffee out West," said Hal.

"Like what?" Ben was curious.

"Well, chocolate, caramel, sprinkles and whip cream. They blend up ice coffee and add all kinds of flavors. But, it ain't cheap. You'll spend your whole paycheck drinking coffee out there. Some coffee drinks cost more than liquor."

"Well, that ain't right. Liquor works quicker than coffee," said Ben. "All I get if I drink too much coffee, is the jitters."

"Well, the way you make it, you'd get a heart attack!" chuckled Hal.

"Oh there you go again, poking fun at my coffee. Well, now that problem's solved, ain't it. Kyle, you go tell your mom, I'm not giving anybody a heart attack from drinking my crude oil anymore. No one need to worry about that ever again. Her generosity is greatly appreciated," said Ben rubbing it in. "Now I got to get to the post office. I got things to do today."

"Watch out for Zelda," said Kyle, talking about the woman at the post office with the evil eye.

"Oh, she don't scare me none," said Ben.

"She's mean enough to scare the hair right off a junk yard dog! The way she looks at you, over those horn rimmed glasses, with her twisted smile. It makes my skin crawl!" said Kyle.

"Boy, she's just got some mean spirits around her," chuckled Ben. "Like attracts like, even in the Spirit World. When a person's angry all the time, or even faultfinding, they'll draw certain evil spirits to themselves. Spirits are attracted to fire and anger is a raging fire."

162

"Is that what it is?" asked Kyle. "Because when I get around her, I cringe."

"Yup, her whole family is like that, with all the gambling and drinking they do. They are pretty much as self-serving and predictable as they come. I don't think they ever paid a kindness to anybody," said Ben. "Kyle, you know what attracts dark spirits to you, don't you?"

"No, not really," said Kyle.

"Well, for starters, anything that poisons the body, like alcohol or cigarettes, brings them on. But, even being in a dark mood can draw them to you. People who are mean-natured, like Zelda, are the best candidates for dark spirits, because their energy is the same. Dark spirits feed off the living. Does that make sense?" Ben waited for the light to go on in Kyle's brain.

"What do you mean, they feed off the living?" asked Kyle getting the creeps.

"Oh, this is a long conversation," said Ben looking at the clock on the wall. "And I got to keep it short because I got to help my daughters plan the boy's funeral. I heard them yelling at me already this morning."

"But, your spirit is fed by a cord of light from Creator. It goes right through the top of your head and beats your very heart. Your heart is the motor and your head is the reins. Does that make sense?" Opening up the drawer, Ben found some paper and drew a stick person, a sun and a line between the two of them.

"Yeah, I guess," said Kyle.

"Well, let's say this sun represents Creator and this cord is the light feeding your soul. Creator don't feed the dark. The dark work is left to the other guy, the one the Christians call the Tempter or Lucifer. So, lets say you do evil things. What happens is, the light slowly withdraws, leaving your body to wither and die. You following me so far?"

"Yeah, I think so," answered Kyle.

"Well, earthbound spirits who raised hell while they were alive, don't get fed light from Creator anymore. So they feed off of the living. They suck off the Light feeding your soul." Ben drew a few evil spirits siphoning off the light from the stick person. "Do you see that? This happens when people are haunted. Dark spirits suck the life force right out of you, like a parasite. That's why you get so tired."

"Whoa, I get it," said Kyle. "Like with Jason. He kept coming into my dream time."

"Oh, he was around you more than that. But, you couldn't see him. You probably heard his voice in your thoughts. Spirits talk to you in your thoughts. Not all of your thoughts are your own," said Ben looking at the clock.

"Oh man, I see it! This makes sense to me," said Kyle. "So how do you get rid of them? I know you got to go, but I want to know."

"Don't be like them, Kyle. Don't be selfish. It's the mark of evil," said Ben as he sat down at the table, looking the boy squarely in the eye. "See, what you speak matters. Because your words come from your heart. If your heart isn't clean, neither are your words. So clean out your troubled heart and don't hate. The dark ones are attracted to hate. Those ghouls are happy when you're miserable."

"Another thing," Ben went on. "Use sweet grass, cedar or sage to cleanse your home. Find a sweat lodge. Go to a Sun Dance ceremony. Clean out your mind, body and spirit. Clean up your house with ammonia. Because dark spirits live in filth. But don't mix ammonia with bleach, ever, because that'll kill you. And most of all, love others like Creator loves you. Without conditions and without exceptions. You might not like them, but you can treat them with dignity and respect. And if you and Hal work the 12 Steps, by the time you get to Step 12, you'll be a hollow bone, like Hal talked about the other night. Then Creator will hold you to Himself and you will never walk alone."

"I couldn't have said it better myself," said Hal.

"There are two roads, Kyle. The High road and the low road, Light and dark. When you serve Creator and others, you are on the High road. When you only serve yourself, you're lined up with the dark." Ben got up from the table.

"I got to go. You'll find a couple AA Big Books in the small book shelf over there. Maybe even a Twelve and Twelve. You can use them. I always wanted to start a book study, but never got much interest. I'll see you later," said Ben as he took his hat off the nail and walked out the front door.

Finding the books on the shelf, Hal laid them on the table. "Well Kyle, you ready to work the 12 Steps?"

"Yeah, I am," said Kyle pondering what just happened. "Ben's really deep, isn't he?"

"Deeper than the ocean's blue," said Hal.

"I've never been to the ocean," said Kyle. "I've only seen it on TV."

"Well, one day, you'll go see it and know what I mean. But, even the midnight sky is deep blue, blanketed with all those stars." Hal slid a copy of the Big Book over to Kyle and cracked it open to page 58, chapter 5, HOW IT WORKS.

"Here, we'll start with 'How it works.' I'll read a page and you read a page. After that, we'll get started on the Steps. You go first, Kyle."

"Oh, why do I got to start reading first?"

"Listen you big whiner, I already did the Steps. It's your turn," smiled Hal.

"I'm not a good reader," Kyle admitted trying to get out of it.

"Uh, listen here, knucklehead. I met guys in the joint who learned how to read out of this book. So get on with it. I won't make fun of you, promise," smiled Hal.

"Oh, yeah, I saw how you and old Ben got along," said Kyle. "Like two old hens."

"You gonna read or what?!" said Hal taking the Big Book and raising it over his head, ready to clobber Kyle with it.

"OK, OK," said Kyle, as he turned to page 58. "Chapter 5, How It Works... Rarely have we seen a person fail who has thoroughly followed our path..."

As they took turns reading, Hal gently corrected Kyle as he mispronounced some words. They read until they got to the middle of page 60, when Hal stopped Kyle after he read (c) That God could and would if He were sought.

"So did you understand any of that?" asked Hal.

"Man, what year did they write this book anyway? Nobody talks like that anymore!" said Kyle mockingly.

"The book was written in the 1930's by an unemployed drunken stockbroker and an addict/alcoholic doctor who admitted, when it came to alcohol, they were beat, down for the count, that they were powerless..."

"Hey, what's up with this powerless crap," Kyle interrupted sarcastically. "Do I look weak to you?"

"The first step says powerless over alcohol, and that's what it means. I don't give a rats ass if you can bench press a gorilla. It's when you partner up with those demons in the bottle, that you're a defenseless drunk. And end up face down in the gutter in a puddle of your own puke. Sound familiar?"

"So, what are you trying to say?" Kyle asked shirking the implication.

"Oh! Come on," said Hal exasperated. "Are you denying you never puked, passed out or blacked out after a good night of partying?"

"Well, yeah but doesn't everybody?"

"No fool! Most people, who are not alcoholic, will generally stop drinking the second they feel tipsy."

"Yeah, well then, more for me," Kyle laughed sarcastically. "Tipsy is when I drink harder."

"Exactly... and after the 3rd or 4th drink, when things start to go sideways, you drink some more, right?" asked Hal.

"Yeah, sure," said Kyle. "What's your point?"

"The point is, non alcoholics don't drink for the effect. They're not looking to get sideways, lose their car keys or not find their way home. They don't puke on their shoes, pee their pants, pass out or even black out. They remember everything that happened and will tell you exactly what you did the next morning when you're nursing a nasty hangover," laughed Hal.

"Oh yeah, I had a girl like that once. It didn't last long," said Kyle.

"Naw, I wouldn't think so," said Hal.

"So, you think I'm alcoholic?" asked Kyle.

"Well, it doesn't matter what I think. Only you can decide that. All I can do is take you through the Steps and help you out that way."

"Oh, I see."

"So, in the first 3 Steps, you're basically trading the demons in the bottle for the Spirit of the Universe. And living a better, honest, purpose driven life."

"That sounds kinda boring," said Kyle scoffed, leaning back in his chair.

"Yeah, trading chaos in for serenity seems boring at first," Hal chuckled. "But I like it better. I usually know where my keys are."

"But, what do you do for fun?" asked Kyle anxiously afraid he'd have to turn into a monk. "I don't want to be like one of them church goers, sitting around, praying all day."

"Yeah, I can see where that'd be a problem. Those tight collars never appealed too much to me either. But if you look here, on page 44, "To be doomed to an alcoholic death or to live on a spiritual basis are not always easy alternatives to face." They thought of that already. Don't worry. I was grateful to not go off in handcuffs anymore."

"Who said anything about an alcoholic death? What the hell does that mean?" asked Kyle obviously agitated.

"Oh, so you never considered passing out and choking on your own puke? That's one kind of alcoholic death. Do you want me to name a few?" Hal was having way too much fun with this. It was starting to piss Kyle off. Kyle threw Hal a dirty look.

"Okay," said Hal with a chuckle. "I'll give you a few examples, so you'll know what's waiting up the road for you, if you be a real alcoholic. That's only fair. Give a man a choice, I say. Choking on your own vomit, well that's always attractive. It happened to a famous drummer back in the '70's. Wrapping your car around a tree and breaking your neck, runs a close second. Getting murdered in a drunken bar fight, that's one of my favorites. Or you can die a slow miserable death where your liver shuts down and all your internal organs fail. Do you get the picture?"

"Yeah, whatever," said Kyle staring at the floor. "That shit don't scare me."

"I'm not trying to scare you," said Hal feeling that he was losing his audience. "I'm giving you your options, because I've never met an Indian who could drink. At least not very well. Do you think you are an alcoholic? Have you ever tried to quit? Is your life is out of control because you drink?"

Kyle thought about it for a minute. "I don't know. Sometimes it goes my way. And other times it goes to hell and shit gets all pushed out of shape."

"Well, if you can't admit you're powerless when it comes to alcohol, you probably need to drink some more," said Hal pushing his seat back. "You might need to get locked up behind a DUI or kill someone, before you can admit that you can't drink without consequences."

"Well, how do you know if you are alcoholic?" asked Kyle. "Is there a test? Maybe I'm not one."

"Actually there is a test, right here on page 44, chapter 4, We Agnostics," said Hal.

"Man, you sure know this book?" Kyle chuckled.

"You'd know something too, if it saved your life," Hal said with a serious look.

"Okay, so what's the test?" asked Kyle.

Hal started scanning and reading to himself. "Okay here it is on page 44. It talks about the distinction between the alcoholic and the non alcoholic. I'll decode it for ya. It says if, when you want to stop drinking, but you can't quit for keeps or when you drink, you can't control how much you drink, then you're probably alcoholic, which is an illness only a band of heavenly Angels can conquer. More or less."

If the look on Kyle's face wasn't so disturbing, it'd be priceless. Feeling under the gun, Hal skimmed a few more pages, before he closed the book and told it to him straight.

"Okay, look," said Hal with all the patience he could muster. "First of all, the only person who can decide whether you're an alcoholic is you. There are definite signs, things that happen to people who are addicted to alcohol and drugs."

"Alcoholics crave alcohol. Once they drink it, it's damn near impossible to stop. For all I know, you might be a potential alcoholic. Maybe you have a few more years of good drinking left, before you end up in jail, the hospital or the morgue."

"Whoa dude, what do you mean the morgue?" asked Kyle thunderstruck.

"Jails, institutions and death. That's the way it goes for

people afflicted with alcoholism. It's not pretty. The car wrecks, the gunshot wounds with blood everywhere. Broken families, divorce, the body's broke down and spiritually bankrupt. Alcohol makes decent people do insane things. People get hurt and some die. Actually, a whole lot of them die. Some more slowly than others."

"Yeah, my mom won't let my dad in the house anymore," Kyle said sadly. "The last time he was drunk, he blew up and trashed the house. He punched my mom in the mouth." The painful memory was evident on his face.

"From my experience, when a woman gets punched in the mouth, it's because what she said, cut real deep. Most murders start out with words. Wasn't that your dad I met at the meeting the other night?" asked Hal.

"Yeah, he's got 2 months sober," smiled Kyle.

"How long has he been out of the house?" asked Hal.

"Almost 2 years," said Kyle looking down.

"And he's only got two months sober. Do you see how strong those demons in the bottle hold on?"

"Yeah, he tried to quit on his own, but it never worked. After he beat up my mom, she called the police and told him to get out."

"Smart woman," Hal commented. "Have you ever tried to stop?"

"Yeah, I had to quit drinking for a while. I almost didn't graduate high school. When the school counselor called my mom, she was so pissed because I was short on credits. I missed too much school in my senior year to graduate with my class. I was truant too many times."

"So what happened in high school?"

"Oh, it was boring. I had to get out of there. Me and my buddies would cut class and get high on the football field. Or we'd end up by the river and get drunk."

"So it never occurred to you that you might not graduate?"

"I didn't really care. It didn't seem important at the time. Who really gives a shit? Everybody here lives on the government dime. It's not like that's going to change. If I marry a Seminole girl, I'll be in good shape. They get some good benefits, like three or four grand a month."

"Back in the day, guys like that were called 'squaw men.' Usually they were white men who married an Indian girl to live off the federal government. You really want to be a kept man, Kyle?"

"Well you make it sound like it's a bad thing," laughed Kyle sarcastically.

Hearing enough, Hal pushed his chair back from the table and walked to the counter to get some more coffee. He felt himself drawn down into the belly of the beast and wasn't sure what his next move would be.

He remembered reading once, that George Washington thought he could solve the Indian Problem by 'civilizing' these freedom loving people'. As far as he could see, the results of this 180 year social experiment with Native People were pretty grim.

It started long before the US government acquired Florida from Spain in 1821. Back then, the white settlers wanted that Native land to grow cotton. The white expansion spread like a cancer through Turtle Island, killing everything in its path. By any means, the settlers drove the Native People off their ancient homeland. After that, in 1830, began the "Trail of Tears" whereby tribes in the Deep South were forced against their will to relocate to federal lands west of the Mississippi River. Thousands died as they trekked over a thousand miles to Indian territory. Bloody wars began as many of the southeastern tribes resisted military takeover.

In 1851, by executive order, which has the full force of the law, the American Indian was forced onto reservations.

Those tribes who refused to obey the Great White Father were slaughtered. This executive order lead to the bloodiest wars between the encroaching Europeans settlers and the Native People. Against their will, tribes were driven from their ancestral lands to desolate areas that didn't grow corn.

After being forced at gunpoint from their land and imprisoned on a federal reserve, the Europeans sought to "civilize" the wayward Injuns by shoving Christianity down their throats. After 180 years, these federal land reserves equaled a communist country dictated by the federal government. Invisible barbwire made of hatred corralled the Natives in. In effect, this wasicu mindset crippled the Native spirit and imprisoned its will.

"You want a warm up?" Hal asked as he realized how deep this malady was in Indian country. But, he had no idea how to reverse the ill effects of reservation life. When he left the rez at 17, he enlisted in the Army and never looked back. Once a year, he'd visit his parents during his rodeo days. But the last time he'd been on the rez was when his mom died about 10 years ago.

"You know, my dad always hunted and fished when I was a kid," said Hal as he poured them both some more coffee. "We'd go out, deep into the woods, find a spot to sit down and wait. My dad had a knack for finding the biggest tree to lean up against. Then we'd settled in to listen to the sounds of the forest. He'd have me close my eyes and listen to every sound. It took a while to train my ears, but pretty soon I could make out almost every sound I heard. The deep woods were so quiet sometimes, hearing a twig snap sent echoes down my spine. But I had to be quiet, not to scare anything off. It taught me important skills, like patience and being aware of my surroundings."

"To hunt, I had to be clear-headed and disciplined. Which ain't easy when those small gnats were buzzing around my head. Shit, some of them crawled right up my nose. Now, I'd scare off the game, if I sat there cursing and swatting mosquitoes."

"Before we set out, my dad offered a tobacco prayer. He'd call on the Spirits for guidance. This gave us serenity in the hunt. When the game showed up, it was a gift from Creator. It made it possible for us to live another day. We never took it for granted. For me, being a good provider, was part of becoming a man. I still fish or hunt when I can. I caught like 5 bass yesterday in the river. Me and Ben had a fish fry last night. We got 3 more fish in the freezer."

"When I was young, the Old Ones drilled into me, that to become a man, I needed to be a good warrior. Protecting our loved ones was part of our traditional culture. They told me to enlist in the Army. I enlisted when I was 17 and been on the road ever since. I had to make my way, wherever I was. Sure, there were times when I was down and out. Especially when I was drunk and lived in a chicken coop. But I couldn't marry a woman to take care of me. What attracted me to Arlene was she had a job and an clean apartment when we met. But, I started working a couple months after I got sober and have ever since."

Feeling lectured, Kyle ire rose into his throat and he lit into Hal. "So what, you think we should go back to hunting buffalo? And drag our stuff all over the prairie?" Kyle goaded Hal. "Or maybe we should wear a loin clothe and ride our painted ponies out to count coup on the Crow?"

"That's not what I said," Hal felt Kyle's anger building.

"Yeah, well I get it," Kyle fumed as he push his chair back from the table and stomped through the kitchen. "I live this reservation life every day. Everyone here is dependent on the government, but we're still starving to death. It's a no man's land out here. There's no shopping malls or movie houses. The damn grocery store is 20 miles away. Try making it there in a snow storm on your paint pony!"

Like flipping the lid off a volcano, Kyle's tirade took life. "When those greedy whites came here, looking for gold, they trampled over our land, killed our people, and destroyed our Old Ways. We're a nation of forgotten people and the Old Ways you talk about are dead!"

"You're wrong, Kyle. Those Old Ways are the heartbeat of our people," said Hal. "Great Spirit..."

Kyle cut Hal off mid sentence. "NO! You're wrong! Those Old Ways are in cardiac arrest! That heartbeat flat lined a long time ago. People don't give a shit about those things any more. It's history!" Kyle's venomous rage exploded. "The real thing, those Old Ones who carried the Medicine Ways, they died and took the Old Ways with them. All we got now is talk!"

"KYLE!" Hal interrupted, but Kyle wouldn't listen. Dumbfounded, Hal sat back as Kyle exploded about how the Old Ways were dead. But what boggled Hal's mind, was that Kyle didn't realize Ben spent the better part of yesterday practicing the Old Ways to cast out earthbound spirits.

"You ever watch television, Hal? You know, the only time Indians are on TV is when they're covered in war paint! Riding bareback on a paint pony and wearing a loin cloth!" Kyle scoffed. "We only make the news when a group of Indians blows up buildings! We're fed up with the white government screwing us out of our treaty rights signed by my great, great, great grandfather! Did you know, two years ago, the power lines went down during a blizzard and the Elders here froze to death. You tell me where Great Spirit was, when my grandmother was freezing in her house? It was the dead of winter. She didn't have money to pay the utilities. Where was your Great Spirit then?"

Watching this volcano erupt, Hal got quiet. The old wooden floorboards quaked as Kyle stomped across the floor. Hal didn't quite know how to answer. How do you explain the effects of a world calloused by hate?

When Mother Earth brings forth her gardens of color every spring, the fields explode in a vibrant blaze of beauty. A rhapsody of wildflowers blankets the prairie. Every bloom

174

blends its color in a majestic rainbow. But flowers don't hate each other for being different colors. Only mankind discriminates by skin color, education or social standing. Indian reservations were the result of such hatred.

"Nobody gives a shit about us," fumed Kyle as his rant went on. "Don't you get it! We don't exist! To the rest of the world, we're invisible. There's no jobs. Last hunting season I worked at the casino. These rich white dudes, all decked out in army fatigues, showed up with their high powered hunting rifles. I watched them strut around the buffet. They were bragging about the deer they shot that day. But they are shooting here, on our land for money."

"OKAY!!! I hear you! I get it!" said Hal trying to get a word in edgewise. "It's hard, damn near impossible, to trust in a God who let you down your whole life. Especially when you feel that He abandoned you. That He let bad things to happen to you and your family. I understand how hard that is. Listen, when I was a little tike, an old nun told me the best I'd ever do, was go to purgatory. And I believed her because she was close to God. I see how painful this is. Our ancestors were a noble people. They roamed the Great Plains, free and brave. And now, 200 years after the whites showed up, we're dying drunk in the gutter and scrambling for money. After the Sacred Hoop was broken at Wounded Knee, they shoved us onto a concentration camp. Now we're crippled by government programs and turned into beggars."

Sitting back down at the table, Kyle put his head in his hands. "The whole thing is hopeless. I read somewhere that before the white man came to America, there were 19 million Indians on this continent. Now there's only about 260 thousand Indians left on Turtle Island. Where did all the Indians go, Hal? That's a lot of missing people since Columbus got here. We lost the war. Since those bastards couldn't kill us all, they shoved us on this prison camp and stripped us of everything. Hell, most of us don't even know our own language."

"War is ugly, Kyle. Europeans brought diseases to our people we never had before. We never crushed grapes. We didn't have small pox. We ate pure food and drank clean water. Look around now and you don't see a pure food in any kitchen. Tell me what plant does Mountain Dew or Coca-cola come from? Today you can't drink out of the rivers, because some industrial plant dumps their chemicals in it," said Hal disgusted.

"Yeah, 200 years ago, our people weren't fat either. But, now we're all dying of diabetes," said Kyle. "It was all about gold and broken treaties."

"You know, I don't know much about treaties," Hal started. "But we don't own the Earth. When I die, the only thing I'll own is my name. For the most part, we can't tell Mother Earth what to do. We don't even own our bodies, because we don't take them with us when we go. What comes from the Earth, stays with the Earth. So I'm clueless why people argue over a chunk of land. In my travels, I learned every pebble is sacred, because it was created by a Power much greater than me."

"Don't give up, Kyle," said Hal intently. "You may think the Old Ways are dead, but I've witnessed their power. Think about the work you, me and Ben did yesterday. The only reason Natives are cynical of our ancient ceremonies is, because they've been influenced by too much white education. But I've seen the power of prayer, Kyle. I've seen Creator move through impossible situations and miracles happen. Can you believe that I believe?"

"Believe in what?" Kyle shrugged. "In a medicine that's grown cold."

"But, that's not true," Hal said digging deep into his soul for answers. "All real Power comes from Creator, Kyle. And it's still here. We are Spirit and to Spirit we will return. How can you deny the power of a thunderstorm? Have you ever watched it sweep over the land and purify everything with all its might? Or the wind, when she works herself into a fury and clears out everything in her path? What about the warmth of a blazing fire? Or the power of rushing rivers after the winter snow melts? We are people of the Earth, Kyle. We have walked with the Power of the Elements for centuries."

In the deep recesses of his mind, a light flickered. Kyle realized he couldn't deny the power of Mother Nature. Sitting there in the kitchen with Hal, it struck him that nobody talked about the things Hal and Ben talked about. After a long moment, Kyle conceded. "Yeah, I can see that you believe. But, what does that do for me?"

"One step a at time, Kyle. One step at a time," said Hal as his soul smiled. His stomach was rumbling. "Hey, I need to get some supplies. Do you want to show me where the supermarket is?"

"There's nothing super about the market on the rez," laughed Kyle. "It's about 20 minutes north of here. Or we can drive an hour into the city, if you want to go to WalMart."

"What? There's no market here, in town?"

"Naw, there's a mini market. But he charges 3 times as much as the store."

"Well, alright, let's go to the market. At least I'll know where things are," said Hal.

Walking out the door, Hal noticed the towering billowy thunderheads painted across a sprawling blue sky. Whispering softly through a few trees, the wind caressed the tall prairie grasses, making them dance to and fro. Hal's truck was packed to the gills with camping gear and old suitcases full of his meager possessions. As he moved a few things into the back seat, it dawned on him, everything he owned was in the cab of his truck.

"So where's home for you?" asked Kyle as he pulled the creaking door shut.

"You're looking at it," said Hal as he revved up the old rumpy motor. "Working rodeos as long as I have, you hardly settle down. Sometimes, I worked different ranches for a spell or two. But most of the time, I keep moving. I'm just a nomad, chasing the buffalo."

"Don't you get tired of going from one place to another?"

"Naw, I get more tired listening to the stale yammer of ungrateful people. Or being tied down to someplace unfriendly. If the people are good, that's different. I had a few good runs out West. I'd stay a stretch of time at a ranch, until the work got sour or the wind told me it was time to go. For the most part, I like to go where I'm appreciated."

As they turned out onto the main two lane highway, the wide undulating prairie opened up. It was speckled with a few farm houses and fields of golden corn.

When they got close to town, there were a number of plain buildings on both sides of the highway. "That's the high school over on the left and behind it, is the community college, where I go to school," said Kyle. "Turn left when you get to the stop light. The store is on the right, just before the gas station."

His old beater truck slowed as they approached the blinking red stop light hanging in the middle of the intersection. Hal put on his blinkers and turned into the left turning lane. The main street was lined with small business on the right and a taco stand on the left. Listening to his stomach grumble, a taco sounded pretty good about now. Turning right, Hal pulled his truck into the market parking lot along side the road. In front of the market, was a homeless man in grubby overalls, stumbling around on the sidewalk.

"Look at that guy," said Kyle in a harsh, callous tone.

Having been homeless himself, Hal was familiar with homeless people. "What's the big deal? Out West, there's homeless people all over. Almost under every freeway off ramp, they got shopping carts packed full of chattel," said Hal.

"Yeah," said Kyle looking at the man in disdain. "But, out West, not every homeless guy is your brother."

"That's your brother?" asked Hal surprised. He watched this drunken Indian stumble all over the sidewalk.

"Yeah," said Kyle horrified by how bad his brother looked. "When Leroy got back from the war, almost a year ago, he was a mess. His team got ambushed. And he was wounded in battle. Most of his buddies died in the ambush."

"Nobody takes care of him?" Hal's heart went out to this drunken soldier, as he parked the truck in front of the store.

"Mom tried, but she don't allow drinking in the house. Leroy wasn't going to stop. He told her point blank, he earned his right to drink. They had a big fight and he bailed," said Kyle. "That's the last time we saw him, until now."

Getting out of the truck, Hal watched as Leroy stumbled down a step and crash landed on his face. Hal rushed over to where Leroy's sprawled body was laying, face down in the dirt.

"Leroy, Leroy, can you hear me?" asked Hal as he got a whiff of the overwhelming stench coming off Leroy's body. From his emaciated condition, Hal could tell Leroy had been roughing it for quite a while. Hal hoisted Leroy up in his big arms and leaned his frail, depleted body against the side of the grocery mart.

"Leroy, my name's Hal. I got your brother Kyle with me. We're going to take you and get you cleaned up. You got it, son?"

Semi-conscious, Leroy eyes rolled from side to side as he groaned some inaudible response. Staring in disbelief, Kyle stood on the other side of Leroy, shaking his head.

"Kyle," Hal's tone was urgent. "You get on the right side and I'll take the left. Let's get him into my truck. He needs help. How far is the VA Hospital from here?"

"The VA, ugh, the closet one is about 2 hours from here."

"Well, that ain't gonna work," said Hal frustrated, thinking on his feet. "Okay, I know what we're going to do. Here, help me get him into the back seat."

"You want me to throw your suitcases in the back of the truck first?" said Kyle. "It's pretty crowded back there."

"No, I'll do it," said Hal. "You stay here and hold him steady."

Not wanting to throw up, Kyle covered his nose, as he held his brother against the wall. Hal made quick work of unloading his suitcases and bedroll from the back seat. He put everything into the truck bed. Then, he pulled a tarp over and tied it all down so it wouldn't get sucked out with the wind. With the back seat cleared out, Hal walked over to where the two brothers were leaning up against the store wall.

"Okay, let's get him into the back seat," said Hal as they got on both sides of Leroy and pulled him up. Draping Leroy's arms over their shoulders, they walked him over to the truck and laid him down across the back seat. "Okay, lean his head up against the sleeping bag. I don't want him to choke on his own vomit," said Hal as he strapped Leroy in with a lap belt, so he wouldn't roll off.

"Where are we going?" asked Kyle as he gently put the sleeping bag under his brother's head.

"Well first, I want to get him cleaned up. From the looks of it, he's been on the skids for a while. There's a truck stop off the interstate. I can get him a shower. He needs liquid and food. My guess is, he's pretty dehydrated. It's sad that we let our soldiers get so pitiful," said Hal watching Leroy through the review mirror.

Backing out of the parking lot, Hal made a u-turn and headed towards the main highway. Hal was no stranger to Twelve Step calls, but this was the worst he'd ever seen. Living on the beach, most winos out West survived the mild winter. But the winters on the prairie were fierce. Hal doubted very much, if Leroy could survive one more season in his condition.

"So what branch of service was your brother in Kyle?" asked Hal.

"He was a Marine, gunnery sergeant. He served about 6 years when he got wounded and the rest of his guys were ambushed. Most of them died," said Kyle.

"That's rough," said Hal. "Did anyone do a healing, a warrior ceremony or anything for him, when he got back?"

"I don't think so. I don't know what that is," said Kyle.

"In the old times, after our warriors returned from battle, we held ceremonies for them. The ceremony cleansed off the evil of war and healed their wounded spirits. That way, they could return to the path of peace. We had special sweat lodges for them. Maybe I can get Ben to fire up his lodge and we could get your brother's spirit back in a good way," said Hal.

"You know a lot about this stuff," said Kyle. "You think you can help my brother?"

"I only know bits and pieces, Kyle. I can get him cleaned up and put some food in his belly," said Hal with concern. "But he's got to want to recover. That part's on him."

Pushing his old beater truck as hard as he could, they drove passed small hamlets and towns until they got to the interstate. "West to Colorado," said Hal to himself.

"Colorado?" Kyle questioned.

"That's the way to the truck stop," said Hal. "It's only a couple miles from here." Turning onto the interstate, Hal drove to the truck stop and pulled into the parking lot. "Wait here, I'll buy a shower and come get you."

Behind the counter stood a teenage girl, bored and listening to the radio. Feeling anxious, Hal waited at the counter, wondering how this was all going to go. Quietly, he made a prayer for help while he waited for the cashier to notice him. As he cleared his throat, she turned around.

"Can I help you?" asked the cashier.

"Yeah, I'll take one shower, a cup of coffee and a bottle of water."

The cashier punched in the amounts on the register. "That will be $7.00."

"I'll need a couple of towels too," said Hal as he pulled out his wallet. After she took his money and put it into the register, she handed him two blue towels and the key for shower #1. "The showers are around back," said the cashier.

Putting the change back into his wallet, Hal noticed t-shirts hanging on the wall. "How much are those t-shirts?"

"Those are $5.00 or you can get two for $9.00," she said.

"I'll take two of the extra large 'NATIVE PRIDE' camouflage shirts with the eagle feather on it," said Hal reaching for his wallet one more time. He noticed all the Native American trinkets and statuettes all over the store.

"Anything else," the cashier said, putting the t-shirts into a bag.

"Yeah," said Hal. "You got some boxer shorts?"

"They're down that aisle to the left," said the cashier.

Walking down the aisle, Hal grabbed a couple packages of boxer shorts. Leroy would need some clean skivvies after he showered. Then he remembered how the old timers in AA gave him orange juice with some corn syrup in it. It helped to stop the shakes, when he first got sober. Hal found the grocery section and got a pint of orange juice and some corn syrup. This would get Leroy's blood sugar up. Hal had some jeans Leroy could wear and some socks. But, nothing felt better than a clean shirt, clean shorts and a shower after you lived on the streets for a while.

Handing the cashier all his packages, she placed them in the bag and totaled Hal's bill. Once the money was exchanged, Hal got his coffee. He looked around to see if he needed anything else. When Hal got back to the truck, Leroy was starting to come around, groaning in the back seat.

The shower house was around back, with individual rooms containing a full shower, toilet and sink. There was a bench to put things on. The blue tiled floors were clean. There was a full soap dispenser in the shower and at the sink. Walking back outside, Hal spied a couple plastic chairs around a table by the fast food restaurant. "That would work," Hal thought out loud.

"Kyle, go get one of them plastic chairs and bring it in here," Hal commanded. Running like a thief in the night, Kyle hustled over to the burger joint, grabbed a chair and brought it in the shower room.

"Great, put it inside the shower and help me get your brother," said Hal. Wasting no time, Kyle moved quick after hearing Leroy groaning in the back seat. He was totally disoriented.

"Where the fuck am I?" hollered Leroy, tugging at the seat belt.

Undoing the seat belt, Hal's compassionate voice gentled Leroy's fear. "Hey buddy, me and Kyle are going to help get you cleaned up," said Hal as he eased Leroy out of the truck. Faltering, Leroy's gait was unsteady. His knees gave way and he started to plummet towards the ground. Grabbing Leroy by his coveralls, Hal put his big arms around Leroy's shoulder. "Hold steady now, Leroy."

Walking Leroy into the shower, they set him down on the bench. "Okay, let's get him down to his skivvies and set him in the chair. Go ahead, untie his boots Kyle."

As Kyle knelt in front of his brother, untying his army boots, a vivid memory flooded into his mind when he was a boy. "He used to do this for me, tie my shoes, when I was a little kid," said Kyle to Hal.

"Life goes full circle, boy," said Hal pulling off Leroy's soiled shirt. On Leroy's shoulder was a large angry scar where the bullet had passed through. Hal's fingers slightly traced over the war wound. He felt compassion for the pain.

"Your brother got shot in the shoulder," inquired Hal.

"Yeah, it passed straight through," said Kyle looking at the scar. "The doctor said he was pretty lucky. It didn't hit the bone." The hot water was already running in the shower, once they got him down to his shorts. Setting Leroy in the shower, he slouched down in the chair. His body was limp and exhausted. He was trapped in a fog of an alcohol induced black out.

"Kyle, why don't you wash his hair, while I get my sponge to lather him up," said Hal. "At least he'll start smelling better. Those pants have been soiled too many times. We'll just throw them out."

"Yeah, he's got clothes at home. I'll get him some things when we get back," said Kyle scrubbing his brother's long, unkempt hair. With sponge in hand, Hal rolled up his sleeves. After he soaked the sponge with warm water and soap, he gently scrubbed Leroy's shoulders and arms. The dirt splattered and circled down the drain. As they scrubbed Leroy's tired body, the alcoholic fog started to lift. The warm water felt good. He tried to stand up from the chair.

"You wanna do it yourself, buddy?" asked Hal watching Leroy try to stand up. Along the shower wall, were handicapped railings. "Here, hold on to the railing, Leroy," said Hal helping Leroy get a grip as his legs teetered a little.

With gratitude, Leroy's bloodshot eyes looked up at Hal. "Thanks," whispered Leroy.

"You got it buddy," said Hal with a voice full of compassion. As Leroy stood up on his own, he pulled the shower curtain closed.

"Hand me the sponge," Leroy said as Hal passed it through the shower curtain. The hot water felt good as his soiled boxers slid down to the floor and Leroy cleaned himself up. Life started to flow through his tattered and torn spirit.

"You got a towel?" Leroy asked as he turned off the water. Kyle handed him a towel through the shower curtain. When Leroy opened the shower curtain, with the towel wrapped around his waist, you could count almost every rib.

"You ready for a good meal?" asked Hal.

"Yeah, when we found you, the buzzards were circling already," said Kyle.

"Shut up Kyle," said Leroy crossing the floor to get dressed.

"Kyle, there's not enough meat on your brother for any self respecting buzzard to want," Hal joked.

"So what, now I got to deal with Heckle and Jeckle?" Leroy scolded as he made it over to the bench to sit down. "Where's my clothes?"

"Yeah, about your clothes, we threw them out, except your boots. I got you a new t-shirt, some boxer shorts and a pair of sweat pants and some socks. You can wear that until we get you home and get some clothes. If that's alright with you?" asked Hal giving him clean clothes to wear. "You need a tooth brush?" asked Hal as he got a new one out of his pack with some tooth paste.

Leroy nodded. He felt raw and out of his element. Not having looked in the mirror for a while, Leroy dared to meet his own gaze as he brushed his teeth. His blood shot eyes stared back at him. His eyes told the tale of the horror he'd witnessed back in the desert of hell. He'd seen a lot for a man not 30 years old.

"Are you up for a good bowl of stew and some corn bread? How is your stomach feeling?" asked Hal.

"Yeah, I could eat," said Leroy meeting Hal's gaze in the mirror.

"There's a pretty good coffee shop about a mile from here. We'll go eat there," Hal suggested.

"That sounds good. Just nothing spicy. I don't think I could handle that right now," said Leroy.

While Kyle brought back the chair to the burger joint,

Hal rearranged his things in the back of the truck. He covered them with the tarp, so nothing would fly out. After both brothers settled in, Hal started the engine and looked up to the sky. He whispered "Thanks" to Great Spirit.

When they got to the coffee shop, it was shortly after the lunch rush. Most of the restaurant was empty. After they found a booth, the waitress brought menus and asked them if they wanted anything to drink.

"I'll take some coffee," said Hal. "And what's your soup today?"

"We have a beef stew with potatoes, carrots and celery. That comes with cornbread," said the waitress.

"I'll take a bowl of that, with cornbread and coffee," said Hal.

"Make that two," said Leroy.

"Make it three," said Kyle.

"Well, so that's three bowls of beef stew, cornbread and coffee," said the waitress. "Anything else?"

"Not yet," said Hal as the waitress left to fill the order. "You might want to go easy on the coffee, Leroy, until you get something in your stomach," Hal cautioned. "When was your last meal?"

"A few days ago, I think. But right now, it's all a blur," said Leroy getting his bearings, back on civilized ground.

"Yeah, I've had years like that," said Hal knowing from experience. "Not the best memories, either."

"So where'd you all meet?" asked Leroy changing the subject. He wanted to get the eyes off him. "I don't think I've seen you around."

"Dad dragged me along to his AA meeting and Hal was the speaker," offered Kyle. "Hal gives a good talk."

"Well thanks Kyle. That's good to know," Hal smiled.

"Yeah, they tried to get me to go to AA, but..." said Leroy.

"Well, you got to be ready for that. It's a whole different life. Before I got sober, I was living or I should say dying in a chicken coop," said Hal. "No chicken's though, just feathers."

The waitress brought 3 coffees, 3 bowls of beef stew and 3 big slices of cornbread and put them down in front of them. "Now let me know if you'd like something else," said the waitress.

"Can we get some water too," asked Hal.

"Of course, and I'll bring some more coffee," said the waitress.

With trembling hands, Leroy picked up his soup spoon. It took concentration to keep his hands steady, so not to spill his soup. When he finally got the soup to his lips and put it in his mouth, he felt the warm soup go down his throat. His belly had been empty so long.

Not saying a word, Hal cut Leroy's cornbread in half and slathered it with honey butter. The butter melted into the warm cornbread as Hal slid it across the table. Leroy smiled in appreciation as he picked up a piece and put it in his mouth. Honey butter on warm cornbread brought sweetness.

"Man, I got a headache," said Leroy after a while.

"You're probably dehydrated," said Hal as he reached into his bag and pulled out the orange juice and corn syrup. He fixed up a glass and pushed it towards Leroy. "Here, this will slow down the shakes and get your body fueled up again."

"I could sleep, after we finish this food," said Leroy feeling tired.

"Drink some water, first son. You're body needs it," said Hal. "Alcohol dehydrates the body, especially the brain."

Watching Leroy finished his stew and cornbread, did Hal's heart good. Homeless and hungry veterans broke his heart. He knew the great sacrifice they made for others. After they finished their meal, Hal paid the check. He left enough on the table for the tip.

"Alright boys, let's go," Hal said as he put his big arm around Leroy to keep him steady. Once Leroy settled in the back seat, with his head on the sleeping bag, he fell into a deep slumber. As the rumpy motor came alive, Hal looked in the rear view mirror and backed out of his parking space. Making the drive back to the rez in silence, they recapitulated over the days happenings. The day had been large and it wasn't over yet.

Sitting on the front porch, Ben watched as Hal pulled the truck up to the house. Curled up in the backseat, Leroy's exhausted body hadn't stirred the whole ride home. The doors of the old truck creaked as Kyle and Hal got out and walked up to the house.

"Well, where you been?" asked Ben as he noticed the deep furrows of concern on Hal's brow.

"It's been a day," said Hal. "Kyle, run home and get your brother some clothes. I don't think he's going to wake up soon."

"Okay, sure. Thanks for doing that for my brother today," said Kyle.

"No worries, but we're not out of the woods yet," said Hal.

"Okay, I'll be back," said Kyle as he went running toward home.

Hal's heavy boots clomped up the porch steps. He looked intently at Ben as he sat down on the other chair.

"Looks like you been of service today," said Ben.

"You ain't kidding," said Hal, worn out from a good day's work. "Leroy is passed out in the back seat of my truck. I think I need to keep an eye on him or he might be headed to the Spirit World prematurely."

"Where'd you run into him?" asked Ben. "I think he's been missing for a year, from what Jed told me."

"He fell down on his face right in front of us, when we were going to the market," said Hal shaking his head. "I ain't seen anything so pitiful in a long time. It reminded me of myself, when I crawled out of that chicken coop, all those years ago. I still didn't make it to the market."

"Don't worry, my daughters made me enough food to last a week. I got a fridge full of food and I don't eat much," said Ben. "The funeral for my grandsons is in a few days. And they're busy planning everything and buying star quilts for the give away. Plus putting together a huge feast."

"How are you doing around all that?" asked Hal with a note of concern.

"How does anyone do around that? All this misery could rip a soul to shreds," said Ben.

"I'm sorry Ben," said Hal.

"Well, what are you gonna do with Leroy?" asked Ben changing the subject.

"I was thinking of setting up my tent down by the river, where we made the fire yesterday. I can keep an eye on him that way. If someone doesn't look after him, he might die of malnutrition. He's as skinny as a rake," said Hal.

Ben's mind started thinking. "Ah, I got a better idea. There's a tipi in the shed, with all the lodge poles too. Elsie's cousin left it here. We could set it up and you can have the fire right inside to keep warm. What do you think of that? We'll put it right behind the house," said Ben.

"That's a great idea," said Hal. "Show me where it is."

As the two of them walked towards the shed, Frank and Ernie pulled up in front of the house and walked over.

"Hey," said Ben waving them over. "You showed up in the nick of time. You want to help set up the tipi in back of the house?"

"Sure, what's going on?" asked Frank.

"Hal's been busy Twelve Stepping since he got here. And we're fixing to open up a rehab in the tipi," laughed Ben.

"Seriously?" said Ernie.

"Well pretty much," said Ben. "Hal fetched Leroy out of the jaws of death today. And he's passed out in the back of the truck. Now, Hal wants to keep an eye on him. So we're setting up the tipi."

"I heard he came back from the war all shot up. He lost all his men in an ambush or something like that," said Frank.

"Yeah, that's what Kyle told me," said Hal shaking his head. "Poor kid. It's such a brainless war to waste our young people on."

"Oil and opium, that's what they're fighting about. I talked to one of my buddies who got back from the Middle East. They are using our military to bomb up all the opium fields, is what he told me. It's crazy to think that war could change the way people have lived after thousands of years," said Frank.

"That's exactly what the Christian soldiers did to the Red man. Take a look around. Look at what happened to our people. They just exchanged the Gatling gun for warheads and we still haven't recovered," said Ben.

"Oh don't get me started," said Ernie, his ire rising.

"Well, if you two help put up the tipi, we'll get this rehab started," said Ben.

"Sure, we'll help out," said Frank. Working together it didn't take them long before the tipi was set up. Finding a rake, Frank cleared the ground inside the tipi.

"You gonna have a fire inside?" asked Ernie. "Because I got a chain saw and there's a lot of wood down by the river."

"Oh that's a good idea," said Ben. "I could use some wood for my wood stove. I'll head out there with you." While Ben and Ernie took off down to the river, Frank and Hal set up the inside of the tipi. Hal's camping gear came in handy, with a cot and bedding too boot. Together with his camp stove and a couple lanterns, it didn't take long before the tipi became suitable living quarters. By the time it was all set up, Kyle came back with a bag of clothes for his brother.

"That's cool," said Kyle as he stepped into the tipi.

"Yeah, this way, I can keep an eye on Leroy and see what he needs. I did some drug and alcohol rehab work out West and learned a few things," said Hal.

"I told my mom what you did for Leroy. She wants to help out in whatever way she can. She said she'd go to the store and get whatever groceries you need. She can cook some of the foods he likes too," said Kyle. "You know, she works at the Health Clinic. If you need something from them, it's not a problem."

"Well that's good to know," said Hal. "If he starts going through heavy withdrawals, we might need to get him treated. But most likely, he just needs some good food and rest. His body is pretty weak and malnourished. Why don't you go check on him. See if he's still sleeping, but don't wake him up, if he is."

As Kyle looked in on his brother, it was obvious that the ravages of war had taken its toll. The strain on Leroy's gaunt face told the story. He wasn't the same young man who went into the military, all those years ago. Combat had aged him. Though Leroy was still passed out in the back seat, he was sweating pretty bad.

The sun was getting close to the western horizon when Ernie and Ben came back with a truck full of wood. Backing the truck up to the shed, everyone pitched in to unload the mountain of wood. Hal had already dug a deep pit in the middle of the tipi to hold a good sized fire.

Being a true mountain man, Hal got out his ax and started splitting wood. With every swing, he brought the ax down hard and precise, cleaving the logs in half. It wasn't long before a contest ensued, seeing who could split the most wood. Filling the wheelbarrow with newly split wood, Kyle worked up a sweat. He ran back and forth, stacking the wood in piles. Soon there was enough split wood to last a while.

Wiping the sweat off his brow, Hal was beat by the time everything was set up. Kyle helped get a fire going in the tipi. It started to feel pretty good in there. Hal set up a bed roll with a warm sleeping bag and some blankets for Leroy.

"You want the mattress you've been sleeping on and put it in the tipi?" asked Ben. "I don't need it and if it makes you comfortable, that's good with me."

"Are you sure?" asked Hal. "I know it goes in the couch."

"Oh that old couch, you can have that too. I hardly ever sit on it."

"First, let's see how long this set up lasts, but I'll take the mattress," said Hal.

"There's an old rug in the shed, you can use. It might make it more homey in there," said Ben.

"Yeah, I'll take that," said Hal. "It'll keep the dust down."

"Well, I'll show you were it is," said Ben walking over to the shed. Rolled up in the corner was a Chinese wool and silk rug with beautiful patterns and vibrant colors. They each grabbed an end and carried into the tipi. When Hal unrolled it, he was amazed.

"Why don't you have this rug in the house?" asked Hal. "It would cover up them worn out, wooden floorboards."

"Oh, we used to," said Ben casually. "Elsie bought it one year at a flea market and we had it in the middle of the floor. But that darn rug had it in for me from the beginning. Every time I got near it, it tripped me."

The idea of a rug with a bad attitude, made Hal chuckle. "So you're telling me, this beautiful, innocent looking rug grabbed your ankles with its tassels and sent you flying across the floor?"

"I don't know what, but that darn rug had it in for me. And never in front of Elsie. She was always gone when it happened," said Ben.

"What, you think maybe the rug was jealous?" snickered Hal playing along. "And it tried to take you out. It wanted to get rid of you when Elsie wasn't looking?" Hal burst out laughing. "That way the rug could have Elsie all to itself."

"Oh, you go ahead and laugh! But wait until that sucker sends you flying! Then, you'll crash through the tipi and land on your ear. You'll see," said Ben.

"Oh you're killing me, Ben. You're killing me. So I got to ask," Hal said laughing. "Did you tell Elsie that the rug tripped you and banished it out to the shed?"

"No it didn't go that a way. She loved that darn rug. But, after she passed away, it tripped me one more time and that was it. I rolled that sucker up and put it away. That way, it wouldn't bother me anymore," said Ben. "You might want to cedar the darn thing off when you get it in there."

"Oh, I plan on it," chuckled Hal as a car pulled up to the house. Not having seen her son Leroy in a year, Vera raced over when Kyle told her the news. The look on her face caused Hal to stop laughing. Between her deep seated frown and furled eyebrows, Hal couldn't tell if she was infuriated or worried.

When he saw his mom drive up, Kyle ran over. "Hey mom, what's up?"

"I came to see Leroy! And see if you needed any help over here," said Vera.

Leaning over slightly, Ben whispered into Hal's ear, "Watch out Hal! Here comes the Cavalry."

193

"You don't say," Hal whispered back.

"Watch how Kyle tightens up," whispered Ben. "Vera's gonna try to control everything."

"Oh, I'm familiar with the untreated Al-anon," whispered Hal. "They are much sicker than us alcoholics, you know."

"Who else would put up with our crap, unless they were sicker than us," whispered Ben.

"Darn right, there Ben. Introduce me, would you," said Hal as they walked over to the car. Rummaging around in the back seat, Vera got out a few pots and set them on the trunk. She cooked enough food for a small regiment.

"Hey there Vera," said Ben as he walked over to the car. "Let me introduce you to Hal."

"Howdy, ma'am," said Hal, taking off his hat.

"It's very nice to meet you, Hal. Kyle's told me a lot about you," said Vera with a controlled smile. "Thank you for picking up Leroy. Where is he?"

"He's still passed out in the back seat of the truck," said Kyle biting his lip. "He's gonna be alright, isn't he, Hal?"

"We'll see," said Hal. "I'm going to keep watch on him tonight..."

Cutting Hal short, Vera's voice was shrill with angst. "Shouldn't we get him to the hospital, if he's comatose and passed out. He might get the DT's and need medical treatment," she said all wound up.

"I understand your concern ma'am," said Hal. "If Leroy gets the DT's, it'll probably be 2 or 3 days after his last drink. Right now, he just seems exhausted and plain starved."

"He never was a good eater," Vera fretted. "He was always watching his weight. He ran track in high school and never had an ounce of fat on him." The fear of failed motherhood was in her eyes. "I made some of his favorite

194

foods that he liked growing up. Macaroni and cheese, some beef stew and some other things."

"Kyle, why don't you take the food and put it in the fridge in the house," instructed Ben gently. Vera's anxiety noticeably jammed Kyle up. Ben attempted to run interference before things got out of control.

As Kyle grabbed the groceries and the pot of stew, Ben followed with the macaroni and cheese. They walked up to the house together.

"Ma'am, why don't you come with me and I'll show you the tipi where I'll keep watch over your son," said Hal gently. Having worked as a rehab counselor, Hal knew that dealing with parents of addicts was the trickiest part of the job. Most of the time, parents hit bottom around their child's addiction long before the addict did. Hal witnessed many wealthy parents throw their hard earned money away on kids who weren't ready or interested in sobriety. It troubled him back then.

But addiction was big business out West. The hillsides of the California coastline were littered with drug and alcohol rehab facilities. Every one of them promised the creature comforts of home, while the addict was weaned from their drug of choice. But sobriety isn't meant to be comfortable. Honesty and truth rarely are. The greed of the fat-takers preyed on the feeble minds of weakened addicts and the driving fear of their parents. This greed finally drove Hal away from drug counseling all together.

"Oh, I'd like that," said Vera.

As Kyle stomped up the porch steps, Ben saw the storm clouds brewing. After he opened the front door and set the pot on the table, Ben fixed his gaze on the fuming boy and asked, "What's on your mind, son?"

"Oh, it's always the same. LEROY THIS AND LEROY THAT! LEROY! LEROY! LEROY! I knew she'd come flying over here the minute I told her where Leroy was. You should have seen her back at the house. First she's pissed that he's drunk! Then she's crying because Hal cleaned him up," said Kyle putting the groceries down with a thud.

"It must be tough always being in your brother's shadow," said Ben prying open the can of worms.

"Shadow!" roared Kyle. "I'm not in his fucking shadow! When it comes to Leroy, I'm fucking invisible. He was the star at this, and the star at that. Then, he gets wounded and comes home drunk. It's like her whole world shattered. When Leroy went into the Marines, it's all she talked about. If he won a track meet, that's all she'd talk about. If Leroy took a shit, that's all she'd talk about!"

"So do you hate him, Kyle? Do you hate Leroy?" asked Ben.

Whirling around, Kyle looked at Ben with the deepest hurt in his eyes. "Naw, I don't hate him. I ..." Kyle's voice broke off.

"But you're jealous, cuz he get more attention than you," said Ben.

"Yeah, I guess," conceded Kyle. "I'm just the after thought. Leroy was the athlete. He was the star who everybody liked. I was the nobody, the fat kid, just like her. I got picked on, bullied by the other kids. He was the All Star in track. It sucked being his younger brother."

"I imagine it would," chuckled Ben. "That's a lot of stress to have as a kid."

"It totally sucks," said Kyle. "You know what else? Leroy doesn't even like the shit she does, hovering over him all the time. He hates it. He runs from her. I think he joined the Marines to get as far away from her as possible. But the longer he was gone, the more she obsessed about him."

"So you never got to be center stage, even when he was gone?" surmised Ben.

"Oh, she'd be nice to me, but not like she was with Leroy. I was the mashed potatoes, but he was the gravy. Mash potatoes by itself is boring, but with gravy, they're good," said Kyle.

"I like mash potatoes with butter, myself," said Ben. "There's more than one way to eat a potato."

"Yeah, like tater tots and French fries," said Kyle.

"You're starting to make me hungry, boy," said Ben.

"Well, we got more than enough food. She'll cook enough food for an army if you let her," said Kyle.

"Well, we'll see how it goes," said Ben. "I wonder how Hal's doing. Let's see what's up with him and your mom." By the time Kyle and Ben went outside, Vera was in her car and Hal was seeing her off.

"You come by any time now, ma'am," said Hal. "I'm sure Leroy will appreciate all the good food you brought by."

"It was nice to meet you, Hal. I'm going to tell the doctor what you're doing with Leroy and see if he has any suggestions," said Vera.

Ben and Kyle walked up as the car pulled away. "How'd that go?" Ben asked.

"It went alright," said Hal. "One thing I learned in my rehab training was everybody just wants to be heard. So I let her talk and say her peace. When she was done, I showed her around. I told her what I thought was going to happen. She told me about the doctor she works for and is going to consult with him about Leroy. The doctor lives the next town over, so it's pretty close."

"Wow," said Kyle astonished. "My mom must have liked you. I thought, for sure, she'd come over here like a steam engine and take over."

"She's just worried, Kyle," said Hal. "All three of her men got smote by the demons in the bottle and she scared. I lost my wife to pills and booze, so I can relate to how she's feeling. She wants to help, but she don't know how."

197

"She tries to control everybody and everything. And if you're not doing it her way, it's wrong," said Kyle exasperated.

"That's what fear does, Kyle. It clamps down on people. Your mom's afraid of losing you guys," said Hal. "But she helped me get Leroy out of the truck and spent a few minutes alone with him. There were tears in her eyes when she came out."

"Oh, so you got Leroy in the tipi?" asked Ben.

"Yeah. Vera, she's a strong woman. Make no mistake about that. She got him on one side and I was on the other. And I tell you what, there is nothing more fierce than a mother bear taking care of her cub," said Hal.

Listening to Hal, a frown crossed Kyle's face. His brother had the spotlight all over again. Kyle felt himself disappearing.

"What's the matter son?" asked Hal noticing Kyle's long face.

"Aw, it doesn't matter. It's the same as it ever was," said Kyle.

"What's the same?" asked Hal.

Ben put his arm around Kyle's shoulders. "Let's put one fire out at a time, okay?"

"Yeah, but it's starting all over again," Kyle whined.

"What's starting all over again?" asked Hal feeling left out.

"Just a little resentment between brothers," said Ben. "Kyle gets left behind in his brother's wake. And Leroy gets the lion's share of Vera's attention. She frets over Leroy, while sonny boy here, disappears into the wood work."

"Oh, it's like that," said Hal nodding his head. "Most of the drunks I know, knocked back a few strong ones while nursing a good resentment. That kind of bellyache kills more drunks than anything else. But we can work on that."

"Yeah, whatever," said Kyle disgruntled.

"Come on, Kyle," said Ben. "Let's go see Hal's new tipi rehab."

As they entered through the door, the fire was crackling nicely and Leroy was curled up on the bedroll. The oriental rug looked a bit lonely in the front by itself. But it felt homey enough.

"Hal, do you want some wood stacked outside the door here?" asked Ernie.

"That'd be right nice, Ernie. It'd save me a trip to the wood shed," said Hal.

"You know what," said Ben as he scanned the inside of the tipi.

"What?"

"I think you need the couch in here. That darn rug looks lonely without it," said Ben. "What do you think?"

"I agree," said Frank. "If you're going to spend some time in here Hal, you might as well be comfortable. It wouldn't take us a minute to move it in here."

"Okay," said Ben clapping his hands together. "That sounds like a plan."

In the West, the sun dipped low in the cloud covered sky, while bright neon pinks, orange and blue colors streaked across the heavens. Ernie and Hal hurried to stack some wood outside the tipi. Soon, a choir of crickets began chirping their evening melody. The men moved the couch from the house and placed it on the oriental rug. Off in the eastern horizon, a slow Grandma Moon rose through the sky. She greeted the Star Nation during her slow ascent. The moon signaled to Frank and Ernie that it was time to go.

Sitting down on the front porch, Hal and Ben took a rest. Covered in sweat, Kyle walked to the house. "You want to stay for dinner, Kyle? Looks like you worked up a good appetite. We got food from your mom," asked Hal. "I'm going to see if your brother is ready to eat something."

"Naw, I got homework to finish," said Kyle shaking his head. "But I'll come by tomorrow and see how Leroy's doing. Thanks for taking care of my brother."

"You bet," said Hal smiling. "I can't keep it, unless I give it away."

"That makes no sense to me at all," Kyle shrugged.

"Oh, you'll understand soon enough. Come by anytime, okay buddy?" said Hal.

"Yeah, sure," said Kyle as he turned and headed for home.

"I'm going to check on Leroy," said Hal, pushing his tired body from the chair.

"You go, I'll see about dinner. You want me to bring you down some or you want to come up to the house?" asked Ben.

"Depends on Leroy. Let me tend to that, then I'll know better," said Hal headed towards the tipi.

Opening up the front door, the kitchen table and counter were full of pots and plastic containers of food. Between his daughters and Vera, Ben was sure not to starve to death. He was grateful they cared enough to cook an old man a meal. Kyle was right, Vera could cook for an army.

Beads of sweat poured off Leroy's face, as Hal went to look in on him. His frail body shivered as the fever worked hard to purify the toxins out of his system. Hearing Leroy's teeth chatter, Hal put a few more logs on the fire. As he wiped the sweat off of Leroy's brow, he was grateful for his work experience in a detox unit. Though most western doctors would have pumped Leroy full of medication, Hal knew from his own experience, how powerful the body was at healing. By the signs, Hal gathered that tonight would be rough.

"You alright there buddy? Can you hear me?" asked

Hal. Leroy groaned in excruciating pain. His head ached so bad, it felt as if someone was beating him with a sledgehammer.

Finding a bottle of water, Hal brought it to Leroy's lips. "Here, take a drink. You are sweating pretty good. I don't want you to get dehydrated," said Hal with compassion as he put his arm under Leroy's head to get some water down. Moments after Leroy took a sip of water, his stomach got queasy and it all came up. Hal grabbed a bucket he'd placed nearby and put Leroy's head over the bucket.

"That's the alcohol poisoning coming out of you," said Hal while he held Leroy's frail body over the bucket. "If you want, we'll take you to the hospital."

"NO HOSPITAL! Keep them pill pushers away from me!!!" scowled Leroy.

"Okay, okay, just checking," Hal said soothingly. "But so you know, your mom plans to talk to the doctor and have him come by. You might need to get checked out by somebody."

"Here have some more water. It's important to keep your body functioning." Handing Leroy the bottle, he took a good swig. This time he kept the water down.

"You feel like eating something? So the walls of your stomach don't grind together. Maybe a little beef broth and bread?" asked Hal as he saw the panic in Leroy's eyes.

"Yes," Leroy whispered, even though the last thing he wanted was food. His life force was slowly slipping out of his depleted body. His heart raced as if it would beat right out of his chest. He'd give anything for a bottle right now, just to get him straight again.

"I need a drink," Leroy uttered in desperation, under his breath.

"I know you do," said Hal gently. "But we're going to ride this one out together, okay buddy. I'll be here all night. You don't have to do this alone."

Warming Vera's beef stew on the stove, Ben walked over to the tipi, to see how things were going. "You doing alright?" asked Ben as he stepped inside and walked over to Leroy and Hal.

"Well, we're going through it," Hal said looking up concerned. "If I can get him to eat something, it might help. Maybe some broth and bread for starters."

Standing over them, Ben saw how pitiful Leroy's condition was. "You want me to bring some food in. I got the pot of stew warming up. I'll bring in a small pot full and set it on your camp stove."

"That'd work. You got some bread? It'll soak up the stomach acid," asked Hal.

"Sure thing, Vera packed a couple of loaves of bread. I got French and a loaf of sandwich bread. Which one do you want?" asked Ben.

"French sounds good. Did she pack any butter?" asked Hal.

"Oh, I got some butter," said Ben. "I'll be right back." Ben hurried to the cabin while a cool breeze came up from the Missouri, stirring through trees. The evening stars twinkled brightly, as the moon traversed across the deep blue sky.

Feeling called to duty, Ben rustled through the kitchen. He looked through every cupboard for a tray to put things on. Finally, he looked in the oven and found all the baking pans. Organizing a cookie sheet with bowls, spoons, a pot of stew and a ladle, he made room for the French bread and butter. As an afterthought, Ben found a coffee mug, in case Leroy's hands weren't steady enough to hold a bowl. Before he walked out the door, he gave the kitchen one more glance, to see if he needed anything else.

"Ah, paper towels," he thought out loud as he snatched the roll of paper towels off the counter. Holding the tray, Ben carefully hustled across the yard. On a small table, he put

202

everything near the camp stove and lit the burner to keep the stew warm.

"Man, that smells good," said Hal as his stomach growled.

"Here, I brought a coffee mug for Leroy. His hands might not be steady enough," said Ben.

"Good thinking," said Hal thankful for the help. "He's already sweated through one tee shirt. Good thing Kyle brought clothes."

"Looks like you done this before," said Ben.

"Yeah, I started out working with homeless kids, getting them off the street and fed. Then I worked in detox for a while. But the all the politics around the treatment center, damn near drove me out. You know, they got all these 'sober' alcoholics running the joint. It's just too many personalities. If I didn't leave, I'd have to drink. So I quit," said Hal.

"I always thought 12 Step work was for fun and for free," said Ben.

"It used to be. That is until the rich and famous wanted to get sober. Then, it became a business, with the pill peddling pharmaceutical companies leading the way. Most counselors got their heart in the right place. But, my boss was a loud mouthed buffoon, with an ego the size of the Grand Canyon. He was a basic 'Know It All.' You know, the kind you want to shut up. Knowing myself the way I do, my character defects would have gotten the better of me, so I left." said Hal.

"Saved yourself a trip to jail, did ya?" laughed Ben.

"Yeah, I don't know what it is with some people. They get a couple letters behind their name and all of a sudden, they're god. It got toxic and that's not for me. I loved the work though. Especially with the wet ones. After 20 days or so, I'd see the lights come on. But most don't stay sober. They go in and out of treatment like a revolving door. Twenty eight days is just enough time to bill the insurance."

"Yeah, I don't know much about that," said Ben. "Most of our drunks die on the street."

"Oh these rich people are dying alright. After they get doped up by the psychiatrist, they end up in high-end sober living house on the beach. Imagine this Ben, you roll up in your chauffeur driven Bentley, to a mansion with 14 bedrooms. It's fully equipped with a gourmet chef and servants. A pretty blonde nurse dispenses your meds three times a day, while another one turns down your bed. And that's not all. There's a swimming pool, tennis court and an outdoor kitchen, all with the view of the ocean," said Hal.

"That must of cost a pretty penny," said Ben. "With all that, who'd want to go home?"

"Exactly what I said," Hal exclaimed. "When you get these ultra rich, down and outs, in these fancy houses, you gotta ask yourself, who'd want to leave? Especially when mom and dad are picking up the tab."

"Do they stay sober?" asked Ben.

"Some do. But, I caught a woman bringing her dealer into the house at 6 am. She was shooting heroin in the bathroom."

"How'd you find that out?" Ben said curiously.

"Blood splatter!" Hal burst out laughing. "There was blood splattered all over the toilet, counters and the mirror. She shot up in the guest bathroom!"

"Maybe she wanted to get caught," Ben considered.

"Apparently so, because she got some of the other housemates using heroin too. They finally ratted her out!" Hal shook his head. "But then it gets even better. Because now getting sober is a business. The owner doesn't want to kick them out, because of the money. Sixty grand a month is a lot of dough per customer."

"That's more money than I get in three years," Ben commented.

"It's a racket. But listen to this," Hal goes on. "One day, this mafia kid moves in. He's got the big diamond studs in his ears and gold chains every where. His daddy owns some big casino out in Vegas. The kid shows up with a couple big brutes to carry in his luggage."

"Well, when I come on for my shift, the kid's sleeping all day. He's up all night. And he's scratching and picking at his skin and his pupils are dilated. And the owner didn't know the kid was shooting up speed balls in the bathroom. It was a real mess. The poor trainee, working the night shift, called 911 because this mafia kid overdosed at 2 am and had to go to the hospital."

"Sounds like a lot of drama," said Ben. "Hey, the stew's ready. You think Leroy's ready for some?"

"Yeah, let me see if I can get him to sit up," said Hal.

"Hey buddy, can you sit up and take in some broth and some bread? It will help get your strength back," Hal coaxed hoping for some signs of life.

Leroy groaned. "Man, I sure could use a drink. My head is killing me."

"Yeah, that ain't in the program for tonight, buddy. But, we got some good stew that your mom made special. All you got to do is sit up," said Hal. "You think you can do that?"

"Sure," said Leroy. "I'll give it a shot." Struggling to get up on his own power, Leroy faltered and collapsed back down onto the bedroll.

"Come on, I got you. Let's go sit at the table. I got a camp chair you can sit in," said Hal pulling Leroy upright. As they walked over, Ben served some stew in the coffee mug. Feeling pretty pitiful, Leroy slumped down in the chair.

Staring into the blazing fire, Leroy wrapped his hands around the mug and put it to his lips. The warm broth thawed out his insides after a few sips. Coming back to life, after being gone so long wasn't an easy journey. Famished, Hal tore off a piece of French bread, dunked it in the stew pot and took a bite.

"Man, I am hungry," Hal said as he scooped ladles of stew into a bowl. "This day has gone nonstop, since this morning." He felt the years creeping up on him as he flopped down on the couch. The warmth of fire felt good. But it could use a few more logs. "I didn't get a chance to ask you about your day, Ben."

"Ah, what's there to talk about," said Ben gruffly as he stared into the fire. "I keep having to bury my grandsons. I don't want to talk about it."

Leroy piped up. "I heard about that on the street. Your grandsons got hit by a drunk woman, didn't they. She sent one flying into a corn field and dragged the other under her car. Man, that's a tough way to go."

"Well, from the looks of things, the Grim Reaper almost snatched you from this world in his boney claws," snapped Ben tearing off a chunk of the French bread. "Here, dunk this bread in your broth and get some food in your belly."

Listening to the fire crackled and spit, Hal and Ben watched Leroy gobble his food down like a starving man. Hoping his food would stay down, Leroy put away two more cups of broth and bread. Hal removed the sweat soaked sheets on Leroy's bedroll and hung them over the couch to dry. The heat from the fire would dry them in no time.

Once they were done eating, Hal found the toothbrush and toothpaste he put aside for Leroy and filled a cup with water. "Here, Leroy, you're teeth will appreciate a good brushing."

Leroy looked up with grateful eyes. "Thanks. I don't remember your name, but you've been good to me. I don't deserve it."

"Oh brother, you deserve it. You gave all you had for this country and it's the least I can do," said Hal. "By the way, my name is Hal."

"Thanks, Hal, and you too Ben. Sorry about your grandsons. I was a couple years ahead of them in school. I remember them though."

"Yeah, I'm ready for some good news. For a change," said Ben feeling downhearted. "I'm plum wore out with all this sad news. I think I'm going to turn in. I had me a long day and you two ought to do the same."

"Good night Ben," said Hal as he put a few more logs on the fire.

"Yeah, good night," said Leroy feeling the life flow back in his being.

As he got to the door, Ben turned and saluted them both before he went out. They saluted him back.

"Ben's a good guy," said Leroy. "I never got to know him much. He was always pretty quiet."

"Yeah, we met back when he was in the military, a long time ago," reminisced Hal. "He wasn't much for talking back then either. I'd have to drag the words out of him. But once he gets talking, he's a good story teller." Before he turned in, Hal wanted to replenish the wood supply. "I'll be right back," Hal said as he opened the door flap.

In the panorama all around him was an endless sky. It was studded with glistening stars as far as his eyes could see. A slight breeze brushed his hair off his shoulders. Over the Missouri, a dense fog gathered while millions of crickets chirped their nightly symphony. His heart felt good, but his body was tired. He looked forward to a good night's sleep. But the way the chips were falling, he wasn't sure if he'd get one. Detox can be tricky. Even when you do everything right, you may not see the whole picture.

As Hal stacked the wood inside the doorway, he thought about getting his hunting rifle and keeping it close in case something unwanted wandered in. While he was at his truck, he found his flash light and a book he'd started reading.

Nothing worked better on restless nights than reading, to lull him to sleep.

The quietude of nighttime soothed Hal's soul after the bustle of a long day. Sitting on his tailgate, he watched the shooting stars and breathed it all in. If he didn't have a job to do, he'd sleep under the blanket of stars next to a roaring camp fire. The stillness of the prairie and the vast star studded sky, penetrated his being. For nothing was heard, save the whining wheels of a lonesome eighteen wheeler traveling down the deserted highway. Traversing the sky, Grandma Moon cast a silvery glow on the rolling hillsides.

The undulating waves of buffalo grass stretched far in all directions. It was much different from the towering Rocky Mountains or the endless stretches of shoreline bordering the Pacific Ocean. The only familiar were the celestial bodies of the Star Nation. Orion, the great warrior of the sky with his arrow and belt, rose in the east. The north star and Big Dipper weren't far from the Northern Cross above him. For Hal, the Earth was his home and doing good was his religion.

Walking back to the tipi, a cold chill crept up Hal's spine. He shivered for a moment as he closed the door flap. The fire glowed softly as Hal put his rifle, book and flash light next to his bed.

Leroy had nodded off in the chair. His limp body was crumpled and curled up. After years on the battlefield, he knew well the constant threat of death and destruction. Living through combat, his sleep was haunted by the looming smell of burning flesh and gunpowder. With a fierce loyalty to his troops, this lone gunnery sergeant barely survived the ravages of war. But, the battle with alcohol would smite him, if it wasn't arrested soon.

"Come on buddy. You'll get a kink in your spine sleeping that way," said Hal lifting Leroy gently out of the chair and guiding him to his bedroll. Full of compassion, Hal was grateful Leroy wasn't another casualty of war.

Many soldiers struggled with the banality of civilian life, once they tasted the bloodiness of warfare. Trained killers rarely come home unscathed. How could they? They've traveled to the edge of the outer reaches of humanity and traded in their innocence. With blood on their hands, they carried the shame of assault on another of Creator's children.

Warriors have an edge most common folk don't understand. They are haunted and hunted by memories of the past. There is seldom peace as they look over their shoulder, for whatever lay in wait around the corner. With heightened senses, particular sounds and smells propel their mind back to horrid places, which are forever etched in their memory of a time gone dark.

Many soldiers believed the political lies and justifications. In the morass of political mumbo jumbo, they lost their sense of right and wrong. Truth and honor become twisted and gnarled as soldiers struggle to fulfill the duties. But, once they're home, the worst of it begins. It starts with the reoccurring nightmares of battles never won. Many soldiers close their eyes only to see the faces of the dead.

Under the weight of pure exhaustion, the soldier dares to sleep. Waiting in the shadows, the dead come flooding into his mind's eye. The torment begins. To speak about the burning bodies, the dismembered corpses only brings the reality crashing into the present. The nightmares persist. So, the soldier remains silent, not wanting to call up the past. He harbors a truth too gruesome to reveal. Yet, the silence strangles him.

Back at home, most soldiers feel misunderstood. Whom can they trust with what they saw, what they experienced? Unfortunately, they are unaware of the spiritual repercussions that war madness brings. The tormented soldier seeks relief by drinking himself into a stupor and praying for oblivion. But, the few hours of oblivion aren't long enough to give him any peace.

Hal settled Leroy back onto his bedroll and covered him

up. Though he'd never been a father, he felt love for this young man curled up under the covers. "Sleep tight, buddy," said Hal tenderly. "We'll see you in the morning." Dosing off, Leroy groaned a reply.

Feeling his bones creak as he pushed himself up, Hal threw a few more logs on the fire, before he called it a night. With his book in hand, Hal curled up on the couch, waiting for sleep to come. After a few pages, his eyes grew heavy. The crackling fire soothed his spirit. It lulled him off to sleep.

All stirred up, Ben fussed around the kitchen putting the food away before he turned out the lights. In a matter of days, his solitary life had completely changed. Like a magnet, Hal drew people to him who needed help.

"Is this what you kept me around here for?" Ben grumbled to Creator. "To get a few more drunks sober, before You let me out of here?"

Having Hal around eased his loneliness. Ben didn't mind. It broke up the humdrum life he'd been living since Elsie died. Nothing drives people away faster than constant moodiness and grief. Ben debated the pros and cons of this new change. He decided it was for the better. It gave him something useful to do, even when he was grouchy.

Before going to bed, Ben took a spoonful of stew and macaroni and cheese. He put it on a little plate. Opening the front door, Grandma Moon was directly overhead. Her light sent silvery shadows across the prairie. Holding the plate, Ben walked out on the front porch. He raised the plate up to Creator and all the helping Spirits and especially to his grandsons who just passed on. With a prayer of gratitude, he offered this spirit plate to his grandsons, who wandered in the world Beyond.

"This is for you boys. I love you both. Be well on your journey to the other side. Aho."

After he placed the plate on the front porch, he sat down on the steps. The Earth was quiet. The wind came to greet him, blowing softly across his cheek.

"Hello Tah-tey," Ben said. Tonight, there was a hollow in his heart. It wouldn't go away. Making funeral arrangements with his daughters tore at the fabric of his being.

Being American Indian, Ben's tolerance for pain was high. How could it not be? But tonight, he reached his limit.

"There is got to be a better way," Ben thought to himself. *"Why would we go through the trouble to be born, only to destroy ourselves? Life had to be more than a mere pipe dream. It had to be."* Deep in the midnight heavens, one lone star twinkled brightly.

"Oh, so you do hear me," Ben said out loud. A faint Voice whispered words he'd heard a hundred times.

"Half measures availed us nothing. We stood at the turning point. We asked His protection and care with complete abandon."

Standing up, Ben felt incensed. He fixed his eyes on the twinkling heavenly bodies.

"Are you accusing me of doing half measures?" he challenged the Heavens. Whipping around his face, the wind made dust flurries in the dirt.

Softly the Heavens whispered their reply. "We stood at the turning point," the still Voice toned. In his mind's eye, Ben saw the Sacred Hoop, the altar of his people. It had been defiled and corrupted, through ways that were not their own. This holy heartbeat of the First Nations People was tattered through war, starvation and neglect. It longed to be repaired and protected. Carried deep within each soul was the boundless heart. This sacred altar was placed where true holiness resides.

Standing on the front porch, Ben searched the heavens. It revealed, in order to restore the altar, the patterns of abuse must cease to be. Once the boundless heart was cleansed of impurities, it would be restored to its original condition. When the altar of the heart was pure, then countless miracles could begin. Every expression of love was a miracle.

The Creator was lonely without His children. His children were lonely without Him. For they depended on each other. This imagined separation caused the soul sickness. The spiritual malady left all of humanity love starved. In effect, His children felt cut off from the Love of their Being. They sought happiness through shallow pleasures. They danced with the spirits in the bottle. Yet in so doing, they made grave mistakes and incurred tremendous debt. It was this unfinished business which forced their spirits to be recycled from one life to another. They had to correct their mistakes and pay their debt. Creator never intended it this way.

Standing on the porch, Ben saw it so clearly. He understood how Mother Earth was a gift for all of Creator's children, to be cherished. Yet Creator's children had turned away from their Source. They forgot who they were. But, how could Ben get his people to wake up?

Facing the wind and the stars, Ben's heart opened and in true humility, before Creator, he asked, "What do you want me to do?"

In the stillness, the moments passed and then the whisper came. "Be of Service," was all it said.

"AH!!! YOU'RE KIDDING!!! That's ALL you got! BE of service!" Infuriated with this simple answer, Ben turned his back on the wind and the stars and stomped off into the house.

"BE OF SERVICE!!! BE OF SERVICE!!! When am I not of service?" The floorboards creaked in protest, as Ben paced across the kitchen floor. "Who else secretaries the meeting around here? Who else makes the coffee, gets there early to set up and stays late afterward to make sure it's all put away? Huh, I ask you, who else? Sure, once in a while, someone will come a few minutes early. But, I do it every week!"

As he ranted and raved, stomping across the kitchen floor, it dawned on him. He lived on a reservation which was

90% drunk. But, he was still sober. The few guys, who showed up at the AA meeting each week, struggled as hard as he did, to maintain their sobriety. While everyone else drank to oblivion through each hardship, it took tremendous courage to say 'no thank you' at every turn. Especially at the holidays, when the wine and the whiskey flowed like Kool-aid.

As he calmed down, Ben realized he survived another hard day. At times, the pain of this life was intolerable. Given his druthers, he just as soon collapse in a heap and pass away from this world. Yet, even though he grieved the loss of his loved ones, he still walked sober. As he flopped into bed, he kept thinking, there must be a better way. Haunted by the answer the Star Nation gave him, 'Be of service,' Ben stared at the ceiling. The wind howled outside. With her sheer force, she blew empty soda cans down the street.

"GOOD NIGHT TAH-TEY!" Ben hollered as he closed his eyes and fell exhausted into a deep sleep.

Hours passed as Grandma Moon traversed across the starry night. Her pale light shone on all life. Her moonbeams flooded through the kitchen window. While the men slumbered, Ben stirred restlessly in his bed. He heard a low wailing sound coming from outside. Groggily, he leaned up in bed and tried to make it out. *Was it coyotes yipping at the moon*? he questioned at first. Yet the more he listened, the more it sounded like a baby crying.

Someone was speaking in low tones outside the house. "*Maybe Hal and Leroy are awake,*" he thought as he tried to roll over and go back to sleep. But the low wailing grew louder. Within moments, it was more insistent. At his wits end, he finally pulled on his jeans and looked out the window toward the tipi. The blazing firelight inside cast shadows against the canvas wall.

"What the heck..." uttered Ben looking out the window. From what he could make out, there were a small group of people standing outside the tipi. Then to his dismay, Ben realized it wasn't people at all. It was spirits hovering near where Leroy's bedroll was. Hal's silhouette was moving inside. He was putting more wood on the fire. Glancing at the clock, it was 3 am.

"I better get out there," muttered Ben to himself as he got his jacket and found his cedar bag. While he quickened his gait across the yard, the whispers of a dozen spirits were carried by the wind. Not wanting to draw attention to himself, Ben barely glanced in their direction, lest they figured out he could see them. He dreaded nothing more than a gaggle of tormented souls spilling their woes to him in the middle of the night. The last thing he wanted was to get caught in the crossfire of unfinished business.

Brushing against his cheek, the wind came up gently, like a loving friend. "Hello old girl, you come to make amends?" Ben chuckled lovingly.

Jostled out of a deep sleep, Hal heard the piercing yowl of caterwauling felines coming from somewhere in the distance. The crescendo of this grief stricken wailing echoed across the prairie. It sent shivers down his spine. Though he'd never admit it, Hal felt a little jumpy. With rifle in hand, he sat up. Outside he heard footfalls crunching across the yard. As they grew closer, Hal lay in wait on the couch, ready for whatever was passing by. All of a sudden the door flap lifted and Hal jumped up, pointing his rifle at the door. "Who is it?!" he demanded in a stern, commanding voice.

"It's me," Ben said as he opened the flap seeing a rifle barrel pointed at him.

"Man, you better be more careful, sneaking up on somebody like that," demanded Hal. "I could have blown your fool head off."

"Yeah, but you didn't," Ben said calmly. "Feeling a little uneasy, are ya?"

"I don't know what. But I woke up about an hour ago. I had this creepy feeling of impending doom. Like some dark cloud descended," said Hal.

"Well, you're close. You got a host of undead standing outside the tipi over there by Leroy," said Ben.

"So that's what I was feeling," said Hal relieved to know what it was.

Trapped in another dimension, beads of sweat covered his forehead as Leroy thrashed about. He tossed and turned in the midst of his tortured sleep. With balled up fists, Leroy snarled out cries of anguish, ready to punch some unseen attacker.

Hal looked at the boy with compassion. "He's had nothing but troubled dreams. You'd think he was being chased by the devil himself, the way he's moaning and yelling out things I can't understand. Do you think we should wake him up?"

"Well, sometimes dreams are strong enough to kill a man," pondered Ben. "But I'm not sure if jerking him out of his dream-time is the way to go."

"What do you suggest?" said Hal scratching his head.

"Well," Ben started to explain. "Our boy's not fighting random demons and deadly spirits. Like the ones who roam the earth from dusk to dawn, searching for living souls to torment, because they were tormented themselves. He's back in the combat zone. He's with the guys he fought with. He's killing the same people he killed all over again."

"How do you know that?" questioned Hal.

"Out there in the moon light, I saw the spirits of the people he killed. I heard a baby crying and saw its young mother holding her child. They were killed by a bullet meant for someone else. Leroy's in the middle of a spiritual warfare. And no human power is going to get rid of that," said Ben, deeply concerned. "Do you have any idea, how many tormented souls wander the Earth after they've been killed in battle?"

"No. I never thought about it," admitted Hal.

"Well, it's a lot," said Ben. "And they're tied to the

215

soldier boys coming home from this damn war. I bet most soldiers, when they close their eyes at night, are thrashing around like Leroy here. So many come home and destroy themselves. They destroy their families and then go off half cocked and commit suicide. It's no wonder. They're going insane because they're haunted and hunted down every night by the souls they killed."

Putting his rifle down, Hal put more wood on the fire. While they listened to the crackle of the fire, the men contemplated on how to rectify this situation.

"I never realized how deep it was," said Hal quietly.

"Oh, it's deep alright," said Ben getting all wound up. "These spirits are caught in the In-between. They're bound to their killer. There's heavy consequences for killing. Even if you're doing it behind the apron strings of a flag. You know that fella Moses, who went on a vision quest and brought down a tablet with the 10 Commandments?"

"Yeah," answered Hal.

"Well one of them commandments was 'Thou shalt not kill!' But them Christian fellas think, if they got a cross and bible in one hand and a Gatling gun in another, they'll be forgiven."

"Oh don't get me started," said Hal. "So what about Leroy? Are we going leave him like this or what?"

"I got some cedar. It might ease things up a bit," said Ben. "What I can't figure out, is why those spirits stayed outside the tipi? Usually if a spirit's going to torture someone, they'll be right where he is. But, all the undead are outside."

"Maybe the fire is keeping them outside," suggested Hal.

"Naw, fire draws all kinds of spirits to it. The cedar will weed them out, and send the unfriendlies on their way," explained Ben.

"Yeah, you're right there. I didn't think about it that way. So, can you get rid of them?" asked Hal, relieved Ben showed up with his cedar bag.

"I can't clean up his unfinished business," Ben cautioned. "But I can show him what he's got to do. That's only if he's willing. He's got to do the work and decide whether he wants to follow my direction. It's always been the way."

Ben walked around the fire sunwise. While he tossed some cedar onto the glowing embers, he sang his medicine songs. The sacred cedar smoke rose through the flames. The spirits moved a distance away, but didn't disappear. Filling the tipi, the cedar smoke enfolded Leroy's troubled, slumbering body. It temporarily broke the stranglehold that the spirits had on Leroy's dream time.

"Yeah, just as I thought," said Ben thinking out loud. "Those spirits are chained to Leroy. He's got blood on his hands. And they aren't leaving until he cleans it up. When Creator said do no harm, He meant it!"

"Well, I'm grateful they weren't in here," said Hal with an uneasy chuckle. "I was jumpy enough with them out there."

"I noticed," Ben laughed and pointing to the rifle leaning against the couch. "But, they didn't come for you. I'd bet my bottom dollar, those spirits want to be set free from Leroy." Then it dawned on Ben as to why the spirits didn't come inside. This was a ceremonial tipi. Years ago, it was used for the Native American Church ceremony. Ben chuckled to himself.

"What's so funny?" asked Hal.

"Well, I just realized why the spirits didn't come inside and it makes perfect sense," said Ben.

"So, what is it? Spit it out already!"

"Well, it's no big deal," said Ben. "But Elsie had a cousin. Derwen, the Oak, we called him. He was a peyote road-man and this was his tipi, the one he used for ceremony. These old lodge pine poles and canvas were blessed up quite a bit. Derwen held many ceremonies in this tipi. So, it makes sense, why something unholy can't enter here, with all that sacred medicine in the poles and canvas."

"What happened to him?" asked Hal.

"Oh, he had some woman trouble and moved out West. He asked Elsie to hold on to it, since he couldn't take it on the bus. So, we put it on my truck and brought it here. I never heard from him again. It's been in the shed for a while," said Ben.

"Speaking of ceremony, we did a warrior sweat up in Montana for me and some of the guys, before I met you. Do you think that'd work for Leroy?" asked Hal.

"Yeah, it might. But it all depends on Leroy. I been in a couple of warrior lodges. I wasn't sitting behind the bucket, though. I think he'd benefit from a warrior lodge. It'd help wash off the war madness from his muddied soul," said Ben.

"Well from the looks of things, now I know why he drank," said Hal. "He tried to blot out all the memories and those spirits."

"Yeah, the lodge will help. But having blood on his hands, he's got to make amends and clean up his unfinished business."

"Why do you say it depends on Leroy?" asked Hal.

"Well, it's like any drunk who goes to AA. If he only goes to drink coffee, gobble down sweets and flirt with the girls, he won't stay sober long. Because he's not doing the deal. With Leroy, he's got to clean up his unfinished business with these spirits. If he doesn't make it right with a sincere amends, they won't leave him alone. Eventually they'll destroy him," said Ben. "Putting someone in their grave is serious business. They'll haunt him with a vengeance. And there's no peace until it's cleaned up."

With a deep sigh, Hal saw how knotted this ball of yarn was. "You know what Ben, I could really use a sweat. Is there an Inipi around here?" asked Hal. "Maybe we could figure

218

something out for Leroy."

"To be honest, Hal, after Elsie died, I quit pouring water. I was so tore up and angry at Creator for taking her away, I said the hell with it all and I quit. Only a few people came anyway. Most don't believe in the Old Ways anymore. To be honest, I haven't been there since before she died. I pleaded with Them to take me instead. I'm not sure if the willows would still hold up," admitted Ben. "If Leroy wants a ceremony, he'll need to offer tobacco."

"Yeah, I can't shove it down his throat. For all I know, he might drink tomorrow. And that'd be it. All this work down the drain," said Hal.

"You're forgetting the point, Hal. And that is, we're still sober. That's why we do this work. It insures our sobriety. After he wakes up, I'm going to thank him, because I don't want what he has. And I've had a rough few weeks," said Ben as he tossed more cedar on the fire.

Hal laughed. "Well, if you put it that way, I don't want what he has either."

"Exactly," smiled Ben. "So it's working. At least for right now, it's working for us."

"I believe that's how it was meant to be," Hal said bowled over. "I read the Big Book so many times, but I see it now. Bill and Bob showed the way for a drunk to stand sober in the face of anything."

"Creator only needs a small opening. Just a touch of willingness and an open mind," smiled Ben.

As the cedar smoke filled the tipi, it drove off the undead. Leroy started to stir, stretching his arms over his head. Slowly, he rolled over to face the fire. "Hey, what time is it?"

"Ah, he lives," said Ben. "It's a couple hours before dawn, give or take."

"How ya doing, buddy?" asked Hal. "You were having

219

some tough dreams."

"Yeah, every time I close my eyes, I see their faces. I have the same dream over and over," said Leroy groggily. "It makes it so, I don't want to close my eyes."

"What's the dream," asked Ben curiously. "And whose faces do you see?"

"It's the faces of the insurgents coming out of nowhere. And every night, I see my team get ambushed. There's all the gun fire and bombs exploding. We didn't expect it," said Leroy.

"Is the face of the woman there, the one dressed in yellow with her baby?" asked Ben.

"How'd you know about that? Nobody knows about that," said Leroy incensed. "What are you, some kind of mind reader?"

"No, but those spirits are right outside the tipi..." said Ben when Leroy cut him off.

"I don't believe in that spiritual crap!" sneered Leroy.

"Doesn't matter what you believe. It's what's true that counts. Ignorance of the law, doesn't mean that you are exempt from it, son. Your true reality is spirit. This body is just a temporary house..." Ben started but Leroy cut him off again.

"If this is going to be some lecture about god, I don't want to hear it," Leroy went off. "If there is a god, I never saw any sign of him. My mom tried to shove Jesus down my throat since I was four. She wanted to save me," Leroy sneered contemptuously. "Save me from what? We already lived in hell. Then, she had this great idea. She wanted me to be a disciple of Christ and devote myself to him. That was enough for me. I couldn't wait to get the hell out of here."

"You didn't mean to shoot her or her baby," said Ben gently, carefully testing the waters again. "They were standing behind a man holding a rifle. He was her husband. The bullet that killed him, passed through his body and shot the baby and the mother too."

"How do you know this?" asked Leroy shaking his head in disbelief. "Who did you talk to?"

"I told you. But you don't want to believe me," said Ben in a quiet calm voice. "They're all waiting outside. The baby cries and the wind carries those cries all over the prairie. You've tried to drown out their voices by drinking. But it won't work."

"I don't want to talk about this. I didn't mean to shoot her or the baby!" Leroy ranted on. "The man was standing out in the open with a rifle. I didn't see the mother holding the baby standing behind him. It's all fucking collateral damage!!! People get caught in the crossfire. You don't want to kill them but you have no choice. Over there, the women carried guns and shot at us too. It's not like the rebels had uniforms on. It's not a damn training exercise!"

"That's mighty fancy language to describe the killing of innocent people, Leroy," Ben started. "When those paleface Christians came over the big water, they carried their holy cross in one hand and muskets in the other. They called our great, great grandfathers heathens to dehumanize us. Those greedy bible thumpers trampled our lands, looking for gold. They invaded our hunting grounds and murdered the buffalo, which we relied on to survive. Only they did it for sport. They pulled off the hides and left the carcasses behind."

"Over a hundred years ago, the Christian soldiers murdered over 300 women and children at Wounded Knee. Were they collateral damage?" asked Ben driving his point home. "Sitting Bull and Crazy Horse were called villains. The white soldiers hunted them down like dogs. In the eyes of a white man, your great, great grandfather was an insurgent. Don't you see?"

"I don't know, man. I don't know. I don't have answers like that. I served my country. We got attacked and I did what I was trained to do. I was just following orders," said Leroy.

"So were the Christian soldiers who killed off my great, great grandfather. It's no different," said Ben.

Leroy looked at Hal with pleading eyes. His brain wasn't ready for any more talk. "Do we got any coffee?" Leroy asked.

"I got a jug of water," said Hal as he poured some water in a cup and handed it to Leroy.

"I'll go make some coffee in my new coffee maker," said Ben headed towards the door. "I got to go stretch my legs anyhow. Here Hal, I'll leave you my cedar bag. I'm not sure if the coast is clear yet." With that, Ben opened the flap and was gone.

"Man, I was not ready for that conversation at all," said Leroy, when Ben was out of earshot. "How did he know about the woman in yellow and the baby? Did someone tell him? Because nobody knows that."

"Ben has a way of knowing things," said Hal sitting down on the couch. "Before you woke up, you were thrashing around, screeching like a tortured banshee. That woke me up. And then something creepy made the hair on the back of my neck stand up. It was a crying sound like yowling cats, but different. I couldn't make it out. Then I fetch my rifle, because I heard crunching sounds outside. That's when Ben shows up. He lifted up the door flap and I nearly shot him. I was that jumpy. That's when he told me that you had a dozen spirits attached to you, a woman and a crying baby."

"I don't know about that. And I got no use for ghost stories, right now," said Leroy with disdain.

"But it's your ghost story, Leroy," said Hal.

Leroy shot him a dirty look. "Look, I'm grateful that you 'saved' me, gave me clothes, cleaned me up and fed me. But, and let me be very clear on this, I AM NOT INTO this spiritual crap! I don't believe in fairy tales! Or happily ever after or ghost stories. I don't want no hocus pocus or any kind of mumbo jumbo. I got enough Christian crap shoved down my throat to last me a few life times."

"Oh, so you do believe in life after death?" asked Hal jokingly, trying to lighten things up. Leroy threw him that same look of disdain.

"Well, you said 'a few life times' right?"

"Yeah, whatever," said Leroy wanting to change the subject.

"So, are you an atheist? You don't believe in God or a Higher Power at all?" probed Hal a little further.

"I don't know. I never thought about it much," said Leroy defensively. "After what I went through in that hell hole, getting ambushed, losing my men. I'd be hard pressed to believe in anything."

"But do you pray?" asked Hal not wanting to let this go.

"What difference does it make if I pray? I don't think it's ever done any good. I was raised in my mother's house. My dad was a drunk and she found some white man's god in the bible. I got dragged around to church on Sunday's and went to their little schools. But praying didn't get my dad to stop drinking or my parents to stop fighting. So yeah, I prayed. It was a long time ago. But, what good did it do?"

"Leroy, do you know why the windshield in my truck is bigger than the rear view mirror?" ask Hal.

"No!!! What kind of stupid question is that?" asked Leroy mockingly.

"It's not a stupid question," said Hal gently. "My windshield is bigger than my rear view mirror, because where I'm going, is more important than where I've been. If I keep looking behind me, I'll miss what's in front of me. Unfinished business can cripple a man. Especially when it rattles around in his mind."

"I just need a good night's sleep," said Leroy giving Hal the brush off.

"I don't think that's too likely, from what I witnessed," said Hal not letting this one slide. Leroy's eyes burned with scorn, as he pushed himself up off the bedroll.

"Leroy, I get you're angry about your parents, the church, Christ, the military and the rest of it. Dragging all those tin cans behind your bumper, it must get pretty noisy in your head. If you want a better tomorrow, you got to cut yourself free. There's another victory coming, son. But you won't see it, until you quit mourning things you can't change. All you got to do, to quit stumbling around in the dark, is turn on the light."

"Now you're sounding like a Sunday morning preacher," said Leroy.

"I'll take that as a compliment," said Hal. "An old hillbilly told me this once. He said Hal, if you always do what you've always done, you'll always get what you always got."

"Was he a preacher?" Leroy laughed.

"No, he was just a sober cowboy," said Hal. "Good man. He had simple wisdom. Speaking of sobriety, isn't your dad's name Jed?"

"Yeah, why? Do you know him?" asked Leroy as his defenses went up.

"Yeah, I met him the other night when I spoke at the AA meeting. He brought Kyle with him. You're dad has 2 months sober, Leroy. Maybe your prayers took a while. But, they took root. Look, I'm not asking you to believe in anything, but just keep an open mind. Ben has knowing, most people don't. He might be able to help you, son," said Hal as he slammed into Leroy's mental granite wall.

Hal suspected Leroy had a bad case of contempt prior to investigation. This contempt kept a man in everlasting ignorance, as the Big Book talked about. Since Hal didn't meet Leroy at an AA meeting, they had no common ground. He didn't know whether or not Leroy wanted sobriety.

"So you're one of those AA guys, trying to get people sober and shit," said Leroy after a while. "Do you go on AA crusades?"

"You make it sound like it's a bad thing," said Hal amused at the challenge. Leroy was no easy sell.

"Yeah, I never liked having something shoved down my throat," Leroy's voice softened up a little.

"I wonder what's taking Ben so long with the coffee? I'm going over to the house and see if the coffee is ready. You want to come?"

"No, you go. I'm going to lay back down for a while. I woke up exhausted," said Leroy as he curled back up under the blankets.

Before Hal left, the cedar bag caught his eye. "*Good idea*," he thought to himself as he tossed some cedar onto the burning embers. After a few more logs, the fire was roaring again. Opening the door flap, the cool crisp air felt refreshing as he started across the yard.

The morning stars sparkled against the deep blue sky as the moon made its way below the western horizon. The only sound he heard was his boots crunching against the gravely soil. Hal shivered as he glanced around the side of the tipi. He wondered if the undead were still dancing there. There was no sense in causing trouble with the Underworld. So, he hurried over to the house. When he walked in the front door, Ben was sitting at the table, sipping his morning coffee.

"Ah, that coffee smells good. Thanks for making it," said Hal as he poured himself a cup.

"How's Leroy doing? Seems like he's going to be a tough customer," said Ben familiar with the contempt for the Old Ways.

"Don't' take this wrong. I'm not criticizing you, Ben. But, you kind of laid in heavy on that kid. Don't you think?" asked Hal.

"Did you want me to lie to him?" asked Ben with his eyebrows raised.

"No, but..." Hal started.

"Look, he's got a closed mind. You run into that a lot around here. It's a spiritual no-mans land, between the fading sunset of the Old Ways and bible thumping Christians," said Ben. "People don't know what to believe, so they believe in nothing."

"I thought it was more 'contempt prior to investigation' myself," said Hal.

"Well, that too. I agree with you there. You can't save them all, Hal. You can't save them all. The biggest error I made, was offering healing to people who didn't think they were sick. They didn't need my services. So I had to let them die. If they get uppity on me, when I'm trying to help, I got to let them go. I ask you this, what honor does a man have if he's forced into something?"

"What do you mean?"

"Well, I think it's better if a drunk suffers the consequences of his actions. That way he'll feel the sting. And maybe, he'll grow up enough to make a better choice. Even the Big Book says you got to want what we have, and be willing to go to any length to get it, before you're ready. I wouldn't worry too much about Leroy though," said Ben.

"Oh, yeah. Why's that?" asked Hal having witnessed a train wreck.

"Well, for one, those spirits ain't done with him yet. By the time they've had their way, he'll be stark raving mad, a plum lunatic. They won't leave him alone. Every time he closes his eyes, he'll see their faces. They're walking through the graveyard of restless souls, which exists in the In-betweens." Ben took another sip of his coffee and stared into the darkness outside the window.

"So what do you think we should do?" asked Hal

breaking the silence.

"Who us? We can't do nothing except offer him another choice," Ben scoffed. "He's a stubborn one. He comes from a family of hard-heads. It's unlikely he'll take advice when he hasn't asked for it. But you watch. After those ghouls prey on him for a spell, he'll either shoot himself in the head or beg Creator for help. Between the baby crying and being sleep deprived, he'll get pushed over the edge real quick. Those spirits will do better job convincing him about the Other World than we ever could." Ben took another sip of his coffee. "But I'll leave the Light on for him."

"All righty then, Mr. Tom Bodette," said Hal. "You gonna call this place the spiritual Motel 6."

"I like 'Camp Sobriety' better. It has a nice ring to it, don't you think," Ben laughed.

"So what's the second thing? You said well for one," asked Hal.

"That's pretty obvious. He's a drunk. It's a battle he can't win in single handed combat. It don't matter how brave he is. Sooner or later, he'll either surrender or die. If he weren't such a Know It All, he'd have seen it already. But, I predict he'll be face down in the dirt before long," said Ben. "You can't teach a fool, who knows it all. They got no humility. I trust the bottle will make him humble."

"So is there anything we should do?" asked Hal, wondering if this trouble was all for nothing.

"Be of service," said Ben who, as soon as he said it, remembered the angry row he had with the Star Nation a few hours ago. Love is the power which straightens out any crooked road and lights every darkened path. The power of Creator is expressed through giving and service.

"Half measures availed us nothing... We stood at the turning point... We asked His protection and care with complete abandon," those words resounded in his being as Ben spoke them out loud.

These simple sentences carried such impact. At that moment, he knew what it meant to be in the flow of Life. This wasn't about him or the heartache. He was given a precious gift. One that others, like Leroy, would die for. And it was meaningless unless it was given away. "Be of service..." said Ben, as he got out of his chair to get his sacred pipe from the cedar box. "I got to go take care of my pipe," Ben said. "You might want to check on the boy and use the cedar."

CHAPTER FIVE: HISTORICAL TRAUMA

In the predawn hours, the sentinels of darkness watched carefully over Leroy's slumbering body. Unwilling to let go of their prey, they stalked Leroy ruthlessly. It was a hellish game of tag. Each one took a turn. Yet, it was Leroy's own pride and ignorance, which kept him vulnerable to the dark whims of the rapacious ghouls who thirsted after his blood. Waiting in the wings, the Spirit of Suicide watched it all. It lingered in the shadows for its chance to entice Leroy into the restless world of the undead.

While his body lay there stiff, his spirit hovered overhead. Leroy's soul was attached by a thin white cord to his corporal body. With every stifled breath, Leroy slipped deeper and deeper into the shadows. From which, without help, he could linger in through all eternity.

These guardians of illusion knew only too well, their only undoing was the Light. For there was no darkness, the Light of Love couldn't drive out. Unless it was kept in secret and away from love's healing grace.

The baby cried and cried, ceaselessly. Hunger waged war in its empty belly. No solace could be found. The mother dressed in yellow, carried the screaming child in her arms. She did what she could to bring it comfort. She herself, hadn't eaten since the day before yesterday. Her husband worked in the vineyard to support his family. He came running into the house, after he heard the gunfire off in the distance. He hurried as he loaded his antiquated rifle. It was their sole source of protection against robbers, who came in the night. They were hungry themselves, ready to rape and pillage whatever they found.

Combing the hillsides for rebel soldiers, Leroy and his team were on patrol. They targeted a suspected band of insurgents who were tucked away in caves in the surrounding areas. Then, his team heard the gunfire. Leroy wasn't afraid to die. His only fear was not doing the job right the first time. Alert and ready, his team stealthily crept through the hillsides. They searched for the source of the gunfire.

Insurgent snipers were everywhere, under the cover of this desert hell. As they came over a small hill, Leroy spied a man holding a rifle. He stood in front of the arched doorway of an earth constructed building. Leroy sent his men ahead. Quietly, he crept to a nearby hilltop to gain a better shot. The wind was in his favor. He took aim through his scope. The shot was clean. He fired and saw his target go down. The man didn't get back up. To his horror, there was a woman in yellow holding a baby. They stood behind the target. His bullet tore through the flesh of mother and child, killing the family instantly.

As his single shot echoed through the countryside, it signaled the rebels of the patrol's location. That's when the ambush began. Out of nowhere, Leroy's team was showered with rocket launched bombs and sniper fire. Bullets rained down through the open field. Leroy got on the radio shouting his team was under enemy fire. Crouching low, he ran to find his team when a bullet tore through his shoulder. It knocked him flat.

A searing, unbearable pain radiated through his chest. The blood seeped through his torn uniform. With his good arm, Leroy broke off a stick and put it in his mouth. Clamping down hard with his teeth, Leroy tried to muscle through the pain. With bare and bloody hands, he pulled himself through the brush, trying to get to his team. But with every move, more blood gushed out. He hoped to find his men alive.

As he lay there on the ground, his shoulder ripped open from enemy fire, the woman in yellow flew up the hill carrying her screaming baby. Hovering over him, she screamed in agony, "WHY DID YOU KILL MY BABY?!!! WHY DID YOU KILL MY BABY?!!! MY HUSBAND WAS A GOOD MAN!!! WHY DID YOU KILL MY FAMILY?!!! WE DID NOTHING TO

YOU!!!! WHY DID YOU KILL MY BABY?!!!"

Her screams were relentless. The baby's cries were earsplitting. With his hands covering his ears, Leroy tried to drown out the agony of her screams. But no matter what he did or where he turned, she was there, fiercely angry. The screaming and crying were never ending.

Feeling like a cold blooded, heartless asshole, Leroy tried anything to ease her pain. "I didn't mean to kill your baby. I didn't see you or your baby in my scope. All I saw was a man with a rifle." But his words were empty. The woman in yellow dogged his every step. Leroy was now the hunted one and somehow he knew in his mind he couldn't kill her again.

In a surreal moment, Leroy could see in all directions. He floated far above the battle zone. Death was everywhere as devils rode on the winds of hate. The smell of burning flesh and gunpowder filled the air. Mangled bodies littered the hillsides. In his team, only 4 out of 11 managed to get away to safety. Barely 19, Tortoise, a new private, was an Indian from the South Eastern Tribes. His legs were blown off from stepping on a land mine. Lingering between worlds, Leroy was powerless to help his men.

"The crack of dawn seems to be taking longer than usual this morning," thought Hal to himself as he put another teaspoon of sugar into his second cup of coffee. He watched through the window as Ben climbed the small knoll, carrying his pipe bag. In these short few day, he'd come to love that crazy ol' coot. "Well, I better get out there and check on Leroy," he said out loud, taking one last swallow of coffee.

As his leather soled boots crunched over the yard, a pale silver moon shone enough moonlight to make his way. Overhead, an owl screeched as it flew towards the tipi. A chill crept down his spine. The prickly cold made Hal shiver. The wind howled low across the prairie. The glow of the fire was almost gone, when Hal realized Leroy was in trouble. As he opened up the door flap, Hal saw Leroy shriveled into a ball, whimpering something about a baby.

"Oh shit, those spirits are at it again!" said Hal out loud as he ran over to Leroy and tried to shake him awake.

"LEROY!!! LEROY!!! WAKE UP!" shouted Hal as he jostled Leroy awake. Within seconds, Leroy's eyes bugged open. His hands lunged for Hal's throat and started to choke the life out of Hal. Adrenaline pumped through Leroy's veins. It gave his frail body the strength of a pit bull trying to bring down a horse. Leroy's thumbs dug deep into Hal's arteries which fed the brain. It almost caused Hal to pass out. Within seconds, Hal's combat training came flooding back. He pried this pit bull's thumbs off his neck. Wrestling on the ground, the two men almost landed in the fire pit. Hal managed to break free from Leroy's stronghold and shoved the boy back onto his bedroll.

"That's why Ben said to use the cedar," Hal laughed out loud. "Boy, if I didn't know better, I'd think you were trying to kill me."

"I was, ya dumb shit! Don't you know not to manhandle someone while they're sleeping? I didn't know who the fuck was trying to wake me up. You can't be as stupid as you look," scolded Leroy.

"Easy now, buddy. There's no need for disrespect," said Hal as he dusted himself off. Hal put more logs on the fire. He tossed cedar on the embers to smudge the darkness away. After a few moments of silence, Hal sat down next to Leroy. "You were wrestling with those spirits again. I heard you talking about a baby. I heard you say it this time."

"Oh, don't start on me again," Leroy cautioned ready to hit someone. "What is it with you guys and all this spiritual crap?"

"I'm just trying to help you, son," said Hal.

"Yeah, well I didn't ask for help, now did I?" sneered Leroy.

"No, you sure didn't," said Hal as he remembered

unasked for advice is seldom heeded. He pushed himself off Leroy's bed roll. "I'll stop wasting my breath, since you seem to know better. It's your life. I wish you luck, battling all this spiritual crap on your own. Let me know how you make out. But, before you head out, tell me what you want written on your damn headstone. At least we'll get that straight," Hal's voice was stern. "Maybe you're one of them hard-heads who has to die drunk, since you don't have one humble bone in that beat up body of yours."

"What, like being a homeless drunk isn't humble enough?" sneered Leroy.

"Apparently not. Humble means teachable and you got all the answers," Hal said sarcastically. "I am a 'recovering Know It All' myself. And from where I standing, you don't know the meaning of the word. You know what I get about you, Leroy? You were a hot shot. A big strong fighting machine, tough and untouchable. And now, you're busy licking your war wounds. You're in a battle you don't even know you lost. That cock-and-bull story you keep telling yourself, won't let you see how low you sunk."

Hal walked over towards the couch. He felt Leroy hateful glare bore into the back of his neck. "Oh, go ahead, hate me all you want. But I know what I see and it ain't pretty," said Hal as he plopped down on the couch. "You know what it is about guys like you? You're so damn proud, vain, and arrogant. But you're living a madman's dream. And you wear it like a badge of honor."

"Go to hell!" Leroy cursed as he pushed himself up off his bedroll. "I'm getting out of here," he said as he bolted towards the door.

"Yeah, where you gonna go? To the same damn rock you crawled out from under." Tall and built like an oak, Hal stood up. The two men faced off in front of the door. Hal's massive chest puffed out as he towered over Leroy. With the fire crackling, they stood there, in silence, glaring at each other.

Unafraid, Leroy stood his ground as the seconds ticked by. The silence was deafening. Then, in a voice thick with unshed tears, Leroy roared. "YOU DON'T GET IT!!! I VOLUNTEERED TO GO ON THAT MISSION. I WAS UP FOR A PROMOTION! BUT I WANTED TO BE THERE!!! WITH MY MEN! I WANTED TO BE OUT THERE! I WANTED TO BE A WARRIOR!!!!"

"Stand down, Sergeant," came back Hal's voice full of compassion.

As the water welled up in his eyes, a small tear rolled down his cheek. But Leroy couldn't let it go. If he started crying now, he'd never stop. So he harbored his pain and held strong, even if it killed him.

"How many men did you lose?" Hal finally asked.

"We started with eleven, only 4 made it back. I couldn't believe it. Tortoise got both of his legs blown off, but he pulled through. Two guys dragged him out of the line of fire. They used tourniquets to tie his legs off so he wouldn't bleed out. We lost so many good men that day," said Leroy as he looked down. He was heart broken from all the pain.

One lone tear rolled down his cheek and fell at his feet. He watched it hit the ground. Putting his big arms around Leroy, Hal hugged him like a bear. Only the fire crackled. Unsure of what to do, Leroy's arms hung at his sides. Men didn't hug in his family. Yet it didn't seem to bother Hal.

"Come on, sit down Leroy. That rock you crawled out from under can wait a few more minutes," said Hal as he pulled Leroy to the couch and they plopped down with a thud.

"You are such an asshole, Hal," laughed Leroy quietly.

"Yeah, it's one of my better qualities," said Hal as he stared into the fire. "You know, you and I are not so different. The first night we were 'in country' we got mortared pretty thick. The air was so heavy there. It was thick and humid. The smoke just hung in the air. I was in my bunk, when we got hit with mortar fire. It hit the barracks and I rolled off my bunk. I was holding my pillow, when I hit the ground. The guy two bunks over from me, wasn't so lucky. He went home in a body bag. I watched a lot of my buddies die over there. I often wondered how it was, I got to live. I got real familiar with the smell of death and the smell of burning flesh. It was everywhere. After a while, I didn't want to know the name of the new guys. Because it was one less person to say goodbye to. There's no joy in killing, Leroy. Even if you're getting paid for it."

"Yeah, I know the feeling," said Leroy. "So what happened to you?"

"Well, I drank. And I drank to get drunk. I wanted out and oblivion worked for me. By the time I was 19, I hit my first jail cell. There were more of them. Then the doctors at the drunk tank said I was alcoholic. That being so, I was a total liability as an enlisted man."

"According to them, I was a hopeless alcoholic. Well, needless to say, I felt doomed and ashamed to my core. When I got out of the service, it didn't much matter to me, if I lived or died. Frankly, death seemed quite inviting. But, I was too great a coward to take my own life. And the feeling of uselessness and despair made me thin-skinned after a while. By the time I reached 30, I was lonely, angry and homeless. And living, or I should say dying, in a chicken coop. I blamed everybody else for my lousy lot in life. Which kept me walking with the demons in the bottle for a long time. Son, I'm offering you a chance at a better life," said Hal. "But there's only one problem."

"Oh yeah, what's that?" asked Leroy taking the bait.

"You gotta want it, Leroy," said Hal with all earnestness. "You have to want to be sober more than you want to drink. Most drunks can put the bottle down for a while. If they got a good reason. But, once you been bit by the hair of the dog, you don't stay stopped for long. You can turn a cucumber into a pickle, but you can't turn a pickle back into a cucumber. That's the way it is for drunks."

"So what helped you?" asked Leroy, now curious about the prospect of a new and better life.

"AA and ceremony. Working them together eased the ache and soothed my soul," said Hal. "First, I had to treat my alcoholism by working a program and helping others. Then I got introduced to ceremony through one of my AA buddies."

"Sound simple," said Leroy a bit more open minded.

"Oh, it's simple, but it's not easy," said Hal knowing from experience. "My mind was all twisted up, witnessing everything I did in combat. Those memories haunted me. Then, there's the night sweats, the nightmares. Every loud noise set me off and I'd relive it all over again. I got diagnosed with PTSD and they wanted to pump me full of meds. But I can't take just one pill. If one works good, a thousand works better. I had a good sponsor in AA and got some outside help. But, combining AA with ceremony, is what healed me," said Hal.

"What kind of ceremony did you do?" asked Leroy.

"I had a buddy, Wyatt, who told me about a Warrior Sweat Lodge. He sun danced for a number of years and he took me to a lodge. The first time I prayed in the dirt, I knew I was home."

Feeling his hopes dashed, Leroy's face sank at the mention of the Old Ways and the warrior sweat lodge. It was incomprehensible to him, how these ceremonies could work at all, when his people barely survived.

Seeing Leroy frown, Hal stopped. "What's on your mind?"

"Ceremony...If they're so powerful, how come we're so poor? I mean have you looked around here? The broken down cars, people out of work. Everybody's living on the government dime. How did this happened to us?" Leroy looked perplexed. "Do you see why I don't believe?"

Hal took a deep breath. He knew this argument well and felt that way himself not long ago. "Oh Leroy, I sat on the same fence. And it was down right uncomfortable. I grant you, it's hard to believe in a God who disappointed me my whole life. But, you're judging the inside of a man, based on his outsides. We're a strong resilient people. Our spiritual muscle is strong, because we took the hard road. For myself, it's a matter of faith. It's not that I didn't believe in a Higher Power. I just didn't think He gave a damn about me."

"That's just my point," said Leroy. "I don't need to rely on something I can't see. I've gotten myself through my life."

"And judging from your condition, you are doing a bang up job," jested Hal.

"Shut up, Hal," said Leroy throwing him a look. "I don't need this shit from you."

"The problem is, you don't know what you need. Since you relied on yourself for so long. But, from the looks of it, your well's run dry. You don't have to figure it out, all at once. Creator's patient. He'll hold supper for you until you show up. He's not going anywhere," Hal explained.

"Yeah, well I'm not holding my breath," scowled Leroy.

"I've met my share of hard-heads like you. Hell, I'm one myself. You know what I think your problem is, it's contempt prior to investigation," said Hal.

"What the hell does that mean?"

"Well, have you been to ceremony?" asked Hal.

"No, but I went to a few Powwows," said Leroy.

"Exactly my point. You're judging it, without ever giving it a chance. Have you been to an AA meeting?" Hal pushed the subject a little further.

"No, but I don't need that crap either. I can do this on my own," said Leroy as his willful rejection and defiance loomed.

"There you go again, contempt prior to investigation. Why do you need to suffer this out alone? What do you got to prove?" Hal asked intently and paused before he shot out the next question. "Are you seeing a pattern here?"

"Okay, so what's your point?"

"You won't be less of a man, if you get help," said Hal gently picking away at Leroy's hostile closed mind.

"Help from who? Ceremony didn't help our people," said Leroy.

"We could hammer this out all day," Hal started. "You know, the downfall of our people didn't happen overnight. The 'Indian wars' started around the year 1540 and didn't end until 1890, after they slaughtered our people at Wounded Knee. That's over 350 years of bloodshed on both sides. Neither side was innocent."

"Honestly, the only reason I think we lost the war, was whiskey. It poisoned the minds of our warriors, making them useless to defend themselves. It's hard to shoot straight when you're drunk. Alcohol was never our medicine. But it's destroyed more of our people than a thousand guns. Once it clouded our minds, we were powerless to fight our enemies."

"Where'd you get all of this stuff?" asked Leroy thunderstruck by this insight.

"I got sober. Then, I had a lot of time to read. I had the same questions you did. After all my studying, I realized the Gatling gun didn't destroyed us, the whiskey did. And we drank it willingly," said Hal.

"I think you're right," agreed Leroy. At that moment, there was a noticeable shift between the two men.

"Leroy, if you put your dukes down long enough, I'll show you what I did to heal my war wounds. And maybe, just maybe, you'll find something to heal your own. I'm not the enemy here," said Hal.

"I know you're not," said Leroy softening up a little.

After a long moment of silence, Leroy looked up from the ground and met Hal's gaze. "So did you do a Warrior Sweat Lodge? And did it work?"

"Yes to both questions," said Hal.

Leroy threw him a look, "Tell me more."

"Well, Wyatt grew up on a rez in Montana. He was a preacher's son, a white man, but his dad ministered to Native people. We went back there and he introduced me to ceremony. Since he grew up around Sun Dance, Wyatt knew the Old Ways. We found a man qualified to run a warrior lodge and offered him tobacco. That's how I asked him if he'd run one for me. He told us everything we needed to do to prepare. After we built the lodge and gathered up fresh stone people, we had the ceremony. The first thing I noticed, after the lodge, was I had a peaceful nights sleep." Stopping himself short, Hal wanted to say, when he humbled himself to Creator, his heart changed. It became a partnership. Whereby Spirit purified him as he worked the 12 Steps and cleaned up his side of the street. After he made his amends, his heart was clean and the Love of the Creator flowed through his being without end. This simple truth filled his heart with joy.

Leroy was quiet for a time, taking in what Hal said. "I can't remember the last time I slept peaceful. I was living in the caves when you found me. The only sleep I got was when I drank. The nightmares were so intense. It got so bad, I didn't want to close my eyes. When you found me, I hadn't slept in a week. I'd do anything to shut off the noise in my head," confessed Leroy.

"I know exactly what you mean, son. I've been there. When you've been in combat, evil sticks to you. It muddies the windshield of your soul. After the sweat lodge, the evil washed off and I felt clean again."

Dawn started to break across the prairie. The morning birds sang their greeting to the sun. A truck pulled up in front of the house and men's voices carried across the yard. Hal and

Leroy heard someone running towards the tipi.

"Leroy! Leroy!" Jed called out as he hurried towards the tipi.

"That's my dad!" Leroy exclaimed as he got up off the couch. The door flap opened and his dad poked his head in.

"Hey, Leroy, look at you!" Jed beamed as he stepped inside and embraced his son. It was a long hug, something Jed learned in AA. Standing there, Hal felt a little awkward. He missed out on fatherhood, having been a rolling stone for so long.

"Hey dad, you know Hal?" said Leroy as he broke the silence.

"Yeah, we met at the AA meeting, what almost a week ago," said Jed. "Frank and Ernie told me you were here, so we brought breakfast. Hotcakes, eggs and sausage. We even brought some coffee if you need it."

"That's mighty nice of you," said Hal. "I could use something to eat."

"So what, you're sober now, huh dad?" Leroy asked his dad.

Jed pulled out his key chain. There were two AA chips dangling from it. "Yup, I got 68 days this morning," said Jed with clear eyes and a peaceful heart.

"Wow that's great," said Leroy smiling at the reunion.

"Yeah, I've been taking Kyle. I'm not sure if it's working yet or not. But he comes with me," said Jed.

"Probably to get away from mom," laughed Leroy.

"Oh don't pick on your mother. She did the best she could with what she had," said Jed. "Well, come on! The food's getting cold. We bombarded old Ben and took over the kitchen."

In the east, the radiant glowing light of morning flooded

over the hillsides as the three men walked across the yard. On the ground, the rays of the sun sparkled in the small dew drops which were scattered over the Earth. Curls of smoke drifted from the smoke stack on the roof. Ben stoked up the fire to heat the kitchen. The small kitchen was quite a bustle as Frank and Ernie kept the breakfast warm. Sitting at the table, Ben drank his coffee, taking it all in.

Hal walked through the front door and looked around at all the commotion. He leaned over to Ben and whispered in his ear. "Welcome to Camp Sobriety."

Ben laughed. "You ain't kidding."

"Hey, good morning Hal," said Ernie stirring some eggs in a frying pan.

"Hey guys, thanks for the spread," said Hal as he got a plate and dished out some scrambled eggs, hotcakes and sausage and poured pancake syrup all over it all. His coffee cup was still on the counter where he left it.

After they made their plates, Leroy and Jed sat out on the front porch. It'd been almost a year since they'd last saw each other. Watching father and son come together, Hal's heart smiled. It was good to see them laughing and enjoying a meal.

"So, how was you're night?" asked Frank to Hal.

"I slept comfortable enough. There was enough wood for the fire, which kept the place nice and toasty," said Hal knowing that wasn't what Frank was asking. But he never liked gossip, so he kept it light.

"Yeah, how'd Leroy do?" asked Ernie getting to the point.

Hal looked at Ben, but Ben kept quiet. "Well, he made it through. He's a tough kid," was all Hal was willing to offer up. "Go talk to him. He could use some sober minded people around."

"That's a good idea. We'll keep him surrounded. It

nearly broke Jed's heart when he disappeared last year," said Frank. "But they're looking pretty happy now."

After Hal finished his breakfast, he washed his plate in the sink and put it in the dish rack. Ben put his coffee cup in the sink. "Hey, go ahead and make yourself at home. You can put the leftovers in the fridge. Vera dropped off food last night, so just make some room. I'm gonna go walk," said Ben.

"Hey, I'll go with you," said Hal.

"Suit yourself," said Ben as he went out the door. Hal walked out after him.

"Hey," said Hal to Jed and Leroy, as he caught up to Ben. "There's some fishing poles in the back of my truck if you want to go catch dinner. The bait and tackle is in the green box."

"That sounds good," said Jed. "I'll see if my boy still knows how to fish."

Ben was halfway down the block, when Hal caught up to him. "Hey, what's you're hurry?"

"No hurry. I just got to stretch my legs. One word of warning," said Ben catching Hal's glance. "Button your lip around here, if you don't want your business all over the street. It's a small town and people like to talk. Leroy's too fragile, to have his business coming back to him from someone else."

"Oh, I agree," said Hal. "But me and the boy had ourselves a good talk. What do you think about running a Warrior's Sweat?"

"For Leroy? He ain't ready yet. He's got to have at least a few weeks sober, before he could handle the heat. I don't think his family ever did ceremony, except a Powwow," said Ben. "Not only that, he has to be willing to conquer himself, to conquer his lower nature. And be humble enough to ask for help. You can't take that away from him."

"I agree. I don't know how we're going to keep him sober. When I walked into the tipi, he was in a fitful sleep again. He was mumbling about a baby," said Hal.

"Well, I told you those spirits weren't going to leave him alone. That mother, she's got a major bone to pick with Leroy. I don't blame her really. If he understood what was happening to him, he'd be shaking in his boots. I've seen this before. Most crazy people are tormented by spirits. They suck the life force right out of them. You won't get an educated psychiatrist to believe that, but it's true."

"Are you saying insanity is caused by spirits?" asked Hal wanting to know if he heard Ben right.

"Spirits with unfinished business," Ben corrected. "There's got to be a good reason for them to go to all the trouble. Take for instance the killing fields like Wounded Knee and Little Big Horn. They're still active with spirits who sacrificed their lives there. I heard their voices echoing in the wind. The land is heavy from all the bloodshed. Mostly because the white cutthroats in charge, turned a blind eye to the killing of innocent women and children. Those tragedies were ignored by the government which committed them."

"Now that's unfinished business," said Hal. "But what about Leroy?"

"With Leroy, all we can do is lay these spiritual tools at his feet. And these matters can't be rushed. It's his choice whether or not he picks them up. He's responsible for making peace with his own soul. We'll give him our best. But you know as well as I do, Hal, we can't keep anybody sober but ourselves." Ben turned off the River Road and down a small dirt road heading west towards the river. "One more thing about those spirits. If you're not careful, they'll come into your dream time and you'll be fighting in the timeless battlefield with the dead."

"Well, I sure as shit don't want that," Hal responded.

"Well, you got the cedar. I suggest you use it," Ben cautioned. "Here, I'm going to show you where the Inipi is. I ain't been over there for a while."

Hal kept quiet about the alligator wrestling he did with Leroy that morning, when he tried to wake him up. Ben warned him to use the cedar to keep the spirits at bay. Now he knew why.

Walking through a rhapsody of wildflowers, they followed a small, winding trail through the fawn-colored prairie. "Over there is the Powwow grounds and my land starts about five feet from where the tall lamp post is to the north. The lodge is near a bluff facing the river," said Ben. They passed the Powwow grounds, which was an arena with wood plank bleachers about 3 tiers high.

Overgrown with buffalo grasses, the deer trail wound around until they reached a plateau which overlooked the Missouri. That's when Hal saw the willows of the Inipi.

His heart sank as Hal walked across the Inipi grounds. It screamed of neglect. The fire pit was overgrown with weeds. The poor willows of the Inipi cried. The willow ribs sagged after a year of hard weather and lack of use. Piled in the center of the stone pit, were the Ancient Grandfathers. They were still there from the last lodge before Elsie died. It felt sad, abandoned and lonely. Scattered along the half moon, was a small pile of crumbled Stone People.

"When did you pour your last lodge here?" asked Hal tenderly as he walked around the fire pit. Ben looked out at the endless sky. His mind drifted back as he sat on a wooden bench overlooking the Missouri.

"It was about a week before Elsie went in the hospital. She sat next to me, right here and put the cedar on the stones. They were the last stones she put cedar on, right there in the stone pit," Ben's voice cracked. It was pained with memories. "Days later, she went into a coma and never came out. I ain't been back here since."

The Missouri flowed wide and calm. Glimmering rays of sunshine sparkled on the waves stirred up by the wind. Hal sat down next to his buddy and they were quiet for a time. Each one lost in their own thoughts.

Not quick to interrupt the stillness, Hal felt Ben's sadness down in his own bones. He was no stranger to grief. Feeling a little awkward, Hal broke tradition and put his arm around Ben's shoulders.

"You know, I got to say this is a right pretty spot for a lodge. If I was the fire keeper, I'd show up with swim trunks on and go for a dive between rounds," said Hal.

"Oh, you don't know the half of it," started Ben. "We'd start the lodge about ten in the morning and be finished come lunch time. Elsie got the feast all organized and we'd be out here all day. Sometimes, we'd watch the moon come up. People brought food for picnics. Heck, in the summer, Frank and Ernie set up a barbeque and we'd roast everything from hotdogs to marshmallows. Then after the lodge, we'd all go swimming. It was a good way to spend the day." Ben let out a long sigh. "Ah, I miss that woman. It's been a thorn in my side, ever since she left. Sometimes my heart aches so bad, I can't catch my breath. Do you know what I mean?"

"Yes sir, I know that heartache well. Looking back now, that's why I was a rolling stone. I went from one rodeo to another. I never wanted to get close to another woman after Arlene overdosed. When I came home from work, she was dead on the bathroom floor. Her face was laying there in her own vomit. No one should die that way, least of all my wife. I tell you what, that guilt burned deep inside me. I couldn't get rid of it. She had 10 years sober. I figured we were cured and didn't have to go to those damn meetings anymore. If I wasn't such an idiot, she'd be alive today." Before he tripped over his heartache, Hal got up and walked around the fire pit. Looking for something to do, he picked up the scattered stones and piled them up.

"What do you got in mind for this warrior lodge?" asked Ben quick to change the subject.

"Well, from the looks of things, we need to go on a stone

run and a willow run. These willows need to get put into the fire. And you probably want to memorialize the stones Elsie last put cedar on," Hal threw Ben a look.

"Well, maybe I'll keep one and put it next to her picture," the old man said quietly. The deep void in his middle tugged at him. Tears were not far away.

Standing up, Ben walked over to the door of the lodge. He got down on his hands and knees and put his forehead to the earth. "Aho Mitakuye Oyasin," he said as he crawled through the door and went sunwise around the lodge. Sitting in his spot near the door, he was quiet while he remembered his last lodge with Elsie.

As he closed his eyes, Ben started singing his medicine songs to the Spirits of the lodge. Riding on the Four Winds, the souls of his forefathers came from the four directions. Ben's voice caroled four songs to Great Spirit. As the Spirits came into the Inipi, the Power of Wakan Tanka filled his heart with Light.

All the while, a searing heat radiated off the Stone People in the pit. Steam rose from the water splashed on the glowing grandfathers. Spirits danced to the heartbeat of Mother Earth. They brought their love and healing to everyone in the Inipi. When the scorching heat became almost unbearable, Ben sang his fourth song to end the round. After his last song, he called out, "AHO MITAKUYE OYASIN!"

Opening his eyes, his gaze was drawn to the stone pit. A small cherry bomb of a stone called out to him. He picked it up tenderly and set it right next to him, in Elsie's place. "I will take you home with me," whispered the old man to the stone.

"FIRE KEEPER!" Ben yelled out.

"Ho!" answered Hal.

"Here, I'll pass these stones out to you. Put them in a pile in the west, so I can give them back to the Earth in a good way," Ben commanded as he handed the Grandfathers out the door. Working quietly, they cleared the stone pit. Hal piled them west of the fire pit. Once they were finished, Ben crawled out the Inipi door and put his face on the earth. "Aho Mitakuye Oyasin," he said as he exited the lodge.

Walking around the lodge, Ben surveyed the neglect. "We'll have to set up a work day and get this lodge cleaned up," said Ben. "Hal, when we get to the house, remind me to talk to Frank and Ernie. I avoided this Sacred Place far too long."

"You got it," said Hal as he pulled some weeds from around the fire pit.

"You think Leroy's wants to do a warrior lodge?" asked Ben. "Because if he does, he needs to get out here and do some work. Nothing tends to a troubled soul better than working with Mother Earth."

"I talked to him about it. But he's a hard sell," said Hal. "He don't believe in the Power of ceremony."

"Yeah, that whole family got Christianized. I don't see what good it's done them," said Ben. "I got nothing against Christ. He was a great Holy Man. But Christians, you can keep them. I never met one of them who could cast out demons, let alone raise the dead or heal the sick. They preach His teachings, but don't do His work."

"Oh don't get me started," Hal started. "I went to that white man church and the preacher called me a sinner. Now, I admit I've made a few mistakes, but that don't mean I am one."

"Yeah," said Ben. "I'm with you there. You know Hal, I read somewhere that Our People have been on Turtle Island close to 10,000 years and it only took the white man a couple hundred to undo our way of life."

"You know, out West, the Klamath tribe was completely terminated by the federal government," Hal started. "Once those missionaries got the Indians properly Christianized, the feds came out, sold off their land and gave those white lumberjacks free reign to clear-cut acres of virgin forest where the Klamath lived for thousands of years. The government wanted to Americanize what they thought were a vanishing people and make them disappear," said Hal shaking his head. "It took over 30 years for the Klamath to get their tribal recognition back from Congress. But, they didn't get back their land." Silence followed.

"I wonder what it felt like to legally cease to exist," Ben thought out loud. "And what kind of people would try to erase an entire nation from the world?"

"I think it started with that fella, Charles Darwin. He told the whole white world that Native people didn't have any religion. He said we were a godless people. Most of those missionaries thought our ceremonies were some kind of witchcraft, devil worship or what have you," Hal said.

"Well, I'd tell them, they're wrong," said Ben quietly looking out on the Missouri. "The guilt of their white ancestors brought on the racism of today, Hal. It's got to get set right, if there's ever going to be peace."

"Have you ever looked at the whole picture, Ben?" asked Hal, taking a moment to stretch his sore back.

"What whole picture are you talking about?" asked Ben.

"Well, when I was in Montana, I found a book. It talked about the Native soul wound and historical trauma. It got me thinking about all the crap our people went through since the Europeans first stepped foot on Turtle Island."

"I'm interested. Keep talking," said Ben.

"Well, it gave good reason for this heartache we carry that won't go away. Do you realize, by the time the massacre at Wounded Knee happened in 1890, we'd fought almost 400 years of war? That's a lot of killing and a lot of dead Indians. Those blood thirsty butchers trampled over our land looking for gold. When they couldn't kill us all, they forced us onto reservations and slaughtered the buffalo. I found out later, ol' Teddy Roosevelt opened up Yellowstone with the last 23 buffalo, probably because he felt so guilty. Buffalo was our main source of food." Hal was passionate about this.

"Go on, I'm listening," said Ben.

"Well, think about it. We're people of the earth. When the government forced us onto reservations, we lost our connection to Mother Earth. That alone ripped the heartbeat right out of our nation."

"I'd agree with you there," said Ben.

"Oh, but it gets worse. Now, the government has our hands tied behind our backs. But, hold on, let me back track a minute. I read somewhere, this British fella Amherst left no stone unturned when it came to exterminating our people. I saw the letters he wrote to some Colonel back in 1763. Amherst planned to kill our people off with small pox. That's when they got the bright idea to infect a bunch of blankets and give them to our people."

"A fatal gift. That was the first chemical warfare," Ben commented.

"You know, those bastards had the vaccine at the hospital, but wouldn't help the women and children. They told them to run for the hills, that way the whole tribe would get infected," Hal shook his head.

In a vision, blistered faces of women and children crowded into Ben's mind. He heard their teeth chattering as they shivered with high fever. Puss seeped from their blistered bodies as their cries of pain pierced his heart. On her wings, the wind carried their pained, confused cries across the land. "Those were our great, great grandmothers and grandfathers, our ancestors..." Ben's voice trailed off.

"Yeah, that fella Amherst wanted to extirpate our people. Kill us off, root and branch," Hal continued.

"He was sick with gold fever," Ben suggested. "They all were. Greed drives the beast in people."

"They wanted to claim our hunting grounds, our land,

for their king." Hal went on. "When Mad King George lost America to Washington, the frenzy for land took off. After that, they slaughtered our people with Gatling guns and shoved us on reservations."

"You ever been to Wounded Knee?" Ben asked quietly.

"Naw, I drove by there. But the air was so heavy, I couldn't stay," Hal admitted.

"They were dancing the Ghost Dance, when those soldiers came. Praying to Tunkashila to bring back their freedom, the buffalo and the hunting grounds. They thought the bullets would fly past them," Ben said quietly. "But they got slaughtered."

"Yeah, about that time, they shot Sitting Bull," Hal commented.

"He got shot by Red Tomahawk and the Indian police at Standing Rock," Ben said. "That day, they killed a holy man, who carried our traditional ways and fought the whites to save our way of life. After that, our people got slaughtered at Wounded Knee and the Sacred Hoop was broken."

"That's when they had us cornered Ben," Hal said thoughtfully. "The winter was brutal and our children were starving. The government had our hands tied behind our backs. We had to rely on a tyrant for our very lives. And those whites showed up with crap grade food and barely any provisions to live by. In return, they wanted the gold in the Black Hills, the heart of everything that is. This is where they broke our back."

"I'd say that sums it up pretty good," said Ben.

"But the story doesn't end there. After we're crippled and begging, that don't suit them either. Because now, we're a burden. So they steal the children and shove them in boarding schools. That way, they can civilize us and kill the Indian all together. After that, they chop off our hair and give us white man names, so we'll be easier to remember. Then, they made us speak their language and stripped away our culture. They brainwashed us to believe our traditions and ceremonies were devil worship. And tried to bleached us white."

"They tried to bleach the red out of the fabric of our soul," laughed Ben.

"Ya think," said Hal. "Is it any wonder why our people are drunk and dying in the streets?"

"Not when you put it that way. You got all that from one book?" Ben asked curious.

"No, more than one," said Hal slowing down. "But the soul wound goes deep, after centuries of trauma. Then, came the whiskey and the bible toting Christians, and it's all downhill from there."

"Very good professor! I hear they got a job over in the history department at the college," Ben laughed.

"Shut up, you old smart ass!" laughed Hal. "Before I throw my shoe at you."

"Historical trauma," said Ben mulling the idea over. "I like how it describes the soul wound. It's a wonder we survived at all. America laid up quite a heavy debt in the Spirit World, with the armies of Native souls they've massacred. No telling how many white soldiers were spooked in their dream time after all the bloodshed. Angry spirits are a powerful force to be reckoned with. You know, Hal, the souls of our ancestors want to return," said Ben with a faraway look in his eye.

"How do you know that?" asked Hal as Ben shot him a look.

"They told me, Hal. They told me," Ben started. "But, they want to live free. Like they did before with Nature, in tune with the Spirit of Mother Earth."

"That's a tough call for an Indian," said Hal having grown up on a reservation. There was no freedom there.

"Well, not all of them came back as the Red Man,"

started Ben with a twinkle in his eye.

"What do you mean?" asked Hal.

"Well, our ancestors, some were born into other races, including white, so they'd live free. They're scattered from shore to shore across Turtle Island. You'll know them by their Eagle Eyes and high cheek bones. They demand to be free. You can see it in their walk. They have a fierce love of Mother Earth and freedom."

"You know that makes me think of Wyatt," said Hal. "The first time I saw him Sun Dance, covered in red paint, I swore he was Indian. Come to think of it, he had high cheek bones and a deep respect for Mother Earth."

"Maybe he's a spirit of one of our warriors who died at the Little Big Horn," said Ben. "Who knows, but it's harder to eliminate our ancestors if they wear a white body in this life time."

"I never thought about that. Out West, many races of people prayed at the Sun Dance Arbor," said Hal. "You think they were our people?"

"Spirit's not tied to color. It's tied to the heart," said Ben. "To a way of life."

"Man, this historical trauma goes deep," said Hal. "Even spirits had to make changes in order to live free."

"I think you're right there. It's a heavy debt that's got to get paid up. When a spirit can't fulfill it's mission in one life, it has to come back and try again," said Ben thoughtfully. "But what did the fella who wrote the book say we should do about it?"

"I don't know. I never finished the book," Hal laughed as Ben shook his head. "But it's somewhere in my truck, if you want to take a gander at it."

"Well, you're a big help," said Ben walking over to check the blankets in the shed. Pulling a blanket out, it had holes eaten through by rodents. "Hal, we got to make a run to the thrift store and get some blankets."

"Yeah, no kidding. I got a canvas tarp in my truck we could use to cover the lodge," said Hal. After a while, they headed back because their stomachs growled.

Walking through town, Hal noticed an abandoned building set back from the street. Most of the windows were smashed and some were boarded up. "Hey, what's that building over there?"

"Oh, that old rat's nest," said Ben. "It's been sitting empty for almost 15 years. Elsie wanted to turn it into a soup kitchen. She cooked extra food for the homeless around here."

"Mind if I give it a look see?" asked Hal.

"Suit yourself," said Ben as they walked over.

"Interesting," said Hal as he walked the perimeter of the building. "They used cinder block construction. That makes it pretty cold in the winter time."

"I can't remember what it was going to be," said Ben. "Elsie tried to find out who owned it, but I wasn't interested. I admit, I didn't pay much attention."

Looking through a broken window, Hal saw an old mattress and a dark sooty corner where someone had built a fire. "Looks like someone's living there already."

"That don't surprise me none. There's plenty of homeless people on the rez," said Ben. "It must get mighty cold in the winter time though."

"Yeah, you'd be protected from the wind, but not from the cold," said Hal. "So whatever happened to Elsie's soup kitchen idea?"

"I didn't pay it no mind," sighed Ben. "She saw a TV show where they did house makeovers and she thought they could do something here."

"I know that show," said Hal as he pulled himself out of the window. "They help disadvantaged people. They'll tear down the old house and build a new one."

"Yeah, that sounds about right," said Ben. "I wouldn't mind setting them loose around here. I bet they'd do wonders on an Indian reservation."

"Ya think," laughed Hal. "I doubt the rest of the world even knows how we live."

"Well, if it ain't on TV, it don't exist," said Ben. "I don't recollect a TV news crew coming through here."

"I bet you're right," said Hal. "I wonder how Camp Sobriety is doing?"

The wind carried the aroma of fresh grill through the air. "Do you smell that?" asked Ben. "I wonder whose cooking barbeque."

As they come up on the house, Ernie was bent over the grill. Mother Earth was bountiful. They were surrounded by the blessings of the Great Mystery.

"What are you grilling, Ernie?" yelled Ben across the yard. "It smells good and I'm hungry."

"Jed and Leroy went fishing and brought back a bucket full. So we gutted them and I'm grilling them up," said Ernie smiling.

"Hal, you're in luck today. Nobody grills better than Ernie around here," said Ben as they hurried to wash up. "Maybe we should warm up that macaroni Vera brought last night."

"Ernie, you want some of Vera's macaroni to go with the fish?" asked Ben.

"Jed and Leroy are already on it," said Ernie as he flipped the fish.

Sure enough, when they walked up the porch steps, the kitchen was a bustle of activity. Ben's heart smiled to see them here. It reminded him of when Elsie cooked and everybody came for dinner.

"What are you looking for?" asked Ben as he walked through the door.

"You got a pot or a frying pan to heat up this macaroni?" asked Jed.

"Elsie kept them hidden in the oven, over there," laughed Ben.

"Oh, right. That's last place I'd look," sighed Jed. "The kitchen never was my territory."

"It was never mine either," said Ben.

Leroy came up to Hal and in a low voice said, "I told my dad about the Warrior Sweat. He wants to know more about it. Can you tell him?"

Jed overheard Leroy and spoke right up. "Hey Hal, tell me about the Warrior Sweat. It sounds interesting. But, didn't the guy in Arizona kill those people in a warrior sweat."

"Oh that idiot," Ben chimed in. "He was trying to make big bucks by imitating our ceremonies. He was never authorized to do ceremony. And those white folks weren't properly prepared. He just sprung it on them. He was a con artist preying on the feeble minded with a credit card. I heard he charged $10,000 for a lodge!"

"No, it was worse than that," Hal said. "First, he put them up on the hill for 3 days, on a prayer fast. Then he shoved 56 people in an 8 round sweat lodge covered with plastic tarps. He plum cooked them to death. They paid him for an E-ticket ride to the Spirit World and some of them got it."

"Didn't he put jimson weed on the stones?" Jed asked.

"Oh, I don't know, cuz I wasn't there" started Ben all lit up. "But that greedy son of a bitch put a price tag to our ceremonies. That drives the sacredness right out of the lodge. Spirits know the difference. His ignorance killed people and dishonored our sacred traditions. I watched the news. That fool played a Samurai Warrior game with those folks and told them 'he was God!' Well, his pride killed 3 people that day.

255

That's a heavy toll for arrogance."

"You ain't kidding," said Hal.

"I'll tell you this, Jed," Ben went on. "The way you know a phony is when they're strutting around like a peacock with their feathers fanned out, telling everybody how great they are. Great healers are humble. There's no fancy show to impress people. They just take care of the healing and go on their way."

"Out West, they got a word for that," Hal started. "It's called 'Spiritual Materialism.' That's a guru who's got a bunch of followers, he wants to control. The easiest prey are the weak and feeble minded. If you notice, he didn't work with the poor. Instead of sharing the truth and being of service, he was only interested in making big money. In my book, I only need to follow the dictates of a Higher Power, not some fool interested in taking my last dollar."

"Well, even Jesus got mad at the money changers and turned the tables over," remarked Jed.

"I read parts of that white man's holy book. When Christ put the mud on the blind man's eyes and helped him see, he didn't charge him. A real medicine man isn't walking around with his hand out. He knows Creator will take care of him," Ben started. "That healing power comes from Creator. It's a gift. When someone uses His power to take advantage of people, bad things happen and the power goes away. Our ceremonies were a gift from Creator. It's not a good practice to charge for them. The whites brought that wasicu mindset to the Red Man."

Watching this conversation spin out of control, Hal pulled hard on the reins to steer it back. "Now Jed, I understand your worries. But I've sat in a hundred lodges. I've gone up on the hill, done a Hanblecha and cried for a vision, close to a dozen times. And sun danced for years. From my experience, I can tell you, it gets hot in the lodge. At times, it's down right uncomfortable. But it's meant to purify us. And nothing gets clean without a little elbow grease."

"So you've done everything they did in Arizona and lived," said Jed. "So what went wrong there?"

"Well, it's the sequence of things," started Hal. "To do a vision quest, which is a four day pipe fast, you prepare for months. Before I went up on the hill, I made 405 prayer ties. That's 101 prayer ties for each of the four directions, plus an extra one for Tunkashila. It took a long time to pray that many prayers and tie them all up on a string. Then, I had to clear the ground at my vision quest site and make it ready. When I did my first pipe fast, I was so broke I made my own star quilt. It weren't much to look at, but I put the effort into it."

"I'd like to see that," Leroy jested. "You sitting in front of a sewing machine."

"You'd be surprised what you can learn, when your willing, Leroy. Now, when Ohiya did his vision quests, he dug a pit and sat in there for four days. Or sometimes he'd do his pipe fast in a covered Inipi. When I was out West, I did my first vision quest out under the trees in a small canyon. It had a creek running through it, with big oak trees. It was a right pretty spot to spend quiet time with Creator and Wyatt's Cannupa. When they put me up on the hill, I put those 405 prayer ties around my vision quest site. Those prayers put up a powerful field of protection. So you're not visited by unfriendlies. And there's four prayer flags, one for each direction hanging from a willow pole."

Hal stopped and took a sip of his coffee before he went on. "I have to tell you this, though. The first time I put the prayer ties around my vision quest site, it fit perfect around the willow flag poles. All the yellow prayer ties were in the east, the black were in the west. All the white were in the south and the red were in the north," Hal boasted for a moment. "After that, I set up the altar with a Waluta. That's an eagle feather tied to an abalone shell on a red cloth. I hung that on a willow pole and put the altar cloth in front of it. That way I had a place for the Cannupa, when I wasn't praying with it.

"It sounds like a lot of prep work," said Jed.

"Well, it is Jed, and that ain't all. Every week, I went to lodge to purify and we brought up food for the feast afterward. Not to mention, there was a give away for the supporters. So before you go up, you know exactly what you're doing and why. Crying for a Vision is a beautiful ceremony. It gives you time in solitude with Creator. It's not an endurance test, like this joker set it up to be."

"But what about the sweat lodge? Didn't he do 8 rounds?" Jed wanted to know.

"Well, that's where this guru went wrong. When you do a vision quest, that's the main ceremony. The sweat lodge is just a dust off, so your mind is cleansed and your vision is clear. It's fairly simple," Hal started. "Before you go on the hill, there's a 2 round sweat. After the lodge, you pray and fast for four days. Now, some people don't go up for four days right off. They might start with one or two. Especially children, who might go up for a night and a day. Another thing, the whole time you're on the hill, that fire stays lit. While you're praying in solitude for the people, they're eating, drinking and praying for you. After you come down, you finish the last two rounds of the lodge. So, there's a total of four rounds in an Inipi ceremony."

"That idiot tried to turn those people into 'Spiritual Warriors' in 5 days," Ben cackled, slapping his knee. "And charging them lots of money to get there. The greedy son of a bitch!"

"What Ben's trying to say is," laughed Hal. "Is we won't be charging ten grand to turn your boy into a spiritual warrior. Ain't that right Ben?"

"No, we won't! And it takes longer than 5 days to turn a lump of coal into a diamond anyhow! It might take two or three life times to do that kind of work," Ben exclaimed with a laugh. "Go on professor, finish telling them about the lodge." Ben winked with a wily smile.

"Well what I was saying was," said Hal as he looked over

at Ben. "You might want to lay off the coffee."

"Oh, it ain't the coffee, Hal," Ben joked. "But, here's what puzzles me. I heard that idiot guru was a preacher's boy. Those Christians had their own Spiritual Warrior. Christ went up on the hill for forty days and nights. When he was up there, he was tempted by the devil and all. So why don't they follow Christ's teachings instead of stealing our Sacred Ways?"

"Christ didn't work with the rich," said Jed having Christianity forced on him. "The love of money is the root of all evil. The rich don't need God. They can buy whatever they want. Christ healed the sick, the poor lepers, all the rejected ones with power of love. But the rich never took to it."

"Well, it's not much different today," said Ben quieting down a little. "Most rich folks would rather step over a homeless man, than buy him a meal, let alone help him out. Christ fed thousands of people with a prayer, a few loaves of bread and some fish. He didn't waste a thing."

"That's true," said Jed having studied the bible. "You ever heard about the one rich man who approached Christ, wanting to be taught?"

"The one Christ told to give up all his belongings and follow him?" Ben replied.

"That's the one. And he couldn't do it. There is that principle, 'to whom much is given, much is expected," said Jed.

"Ah.... we could change the world," said Ben. "With some resources. You know there's enough food on Mother Earth, that no one need go hungry? It's the greed of a few that causes the suffering of many."

"I know, Ben," said Hal having witnessed the selfishness of the wealthy on the West Coast. "But some people teach you how to be and some people teach you how not to be." Stopping to gather his thoughts, Hal lit a piece of sage to clear out the negative energy. "I don't want this bozo's mistakes to bleed into our ceremony."

After the negative energy cleared out, Hal resumed his talk. "Now I was taught the Inipi, which is our purification right, is an ancient ceremony. Our people are a warrior society. After battle, our warriors needed to cleanse. They sacrificed their innocence by doing and seeing things they'd rather forget. War madness takes a toll on the spirit, especially if you've got blood on your hands. In the lodge, we ask Creator for forgiveness. And He washes us clean from the ravages of war. It's a safe place to make amends for the harm we've done to another," said Hal, trying to keep the conversation focused. "Does that make sense?"

"Yeah, I guess. We didn't go to ceremony, my wife being Christian and all. As a family, we went to a few Powwows but that was it," said Jed.

"I didn't grow up around ceremony either," explained Hal. "My buddy Wyatt took me to my first ceremony and he was a white guy. I never realized how 'dirty' I was until I was washed clean."

"Since you're not charging ten grand, what does it cost?" asked Jed wanting to know the charges up front.

"UH..." said Hal with his hands in the air, when Ben interrupted.

"It'll cost your heart and soul," said Ben. "You're not bowing before me or Hal here. We never claimed to be gurus. You're bowing before Creator and asking Him for help. Sure, some things cost money. Like blankets from the thrift store and food for the feast. But it seems Vera likes to cook."

"Would my mom come?" asked Leroy. "If this is a warrior sweat."

"That son, is up to you," said Ben. "When people pray for each other, it blesses them too. There's power in numbers. Your parents had fears when you were in combat. Those fears would get cleansed too. Whether or not your mom opens her mind to these Ancient Ways, is up to her. Kyle can come too, if he wants. Chew on that and let me know what you decide."

260

"Talk about the power of prayer," started Hal. "You know, I read somewhere that in World War 2, the German Luftwaffe got defeated because ol' Churchill had the English people pray every night. It was their secret weapon. The second Big Ben struck nine o'clock, the whole nation went into a heartfelt moment of prayer."

"What, you think some miracle stopped the German air force?" scoffed Leroy.

"Do your own research," said Hal. "All I know is, they called on the Higher Powers and the Nazi pilots turned around and flew off. Then the Germans lost the war."

"I think it sounds good," said Jed staying out of the battle zone. "You ran a sweat here for many years, Ben. And you and Hal have been sober for long time."

"Speaking of sobriety, Leroy," started Hal. "You still need to treat your alcoholism. The Inipi can ease the PTSD, but you're an alcoholic. Maybe you can go to meetings with your dad."

"Who said anything about meetings?" Leroy rolled his eyes as his defiance reared its ugly head. "I'm not going to a program started by some white guys."

"You're not getting it, son," started Ben. "The anti-venom comes from the snake that bit ya. Alcohol came from the whites and killed them off for centuries. Creator don't give a lick about the color of a man's skin when He gives a remedy. All He needs is an opening. Someone who's willing to receive what He gives them."

"Nobody's shoving program down your throat," said Hal. "But we don't want you to die, because you're a knucklehead who won't ask for help. There's an ocean of alcohol on this rez and everyone's drowning in it. We've got your back, Leroy."

"You forgetting something Hal, and it's the most important thing," said Ben as he was struck with a thought.

"What's that?" asked Jed.

"Well, when Hal and Kyle snatched Leroy's unconscious body from the jaws of death and dragged him over here. We didn't ask him if he wanted to quit drinking. There's a requirement to join AA. And we don't know if he meets the requirement," said Ben.

"You have requirements to join AA?" laughed Leroy, thinking Ben was pulling his leg.

"Yup, we do. In order for this organization of victorious losers to work, it has rules to follow. We all had to fulfill certain conditions to get sober and come back winning. To get something better, we gave up alcohol. Our job is to carry the message. But you have to fulfill your end, if you want to join up with us," said Ben leading the horse to water.

"Okay," said Leroy playing along. "What are the big requirements to join AA?"

"Well, the third tradition says, the only requirement for membership is a desire to quit drinking. That's what it takes to join AA. Only you can decide. It doesn't matter what your dad, me or Hal wants. So the big question is, do you have the desire to quit drinking?" asked Ben. "Because your other options are go insane or die. You got pretty close to both."

The room fell silent. Leroy stared at his shoes. Ben sent a knowing glance at Hal. He felt Leroy was being ganged up on. "Hal, I think all this pushing is too much. Will you take Jed outside and let me talk to the boy alone?"

"Sure," said Hal. "Let me just fill my coffee cup. Come on, Jed. Let's go see how the fish are frying."

After they walked outside, Leroy looked up from his shoes. "Thanks," he said.

"Yeah, I had a feeling it was too much," said Ben. "No one can be pressured into sobriety, son. You either want it or you don't. It doesn't matter how many people want it for you. I've seen it over and over. A man gets sober because his wife left him. But the in the long run, it don't stick. He's got to want it for himself. I'll say one thing though, you need at least 30 days sober and a few more pounds on your scrawny body before I'll run a warrior lodge. Your bag of bones won't hold up in the heat. And I don't invite drunks into the lodge. Especially if they've been drinking."

"I understand. I just don't want to disappoint my dad," said Leroy staring at his shoes. An old heaviness was around Leroy's heart which was obvious to Ben.

"Tell me about that," said Ben.

"Ever since I was a kid he pressured me to BE A MAN, BE A MAN! I did everything he asked, but it wasn't enough. After a while, I gave up. He'd find a mistake and that's all he saw," said Leroy. "He wanted me to be perfect, but he wasn't."

"Perfectionism drives love right out the window. Especially when you're surrounded by faultfinders," said Ben.

"One time, I couldn't take out the trash right," sneered Leroy.

The boy's hurt was dripping through the pores of his skin. "There's lots of different kinds of men, Leroy. Not just one," said Ben. After a moment, Ben looked at Leroy intently and asked, "Do you trust me, Leroy?"

"Yeah, sort of. Why?" asked Leroy, confused, looking up from his shoes.

"Well, there's something I want to see. I need to know if you trust me enough to take a look. I'm not going to hurt you," said Ben. "But, I have a feeling about something." Leroy shrugged.

Ben put the candle on the table and lit a piece of sage. The smoke curled and spread out through the room. He stood behind Leroy's chair. "Okay, now I want you to take a few deep breaths and let your body relax."

Ben placed his right hand on Leroy's heart and the left hand on his back. He felt every in and out breath Leroy took as his body relaxed. Closing his eyes, Ben let his mind go blank. The room became very still. Only the tick tock of the clock was heard.

Then, a picture formed in Ben's mind. A small boy sat on his knees on the back porch, just outside the back door. In front of him was a dark object about the size of a pillow. It looked burned, like a large chunk of charcoal. The boy's sadness was overwhelming as if he lost a best friend. But, his tears were stifled and choked down. He didn't want to show his pain. 'Don't dare cry' was the message. Ben took his hands off Leroy and sat back down in his chair.

Leroy opened his eyes. The few moments of stillness pierced his heart. "What just happened?"

"Well, I'll tell you what I saw and you tell me what happened," said Ben.

"Okay," said Leroy wondering what this was leading up to.

"When I put my hand on your heart," said Ben in a gentle voice. "There's a heaviness. A deep sadness. And then this picture formed in my mind. There was a small boy. He was sitting on the back porch on his knees in front of something. It looked like a pillow made out of coal. The boy was sad, like he lost his best friend."

Old memories flooded back from his childhood. "That was my dog pillow. I slept with it and dragged it around everywhere. I was five years old, getting ready to start school when my dad called me to the back porch. He'd been drinking. My dog pillow was on the concrete step, outside the kitchen door. I went to pick it up and hold it. But, dad said no. He poured gasoline all over it. Then, he took a match and threw it on my dog pillow. It burst into flames." Leroy stopped as the memory flooded into his mind.

"I watched it burn. Flames were all around it. I stood there screaming when the dog pillow sat straight up and looked at me. I screamed and screamed. I almost picked it up through

264

the flames, but dad held me back. He told me to stop crying. I fell on my knees and watched it burn. After the flames died out, my dad walked away and left me there," said Leroy as the heartache got stuck in his throat. Ben sat still, knowing there was more.

"When mom came home, she found me outside on the step. She saw the burned pillow. She pulled me up on her lap and asked what happened. I told her dad burned it. That's when she found him drinking behind the shed. They had bad fight and he stomped off. Before he left, he hollered at me and said he was going to make me a man, if it was the last thing he did. I never cried after that day."

Ben sat at the table and absorbed what Leroy said. Knowing Jed most of his life, Ben had information that Leroy probably didn't know about his dad. "No one can be a true man without a heart, Leroy. But now I understand why your dad feels so guilty. That was your first cut and he did it to you. He broke your young heart. And he doesn't know how to take it back."

"Hmm," Leroy sighed. "Years later, he took me hunting. It was his way to show me how to be a man. He saved money to get my first hunting rifle. Later, when Kyle was born, dad never took away his favorite blanket. I think mom would have killed him. Kyle dragged his dirty old blanket around forever," said Leroy shook his head. "Mom washed it so many times, that it just shredded. But he couldn't sleep without it."

"So your dad replaced your dog pillow with a gun," said Ben.

"I guess so. I never thought about it that way. You know what's funny, I used to sleep with my M16," said Leroy. "So yeah, I guess he did."

"A lot of us did, boy. A lot of us did," said Ben. "I think your dad was afraid you'd turn out like his younger brother Rudy."

"I never met Uncle Rudy. Grandma told me stories

265

about him before she passed. I think she was heartbroken that he left," said Leroy.

"Yeah, it was a hard story," said Ben.

"Did you know Uncle Rudy?" asked Leroy.

"Oh yeah. Elsie babysat for your grandma. She worked as a cleaning lady when the boys were small. That's what the boarding school taught her to do back then. Either be a seamstress or a cleaning lady. I knew Rudy. He stuck close to Elsie though. He was her biggest helper," said Ben.

"What happened to him?" asked Leroy.

"Well, I'll give you the short version. When Rudy was little, maybe 3 years old, your grandma found him waltzing around in her church shoes. Well, Jed saw this and made fun of him. That's why Elsie started watching him. Jed beat Rudy up and it got bad."

"So Rudy was gay?" asked Leroy never hearing this before.

"Twin Spirits, a Winkte boy. No one understood him in your family," said Ben. "See Winkte are female spirits who take on a male body. They have both female and male elements in them."

"I don't get that spiritual stuff, like you do. I'm trying to understand, but I can't wrap my mind around it," said Leroy.

"Your dad didn't either. It's no mystery to me. Do you want me to explain it to you?" asked Ben not wanting to push anything on Leroy.

"Yeah, I'll listen," said Leroy.

"It's not a difficult teaching. You see, spirit is what's left when the physical body is removed. When you pass away, what belongs to spirit, goes back to spirit. What belongs to Earth, goes back to Earth. Your body is a house for spirit. And without spirit, your body is lifeless. Does that make sense so far?" Ben asked.

"Yeah, like electricity flowing through a lamp. Without a current, it don't light up," said Leroy having studied electrical engineering.

"Exactly, I couldn't have explained it better. Now, here's the next part. Spirit is always growing and learning. Mother Earth a big classroom. To survive, you got to bring your best game to the world of duality. There's no rules on Earth, so it's a tough planet to live on. For centuries, female spirits had the toughest go of it. If they were born in the Orient, they'd be left on the rocks to die. Or sold into slavery or prostitution. It's not easy for girls to live on this lawless planet. If a female spirit wanted a shot at decent life, she took on a male body. It's a hard teaching, but each lesson brings richness to the soul. And that's why we are here, to enrich the soul."

"So Rudy was Winkte and my dad bullied him," said Leroy finally getting the picture. "And because Rudy was gay, dad had to make sure I was a man."

"Well, his fear drove him to make you a man," said Ben seeing the light go on in Leroy's eyes. "There was nothing wrong with Rudy. Your father was afraid, because he didn't understand and made it wrong. Lack of understanding causes a lot of pain."

"So my dad didn't want me to be soft. He drove me to be a man and I got so hard, I almost cracked... to please him. All because Rudy was gay," said Leroy starting to understand.

"Pretty much," said Ben. "Fear drives a man to do crazy things."

"So what happened to Rudy?"

"Well, Jed and Rudy got into a big fight on the schoolyard. Rudy had to get his eye stitched up at the clinic. That night, Rudy packed a suitcase and boarded a Greyhound bus headed west. He was 17 years old. I thought your grandma would die," said Ben as he recalled standing at the bus depot with Rudy. "I think Rudy needed to find his own kind."

"You know, my dad never talks about Rudy?"

"I can't imagine why he would. I think you're dad was afraid that Rudy was contagious," laughed Ben. "Like it was something in the water."

"So are all gay men Twin Spirits?" asked Leroy.

"Well, I couldn't say for sure," said Ben. "I haven't met them all."

"Hey! You hungry yet?" came a yell from outside the door. It was Hal with two plates full of fried fish. Opening the door, Ben let Hal in. The fish was fried up perfect. Hal set down the plates on the table. "Let's eat!"

CHAPTER SIX: UP IN SMOKE

It was Friday night. Bored out of his mind, Kyle lay on his bed, staring at the ceiling. The last nine days, he hadn't drank and made it to school every day. Ever since Leroy got back, his parents flitted around him. Kyle felt invisible all over again. Stewing in old resentment and living in his brother's shadow made him miserable. The more he thought about it, the angrier he got. But now, he didn't have a drink to buffer the anger. It rattled around in his head. His mind boiled over like an angry cauldron. Desperately wanting to escape, he went in the living room and flopped on the couch. He turned on the TV. In nine hundred channels, there was nothing on. He hated this life.

About 10:30 pm, the phone rang. Kyle got up to answer it. "Hello?"

"Hey Kyle, it's Charlie. Where have you been? I haven't see you around lately." Charlie and Kyle grew up together.

"Yeah, I'm busy with school. I'm thinking about going full time. I want to get my grades up to go to the university," said Kyle wanting to sound like he was doing something important.

"Well, okay. Listen, me and Jimmy are going to this party. We got room in the car if you want to go," said Charlie. "I think Darlene is going to be there."

"Oh, she's pretty," whined Kyle. "But she doesn't know I exist. She's only got eyes for football jocks."

"Well, you want to go or not?" asked Charlie getting impatient.

"Yeah, I'll go. Come by and pick me up," asked Kyle.

"Just walk over here. I'll wait for you," said Charlie as he hung up.

Swinging into action, Kyle dug though a pile of dirty jeans, looking for the cleanest pair. There was a clean shirt under a stack of half folded laundry. Even though Darlene never gave him a glance, he wanted to look good if she was there. For a second, drinking crossed his mind. He decided he'd stick to beer. No whiskey. It clouded his brain, but he figured beer wasn't as bad.

Brushing his teeth, Kyle looked at himself in the mirror. This fat face stared back at him. He loathed his fat face. Somewhere in his body, was another guy. A thinner, more handsome guy. Someone Darlene would look at. Indians weren't always fat, he told himself. Look at our ancestors. They were lean and strong. But back then, there was no Velveeta macaroni and cheese or Mountain Dew to wash it down with. No, his ancestors ate buffalo meat and berries. They rode horse and lived off the land. Someday things would be different, he kept telling himself. After he combed his hair, he found a jacket and hustled down to Charlie's house.

On this moonless night, millions of stars twinkled across the endless sky. A cool breeze whipped up from the Missouri as Kyle hustled the three blocks to Charlie's house. When he got there, Charlie and Jimmy were sitting in his mother's car. They waited until Kyle got in the back seat to start the engine.

"Hey dude, what's up?" asked Charlie. "I think Jeannie wants to come. I was waiting for her. But if she doesn't get here in 5 minutes, we'll go without her."

"Why don't you just drive by her house. She might be on her way," said Jimmy, not wanting to wait.

Charlie backed out of the driveway and headed to Jeannie's house. They found her walking, two blocks down. When she got into the back seat next to Kyle, their eyes met. They both remembered the AA meeting and their shares about Jason. It was uncomfortable memory, but neither one said anything.

"So who's party is this," asked Jeannie.

"It's at Alan's house," said Charlie as he took a swig from a small pint of moonshine. "His parents left for a couple weeks. So he's man of the house."

"Doesn't he have 4 younger sisters?" asked Kyle wondering if they'd be there.

"Yeah, but I think they got farmed out to his aunt's house. So it should be alright," said Charlie driving through the neighborhood.

Pulling up to Alan's house, an old clunker was parked in the driveway. Music streamed out the front door and all the lights were on. Inside the house were a few people sitting on the couch. Some milled around the kitchen. Empty pizza boxes cluttered the kitchen counter. The trashcan was full of empty beer cans. Alan walked out of the back bedroom, as Kyle opened the fridge looking for beer.

"Hey man, sorry, we ran out of beer about a half hour ago," said Alan as he filled a cup with water from the faucet. "I haven't seen you around, Kyle."

Disappointed, Kyle closed the fridge. "Yeah, I've been busy with school."

"I heard you found Leroy. They got him set up in a tipi at old man Ben's house. Didn't he disappear a year ago? We thought he must be dead," said Alan.

Striking a raw nerve, Kyle was in no mood to talk about his brother's brush with death. He wanted out of that noise for a while. A moment later, Pete stumbled out of the back bedroom. "Hey Kyle, where you been duuuude? We saw your brother down by Kelly's the other day. I guess he came out of hiding, huh?"

Pete staggered across the kitchen to the fridge. He opened the door looking for beer, but it was empty. Kyle mumbled something, but Pete didn't pay attention.

"Shit, we're out of beer. Dude! We need to go on a beer run. Kyle, here, you drive my car." Pete shoved his hands in his pocket and found his keys. "Come on, let's go."

In high school, Pete was the cool guy. He always had a girl on his arm and could get whatever he wanted. Alan was his faithful sidekick. They went everywhere together. Tonight was no different. Feeling out of place, Kyle lumbered behind Alan. They trailed after Pete, who stumbled down the driveway. Pete's car was a beat up, old Lincoln. The sagging bumper was tied on with a bungee cord. Cracked and torn, the maroon leather seats were covered with old towels.

"Hey Kyle, have you ever driven my ride before?" asked Pete leaning over, exhaling his whiskey breath all over Kyle. "Cuz you got to pump the gas a little when you start it. Otherwise it dies out. It still runs good for an '87. But doooon't FLOOD it! Or we'll never get it started."

As Kyle got in the driver's seat, he had a bad feeling about this. Pete road shotgun and Alan got in the back. Pumping the gas, the old Lincoln started right up. As they headed toward the main highway, it was already after midnight. The only liquor store nearby was owned by a white man who charged double for everything. Kyle didn't think it'd be open. But that's where Pete wanted to go. The store was about a mile up the main highway, in the middle of nowhere. When they got there, it was closed and the lights were out.

"AH, shit, what do we do now?" said Pete getting out of the car. Kyle watched him stumble around the small dirt parking lot. He looked at the gas gauge. It was on empty. The next liquor store was off the rez about a half hour away.

Feeling pretty thirsty, Pete's buzz was wearing off. He was determined to get something to drink. Opening the trunk, he fished around until he found rope and a crowbar.

"Hey, I got an idea," said Pete all lit up. "We'll tie this rope to the stock room window and pull the window cage off. Then, Alan and I can grab a case of whiskey and we'll get out of here. Kyle, I'll tie this rope under the back bumper and you punch the gas when I tell you. Got it?"

Feeling nervous, Kyle hesitated. In his gut he knew this wasn't a good idea. "I don't think..."

But Pete whirled around and cut him off. He wouldn't allow Kyle to question his authority. Like a vicious hellcat, Pete turned on Kyle. "Who paid you to think, Kyle?" Pete sneered as he got up in Kyle's face. Kyle backed away for a moment.

"What? Are you chicken? I always figured you for a pantywaist pussy. You're not eagle-hearted like your brother Leroy. You got a puny chicken heart. You're just a big fat Pillsbury dough boy," Pete taunted Kyle as he poked him in the chest. Standing in the shadows, Alan snickered and grabbed the crowbar.

Pete's words sliced through Kyle like flaming daggers. They burned deep in his soul. Trembling with rage, Kyle's stood silent with clinched fists, feeling his blood boil. Some unseen force kept him from punching Pete in the mouth.

Seeing Kyle's balled up fists, Pete laughed. "What, you think you're going to punch me, Kyle?"

Like a stone, Kyle said nothing. He glared at Pete, filled with hate. Returning the stare, Pete didn't back down. After a few seconds, Pete stepped back from Kyle.

"Yeah, I didn't think so. Kyle, get your fat, candied ass back in the car and do what I tell you to do. Got it?"

Mocked and bullied, Kyle felt defeated as he slunk down into the driver's seat and started the engine. He was nothing but a big jelly fish. No backbone. Even though he outweighed Pete by 80 pounds, Kyle lacked confidence. He could have crushed him with his butt cheeks alone. But Kyle never learned to stick up for himself. The King of Nothing, here he was, hanging out with drunks and robbing a liquor store in the middle of the night. 'Boy mom would be proud,' he thought as a dark cloud descended on him.

Busy prying the window grate off the wall with the crowbar, Alan couldn't see well without much light.

273

Determined to keep the party going, Pete tied the rope under the back bumper and to the window grate with a few good knots. "OK KYLE! PUNCH THE GAS!"

Stomping on the gas pedal, the Lincoln V8 engine roared as all 225 horses powered into action. It fishtailed all over the dirt parking lot as Kyle clutched the steering wheel. He felt the Lincoln's rear end lift off the ground several times. The rope pulled taut as Lincoln tugged hard on the window grate. The tires spun on the dirt, kicking up great clouds of dust. It pulled and jerked, when suddenly the entire window tore away from the wall. It bounced behind the Lincoln, as the car launched forward like a rocket. The car swerved and skidded across the dirt parking lot. Kyle stomped on the brake before the Lincoln plowed into the cornfield.

Getting out of the car, his heart pounded out of his chest. Kyle turned to look at the gaping hole torn out of the building. Adrenaline and dread surged through his shaking body. He saw this madness with sober eyes.

In the middle of the parking lot, Pete and Alan did a victory dance. With a war whoop, they scrambled into the liquor store through the gaping hole. Once inside, the temptation to grab everything they could, was irresistible. They filled their pockets with cigarettes.

Lighting up a cigarette from a carton he just shoved into his jacket, Alan took a long hit, letting the smoke fill his lungs. His stomach growled as he spied the deli full of roast beef, ham, turkey, all kinds of cold cuts and cheese. He walked behind the deli counter and opened the window to the cold case. Finding a roll, he piled it high with different meats and cheeses and made a colossal sandwich. Living on government handouts and welfare, his family didn't have the money for anything more than cheap white bread and baloney. So this was a feast.

Anxiously waiting in the car, Kyle kept the motor running. Beads of sweat poured down his face. Kyle thought Pete would just grab a case of whiskey and they'd get the hell out of here. Now he wondered what was taking so long. He sure as shit didn't want to end up in jail for being the driver of the getaway car.

Getting out of the car, Kyle untied the rope from the bumper. He rolled it up, throwing it in the back seat. Large shards of glass from the broken window were strewn everywhere. Down the highway, Kyle saw headlights coming towards them. He hid behind the building until the car drove past. Fear gripped him.

On a scavenger hunt, Pete found an expensive bottle of brandy behind the cash register. He uncorked the bottle and the rich aroma flooded his nostrils. When he put the bottle to his lips, he poured the smooth liquor down his throat. He felt the familiar burn. "Whew! That's good shit!"

After Alan finished making his sandwich, he took a big bite. The roast beef melted in his mouth. He savored every bite. Finding the deli paper, he wrapped up slabs of cold cuts and shoved them into a brown paper bag. He took a swig of whiskey to chase down his sandwich. Sitting on the counter, his feet swung back and forth, while he enjoyed his meal.

Surveying the store, he wanted to fill as many paper bags as he could. Then, he'd have groceries for a week. After he finished his sandwich, Alan grabbed a stack of paper bags and filled them with everything in reach. Then, he passed the bags through the gaping hole in the wall and yelled at Kyle to put them in the car.

Still busy with his brandy bottle, Pete saw Alan filling up bags and filled a few of his own. But the spirit of brandy assumed control. Under its influence, Pete's mind started to swirl. His feet were unstable as he stumbled all over the store.

Looking in the rear view mirror, Kyle saw Alan waving at him through the hole in the wall. Another car drove passed headed down the highway. Fear gripped Kyle's insides and he started to freak out. He thought it was the police. With his heart pounding, Kyle ducked until it passed by. Getting out of the car, Kyle ran over and saw the bags full of booty. He wanted to get out the hell out of there. So he backed the car up and shoved all the bags in the trunk.

"Come on, man! Hurry up. I don't want to get caught out here," shouted Kyle through the hole in the wall. But, Alan and Peter were no longer in this world. They were enchanted by spirits in the bottle and danced in another realm.

Howling across the prairie, strong gusts of wind rustled through the corn stalks. The street light overhead swayed in the wind. A chill crawled up Kyle's back. At that moment, he heard Ben's voice as plain as if he was standing next to him. "The spirit of Freddy Kruger is in that bottle boy!"

His heart pounded through his chest as Kyle panicked. He paced back and forth outside the torn out window. As he looked up, a shooting star crossed the heavens. From under the eaves of the store, a lone owl hooted. Hearing its call, Kyle looked up as a large horned owl swooped down over the cornfield looking for mice. A shiver went up his spine. In his gut he knew this was an omen, a warning. "Choose," the wind whispered through the cornfield.

As he staggered around, Pete heard Kyle screaming to hurry up. "What's that asshole worried about?" Pete scoffed. "There's only four cops on this whole reservation. They're not going to show up here in the next few minutes. Hell, it takes them over a half hour to show up if you have a real emergency."

Like a buccaneer stockpiling his treasure, Alan muscled a case of whiskey through the gaping hole. He let the box slide out of his hands, onto the ground. As he turned around to get another case of 100 proof vodka, the cigarette dangling from his mouth fell under the vodka racks. It lay smoldering, its red cherry glowing.

Dancing through the store, Pete came up behind Alan. Off balance, he tripped over an empty box and dropped his bag of booty. As he fell forward, he crashed into a rack of 100 proof vodka. He was startled by the clatter as the bottles of vodka crashed to the floor. Without thinking, Pete hurled himself out through the gaping hole. Broken glass lay everywhere as vodka flooded the floor. Within seconds, the alcohol fumes reached the smoldering cigarette and exploded into flames.

Too drunk to react, Alan stood there, surrounded by flames. As the flames shot up, empty cardboard boxes caught on fire. All around him, bottles of booze burst from the heat. Watching from outside, Kyle panicked. He screamed at Alan to get out. But Alan was confused.

In an instant, Pete was struck stone cold sober. He saw the flames surrounding his buddy. Without thinking, he dove back in the gaping hole to pull Alan out. By this time, Alan was engulfed in flames. His pants caught on fire and he screamed as the flames burned his skin.

Frozen in fear, Kyle stopped cold when he saw the headlights of another car. It slowed as it drove past the liquor store on the main highway. The driver saw the flames and made a U turn. Kyle's heart stopped as it pull into the parking lot.

In the meantime, Pete struggled to get Alan out of the burning building. The blazing heat and flames singed his hair. With no time to lose, Pete yanked Alan out of the fire. He rolled Alan around in the dirt, putting out the flames. While this nightmare unfolded, Kyle bolted into the cornfields. The last thing he wanted was to get caught.

Running like a madman, sweat poured down Kyle's face. He tore through the cornfield like a bull being chased by lions. His massive body left a trail of crushed corn stalks in its wake. Moments later, sirens screamed down the highway as fire trucks thundered onto the crime scene.

As he zigzagged through the cornfield, Kyle was stabbed with pangs of guilt for leaving his friends. But, he wasn't willing to go to jail for breaking into the liquor store. Hell it wasn't his idea! He just drove the car, because Pete was too drunk.

But he couldn't escape hearing Alan's screams echo

through his mind. The horror of it all pierced his soul. In his mind's eye, he saw the flames leaping around Alan's body. Somehow he knew this would go bad. He knew it in his gut. Why did he ignore his gut feeling? He knew why. He didn't want them to think he was a coward. Shit, he really messed up this time. More than ever, he wished he was invisible. He wanted to disappear in the woodwork until this whole thing blew over.

Gasping for air and out of breath, Kyle didn't stop running until he was down by the River Road. Sweat poured off his face. His clothes were fully soaked through. His heart pounded through his chest. Finally, he collapsed by the side of the road.

Suddenly, Kyle heard whispering through the cornstalks as they swayed in the wind. Then, from the distance, Kyle heard Ben's voice again. "The spirit of Freddy Kruger is in that bottle, boy!"

A movie played in his mind. This time he could see it. It was so obvious how his friends were possessed by something. Under the influence of the spirits in the bottle, they were driven to do things they'd never do, if they were sober. Pete was studying to be a fireman. He dove back into a burning building to save Alan's life.

But, they wouldn't have been there if it wasn't for the craving. The driving need to satisfy an unquenchable thirst. Then, it struck Kyle like a thunderbolt. Had he drank tonight, he'd be inside the burning liquor store screaming. He shuddered at the thought. For the first time, he was grateful to be sober.

Looking into star filled heavens, he was overcome by this intense feeling of awe and gratitude. With a deep knowing, a sense of truth, he saw things he'd never considered before. Maybe Ben wasn't as crazy as he thought he was. If he was drunk, he wouldn't have heard Ben's voice in the cornfield. When his heart stopped racing, he dusted himself off and headed toward home.

Not knowing why, Kyle turned down the road towards Ben's house. It was close by. By now, it was probably two or three in the morning. Though he didn't want to wake anybody, he didn't want to go home either. He was afraid the police would be waiting outside his house if he showed up there.

The screaming sirens of fire trucks and emergency vehicles roused Hal from a peaceful sleep. Getting out of bed, Hal went outside. He looked towards the direction where the sirens came from. On this moonless night, he saw the flames shoot up right to the sky. When he realized that sleep would be impossible, he opened the tailgate of his truck and sat down. Hal watched as the fire raged out of control less than a mile away.

The sirens kept coming as the fire trucks, an ambulance, the sheriff and fire marshal rushed to the liquor store. It was now fully engulfed in flames. Every bottle of liquor exploded in the store as the fire roared out of control. Pete barely got Alan out in time. He dragged Alan's smoldering body away from the burning building. Alan screams eventually turned to whimpers as Pete cradled Alan's head in his lap. When the ambulance arrived, the EMTs cut Alan's pants away to assess his burns. They began to treat his wounds there.

The Fire Chief, Capt. Nelson bellowed orders to his men. He was afraid that if the wind picked up, the whole cornfield could be ablaze in seconds. The sheriff shined a light in Pete's eyes. It was obvious he was drunk. His hands were slightly burned. The hair on his arms was singed off from dragging Alan out of the flames. Both Alan and Pete were rushed to a hospital burn unit an hour away by ambulance.

While the ambulance roared down the highway, Pete sat in the back with Alan. He kept seeing Kyle's face in his mind's eye. When Kyle dared to question Pete's authority, he got enraged. Yet in the blurry recesses of Pete's mind, he sensed Kyle was right. Much to Pete's chagrin, this was a bad idea.

Unable to sleep with all the commotion, Leroy and Ben joined Hal on the tailgate of his truck. They watched as the flames shot up against the star studded sky. The wind, who delighted in gentle breezes during the early morning hours, was still and quiet. She held her breath so the whole town wouldn't go up in flames.

Up the road, something moved. It caught Leroy's trained military eye. "Do you see that over there? I see somebody walking," said Leroy out loud. Ben and Hal strained their eyes. They saw a shape lumbering down the River Road.

"I can't imagine who that'd be, at this time of night," said Ben as a thunderous explosion came from the liquor store. A huge fire storm lit up the moonless sky.

The blast rattled Leroy to the bone. Smoke filled his nostrils as his mind flooded with memories of combat. Jolted back to the front line, his heart raced and breathing quickened. Within seconds, Leroy's mind was trudging through the outback, carrying his pack with his M16 in his arms.

"Well there goes the propane!" Hal shook his head. "It's a little late for the fourth of July." Glancing over at Leroy, Hal knew something was wrong from the faraway look in his eye. "Hey buddy, where'd you go? Come on back," said Hal gently as he put his hand on Leroy's shoulder.

As he snapped back to the present moment, Leroy shook off the violent memories. "Hey, I'm going to check out who's walking down the street." He slipped off the tailgate and walked towards the lumbering shadow.

Hearing the explosions, Kyle felt pangs of guilt. There'd be hell to pay for breaking into the liquor store. All he wanted to do was crawl into a hole and disappear. His name was mud, now that Pete and Alan were in trouble. Lost in the doldrums, Kyle heard Leroy calling his name.

Leroy recognized his brother's shamefaced shuffle as he quietly moved toward him. "Hey Kyle, is that you?" Leroy called from across the street. "Dude, what are you doing down here? Did you get dumped or something?"

"Oh, it's worse than that. I did something stupid," Kyle admitted.

"Alright, who is she this time?" Leroy laughed. "Is it Darlene? You know, she's nothing but trouble. She checks a guys bank account before she goes out with him. I know you've had a hard crush on her since junior high."

"No.... I wish I got dumped by Darlene," Kyle groaned. "It's worse. I really screwed up this time."

"Hey Hal, Ben, look who I found. It's Kyle," shouted Leroy across the street. "Come on, man. Don't look so blue. It can't be that bad."

"Oh yeah, it is," alluded Kyle as they both walked across the street.

"I think I better get some coffee on," said Ben to Hal as the boys came walking up. "It could be a long morning."

"Good idea," said Hal watching their silhouettes walk up against the dim light of the street lamp. "Hey Kyle, you need directions or something? I know you live a few blocks up that way."

Flopping down on the back of the tailgate, the old truck creaked. Kyle looked pretty deflated.

"You gonna spill or what?" prodded Leroy, nudging his brother.

After a long silence, Kyle uttered a few words. "See the fire over there?"

"You mean the one that's lighting up the whole eastern sky?" laughed Hal. "I'm sure it's the only fire around for miles."

"Well... I was there," Kyle admitted.

"No shit! You blew up the liquor store! That greedy son of bitch had it coming! Gouging people the way he did. What the hell happened?" asked Leroy.

"No, I didn't blow it up," scowled Kyle hanging his head. There was a long moment of silence and then, talking a hundred miles an hour, he just spilled.

"We were at Alan's. But they ran out of beer. So Pete wanted to go on a beer run. He told me to drive his car to the liquor store, but it was closed. Then, Pete wanted to break in and get a case of whiskey. I said it wasn't a good idea. But Pete got in my face and said I had a chicken heart. He wanted to tear out the window with a rope tied to the bumper. I punched the gas and the window tore out. They went inside and a fire broke out. Alan got caught in flames and Pete pulled him out the window. I ran out of there before the cops came, so I must be chicken."

Hal chortled. His laughter was contagious. Tears were streaming from his eyes and he slapped his thigh. "Oh Kyle, second hand experience is plum worthless! You only learn when you get burned yourself. It's a darn shame that it's got to be that way. But I tell you what! You're writing a fine AA story! It'll outrank your brother's soon, if you keep this up. I swear I heard it all now."

Still smarting from Pete's rampage, Kyle's blood boiled over. He spun around and screamed at Hal. "I'm sick of measuring up to Leroy. I lived in his shadow my whole damn life! Everyday it's Leroy this and Leroy that! I'm always the fucking nerd! He's always the fucking hero! The fucking KING of the track team!"

"Whoa, there cowboy. I'm not putting you in the ring against your brother. But there ain't a pancake too thin that doesn't have two sides. We were just wondering what caused the fireworks," said Hal trying to calm things down. "Then you come up street and now we know. It's a good story though."

"You really feel that way?" asked Leroy thunderstruck by Kyle's angry tirade.

"Yeah, I really feel that way. Does that surprise you?" Kyle asked still seething with rage. "You're the one, always getting the glory! With mom it's always Leroy this and Leroy that! I'm sick of it!"

"No, I meant the nerd part. I thought you were more of a geek," Leroy laughed poking fun at his brother.

"Shut up asshole," laughed Kyle.

"I CAN FEEL THE LOVE!" said Hal waving his hands in the air. "I CAN FEEL THE LOVE! I'm going inside and get some coffee. Ben's getting better at making it."

"What's the big hullabaloo?" asked Ben walking up from behind. He held a warm coffee cup in his hands. "Who's the asshole?"

"They both are," said Hal. "They're just taking turns."

"Well, I got some good coffee brewed up in the house, if you all want some," said Ben. "Thanks to that wonderful contraption."

CHAPTER SEVEN: NEW YORK CITY

Days slowly crept into weeks as Leroy stayed on at Ben's. It was simple living, there in the tipi with Hal. To keep the tormented spirits at bay, Hal made sure there was always enough cedar. This way, Leroy had a few nights of restful sleep. But they weren't out of the woods. Not by a long shot. After some good meals, the color came back to Leroy's face. He managed to put a few pounds back on.

Frank, Ernie and Jed came by often. Most nights, they sat around the fire telling stories. Their laughter was contagious. Through their storytelling, each man saw how they were enchanted by the spirits in the bottle. Slowly, Leroy learned the meaning of fellowship. After hearing all the stories, he didn't feel so alone. Along with a good meal, Leroy learned the value of community. The tipi became a safe haven. The Spirit of Sobriety kept a close watch over them all.

After countless brushes with death, the men were grateful for their very breath and heartbeat. With a humble prayer, they called on Great Spirit and the Spirit of Sobriety to wrap them in Their loving arms. The Higher Powers kept them warm and away from harm. A brotherhood of sober warriors united around a coffee pot. Coaxed by his dad, Leroy went along to a few AA meetings. But, he was still skeptical of anything two white men put together.

Late one afternoon, Hal and Ben sat on the front porch, when Leroy and Jed came walking up.

"Hey Jed," said Hal getting up to shake his hand.

"How are you two today?" asked Jed.

"Can't complain," said Ben sensing a purpose for this visit. "What's on your mind?"

From his pocket, Leroy produced two pouches of tobacco. They were wrapped in bandanas with a sprig of sage.

He presented them to Hal and Ben. "I'm here to ask if you'll run a warrior lodge for me? I think I'm ready."

"How many days sober you got, Leroy?" asked Ben leaning forward, looking the boy over as if he were inspecting a horse.

"38 days today," said Leroy as his father beamed. "And I couldn't have done it without you and Hal and Camp Sobriety here."

Hal chuckled as he looked around at what they had created, one drunk working with another.

"Well that's good. You finally got the cotton out of your ears," said Ben. "What are you weighing in at?"

"I think I'm at 155 pounds, right now?" said Leroy.

"Hell, you barely weighed a buck twenty five, when we dragged you off the street," said Hal. "Nothing like your mom's cooking. What are you about 5 foot, 10?"

"Yeah," said Leroy holding the tobacco in his outstretched arms.

"Now, if I accept this tobacco Leroy," said Ben earnestly. "There are some conditions you'll have to accept and things you'll have to do. I won't take no back talk. Is that understood?"

"Yes sir," said Leroy.

"No need to call me sir," said Ben softening up. "You see son, by offering me this tobacco, you're asking for a prayer and a ceremony to hold the prayer. Spirit sees the truth of your intention. And prayer is the way of miracles. But, for that healing to happen, you must prepare. And purification is necessary first."

"Now, that's what the Inipi does. It purifies our being, when we humble ourselves in prayer. Then, Creator can undo the past and wash the blood off your hands. Understand, when Creator releases your imprisoned mind, it don't take Him no time at all. He can do it in a holy instant. Then, He'll give you a clean slate so you can move forward. But He won't do it unless you ask and cooperate with what's required. And most important, don't doubt, when you ask Creator for help. Doubt throws a wet blanket on the Sacred Fire of Life. Doubt smothers your prayer, so all you get is smoke and ash. Do you understand?"

Forever changed by the horror he'd witnessed on the killing fields, Leroy struggled with his heavy burden. The smell of burning gunpowder and memories of combat were pressed into his mind. Every night he was haunted by their faces and the mangled and bloody bodies. He felt older and hollow inside. Desperate to be released from this weight, he'd do anything. "I think so," said Leroy.

"Well, that's good enough for now," said Ben assessing the situation. "I'm going to give you some instructions and if Hal accepts, you can get started. If Hal doesn't accept, you got to find someone to complete the mission I'm giving you. Is that agreeable with you?"

"Yeah, sure," said Leroy not understanding what the mission is. Hal's ears pricked up too, since Ben was putting him to task.

"Snake medicine helps you shed the skin of your past. It clears out the clutter so you can move forward. That ball and chain keeps you shackled and stuck," said Ben. "Since you and Hal got to know each other pretty well, I'm asking you to work together on the first eight steps of the AA program before we do the lodge."

"WHAT!" bellowed Leroy with indignation. "I came here asking you for a ceremony, not to work the damn AA program!"

Leaning forward in his chair, Ben spoke in a low, stern voice, "I don't give a damn, what you think about AA or white people. I've known enough hardheaded idiots who'd rather die, by turning their cars into a heap of scrap metal and melted plastic, than get sober in AA. Trouble is, they take innocent lives with them."

"Now if you want freedom, Leroy, you'll do what I say. NO BACK TALK! If you want to do things your way, go ahead and do it. But leave me out of it. I'm not interested in doing something half-cocked. Because anything less than 100% commitment is pure hell. The choice is yours. Me and Hal are free men. We've done our work and we can sleep at night. I can't say the same for you. Either you're in or you're not. You decide."

Feeling the wind go out of his sails, Leroy was stuck between a rock and a hard place. "But Hal never said anything about AA or the steps when he did his warrior sweat."

"Ah, you forget Leroy. I was already in program, when Wyatt took me to ceremony. I knew him from my men's AA meeting. I don't remember what step I was on, but I did do my inventory," said Hal giving Leroy a gentle nudge. "It's not the cards you're dealt in life that matter, son. It's how you play them. We're just trying to keep you in the game. Don't you see, surrender isn't giving in. It's coming over to the winning side. I'd be honored to work the steps with you, all 12 of them."

"Just try it, Leroy. It worked for me," said his dad trying to coax Leroy.

"Stop twisting my arm, dad! You're always pushing me! You've been pushing me since I was five to be a man, when you didn't know what it meant yourself," Leroy snapped, digging his heels in.

Ben had just about enough of this bullshit. He wasn't interested in spoon feeding another hard-head recovery. Hitting bottom on the rez, wasn't like hitting bottom in the white man's world. On the rez, most drunks died on the street.

In the white world, an educated drunk in a three piece suit, might chip the paint on his fancy car in a fender bender. Then, after he gets busted with a DUI, he writes a fat check to the judge. That way, he'll avoid jail time. After that, he'll go to a fancy $100,000 a month treatment program, loaded up with pill pushing psychiatrists and chauffeurs. While he takes a medical leave from his corporate job and enters treatment, he cheats on his pretty wife with an oversexed, out of town crack whore. All under the noses of 'trained professionals.'

Now and then, Ben felt sorry for the celebrities. Their dirty laundry was plastered all over tabloids at the grocery mart. All that money couldn't buy them anonymity or peace of mind. Like Humpty Dumpty, once their egg cracked, all the king's men couldn't save them. It was tragic when gifted celebrities died an alcoholic death because they couldn't get sober in the treatment centers. But it said in the Big Book that probably no human power could fix the alcoholic obsession.

While he sat there on the front porch, staring out into the vast prairie, a young woman, a gifted black singer came to mind. Her dance with the demons, cut her life short. That deadly dance left her daughter without a mother.

No, to hit bottom on an Indian reservation, you had to be tough. Most Indians existed far below the poverty line. With no jobs, most Natives were lucky if they had a moldy, water damaged, crowded house to call home. Even if it was only to keep them out of the cold winter winds.

For the Red Man to hit bottom, it took something much deeper than losing his ladylove, an empty bank account or a bent fender on the old rez car. It required a change of heart. Not just any heart, but a heart hardened through centuries of intolerable, bone crushing pain. A heart gone numb, because nothing more could be taken away. But how to get an a tough, hardheaded Indian to change his heart? That was the question.

Being all powerful, there was no situation Creator couldn't fix, if His children would only turn to Him. Yet Creator never comes uninvited. For His children had free will and choice.

A few hundred years ago, there was no such thing as a poverty line on Turtle Island. Mother Earth was bountiful. This noble nation of people roamed the Great Plains in total

288

freedom. Creator provided all they needed. They never thought of themselves as poor. They shared all they had. Their very survival depended on each other's generosity. Selfishness meant extinction. Even the Old Ones took their leave, when the time was near. Teaming with life, Creator gave them all of Earth to roam.

But then a new religion came to Turtle Island. The railroad tracks of their whiskey ways and the Gatling guns cut deep scars upon the Earth. Soon barbed wire fences divided the land. From then on, the white man claimed to own, what his soul could never take with him. No man leaves the Earth with any worldly possessions, save his name written on a headstone in a cemetery.

Greed, envy and selfishness became the new religion. Behind gunpowder, it spread across Turtle Island in a fury. Hunger for gold and land ownership forced the Natives farther and farther away from their homeland. The firewater spirits wreaked havoc upon an unpolluted people. It weakened their backbone and infected their mind. It corroded the Native spirit.

The Ancient Ways almost disappeared as the Christian soldiers forced their ways upon the First Nations People. The Indian people lost themselves and everything dear to them over a century ago. Stripped of their way of life, they were turned into beggars. All they were left with was government handouts. And the spirit they were created with. But, even their spirit was tattered.

Fixing his eyes upon Leroy, Ben sized up whether his words and effort were worth the trouble, before he launched his comeback. But the boy had done what he had asked, by not drinking and putting on some weight. He had to give him that.

"Leroy, right now the chip on your shoulder is so big, you couldn't fit your fat head through the Inipi door," said Ben leaning back in his chair, familiar with this struggle. "Your problem is you still want to have it your way."

Leroy started to protest, but Ben shut him down. "I said NO BACK TALK! Are we clear on that?"

Leroy nodded his head, as he looked at the ground.

"This is the problem, Leroy. There's no quick fix for what you got. I can't cut this illness out of your head and no pill will chase away those angry spirits. You have a spiritual malady. It's a disease only Creator can heal. Those 12 Steps are tools to help you clear away the wreckage of your past. That's what the first nine steps do. Once all the nonsense is gone, Creator can heal you in an snap. He can remove the madness from your mind forever."

"But you got to get your fat head out of the way. And you have to prepare, son, without skipping any steps. There'll be times you'll be tested, Leroy, fighting tooth and nail, not to take a drink. That's called white knuckle sobriety. It's where all you can do is sit on your hands, because to drink is to die. Are you following me so far?" Ben asked in all seriousness.

Looking intently at his copper colored knuckles, Hal kept making a fist, then letting it go. Then making a fist and letting it go. He started to chuckle a little.

Distracted by Hal's laugh, Ben turned to Hal. "What's so funny?" asked Ben breaking stride.

"Well personally, my knuckles always stayed brown," said Hal half serious with a wily smile. "I guess if I balled them up enough, they'd get tan. But I never had white knuckles. Here you try it, make a fist and see if your knuckles go white."

Flustered, Ben swatted at Hal's fists. He threw him a look for being a troublemaker. "Hal, you're a pain in the ass!"

Trying hard to stifle a laugh, Leroy and Jed both looked down. But after a few strained seconds of silence, they all burst out laughing. Then it dawned on Ben. As a rodeo clown, Hal's job was to distract the bull, so the cowboy didn't get gored. It took the harshness out of a deadly reality.

As they settled down, the mood was much lighter.

Retaking his stand, Ben looked at Hal. "Are you done yet?"

"What do you mean?" asked Hal ignoring the obvious.

Shaking his head, Ben chuckled, knowing he was being duped. "This ain't my first rodeo. I know a clown when I see one."

"Oh, that," smiled Hal. "I didn't want the boy getting run through by those horns of yours."

"So you thought I was bullish," said Ben taking it in.

"Well, your horns were pointed that a way," said Hal still smiling.

"You want to finish this talk for me?" Ben suggested, testing the waters.

"Naw, keep going. You're doing a good job. Except for the white knuckle part. That probably don't apply to Indians," chuckled Hal.

"Well, I'll certainly keep that in mind, next time I give this talk," said Ben shaking his head. "So where was I?" They all held up their fists, showing their copper colored knuckles.

"Oh right, white knuckles," said Ben taking back the reins. "There's no harm in fooling around. Laughter is good medicine." Ben took a moment to recapture his stream of thought. "To drink is to die, that's where I was. Do you get what that means?"

"Yeah, I was pretty much there," said Leroy.

"Exactly. Now you're recovering, but nowhere near out of the woods. And that's why I'm talking to you this way," said Ben trying to spur Leroy out of his ignorance. "Until you surrender, the spirits in the bottle will stalk you like a hoot owl after a mouse. Its powerful wings are so silent, you won't hear it, until it swoops down and grabs you with its talons. Those hungry spirits won't be satisfied until you're dead. They want you on their side. Are you with me so far?"

"Yeah, I've been there," admitted Leroy.

"We all have, son," said Ben. "First understand, alcohol came from the white man. So Creator gave Bill W. a healing medicine through the 12 Steps. For this to work, you got to have an open mind. You got to wipe clean everything you think you know and come with a willing heart. But know this, Leroy. Hardheaded, 'Know It All's' rarely make it around here. Once you get this, we can go to work. After that, a change can come."

Ben leaned forward. His voice got soft. "Most nights, when I close my eyes, I hear those hungry ghosts yowling outside the tipi. The Grim Reaper is waiting for you in the shadows. Is that the way you want to live?"

Knowing his stubbornness wasn't serving him, Leroy sat silent for a long moment. His mind flashed back to his drunken, pathetic state that morning when Hal's truck pulled in the parking lot at the grocery mart. Ben was right about the Angel of Death dogging his every step. Many nights he whispered to Leroy that his time was near. Did he want to go back to a life of drunken emptiness? Hell no! This time he wanted to live. Leroy thrust the tobacco at Hal and Ben. He looked at them both and said, "I'm in."

Taking the tobacco from Leroy's hand, Hal sprung from his chair and gave him a big bear hug. Ben's heart smiled down deep in his being, knowing Leroy might have a chance. Smiling from ear to ear, small tears welled up in Jed's eyes.

As Ben took Leroy's tobacco, they shook hands to seal the deal. "Well, first we'll need a work party to clean up the lodge," said Ben.

"And new willows and new stones too. That old lodge needs to get retired," said Hal. "We probably need quite a bit of wood split too."

"Yeah, you're probably right there," said Ben. "We'll put her in the fire, when we build the new lodge. Leroy, do you own a Big Book?"

"Not yet, but I can get one," said Leroy.

"That's alright. I got one you can have," said Ben as he got up to go into the house.

Near the window, on a small book shelf, Ben had a spare Big Book. As he reached for it, his elbow knocked over a picture of Elsie and their children. It toppled to the floor. Bending over, he picked up the picture and held it in his hands. Memories of that day tugged at his heart. As he closed his eyes, a faint smell of Elsie's cooking wafted through the room. In the echoes of his mind, he heard her voice calling everyone for dinner. "Where are you, my girl?" Ben whispered out loud. It seemed a life time ago, when she was next to him.

After she passed away, she visited him often in his dream time. Every night when he closed his eyes, he looked forward to seeing her again. Once in a while when the moon was full, he'd find her spirit down by the river or sitting on a bench. She always waited for him. Once in the early morning hours, Ben felt her spirit lay down in the bed next to him. That always gave him a start. Many times he thought to himself, if he only kept sleeping, they'd be together.

But the sun rose in the east, flooding the morning light through the window. His eyes continued to open. At night, when he closed his eyes, he called out her name. He searched for her face, hoping to hear her voice once again.

Jarring him out of his daydream, the front door opened. Hal's big boots stomped across the wood planked floor. "Hey Ben, I'm going with Leroy and Jed down to the sweat lodge site. We'll start straightening things up down there. Do you want to come?"

With the photograph still in hand, Ben's mind snapped back to this moment of now. "Sure," Ben replied.

"What ya looking at?" asked Hal.

"Oh, a picture of Elsie and the kids. It seems so long ago. Almost another life compared to now," said Ben as he set the picture down on the shelf. "Here's a Big Book for Leroy. I want him ready to make amends by the time we fire up the lodge. He's mighty stubborn, so I don't envy you none."

"Well, that's step 8," said Hal out loud.

"He's got to admit his part in things. And clean up his side of the street. If he makes a sincere amends, I think those spooks will leave him alone," said Ben.

"Oh, I see where you are coming from," said Hal as he started to understand Ben's plan. "By him working the Steps, he'll have a clear idea of his wrongdoings. Then, come time for the sweat, his amends will send those spirits home. I wondered why you got so stiff in the joints out there."

"Yeah, but this is the problem," said Ben searching for his jacket. "They've got to be sincere amends. Spirits know the difference. Unless they clear up the harm on both sides, Leroy and those spirits are tied to each other. Leroy's so hardheaded, I'm not sure how this will go. Like I said, I don't envy you."

"Well, thanks for setting me straight. That lodge will fail if he's not ready to make amends," said Hal understanding.

"The Inipi would never fail. It'd clear away what it could," said Ben thoughtfully. "Fail is the wrong word. For Leroy, it'd be a test drive. I'd rather do it right the first time, rather than have him repeat it again. That's why I'm counting on you. He's got to understand Creator never gave us permission to kill. Even when we're at war. The spiritual consequences are too great."

"Has his family ever sweat before?" asked Hal not knowing the history.

"No, and that's the other problem," said Ben. "Vera's so deep-rooted in her Christianity, she may be the fly in the ointment on this run. Not only that, but she works for a white doctor. And all the western medicine don't do shit for a spiritual malady. The spirits had themselves a good laugh, when they used that psychology on us patients in the Army hospital. Those white coats stood around, making their important notes, while the nurse gave out her little pills to

294

everybody."

"My buddy Elmo got shot full of holes. Sometimes he'd have fits. He'd be talking to himself. Truth be told, it was the spirits he was talking to. But he couldn't see them. He just heard their voices. The doctors called him delusional and gave him more pills. Now mind you, these weren't loving spirits. The confirmed kills of combat soldiers never are. Most nights, they'd taunt the combat warriors, giving them no peace, till they cried," Ben reflected.

"What did those doctors diagnose you with?"

"Oh, me. I was just a drunk. I wasn't about to tell them I saw spirits. They'd lock me up for sure," said Ben. "When I was little, my dad warned me never to talk to spirits in front of people. They'd call me crazy. I don't need to talk out loud for them to hear me, anyhow. They hear my thoughts. That works best most of the time."

"Well, come on, Ben, we're burning daylight. They're waiting," said Hal holding Leroy's Big Book.

Overhead, the sun moved towards the western skyline. With every passing day, Jed slowly recognized his son again, the parts not destroyed by alcohol and combat. But, there were still some glaring places in Leroy's character.

Barely three months sober, Jed wanted to help his son. Deep inside, he had a gnawing guilt about how his drinking affected his family. He wanted to make right the harm he'd done. Seeing how withered, gaunt and shrunken Leroy was a month ago, shook Jed to his core. Afraid to lose his son again, Jed wanted to help his son escape this dismal reality.

"Here Leroy, this is your Big Book. We'll get started on it tonight. How does that sound?" asked Hal handing Leroy his book.

"Sounds alright. Thanks, Hal and Ben," said Leroy. He felt genuinely grateful this nightmare was coming to an end.

Gentle breezes whistled through the branches of the

cottonwood trees down by the river as the descendents of Sitting Bull, Gall and Red Tomahawk walked through the tall buffalo grasses. The heartbeat of their great, great grandfathers whispered in the wind. As he walked, Leroy opened his palm over the tips of tall grasses. He let it tickle his hand, like when he was a kid.

When they approached the Inipi, the neglected sagging willows cried out to Ben. Kneeling down next to the lodge, Ben's gentle hands touched the willow frame. He whispered an apology for abandoning the Inipi after Elsie died. In her loving way, the wind came up behind him and caressed his cheek with her gentle breezes. Ben's heart smiled as good memories of earlier days filled his mind.

As he stepped onto the neglected Inipi grounds, Leroy stopped in his tracks. A look of scorn furled his brow. He felt betrayed as he looked around at all the weeds, the scattered rocks and the drooping house of sticks stuck in the ground. It was nothing like the grand Native American cathedral he'd imagined while listening to Hal's stories of ceremony and healing. With his hands shoved down deep in his pockets, a deep scowl creased his forehead. He stared at the Earth, kicking dirt clods with his boots.

"Well, as you can see, it needs a little work," said Hal to Jed and Leroy as he bent over, pulling out some of the weeds.

After a long moment of silence, Leroy spoke. "What is this place?" he asked disdainfully, looking up from the ground.

With weeds in his hand, Hal looked up. He caught the foul mood Leroy was in all of a sudden. "This is an Inipi, Leroy. That's the fire pit. That mound of dirt is the altar and this is the house of the Stone People. It ain't been fired up in a while and needs some good cleaning. But, this is sacred ground."

Shaking his head, Leroy scoffed. "That's it? That's all there is to this sweat lodge? Just a small frame of sticks and a weed covered fire pit?"

"Leroy, I don't know what bitter-root you're chewing on, but there's no need for that tone of voice around here. The Red Road is a humble way. But, it is a powerful one," said Hal. "Until you pray in the dirt and feel the love of Mother Earth as she holds you close to her heart, you won't know that."

The doors of his closed mind slammed shut. Leroy didn't hear a word Hal said. "I don't think this is my way. It may be yours. But, I don't think it's going to work for me."

"There it is again, Leroy," said Hal standing straight up. "Contempt prior to investigation. You ain't tried it, but you've decided it won't work for you. How many times have we hit this wall? What are you so afraid of?"

"I'm not afraid," said Leroy crossing his arms over his chest. "I did three combat tours before I got shot."

"Oh yeah you are, Leroy," said Hal as Ben tapped him on the shoulder.

"Hal, the boy ain't ready yet," Ben said quietly. "He hasn't done the work. He's dry as a bone."

"You're right Ben," said Hal as he backed off.

"What do you mean, I'm dry?" asked Leroy defensively.

"It's not an insult, like you're taking it, son. But there's a big difference between dry and sober," Ben started. "But you won't know that until you worked the Steps. Sobriety is a spiritual change."

"Oh, here we go with the spiritual business again," said Leroy. "Why can't I just quit drinking? Why this big push to get me to believe something I can't see?"

"You're not the first alcoholic who tried to stop drinking without spiritual help," said Hal. "Out West, there's a treatment center which used psychology and positive thinking to get people to stop drinking. The problem is, most couldn't stay stopped for long. I've got nothing against positive thinking. But, as a remedy, it's not strong enough for a deadly disease like alcoholism."

"Leroy, I've known your family since your dad was a little boy. When was the last time you had 38 days sober?" asked Ben.

Looking out at the sky, Leroy pondered. "Maybe boot camp? No, we had a party. Maybe high school, when I was training for track, but I can't say for sure. It's been a long time. I started drinking in elementary school, like 4th grade."

"I didn't know that," said Jed shocked. "Where'd you get drinks in 4th grade?"

"You," said Leroy accusingly. "I'd finish off the beers you left sitting on the kitchen counter. Or when you'd have your parties, me and Kyle finished off everybody's drinks."

"All that time I thought I was going crazy. I'd put a beer down and turn around and it was empty," said Jed. "Kids..."

"Now, listen up a minute Leroy. A spiritual way of life ain't for everyone. Unless they have a problem only Great Spirit can cure. I had no use for ceremony before Hal came to the VA. I was as hardheaded as you," Ben began. "You didn't know me back then, but I wanted no part of the Old Ways. I had no use for them."

"Well, what changed for you?" Leroy looked at Ben.

"I got offered another choice," Ben said. "I owe it all to this big galoot here. If he hadn't showed up, needing to preach sobriety at someone, my life would have turned out much differently."

"Yeah, he does sound a lot like a preacher," laughed Leroy.

"I'll take that as a compliment," Hal retorted.

For a split second, Ben saw an opening in that closed mind of Leroy's. "You know, by the time I was in the Army hospital, I drank every day," started Ben. "The doctors there, told me I was a chronic alcoholic. I couldn't control my drinking and I was barely 20 years old. It didn't matter how bad it got, I still drank. Those white coats said there was no hope for me."

"Now, I've known about spiritual matters since I was a child, but it didn't cure my alcohol problem. When Hal came with Wyatt to the hospital to give their talk, I saw something in him that I didn't have. Hal had peace and he laughed a lot. He talked about ceremony and AA and how it changed his life. We'd traveled a similar road, but he was happy and I wasn't. And that's when I wanted what he had. Not the outside things, but the inside ones. I wanted peace. In order to have peace, I had to take what I knew about spirit and turn my life over to the care of a Higher Power."

"I don't know if I believe in a Higher Power," said Leroy after a few moments. "After everything I've seen."

"Well... that explains all the resistance," said Hal. "But I thought you were raised Christian."

"We were," said Jed. "Or I should say my wife and kids were. I thought they were a bunch of hypocrites. They were always drinking wine at bible study. Then, they'd say one thing and do another. Most never kept their word. Heck even the pastor of our church was a drinker. I've seen him drunk more than once."

"Well, when it came to the spiritual stuff, I took it piecemeal myself," Hal began. "I was skeptical about any power I couldn't see. But Wyatt explained there many powerful things that are invisible to my eyes."

"Take for instance, the rays of the sun," Hal started. "Now, too much sun will make a desert. Or if there isn't enough sun, nothing will grow. I can't see the air. But try living without it. I can't see water evaporate off the ocean. But I can see the Thunder's rain clouds storming across the sky. I heard them roll through the canyons of the Rocky Mountains. I've seen white lightning strike the mountains and split a tree in half. I don't know how to make a rainbow, but I saw a double rainbow traveling through Utah."

"One day, at the ocean, Wyatt told me to go in the water and control the waves. Well of course, I couldn't. And the ocean had a good ol' time knocking me around like a prize fighter. Of course, we had a hurricane down in Mexico that day. So the waves were gigantic. I can't make a tree, or even the seed a tree grows from. But if I put a seed in the dirt, Mother Earth will bring that seed to life. I can't make the sun rise or set when I want it to. So I started with the Powers of Nature as my Higher Power, Mother Earth, Father Sky, the Star Nation, the Thunder Beings."

"But I thought you said it was a Power that provided what I needed," said Leroy.

"What, Mother Earth doesn't provide everything you need?" asked Hal. "Think about it. Everything you eat, what you wear, the gas you put in the car, the steel the car is made out of, everything comes from Mother Earth. There's nothing she doesn't provide for you. She is a Creative Intelligence. You put a seed in the ground and she gives you a tree. The tree gives you apples and the apples give you more seeds. Can you do that?"

"I never thought about it like that," Leroy pondered. "But what about God?"

"The relationship you have with Creator is personal, Leroy. But like any relationship, it starts with 'hello' and goes from there," said Hal. "It's not as difficult as you think it is. Creator wants to know his children and wants his children to know Him."

All this talk percolated into the ground waters of their minds. The men got quiet for a while sitting in the late afternoon sun. Along the river, the wind whistled through the trees, while Ben was busy pulling weeds and tending to the lodge he'd let slip by.

Letting his mind wander off, Jed remembered a dream he had the night before. "I had a drinking dream last night. It was so real, I felt the whiskey burn down my throat. I actually woke up scared, thinking I went out and drank."

"Those spirits in the bottle are calling you," said Ben stooped over, piling the Stone People around the half moon near the fire pit.

"I guess so," said Jed. "The bottle whispered, 'I know you miss me.' I said 'I do miss you, but you're trying to kill me! Funny thing, that bottle was curved just like a woman."

"Those spirits are crafty. They'll do anything to get you to fall off the wagon," said Ben concerned. "They know a man's weaknesses. That's how they wear you down. You're being put to the test."

"Well, I'm not giving in today," declared Jed with conviction. "I took my 3rd step with my sponsor the other day. Just for today, I am free."

"That's why they're testing you. They want to see if you really meant it when you took your 3rd step. They're not ready to let go of you yet," said Ben with understanding. "Be mindful Jed, they'll set you up and snare you back in their trap."

"When I had those drinking dreams, I fell off the wagon. It didn't take but six months for me to lose my wife, job, home and everything," recollected Hal.

"That sounds like an old Hank Williams song," said Ben. "You know where the redneck Romeo loses his woman, his truck, his dog and his horse. Then, he's nursing his heartache with a shot of whiskey."

"I'm quite familiar with ol' Hank," said Hal. "Listening to him made me mighty thirsty. After I got sober the second time, I stopped listening to country music all together. It's drinking music, if you ask me."

"You know if you play a country song backwards, the guy gets back his wife, his truck, his horse and his dog," laughed Leroy chiming in after a long silence.

"Oh well, look who's finally got his sense of humor

back," laughed Hal. "Welcome back buddy."

"Sorry about earlier," apologized Leroy.

"No worries. We'll get all the chinks in your armor worked out when we do the Steps," said Hal. "Did I ever tell you how they took care of drunks back in the Old Testament?"

"I don't think so," said Leroy.

"Well, look it up in the bible. I think it's in Deuteronomy 21:18. If you were a ornery drunk, your parents ratted you out to the town council. The town's people dragged your sorry ass to the gates of the city and stoned you to death. Those folks were serious about getting rid of the evil in a man in those days."

"Sounds brutal," said Leroy. "Glad I wasn't around then."

"Maybe you were, since our souls get recycled from one life to another," said Hal. "You know, some tribes are banishing drunks and drug addicts from tribal lands after they get convicted. It getting so bad. Once they lose their tribal membership, those repeat offenders become the walking dead. The tribal government don't want those mean-spirited drugs on the rez anymore or the trouble they bring."

"Well, look around," said Leroy. "There's an ocean of alcohol all over the rez and we're drowning in it."

"Did you hear about the Indians up near Vancouver, Canada on Alkali Lake? That reservation's mostly 90% sober now. It used to be 90% drunk," said Hal.

Deep in thought, Ben held one of the Stone People in his hand and cogitated on what Hal said. "You know Hal, our ancestors used stones to rid their hearts of evil. They just did it differently. With a tobacco prayer, our ancestors placed the Stone People in a sacred fire, where they were purified in their own ceremony. Then, while the stones got restored to their original condition, our ancestors made the Inipi ready. They covered it with blankets and smudged the whole area."

302

In his mind's eye, Leroy imagined what Ben was talking about. For a moment he set aside his prejudice and listened to what the old man had to say.

"Now, when the ancient grandfathers were glowing red hot, they were ready to purify the people," Ben went on. "After everyone smudged off, they crawled into the womb of Mother Earth. Then, the fire keeper brought the grandfathers into the lodge. The doorman placed those grandfathers in a cradle in the center of the Inipi. Since they were purified, those grandfathers could bless up the people. Through steam and heat, the people were brought back to their original condition."

"You see, Leroy, Creator rids our hearts of evil, when we offer our prayers to Him and ask for healing. He sends Spirit-helpers to hear our prayers and those holy messengers carry our prayers to Creator. That's how we get doctored in the Inipi."

"When we give our greatest woes to the Stone People, they can handle it. Because they've been here for all time. They're the backbone of Mother Earth. They've seen every birth and death."

Holding the stone in his hand, Ben looked up at Leroy, emphasizing the point he wanted to make. "Now, when the man behind the bucket pours water on the hot stones, that steam carries our prayers up. The breath of the Stone People purifies our souls. In the Inipi, we work with the oldest beings on Mother Earth, the four Elementals: Fire, Water, Air and Earth. They're powerful Spirits. With their help, we're restored to our right mind and live to serve the Creator another day. I like the Old Ways better," said Ben. "Nobody has to be stoned to death or die to have evil removed. But they have to do the work and be willing to give it away."

Listening to Ben describe the Inipi ceremony, Leroy saw it with fresh eyes. An ancient knowing stirred in his heart as Ben spoke of the Old Ways. Touching the Earth, Leroy felt its sacredness and saw it come to life.

"So that's what this place is," said Leroy with a tone of wonder. "I see it now. But you're right, Hal. It needs work."

"Ya think," Hal smiled. "So you want to do this, Leroy?"

"Yeah, I do," said Leroy meeting Hal's gaze with a smile. "When Ben explained it, I saw it in my mind's eye. It sure sounds a lot better than how they did things in the Old Testament."

"Yeah, getting stoned to death for being a drunk is pretty severe," said Hal. "So is getting banished. I'm glad I found AA and ceremony. I'm a much better man."

Wispy clouds covered the late afternoon sky as the sun neared the western horizon. With her paint brush, the wind and the Angels of the clouds splashed neon colors across the heavens. It made for a glorious sunset. A cool breeze came up from the river's edge. Ben felt a chill as the setting sun made way for nightfall.

"Well," said Ben as he pushed himself up off the ground. "I'm glad we had this talk and cleared a few things up. I'm ready to head back to the house. We'll get a work party over here. Frank and Ernie got a truck. Maybe they'd be willing to go on a willow run or fetch some new stones."

"That sounds good," said Hal. "You know Leroy, you might read up about those Indians on Alkali Lake. Getting a whole reservation sober is a big job. But they did it with the same tools I'm going to show you."

After a good dinner, Hal and Leroy set to work on the Big Book, reading paragraph after paragraph. Delving into the twisted nooks and crannies of the alcoholic mind, Hal's drunken stories made the Big Book come alive.

A glimmer of hope held Leroy's hand. He saw the light at the end of the tunnel. This time, it wasn't a train. For Hal, nothing was more wonderful than a willing student. After they finished the first chapter, Hal closed his book. Staring into the fire, they took in all they had read.

"That's sad about the guy committing suicide in Bill's home," said Leroy after a while. "I was there, so many times, wanting a way out."

"Oh, the spirit of suicide waits outside the barroom doors for most drunks," said Hal wistfully. "It likes to get you when you're alone. It'll whisper in your ear. It fills your head with empty promises. It says if you drink wine and take these pills, there'll be no more pain. Arlene, my wife, committed suicide. The death report said it was an overdose. But she was really down about losing her sobriety. She tried getting sober. But those demons wrestled her down like a shifty eyed croc with his jaws clamped down tight on a water buffalo. The hardest thing was, she blamed me for making her drink. I told her we had this problem licked."

"Sorry to hear about your wife," said Leroy feeling Hal's pain.

"Oh, Leroy, I was a fool, an ignorant one. I had no idea how good I had it. But see, nothing inside me had changed. I never sat down and worked the Steps like I'm doing with you. All I did was go to meetings and not drink. I was still running my game, looking like the big man. The way I always did," Hal sighed.

"Without a Higher Power, I was still hungry inside. I wanted something. But, nothing on the outside completed me. Since I never surrendered, I finagled Arlene and the world to give me what I lacked. And I screwed it all up. I only loved her to get something for myself. That's not love, boy, that's just plain selfishness."

"Is that how you ended up in a chicken coop?" asked Leroy.

"No, that was before I came to AA the first time. Though, once Arlene died, I ended up on the streets again. My damn pride wouldn't let me go back to a meeting and face the people in AA. I knew they'd blame me too. Never mind the dirty looks, the snickers and whispers when I walked by."

"Of course, it was all in my head. Truth be told, I never gave those kind people in AA a chance to say one damn thing to me. I was busy washing down my guilt. I drank with a vengeance. For two years, I danced with those demons again, until it damn near killed me."

"You think it was your fault that your wife died?" Leroy asked seeing how tortured Hal was. "You met her in AA, so she was an alcoholic too, right? You didn't hold a gun to her head and make her drink? She could have told you to go to hell."

"Yeah, she had a choice, Leroy. We all do. But there was a fatal flaw and I used it to kill her. See, she loved me and I let her down. She loved me and I let her down. I lassoed her heart with my honeyed words and she gave her trust to me. Then, I went out to play with the demons again. And I told her she should too. She believed her man wouldn't steer her wrong. So, she followed me to the gates of hell. Until it was too late to turn back. After that, she couldn't find her way home. And I've got to live with that. This is a fatal disease, Leroy. And I brought the demons back into our home and she died."

Getting up, Hal threw some cedar on the embers to dispel this overwhelming sadness. As Leroy stared into the flames, he finally understood why Hal took this so seriously. After a long silence, Leroy looked at Hal standing there, with the cedar bag in hand. "So how'd you finally forgive yourself?"

When Hal looked at Leroy, his eyes welled with tears. "I danced, Leroy. I danced." Hal opened his shirt. His chest and his back looked like he'd been pumped full of bullet holes.

"You see my chest and my back. Each one of these scars is where I pierced up to the sacred Tree of Life or dragged a buffalo skull around the Sun Dance arbor. Every piercing was for Arlene. That's how I made amends to her. I sacrificed my flesh, my hunger and my thirst every year at Sun Dance. It was the only thing which was truly mine. It was the only thing I could give her. Then, in the last sweat lodge of the dance, the Sun Dance Chief looks right at me. He says 'Hal, you're forgiven. Arlene forgives you. Go in peace.' After the lodge, I asked him how he knew about Arlene. I hadn't told anybody there about her. He said he didn't remember saying anything to me. Sometimes spirits spoke through him. But he was grateful if it gave me peace."

Listening to the crackle of the fire, a warm silence enveloped the men as they took it all in. "Well Leroy, you had enough for one night? I didn't mean to go on about Arlene. I don't even remember what got me started."

"No, it's all good," said Leroy. "It was the suicide in Bill's story that brought it up. But Hal, your stories make the book real for me. They make it come to life. Reading the book is good. But listening to you talk about AA and ceremony, it hits home and I hear it."

"Well thanks, Leroy. That's why we do this thing, one drunk talking to another. The laughter in the healing halls of AA fed my soul. Hearing other people's stories, I stopped taking myself so seriously. But, the real magic happened after I worked the 12 Steps. That's when the heartache started to ease a bit," Hal paused. It was a long road from then to now.

"It was the first time, I was free," said Hal closing the Big Book. "Come to think about it, I never knew unconditional love until I walked into AA. It fed my inner man."

"I never thought about the inner man," contemplated Leroy. "I was too busy trying to be a man."

"Well, that's part of the journey," Hal went on. "Now mind you, I was a love-starved drunk when I walked in. It took a lot of work to change that. Does that make sense?"

"Yeah, I follow," said Leroy.

"Okay, good. The trouble is, people get stuck somewhere between the ceremony and the prayer. Or between going to meetings and working the Steps. One feeds the body, the other feeds the soul. For it to work, you gotta feed both. One is external and one is internal. Ceremony and AA work better when you put body and soul into it. Do you see where I'm headed?" asked Hal.

"Yeah," started Leroy as he contemplated his inner man. He'd never paid much mind to the matters of the heart, until now. "Without heart, you're traveling on empty roads going nowhere. And it doesn't matter how much stuff you have, because you're not growing. Everything man-made either dies or breaks down."

"Exactly," said Hal glad Leroy was paying attention. "But most people waste their life, chasing after things that just collect dust. All the meaningless chattel eventually becomes a ball and chain. After Arlene died, I packed a few things and donated the rest. None of it mattered to me anymore because the heartbeat of our home had died. Everything we collected was chocked full of painful memories."

"That'd be tough," said Leroy. "Before I enlisted, there was a girl I thought was the one. I couldn't stop thinking about her. So in Boot Camp, I decided to ask her to marry me. I spent 2 paychecks to buy her a ring. When I got home, I found out she'd hooked up with another dude. That ring didn't mean shit to me then."

"It's just stuff," said Hal knowingly. "But, that must have hurt. How'd you find out?"

"It's a small town, people talk," said Leroy. "That's why I signed up for so many tours. I wasn't ever coming back."

"You run into her yet?" Hal asked.

"No," said Leroy, not wanting to talk about it.

"You still got some heat there, I can tell," said Hal.

"Oh there's heat," said Leroy with an twinge of smoldering heartache. "From what I heard, she played me the whole time. Some girls get off dating the captain of the team. It was all a status thing."

"Oh that's right, you were the captain of the track team. Kyle had a problem with that, the other night," chuckled Hal.

308

"Kyle," said Leroy shaking his head. "Kyle was a mama's boy. He doesn't even know how easy he had it, growing up. Mom smothered him. Probably cuz she couldn't catch me."

"From what I understand, Kyle had a few bumps of his own. But, you can ask him about that some time," said Hal.

"Try getting shot at," said Leroy scoffing.

"You forget son, I've been shot at. But pain is pain, whether it's emotional or physical," said Hal. "Did you two compete all the time?"

"I don't know," said Leroy. "It didn't seem like competing. But I guess in one way it was. He always whimpered around, whining about something. Mom would shove a cookie in his mouth to keep him quiet. Now he's huge."

"Many people use food to numb emotional pain. Especially if they get hurt as children." Hal wasn't sure if Leroy knew his brother got raped by Jason as a child. But he wasn't going to let on what he knew. Peeling onions was tough business.

"You know something don't you? Did something happen to Kyle?" said Leroy leaning back, fixing his eyes on Hal.

"Yeah, you're brother has some heartache. But I don't take to gossip. So ask him yourself," said Hal. "He's pretty brave. I got to give him that."

"Okay, I'll ask him. So does what I tell you stay between you and me?" asked Leroy, not sure if he could trust Hal.

"Leroy, I'm just a new set of eyes on an old story. The things I've heard here so far, I've heard in AA meetings all over the country. The betrayal, the heartache, lust, greed and vengeance. It's not new. It's the human condition. But you can bet your bottom dollar, I won't put your business out on the street. In AA's Twelve Traditions, anonymity is the spiritual foundation of the whole program. What you say to me, stays with me."

"Now if you don't trust me, there are meetings all over

309

the globe. And you can call a sober alcoholic in New York City and tell him you business, if you feel safer," said Hal compassionately. "See, there aren't any skeletons in my closet, which can't be let out. Everything I've done, I admitted to Creator and another human being. I've cleaned up my side of the street, so I am free."

As Hal's words sunk in, the idea of calling someone in New York City appealed to Leroy. But, there was something about Hal he trusted. "So do you have the number of someone in New York City? Someone I can tell my business too."

"No, but there's a public phone over at Kelly's Tavern. For a quarter, the operator will give you the number of AA's Central Office in New York City," said Hal.

"You got a quarter? I'm fresh out," laughed Leroy pulling his empty pockets out of his pants. "It might take two quarters to call New York City."

Reaching in his pocket, Hal fished out his last bit of change. He handed it to Leroy. "There, now go make your call," said Hal with his eyebrows crunched together. "I'll walk over there with you. I need to stretch my legs."

"Dude, I was just pulling your leg. You're way to easy."

"I wasn't pulling yours. I want you to make the call and find out the number to AA Central Office in New York City." Hal stood up and stretched his arms over his head. The days were long but the years were short. "Come on, wise ass! Let's go!"

"I was just kidding," said Leroy protesting.

"Don't make me pull you up by your ear, Leroy. Cuz I will," said Hal towering over Leroy. "And bring your Big Book 'cause you're gonna write the phone number right there on the first page."

Opening the flap, the cool night air was brisk. It felt good to stretch his legs. A short walk for a cup of coffee and a slice of pie whet Hal's appetite. "Leroy, I'll tell you how it's gonna go. After you're half way through the Steps and shared your darkest secrets, they won't have power anymore. Your character flaws, which are obvious to everybody else, you'll let go of. Because they stopped working."

"After that, you'll tell your own story. And it won't matter who knows what. Because it ain't a secret anymore. All the heat will be gone. After that, when you tell the worst of it, you'll laugh. You'll finally see the comedy in the tragedy."

"But the best part is when some lonesome loser comes up to you after the meeting. He'll shake your hand and say thanks for sharing your awful secret. Because it's exactly what he's going through. And now he doesn't have to blow his fool head off in shame." The night air felt good as Hal's boots crunched down the gravel walkway.

"That's how it happened for me. Your dark secrets, the ones you thought you'd take to the grave, will save someone's life. Because it's eating their guts away. Once you say it out loud, it loses its power over you. I've seen it over and over. In the Big Book, it promises that no matter how far down the scale we've gone, we'll see how our experience benefits others. Pretty soon, you'll share your dirty laundry from the podium and help someone else with theirs."

"Do I really have to call New York City?" Leroy barely heard a word Hal said. He may as well have talked to the wind. All Leroy could think about was feeling humiliated, by calling some stranger in New York.

"YUP!! And that's the first thing we're gonna do. I wanna make sure your dialing finger ain't broken. That way, when you're in trouble, you'll be able to pick up that 800 pound phone. Once we get that squared away, we'll get some pie and coffee," said Hal.

Pie and coffee sounded good. "Now you're talking," said Leroy looking to fend off embarrassment. With his Big Book under his arm, he followed along. "What did you think about the headstone Bill saw at the Winchester Cathedral?"

311

"You mean about the soldier dying from drinking a cold beer?" asked Hal.

"Yeah," said Leroy.

"Pretty telling," said Hal. "Hold on a minute, I got to get something out of my truck."

The night sky twinkled full of stars as Grandma Moon coursed her way through the heavens. At the truck, Hal fished some money from his bedroll. He needed to make a run soon to replenish his supplies. He shoved a few dollars in his pocket and closed the truck door.

"Okay buddy, let's go make that call," said Hal. "This is a good lesson to get out of the way."

Leroy squirmed at the thought of calling someone he didn't know. "What do I say to the guy who answers the phone?"

"Heck, I don't know," Hal shrugged. "Ask him if they got any sober American Indians you can talk to," said Hal. "Tell him there's only one meeting out here a week with the same 5 or 6 guys. If a couple of them die off, it will be slim pickings."

Bounding up the steps, Hal opened the door. Cigarette fumes greeted them as they stepped in the door. "Ah, I still can't get passed that smell," said Hal.

"The cigarettes or the smell of greasy hamburgers?" asked Leroy.

"Naw, the cigarettes," said Hal a little frustrated. "Out West, they banned smoking in public places. I quit smoking some years ago. Walking in here, I might as well suck on an exhaust pipe."

"Well, if the smoke bothers you, we don't have to do this," said Leroy seeing a way out.

"Oh no, you're doing this. Nice try, French fry," Hal laughed. "Here, I thought you weren't afraid of anything. But, you're squirming like a worm on a fish hook."

Without a word, Leroy puffed up his chest out and walked straight to the phone booth. Fishing through the change Hal gave him, Leroy put a quarter in the pay phone. As he pushed zero for the operator, his stomach fluttered. "Hal, you got a pencil to write down the phone number?"

Moving quick, Hal rushed over to the counter and asked the girl for a pen. As he walked back, Hal handed it to Leroy. Pen in hand, Leroy cracked open his Big Book, ready for the number.

"Operator," said a woman's voice over the phone.

"Hello operator, can you give me the number to New York City's AA Central Office?"

"Just a minute," said the operator. "That was New York City's Alcoholics Anonymous Central Office?"

"Yes ma'am," said Leroy.

"Okay now, here's the number. It's 212-647-1680. Do you got that?"

Leroy scrawled the number down in his Big Book. "Could you repeat that?"

"Sure, it's 212-647-1680," said the operator.

"Okay, got it. Thanks very much," said Leroy as he hung up the phone. Hal waited nearby when he saw Leroy hang up the phone.

"You got the number?" Hal asked as Leroy held up his Big Book with the number inside.

"Good, now dial it up!" Hal commanded.

"That will be 75 cents for the first 3 minutes," said the automated phone voice. Leroy fished out 75 cents and put it in the pay phone. Holding his breath, it rang 3 times. He felt completely awkward calling total strangers in New York City.

"AA Central Office, Bernie speaking. How can I help you?" said a voice with a heavy New York accent.

"Oh hey, hi. I was wondering if you got any sober American Indians I could talk to?" asked Leroy. His voice was shaking.

"So you want a sober Native, huh?" asked Bernie curiously. "That's the first time I ever heard that one. And I been answering these phones for years."

"Well, there's a first time for everything," said Leroy awkwardly.

"Can I ask why it needs to be a Native? I got lots of sober guys here," asked Bernie.

"Well, I live out on the reservation," started Leroy. "We've got one meeting here a week with the same 5 dudes. My friend thought it'd be good to have another person to talk to, so my business don't get spread all over the street."

"Smart man, your friend," said Bernie. "I used to know a guy, Native, out in California. He was a real wiz with horses. He had this one long braid down his back. Big guy. He said he was from Canada. And I think he was somehow related to Sitting Bull."

"Yeah, lots of our people fled to Canada, to escape the Gatling gun," said Leroy feeling calmer.

"Yeah, what they did to the Indians, that was a real shame," said Bernie. "I think Indians were the most misunderstood people. I went to a sweat lodge once. We had some guys from our men's meeting who used to go. One night, they dragged me along, but I couldn't stand the heat. You know what they say, if you can't stand the heat, stay out of the kitchen. I'm trying to remember. What was his name? He had a tough time after he lost his wife. It was real sad what happened to him. I don't know if he ever got over it. Hold on a second, would ya, kid?"

"Sure," said Leroy as he glanced over at Hal, with his long braid going down his back. Leroy wondered if the guy Bernie was talking about, was him.

"Hey Sweeney, the kid on the phone is calling from an Indian reservation. He wants to know if we got any sober Natives he can talk to. You got any ideas?" echoed Bernie's voice in the background.

Leroy heard a muffled response from whoever Sweeney was.

"Do you remember the Native guy, out in California? He was real good with horses. I must be getting Alzheimer's," said Bernie to Sweeney. "Remember he worked on the movie set with us. He took care of the horses. I can't remember what movie it was now either."

"Dances With Wolves. Hal, his name was Hal," Sweeney's deep voice echoed in the background. "Give the kid your number. Have him call back tomorrow. I think Gladys is an Eskimo. But I don't know if she wants to give her number out. We got more Puerto Ricans than Indians here," said Sweeney to Bernie.

Waving at Hal, Leroy cupped the phone. "Hey do you know some guy named Bernie. He went to a sweat lodge in California. Did you handle horses for a movie?"

"What? You got old Bernie on the phone?" chuckled Hal surprised. "It's a small world, buddy."

"Hey kid, you still there. Sorry, I wanted to see who we could get to talk to you. Let me give you my number and you call me back tomorrow. I got a few people in mind. But I don't know if they're Native American, you know sober and all," said Bernie. "You got a pencil?"

"Yeah, sure. But I think you got to say hello to someone first," said Leroy as he handed the phone to Hal.

"Hello," said Hal. "Bernie, ya old dog! It's Hal. What are ya doing in New York City?"

"You mean Hal, the Indian with the long braid?" asked Bernie a little confused.

"The one and only," said Hal beaming, like he was

315

talking to his best friend. "So why did you leave California?"

"Oh you know, it's the land of nuts, fruits and flakes out there. Once the money dried up, Sweeney and I decided to go back to our roots," said Bernie. "We were never really cut out for the California lifestyle. Don't get me wrong, I loved the weather. But, sometimes I got homesick for a real slice of pizza. And they got no business making bagels out there."

"You got old Sweeney with you? Well I'll be," said Hal. "It's old home week."

"Hey Sweeney, I got Hal the Indian on the phone. Pick up the other line," hollered Bernie across the small office.

"Hello," said Sweeney in his deep gravely voice.

"Hey Sweeney! Is that you, you ol' skinflint," said Hal laughing.

"Hal, what's shaking," said Sweeney. His deep voice was a little shaky. "I thought Bernie was talking to some Indian kid who wanted to talk to Natives in New York."

"He was talking to my buddy Leroy, here. You probably got what, about 100 years sober now. Heck, you were an old timer when I came in," laughed Hal.

"Don't laugh," said Bernie. "Old Sweeney here, he's what 92. He's been sober 54 years. His mom finally passed on and left him a boat load of money. Today he's got more money than god, but he's still shopping at thrift stores. Go figure. He's still chasing the girls at the Friday night young people's meeting. And in spite of everything, he's sharp as a tack."

"Oh that don't surprise me none. He was a hound dog, if I ever met one," laughed Hal. "A penny pinching hound dog, but still a hound dog."

"I've been sober 57 years," Sweeney's deep voice corrected Bernie. "Bernie was never much good at counting. So what are you doing out in Injun country, Hal. Bernie was saying the kid called from the reservation."

"I was passing through, coming from Colorado. I just finished a rodeo when I remembered Ben lived out this way. I found out they had a meeting and Ben headed it up. Right now, I'm living in a tipi along the Missouri River," said Hal.

"You never were much for settling down," Bernie broke in.

"I tried it once. Weren't much good at it," said Hal.

"You mean, you don't take a nibble when a plate of cookies is passed your way?" asked Bernie.

"Ain't got much of a sweet tooth these days," said Hal knowing they weren't talking about cookies.

"Is that Ben, the Indian fella you broke out of the loony bin?" asked Sweeney.

"Boy, you got a good memory Sweeney. Yup, ol' Ben's doing good. But they got a bad drinking problem out this way. There is an ocean of shipwrecked drunks here. It's worse than Venice Beach on a hot summer day. Trouble is, there's only one AA meeting a week. So there's not much recovery," said Hal.

"Well why don't you start a couple more meetings, Hal. You know, throw in a book study and change it up a little. Heck Bill and Bob started with no meetings at all. They were pulling drunks out of hospitals to carry the message," said Bernie. "We got meetings around the clock out here. But, it wasn't always that way."

"That's not a bad idea, Bernie. Remember the meeting we had, with the guys, where we'd barbeque steaks afterward?" reminisced Hal.

"That was at Delbert's house. But he died, you know," said Bernie. "He wouldn't let go of his cigarettes. He got married. I think it was a year before he took ill. He passed real fast after that. His poor wife. She was so upset."

"She was more mad than upset, Bernie," interrupted Sweeney. "She'd been on him to quit smoking since they'd met. But he was a stubborn goat and dug his heels in. He didn't want a woman telling him what to do."

"I remember some fool took Delbert's seat in a meeting once," said Hal.

"Oh, that was a big mistake," said Bernie interrupted. "You know, people get real attached to their chairs in meetings. We almost had a fight here, up the street in one of the Burroughs. You'd have thought it was starving men fighting over food. I've never seen such a commotion," said Bernie.

"PLEASE DEPOSIT 75 CENTS FOR THE NEXT 3 MINUTES. PLEASE DEPOSIT 75 CENTS FOR THE NEXT 3 MINUTES" said the automated phone voice as it started to beep. Hal dug in his pockets for some change.

"Leroy, you got 3 quarters?" shouted Hal across the small waiting area. Leroy brought over all the change he had. Hal plunked quarters into the pay phone before it hung up.

"You on a pay phone, Hal?" asked Bernie.

"Yeah, I don't have a telephone in the tipi," said Hal.

"Oh, I thought you were kidding around about that," said Bernie.

"Naw, it's true," said Hal. "Me and Leroy are camped out in Ben's tipi. It's got a nice fire in the center. It keeps us good and warm."

"Boy, you really are in Indian country. Well, you let us know if we can help out in any way. I can get old Sweeney here to donate some Big Books and mail them out to you. He's good about stuff like that," said Bernie. "The old guy just nodded off in his chair. He likes doing the phone calls, you know. It keeps him from getting bored at home. Here let me give you my phone number, in case I'm not here to answer the phone. You got a pencil?"

"Leroy, give me the pen and your Big Book so I can write down Bernie's phone number," said Hal as Leroy brought it over.

"Okay, here's my number, 212-555-2012. You have Leroy call me tomorrow. I'll see about getting some phone numbers for him. No one's asked me for sober Natives before, but I'll see what I can do. You'll tell him, right Hal?" said Bernie.

"Yeah, Bernie. I'll tell him. Or better yet, he's standing right here. You finish up with him and I'll call you tomorrow," said Hal as he handed Leroy the phone.

"Hello," said Leroy.

"Yeah, listen Leroy. I'm going to find some numbers for you of sober Natives. We got one woman here. She's an Eskimo. Her name is Gladys. But I got to ask her before I can give out her number. You understand," said Bernie.

"Oh yeah, sure. That'd be great to talk to other people. Thanks a lot Bernie. Hal wrote your number down. So I'll call you tomorrow," said Leroy.

"Oh, you know what? I just thought of something. There is a Native American AA fellowship. I saw them on the internet. Hold on a second, I think I wrote it down here the other day. Oh yeah, here it is. Their website is www.naigso-aa.org. They do their whole meeting in a circle with an eagle feather and some sage, from what I understand. Let me see if I can get you that information too. Do you got a library close by or a Starbucks so you can hook up to the internet?" asked Bernie.

"No, on the rez we got nothing but a few bars, lots of churches and there's a grocery mart about 20 miles away," said Leroy. "You got to drive about an hour before you get to a Starbucks."

"You don't got a mall or anything? I never realized it was so remote," said Bernie. "I'd die without my coffee and a bagel in the morning. We got a Starbucks or some kind of coffee shop on almost every corner out here."

"Hey, but I can go visit my mom's house and get on the internet there. So if you get me that information, I can look it up," said Leroy.

"Okay, so I'll find this out for you. It's good meeting you, Leroy. You're in good hands with Hal. We go way back. So call me tomorrow, okay," said Bernie.

"Yeah, Bernie. Good to meet you too. I'll call tomorrow. Good night," said Leroy thunderstruck as he hung up the receiver. This was the most awkward thing he'd ever done sober. But it turned out good. He couldn't wait to see what numbers Bernie came up with and talk to other sober Natives across the country. Then it dawned on him. There were sober people all over the world.

"You ready to go have some pie, Leroy?" said Hal standing in the waiting area.

"You didn't tell me you were in a movie. Hey 'Dances with Wolves' was a pretty big hit back then," said Leroy nudging Hal with his elbow.

"It weren't no big deal. I just tended to the horses," said Hal shrugging it off.

"You didn't get in front of the camera, not once?" asked Leroy.

"Well, for a second," Hal admitted. "They needed a lot of extras. So when I wasn't tending to the horses, I'd stand around looking like a fierce warrior." Hal laughed as he puffed up his chest. "But you won't get any money for my autograph."

"So what's the story on Bernie and Sweeney?" asked Leroy as they sat down at a table. The waitress came up and put down some menus.

"That's alright," said Hal. "We're just here for a slice of pie and some coffee."

The waitress glanced over to the pie case. "Tonight we got apple, cherry and pumpkin. There might be one slice of banana cream left, but it's pretty beat up."

320

"I'll take the apple, hotted up, a' la mode with vanilla ice cream," said Hal. "And a cup of decaf. Otherwise the sugar and caffeine will keep me tossing and turning all night."

"I'll have what he's having," said Leroy. It'd been a while since he went out to get something to eat. Thirty eight days sober and he felt like a human being again.

"Bernie and Sweeney, now that brings back some memories," said Hal reminiscing. "Bernie was always looking to make some fast cash. He was a real go-getter. That's how I got dragged onto the movie set. It was one of Bernie's get rich quick schemes. Sweeney came from big money back in New York. But his father disowned him because he was a drinker and married outside of his tribe."

"Wait, I thought these guys were white?" asked Leroy. "What tribe?"

"Well, I didn't know this. But some factions of the Jewish faith are fairly tribal," Hal explained. "They don't want their blood mixed with anybody impure. No half breeds. Behind his father's back, Sweeney went off and married a Catholic girl. That brought the house down in his family."

"That'd be like me marrying a white girl," Leroy understood. "I don't think I'd hear the end of it. My mom had girls lined up for me to marry before I went in the service."

"No kidding," Hal nodded his head. "Well, add that to the shame of being alcoholic. Sweeney's father, the money mogul, couldn't stand it. So, with no uncertain terms, he told Sweeney, either get divorced or you're out of the family. Sweeney wouldn't do it. His father was a mean, controlling bastard, who always bought his way through life."

"Well, when the Catholic girl realized Sweeney was broke, she took off and got the marriage annulled. Even though Sweeney was off the hook, his pride wouldn't let him go back and beg his father's forgiveness for straying from the family traditions. So he moved to California. If you're going to be homeless, it's not as brutal as New York winters."

"Back in the Old Testament, they'd have stoned him to death," observed Leroy.

"Rightly so, rightly so," said Hal grateful Leroy was paying attention.

"So he went from having everything to having nothing?" asked Leroy.

"Life is a roller coaster," Hal contemplated. "But, losing money is nothing, compared to losing your soul, Leroy."

"I wouldn't know," Leroy jested.

"Well," started Hal as he contemplated on how to say this. "When the spirit of lack takes root, people who live in fear, sell out. Sweeney finally had a chance to man up and he took it. He'd rather make his way with Creator's help, than live at the mercy of his father. I respected him for that. He was humble, but grateful at the same time, because he didn't lose himself."

Carrying a tray with 2 cups of decaf and hot apple pie a' la mode, the waitress set them on the table. The smell of warm apples and cinnamon filled Hal's senses with pure joy. He bent over the plate to take a whiff of the pie. It was bathed in vanilla ice cream. "Ah, now that's a slice of heaven, right there," said Hal carefully extracting his first bite.

"Now about the first step," said Hal between bites. "Bill's story pretty much sums up the whole program. The first step is the only one you have to do 100% for the rest to work. When I got to AA, there were 3 things I was powerless over."

"What were they?" asked Leroy, curious.

"Tequila, red heads and chocolate chip cookies," said Hal, his eyes sparkling. "Before I got sober, I'd pour tequila on my pancakes in the morning to stop the shakes. But nothing spelled trouble like a red head with fiery blue eyes, wearing cowboy boots. When she glanced my way, I'd go weak in the knees. And then came Arlene's chocolate chip cookies. I couldn't eat just a couple of them. Once I got started, I ate the whole damn batch. If she was making the dough, when I got home from work, they never make it into the oven."

"Didn't you get sick eating all that dough?" said Leroy shaking his head.

"A belly ache never stopped me. Hell, fiery red heads made me heartsick and I couldn't drink tequila without puking. But it never stopped me," said Hal. "That's what powerless means. You'll do it no matter what the cost."

"I've been there," said Leroy.

"I know you have," said Hal compassionately. "Well, the second half of Step One, is admitting your life is unmanageable. Hell, a month ago, you were scrawnier than a scarecrow and smelled of dead goat. This should come easy for you."

"Shut up, Hal," Leroy smiled knowing it was true.

"Listen," said Hal leaning forward. "This is the only step you've got to take with NO reservations. Because if you still think you can drink, you'll do a half-assed job of the rest of the steps."

"I see that. I do," said Leroy meeting Hal's gaze. "Once I got started, I could never control how much I drank."

"That means come hell or high water, you know you can't drink. NO MATTER WHAT," said Hal with all earnestness.

"No matter what," said Leroy letting the words sink in.

"Well good, glad we got that out of the way" said Hal. "That's one Step down, eleven to go. Welcome to the 'NO MATTER WHAT' CLUB."

CHAPTER EIGHT: NINETY DAYS

It was late afternoon, when Hal and Leroy walked towards the Community Center where the AA meeting was. The small prairie town was quiet, except for a few barking dogs who raced after the cars.

"Now Leroy, this is a tender subject and I never liked talking about it much. But I'll give it to you straight. I may be dead wrong on the whole thing. But, I'd much appreciate you hearing me out before you set your mind against what I got to say," said Hal squirming in his boots.

"Sure Hal. What's so serious?" asked Leroy as they walked along River Road. Leroy had 90 days sober and they headed to the AA meeting so he could take a chip.

"Well, first of all, today I go to AA to treat my alcoholism and to be of service," Hal started uncomfortable. "But it wasn't always that way. See, in California, AA has many pretty little lassies there. Well, they dressed up like Burlesque show girls at meetings. It's troublesome because it makes a man think of entirely different things," Hal cleared his throat. "Rather than treating his sobriety."

"Are you talking about sex?" laughed Leroy sensing how awkward this was.

"Well, when some of the birds and bees get to AA, they're more like bone picking vultures and angry hornets. Those hellcats can be down right vicious! They're out for blood, because they've been hurt. Never mind that you got a room full of wounded warriors and love starved damsels in distress." Hal shook his head.

"Sounds like you had some experience," Leroy laughed.

"Well," said Hal clearing his throat. "The combination just makes for a mess. This shit's got more layers than a prize onion at the county faire, Leroy. And don't forget what some of these 'not so fair maidens' did to get their fix. It's not a pretty site. Nothing twists a man's mind more, than loving a crazy woman. What I'm trying to say is, it'd be better if you left your pecker in your pants when it came to the ladies in AA. You'll stay sober longer." There, he said it as he sighed with relief.

"So that's your best relationship advice," Leroy chuckled in disbelief. "Keep my pecker in my pants?"

"Look Leroy, when I got sober, the old timers told me point blank that my picker was broken. And it's safe to say, I'm not any good at relationships," admitted Hal sincerely. "But alcoholics remind me of dented cans. They've been kicked around all over the place. Most of these scoundrels are devoid of any moral fortitude. When they walk into AA, they're hurting, lonely and looking like forty miles of bad road. Oh, they'll clean up, after a clean shave and a few weeks of not drinking. But that don't take the dents out of the can."

"That sounds attractive," Leroy chuckled.

"That ain't all," said Hal. "When these wolverines get a couple bucks in their pocket, they'll buy some fancy duds and try to get laid. It boggles my mind. The same scroungy drunk, who stood on street corners and couldn't get a stranger to put a dime in his cup, is looking to bed down with a hussy, who sold her soul to the devil to get her fix."

"Well shit Hal, if you put it that way," said Leroy laughed. "It sounds like a match made in Heaven."

"Or hell. You go ahead and laugh now," said Hal shaking his head. "But wait 'til you're doubled over and miserable because you let some trollop play with your heartstrings. Men lose their sobriety over this bullshit. Don't get me wrong. It cuts both ways. I've met my share of predators in AA. These scoundrels prey on women with their honeyed talk, never meaning a word of it. Just know, wounded people walk into AA, Leroy. So don't go tipi-creeping with some newcomer girl."

"So how do you know if you're being played?" asked Leroy familiar with the burn of betrayal.

"My best advice is to interview them. Ask questions and watch if their words match their actions. See if they walk their talk," Hal offered.

"So, what would you ask," wondered Leroy.

"Well, for starters, do they work a program? Are they pounding the dents out of their can? A telltale sign they're not, is if they're still blaming everyone else. I don't go to AA to get laid, so it's not my problem." Hal straightened up. Experience was the best teacher, but he'd hoped Leroy had some sobriety under his belt first.

"Okay, let me shoot it to you straight," Hal whispered not wanting the wind to hear. "A loved starved girl who's oversexed, might be fun for about 20 minutes. But, from my experience, those empty nights, turn into lonely weeks. Lust makes a poor substitute for love. At the end of it, she'll just boil your bunny and make you pay. So, I'd suggest that you take your time before you dive in. If you follow my drift."

"Oh, I hear you loud and clear," said Leroy realizing he spent years fighting a war in the desert because some girl betrayed him.

For weeks, Hal and Leroy worked the Steps like two furious madmen. After he finished his fourth step, Leroy saw his faulty thinking. It caused him to make foolish choices without knowing the whole truth. For the most part, he saw how the demons in the bottle, crippled him. Anger and resentment influenced most of his life changing decisions.

"Look, I'm not telling you what to do, Leroy. You're entitled to the dignity of your own lumps," Hal gathered. "Most of us pay better attention after we burn our hand on a hot stove. But I'd be remiss in my duties if I didn't teach you some good manners. At least this way, you can walk like a man."

After walking this stretch of road together, there was a true kindheartedness between them. The wisdom of a sober Elder gave Leroy insight, he'd never have considered on his own. "Thanks Hal. I hear what you're saying," said Leroy. "All your stories help me see."

"Well I'm glad I'm not wasting my breath," chuckled Hal. "Talk about a dented can, I knew this woman in AA. She wasn't pretty, but your guts didn't sour to look at her. But boy, she was troubled. Most women are, who come to AA. Her daddy was a violent drunk and beat her but good. On top of that, she got raped by her babysitter at a young age. By the time she came to the program at nineteen, she was a mess. Her rage left deep creases in her forehead. Even though she worked the Steps, she couldn't get sober for a couple years. To make matters worse, she'd eat a truck load of food and puke it all up. Sometimes it took her all day."

"This is all in one girl?" Leroy.

"What, you think I'm making it up?" asked Hal with his eyebrows raised.

"No, not exactly," said Leroy seeing how deep the sickness was.

"Well, that ain't all. This girl was one big minefield of hurt. She had tried to kill herself since she was five. After she got messed up with the wrong fella, she crashed her truck into a tree on purpose. When she showed up at the meeting, her face was all banged up. It looked like someone took a baseball bat to her. It was a real mess. But, she hooked up with a good woman in program and worked the Steps. It took a while, but she finally surrendered to a Higher Power. After that, the alcohol problem vanished and the food got under control. But like every woman, she wanted a relationship. And that hunt damn near killed her. One afternoon, she tells me she wanted to be part of the 4H club."

"The one for kids?" Leroy asked not sure if he really wanted to know.

"Naw. House, husband, horse and Harley. The Four H's," Hal explained.

"Oh," said Leroy.

"Well, I warned her. The trappings of the ego usually bring pain. But, she wouldn't listen. She was on a mission, looking for a dime store Romeo with all the fixings. Of course, he had to be sober. So she found a sober Latin lover with a Harley, who owned a house," Hal continued.

"That's 2 out of the four," Leroy figured.

"Yup, all she had to do was turn him into a husband and get a horse." Hal laughed.

"So she found what she wanted?" asked Leroy.

"Oh, she found what she wanted alright. But there was a problem. In her hurry, she never completed Steps Six and Seven," said Hal.

"What do you mean?" asked Leroy.

"Well, the poor girl was bedeviled," Hal went on. "Rage and jealousy ran deep in her veins and she threw a good temper tantrum."

"So what happened?" Leroy asked hanging on.

"Well, being that she was desperate for love, every time Creator showed her a red flag, she'd paint it green. Her dime store Romeo was addicted to porn. He spent hours looking at smut on the computer. And he liked to talk dirty to strange women on the phone," Hal continued.

"EEW! OUCH!"

"Yeah, it was sad, but she thought she could fix him. My best advise was to run like hell. But she was determined. Her clock was ticking, so she dragged his sorry ass to counseling. Well, as fate would have it, the fool proposes and buys her a fancy diamond ring. By now, she's down for the count. There was nothing I could do. Her dreams were in hand. A few months later, she finds that son of a bitch in the bathtub with a 20 year old South American gal who's after a green card."

"Ouch!" said Leroy. "That must've hurt."

"Ya think? Well, here's the kicker," laughed Hal. "That

night, that redheaded dynamo had cowboy boots on. Those shit kickers did a lot of damage. Bella turned into the Tasmanian Devil and glass flew everywhere."

"Hell hath no fury like a woman scorned," said Leroy.

"You ain't kidding. That night, she lost everything to an illegal alien shining her man's bumper, for a green card." Hal shook his head.

"You said she was sober?" asked Leroy surprised.

"Oh yeah, Bella had 22 years when she went to jail. But, she skipped a couple important Steps and it cost her." Hal shook his head. "Jealousy, rage and lust are a deadly combination. Without friends in AA, she'd have been out on the street. After she got out of jail, she thoroughly worked Steps Six and Seven. She wasn't going to let anyone do that to her again. It was a painful lesson, but she didn't drink."

"That's a hard lesson."

"It's damn near impossible to reform a drunk on self will. But, many do get transformed by Creator's love through working the 12 Steps," said Hal.

"What happened to him?" Leroy asked.

"Who knows," Hal shrugged his shoulders. "He disappeared after a while. On page 70, the Big Book says if we don't change our behavior and keep hurting other people, we'll probably drink."

Walking through the parking lot, they saw the same old junk cars and trucks. "Well, looks like the usual suspects are here," said Hal. "You ready to take your ninety day chip, Leroy?"

Standing outside the door, Leroy felt how 90 days sober made a difference in his life, along with the love of a few good people. For their generosity and unselfishness, he felt grateful. "Thanks Hal," said Leroy. "Thanks for pulling in the parking lot with my brother that day. I doubt I'd be standing here, sober, if you hadn't showed up."

329

"Creator has plans for you, son. I'm simply a messenger," said Hal. "I'm just glad I showed up on time."

"Yeah, me too," said Leroy as they walked into the AA meeting.

As he greeted everyone at the door, Ben spied Hal and Leroy ambling through the parking lot. There was an easiness between them, Ben hadn't noticed before. Having witnessed Leroy get sober, it reminded him of a chick hatching out of an egg. As it pecked its way out, it built up the stretch necessary to confront life.

"Hey Ben," said Hal. "Our boy's got 90 days today."

"He's looking better than when you found him," said Ben, giving Leroy the once over. "Say Leroy, how about you lead the meeting tonight?"

"What!?!" said Leroy in shock.

"That's a great idea," said Hal. "Hey Leroy, I was told never to refuse an AA request."

"Well, what do I have to do?" asked Leroy in full hesitation.

"It's easy," said Ben reassuringly. "You sit up front, read a few things, tell your story for 20 minutes and then pick people to share. You've watched someone else do it."

"But what do I say?" Leroy cringed. He hated feeling on the spot.

"You tell them what it was like, what happened and what it's like now," said Hal. "Like it says in the Big Book, we shared our experience, strength and hope. And from where I'm standing, a near dead, hopeless drunk walks sober. Listen son," said Hal as he put his arms around Leroy's shoulders. "Courage is when your scared out of your wits, but you saddle up anyway."

The butterflies in Leroy's stomach went on full frontal assault. "I've never talked in front of people before," said Leroy in a quiet whisper, not wanting anyone else to hear. It was this kind of toe-curling awkwardness he'd just rather avoid.

"Come on, son. You can do it," said Hal slapping Leroy on the back. "I've got faith in you. Look, after you give your pitch, you'll realize you didn't die. So get on up there."

If he didn't trust these two men with his life, he'd turn around and walk straight out the door. He never liked talking in front of people. "Okay, I'll do it," said Leroy with a hint of trepidation.

Leading him to the front of the room, Ben gave Leroy the meeting format. "You want a cup of coffee, cream and sugar?" asked Ben as Leroy sat down. "I found, my hands don't shake so much, if they're holding onto something."

"Yeah, that's a good idea," said Leroy as he watched everybody mill around the room, talking and getting food at the back. Seeing his son sitting up front, Jed and Kyle came walking over.

"You leading today?" asked Kyle.

"Looks like it," said Leroy with a grunt.

"Well, you look better," said Kyle "And you don't smell like a dead goat."

"Shut up Kyle," said Leroy as he softened. He remembered when Hal and Kyle dragged him off the street. "Thanks for that," Leroy said.

Beaming at Leroy, Jed couldn't be happier with both his sons at the meeting. "Oh, I'm glad to see you sitting in that chair, Leroy."

"Yeah, Ben snagged me at the door," said Leroy.

"Ah, good man, good man," said Jed. "We better go take our seats Kyle. They're about ready to start."

Ben eyeballed the clock as he handed Leroy a cup of coffee. Taking a sip, Leroy felt the warm creamy coffee go down his throat. The room smelled of smudge as Frank walked around the room sunwise with the sage. As the meeting settled down, everyone took their seats. Leroy looked out at the faces. He realized many of them had stopped by Ben's to visit or help out. In some way, he knew them all.

Calling the meeting to order, Ben handed out the readings. A calm came over the room. As the literature was read out loud, Leroy sat in a daze. A gentleness soothed each tattered soul as the Spirit of Sobriety stretched her wings across the room and enfolded them in a loving embrace.

Ben nudged Leroy with his elbow. "Leroy," Ben whispered. "Come back to Earth, boy. It's time to tell your story."

Jolted back from far away, he shuddered. "What do I say?" whispered Leroy.

"Just tell the truth," said Ben. "It's the easiest to remember. What it was like, what happened and what it's like now. Start with your name. Breathe."

"Oh yeah," said Leroy as the motor in his heart clicked into gear. Looking into the sea of expectant faces, he swallowed hard, choking down his nervousness. "My name's Leroy and I'm grateful to be sober today."

"HI LEROY!" came back the voices of the room.

"I didn't know I was going to be speaking tonight. Which was probably a good thing, since I don't like talking in front of people."

A few heads nodded in agreement.

"About 3 months ago, Hal and my brother Kyle pulled in the parking lot of the grocery mart. Hal said I was scrawnier than a scarecrow and smelled like a dead goat. I admit, I was pretty far gone. I couldn't remember my last meal. It was hard to hunt when I was drunk. My hands shook so bad, I couldn't shoot a cottontail. After not eating for days, I lost my patience. It got pretty ugly. Stumbling around, I couldn't sneak up on anything. Most of the game ran away. To stop the shaking, I spent my last money on this rock-gut which burned my insides. Honestly, I knew I was dying. But, I didn't want to die alone, out in the caves."

"There were some dark moments. I seriously thought about taking my life. Sitting in that cave, I had just enough wood to stay warm for the night. But I didn't have the energy to do it anymore. This thought kept pressing in my mind. It told me to use my last bit of ammo and shoot my head off. I dozed off with my rifle in my hand, when I had this dream."

"All I can remember is that I was sitting around this fire. This old man comes up to me. He tells me that if I take my life, I'll have to come back and do it all over again. He says the lessons will be harder in the next life. Then he asked me if I want to repeat this life all over again? I told him 'no way.' He said 'good.' When he was walking away, he turned and said "Don't worry, they're sending reinforcements.""

"The next day, I crawled out of that cave. That's when Hal and Kyle loaded me in his truck. But, I don't remember much else about that day."

His butterflies settled down as he took a sip of coffee. "The next thing I know, I'm in a tipi with a snoring bear. My nerves were shot. Sleep was impossible. Every time I closed my eyes, I saw the faces of my men...," Leroy voice trailed off as he paused. Those memories were still raw and packed with charge. He didn't want to fall apart in front of everyone.

"Breathe," Ben whispered in Leroy's ear.

Leroy met Ben's gaze. The room was still. A slight breezed came through the door. Leroy took a deep breath. As he exhaled, he found the words to keep going.

"All I wanted to do was get the hell out of that damn tipi and get a drink. My head hurt. My hands were shaking. But, every time I tried to leave, this damn grizzly stood in the way. I never hated anybody so much in my life. I let him know it too. He stood between me and only thing I wanted. A damn drink! At least then, I'd drown out the voices in my head, so I could sleep. I just wanted to sleep."

A calmness came over him as his story poured out. "But that ol' grizzly turned out to be a great friend. And I know I'm alive today because he showed up in the parking lot at the grocery mart. A couple weeks ago, I finished giving away my inventory. It was the first time I ever told anyone the whole truth. I didn't know it but Hal's also a bone-picking buzzard," Leroy said with a chuckle.

"I'll take that as a compliment," Hal's voice boomed across the room as everyone laughed.

"There was no pulling the wool over his eyes," Leroy chuckled. "When he went through my inventory, he picked the meat clean off every bone. If he wasn't satisfied with what I wrote, he'd get out his pen and mark up the page. He forced me to dig deep and look at it from a different angle. The Big Book talks about doing a thorough job. But, the guys who wrote the book, never met Hal."

"If I didn't know better, a couple times, I thought he'd turn me upside down and shake it out of me. Especially, if I didn't do a good job." Leroy laughed poking fun at his mentor. Hal beamed as if it was the best compliment he ever got.

"After I wrote everything down, Hal pointed out I was always running from something. I couldn't put my finger on it. Hal said it was fear. But not every fear has a name. The fear settled in my soul and I didn't want to hurt. So I ran. And I kept running. That's probably why I took up track in high school."

"It's hard to say when the trouble started. I just knew I didn't want to be like everyone else. But, alcohol was always around. When my dad wasn't looking, I'd snag his beers off the counter. After I got good at that, I finished off everyone's drinks at Christmas. Sometimes I got caught. But most of the time, the grown ups were too drunk to notice."

"When I got older, My dad took me hunting. It took a lot of patience to track an animal for days. By watching him, I learned how to gauge the wind and see if it blew in my favor. Sometimes we'd sit under a tree for hours, just waiting. We'd have to be quiet, so as to not scare anything off. Then at night, he'd show me how to make a fire without matches. Later I found out, he always carried a book of matches with him. He just never told me."

"When I was 14, he told my mom we were going hunting for a week. But on this trip, he left me alone. I had a bedroll, some pemmican, my rifle, a buck knife and a canteen with water. This was my test to see if I was going to be a man or not. He said he wouldn't be far off. But I better not to come find him, unless I was going to be eaten by a bear."

"I remember watching him walk away into the trees. He wore moccasins when we were hunting, because they didn't make a sound when he walked. There was nothing he couldn't sneak up on. It was already late afternoon, when he left. So I figured I better find a good spot to set up camp. I had mixed feelings. Mostly, I didn't want to let him down. I'd prove to him I was a man. I wanted to show him that I was the best. From then on, I had to be the best at everything. That drove me for the rest of my life. It didn't matter what it was. I'd be the best at it."

"After doing my inventory, I found out that being the best was a long ladder with no end. You never get there. And there's always someone better." As he recalled these memories, they played like a movie in his mind.

"That first night, I worked hard to get a fire going. After I gathered up dry twigs, some grass and bark, I made a small fire pit. I was grateful it hadn't rained. Wet kindling makes it a lot harder. Along the river, we found some of flint. I had a buck knife and used it on the flint to get a spark. When I saw the first curl of smoke, I did a victory dance. Then, I almost smothered the flame, because I piled on too many twigs, but caught it in time. At that moment, I knew I was a man because I started a fire. I got more wood and kept it going all night. Once the fire was lit, I laid out my bedroll, sipped my water and ate a little pemmican. I was hungry, but I had to make it last."

Nothing stirred, as the room listened. Feeling at ease, Leroy took another sip of his coffee. Leaning over, Ben asked if he wanted a fresh cup. Leroy nodded yes.

"Well, next to the fire, I was warm enough in my sleeping bag, but I didn't sleep. The night was full of sounds, crickets and bullfrogs. Then the coyotes started howling. That kept me on edge and awake. I heard every twig snap. The owl hooted and I was afraid it was a bad omen. Then, out of the shadows, I heard something coming towards me. I got out my rifle. I'm staring hard in the direction where the sound is coming from."

"Then, behind the tall grass, comes this masked bandit. It's a mother coon foraging for food. She comes closer to the fire and sits up on her hind legs. I swear she asks me if I got something to eat. I found a piece of jerky and handed it to her. She sat there with me around the fire and ate it. When she was done, she whispered 'thanks' and scampered off. Sometime before dawn, my eyes felt like sandpaper. I couldn't keep them open any longer. I nodded off, until the sun woke me up."

"That morning, my stomach was growling. The only way I'd eat was if I killed something. So I buried my fire and went hunting. I found some berries to keep me going. But I kept tracking, looking for real food. After a while, I spotted a squirrel. But it didn't hold still long enough to get a shot.

Then Creator gave me a break and I spotted a rabbit. I got it with one shot. I was determined, because I was becoming a man. Afterward, I found a camp site and I started my fire. I skinned the rabbit and hung the skin up to dry. With my buck knife, I sharpened a twig and skewered the meat on it. I was starving. By nightfall, when I laid out my bedroll, I slept like a log. The next few days, I got better at making a fire and hunting."

"When my dad finally came to get me, I expected him to tell me I did a great job. But he didn't say a word the whole way home. Staring out the window, I got pissed. I couldn't look at him. I thought I failed. The one man I wanted respect from, said nothing. He never talked much anyway. That was the longest ride home."

Listening to Leroy tell his story, Jed remembered the ride home. He wanted to reach over the vast stillness between them. But he couldn't. The words got caught somewhere below his Adam's apple. As a boy, Jed's grandfather left him out in the woods to fend for himself. He was expected to learn these things. Hunting wasn't a sport. It was a necessity. That's how men kept their families fed.

"In high school, I drove myself to be the best. Being a fast runner, I got to be the captain of the track team. I had the right girl and I drank. At first, I could hold my liquor. I wasn't going to be a bleary-eyed drunk like the fools who stumbled down the street."

"When the war started, I signed up. I had something to prove. Our people had warrior societies and I was determined to be the best. After I went to Boot Camp, I knew one thing a man needed, was a good woman. There was a girl, I dated back in high school and I decided to ask her to marry me. When I came back, she'd already met someone else. The next day, I was back on the bus and never looked back. I was still running."

"Turns out everything my dad taught me as a hunter, made me a good warrior. In the back country, I sensed things before they happened. This kept me and my men out of harm's way. But I still had something to prove.

'With every confirmed kill, the ache inside grew bigger. The more holes I blew in the enemy, the bigger the hole got in me. Everything I did to them, I did to myself. Pretty soon, I was numb. And I drank hard. I believed that by killing the enemy, I was doing our country a service and being a man."

"One day, Ben pointed out, our ancestors, the great chiefs like Sitting Bull, were the enemy of the US government.

Just like the desert warlords are now. Our people were the insurgents, the rebels and the barbarians. I can only imagine what it felt like to be hunted down like prey, our women and children slaughtered."

"On my last patrol, my team got ambushed. Most of my men died. I never saw it coming. A bullet blew through my shoulder. I lost a lot of blood. I barely remember getting dragged out of the line of fire, when a chopper came. When I woke up in the hospital, they told me what happened. I was being sent home."

"Laying in that hospital, I felt I had failed my men. I couldn't desert them. And I didn't want to go home. So I drank to drown the memories and the pain. When I closed my eyes, I saw their faces. I heard their screams, the gun fire and the exploding bombs. There was a woman in yellow and a baby crying. It was horrible. The only way to sleep, was to mixed alcohol with the pain killers."

"When I got discharged, they said I was a hero. But I didn't feel like one. I wondered why I was allowed to live. My men gave the greatest sacrifice, but I was still here. I let them down. I lead them into harm's way. Night after night, I went over it in my mind. How could I not know? What did I miss? I prided myself on my tracking skills in the back country. But I was bested and it burned a hole in my gut."

"When I got off the bus, in my uniform and carrying my duffel bag, my mom was waiting for me. She cried. She was glad I was home. But," Leroy shook his head. "The boy she sent off to war, wasn't the same man who came back. I was angry and mean. I didn't want to be. But I couldn't handle it. People didn't know what they were talking about. The news was full of shit. When I wore the uniform, I stood for something. I had a purpose and knew what I was here to do. Once I took it off, I lost that. Wearing jeans and a tee shirt, somehow, everything I'd done didn't matter. People asked me questions, like did I kill anybody? I just looked at them like they were stupid. I couldn't handle being a civilian. So I

338

drank. Hard."

"What I saw in the desert, changed me forever. It sounds impossible, but there are people living across the world that make us Indians look rich. In Iraq, gangs of orphans search minefields for unexploded mines to sell to arms dealers. Some had their arms blown off. In Africa, starving kids die in their mother's arms, skin and bones. When I got back to America, the land of the free, nothing made sense. How could anyone complain if they had food and clean running water?"

"Before I came home, my parents split up. My mother loves me, but she got in the way of my drinking. Those four walls closed in on me. I couldn't handle it. So I packed my duffel bag with hunting gear and left. What I learned in combat, didn't mean shit in the free world. I made sure I brought enough bourbon with me. I told my mom I was going hunting. I never came back. That is until Hal and Kyle found me, half starved and almost dead."

"I'm not proud of leaving the way I did. I never considered anyone else in my decisions. I only did what was best for me. Or so I thought."

"One day down by the Missouri, Hal was talking about Step Two and finding a Power greater than myself. He told me to get in the river and make it stop or go the other direction. I thought he was crazy, but I went along with it. Of course, I couldn't stop the river."

"Then he said I was standing in the same water dinosaurs drank millions of years ago. Now T-Rex was definitely a weapon of mass destruction. And it took a Divine intervention to get rid of them. Hal tells great stories. He said a Heavenly Body crashed into Mother Earth and brought on the Ice Age. It froze those lizard brained monsters out. So if Creator could do that to save Earth, why couldn't He help me stop drinking?"

"I didn't have an answer for him. I still don't. All I needed to do was ask for help. As I dried off, the sun was shining just right on the Missouri. Though I couldn't see the water evaporating, I could see the Thunders. There was a rain storm brewing up north. In that second, I saw the perfection in Mother Earth. And it worked whether I said so or not."

"Another thing Hal said was that my big shot-ism, was my self importance rearing its ugly head. Halfway through my 5th Step, he stopped me flat. He said, "Everything you've done, is about puffing up your puny self and that bores the crap out of me. Name one thing you did for someone else, where it wasn't about you getting credit.""

"If he wasn't almost twice my size, I'd have belted him. I felt slapped, especially after I served my country. I thought I was pretty generous. But I couldn't name anything I did, where I didn't get credit. After that, he gave me a mission. Every day, I had to do someone a kindness, without getting caught. Nobody could know about it. If anyone found out, it wouldn't count. I was used to impossible missions. Hell, I thrived on them. But this was covert and I couldn't get credit. I wanted him to tell me what to do. But all he said was, find some need and fill it. I argued, but he shut me down quick. He said, "What, you don't know anybody who needs anything?""

"On the top of page 20 in the Big Book, it says, our very lives depend on our constant thought of others and how we can help meet their needs. It's the craziest mission I've ever been on. I had to pay attention to what people needed and help them out on the sly. I can't say anymore about it. Or none of it will count."

"After that, Hal told me that each of us was born with a gift, something we bring to the table and I'd damn well better go out and find mine. Whatever it was, I had to use it in a good way. Because if I didn't find it or used it selfishly, it'd eat a hole in me. Then, he said if I wasn't such a pig headed, trophy collector, I'd have found my gift already, and made a real difference in the lives of others."

"What I got from his tongue lashing was, I had to treat my alcoholism daily and be of service to Creator and my fellows. That a good man is the best I'll ever be."

"I have ninety days today, clean and sober. Sometimes that firewater still calls my name, but I don't answer. I ask Creator to see me through the day. I'm not done yet. There's a lot cleaning up to do. But I'm not feeding my soul junk food. Hal told me only fools feed on trash. I worked the 12 Steps with this pit bull, who won't let me slide on anything. Finally, I can say, I'm coming to know myself."

"On page 28 of the Big Book, it says no matter who we are, what color our skin is, we are all children of a living Creator. I can see that today. I had a hard time with the white man's god. From what I saw, there was nothing holy in what the white man did, especially to our people."

"But sitting on Mother Earth, I witnessed how she fed her children. She provided everything. I saw the heart of a living Creator at work. The sun shined on everyone, good or not. When the rain fell from the sky, it blessed everything on Earth. What would the rain do, if it had no one to bless?"

"One last thing Hal told me is that sobriety is a gift that takes sacrifice. First, I had to give up drinking. But more than that, I had to give up my closed mind and become teachable. I don't know everything and that's okay. Lots of people have good ideas, but they're afraid to act on them because of what others might think. Or that they're not good enough."

"But then he told me this. When my mind wasn't disturbed anymore, the peace of Creator could flow through me. The whole purpose of working the Twelve Steps, was so I could have a peaceful mind. That way when Creator spoke to me, I could hear him."

"I don't know if anything I said tonight made sense," said Leroy looking at the faces in the room. "All I know is that 91 days ago, I wanted to die. And today, I walked into this room a sober man. Most of all I want to thank Ben for letting me stay in his tipi and drink his coffee. My little brother and Hal for not letting me die. And Hal for putting up with me as long as he has. Thanks everybody for all your prayers and help. I think that's all I got to say," said Leroy.

The whole room burst into war whoops and applause. With a shit eating grin, Hal leaped from his seat and cheered. All the trophies in the world, didn't come close to how Leroy felt. He finally belonged.

Ben listened to every word Leroy said. When a person was purified of all flaws, they could move mountains. Because then the love, wisdom and power of Creator flowed through them like a hollow bone. From Leroy's words, Ben knew his faith had changed. His heart wasn't calloused and cold, like the first night in the tipi. Leroy still had work to do. But, Ben could see him moving mountains if he stayed sober and gave it away.

After the meeting was over, Ben walked over to Hal. "Leroy's ready, Hal. Frank and Ernie can help me go get the willows, if you take Leroy on a stone run. You've done some good work with him, Hal. It wasn't but a few weeks ago, I thought it was hopeless."

"Thanks Ben. At least, now I know the boy was listening. I never done so much alligator wrestling in my life," said Hal.

"From the sound of it, you've got quite a few animals as your totems," laughed Ben. "Grizzly bear, buzzard and a pit bull, from what Leroy told."

"Whatever gets the job done, I suppose," said Hal shaking his head. "It's all strong medicine."

"Oh, yes it is. Ah, before I forget. I was at the post office this morning. You got a few boxes there from New York. There was a name 'Sweeney' on it. Does that sound familiar?" asked Ben.

"Oh, don't you remember old Sweeney, out in California? He was an old crawdad then," said Hal. "Bernie must of cajoled him into sending us some AA supplies."

"The one who's dad threw him out from New York? I do remember him. How did you chance meeting him again?" asked Ben.

"It's a long story. I'll tell you on the way home," laughed Hal. "Let's close up shop."

CHAPTER NINE: STONE RUN

Sitting at the table, drinking his coffee, Ben gazed through the kitchen window. The morning glow lit up the hillsides in the east. It wouldn't be long before Hal's heavy cowboy boots clomped across the front porch and he'd bust through the front door, wiping the sleep out his eyes, the same way he'd done every morning so far. Ben expected Frank and Ernie would roll up soon to go on a willow run for the new lodge build.

Enjoying the stillness, Ben's mind wandered as fingers touched the beaded tobacco pouch Elsie made him years ago. He'd use the tobacco later. It was an offering for the willows they'd harvest for the new lodge build. The quiet of the morning was Ben's favorite time. The solitude gave him a moment to sort things out before the days happenings. Jed, Kyle and Leroy were going with Hal to fetch the stones, a few hours away.

Though Ben never considered himself a saver of souls, he knew Leroy needed a healing. From where he stood, only faith and ceremony could accomplish this miracle. Hal and Leroy had done most of the groundbreaking work, by doing the first 8 Steps.

To make a thoughtful adult out of a self-centered alcoholic was hard. Let alone, teach a knucklehead to be accountable for his actions. Or to be willing to face the consequences for his choices in life. Sometimes this took years. How do you get someone, who is only interested in themselves, to look out for the needs of others? Most were concerned only for the instant gratification of their base appetites.

For Ben, the hardest thing about this work, was knowing what needed to be done, but not being able to convince anyone else of it. So much unnecessary suffering could end if the Old

Ways were practiced again.

When a man's mind is pure, it's strong. A pure mind knows the truth. A mind clouded with anger, envy and hate makes bad decisions, which more often than not, leads to destruction. The people needed their Medicine Ways. They revealed how their spirit mind was clouded. When healing blew the storm clouds of hatred away, then, the integrity of the mind could be restored. Integrity is when your words matched your actions, when you walked the way you talked.

Today, most people trusted the western ways of science. They wanted to take a pill to mend their broken hearts or a surgeon to cut away their tattered souls. A chemical peace of mind. But true healing is a labor of love and truth. Ben rarely met a head doctor who'd confront his patients with the truth. Especially, if the truth threatened his pocket book. All the pills in the world won't chase away a relentless spirit. But try telling anyone that. Desperate people want the easier, softer way.

When the past is released, forgiveness becomes possible. The Spirit of Healing reveals the ugliness locked away in the dark and brings it to the Light. It was simple. But few people truly had the courage to confront the demons they kept locked in the dark. A sick mind twists the truth to justify the wrongs it committed against another.

Ben glanced at the clock. Clomp, clomp, clomp, went the boots on the front steps. "Right on time," Ben smiled to himself.

Feeling haggard, Hal clutched his back as searing pain shot up through his spine. Climbing the porch steps, all his grouchiness thundered up in his voice. He turned towards the tipi and bellowed. "Come on Leroy, GET UP! We're burning daylight!"

"Morning Ben," said Hal as door blew open. He hobbled to the coffee pot, yawning and stretching. "Man, waking up Leroy, was like waking the dead this morning."

"The dead aren't that hard to wake up," Ben smiled. "If

345

you know how to do it."

"Oh you know what I mean," said Hal throwing Ben a look.

"You think he's having second thoughts? You know, every time something good wants to happen, something bad tries to get in its way," observed Ben. "He might be backsliding. Fear does that."

"That lily-livered, chicken-hearted, son of a bitch better not change his mind this morning, after all the work we put in," cursed Hal as jolts of pain shot through his back. Stepping back, he thought back to what Ben just said. "Hmm... That's another way of quoting Newton's third law of physics."

"Oh, what's that?"

"For every action, there's an equal and opposite reaction," quoted Hal.

"Well, okay PROFESSOR! Then, you probably know this too," Ben chided.

"WHAT?"

"The only reason we work with others is to stay sober ourselves," Ben smiled.

"Oh don't you start quoting the book at me," Hal snapped back, stretching his back side to side. "Ah, I got a kink in my back," Hal grimaced in pain. "It must have caught a draft."

Getting up from the table, Ben went to the bathroom. He found an ointment good for sore muscles. "Here, try rubbing some of this on your back. It heats up and might take the chill out. Just don't get it in your eyes or any place that's sensitive."

"You mean, like my balls?" laughed Hal remembering a vindictive ex-girlfriend. She lured him over, with the promise of a good rub down, only to pour a flaming Chinese eucalyptus concoction all over his nuts. But, that happened way before he was sober.

"Sounds like you had that done before," laughed Ben.

"Oh, yeah. But I probably deserved it," chuckled Hal. "I guess, I wasn't always a nice guy."

"I can't imagine," said Ben with a sideways glance.

"Well, I only slept with her when I was drunk," said Hal while he rubbed the ointment on his back.

"How often were you drunk?" Ben queried.

"Back then, damn near all the time," Hal shook his head. "Hell, I met her in a bar. She took me home. Somehow she got it in her head that I loved her. When she figured out I wasn't the one, she lured me in for the kill. I have to say, it was brilliant on her part. Most girls just scream bloody murder. They slam the car door, with steam blasting out their ears, while those sharp heels go clickity-clack down the street. Not this one. That little apple-polisher planned the whole damn thing. Right down to the candles and all. Being drunk, I didn't know what she rubbed me down with, until it started burning."

"OH!!! That smarts," laughed Ben.

"Oh that ain't the half of it," said Hal, stretching out his sore back. He let the ointment work in. "I didn't know that little spitfire was out to get me, until she started laughing. That's when I saw red. I tore out there and drove home with my nuts on fire." Ben let out a good laugh.

"Talk about needing a cold shower," Hal laughed. Sitting on the chair, Hal put his head on his knees to stretch out his back. Then, Leroy walked in the door.

"Morning," said Leroy as he got a cup of coffee. "What's the matter with you?"

"His back's hurting him," said Ben. "He's a bit grouchy this morning. So mind your step."

"You still want to go, Hal? If your back's hurting, we can go another time," said Leroy.

347

"You're not backing out on me now, are you Leroy?" asked Hal a little testy.

"No, but if you're in pain," Leroy started.

"Listen, busting broncs and riding bulls tweaked up my back. But, I don't let a little pain stop me from getting the job done," said Hal stiffly. "As far as I'm concerned, we're still on. Once this ointment takes the chill out, I'll feel better."

"When dad's back went out, Mom heated up a wash cloth on the stove. She'd put them on his dad's back. Maybe that'd help," said Leroy.

"That's a good idea," said Ben getting a wash cloth and heating it in a pot of water.

"You know what Leroy, walk my back," said Hal getting out of the chair. He walked over to the wall where the couch used to be. "I'll lay down and breath out. Then, you walk up and down my back, with your feet facing to the wall," said Hal. "But, take your shoes off."

As Leroy walked Hal's back, he heard the backbone popping into place. Then, Leroy put hot wash clothes on Hal's worn out back. The steam loosened the sore muscles. Hal was almost smiling again. A half hour later Kyle and Jed showed up.

Getting up off the floor, Hal stretched his arms out. He twisted around to loosen up his back muscles. Ben glanced at Hal's tee shirt and tried to make out what it said. "What's that say on your shirt?"

"Oh, this old shirt. I dug it out of the bottom of my suitcase. I'm running out of clean clothes," said Hal as he pulled the shirt out from his chest to read it.

"NEVER TRY TO TEACH A PIG TO SING! IT WASTES YOUR TIME AND ANNOYS THE PIG!" Leroy read it out loud and started laughing.

"Oh yeah," said Hal. "I remember when I bought this. I was working with a bunch of knuckleheads out West. They

348

never did get it though."

"That's some good wisdom," said Ben with a knowing smile.

Rising above the hillsides, the morning sun promised a beautiful day. Hal went out to his truck to check on his cash supply. Thumbing through his money, his bankroll was pretty thin. Maybe enough funds to fill the tank and get a few groceries. He hadn't worked a day for pay, since he got there.

"Well Creator," he whispered. "Looks like we got to find some work." Since he got sober, Hal lived one day at a time. Most all his needs were met, one way or another. He trusted his Higher Power to see him through.

With his coffee mug in hand, Ben stood on the porch and watched the men depart for the stone run. He was thankful Hal recovered from his backache. Otherwise his foul mood may have chased the Spirits of the Stone People away.

After Hal made some space, Leroy and Kyle took the back seat of the cab. Hal got behind the wheel of the truck and started the rumpy old motor. His foot tapped the gas, to keep her going. Jed rode shot gun. On the bench seat between them, Jed put an ice chest full of sandwiches Vera made, along with some cold Mountain Dew.

The morning air was cool and crisp. The highway opened up as Hal's old truck rumbled through the prairie. Under a cloudless sky, they headed for the interstate. They passed through several small towns and hamlets. Most intersections were empty as Hal slowed to 25 miles an hour because a single traffic light blinked red. The lonesome blinking light hung in the middle of the intersection.

With miles of countryside ahead, Hal's mind wandered off. He never intended to stay this long. He was glad to be of service and see this family come back together. The road felt good this morning. He rolled down the window and hung his arm out. His thumb hung on to the wing window frame. The open road always lifted his spirit, no matter how tattered he

349

felt. Though his life was held together with duct tape and baling wire, his Higher Power never failed him.

After a while, Kyle perked up in the back. "Hal, do you know what a Heyoka is? I was doing research. It said Sitting Bull was a Heyoka. But, I haven't found much on the internet about that."

Looking in the rear view mirror, Hal saw the eager expression on Kyle's face. What a different kid he was, from the one he'd met the night he lead the meeting. "Well I'm no authority, but from what I understand, they're Sacred Clowns whose medicine comes from the Thunder Beings. If that helps you out at all," said Hal turning back to the road.

"Yeah, okay but what do they do?"

"Well, my buddy Ohiya was Heyoka. We had plenty of long talks," said Hal. "I could tell you what he said."

"Is he the one you shared about in your talk at the meeting? The guy who got murdered in the county jail in North Dakota?" asked Jed.

"Yeah, you remembered. He was a Sun Dance Chief I supported a few times. He taught me that each of us is a pipe carrier because we are children of Creator. The sad thing is, even though everybody is called, only a few choose to listen," said Hal thinking back to all the fire place conversations. "Well, let me start this off right, Kyle. Because then you'll see the big picture."

"Sure," said Kyle. Hal was full of good stories.

"Alright, how I should I start this?" said Hal thinking out loud. "Okay, Heyoka medicine comes directly from the Thunder Beings of the West. The Thunders are servants of Creator. Their medicine is for purification, like how the world feels fresh after a thunder storm. Heck, even a lightning strike cuts right through the dark."

"What about a hurricane?" Leroy queried.

"What about it?" Hal asked back not understanding.

"Well, it's pretty destructive," Leroy asserted. "It makes a mess."

"Yeah, that means there's major clean up involved," Hal offered. "Mother Earth is the only girl I know who can close up the New York Stock Exchange for two days with a rain cloud."

"I remember that rain cloud you're talking about," said Jed. "It was more than 850 miles wide."

"Well, this priest from Peru told me there were a lot of practitioners of the dark working their black magic in New York City," Hal's eyes lit up. "From what he said, they got word 3 years before that hurricane hit, that this storm was coming."

"So, they got fair warning," Jed surmised.

"Well, it'd take a storm cloud that size to clean up dark medicine," Hal said.

"Well, look at hurricane Katrina," said Jed. "They got all that Cajun voodoo down there."

"That's strong purification," Hal agreed. "Not only that, there was a lot of slavery and whatnot going on in that neck of the woods. When those Nature Spirits work themselves up into a frenzy, there's major clean up involved."

"What Nature Spirits?" Leroy scoffed.

"Well, the Elementals," said Hal. "The Beings of Fire, Air, Water and Earth. They're the oldest Beings on the planet and work for the Higher Powers to keep the balance on Earth. Nothing works faster or more efficient than the Powers of Nature. When those crooked farmers grew that poison crop of corn, laced with pesticide, well, Mother Earth answered that with a drought. Then, once everything was dried up, lightning struck and burned those poison crops to the ground. Then came a flood and that farmland was buried under tons of silt. When Mother Earth wants to balance the scales, she's a powerful force to be reckoned with."

As Leroy listened, his mind flashed back to a day of intense battle in that desert hell. Something happened there,

351

that day. Hal's words started to make sense. Mother Earth wasn't a benign chunk of dirt. But, rather a powerful Being who wouldn't tolerate being overrun by dark forces. That hellish morning replayed in Leroy's mind as he recalled his team being under heavy fire.

The smell of burning flesh and smoke hung heavy in the air. Hidden from men's eyes, behind the veil, the demigod of war raged on the battlefield. His hellfire sparked the forces of hatred. An unholy wrath burned hot in the hearts of men.

The tide of war rushed across the land, baptizing the Earth with blood. With triumph in their eyes, gloating demons rode on warheads, which opened the doors of hell. Their astral disease spewed forth, seeking refuge in the evil of men's beings.

This shrieking desert hell was riddled with shellfire. With few places to hide, flames swept across the killing fields. Mother Earth was stained with split blood caused by the guns of men. Their cries of pain and fury pierced Her tender soul. Love was dying and peace was dead as men rushed to wreak destruction upon their earthly brothers.

Shocked out of life by this murderous assault, the torn and mangled souls of newly dead soldiers wailed with anger, grief, love, uncertainty and despair. The bands of Spirit-helpers who sought to help them, were attacked by beings of evil who made war in the astral regions.

The souls of murdered men tore at the living soldiers as they entered the battlefield of Spirit World. Entangled in this region of torment, many souls remained below. They were spun round and round in a violent whirlpool created by an army of once human, angry beings who'd died at the hands of war.

Away in the trenches, a few soldiers waited and prayed. They knew Creator dwelled in the hearts of all men, though in some, He lay asleep. All around them, bombs exploded, filling the air with smoke and ash. Prayers were whispered in anguished moments. "Help me, PLEASE!," they cried. There were no atheists in foxholes.

Prayer is a powerful, far-reaching force, where the heart of the created communes in sacred silence with the Creator. The Angelic Host was bound to the Universal Law: 'the Call for help MUST come from the realm where the help is needed.'

Above the battleground, stood strong-hearted souls who committed themselves to peace. In the silence, they centered the force of their will to reduce the pressure of the feverish war-madness that surged across the land.

Holding back the dark forces from the outer stars, these angelic soldiers of mercy stood their ground against the devils of war. Their outpouring of love slowly melted the sharp-edged forces of hate. When love and faith grew stronger on Earth, the need for armies would grow smaller and war will come to an end.

In a holy instant, a strong momentum gathered in the ethers. The wind pulled all her strength from the four corners of Earth. In a flurry, a huge windstorm came up and drove those devilish beings back to the bowels of Earth. Rising a thousand feet in the air, the fine desert sand blew so strong that nothing was seen. Within seconds, everything was covered with dust. The fighting ground to a stop. For hours, not a shot was fired. War-weary, the soldiers fell back into the trenches for a long night of rest.

Seeing all this in his mind's eye, a new understanding came over Leroy. "I get it," said Leroy.

"Good," Hal went on. "Now, let's see. Where was I?"

"Heyoka," Kyle chimed in.

"That's right," said Hal as he collected his thoughts. "Okay, the fella who carries this medicine, is chosen by Spirit. He has a dream or a vision about thunder storms, a Thunder Bird or the Wakinyan Oyate. Something like that. Does that make sense?"

"So what, the guy dreams about a thunderstorm and

353

then he's a Heyoka?" asked Leroy.

"Well, not exactly," Hal started. "There's some learning involved. From what I understand, if you're called, you were probably Heyoka before you were born. The Thunders just come to remind you of what you signed up for. Ohiya said a Spirit came to him when he was a little guy. This spirit stuff isn't an exact science."

"So what do they do?" asked Kyle.

"Well, the long and the short of it is, they heal things," said Hal. "The Medicine Ways of the Thunders involves working with Spirit-helpers of the West. Ohiya gave me a couple of brief descriptions. These are aspects of those chosen to work with the Thunder Beings. Are you with me so far?"

"Yeah, I'm listening," said Kyle.

"Good," Hal started. "Well, first there are the "Clowns." They make fun where there isn't any. Most people are familiar with these guys. Next, are the "Winktes." They bring female energy, which helps balance out masculine energy. Then, we got Iktomi, who is a 'Spider Being.' He's a trickster who play tricks with people's faith. Now, the "Fools" try to get in the way of whatever you're doing to distract you, on purpose. Then, there's the "Backward Ones" who are inexperienced and mischievous. They play around, mock others and pretty much disrespect every thing around them. And then there are the "Mindless" who blindly follow instructions to hurt, maim and kill the innocent."

"Wow, where did you get all this?" asked Kyle astounded.

"Well, Ohiya was a Heyoka. He worked directly with the Thunders. We traveled for days going from one Sun dance to another. That gave us a lot of time to talk. He said the internal medicine way of the Thunders is the most difficult to work with."

"Hmm," acknowledged Kyle.

"See, when Ohiya was a child," Hal went on. "He dreamt about thunderbolts and white lightning. The Spirit-helpers of the West brought him a vision. Since he was pure and young, he was approached by a Spirit who guided him. Does that make sense so far?"

"Yeah. When I read about Heyokas, it said they walk backwards. They'll do crazy things. Like, in a blizzard, they'll walk around in their underwear and complain about how hot it is. I don't get that at all," said Kyle.

"Oh, I see where you're coming from," said Hal. "Heyoka medicine is also about healing and reversals. When the Indian nation was down and out, freezing and hungry, those Sacred Clowns did funny things to make people laugh. I bet you didn't know this, but laughter chases dark spirits away. It's powerful medicine helps people get their spirits up. That way, they'll find the courage to keep going."

"So what, they're jokers?" asked Leroy stifling a yawn.

"Well, we call them clowns. But, not the way you're thinking. See, I was a rodeo clown. I had a goofy outfit with a big red nose and frizzy hair. My job was to distract the bull long enough so the thrown bull rider didn't get gored. A Heyoka clowns around to save the people from the spirit of despair. Especially when they're starving in the middle of a freezing winter."

"But it's more powerful than that," said Hal excitedly. "A true Heyoka, worth his salt, can actually reverse a disease."

"What, like cancer?" asked Leroy.

"Yeah, like cancer. Cancer is a beast, Leroy. Its spirit is nothing but piles of self-hatred. What most folks don't understand, is every cigarette or poison they take in, fuels the beast. When that beast finally breaks out in the body, it's been a long time in the making."

"So, how does a Heyoka fix that?" Leroy asked.

"Well, from what I understand, he'll speak to the spirit of

cancer and find out how to reverse the contract the person made with it. Here, he'll try to save a life by reversing the practice of self-hatred. Laughter helps. True Heyoka medicine is much deeper than walking backwards in your skivvies through a snowstorm."

"I never thought about that," said Jed. "Our people thrived on laughter. We've shed more than our share of tears. But laughter got us through. It kept our spirits up when times got hard."

"Laughter is powerful medicine. It breaks through the stranglehold unhappiness has on people. That's why we tell our stories at AA meetings. Most people laugh at the crazy antics we do when we're drunk. Actually, there's a comedy inside the tragedy," said Hal. "It lets the new guy identify with the people in the room."

"I think you're right about that," said Jed. "Stories bring us together."

"The other thing Kyle," said Hal looking in his rear view mirror. "Indians of the Great Plains had a warrior society. Here's where a Heyoka played an important roll. They were the Dog Soldiers. They went out in battle and fought tooth and nail. They'd get that crazy look in their eye, scare off the enemy and come back unscratched. Heyokas also had another job, but it wasn't very popular. Have you ever been to Sun Dance?"

"Yeah," answered Jed. "I don't know if the boys remember, but I got invited one year by my buddy who sun danced. He asked me to support him. I brought the boys with me. But when Vera found out, she got upset. At least they went one year."

"Okay, at least you'll know what I'm talking about," Hal started.

"Mom was afraid to get in trouble with that Christian preacher," Leroy scoffed. "He never thought much of ceremony and didn't want his sheep to stray."

"Well, I supported at this one Sun Dance. On the third day, they did a Heyoka round. By then, the Sun Dancers had fasted 3 days without food or water. They were pretty well tied to the Spirit World. I'll never forget how those clowns went around the arbor with ripe watermelon and dripped it on the dancers heads. They tried to pull the dancers off their prayer. It was a true test of strength and determination," said Hal.

"I don't get that," said Kyle.

"Well, let me put it this way," Hal began. "Say, you're a warrior and you get captured by the enemy. Chances are, you'll be starved and tortured. Your only strength is in your prayer. Sun Dance is a warrior ceremony that pushes a man to his limit."

"How so?" asked Jed.

"Well, for starters, it's hot and the days are long. For four days, the sun dancer doesn't eat or drink. During the dance, he's either pierced to a tree or dragging buffalo skulls around the arbor which are pierced to his back. By the third day, his back aches, he's tired and his feet hurt. The drum keeps pounding and he's dancing in the hot sun."

"It's one thing to pass a test when you're strong and your shields are up. But try staying true to your prayer when your ass is dragging, your muscles are tired, you're hungry, thirsty and your feet hurt. From where I stand, that's true grit," said Hal.

"That's true," said Jed, following along.

"Now, listen up because this is key," Hal went on. "The most important part of Heyoka medicine is revealing a warrior's weaknesses. It shows them where they're soft. It's not done to humiliate them. It's done for healing."

At this point, Hal got Leroy's attention. Being a warrior was important. It's where he felt his best. He wanted to know more about it. "How does that work?" Leroy asked.

"Well, our people had a warrior society. It was an

357

important part of becoming a man. Before going to war, you needed to know a man's Achilles' heel. On the battlefield, a stupid mistake could get you killed. Or worse, you'd lose the war. So you needed to know if the guy fighting next to you, toting an M16, was a spineless jellyfish or a raging hothead. Because on the killing field, his weakness could put you in shackles or leave your people vulnerable or dead."

"Yeah, I know that one," said Leroy reflecting back to his last battle. "I could have used some extra training that way."

"War is hell, Leroy. But understand, this is where Sun Dance is the testing ground, on every level," explained Hal.

"You mean with the fasting and piercing?" Leroy inquired.

"Yeah," agreed Hal. "It takes all that into consideration and puts it into a prayer. Which, if you haven't figured it out yet, is where the Power comes from. This way, if your caught with your shorts down, your mind will stay strong."

"If your mind is strong, you can handle anything," said Jed knowingly.

"No kidding," said Hal. "But see, this is where the Power is. When a Heyoka reveals a warrior's weaknesses at Sun Dance, it can be healed right then. It's a different way of doing Steps 6 and 7 in the Big Book."

"What?" asked Leroy having done his Seventh Step prayer a couple weeks ago. "What do the Steps and Ceremony have in common?"

"Ah, a lot," smiled Hal inwardly. He was glad Leroy paid attention. "When someone is a dented can, they've usually got bad manners. Maybe they grew up that way, but they offend everyone around them."

"That drives all their good away from them," added Jed.

"Exactly," agreed Hal. "I knew a loud mouth who lost a job, because he never shut up. His damn self-centeredness drove everybody nuts. He went to AA, but never worked the steps. His jaw kept flapping, but he said a whole lotta nothing."

"I've know people like that," said Jed shaking his head.

"Yeah, duct tape would've helped," laughed Hal. "Now, this guy was such a blowhard, he'd have you believe that he was born in a log cabin that he built by himself."

"Did he grow the trees by himself too," laughed Jed.

"OH, ALL OF IT!!!" Hal laughed. "He milled the wood, mined the iron! Milled the steel! Yeah.... Truth be told, he wasn't worth the gunpowder it'd take to blow him up."

Jed laughed. "It takes all kinds, don't it."

"It's a big world out there," Hal sighed as he remembered the point of this conversation. "Now, Leroy, both ceremony and the Twelve Steps are a process of purification. If you do them right, they'll lead you to your highest and best self."

"Well Hal, you're the blacksmith of the 12 Steps," Leroy laughed. "If I didn't know better, I'd say that you pounded out dented cans for a living. We always had a blazing fire, heat and a lot of pounding."

"I'll take that as a compliment," Hal paused, thinking how explain this. "Okay, Ohiya was a Sun Dance Chief. Before he died, he had things he wanted to do. After dancing for 35 years, he wanted to write a book on the Old Ways and how they came to him. At his last Sun Dance, he invited a camera man to take photographs. That way, he'd document this knowledge so it wouldn't be lost. He looked for an apprentice dedicated enough to follow him to every ceremony."

"I thought taking pictures of ceremony was taboo," said Jed.

"Well, it is. Unless you're walking backwards," Hal explained.

"So you're saying the traditional rules didn't apply because he was Heyoka?" asked Jed having spent a little time around ceremony.

"Yes and no. Traditional rules don't really apply to those who walk backwards. But fear is a weakness. And most of the traditions around cameras were based on fear," said Hal. "Now those are Ohiya's words, not my own opinion."

"Yeah, people were afraid the camera would steal their soul," Jed agreed. "But also, many traditionalists are opposed to whites imitating our ceremonies. If they film them, what's to stop them from turning around and using our ceremonies for money? Like the guy in Arizona who killed those rich people?"

"Jed, we're powerless over what other people do. How do you stop a guy who throws blankets over a bunch of sticks and crawls in with hot stones to pray, in his own backyard? The guy in Arizona is a textbook example of what not to do. And now he's doing jail time for that."

"It's about time," said Jed.

"Ya, think? Now, some traditionalists are opposed to whites attending our ceremonies," said Hal. "I don't agree. Ohiya didn't either. He told me straight up that his grandfathers and uncles passed ceremony onto him to pray with all people. Everyone was welcome to the ceremonies he conducted. The Spirit who helped Ohiya, taught him to keep the altar open for all people."

"Hmm," said Jed thinking about Ohiya's defiance of tradition.

"Look, Jed, I don't know if you remember my talk, but it was a white guy who brought me to ceremony. So for me, it's basic. It's about the prayer and nothing more. Creator don't see color when He's hearing our prayer."

"Yeah, I see the dilemma," said Jed. "It's about the prayer and we're all free to pray in the manner we choose."

"Well, chew on this for a minute," started Hal. "You're working the 12 Steps, with a few months sober under your belt. Your boys are here with you sober, working the same 12 Steps.

What if Bill W. and Bob and the old timers of AA, decided there was another requirement for membership to AA, other than a simple desire to quit drinking?"

"I'm not following you," said Jed.

"Well, what if they decided, they didn't want rednecks, convicted felons, atheists, beggars, hookers, nut house inmates or truck drivers. They only wanted upstanding, real alcoholics, like doctors and stockbrokers with a padded expense accounts," said Hal. "Think about it. Indians wouldn't make the cut. If someone hadn't carried the message to us, we wouldn't be sober today."

"Yeah, I see your point," said Jed cogitating on their sobriety.

"Have you read the third tradition in the Twelve and Twelve yet?" asked Hal.

"No, I only have a Big Book, but the traditions are in there. Isn't the third about the only requirement for membership is a desire to quit drinking?" asked Jed.

"Yeah, but if you read the third tradition in the Twelve and Twelve, the early groups of AA were terrified of inviting of bunch of hooligans and criminals into their homes. They only wanted respectable alcoholics. The main office had every group send in their rules for membership. After they read the rules that each group put together, they realized, no one could be a member of AA. Especially, if they bought into their fears," said Hal. "Go ahead, read about it. When we get back I got a copy you can look at."

"When I was a young man, I went with my father into town. There was a tavern called the Kadoka Bar. On the front door it had a sign. "No Indians or dogs allowed," recalled Jed.

"Yeah, I ran into that before. When I was an enlisted man, there was a guy from the southern tribes who told the girls he was Italian. Hatred and fear makes you lie about who you are," said Hal.

Considering all they'd talked about, Jed grew silent. He realized fear was the corroding thread of all people. "So what happened with Ohiya and the cameraman Sun Dance?"

"Oh, the Heyoka Sun Dance," Hal started. "Yeah, well... that was a good one. Ohiya had planned it for years and finally pulled it off. One dancer knew a camera buff who did great work. He agreed to travel to Ohiya's Sun Dance to shoot it. But there was a problem. Ohiya knew it going in. His head dancer had a bad temper. People were afraid of him. The guy was explosive and it was a small dance."

"How did Ohiya handle that?" asked Jed.

"It got pretty interesting, I'll give you that. It started with a few glitches. No big deal. But, by the third day, when Ohiya wore his silver skirt in the arbor, that Heyoka medicine kicked in full force. The head dancer lost his top and started hollering at people. Then he pointed his eagle fan at the cameraman. At one point, he just went off like a madman."

"I heard if you point an eagle feather at someone in anger, you could split them in two," said Jed.

"Yeah, imagine what pointing a whole eagle fan at someone could do," remarked Hal. "Well, it got interesting. The dark underbelly of the head dancer and his buddies showed up. They circled the cameraman and threatened to destroy his camera. Luckily, Ohiya got there in time to break it up. I'd never seen him so pissed. I thought, for sure, it'd come to blows. After the commotion died down, Ohiya had enough. Spirit guided him to put the whole arbor into the fire. The dance ended on the third night."

"But why would Ohiya choose this head dancer, if he knew he'd fly off the handle like that?" asked Jed. "It seems like a bad choice."

"You'd think so, if you weren't of Heyoka mind," said Hal. "A few days after the dance, most of the crew had cleared out. I sat down with Ohiya. You could say I was puzzled. So, I asked Ohiya about it. His eyes twinkled when he said the cameraman was the Heyoka. The whole purpose of that Heyoka Sun Dance was to draw out the dark underbelly of the head dancer and expose it."

Thunderstruck, Jed chewed on that for a moment. "This Ohiya was a real mastermind, wasn't he? He set it all up to expose the head dancer's character flaws."

"Oh Jed, if he was here, Ohiya would tell you that Great Spirit is the real mastermind. It's a brutal way to get your Sixth and Seventh Step done. Though, I thought it was brilliant, myself. Ohiya said he'd let his head dancer stew on it for a year. Then they'd get together and talk, to clear things up," said Hal.

"So did they clear things up?" asked Jed. "I expect that wasn't a fun conversation."

"No, they never did. Ohiya died that winter," Hal's voice faded off.

"This is the guy you said got murdered in the county jail in North Dakota?" asked Jed.

"Yup," said Hal. "He got arrested and was dead three hours later. He never saw the judge. Never got sentenced. Nothing. Oh, they covered up real good. They made it look like suicide. But being a Sun Dancer, Ohiya would never do that. He believed suicide was a cowards way out. Did I tell you he was also a Hereditary Chief? Both his parents came from a long line of chiefs. Since his older brothers were all dead, that honor got passed onto him."

"It don't seem like he was someone who would commit suicide," Jed pondered. "The way I heard it was, if you commit suicide, you had to come back and do the whole mess over again. I'd rather get it right the first time."

"Yeah, me too. But I can't say that suicide never crossed my mind," said Hal thoughtfully. "After Ohiya died, my sun dance brother, White Feather went to see a Yuwipi man. He passed him some tobacco and asked how Ohiya died."

"What did he say?" asked Jed.

"The Yuwipi man told him that Ohiya got murdered by two men and they covered it up," said Hal. "He also said Ohiya had some woman trouble. He was probably messing with something he shouldn't. White Feather never gave any the Yuwipi man any details. He just let the Yuwipi man talk."

"That gives me an uneasy feeling," said Jed setting his jaw.

"Me too, Jed." said Hal staring out the window. He felt the cool air on his forearm and wondered how this would get set right.

Staring off into the distance, Hal's mind wandered off. In his mind's eye, he pictured Ohiya running across the sun dance arbor, that last day dressed in his silver skirt. The whole experience lay heavy on his mind.

Off on the distant horizon, storm clouds started to brew. As his mind wandered, Hal heard the big drum pounding. "WA-KEE-YA" whispered the wind. A shiver crawled down his spine.

Moving and swirling, the thunderheads formed an ominous backdrop against the endless sky. In the far corner, came a flash of white lightning. Dancing across the top of the Thunders, Hal spotted the spirits of several fancy dancers. With flashes of color, they whirled across the top of the storm clouds.

In Hal's mind, the drumbeat got louder and louder. Carried on the wind, he heard their voices singing. In his hand, one of the Thunders held a lightning bolt. He raised it above his head and sent it flying to the ground. It crashed onto Earth as the roar of thunder shook the land. Then, from the center of the circle, came a dancer dressed in a silver skirt. He was walking backwards.

Clashes of thunder and white lightning coursed across the darkened sky. The wind was in full fury. Tumbleweeds flew across the highway. With his long hair blowing behind him, Ohiya danced across the storm clouds dressed in his silver skirt. He was surrounded by his brothers, the Wakinyan Oyate.

Dressed in their full regalia, the Thunders danced as the big drum pounded thundering across the heavens. True to his Heyoka nature, Ohiya danced backwards. Flashes of lightning trailed behind him as his silver skirt reflected the light. With every footstep of his intricate dance, his movements reversed negative conditions, the evil man had done. The intense power of the rain washed away the darkness.

On the highway, hail and rain pelted the windshield of Hal's truck. His windshield wipers squeaked as they pushed the water from side to side. The Earth mother was purified. All discord and unhappiness was removed.

"Thanks for remembering me," whispered Ohiya's voice on the winds. The rays of the sun broke through the clouds as a rainbow crossed the highway.

"Did you see that?" asked Hal wondering if anyone else saw his vision.

"That was a great thunderstorm," said Jed absently staring out the window. The boys were asleep in the back. On the side of the highway was a sign. "DRIVE CAREFULLY!!! IT'S NOT ONLY CARS THAT CAN BE RECALLED BY THEIR MAKER."

As they passed through the storm, blue, crystal clear skies awaited them on the other side. The heat from the blazing sun burned the rain away. Steam rose from the blacktop. It wasn't long before Hal spotted the exit off the highway.

"Oh, there it is," said Hal. Putting his blinker on, Hal pulled over in the right lane behind the eighteen wheelers. While they ambled along, the sun climbed a third of the way across the heavens. Hal pulled off the interstate onto a dirt road in the middle of nowhere. Every joint squeaked as the truck lurched down the rough road pitted with potholes. Being tossed from side to side, shook Leroy awake.

Scattered all over the low sloping hillsides lay the ancient grandfathers. Before history began, these stones were fiery tear drops from Father Sun. As Mother Earth gave birth to life, Father Sun rejoiced. Reigning down with love, his fiery golden tears splashed onto her green celestial body, filling her caverns with golden light. Eons later, these droplets of molten rock waited to be invited to ceremony and become fiery golden light once again.

The truck bounced a few more times before Hal parked along the dirt road. The doors creaked as they got out and stretched their legs. As the sun warmed their faces, a cool breeze came down from the north.

"How'd you find this place?" asked Leroy looking around at all the stones.

"Someone showed it to me on the way back from another dance. We've picked up stones here before," said Hal as he stretched his back. He was grateful the ointment worked. Otherwise he'd still be grouchy.

"Now, let me explain a few things. Don't go hurling stones in the back of the truck," said Hal bending over to pick up a stone. As he held the ancient one in his hand, a calm come over him.

"Now, this is your oldest living relative," Hal began. "These grandfathers are the backbone of Mother Earth. When you find one that calls to you, take a pinch of tobacco and make a gratitude offering. You're thanking this relative for helping you in the Inipi."

"Keep in mind, we're removing this stone from its home and bringing it back with us. So pray with gratitude to the spirit of these ancient ones and place them gently in back of the truck. The teachings of these ancestors help us to live."

Leroy got that look on his face again. This time Hal noticed it. "WHAT?"

"You really think a rock has a spirit?" Leroy's mind was bending with all this spiritual mumbo jumbo.

"OH, we're back here again," acknowledged Hal. "Listen, everything's got energy. Even science will tell you that."

"Right," Leroy acknowledged.

"Well, the way I see it," Hal continued. "Energy is just another name for Spirit. So if this stone has energy, it's got Spirit."

"That's simple enough," agreed Jed.

"HMMM," Leroy cogitated on all of this information.

"Don't get your panties in a knot, Leroy. Just keep your mind open to the possibility that there's a Greater Intelligence working here. See, when you practice the Old Ways, your spirit will wake up."

Leroy threw Hal a look he was familiar with. Contempt prior to investigation reared its ugly head again.

"I'm not done," Hal said. "After that, your heart will be strong and your mind will get peaceful. When your mind's quiet, it's possible to ride out any storm. This way, you're not letting outside conditions twist up your insides. It took me a while to walk with the Power of Great Spirit. Most good things I know came from the ancient ones. One elder explained it this way. He said we're all related. What the two-leggeds breath in, is what the trees breath out. We're here to be helpful each other."

None of this spiritual talk sunk in with Leroy very far. But he listened out of respect. One thing Hal pounded into his thick skull was having respect for All That Is. Even things he didn't understand.

"How many stones do you want?" asked Leroy when Hal was done explaining.

Hal sighed a breath of relief. He wasn't up to alligator

wrestling today. "I figure, if we get 25 a piece, that'd make for a good stone run. Make sure you pick stones somewhere between the size of a good cantaloupe but smaller than a watermelon. You got to be able to pick it up on the end of a pitchfork, without breaking your back. Understood?"

"Yeah, we got it," said Jed as they went off in different directions. Moving through the stone patch, Jed heard Hal singing Sun Dance songs. Jed held a pinch of tobacco in his hand and made a prayer. He was grateful to be here with his boys. Afterward, he sprinkled the tobacco on the stone and gently gathered it up.

Racing off like a jack rabbit, Leroy chased down stones in a fury. As he held it in his hand, he tried to imagine that this pockmarked stone had a life force, but the realization came hard. With every prayer, his hard shell of contempt chipped away. His mind began to wonder how life all began. Whose story was true? Did we evolve from the apes? Or was there really a garden of Eden? While his mind raced with inquiry, he never lost sight of his mission and brought in as many stones as he could.

Kyle's mind was filled with Heyoka stories as he toddled off to gather stones. Carrying the stones to the truck, sweat poured off Kyle's brow. Since he started school, he spent a lot of time in front of the computer. This was the first exercise he'd gotten in a while. His cheeks were flushed red as he loaded his last stone in the truck. It felt good to be out here with his family and Hal, getting fresh air.

Standing behind the truck, Hal counted the stones. Kyle laid his last one down. "Well Kyle, that makes 99. One more and we got an even 100," said Hal.

"Back there," said Kyle as he wiped the sweat off his brow. "Was one that talked to me. It was pretty big, so I didn't think you'd want it."

"Well if it spoke to you, I'd bet it wants a ride to ceremony," laughed Hal. "Can you find it?"

"Oh, I know where it is. I passed it by every time. But I don't think I can pick it up," said Kyle. "It's pretty big."

"Well, come on and show me then," said Hal as the two of them walked through the stone patch. In the middle of the field, was a great grandmother. She was the size of a good Mexican watermelon.

"Well that's a real Bertha, Kyle. We had one that size in the lodge before. You got some tobacco?" asked Hal.

Surprised, Kyle reached for his tobacco. He offered it to Bertha. In a whisper, Kyle leaned over and told her thanks for all her help. As Kyle placed the tobacco on the stone, Hal stood on the other side. But as Hal leaned over, a searing pain shot through his back and he thought better of it.

"Hey Leroy, come here and help Kyle with this stone, would ya?" called Hal to where Leroy and Jed were standing. They both walked over.

"I thought you didn't want any that big," said Leroy when he caught sight of Bertha.

"Yeah, but this one's a talker. I think she wants to go," said Hal. "But if I pick her up, it'll be a long ride home with my back. If you each take a side, you can walk her over to the truck."

Looking up at Leroy, Kyle suddenly felt inferior. It was an old feeling. The one where he never measured up. Usually he'd give up and let someone else do it, but not this time.

As he watched, Jed noticed Kyle's hesitation and started to step in to take his place. Before Jed could move, Hal caught his arm and whispered to let the boys work it out.

"Okay Kyle, we'll pick it up together on 3," said Leroy taking charge. As he started counting off, they squatted facing each other. With their hands gripped tight around her jagged edges, they lifted this 100 pound grandma off the ground. Each step was deliberate as they wrestled her over to the truck. Close behind, Jed and Hal made sure the boys didn't stumble.

As the boys gently lifted Bertha onto the tail of the truck, Jed and Hal lent a hand.

"Well, I don't know if she'll make it into the fire," said Hal. "But she's a beauty."

"What are you going to do with her?" asked Leroy knowing it'd take a mighty strong man to lift her on the end of a pitch fork.

"I'm not sure, but she's coming with us," said Hal.

"Hey, you hungry?" asked Jed. "I got sandwiches that Vera made this morning."

"Oh, that sounds great," said Hal. "We'll have a tailgate picnic in the valley of the stones."

When their bellies were full, Hal closed the tailgate and secured it so it wouldn't come loose. As they headed back, Kyle and Leroy were lulled to sleep by the open road. An hour from home was the only big town with a WalMart. Needing supplies, Hal pulled into the parking lot and maneuvered the heavy load off to the side to avoid speed bumps. This way, the stones wouldn't jump in the back of the truck.

"Where are we?" said Leroy in a groggy voice.

"WalMart," said Jed as he reached for his wallet. "Hal needs supplies. You staying in the truck?"

"I don't know, I want to stretch my legs. Old Bertha worked my muscles," Leroy yawned.

"I didn't know I had all the muscles I'm feeling," said Kyle rubbing his arms.

"Try getting off the couch," said Leroy sarcastically.

"Shut up! Leroy," Kyle snarled.

"Oh yeah, make me dough boy!" scoffed Leroy.

"Hey! Knock it off," said Jed sternly as he turned around facing his sons. Getting out of the cross fire, Hal opened the creaking door. Hal surveyed the truck bed.

Everything looked good. Jed got out and approached Hal.

"Here, I want you to have this," said Jed as he pressed $50 into Hal's hand. "I wish it was more. I appreciate you all you've done with Leroy. I prayed a while back for Creator to send reinforcements. I hadn't seen Leroy in a year and Kyle was a mess. And now I got them both back in my life. Neither one of them is drunk. You had a lot to do with that. Thank you."

Looking in the palm of his hand, a large smile spread across Hal's face. "Well Jed, it seems both our prayers were answered. I was plum out of cash," Hal laughed. "Look, I just go where Creator sends me. Working with the boys, was my pleasure. It does my heart good to see them get sober. Listen, I'm running in to get supplies. I'll leave you to deal with Heckle and Jeckle."

"You got it," said Jed.

Walking through the double doors, Hal stood inside this sprawling department store. It was so large, he didn't know what direction to go first. He only needed a few sundry items and food. After searching down endless aisles, he finally found soap, toothpaste and a few groceries. He stopped for a moment in the cheese section. There, he found a round loaf of smoked Gouda cheese.

"Road food," Hal said out loud. Ohiya loved Gouda with crackers when they were on the road. *"Here you go, old buddy. I'll get you some for the spirit plate,"* thought Hal as he spoke to Ohiya in his mind. IIe placed the Gouda cheese and crackers in his cart.

By the time he ambled to the check out, Hal felt plum tuckered out. While he waited in line, he heard a familiar voice from the next check stand over. But he couldn't place from where.

"Honey, go find Emma! Make sure she hasn't found the only heroin addict in the Midwest," said the man gruffly to his wife as she walked away.

'*Emma*' thought Hal. '*Where do I know that voice from?*' Peering over the aisle, Hal spied a man with gray long hair. It was pushed down by a baseball cap and curled at the collar of his white IZOD shirt.

"Mr. Lewis?" said Hal hesitantly as the man turned around.

"Yes?" said the man with a pinched expression as he gave Hal the once over. Squinting behind his glasses, a look of recognition crossed his face. "Hal, is that you?"

"Yes, sir, it is," said Hal with respect.

"Ah, you don't have to call me sir. Those days are long past," said Mr. Lewis, as the two men shook hands. "Call me Roy, please."

"Okay Roy, you can still call me Hal," laughed Hal.

"Oh I remember that about you. You were always good for a laugh. How are you? And how'd you wind up in this godforsaken place?" said Roy.

"I drove up from Colorado and ended up stopping to meet a friend. I've been here for a few months now," said Hal. "I did some rodeo work in Colorado."

"Oh, how's that going? As I remember, you were one of the best horse whisperers I'd ever met. Are you still working with horses?" asked Roy

"Don't know much else I'm suited for," said Hal. "I worked for a short spell in drug rehab out West, after I worked on your ranch. But horses are my first love."

"Oh, drug rehab," groaned Roy. "That's a big racket right now in Malibu. I've never seen more mansions turned into rehab centers. They're charging $100 grand a month so your kid can watch their flat screen TV and get shuffled around to AA meetings and do art therapy."

"Sound like you got some experience, there," said Hal concerned.

"You remember Emma, my sweet little angel who rode on the white stallion with me?" asked Roy.

"Of course I remember Emma. I taught her to ride bareback around the ring," said Hal. "What happened?"

"She got mixed up with some wanna be gang bangers who made their nest in our gated community. It turns out the drug dealer lived in our neighborhood, right up the street," sighed Roy. "But we got him arrested. He was dealing to minors at the high school."

"Yeah, those drug dealers sure do like gated communities," said Hal.

"Well, Emma got strung out on heroin. It was bad. I was afraid we'd lose her. That's why we're out here. My brother's got a spread on the Missouri River. We bought the 60 acres next to him down on River Road near the reservation," said Roy.

"Sorry to hear about Emma. Heroin's tough to get clean from," said Hal.

"You're telling me," said Roy. "Listen, my horses are being shipped in about a week. Are you looking for work? I could use someone I can trust out here."

"As a matter of fact, I am. Where abouts on River Road are you?" asked Hal smiling inside at this stroke of good fortune.

"Well, the closest place is Kelly's Tavern. We're about 15 miles from there. It's in the middle of nowhere. But I had to get Emma away from that drug environment. She was in a coma for 48 hours from a drug overdose. I nearly lost my mind. I can't lose this kid," said this father as his voice choked up. "Ah, here they come now. Don't tell her what I told you. She'd have my head."

"No worries. I'm familiar with the drill," said Hal as he saw Emma and Roy's wife, Sally walk up.

Hal fixed his eyes on Emma, like he used to when she

was up on the horse. She was a little sprite back then. Her bouncy blonde head chattered away, until she caught his eye.

"HAL!!!" Emma squealed as she ran up and threw her arms around him.

Hal blushed as she planted a kiss on his cheek. "Hello there little girl," said Hal sweetly. "You're almost all grown up."

"I turned 19 last week!" Emma squealed. "I can't believe dad found you in WalMart! God must be listening to me. I told Him I can't stand this place. There's not one familiar face. And here you are!"

"I asked Hal if he'd come work with the horses," said Roy to Sally and his daughter.

"Oh, would you Hal? Please don't say no. We don't know a soul out here, except for Uncle Harry. Oh mama, we should have Hal over to dinner," squealed Emma. "You will come, won't you Hal?"

"Don't know how I'd say no to that invitation, Miss Emma," said Hal in a gentle voice.

"Well then, it's all settled," said Emma. "I still have the Arabian you trained me on."

"Ernie, what he must be about 24 years old by now," said Hal. "He was a fine horse. He loved to run."

As they waited in line, Emma chattered away. She filled Hal in on every detail of her young life. As he stood there, Hal realized he'd missed this little chatterbox since he left the West Coast. All time stopped as he listened to her zany adventures.

Walking towards the exit, Roy reached in his pocket for his wallet. He pulled out a couple of his business cards. "Hal, here's my card. Do you have a phone where I can reach you?"

"No, I don't but I'm not far from Kelly's Tavern. They got a pay phone there. I can call you tomorrow," said Hal.

"Oh then you're close by," said Roy looking relieved. Knowing he could trust Hal, eased his mind. "Listen, if you

374

know anybody who'd work cleaning stalls and feeding the horses once I get them out here, let me know. But I don't want any drinkers or dope users and I will drug test."

"I'll ask around," said Hal taking Roy's card and putting it in his wallet. "I'll be in touch." Roy and Hal shook hands. Emma gave Hal another hug. Walking away, Roy and Sally were happy to have found Hal in WalMart.

Shaking his head, Hal started whistling an old show tune as he walked back to the truck. Who'd a thought, here in the middle of the prairie, he'd run into one of the best horse ranchers in California. Little Emma doing heroin didn't set well with him. But they'd have time to talk about that.

By the time they got back to the house, it was early afternoon. Everybody was down by the Inipi site, getting the ground ready for the new willow. After he put the groceries away, Hal drove his truck close to the lodge. Tucked under some scrubs was a little red wagon. '*We could of used that today,*' he thought.

Hearing Hal's old truck rumble up, a bright smile crossed Ben's face. "*Right on time,*" Ben thought as he leaned into Hal's window and looked in at the tired, happy faces.

"You had a good run?" asked Ben.

"We did real good," said Hal. "Go have a look. We've got a hundred stones."

"Well, that will last us a while," said Ben pleased. "A few of the guys cleared the fire pit and took down the old lodge. I'll get them to help unload the truck, before we build the new lodge. I figure we can have a sunrise sweat for Leroy tomorrow."

"That sounds good," said Hal. "I need a hot one."

"Leroy," said Ben. "You ready to sweat tomorrow morning before sunrise?"

"Yeah, that's why we did all this, right," said Leroy.

"Well, then we got to talk about a few things. And if your mom's coming, you need to let her know," said Ben.

"I'll do that," said Jed. "I'm going by there after we get done."

It didn't take long for the men to unload the truck and put the ancient ancestors near the fire pit. While the men prepared the ground, the willow were soaking in the Missouri. Soaking made the willow bark easier to peel off. They'd use strips of willow bark to lash the willow spines together. Rebuilding the dome shaped Inipi took a while.

Before they rebuilt the lodge, they replaced the four willow flag poles in the four directions along the outer perimeter. Ben smudged a foot wide piece of yellow cloth with sage for the east flag pole. Then, he smudged a handful of tobacco and prayed, calling on the Higher Powers to bless and protect this sacred place. Placing the tobacco on the yellow cloth, Ben folded it over, making a prayer flag. Next, he took a strip of yellow cloth and tied the flag to the top of the willow pole. He made prayer flags for the south, west and north, as well. These prayer flags were placed in the four directions around the outer boundary of the Inipi site, creating a sacred circle.

In a few large strides, Hal walked across the earthen circle where the Inipi would be rebuilt. He planted a stick in the center. Then, he tied a 7 foot string to the stick. Holding the end of the string, he walked the border of the earthen circle. He measured the inner width of the Inipi from the center of the stone pit. This marked the outside border where the willows would go. This way, there'd be enough room for people to sit around the stone pit.

After Hal walked the perimeter of the earthen circle, he came to the east door. In a straight line, from east to west, was the east flag pole, the fire pit, the earthen altar, the east door of the Inipi, the stone pit at the center of the lodge, the west door of the Inipi and the west flag pole. This followed the path of the sun. On the east side of the fire pit was a half moon formed from the earth taken out of the fire pit.

Lying between the fire pit and the east door of the Inipi, was an earthen altar. This mound of earth came from inside the lodge. It was taken out of the stone pit, in the center of the Inipi. During the ceremony, the Cannupa and other Sacreds would be placed on the earthen altar. On the altar was a pipe rack made from willow. In the center of the earthen altar stood another longer forked willow with two branches. This forked willow represented the Tree of Life. The fork represented the world of duality, Light and dark, the good and the not so good.

Hal stood with his feet a shoulder's width apart in the east door before the willow spines were planted and faced the west. "Okay, Leroy, I want you to stand opposite of me in the west. We'll measure how wide the east and west doors will be. After that, we'll measure the north and south doors. About where your feet are, is where we'll dig the holes for the doors. You should be able to get your shoulders through the door with room to spare. One day, you'll build an Inipi by yourself."

At the river, Jed and Kyle peeled off the willow bark and placed it in a water filled bucket to keep the bark moist. The bark would be used for lashing the willows together to form the dome of the Inipi.

Frank and Ernie dug the first 8 holes around the earthen circle. They were evenly spaced to mark the four doors of the four directions. Between the doors, they dug another 8 holes, evenly spaced for the support willow spine. In all, sixteen fresh holes were dug around the lodge to place the willows in.

Before each willow spine was placed in the hole, Ben prayed with tobacco and placed it in the hole. He called on Great Spirit to send His Spirit-helpers to bless and protect this sacred place.

Afterward, the 16 willow spines were placed in freshly dug holes, framing the earthen circle. The earth was packed around each one. This is where the tender work of building the Inipi began. The men gently coaxed the willows to bend by placing their hind foot at the base of the willow. Gently, they bent it over their back, ever mindful not to pressure the willow too hard or it would snap. Broken willow wouldn't hold up the blankets and tarps.

In the West, Leroy gently bent a willow spine towards Hal, who bent his willow spine from the east. Once the tips of the willow overlapped, Ernie quickly lashed them together with the wet willow bark. After they finished the east-west doors, Hal and Leroy moved towards the north-south doors. Once the 16 willow spines were lashed together with strips of willow bark, it formed the top of the dome. If the willows were forced to bend too fast, they'd split and another willow had to be put in it's place.

After the willow dome was formed, three willow ribs were added around the body of the Inipi and lashed to the frame. This created the womb of Mother Earth. In the center of the Inipi, over the stone pit, Ben lashed a small circle made of willow branches to the top of the dome. Within the circle, the pattern formed an eight-pointed star. Now, the Inipi was connected to the star fire from home in the Star Nation. While Ben put on the finishing lash, he looked over his shoulder to the west. The endless sky was ablaze with color as the sun began to set.

There was an abundant wood pile stacked near the fire pit. Jed presented Ben with a new pitch fork for the fire. He'd noticed the worn condition of the old one. Like a precious stone, Bertha was placed in the center of the half moon crescent which went around the east side of the fire pit.

After a long day, Leroy, Hal and Ben were in the small kitchen having dinner. From his pocket, Leroy pulled out a CD. He bought it from a big drum group standing in front of WalMart. They'd run out of money on their way to Montana and were selling their CD for $5.

"Hey," said Leroy holding the CD. "I got this from a drum group in front of WalMart. Trouble is, I don't have a CD player."

"Let me see that," said Ben looking at the cover of the CD. "I think there's a player on the top of the book shelf over there. One of my grand kids left it here."

"WAKANKDISKA," said Hal reading the label.

"It means WHITE LIGHTNING," said Leroy as he plugged the CD player.

"I know what it means," said Hal. "I knew a drum group out in Montana. Were these guys standing outside WalMart?"

"Yeah, I ran in to get a slice of pizza, but bought this CD instead," said Leroy. "They were pretty desperate to get home."

After Leroy put the CD in the player, the small kitchen was filled with Big Drum music. Standing near the sink, Ben's feet started moving in intricate movements. The old wooden floorboards creaked in time as his feet glided across the floor. He remembered the steps of all the dances he'd competed in.

"Hey Ben, I didn't know you could move like that," said Leroy.

"Old Ben here was a fancy dancer. He won big competitions at the Powwow," said Hal watching Ben's steps.

Intrigued, Leroy got up and followed Ben's steps around the kitchen. The song moved through his soul. He watched Ben's intricate dance steps.

"Follow me this way," said Ben instructing Leroy on how to do it. "Listen with your heart, not your head. Let your feet follow the heartbeat of the Mother. Your feet are dancing with her heart now."

CHAPTER TEN: WARRIOR INIPI CEREMONY

I AM...

I AM the storm, the sun
The flowers that come
From spring rain, April showers
I AM the thunder, full of power

I AM the seed, the Earth
The cycle through death and birth
The wind that shakes acorns free
The stillness where souls long to be

I AM the rainbow, each and every hue
The deepest shades of violet and blue
I AM the darkness, the Light
Snow geese in flight

I AM the majesty of mountains blue
The heart that beats true
The courage of undaunted love
The song of Angels high above

I AM this and so much more

Knocking patiently on Heaven's door
Don't limit me or make me small
For that is not my truth at all

I AM the eagle's breath
On a cold September morn
I AM a baby's smile
Three days after it's born

I AM the eye of the heart
That sees into your soul
I AM the lover's kiss
And the heart he gently stole

For this I AM and please remember
Some holy night in December
When hearts are high, spirits soar
Perhaps you will think of me once more

Walking out into a field of tall grasses, Ben spied an enormous oak tree. Having lived more than a century, its mighty trunk was wide. It provided shelter for all the Creatures. As he walked towards the oak, Ben saw a precious bear cub tangled in the outer limbs. It cried out as it made its way through the branches.

Perched nearby, on the oak's outer limbs was a golden eagle. When Ben walked near the tree, an eagle feather fluttered towards the ground. As Ben bent over to pick up the eagle feather, three more golden eagles and a white eagle swooped down low, close to the Earth. Turning around, Ben watched them land. Quietly he walked up behind the white eagle. It was a large raptor, with all white feathers.

Ben stood behind it. Then gently, he embraced the white eagle, placing his right hand under the talons. His left hand was near the eagle's beak. Whispering in the eagle's ear, Ben asked, "Will you be mine?" Taking Ben's forefinger in his beak, the eagle gently squeezed his reply, "Yes."

The moonlight shone brightly through the kitchen window as Ben opened his eyes. He still felt the eagle's talons in his right hand and the soft down feathers on his cheek.

As his spirit settled back into his body, he returned to consciousness. While this powerful medicine dream lingered, Ben reached over to Elsie's side of the bed. Often, he told her all his dreams. But her pillow was empty. He remembered she was gone. "Where are you, my ladylove?"

In the wee small hours before sunrise, the morning stars sang in their celestial choir. While the Star Nation took notice, Frank and Ernie pulled up at the Inipi site and left the truck headlights on. Patches of deep mist still clung to the Missouri as the wind came to push it away. The two men got ready to keep fire for Leroy's warrior lodge.

"It's kinda chilly this morning," said Frank as he put on an Pendleton jacket.

"I like it," said Ernie as he pulled his sweatshirt on.

With his flashlight upon his forehead, Frank raked the ground around the fire pit. For Ernie, building a fire came second nature as he carefully laid down four logs in a north-south direction. On top of those, he placed four more logs in and east-west direction. Circled around the fire pit lay the virgin Stone People. Ernie would place them in the sacred fire after he made a tobacco prayer for each one. This way he prepared them for their purification ceremony. Gently, he stacked the stones on top of the wood base. Afterward, he placed more logs around the stones, until they were completely

382

covered. The structure of wood looked like a tipi.

Before he struck the match, Ernie took some tobacco and made a prayer. It was the first prayer of the ceremony. Afterward, he put the tobacco on the kindling and struck a match, lighting the Sacred Fire. While the fire began to burn, he sang a song to the Stone People, thanking them for their blessing.

The moonlight danced across the waters of the Missouri. It enchanted the souls of those yet to awaken, to the peace deep within. An early morning symphony caroled with its choir of crickets and the occasional low croak of bullfrogs. Together, they all sang in chorus along the river bank. Sound came from every direction. Its melody was all encompassing, beautiful and peaceful.

Hunkered down in front of the fire, Hal, Leroy and Jed waited in quiet anticipation, while Ernie fanned the flames. The purification ceremony for the Inyan Oyate had begun. While the Stone People were brought back to their original condition, Hal kept his sights to the mission ahead: freeing a warrior from the mistakes of his past.

Frank and Ernie had kept fire for Ben for many years. The movements of the fire place were worn deep into their souls. Though the fire hadn't singed the hair off Ernie's arms since Elsie passed away, he made the sacrifice willingly. He was grateful to be at the fire place again.

As the fire moved slowly through the wood shaped tipi, Hal placed his worn hand drum next to the earthen altar. The heat would tune it up. The wind gently swayed through the eagle feathers hanging from the forked end of the willow Tree of Life. The forked end represented the dual nature of life, Light and dark, the good and the not so good.

On the altar, Ernie placed the buffalo skull facing the fire. On each side of the east door, he placed deer antlers so no one crossed the spirit pathway. There were several buckets of water standing ready. Once the fire was lit, Hal took his eagle fan and smudged the entire area. He invited all the loving spirits to stay and gave notice to the disgruntled ones to make their way elsewhere.

Once the area was clear, Hal sat down next to Jed and Leroy huddled around the fire. "Now I want to explain a few things, so you understand the movements of Spirit around the Inipi," said Hal in a low, gentle voice. "See those willow flag poles in the four directions around the lodge and the fire place?" They nodded.

In the four directions on the outer perimeter, stood four willow flag poles. Near the top, was a colored piece of cloth, which held a tobacco prayer. The colors represented the Four Elements: Earth, Fire, Air and Water. The four elementals were the original entities who first came to earth. They were the original inhabitants.

"Well," Hal went on. "In those cloth bundles at the top of the pole is a tobacco prayer. The prayer asks the Spirits to protect this sacred place. Once we're inside those flags, we need to be respectful and mind what we say. After that fire is lit and the spirits are called, everything we say is a prayer. And if you start talking about Beelzebub, well, he'll show up to. Cuz you invited him."

"What do you mean?" asked Leroy in disbelief.

"Well, let me tell you a little story," Hal started. "A woman friend of mine, was studying this African-Cuban religion. One night, she's at a woman's lodge. Before the Inipi, she's sitting around the fireplace talking to her friends. Thinking nothing of it, she speaks the name of the trickster god from Africa. It didn't seem like a big deal. That is, until she sat inside the lodge and the stones came in cold. Then, it struck her. She called this trickster's name. I know it sounds crazy. But by the second round, those girls were freezing inside the Inipi. And it never warmed up. So be mindful of whose name you speak when your around the fire place."

"What, you think this trickster god showed up and made

those stones grow cold?" asked Leroy disbelieving.

"I can't tell you if the trickster did it or not. But she called him and that's what happened. A trickster spirit could do that," Hal explained.

Leroy scoffed.

"Look Leroy," Hal started. "When Ernie made the first tobacco prayer and lit the fire, I'll guarantee you he called on Great Spirit and the Spirit-helpers."

"But that don't explain a trickster," Leroy held his ground.

"Look, all I know is, she called his name and the stones came in cold. They were in a blazing fire, just like this one. So you figure it out," said Hal sternly not wanting to alligator wrestle with Leroy this morning.

"I believe that," said Jed after cogitating on it for a minute. "Those Africans do their ceremony with drums and fire, the same way we do. We were both tribal societies. So it makes sense. If you call their god around a fire, he'd show up. But you just mentioned Beelzebub, you might need to take care of that."

"Um," sounded Hal in agreement. "Well, you probably right. I'll take care of that." Hal lit some sage and smudged off.

"Okay, that leads right into the next thing I want to say. See from where big Bertha is sitting in the middle of the half moon in the east?" Hal pointed and they nodded in agreement.

"Well, from Bertha, across the fire, over the altar and through the east door is the Spirit Pathway," pointed Hal in a sweeping motion. "The reason Ernie placed antlers on each side of the doorway, is so we don't cross the Spirit Pathway once the fire is lit. You can go around the lodge or around the fire, but don't cross between the fire and the east door of the Inipi. I don't want to perform an exorcism, if you collide with a spirit moving along this pathway," said Hal with a smile.

Mesmerized by the fire, Leroy had a far away look in his

eye. He contemplated whether any of what Hal said was true. All this talk about spirits and tricksters pressed into a painful, disappointed place that Leroy shut off long ago. Hal may as well have talked about the Easter bunny or Santa Claus. Leroy knew they didn't exist since he was eight years old.

"Earth to Leroy, Earth to Leroy," said Hal jokingly.

"Yeah, I'm listening," said Leroy a little edgy. "So this is a stupid question, but do you believe in Santa Claus?"

"What kind of question is that?" Hal asked wondering where he found this knucklehead.

"Well, if I'm gonna believe in spirits, I may as well believe in Santa Claus," said Leroy. "And I said goodbye to that dude a long time ago. If I believe a trickster can make the stones go cold. Then, what about the fat man in the red suit who comes around every December with his flying reindeer?"

"Oh that's my fault," Jed groaned. "Leroy caught me putting the presents under the tree late one Christmas Eve. I was drunk . Vera convinced the kids that Santa came Christmas eve, leaving presents for them to open on Christmas morning. I was too drunk to be quiet and Leroy heard me," Jed explained turning to his son. "You must have been about eight years old. I'll never forget the look on your face. You thought you finally caught Santa Claus. But, instead you saw me stumbling around with presents and my whiskey bottle. You were so disappointed. It ruined Christmas forever after that."

"Caught you red handed, did he," said Hal seeing the dilemma. Many children suffered at the hands of drunken parents. Hal reckoned, most personality disorders that kids were diagnosed with, resulted from having their innocence pummeled out of them through neglect and abuse. There's no trust in an alcoholic home. Trust takes years to build and a second to destroy. Drunken parents rarely keep their word.

"Afraid so," said Jed realizing how an awful moment jaded Leroy every Christmas thereafter.

For the longest time, Hal couldn't make head or tails about where Leroy's spiritual bankruptcy stemmed from. But he could see it now. "So you let one rotten moment of your dad's drunkenness turn you off from the Spirit of Christmas forever?"

"They lied to me," said Leroy in a soft voice. "And if they lied to me about Christmas, then I figured they lied about God, Jesus Christ and everything else. After that, I decided if I couldn't see it, I wasn't going to believe it."

"So that's the chicken bone you're choking on, Leroy?" asked Hal seeing how old his wound was. "That's a big decision for a little boy to make. But ignorance of the law doesn't mean you're exempt from it."

"What's that suppose to mean," said Leroy a little edgy.

"Well, closing your mind to the Spirit of the Universe, because your dad was drunk, doesn't mean there's no Spirit of the Universe. For all I know, there's a heavenly band of Angels coming to set you free right now. But you're too blinded by hate to see them," Hal said as Leroy started to protest.

"Who said anything about Angels?"

"Well, you can call them Spirit-helpers or Spirit-guides. You'll hear their voice whispering on the wind, if you got ears to hear," Hal continued. "It's not about what you can see, taste or touch. With Spirit, you'll feel it stir down deep right here," said Hal pointing to Leroy's gut. "The love of Creator carries you through the hard times, even when you're in the belly of a whale and can't see your way out."

"As far as Christmas goes..." Hal went on. "Since I've been sober, if there was an AA meeting nearby, I was never alone on Christmas. I don't know if there's a bearded fella riding around the heavens on a sleigh with 8 reindeer. But the Spirit of Christmas and thanksgiving have been in my life since I got sober."

"So Santa lives in AA?" Leroy jested sheepishly.

"Naw, it's more than that," Hal said. "It's the Spirit of

Christmas, where getting is meaningless and giving is all. When I give, my heart feels full. When I'm thinking about myself, what I'm going to get or what I didn't get. It's never enough and I'm miserable. It's as simple as that."

After Hal finished talking, Ernie came over with a charcoal paste. He handed it to Hal. "Ben wants you to paint Leroy's face with this," said Ernie as he handed Hal the black paste.

"This is for the blood on your hands, Leroy," said Hal as he put his fingers into the black paste and smeared it across Leroy's face. "Creator will wash you clean from that shame inside the Inipi."

Soft moonlight lit the driveway as Vera and Kyle rushed to put the food for the feast in the car. Vera was a little frantic this morning, going to her first Inipi. But she trusted Ben. He explained the workings of the Inipi to her. She'd sit right near him and he'd guide her through. When she asked about praying to Jesus, all Ben said was to quietly invite Christ in the lodge. Leroy needed all the help he could get. But not to evangelized anyone. Watching the change in Leroy was profound. His smile made her heart jump. Vera loved her sons. Their sobriety was a prayer answered.

Walking down the dirt road with his flash light, Ben's breath made steam as he headed towards the Missouri. When he crossed the Powwow grounds, Vera and Kyle drove up fast. A cloud of dust kicked up behind their wheels.

"Morning Ben," Vera waved as she got out of the car. She wore a short sleeved dress which covered her body down to her ankles. A few days before, she found the dress at the local thrift store. Ben waved and waited for them to catch up.

"How are you this morning?" asked Ben as Vera and Kyle walked up. Seeing them come to an Inipi was something he never expected to witness. Especially with Vera's staunch Christian views.

"We're good," said Vera a little out of breath. "I have all

kinds of breakfast food in the backseat of the car."

"Oh, that's good," said Ben as they headed down the trail. "Nothing tastes better than good food after a lodge. I'll have Ernie get it after the third round."

A cool breeze greeted Ben as he walked towards the blazing fire. "Good morning Tah-tay," Ben whispered as her spirit twirled a whirlwind of ash around the fire pit. Ben warmed his hands by the fire. It felt good to be here this morning.

"Morning Ben," said Ernie as Ben walked up.

"Hey Ernie," said Ben shaking Ernie's hand. "Good fire. The stone's are showing. You don't want to let their backsides get cold."

"I'll get on that," said Ernie as he covered them with wood. "They'll be ready in ten minutes or so."

"Thanks for taking care of the fire this morning," Ben smiled. "Vera's got breakfast in her car. Maybe you and Frank can get it out about 3rd round."

"Sure thing," said Ernie. "She's a good cook."

Walking around the fire pit, Ben greeted everyone before he sat down with the family to talk. The warmth from the flames felt good as he looked onto their expectant faces. He wanted to make sure they understood the movements of the lodge before they went in. The crackling fire dispelled the darkness around the fireplace. As he sat down, Ben felt Elsie's spirit nearby.

"Hal," said Ben motioning for Hal to come over.

"Yeah," said Hal.

"You know the pipe loading song?" asked Ben meeting Hal's gaze. Elsie always sang it for him.

"I wouldn't be much of a Sun Dancer, if I didn't," chuckled Hal. "I know a few other songs if you want help singing in there."

"That's good to know," said Ben. "How about you set the stones for me this morning."

"I'd be honored," said Hal feeling this ceremony come alive.

"Well then, I guess we better get started," said Ben.

In the last hour before dawn, Ben made his way around the fire. He stood in the fire pit in front of the earthen altar. The air was crisp. All along the river, the crickets chirped away before the night slowly gave way to first light.

"Morning everybody," Ben started. "Thanks for getting up so early to help Leroy with his prayer. We're starting before sunrise. The dark surrounding us represents what we don't know. When we drift away from Creator, we live in the dark. But every morning, sunlight overcomes the night. Its light casts out the shadows. In the Inipi, the love of Creator cleanses our hearts. What happened to Leroy during the war, will be cleansed. In a humble way, we ask Creator for a healing for Leroy and you, his family. I know you suffered too."

"In a moment, I'll load this sacred pipe. When Hal starts singing, think about your prayers. If you want, take a pinch of tobacco and pray with it. Then, give the tobacco to the fire. Go ahead and greet the fire and the Stone People. The stones came a ways to be here. They're our oldest living ancestors. They've been here since the dawn of time. They can handle all our sorrow and concerns. They've seen every tragedy and miracle. Right now, the grandfathers are in their ceremony, being purified by fire. When they come in the lodge, you'll give them your prayers. Then, I'll pour water on the stones and the steam will carry our prayers up."

"The stones are our oldest living ancestors, but so is the fire, the water and the air. In the Inipi, we work with the Four Elements. Without them, it'd be impossible to have life on Mother Earth. I know you can only live about six minutes without air. And maybe four days without water. But without fire from the sun, nothing on Mother Earth would grow. So we honor the Nature Spirits. They're the oldest living relatives here."

"Now, Hal brought me to my first Inipi. I'm honored to have him place the stones. Since we fulfilled our Sun Dance commitments, we're allowed to carry out this ceremony. We were taught by the Elders. They were brave enough to carry the Old Ways through the dark times, when the US government made them illegal for us to practice. That being said, I'm not a priest. Whatever wrongdoing you've done, is between you and Creator. I'll sit behind the bucket and run the ceremony."

"We'll have four rounds. When the door's closed, I'll sing medicine songs. That's a good time to pray. Creator knows what you need, so pray hard. After I sing about 4 songs, the door will open. Now, it's going to get hot in there. So if you're having a hard time, get close to the Mother. Lay down on her and breathe in the cool air. She'll take care of you. Ernie tells me the stones are ready, so let's get started."

Before Ben got there, the men covered the lodge with blankets and canvas tarps. Ernie crawled inside the Inipi to make sure no light came in. Everything was ready to go. Ben opened his battered suitcase and got out his Cannupa. As he knelt before the earthen altar, the firelight reflected in his spectacles. He placed the pipe stem and pipe stone bowl on his altar clothe. Next to it, he put a braid of sweet grass, Chanshasha (a red willow bark mix) and his eagle bone whistle. Ernie filled an abalone shell filled with a layer of dirt and hot coals. He carried it over with deer antlers and placed it near Ben. When Ben put the sweet grass on the hot coals, the smoke curled through the air. It gave the air a sweet honeyed scent.

With the smoke from the sweet grass, Ben carefully smudged off his Sacreds before loading his Cannupa. Then he took his eagle bone whistle and called to his ancestors of the four directions.

With drum in hand, Hal started singing the pipe loading song. "Kola lecel lecun wo, Kola lecel lecun wo, Kola lecel lecun wo, Hey..."

With each pinch of Chan-shasha, Ben honored one of the directions and called on Creator for help. He made prayers for Leroy, his family, the spirits of Leroy's fellow soldiers and the spirits of those Leroy killed in combat. Ben asked for healing and forgiveness.

To repair the damage done, a sincere amends must be made. It had to be more than words. There had to be a change of heart. From experience, Ben knew, the words "I'm sorry" didn't mean much. Especially from alcoholics. Most of the time, those shallow words were just another invitation to do the harm again.

To achieve healing, forgiveness was necessary from both sides of the veil. Each party had to accept responsibility for the harm they created. After forgiveness was granted, Great Spirit could restore His children to the way they were, before the doctoring was needed. When Creator undid the past through forgiveness, He released the future and cleared the debt His children had accumulated. This healing happened in a twinkling of an eye.

By working the first 8 steps, Leroy prepared himself to make amends and clear away his wreckage. This left the last step to Creator. For the miracle of healing to take place, purification must come first.

While Hal sang the pipe loading song, Leroy held the pinch of tobacco in his hand. Staring into the fire, he watched the flames devour the wood. As the logs crumbled to embers, a few glowing stones were visible. His prayer for healing was great. He whispered to Creator. Recognizing one of their own, the Warriors from the Holy Realms, answered the call.

Once the Cannupa was loaded, Ben offered it to all the directions and placed it on the pipe rack. Swaying in the breeze, several eagle feathers hung from the Tree of Life. Hal finished his song and they shook hands. It was good.

"Okay everybody," said Ben as he pushed himself up. "Time to change into our sweat clothes. I'll be right back and then we'll go in."

After changing into his shorts, Ben took a pinch of tobacco and greeted the fire spirits and the stones. Then, he tossed it into the flames. Everyone was lined up, ready to go in.

"Vera, follow me in, on your hands and knees when I call for you. Leroy, you come in next and sit opposite of the door. Jed, you'll be on the other side of Leroy. And Kyle, sit between your dad and Hal. There'll be plenty of room to stretch out," said Ben giving his last minute instructions. Standing by the door, Ernie smudged everyone off as they went in.

As the sage smoke curled around him, Ben knelt down at the door. His forehead touched the Earth. He whispered 'Aho Mitakuye Oyasin' and crawled clockwise around the womb of Mother Earth. Taking his place by the door, he felt Elsie's spirit settle in next to him. A warm smile filled his innards as he touched the cool Earth where Elsie took her place. "Well old girl, looks like I'll have to ask Vera to put cedar on the stones, since you're out of body right now," Ben whispered out loud. "But don't fret. You're still my girl."

"Ernie, send in Vera and everybody else," called Ben out the door.

Feeling a little awkward, Vera walked up to the Inipi door. Ernie smudged her off from head to toe. The firelight guided her as she knelt down and put her head on the Earth. "Aho Mitakuye Oyasin" she said, honoring all her relatives. She crawled clockwise around the lodge to where Ben directed her to sit. The Earth felt cool against her knees and hands. After everyone took their places, a calmness settled into the lodge. Hal took his place opposite Ben on the other side of the door.

"Ernie," called Ben. "Hand in the cedar and the antlers." Holding onto the antlers, Hal passed on the cedar bag until it came to Ben.

"Now Vera, Elsie always put cedar on the stones. I'd like to ask you to do it. Just take a pinch and put it on the stone after I touch it with my pipe. Will you do that?" asked Ben.

"Of course," said Vera feeling honored.

"After all the stones come in, save a pinch of cedar. With that, you'll give a blessing to our fire keepers. They gave up their seats in here to take care of us," instructed Ben as he circled the cedar over the stone pit and handed it to Vera.

"Alright Ernie, hand in my Cannupa and bring us seven," said Ben. Ernie took the prayer filled sacred pipe from the earthen altar and handed it to Ben.

With a pitchfork, Ernie took the glowing grandfathers from the fire. After Frank dusted them off with a whisk broom, Ernie brought them to the door. Silence filled the Inipi.

With his charcoal painted face, Leroy stared at the fire and watched the stones come in. His guts churned with raw emotions as he anticipated what was coming. A powerful heat radiated off the stones as Hal placed them in the stone pit. With the antlers, Hal tenderly picked them up from the pitchfork. The first stones he placed in the four directions, East, South, West and North. Then one for Father Sky, the next for Mother Earth and the seventh stone for the sacred place within, the heart of the Wakan.

Ben gently touched his Cannupa to the stone. Then Vera placed a pinch of cedar on each one, whispering "Aho Mitakuye Oyasin." The cedar crackled and popped. Its smoke curled around the lodge. After all the stones came in, Ben handed Ernie his Cannupa and the cedar bag. Hal passed out the antlers.

"Okay, Ernie bring me the water bucket and my dipper," said Ben. Ernie placed the sacred pipe on the altar and handed in the bucket. Together, Hal and Ben grabbed handle. They brought the water bucket over the stone pit, touching the bottom to the glowing ancestors. A bit of water splashed over the sides onto the glowing stones. The water spit and sputtered, shooting hot steam into the air.

"This is the water of life, Mni wichoni. Without it we wouldn't live," said Ben as he filled the dipper. Pouring it back into the bucket, the water sang its song. "It's the first medicine given to our people. When I pour it on the grandfathers, its spirit rises as steam. Take it in. Through the breath of the Stone People, Great Spirit will give you strength and cleanse you of impurities. Ask Him to take away the sickness from your body and mind. Ask Him to bless your life. Give thanks to the Spirit of Water for all the thirsty moments it has quenched." For a moment, a peaceful silence filled the lodge. The only sound was the water singing.

"Ernie, Frank poke your head in here," said Ben. As they knelt at the door, Ben whispered to Vera to give her blessing.

"Frank, Ernie, I've known you all my life. Thanks for getting up early, starting the fire and making this ceremony ready for Leroy. Most of all, thanks for your sobriety and helping my sons and husband with theirs. May God bless you always," said Vera putting cedar on the stones. Its smoke curled through the air. With his eagle fan, Ben blessed the fire keepers with the cedar smoke.

While the door was still open, Ben filled the dipper and splashed water on the stones. Searing steam filled the Inipi as water bubbled and gurgled against the glowing stones. "Okay, pass in my drum and close it up," called Ben to Ernie.

With the door closed, Leroy only saw the glow of the grandfathers. Their radiance cast a soft light on everyone. Suddenly, Ben splashed dipper after dipper of water on the stones. A sizzling heat filled the Inipi as the water boiled and sputtered. Everyone was blessed with the breath of the Stone People.

"Thanks everyone for coming to help Leroy with his prayer," Ben started in a gentle voice. "He's done a lot of work to prepare. This is a day of reckoning. A day of settling accounts. Warriors have a special place with our people. They sacrifice their innocence by being forced to see and do things they'd rather forget. The madness of war pollutes their souls and casts a dark shadow over their lives." Ben tossed more water on the stones. The steam filled Leroy's nostrils as he stared at the stones, listening to Ben's voice.

"Now, all this hate weakens a warrior's spirit. It opens an ugly door, letting in harmful elements, that come through and enter the body. That heartache he carries from past mistakes, is like a magnet. It draws the same lesson to him over and over. He's bound to make the same mistake, unless he cleans it up. Understand?" Ben emphasized. "If he doesn't, the spirits of depression and alcohol hover around him. Their whispers are a death song."

"This new lodge, with her virgin stones and fresh willow, was built to let Creator cleanse our souls of harmful poisons. When we clean up our side of the street, He makes us new." Splashing more water on the stones, Ben pondered how to ease the newcomer's fear of this Old Way of prayer.

"Within our hearts, is a sacred fire. It never dies. It is the heart flame of Creator. It is what He sees when He looks at us. When we dishonor Him by harming His children, a wet blanket smothers our sacred heart fire. Our light grows dim. Shamefaced, our heart is heavy with a blanket of wrongdoing."

"This blanket of shame makes us vulnerable to wicked forces we can't see. The hell hounds of the underworld dog our every step. Their jaws clamp onto our souls and drag us down by filling our hearts with hate and despair."

"But there is a solution," Ben paused wondering if he'd gone overboard. "That's why we're here. To reckon our accounts, we must right the wrongs we've done others, not just with words but with actions. Everything we do to someone else, we do to ourselves. The Spirits know about our wrongdoing. So does Creator."

"Now Leroy, the work in front of you, is between you and Creator. The souls of your team are here, as well as those you killed in battle. This is a chance to right a serious wrong. Understand, for this to work, your amends better be sincere.

Because unlike humans, spirits can't be fooled by whitewash. Ever since Cain and Abel, men have had blood on their hands. Yet Creator never gave us permission to kill anybody. The black on your face is for the shame you did to the Great Mystery. As warriors, sometimes our choices get pretty narrow. Often it's kill or be killed. Many are haunted by their past. But, only those who carry battle scars, know the meaning of peace. This is your chance Leroy, to make it right. Make good use of it."

"In this Inipi, we'll have four rounds. I'll sing four songs each round. Maybe more, if I feel like it. This round will be for the brothers you lost in battle. Just speak to them, as if they were sitting right in front of you. Feel whatever guilt you've shoved away. Let the heartache bubble up from deep inside, so it don't hold you back anymore. Give your heartache to the grandfathers. They can handle it. Your brothers on the other side feel the grief, remorse and pain you carry. It ties them to you through a dark cord. After you make a sincere amends, let go of the grief. Ask Creator and the Spirit-helpers to cut the dark cord that binds you together. This will let your brothers fly free."

"The second round, will be for those you killed in battle. Now, it don't matter if you meant to kill them or not. Collateral damage is still killing. When we kill someone, we rob them of their chance at life. Souls wait in long lines to come here to complete their divine mission. Bear this in mind, when you ask for forgiveness. Clear away this unfinished business with a true amends. Only forgiveness will do the job. Again, ask Creator and the Spirit-helpers to cut the dark cord that binds you together. This allows these spirits to go home."

"The third round is a giveaway round, a lot like AA's Step Seven. We'll dedicate it to healing the harm you did to yourself and the pain you caused others. This is a living amends. Here, ask Creator how to right your faulty thinking and any wrongdoing. Ask Him to remove your bad habits and shortcomings and replace them with a good way of life. After you make your amends, you'll walk a free man. You'll finally be unchained from the mistakes of the past."

"The fourth round is for thanksgiving. Creator gave us life and we came here to try it out. It doesn't matter if you like the way it's going. It matters how you choose to live. There are only two paths, service to self and service to others. Which did you choose? From where I'm sitting, the self-serving are fairly predictable. In most cases, unhappiness comes from selfishness. These two paths lead in opposite directions. Choose your path and walk in gratitude for another day of living."

"Creator won't render us clean as snow without our help. He'll clean out the hate, indifference, arrogance and despair, if we ask. But, we got to do our part. After that, we'll walk in strength and beauty."

"Now, a disturbed mind can't hear Creator's voice. It's got static like the old AM radio. After He cleans us up, we'll have new eyes. Our hearts will be tender again. Ask Creator to surround you in the mantle of His Love. That way you'll be forever protected from the shadows."

Pouring more water on the stones, Ben listened as they sizzled and gurgled. The breath of the Stone People filled the lodge. Ben called on the Higher Powers as he picked up his drum and kept time with the heartbeat of Mother Earth.

"Wiyohpeyatakiya etonwan yo," Ben sang as he called in the spirits of the four directions. His medicine songs were carried by the four winds. His voice called to the Heart of Creator.

Closing his eyes, Leroy saw the faces of his men. In his mind, he was catapulted back to the battlefield. He heard their anguished cries as the bombs exploded and gunshots echoed through the hills. The smell of burning gunpowder and fresh blood filled his nostrils as he walked through the killing fields.

Leroy forced himself to stay focused and remembered what Ben told him to do. Make sincere amends. Memory after memory flooded through his mind. Leroy saw his men stand in front of him and felt overwhelmed with grief. He reached out to each one, whispering words of solace. He apologized for putting them in harm's way, for not seeing the danger lying in wait for them. He felt responsible for their lives. They trusted him.

Salty tears flowed down his cheeks. He tasted the charcoal on his lips as the pelting steam washed it away. With each amends, the unfinished business between them cleared. His heart began to feel lighter. His men smiled with relief. Their earthly mission was completed. Before they departed the Inipi, they saluted Leroy. He saluted back. Turning around, they walked into the mist. Sobbing quietly, the pain in his heart eased. He could finally let his men go. He asked the Higher Powers to cut the cords and they went home.

As the spirits of these brave warriors soared out the door, Ben poured more and more water on the stones. He honored their release. Outside the West Gate, waited grandparents, Elders and Spirit-helpers. They came to guide the departed soldiers home. As they moved towards the Higher Realms, the anguish from their earthly lives faded away. They were embraced by the Love of Creator.

The pressing heaviness in the lodge began to ease. Ben finished his fourth song. Opening his eyes, Ben emptied the bucket of water on the stones. A rush of searing steam filled the lodge.

"Is everyone okay," Ben asked as the water gurgled.

"Yeah" was the general response.

"Okay, let's open the door," said Ben as they shouted "Aho Mitakuye Oyasin!"

Hearing the last song end, Ernie waited nearby. Stars twinkled high above. There was no sign of morning yet. When he opened the door, clouds of steam billowed out. Ben passed the empty bucket to the fire keeper. The cool air rushed in. Everyone found a little relief from the heat.

"Well, now that we got the door open. This is a good time for anyone to express themselves," said Ben.

Vera had drifted into the deep silence. The cool air slowly brought her back. As she sat on the Earth inside the lodge, she felt she'd finally come home. "Aho Mitakuye Oyasin," Vera said to get Ben's attention.

"Yes Vera," said Ben acknowledging her.

"Ben, I want to thank you and Hal for the hard work it took to put this ceremony together. All my life, I've been afraid to come here. Our minister called these Old Ways 'pagan rituals.' When I went to boarding school, they forbid me to speak our language. In here, I heard the songs my grandmother used to sing..." Vera's voice choked up. She stopped a moment. "Hearing those songs, touched me. Elsie invited me so many times. And I'm sorry now I didn't come. She was a good friend to me. Praying in here with you, Hal and my family, I feel at home. I can't remember the last time we prayed together, but it touches my heart. My soul feels fed. Thanks for doing this for Leroy and our family."

"You're welcome Vera," smiled Ben. It was a miracle for him to be sitting here this morning too. "Speaking of being fed, my stomach is starting to growl," Ben started to chuckle. "And it reminds me of a story about an Indian walking through the desert. He's hungry and finds a turtle. So he tucks it under his arm to make some turtle soup. When he gets to his buddy's house, he asks if they can cook it up. But the wife is out and she doesn't want her husband heating up the house. So the men put the turtle in the microwave and turn on the dial. Now you can imagine how dizzy that poor turtle got, spinning around and around."

"After a minute, the men hear a loud knocking sound. They start to look around, but they don't see anybody. But then it comes again. So they head over to the microwave and open the door. As the door opens, a burst of steam pours out and the turtle shouts "Aho Mitakuye Oyasin!"

A few knowing chuckles lightened the mood. To keep the ceremony moving, Ben hollered. "Fire keeper! Hand in the antlers and my cedar bag."

Ernie set the antlers by the door and handed Hal the cedar bag. It went around the circle to Vera. Before the new stones came in, Hal moved the grandfathers around in the stone cradle to make room for the next seven stones.

As cool air flow in, Ben took a moment to explain some things. "Now there's a sacred pipe loaded on the altar and all our prayers go into the Cannupa. After the third round, we'll smoke the Cannupa. The smoke carries our prayers to Creator. About eight hundred years ago, the Cannupa was brought to us by White Buffalo Calf Woman, Pte San Win. It is a way to communicate with Creator. After the Cannupa is lit, we'll pass it around for everyone to smoke."

"Now if you never smoked a Cannupa before, you hold the bowl in your left hand, which is closest to the heart. You hold the stem in your right hand. Take a few puffs and bless yourself off with the smoke. Then, pass the Cannupa with the bowl facing towards the stone pit. Keep your hand on the bowl as you pass it. We don't want the pipe to come apart until it's fully smoked," said Ben ready to start the next round. "I loaded the Cannupa with a red willow bark mix. There's no funny smoke in the pipe. So don't fret about that."

"Fire keeper, bring us seven," called Ben. With a pitchfork, Ernie pulled the grandfathers from the fire. Frank dusted them off with a whisk broom, removing the ash. With a keen eye, Leroy watched every movement of the lodge, taking it all in. Still a little misty eyed, Leroy barely recovered from the last round. With gritted teeth, he anchored himself to the Earth. Seeing his buddies again, tugged hard at his heart. But this round was for the people he'd killed. He wasn't looking forward to making those amends. Even though Ben explained it, it didn't make it any easier.

As Hal set the last stone down, a yellow blast of fury whooshed passed Ben through the open door. Feeling the impending storm, Ben heard the wailing of a hungry child. '*This is going to be a tough round*,' Ben thought to himself. It was a challenge to make amends to those caught in the timeless In-between. Spirits who were offended tragically in life, often remained stuck until the wrongs were righted.

After the water was brought in, there was a quiet moment. "Okay, close it up," Ben called. As the door closed, Ben wanted to fortify Leroy for the mission at hand and help him make amends to the hungry ghosts on the battlefield.

"Welcome to the second round," Ben began. "It's feeling lighter in here already. This round, we're gonna call on the Spirit of Forgiveness and clear up the unfinished business with those stuck in the Spirit World. On the battlefields, there are some hungry ghosts. Some of them have been there for centuries. They got twisted around by war madness and their lives were cut short."

"If you take a walk through a military graveyard and you'll see it's filled with 18 and 20 year olds. It's a shame to lose our young ones. There's no need to get defensive, but most people only blame the other guy. Blame don't fix a darn thing. It's easy to justify killing, when you're being shot at. But in Creator's eyes, we are all His children. He never gave us permission to kill anyone."

"If people could only see through the Veil, they'd see the lost souls of every war. They wander the Earth, seeking justice or revenge. The fury they feel, trapped in the In-Between, lays a heavy burden on the living. Since they were tortured, those hungry ghosts turn their wrath on us. And we are bedeviled with sick emotions, which only an act of forgiveness can heal. If we want peace, we can't skip this step."

"When we face those we harmed and make amends, it is an act of true courage. Nothing short of true forgiveness will work. As I call on the Higher Powers, I ask each of us to pray for a healing for our enemies. Then, we'll all be free."

Filling his dipper several times, Ben splashed the water

on the glowing grandfathers. Billows of steam and sharp heat filled the Inipi. The lodge was crowded with spirits. Ben felt behind him for his drum and began singing his songs of healing and forgiveness.

As Leroy stared at the glowing stones, the searing heat pelted his body. Steam flooded into his nostrils with every breath. Gathering his courage, Leroy closed his eyes to face the spirits of those he killed. 'Sincere amends' were the words he kept repeating to himself.

Storming her way through the crowd of spirits, a fierce anger radiated from her eyes. She stood in front of Leroy, the moment he closed his eyes. "Why did you kill my family?" the woman in yellow demanded as she held her hungry baby in her arms. "We did nothing to you! My husband was a good man!"

Taking a deep breath, Leroy met her angry gaze. Her pain and anguish were tangible as she rocked her screaming child. Nothing justified taking their lives. Especially when they had no way to defend themselves. "I never meant to kill you or your family," he started as the heartache well up deep within him. "If I could take it back, I would. I became a warrior to defend women and children. Not to kill them."

"All I saw was a man standing with a rifle. I thought he was a rebel, not a husband defending his family. I took your life and the lives of your loved ones, without permission. I am truly sorry. I pray you can forgive me, so we can live in peace. What I did was wrong and I want to make it right. Please forgive me," said Leroy humbly hanging his head.

Feeling Leroy's genuine remorse, her anger softened and the young babe stopped crying. Her husband stood behind her and the child. A soft glow of light surrounded them.

Leroy whispered a prayer for their souls to be released. With a sword of blue flame, the Warriors from the Holy Realms cut dark cords between them. The Spirit of Forgiveness enveloped them in a loving embrace. Compassion filled Leroy's heart as he watched them disappear into the mist.

The lodge felt lighter as Leroy made his amends to the warriors of the desert. When he was finished, he whispered to the Warriors of the Holy Realm, "Cut the cords of darkness that bind me to these people. Set us free and take them home. Heal our hearts and set us free. Aho Mitakuye Oyasin."

Standing ready, the Warriors of the Holy Realm, drew their swords of blue flame. Unsheathed, the flaming blue sword glowed as it severed the cords of darkness between them. These dark cords sizzled like a fuse of dynamite. They burned away until they existed no more. Afterward, the spirits of the soldiers were enfolded in purifying Light. They were guided home, where they could heal from their weary life experience."

Ben kept singing until each warrior's spirit crossed through the West Gate into the hereafter. Splashing dipper after dipper of water on the stones, Ben didn't stop until the bucket was empty. The inescapable heat humbled everyone in the lodge. The breath of the Stone People forced a surrender. It broke down the hardness in their hearts. When the last spirit left, Ben finished up his songs and laid his drum down behind him.

"Is everyone okay," asked Ben hearing Vera whisper 'yeah,' as she gasped for air. Her face lay on the Earth.

"Okay, let's open the door," said Ben. In unison, they all shouted "Aho Mitakuye Oyasin!"

Firelight illumined the inside of the Inipi as Ben passed out the bucket. Billows of steam flooded out the door. "Ernie, give us a back door," called Ben out of compassion. Ernie hoisted up the blankets in the back. A cool breeze came up from the Missouri, blessing everyone. Vera's face was crusted with mud as she sat up. The cool air brought her back.

"We're halfway through," said Ben. "And there's been some good movement in here with all your strong prayers. Now, that we got the door open, Leroy, do you have anything you want to say?"

Coming out of another world, Leroy felt humbled by the last two rounds. The hard crust around his heart gave way. As it crumbled, he could take a full breath. Once he got his bearings, he saw how the firelight illumined everyone's face.

In this sacred circle, he sat with his loved ones. He looked around the lodge at his mom and dad, Kyle, Hal and Ben. Every one of them walked with him through these last few months of sobriety. The Spirit of Gratitude overwhelmed him for a moment. "I was never much good at talking in front of people. But I know without each one of you, I wouldn't be sitting here today."

A tenderness washed over him. He looked at his mom, sitting there in the dirt. Her face was smeared with mud. "Mom, I know I owe you and dad a great amends for what I put you through. I was away for so long. When I got wounded, nothing made sense. When I wore the uniform, I had a purpose. It all got ripped away when that bullet tore through my shoulder. When I got off the bus, I didn't fit here, in this life anymore. After years of combat and carrying a pack, I couldn't see myself flipping burgers. Civilian life doesn't make sense when you've seen war and hell up close. All I wanted to do was forget. But I couldn't. Disappearing like I did, was wrong. But honestly, I felt better out there, than I did with people. So please forgive me for putting you through hell, not knowing if I was alive or dead."

Tears welled up in Vera's eyes as she reached over and squeezed Leroy's hand. "I love you Leroy," she whispered as all the tension of the last few years melted away. Being a good Christian woman, she tried to hold her family together through all the drinking. But her remedies were no match for the cunning spirit called alcohol.

As their eyes met, Jed's words got caught somewhere between his heart and his throat. Leaning over, Jed wrapped his arm around Leroy's shoulders, in a manly shoulder hug.

Staring at the stone pit, Kyle felt small next to the big things his brother had done. Having a brother with a purple

405

heart, was hard to compete with, let alone measure up to.

With different eyes, Leroy saw his little brother. "Kyle, I haven't been the best older brother," Leroy met Kyle's gaze. "Hal pointed out how pigheaded I was, that I always wanted the limelight to myself. It wasn't a pretty picture. I saw how much I ignored my little brother. I left you in the dust, when all you did was look up to me. I was too busy trying to prove I was a man. I didn't see how selfish I was. If it's any consolation, you were more book smart than me. If it wasn't for you and Hal, I doubt I'd be here. I hope you let me make it up to you and forgive me for being such a selfish, nearsighted jerk. Those are Hal's words, but I know they're true. I don't want to be that guy anymore. Thanks Kyle for coming today. I love all of you."

Twisting a small twig in his hand, Kyle stared hard at the stone pit, not wanting to meet Leroy's gaze. His brother's words didn't fix the years of hurt. His fists clenched as Kyle's anger boiled up in his throat. After living in Leroy's shadow his whole life, he struggled with the ball of hate swirling in his heart. Even now, Leroy was the center of attention and Kyle didn't feel all that forgiving. In fact now, with the cat out of the bag, Kyle wanted to let Leroy have it.

"Kyle, you got something you want to say to your brother? This is a safe place to let it go," said Ben gently, seeing Kyle's cauldron boiling.

With balled up fists, the hurt came unleashed and spewed out of his mouth. "Words don't mean shit, Leroy. You've wiped your feet on my back since you won your first trophy. And yeah, you left me behind to EAT your dust. Even now, you've got the spot light. It's always about you. You want everyone to just forgive and forget. But you're right. You did trample all over me. You called me fat, chubby boy, loser and whatever else growing up. I hated you. You think you're so much better than everybody. Mister track star, CAPTAIN of the track team," Kyle sneered finally saying how he felt.

"And yeah, I'm fat and you're not. But you were never

around when I needed an older brother. Bad things happened to me. And I had no one to tell it too. I had no one to protect me. Where were you when I needed you? Where were you when I got raped by Jason when I was a little kid."

Shock waves trembled through the lodge, as Kyle's loaded gun exploded. Vera gasped in horror as Kyle's hurt and ugliness oozed into the stone pit. Completely caught off guard, Kyle's words struck Leroy like a sledge hammer. "You got raped by Jason..." Leroy repeated out loud.

"Yeah! And he was you're friend! And you brought him to the house and he got me drunk in the trailer. I was just a little kid. But my big brother was busy chasing his own tail!" Kyle's hurt spilled out.

"Dude, I'm sorry. I never knew...," said Leroy dumbstruck. "He had problems, but I didn't know that." A fierce anger ignited in Leroy as he thought about Jason hurting his brother. "If he wasn't dead, Kyle. I'd make sure, he'd suffer a long, miserable death."

"Fire keeper!" hollered Ben out the door. "Close up the back door and hand in the antlers and the cedar."

An painful silence enveloped everyone as Ernie handed in the cedar and antlers. Frank closed the back flap. Before it spun out of control, Ben took back the reins.

With the antlers in his hands, Hal felt uncomfortable as he rearranged the stones. He made space for the new ones coming in. The pain visiting this family would overwhelm anyone if they didn't have a solution. Hal was grateful it all came out in the lodge and not on the street, where it could do more damage. Having stayed quiet, Hal felt compelled to speak. "Aho Mitakuye Oyasin," Hal said. "Permission to speak."

"Yeah," answered Ben.

"First of all, I'm honored to be here and witness this good healing. My work with Leroy, kept me sober one more day. Leroy single-handedly made drinking look real unattractive," Hal jested. "But it's easy to lose your way with all the juke joints and lower companions. Most of us end up doing things, we'd never do sober. It takes courage to change. But true courage is usually spurred on by deep suffering and pain. My mentors said hatred is love disappointed. And twisted, sick alcoholics disappoint everybody. Most of all, they disappoint themselves."

"I learned the hard way, that we're all entitled to the dignity of our own lumps," Hal went on. "With faulty thinking, we make bad choices. From that comes hard lessons. Usually, the self-loathing an alcoholic feels is so thick, you can cut it with a knife. We're thin-skinned, tenderhearted people, who take everything personal," Hal cleared his throat.

"That being said, it's hard to walk around a world, calloused with its own hate. Before I got to AA and ceremony, I believed that what other people said about me, was the gospel truth. I was sure they were right. It made me restless. I'd toss and turn at night, waiting for the dark dragons of my past to show up and fry my ass. All that fretting made it hard to live in today. I never met Jason. But, from what I witnessed with Ben and Kyle a few months back, I know he was wounded. The trouble was, he infected other people with his sickness. The same way it was done to him. That's not an excuse, but it does explain things," said Hal.

"Now what we got right here, is a solution," Hal continued. "And we can't fail if we seek the truth. Ask Creator to reveal the truth, before you judge a situation. While we're praying in the dirt, ask for forgiveness and healing, all the way around. Don't leave anybody out. Everyone here has been wounded. When those ghouls in the bottle have their way, families are torn apart and lives are destroyed. But what we're doing this morning, by taking care of this prayer, is a solution. We need to stay focused on what we came here to do. That's all I got to say."

"Fire keeper! Bring us seven," hollered Ben, grateful Hal

backed him up. As the glowing stones came into the lodge, Hal placed then into the stone pit. While Vera took care of the cedar, Ben cogitated on how he wanted to direct this next round of healing.

"Most of us only know the dark side of alcohol," Ben started. "But alcohol also has a good side. It's a medicine. Let's say I shot Hal in the foot," Ben chuckled a moment.

"Oh, I see how you are," laughed Hal.

"Let me finish," said Ben. "I'm not done. Now, if I poured alcohol into the wound, it'd clean it out. That's its medicine. That's the proper use for alcohol."

"But drinkers make a different bargain with those spirits in the bottle. We want the whiskey spirits to show us a good time and make us happy when we're feeling low. So we uncorked that whiskey and let her rip. Those whiskey spirits keep their side of the bargain and ease our pain for a while. Most of the time, they take over our bodies and we go off on a wild ride. But then it comes time to pay up. And most drunks never read the fine print. But that whiskey is a spirit and it wants our spirits in return. That's why most drunks around here paid with their lives."

"In this round, let's strike a new bargain with those spirits in the bottle. I'll pass this cedar around again. If you want, take a pinch and offer it to the firewater spirits. Ask them to strike a new deal. Maybe that way, you'll keep your life."

Once the stones were in, Ben passed around the cedar bag. Everyone took a pinch. "Fire keeper, bring me the bucket and then close it up," Ben called, after the Sacreds were passed out.

As the door closed, all was dark in the womb of Mother Earth except the glowing stones. Ben splashed several dippers of water on the grandfathers. The lodge filled with searing heat. Gurgling, sputtering and hissing, the choir of ancient ancestors commenced their song. A gentleness filled the lodge.

Each one settled back into their prayer. Pounding gently on his drum, Ben's voice prayed in song to Creator. "Wani wachi yelo Ate oma kiyayo..." Father, help me I want to live.

With cedar in hand, whispers from the past flooded into their minds. Everyone revisited their experiences with the demons in the bottle. Burned into his memory, Kyle recalled storming through the cornfields like a raging bull, the night the liquor store exploded in a ball of flames. Had he drank that night, it could have turned out a lot differently. Now he felt grateful he didn't end up in jail or worse.

Battle-scarred and tattered, Leroy's mind flashed back to his last days in the wilderness. All alone, he battled the ferocious demons of his past. With his unaided will he almost lost the war. His mind was weak from starvation. His drunkenness scared off all the game. Living off the land, he found shelter in wind burrowed cave. When Hal and Kyle found him, he looked like a crazed mountain man.

Etched firmly in Jed's consciousness was the drunken night he spent in the county jail. Vera had a knack of saying the wrong thing at the wrong time. But his short temper got the better of him. That night, in a fit of rage, he'd trashed the house and punched Vera in the mouth. He warned her to keep her flapping jaw shut, if she had nothing good to say. When he came to the next morning, he was in the county jail. Somehow, he knew that moment marked the end of their marriage. He lived outside the house ever since.

Smitten with sorrow, Hal's mind was jolted back to Arlene's funeral. In his mind's eye, he could see her willowy body laying in the casket. It still sent shivers down his spine. As he looked back, his heart was riddled with pangs of guilt. At the viewing, he showed up drunk and shot his fool mouth off at everyone like an asshole. A drunken fool, he slunk out of there with his tail between his legs. It took years for the pain to ease.

Carved in the deep recesses of her mind, Vera's recalled her father's drunken face when she was a little girl. He had a whiskey bottle in his hand. His face was twisted in pain as he stumbled through the kitchen. He threatened to blow his head off with a hunting rifle. Her mother fiercely wrestled the gun from his hands. He collapsed in a corner, a broken man. Seeing him that way, scared Vera to death. Shortly afterward, Vera was sent away to the Indian boarding school. His tortured spirit couldn't handle this life. He drank himself to death before she came back home. She never saw him again.

With her eyes fixed on the glowing ancient grandfathers, Vera called to her dad's spirit. A warmth filled her heart as his spirit entered the Inipi. Years of pain were harbored in her heart. Salty tears rolled down her cheeks. She told him how much it hurt her to see him tortured like that. "Papa," she whispered. "I didn't know how to help you. I didn't know how to fix our family. I miss you so much. You would be so proud of your grandsons. Leroy came back from the war and Kyle wants to go to college." What she didn't know was, her father's spirit was with Leroy every step of the way. He watched over him and Kyle, both.

Holding the cedar in her hand, Vera fiercely told the demons in the bottle not to hurt her loved ones anymore. The spirit of a powerful mother bear welled up inside her. She'd do anything to protect her cubs. Adamantly, she called on Great Spirit to heal her family from this deadly disease. With firm resolve, Vera offered the cedar in exchange for her son's lives. Using her motherly authority, she called on the Higher Powers to cast out these demon spirits from her family and protect her sons from harm. When she felt satisfied with her petition, she put the cedar on the stones. It crackled as the smoke curl up.

Hearing their whispered prayers, Ben filled the dipper and splashed more water on the stones. Then, in a moment of kindheartedness, he showered everyone with water. The cool water splashed across the lodge. Ben heard sighs of relief and happy war whoops. The love of Creator reigned down inside the Inipi. The chains of bondage to the demons in the bottle, were smashed to smithereens as everyone gave their cedar to the stones.

Feeling as light as an eagle's breath, Ben stood on his knees and raised his hands to the heavens. "This is a song for prosperity, to the spirit of the Buffalo Nation. Pray hard, relatives. Pray hard."

"Tatanka OH YA TAY KEE HAA..." his powerful voice carried his song on the four winds calling to the spirit of the Buffalo Nation.

Deep in prayer, Ernie warmed his hands around the fire as he heard Ben sing the buffalo song. Under the silvery moonlight, the earth began trembling slightly under his feet. As he turned towards the rumbling, the spirit of a thundering buffalo herd stampeded over the eastern hillsides.

Inside the Inipi, as Ben sang to the Buffalo Nation with all his heart. By his third refrain, one big wooly boy stuck his gigantic head through the wall of the Inipi. Ben turned to his right and looked into the soft, brown spirit eyes of his buffalo brother. He felt himself drawn into the soft brown pools. For a moment, their eyes locked as they peered into each other's soul. A deep smile filled Ben's heart as he met the spirit buffalo's gaze. Then, this big wooly boy exhaled his smoky breath. It filled the lodge and blessed everyone.

In his mind's eye, Ben saw the herd of spirit buffalo grazing all over the prairie. His heart was thrilled by their coming. With great heart, his voice boomed the last verse to the spirit of his buffalo brother. Oh this life felt so, so good.

Outside, next to the fire, Ernie watched in awe. After the thundering stampede of spirit buffalo stormed over the hillsides, his big wooly brothers scattered all over the prairie. The largest spirit buffalo stood sentry facing north, while others grazed. Their smoky breath steamed from their nostrils as it hit the cold air. When they got close to the lodge, they settled down.

Occasionally, his wooly spirit brothers stopped grazing, lifted their gigantic heads and looked over at Ernie. One big boy walked right passed him, just north of the fire place.

Slowly, its massive body lumbered towards the Inipi. Ernie stood there, in awe, watching as the spirit buffalo poked its big wooly head into the lodge.

"Did you see that Frank?" Ernie asked all a twitter.

"See what, Ernie?" said Frank fully absorbed in whittling a piece of wood with his buck knife.

"Oh nothing," said Ernie looking towards the north. He wondered if he just had a vision.

With the water bucket empty, Ben wiped his brow. Droplets of sweat poured down his face. "Is everybody okay?" he asked. He heard a few murmurs. "We were blessed by the Buffalo Nation," Ben started to mention. He wondered if anyone else saw the big wooly poke his head in the lodge.

"Okay, let's open the door!" Ben directed as they all shouted "Aho Mitakuye Oyasin!"

Hearing them call, Ernie rushed over to the door and lifted up the flap. The steam billowed out as Ben handed out the bucket. Tiptoeing over the eastern hillsides, the first rays of sunlight streamed into the Inipi. Ernie took the bucket and filled it back up with water. There was one more round of stones in the fire. Frank covered them with a few logs to keep the fire burning.

"Fire keeper," shouted Ben. "Give us a back door."

Rushing to the back of the lodge, Ernie lifted up the blankets and propped them up with a shovel. He was so excited by his vision, he could hardly wait to pull Ben aside to tell him about it. He'd kept fire for years. In that time, he'd seen many whirlwinds around the fire place. He'd even had many powerful medicine dreams. But this was the first time he'd seen a herd of spirit buffalo stampeding across the prairie. The spirit of the Buffalo Nation responded to the big heart of Ben's song.

Battered by the heat, Leroy put his face on the Earth. He felt fully humbled. Something inside him finally surrendered.

The battlefield in his mind was completely quiet. He was at peace.

"Well," said Ben gathering his thoughts. "We have one round left. Thanks to everyone for hanging in there. I'm going to bring in the Cannupa now. We'll smoke it while the door is open. If you haven't smoked a sacred pipe, you hold the bowl in your left hand. It's closest to your heart. Hold the stem in your right. Take a few strong pulls and pass it to your left. Always keeping your left hand on the bowl. All the prayers we said this morning are in the pipe. It's been on the altar the whole time. After we fire it up, that holy smoke carries our prayers to Creator." Ben turned his head towards the door. "Fire keeper, close down the back door and hand in the Cannupa."

Getting on his knees, Hal was ready when Ernie passed in the Cannupa. Ernie struck a wooden match as Hal cupped the flame so the wind wouldn't blow it out. Hal took a few strong puffs. First, he blessed off the pipe bowl and stem with the holy smoke. Afterward, he blessed off himself. Next, he blew some smoke at Ben and everybody in the lodge. Then, Hal passed the sacred pipe to Kyle. The embers in the pipe bowl glowed red as Kyle drew in the sacred smoke.

As Leroy held the Cannupa in his hand, he felt a strong bond to the traditions of his people. Its memory echoed through his soul. His heart was filled with an old yearning. Sometime, in a lifetime past, he'd walked the Red Road of his ancestors. As he pulled the sacred smoke through the stem, he knew these Old Ways held answers to everything he'd ever wanted to know. After years of wandering through deserts of unfulfilled promises, he finally came home to pray in the dirt with the spirit of his ancestors.

By the time the Cannupa came to Ben, there were a few puffs of smoke left. After he finished the holy smoke, he blew the last charred embers into the stone pit. Ben handed the Cannupa out to the fire keeper, who placed it back on the altar.

"Ernie, hand in the antlers and the cedar. Bring us all

but one," called Ben.

"Well, we made it to the gratitude round," Ben started. "The last 3 rounds, we've said 'PLEASE' and now we get to thank Great Spirit for our life. Maybe you don't like the way yours is going, but at least you have one. A wise man once said, 'There's good news and bad news. The bad news is, if you don't like your life, you prayed it this way. The good news is, you can pray it another way."

"Now an elder told me, the root of all unhappiness is selfishness. This is a good time to let that go and learn to walk in humility. Being humble doesn't mean walking around with your chin dragging in the dirt or feeling humiliated. It's about being right sized. We don't own a thing on this earth, not even our body. Everything we have, including our breath, is a gift from Creator."

"Looking back, my greatest teachers were people who tried to kill me. So, I'm grateful for my enemies. If they hadn't challenged me, I wouldn't have grown. Every test forced me to dig deeper to know the power of Creator within myself."

"I'm grateful to the Old Ones who carried our ceremonies through the dark times, when the US government made them illegal. Many teachers took their wisdom, knowledge and traditions home to the Great Beyond. They couldn't find a disciplined student willing enough to learn these Old Ways."

"To walk in a sacred manner, is to know the Power of Creator and become dreamers with eyes to see. Listen to your heart," Ben said finally. "It knows why you're here. I don't mean to preach a sermon, but nobody's going to clean up our mess. It's up to us. We're the ones we've been waiting for. Now, I never had much use for willpower. But, when we discipline the body, we are feeding the spirit."

The rubber soles of his boots smoldered as Ernie pulled the last stones out of the fire place. Rays of morning sunlight flooded through the open door, illuminating the faces inside the lodge. Leroy's charcoaled face was almost cleansed by the breath of the Stone People.

Ben decided to give Leroy some last instructions.

"Leroy, this next round, take the water in the stone pit and scrub the blood off your hands. The water's been prayed over for three rounds. It's sacred. Careful of the hot stones," Ben cautioned. "After that, scrub off the blood splattered on your body during combat. That hate put dark spots on your Light Shield. But, it'll get cleansed as you do this. Don't forget to thank Creator for cleansing the shame of killing from you. Now all these spiritual tools are laid at your feet. It's up to you to use them in a good way. Do you understand?"

"Yeah," said Leroy, humbled by all he'd experienced. "I hear you. You and Hal gave me lots of good tools. Sitting here, I figured out the only good use for anger is to keep another injustice from happening. That's why I became a warrior. But I made a lot of mistakes and blamed other people for what was wrong in my life. Thanks for giving me another chance to become the man I've always wanted to be."

The end of the pitchfork came through the door, as Hal picked up the glowing stones with the antlers. Vera watched the cedar smoke curl in the air when she placed it on the stones. Her heart was full of gratitude, hearing Leroy talk that way. The Spirit of Sobriety blessed her family. Praying in a humble manner was genuine and personal. At last, her soul felt fed. No one preached at her or called her a sinner.

After the last stone came in, Hal handed out the antlers. Ben passed out the cedar bag. "Fire keeper," called Ben remembering Vera's food in the back seat of her car. Ernie knelt down by the door, waiting for instructions.

"Hey, did you get the food out of Vera's back seat?" asked Ben.

"Oh, yeah. We're on that already. It looks like a good spread too," said Ernie. His stomach growled. Inwardly, Vera smiled at Ernie's appreciation.

416

"All righty then, hand in my bucket and let's close it up!" said Ben reaching for his drum. As the door closed, they were enveloped in the womb of Creation. Ben filled his dipper and poured the Mni wichoni, water of life on the grandfathers.

"Welcome to the going home round. Pray hard relatives, pray hard," was all Ben said as he sang songs of gratitude. Searing steam filled the lodge from the breath of the grandfathers.

His chains of bondage were broken and busted. The hungry ghosts from the killing fields had left. Leroy's heart pain melted into the Earth as he thanked Creator for a second chance. In the sweltering heat, Leroy scrubbed himself clean with the gritty sacred waters. The drama of the spirit battlefield was over. His heart felt lighter and his spirit soared free. Clean, he finally felt clean.

As They heard the songs of thanksgiving, the Higher Powers heeded the call. They swept through the Inipi and cleared away the wreckage of the past. The dirges of loneliness and despair sung by earthbound spirits were silenced through mercy. A blanket of Peace replaced the sorrow. Invited back through gratitude, the Spirit of the Most High walk alongside the children of Earth. All the while, the demons in the bottle and all their relations slithered away and relinquished their reign of terror.

Melting into the coolness of Earth, Vera's body gave way to the pummeling heat. Hearing Ben's songs soothed her soul as she listened to the ancient language she was forbidden to speak at Indian boarding school. As a child, she was forced to turn her back on her culture. This cruelty created a deep ache in her heart. She shoved the pain away under layers of fat. Yet, here they were. Those Old Ways greeted her again. This way of life wasn't dead. It waited for her to pick it up again. Misty eyed, she sang along, remembering her grandmother's songs from long ago.

"We have one more song to go relatives," said Ben as he took a moment to reflect on all that happened. "Leroy, the

417

Higher Powers washed the blood off your hands. But there's a condition They're asking of you. Are you listening to me?"

"Yeah, I hear you Ben," said Leroy. "What's the condition?"

"I was told, the Higher Powers and the Spirit of Forgiveness fulfilled your prayers. They washed the blood off your hands. Now, They ask that you help every soldier you can, to wash the blood off of their hands."

"How do I do that?" asked Leroy overwhelmed at the mission.

"The same way it was done for you," said Ben. "We'll talk more later. All you got to do is tell Creator you'll help other soldiers, the same way you were helped. You'll join a battalion of Light for the soldiers coming home. It's an honor if you ask me. I'll sing a song or two, while you take care of your prayer with Creator, got it?"

"Yeah, I do," said Leroy feeling humbled and overwhelmed.

As Ben finished up his songs, Leroy joined forces with the battalion of Light. Hal and Ben were examples of men who came before him. For all the help he'd received, he knew it was his turn to give back. *Freedom ain't free*, he thought. There are sacrifices to be made. Sometimes huge ones, for a drunk to walk sober.

There was a time, not so long ago, when his people walked close to Mother Earth. Each breath was a prayer. But since the days of the Gatling gun, their faith which saw them through difficult times, had faltered. The spirit of doubt wove its corrosive thread into the blanket of their soul. It sought to unravel even the most devout with its whispers of fear and damnation.

Once the back of the Sacred Hoop was broken, the spirit of despair aligned with the demons in the bottle. Their ugly victory was assured as they tempted the people with empty promises. Drunken shallow pleasures temporarily soothed the wounded hearts, helping them forget the pain of defeat. Mean-spirited drugs and an unholy pipe ravaged their bodies and hollowed their soul.

But the Spirit of Sobriety never gave up. It waited for any whisper, for anyone asking for help. When It was asked, the Spirit of Sobriety lifted up chins, ground so long down into the dirt. Each victory restored sobriety to a nation who'd never known drunkenness prior to the arrival of sailing ships from foreign lands.

"Is everyone okay?" asked Ben as he finished his last song. Through the steamy darkness, Ben heard murmurs saying 'yes.'

"Leroy, thanks for coming into my life. You gave me a reason to fire up this Inipi again," Ben started. "After my Elsie died, I told the Spirits I wanted to go home. But they told me I wasn't finished yet. I still had work to do. But nothing mattered enough to me. That is until that big Indian sitting across from me, stood in the doorway of the AA meeting. It don't surprise me none, that Spirit sent Hal to do a job, I couldn't get behind anymore. I haven't felt this good in a long time. And it's all because Hal pulled you out of the dirt and we started Camp Sobriety in my yard."

"I was just trying to be useful," said Hal wiping the sweat from his brow.

Not sure what to say, Leroy whispered, "You're welcome."

"Now Leroy," Ben continued. "There is no worse tyrant than the demons in the bottle and all its relations. Anger, greed, lust and doubt are waiting around in the shadows. They're ready to trip you up in your new found sobriety. Many times I've seen those gruesome spirits, with their long fangs and crooked smiles, hanging around, dripping with temptation. But I tell you what, nothing forces a man to master his own will, than facing someone who's trying to kill him.

Either you'll become impeccable in your walk on this path of wisdom or you'll die. There's no better way to get to know yourself and all your strengths and weaknesses. With a sober mind, you'll face and bear the unknown. Consider yourself one of the lucky ones, Leroy, because you faced the darkest night of your soul and lived."

"One last thing Leroy, before I open the door," said Ben. "I want you to consider this. When we walk in the sunlight of the Spirit, we are protected against these dark invaders. But the trouble comes when we're arrogant or think we're untouchable. That can be our undoing. Most times, our foolish pride leads us to a horrendous death. A true warrior is humble. He finds peace in the chaos, because he knows it's only a test. He sees the dragon coming and stands prepared, with Creator by his side," said Ben knowing that evil triumphs when good men do nothing. And he was sitting in this lodge with a few good men.

"Okay everybody, let's open the door!" said Ben as the whole group responded with "AHO MITAKUYE OYASIN!"

"Give us a back door!" called Ben out of compassion after the front door opened. The rays of sunlight streamed through the door. Cool air blessed everyone.

"Is everyone okay?" Ben asked hearing their murmurs. "Thank you for staying in all four rounds and keeping this prayer strong. We did good work here today. Let's go out and drink some water. For the next four days, the Spirits will be working on our prayers. Take a pinch of tobacco and give it to the fire. Thank the spirits for all their good work. It's been a blessing to pray with all of you," said Ben. He knelt down and whispered "Aho Mitakuye Oyasin" and crawled out the door.

Standing up, Ben turned around in time to hear an eagle cry as it swept across the Missouri. It was looking for its breakfast. Its broad wings beat on the wind as it swooped down low over the river.

"Well, I'd say we've been blessed already," said Ben

quietly to Ernie who helped him out.

"I'd say so," agreed Ernie.

Leroy's heart felt as light as a feather as he crawled out the door into the sunlight. After shaking everyone's hand, Leroy turned around. The sunlight glinted on the waves of the Missouri. It called to him. His eyes twinkled with mischief. A wry smile crossed his face. As he rolled up his towel, Leroy looked at his not so little brother. SNAP! Went the towel on Kyle's thigh.

"OUCH!" cried Kyle caught unaware.

"Come on Kyle!" said Leroy as he let out a war whoop. He ran down to the river. Rubbing the sting on his leg, Kyle chased after his older brother and tackled him in the water. While her boys ran hollering down to the river, Vera walked over to her husband, Jed and gave him a hug.

Hearing all the commotion, Hal chuckled as he sat next to Ben around the fire place. "Boy, I wish I had that energy again," said Hal looking towards the river.

"Oh that," said Ben glancing down at the river. "That's pretty common round here in the summer months. Winter not so much."

"That must have been nice," said Hal looking around.

"It was," said Ben. "We can start it up again, if enough of them are willing."

"That sounds good to me," said Hal feeling clean. "Oh, I didn't tell you, but I might have a job working a ranch down the road from here."

"How'd that come about?" asked Ben curious.

"I run into a fella I worked for out in California, at WalMart. He just moved his family out here and needs some ranch hands. He's looking for a horse trainer and I can help him out that way. My wallet was getting thin anyway," said Hal.

Smiling, Ben nodded his head, "Good job."

Ernie came over and sat with the two men after putting a couple small logs on the fire. "I got the spirit plate ready to go, whenever you're ready," said Ernie.

"Let me go get changed out of these wet clothes," said Ben getting up. "Then we can eat."

Ernie walked with Ben over to the men's changing area. He whispered real low, not wanting anyone else to hear. "Ben, when you were singing the buffalo song, they came storming over the hills. One of them walked right passed me and stuck his head in the lodge."

"Oh, you saw them too. I thought I was the only one. That big boy blessed us off with his smoky breath," said Ben smiling.

Soaking wet, Leroy and Kyle raced back from the river, teasing each other. After everyone changed out of their wet clothes, Ben called them in a circle to pray over the food.

Holding the plate up to the Great Mystery, Ben prayed in the ancient language of his people. Grateful for the Old Ways and the food they were about to eat, Ben thanked Creator and the Spirit-helpers for healing Leroy and his family. With a full heart, he was thankful for this sacred fire place and his community. Afterward he handed the Spirit plate to Ernie and hollered, "Let's eat!"

After he filled his plate, Hal found a place next to Vera. "How'd you like the sweat, Vera?"

"It was good," she said. "Hot, but good."

"Would you do it again?" Hal asked knowing her Christian beliefs.

"Yeah, I think so, I felt good in there." After a quiet moment Vera looked at Hal. "Thanks for all the work you've done with my sons. It feels good, seeing them goofing off down at the river," she sighed. "It's good to have my sons back."

"I was just trying to be useful, Vera," said Hal between mouthfuls. "The only way I get to keep it is, if I give it away."

"So, do you have anything in your bag of tricks for fat people?" asked Vera half kidding.

"Well, I lost about 70 pounds myself," said Hal.

"That's about how much I have to lose. How did you do it?" Vera asked.

"Well, AA has a sister program called OA with the same Twelve Steps. But managing food is a lot harder than giving up drinking," said Hal remembering the food plan called 'Grey Sheet.' "With drinking, you put the plug in the jug. But with food, you have to take the tiger out of cage 3 times a day. Getting abstinent from compulsive overeating is the toughest thing I've ever done."

"I know what you're talking about. I've tried dieting, but it never worked. But I never heard of OA," said Vera.

"Oh, it's really called Overeaters Anonymous," said Hal. "I met a woman there who used to weigh close to 400 pounds. Her name was Natalie. At the meeting, she passed around a picture of herself when she was at her top weight. I think she only weighed in at a buck twenty five when I met her."

"That's a lot of weight to lose. I'll look it up. If it worked for you, I can do it too," said Vera happily. "And she kept it off all that time?"

"Yes ma'am, she did. She was the size of a refrigerator at her top weight. But she trimmed down and lived a healthy life for over 20 years," said Hal remembering the small room with cruddy green carpeting where the OA meeting was held.

Ben sat down next to Vera with a braid of sweet grass and a small bag of cedar in his hand. He set them down beside her.

"What's this for?" Vera asked acknowledging Ben.

"Well, you and Kyle are clean, but I don't know if your

house is. Have you ever blessed off your house?" asked Ben.

"No, I can't say that I have. But I've used sweet grass before," said Vera.

"Well, when a house is riddled with alcoholism, it collects dark spirits and negative energy. These are tools to help you clean out your house," said Ben. "See most people don't know about the spiritual nature of alcoholism. Even if they stop drinking, there are still dark spirits hanging around, to tempt them back. Drinking attracts negativity. Even cigarette smoke attracts dark spirits."

"Oh, I didn't know that. I'll make everybody smoke outside from now on. So how do I do a house blessing?" Vera asked intrigued.

"It's pretty simple," Ben started. "I usually start with 3 white candles and put them in the main room of the house. When you light them, you can say "Father, Son, Holy Ghost" because of your Christian background. Then, smudge the whole house clockwise with cedar or sage. Ask Great Spirit to send his Spirit-helpers to bless off your house and remove anything that isn't sacred. But make sure you get into the nooks and crannies."

"Oh, He might kick me out too though!" Vera laughed.

"Well, that remains to be seen," Ben smiled. "We're just here for a short time anyways. Now, there's really just 3 basic steps to blessing a house. First, you want get rid of the unfriendlies and sweep out the mess they made. After that, you invite the loving Spirits in to take their place."

"You know, I've felt things," Vera whispered. "I always knew when Jed was drinking. It was like a dark blanket covered the house. Is it alright to ask Christ for help?"

"Of course, He's a powerful cleaning agent. That holy book is an instruction manual on how to cast out dark spirits. It's good to do this once in a while, because those unfriendly spirits are familiar. They'll keep coming back. After the dark spirits are cleared out, smudge the house with the sweet grass. Ask the Higher Powers to fill in the space where the negative energy was removed. That way, when those intruders come back, looking for a place to roost, there'll be a no vacancy sign up. Do this every day, for four days and the house should be good. You might try cleaning the floors and counters with ammonia. Dark spirits hate the smell of clean. Do you got any holy water?" Ben asked.

"No, why?"

"Well, If you mix some holy water from the church with the ammonia, it'll give it an extra boost."

"Oh, sure I can do that," said Vera grateful for the instruction.

"By the way, you'll know you did a good job when all the smoke alarms go off," Ben chuckled.

"Oh, okay," Vera said thoughtfully.

After the feast, Leroy went to find his bag of clothes. He'd prepared a giveaway for everybody who helped him with his prayer. Hal explained that a giveaway was part of ceremony. It was good to spend time making something to give to everyone. One day, while Leroy helped Hal clean out his truck, he found a few pieces of pipe stone in a box. Leroy asked Hal what he used the pipe stone for. Hal said he carved things with it. Leroy tried his hand at it. He made several small carvings for everyone at the ceremony.

Surrounded by people who loved him, Leroy stood in front of the fire place and waited to get everyone's attention. "Hey everybody," said Leroy loudly. When all eyes turned towards him, he took out the carvings from his bag. They were bundled in cloth and sage and tied with ribbon. "I want to say thanks for helping with this prayer today. I feel like a free man. I'm grateful for all your help. Hal told me a giveaway is part of ceremony. So I carved a few things to give everyone."

With that, Leroy walked over to his mom and handed

her a heart carving. It was the first one he'd made. "Mom, you're the heartbeat of our family. Sorry I was such a knucklehead, like Hal would say. Thanks for praying with me this way. It means a lot to me," said Leroy as he gave her a hug. Teardrops trickled down Vera's cheeks as she embraced her son.

As Leroy walked around the fireplace, he handed out his carvings and thanked everyone for their help. His heart felt moved. Standing in front of Hal and Ben was the hardest. They'd done so much work together. As Leroy handed Hal his bear carving, Hal stood up and gave Leroy a bear hug.

"Listen little buddy, don't forget what it took to get you here," said Hal towering over Leroy. "Spirit ain't done with you yet. You'll be a lot of help to men and women coming home from the war."

"I second that," said Ben as he shook Leroy's hand.

"Thanks to both of you," said Leroy grateful for a second chance.

It was barely passed noon when Hal got back to the tipi and put his head down on his pillow. Within moments, he was snoring like a happy grizzly bear, who enjoyed a well deserved nap.

Jed didn't want to waste a moment of this fine day. He took the boys fishing and planned to have a fish fry with Frank and Ernie later on.

Armed with cedar and sweet grass, Vera felt empowered as she drove home. With a fierce determination, she was ready to cleanse her home of anything unwanted. For years, she felt a shadowy presence covering her family, but didn't know how to get rid of it. After she read the Bible passages where Jesus cast out demons, she lit 3 white candles anointed with a little olive oil.

As she stood in the middle of her living room, Vera called on Great Spirit, the Higher Powers, Jesus Christ and all the Archangels to sweep through her house to remove everything unholy. Slowly, she moved from room to room, fearlessly casting out every ghoul with the cedar smoke. When the dark energy shifted, she opened the window shades. Rays of the sunlight streamed into the house. "Light casts out all darkness," she said as the sunlight streamed through.

Once she chased out the unwanted ones, she held the burning sweet grass braid in her hand. Vera invited in Christ and her loving ancestors to take the place where darkness had resided. Afterward, she washed down the counters and floors with ammonia mixed with holy water. It gave the house a blessed cleansing.

It took a couple hours of good cleaning. But when she was done, the shift in energy was tangible. Now, she finally had spiritual tools to keep the darkness at bay. While she cleaned, a bible passage in the book of John kept crossing her mind. She finally understood it. "Whoever believes in me and the works that I do, he shall do also. And even greater things shall they do."

Christ wasn't a spectator, watching other people perform miracles. He was the change agent. He taught others how to be active in their spiritual lives. That night when she read the Bible, she understood it was a teaching manual. She was now ready to learn. A new fire sparked in her being, after watching the miracles which happened that morning She heard the call of Creator and answered yes.

After a good nap, Hal walked down to Kelly's Tavern to use the pay phone. Putting the quarter in, he squinted as he tried to read the small numbers on Roy Lewis's card. Then, he dialed the number.

"Roy Lewis," said Roy answering the phone.

"Hey Roy, it's Hal," said Hal.

"OH Hal, perfect timing. My horses are arriving tomorrow, in the morning some time. Do you think you could make it down and help me out?" asked Roy.

427

"What time are you thinking?" said Hal.

"I have to call the driver to find out for sure. But if you could make it by say 7:30 or eight tomorrow morning. My address is 1122 River Road. It's only about 11 miles from Kelly's. I clocked it yesterday," said Roy.

"You were up here yesterday?" said Hal curious.

"Yeah, I took Emma to get a cheeseburger. She's feeling culturally deprived without greasy French fries," Roy chuckled.

"Yeah, I bet. That little girl had a far different life in California," said Hal.

"Yeah, well I don't feel bad getting her out of there," said Roy.

"No, you made a good decision. Listen, you still looking for a ranch hand?"

"Yeah, you know somebody?" asked Roy.

"Well, I got someone in mind, but I don't know for sure. I'll bring him around tomorrow, if he wants to come. We'll see how it works out," said Hal.

"Great, call me if something comes up. Otherwise I'll see you in the morning," said Roy. "Okay?"

"You got it," said Hal. "Talk to you later."

Hanging up the phone, Hal felt a calm wash over him knowing he had work starting in the morning. He could hardly wait to hear all the adventures that blonde chatterbox would tell him. Emma won his heart when she was 4 years old, when he saw how natural she was riding the big white steed with her dad.

The wind blew some gentle breezes in the late afternoon as Hal walked back to the tipi. When he opened he flap, Leroy was sitting on the couch covered in red dust. He was carving on a piece of pipe stone.

"Hey Hal, did you have a good nap?" asked Leroy

428

working hard on a small figure. "It sounded like a grizzly bear got loose in here."

"Yeah, I did. Thanks for asking," Hal said climbing through the door. "So Leroy, how do you feel about shoveling horseshit?"

Hal burst into a deep belly laugh. The look on Leroy's face was priceless.

CHAPTER ELEVEN: SUN DANCE

Buffalo, sweet buffalo
Days of prosperity, where did they go?
I long to see you roam the plains
It is with bounty that you came

Shelter and clothing for those I love
A smile from the Heavens up above
Courage and laughter round firelight
A sky full of stars burning bright

We search deeply within our souls
To ask the question now so bold
How do we become proud people again
Who followed their heart, listened to the wind

The time is now to gather together
To pass the sage and the eagle feather
To call on blessings, abundance and love
To ask for help from our Brothers of Love

We stand with courage, proud and strong
We lift our souls up with our song
To call back the abundance of the buffalo
And return to the days we used to know

As Vera read her Bible with new eyes, she realized something she'd missed listening to the Christian minister all these years. The point of Christ getting nailed to the cross, wasn't in the crucifixion. It was in the resurrection, when Christ arose from the dead. They weren't two separate events. But one that lead up to the other.

In her church, there was a tall statue of Christ hanging from the cross over the pulpit. The church seemed only to focus on sin and the crucifixion. This kept the people in fear of an angry God. But Jesus the Christ revealed the truth of who we are. Our truth was Spirit. Vera witnessed the rebirth in her sons and her husband through their sobriety. Ceremony showed her the power of directed prayer. Her family was reborn, because they got active in their spiritual life.

Over the next few months, Hal explained to Vera, how he utilized ceremony to work the Eleventh Step of his AA program. All of the Twelve Steps were necessary. The first three steps were the foundation. Steps Four through Nine were a clearing process. When the mind, body and spirit were clean, then the Power of Creator flowed through unimpeded. Steps Ten through Twelve were the maintenance steps, keeping the conduit of the heart open.

When used together, Ceremony and the 12 Steps were the most powerful combination Hal had ever witnessed. They had a common goal. As a sun dancer, he was in service to his community. As a sober member of AA, he carried the message and tried to help other alcoholics. Service was the common thread between both ceremony and AA.

After listening to Hal's stories, Vera found enthusiasm to change her life in a good way. Hal got her in touch with a few women he'd known back in OA. It didn't take long for her to see, how she used food to numb her feelings, the same way her husband had used alcohol. Walking in a Sacred Manner wasn't easy with all the temptation around, but it was worth it.

The women Vera connected with in OA were heartfelt women. They knew the struggle of putting food in its proper place. After several phone calls, they gave her courage to start her own OA meeting. Soon a few of the women in the village noticed Vera's weight loss. Some of them got curious and started to come around.

One day, after Emma got done with her riding lesson with Hal, she walked over to the barn. Leroy was knee high in horse shit, mucking out the stalls. Standing in the doorway, Emma watched how his bronzed, muscled arms sent that horseshit flying. She was curious as to who this long-haired, pony-tailed hottie was, who worked on her father's ranch.

Leroy didn't want any trouble with Roy or Hal. He barely looked up, as Emma perched herself on the railing of the stall. He hoped she'd go away. But she didn't.

"Hi, I'm Emma," she said twirling her blonde hair with her finger.

"Hey," said Leroy hardly glancing in her direction.

"You're Hal's friend from the reservation," said Emma. "He said you just came back from the war."

"Oh yeah, what else did he say about me?" said Leroy wiping sweat off his brow.

"Oh, not much," Emma said coyly. "So do you ride horses?"

"Yeah," Leroy chuckled. "Every Indian rides horses. They were part of our culture as far back as I can remember. Hal has me exercise the horses a few times a week."

"Yeah, I think the Spaniards brought them over here," said Emma. "If I remember my history right."

"So what brings you out to the prairie?" asked Leroy resting his chin on the pitchfork. "Hal said he knew you from the West Coast. That's a big change."

"My dad," Emma groaned. "He thinks I'll end up dead if

I stay out there."

"Sounds pretty serious," said Leroy.

"Oh it was, I guess. I kinda OD'd and it freaked him out," said Emma looking down. "Now he's the great rescuer, trying to save me from myself."

"That'll do it," said Leroy, knowing from experience.

"Well, he's the one who found me. I guess if he didn't, I'd be dead," said Emma. "Now he checks up on me all the time. When we first moved here, he opened up my mail," Emma whined. "He thought my dealer would send me dope."

"Yeah, my mom has a hawk-eye like that," said Leroy. "So do you go to meetings?"

"I did out there. But every time I made a friend my age, they got loaded. My dad did an intervention and shoved me into treatment. The shrink put me on meds and tried to tell my dad I was a nutcase. After taking those meds, I was a zombie."

"Yeah, they tried to do that to me," said Leroy. "I told Hal I didn't want no pill pushers around me."

"Well get this," Emma said. "One day, my dad counts my meds. I was taking 11 different pills a day, morning, noon and night. He was pissed!!! He flew off the handle at the psychiatrist. He said that son of a bitch must be working for the pharmaceutical companies! He put me in treatment to get off one drug and the shrink put me on eleven more. It was crazy. His brother, my uncle, lives out here. My uncle thought it might be good to get me out of there. So we moved to the middle of nowhere. My dad thought if he got me away from the dealer, I'd live."

"Yeah, Hal calls that a geographic," chuckled Leroy. "They only work for a while, but you always take yourself with you."

Thunderstruck, Emma looked at Leroy and started laughing. "That's so true! It doesn't matter where you go, there you are!"

"So how long you got clean?" asked Leroy curious if she'd used since her overdose.

"Oh, I've been clean since I got out of the hospital. Almost 6 months now. I spent 2 months in treatment and we've been out here 2 months. I couldn't believe my dad found Hal at WalMart. I was losing my mind. It was like God answered my prayer," said Emma.

While Emma rambled on about her crazy escapades, Leroy recalled the big talk Hal gave him about keeping his pecker in his pants with the women in AA. As cute as she was, Leroy realized that what Hal had said made some sense.

Over a few months time, Emma and Leroy became friends. After he finished his work around the ranch, they often went riding along the Missouri. Hal finally convinced Roy to bring Emma to an AA meeting, so she could treat her addiction.

Gripped by a bone-crushing fear, Roy was compelled to hold his daughter captive in a self made prison on the prairie. The afternoon he found her passed out with a needle dangling from her arm, forever changed his life. She was near death.

After that, he was like a pit bull. He kept watch over anyone who came near her. He spared no expense to keep his daughter safe and alive. But the more he controlled Emma with his iron clad fist, the more she rebelled. His death grip was suffocating their family.

Being privy to all sides of the story, Hal coaxed Roy to go to an Al-anon meeting. There he could deal with his pain around Emma's addiction. Hal's training as a drug and alcohol counselor came in handy. It was another way he felt useful.

Even though his bones creaked, Hal felt his best in the saddle of a horse. It was a godsend to be working for Roy again. Most nights Sally, Roy's wife, invited Hal and Leroy to join them for dinner. Some nights they did and there was a lot of laughter around the table.

True to his word, Leroy went with Hal to the VA hospital

once a month to carry the message of sobriety. Eventually Hal convinced the director of the VA to allow Inipi ceremonies for the wounded warriors on the VA grounds. Many spirits were released and lives were healed from the madness of war.

Late one afternoon in mid spring, Hal's feet got itchy. Being nomadic by nature, he felt he'd been in one place too long. The call to go out on the open road came on strong. It wasn't that he didn't like what he was doing. It's just how Spirit moved in him. The big drum was calling him home. Cogitating, he sat on the front porch when Ben walked up.

"What's on your mind, Hal. I can feel the wheels turning," said Ben as he sat down. They had come to know each other pretty well.

"I'm not sure," started Hal. "I just got that feeling. Maybe it's time to go. I can hear the big drum beating."

"Sun dance season's coming up," said Ben. He knew the feeling too.

"Yup, that could be it. I've been dancing a lot of years, Ben. It gets in a man's blood. I got a mind to call a buddy in Montana and find out when Tree Day is."

"Maybe you should take Leroy along," Ben suggested. "Being that he's been your fire keeper at the VA."

"Yeah, I was thinking about that too. He's doing a good job at the fire place," sighed Hal. "I've grown mighty fond of that kid. I never had a son, but I'd adopt Leroy as my own."

"Well, it seems the feeling's mutual," said Ben. The wind stirred through the tall grasses as they stared out at the prairie. In the long part of the afternoon, the sun was high in the endless sky. All was quiet for a time. They sat in silence for a long moment

"How do you feel about taking a road trip?" asked Hal as he caught Ben's eye.

An old excitement stirred in Ben as he thought about dancing in the arbor again. "You know, before Elsie passed,

435

she mended the holes in my moccasins," Ben smiled. "I came home one afternoon and she was busy putting new leather on the soles. I asked her what she was doing. She just said I might need these again."

"Ah, a Spirit must have whispered in her ear," said Hal.

"True, true," said Ben. "Well, how you gonna break it to Leroy?"

"I'll just tell him it's part of his Warrior Training," said Hal. "That hard-head will gain a new appreciation after four days of ceremony."

"I'd say that's true too," said Ben.

"Well, I'm gonna walk over to Kelly's and use the phone," said Hal as he pushed himself out of the chair. "I'll come back and let you know when Tree Day is."

Within a few weeks time, the men were ready to travel. Leroy had never seen Hal so excited. Most afternoons, Leroy listened while Ben and Hal told stories, filling Leroy's mind with the wisdom of the Sun Dance trail.

The morning they headed out, Hal packed the truck with all the camping gear. Afterward, he tied down a tarp to cover it all. That way, nothing flew out. To avoid the scorching summer heat, they left before the break of dawn. Getting out on the open road, did Hal's heart good. The morning air was cool, as Hal rolled down the window.

After a good days drive, they arrived at the Sun Dance site two days before Tree Day. The whole camp was busy making ready for the dance. During the first four days of purification, the sun dancers and supporters worked alongside each other. They prepared the Sun Dance arbor, built the sweat lodges, assembled the tipi and the main kitchen. Every morning and evening, there were Inipi ceremonies. The entire area was cleansed before the Sun Dance began.

The Inipi ceremony prepared the sun dancers to enter the world of spirits and begin their fast. During Sun Dance, the dancers were isolated from the community supporters for four days and nights. They'd refrain from taking in food and water. Most of their communication would be through prayer with Creator.

The Sun Dance arbor was at the end of camp. This large Sacred Circle was bordered by stones. The stones were painted the same colors as the medicine wheel, honoring the four directions. In the center of the arbor was a deep pit. This pit would hold a cottonwood tree, once it became the Tree of Life. From the stone border to the center where the tree would stand, was about 30 feet, give or take.

In each of the four directions along the stone border, was a gate. It was marked by two long painted willow poles on each side of the gate. The colors of the gate and prayer flags went along with the four directions, red for north, yellow for east, white for south and black for west. Each willow pole had a long tobacco prayer flag. The prayer flag was made from colored cotton fabric and tobacco.

Behind the arbor was the section of camp chosen for the sun dancers. They'd be isolated from the rest of the community while they were in ceremony.

Everywhere it was a bustle of preparation. It didn't take long for Hal to put Leroy to work, tending fire and chopping wood. Soon the bandana Leroy wore to keep the hair out of his eyes was saturated in sweat.

During the four days of purification before Tree Day, the men were busy building a shade arbor in the southern section of the sun dance arbor. Here, the big drum was set up, along with a place for elders to sit in the shade.

Out of respect, the women all wore long skirts and shawls to cover their shoulders. Some went out to gather sage and mugwort. The main kitchen was bustling with people preparing food for the helpers during the day.

Other supporters and sun dancers prepared the Sun Dance arbor. They painted chokecherry sticks red and prepared 405 prayer ties. Afterward, the prayer ties were tied to the chokecherry sticks. After the Tree of Life was put up, 101 chokecherry sticks went in each of the four directions around the stone border, with one extra.

As Leroy watched this ceremony come together, he noticed such cooperation. Everything had a purpose. There was great attention to detail. This land was being made sacred to prepare for the most important ceremony of their new year.

A day or two before the full moon, came Tree Day. For the First Nations People, the cottonwood tree was especially sacred. If you snapped off a top branch, or cut it with a knife, you'd find a five pointed star hidden inside. Some believed that this is where the stars hid during the day. It was a reminder from the Star Nation, that we're all one.

Days earlier, four scouts were sent out to find the best cottonwood tree. These scouts were good men. It was a great honor to be selected as a scout. When the scouts returned to camp, they announced they found an enemy. Then, on Tree Day, the warriors, the Sun Dancers, went out with the women to where the enemy was discovered. As they crossed a stream, the medicine man made prayers to the spirits of the water. A scout pointed out the cottonwood tree. Then, the warriors rushed the tree, counting coup on the enemy.

Afterward, the Sun Dance Chief offered his Cannupa to Heaven and Earth. He touched the stem of his sacred pipe to the tree in each of the four directions. He started in the west and moved sunwise to the north, east and south around the tree. Afterward, he lit his Cannupa and had a good smoke.

Before it was sacrificed, the cottonwood tree represented the enemy, whose callous indifference, diseased thinking and toxic poisons harmed the people. Under the direction of the medicine man, four young maidens struck the tree with a brand new ax, on each of the four directions. With their purity, the tree was sacrificed. Afterward, the tree was cut down by the sun dancers. A woman struck the last blow. As the tree fell to the south, the women let out a shrill cry for victory. The warriors sang their victory songs.

After the victory, the cottonwood tree transformed into the Tree of Life. It was not allowed to touch the ground. As it fell, it was caught by 20 pole bearers. Special sticks were used to carry the tree. No one was allowed to touch the tree, walk in front of it or step over it. The enemy was subdued. In a great procession, the victors carried the sacred tree back to camp. It never touched the ground.

In great anticipation the entire camp awaited the tree's arrival. Busy chopping wood, Leroy felt a hopeful charge go through camp like a lightning storm. In the center of the Sun Dance arbor, a large pit was dug out where the Tree of Life would go. All was made ready for this sacred ancestor, the cottonwood tree.

By mid afternoon Leroy heard the war whoops. Excitement charged through camp as the sun dancers carried the tree into the arbor. Both sides of the dirt road were lined with supporters. They sang and cheered as the tree was carried in.

Hal explained the moment the tree was cut down, the enemy of the people was captured. After the sun dancers carried the tree to the arbor, it would be adorned with prayer ties. An eagle feather was tied on the highest branches.

Watching the sun dancers carry the cottonwood tree, Leroy was overcome with a deep emotion. Their voices were carried in song as they prayed to Tunkashila. Along with the head dancers, the lead singer walked in front of the procession. The big drum started pounding in the shade arbor at the south gate. Something in Leroy's soul stirred as he recognized this sacred moment.

In the bustle of all the activity, Hal and Ben found Leroy. In their hands, they carried bundles of prayer flags they'd made in camp the night before. "Here ya go, buddy," said Hal handing Leroy his prayer bundle. "There'll be a time after they get the tree situated on those blocks, when we get to put our prayer flags on the tree."

Leroy held his bundle of prayer flags in his hands. Most of his prayers were for the men coming home from the war which still raged on in the desert, half a world away. His life had changed so much since Hal and Kyle pulled in to the grocery mart parking lot. Now it was his turn to give back.

The lead dancers lead the procession through the east gate of the sun dance arbor. Here, the tree was placed on blocks of split wood. The base of the tree faced the center of the arbor towards the big hole. After it was adorned with prayer flags, the dancers would stand the tree up. As soon as the big drum settled down, an elder named Larry stood in front of everyone by the south gate.

"That's my buddy, Larry," whispered Hal in Leroy's ear. "He's been sober longer than most people I know."

"It's good to see everybody here," Larry started, looking into the sea of faces. "I want to welcome everyone to this ancient ceremony and the beginning of our new year. Some of you know, I grew up on the reservation. Back then, our ceremonies were illegal, outlawed by the US government! Our people went to jail for praying in the arbor or in the sweat lodge. There was no freedom of religion for the Red Man."

"Most people don't know the history of our people or the sacrifices our ancestors made, so we could pray here today. After we lost the war, many went into hiding. Some sacrificed their lives to keep this ceremony alive. You see, when the white government figured out they couldn't exterminate all of us, they took away our horses, outlawed our ceremonies and forbid us to speak our language. Our medicine men, who didn't conform to the white man's ways, were locked up in insane asylums because they talked to the wind and parted the clouds when the Thunders came. One of my great grandfathers died in that horrible place." Larry got quiet for a moment as the impact of his words took root.

"The US government was afraid of the power in our

sacred pipe. To keep us small, they forbid us to pray to Creator in our language. They ripped us away from Mother Earth and confined our people to reservations. After that, the government put the missionaries in charge of the food rations. If you didn't get with their program, they didn't give you any food. Our children were starving. I read some where that they killed over 64 million of our sisters and brothers since Columbus sailed here," Larry paused a moment.

"Now it's hard to imagine, with all the cities and highways, but before Columbus, our people roamed freely over all this land," Larry stretched out his arms encompassing the wide open spaces. "So just imagine how our ancestors felt when the white government tried to make them to live in cold concrete cities and assimilate, so we could be like them. The white government broke every treaty they ever made with our people. After Wounded Knee, our holy men went underground for almost a century to keep our ceremonies alive. Without them, we wouldn't be standing here today, praying in this ancient way."

Larry stopped and look into the eyes of the people circled around him. "We owe them our gratitude. Someone cared enough about the next seven generations to keep our language and ceremonies alive, against all odds."

"In the summer, when I was a boy, I remember my dad and my grandpa left early in the morning and went off in different directions. This way, nobody would catch them. They'd put up the Sun Dance arbor in secret places. During the day, the sun dancers prayed and danced. At night, they'd come home like they were coming home from work. Nobody talked about what they were doing. They were afraid. If someone found out, they might turn up dead. Some of our medicine men got caught and spent thirty years in prison for praying to Great Spirit. Growing up in fear, kept the people silent. That way, nobody would catch on."

"Almost a hundred years after the massacre at Wounded Knee, President Carter signed into law, the American Indian

441

Freedom of Religion Act in 1978. Now, even though the silence is broken, some of the fear is still there. People are still afraid to talk about ceremony. That fear, along with all the spilt blood of our people, lays a heavy blanket on the land."

"Out on the West Coast and in upstate New York, I met white men who were sun dancers. Some traditional people may not agree with me, but I think it's time to share the Old Ways with our brothers and sisters of the four directions. 'Mitakuye Oyasin' means for all my relations. The four races of people are represented in our medicine wheel. Many people are called to the Old Ways to pray. When the eagle of the north flies with the condor of the south, the people will awaken."

"Now, my dad never gave me a choice if I wanted to go to ceremony or not. My whole family went and so did all us kids. That's the way I raised my sons. So I honor those elders who faced prison sentences and carried these ceremonies for the future generations. They refused to let them die."

"Okay, now that I gave you a bit of history of Sun Dance, there's a few rules I want to go over. Then, we can get the tree set up. Except for a few elders here, there are no shoes allowed in the arbor. Now, since I got to elder status, I'll be walking around with a cedar can, wearing my white tennis shoes. But everyone else needs to be barefoot or wearing moccasins. Also, we don't wear jewelry or anything made of metal in the arbor. If you got glasses, like me, just put a bit of red cloth beside the rim of the glasses and that will make them okay."

"On the Sun Dance grounds, NO drugs or alcohol is allowed. Most people don't understand this, but those mean-spirited drugs block your connection to Creator. They keep you from doing what you came here to do. Once the dance starts, smoking tobacco, eating or drinking needs to be away from the arbor. It will be hard enough on these dancers, when they smell the bacon frying every morning. We don't need to make it any harder on them by eating or drinking in front of them."

"Now, I don't want to have to say this, but..." Larry started. "You all came here to support. In the morning, when our singers go out to wake you up, we need you to get down to the arbor. Be ready to start the day praying. That's what we're here to do. If you wanted to be comfortable, you could have stayed home, sat in your Lazy Boy and watched TV. This cottonwood tree sacrificed its life, so we could have a Sun Dance. Our dancers are sacrificing their hunger and thirst for the people. They need to see you out here, praying with them. Make sure you drink plenty of water, with them in mind. We'll be eating and drinking for them, while they're praying and fasting for us."

"When the main helpers let me know they're ready, we'll call small groups of people to put their prayer flags on the tree. Just be careful about putting too many prayer flags on small branches. We don't want them to break off and your prayers to hit the ground."

In the middle of his talk, a pretty woman walked up to Larry and whispered in his ear. He smiled at her and said thanks before he turned around. "Now, I was just told that we need to cover a few more shifts for the east gate."

Hal nudged Leroy, "What do you think buddy?"

"Yeah, sure. What do you have to do?"

"It's a gravy job," whispered Hal. "You just make sure no one crosses the spirit pathway on the east gate and keep the cedar can going."

"Okay," whispered Leroy.

"Hey Larry," Hal called out.

"Hal, good to see you," said Larry.

"Yeah, it's good to be seen. Listen, me and my buddy Leroy here, will take a shift at the east gate," said Hal.

"Well, go talk to my wife Katerina after the circle breaks. She's keeping the shifts together," said Larry.

"Well, I'll be..." whispered Hal to himself. "Larry married that girl..."

443

While Larry finished speaking, the sun dancers and main helpers situated the cottonwood tree in the middle of the arbor. The dancers tied ropes high on the trunk of the tree. During the ceremony, they'd use the ropes for piercing.

When they were ready, the helpers directed folks to the tree to hang their prayer robes. Each person had 7 prayer robes, made from a piece of colored cotton fabric which held a tobacco prayer. The colors represented the seven directions: north, east, south, west, Father Sky, Mother Earth and the Wakan which lies within.

The afternoon sun bore down heavy as the men waited in the shade arbor. "Now, listen up Leroy. After you put your prayer robes on the tree, we'll be praying for four days. We're calling on some big medicine during this dance."

"Are you going to dance, Hal?" Leroy asked as he looked up at him.

"Yeah, more than likely," Hal started. "I'll probably drag buffalo skulls around the arbor a few times."

"What about you Ben, are you going to dance?" asked Leroy.

Lost in thought, Ben took in all the sounds and smells of the dance. The cedar smoke and the sound of the big drum soothed a place deep inside him. He and Elsie had traveled to sun dance for many years. During his sun dance pledge, she was there to support him. After he pierced to the tree, she stood behind him. One year, she went on her moon time and spent most of the dance sequestered in the moon lodge. It was the loneliest dance Ben ever had. Now, he looked for her in the sea of faces. *Elsie, where are you my girl?* Ben thought to himself.

"Where'd you go Ben?" Hal nudged.

"AH, I was looking for Elsie. She stood behind me after I pierced to the tree," sighed Ben. "But, I don't see her anywhere."

Leroy threw Hal a concerned look, but didn't know what to say.

"Don't worry, old buddy. She'll be here. If you want to pierce up, Leroy and me will stand behind you," said Hal lending support.

"I don't know just yet," said Ben. "I'll have to see how Spirit guides me."

When they made it up to the Tree of Life, Leroy held his prayer flags in his hands. As he tied each one to the branches, he remembered the men he lost that fateful day. The wind danced through the leaves as people tied their prayer robes to the tree. Everyone was in good spirits. There was laughter in the Sacred Circle.

At the fork of the cottonwood Tree of Life, the main helpers tied a bundle of chokecherry branches to honor them. Before grocery stores, the chokecherry was an important fruit for the people. It was slowly disappearing. Now, what few chokecherry's were left, didn't have much meat on them.

Afterward, the Sun Dance Chief brought the traditional silhouette of a man, a buffalo and an eagle wing into the Sacred Circle. He tied this all to the branches on the Tree of Life. The man represented all of humanity. The buffalo was sacred for the people. It sacrificed its life to feed the people and supply all their needs. The eagle wing would fly on the four winds and carry the prayers up to Creator.

Next, row after row of colored prayer ties were wrapped around the tree trunk. Once the prayer robes were tied, the supporters moved out of the arbor.

After the tree was adorned, three women elders came out into the Sacred Circle with the Sun Dance Chief. In their hands, the women held sacred foods: buffalo meat, corn, berries and a bag of buffalo fat. These foods sustained the First Nations People before the Europeans came across the big waters. They offered the sacred foods to feed the Tree of Life during the dance. After the foods were placed in the pit, the

445

sun dancers were ready to hoist the tree up.

The arbor grew quiet as Sun Dance Chief and the main helpers directed the sun dancers on how to hoist up the tree. Every sun dancer held his rope in his hand. When they got the signal, they pulled the tree up all at once.

When it was standing, they rotated the tree four times with the ropes, until it stood straight up in the pit. While the sun dancers held the tree in place, men shoveled the dirt back into the pit. They packed down the dirt, insuring the tree stood straight.

A slight breeze tickled the leaves of the tree as Hal, Ben and Leroy stood outside the stone border of the Sacred Circle, watching. During the dance, the supporters would stand there. The branches swayed as the wind blessed the prayer flags. It was beautiful. All those prayers placed on the Tree of Life, held so much love.

"Okay buddy," started Hal. "Being this is your first dance, I want to tell you a couple things. Tonight is the dancer's last meal. Starting tomorrow, whatever we eat or drink, we'll do for them. They'll start their prayer fast after midnight."

"So they don't eat or drink for four days?" asked Leroy.

"No food," said Hal. "Sometimes they'll make a sage tea. But those dancers are tied to the Tree of Life and Creator, so they'll get what they need from Him. The other thing is don't stare at the dancers or catch their eye. Once they're tied to the Spirit World, they've got spirit eyes. You don't want to knock them off their prayer. Larry tells everyone to look at the tree. I spent most of my time in the arbor. But this time, I might dance a day or two. The dancers do notice when people are in the arbor, so it does make a difference. We're all praying for each other."

"I don't think I've ever gone that long without eating," remarked Leroy.

"Well, this is a warrior ceremony," Hal started. "If you were captured by the enemy over there in the desert. Chances are, you'd have been starved, tortured and not given anything to drink."

"Yeah, thank God that didn't happen," Leroy sighed.

"Yeah well, this ceremony takes all that into account. The only difference is, here, you're praying the whole time. Remember how I told Kyle about the Heyoka?"

"Yeah," said Leroy.

"Well, at Sun Dance, he does his best work, showing these warriors where their weaknesses are," Hal said. "Oh and one last thing. This is important. If for some reason, someone starts yelling at you about something. Don't engage. Just let them say their peace and answer OK. You got that? If you got a problem, let me know and we'll get it handled. We don't want to stir up a bunch of negativity here."

"You know," said Ben. "There's something else you should know. This is a sacred place. Don't kill anything. Not a spider, a fly or mosquito. And don't throw water through the air or shake the blankets out."

"Why not?" asked Leroy.

"Well," Ben started. "By throwing water, you'll call on the Thunders. As much as I love Tah-tay, if you shake the blankets out, she'll bring on a wind storm."

"You believe that?" asked Leroy.

"I know what I know," said Ben, leaving it there.

Once the Tree of Life was in place, the supporters put the finishing touches around the arbor. The three men helped put 405 prayer ties around the stone border of the Sacred Circle. Each prayer tie was attached to red painted, chokecherry stick. There were 101 prayer ties for each direction, with one extra one.

According to a medicine man's vision, there were 101

spirit helpers who took care of each of the four directions. Each prayer tie was for one of the Spirit-helpers of that direction, with an extra one for Great Spirit.

It turned out, the men were camped close to Larry and Katerina's tipi. After dinner, they paid Larry a visit. Talking to Katerina, Hal found out when their shifts were for the east gate. It was the night before the dance. Everyone stopped by to visit. It was a busy night. As Leroy sat and listened, he was blessed with the wisdom of sober elders. They told stories well past sunset, which was after 10 pm.

Before daybreak, a group of singers circled around camp. With a hand drum, their morning songs signaled the crack of dawn. The fire was already burning for the community Inipi. Hal, Leroy and Ben hustled down to the lodge, before the dance started. By the time they lined up, the women were already going in.

It'd only be a dust off sweat. First, the women would sweat two rounds. Then, once the lodge was all warmed up, the men would sweat two rounds. This way, everyone was clean before they got down to the Sun Dance arbor.

As it turned out, Hal and Leroy had the second shift guarding the east gate. After the lodge, they hustled down to the arbor. When they got there, a helper with an old coffee can of smoldering cedar, smudged them off. Sometime after midnight, two people manned the east gate. Hal and Leroy relieved them of their post.

Directly across the arbor, by the west gate, was the Inipi for the sun dancers. Cedar smoke wafted through the air as Leroy walked around the Sacred Circle. Passing the west gate, he saw the dancers milling around the fire place. They just finished their morning lodge. The sacred fire would be ablaze the whole sun dance.

When Leroy got to other side of the east gate, the coals in the cedar can were barely going. He tossed some fresh cedar in the battered coffee can and shook it up a little. The cedar popped as the smoke wafted through the air.

"Hey Hal, how do I get fresh coals? These are almost out."

"Bring the fire keeper from the dancer's lodge your coffee can. He'll replace them" As Hal laid a blanket down, he muttered to himself, "I wish I'd thought of bringing my chair down here."

"You want me to run and get it?" asked Leroy looking across the Spirit Pathway between them. "It won't take me long."

"Yeah, I can hold out for a while. I just don't want my back to start aching. Ask the fire keeper to bring me some fresh coals while you're at it and another pile of cedar too," said Hal. "I'm almost out." At that moment, Ben showed up. He set a blanket down for himself under the shade arbor near Hal.

"Hey Ben, will you sit here, while I go get Hal's chair? If his back starts hurting, he'll turn into Mr. Grouchy Bear," said Leroy as Hal threw him a look.

"Yeah, just give me a minute," said Ben as he started walking around the arbor. The smell of cedar brought old memories into his mind from sun dances past. The Tree of Life swayed in the breeze. Ben was in high spirits. He wore his moccasins which Elsie mended just months before she passed. Her bead work was flawless. Leroy met Ben at the north gate as he went to fetch Hal's chair.

"Hurry back," said Ben. "You don't want to miss this."

While the dancers lined up south of the west gate, Leroy hurried by and found a fire keeper named Issac. He asked for some fresh coals. The fire called to him as he watched the flames conquer the red cedar logs. At that moment, the lead singer pounded hard on the big drum. The sound echoed through camp, letting everyone know it was time to start. Back at his tent, Leroy throat was parched. He drank a huge swig of water, knowing the dancers hadn't had water since midnight.

He found Hal's good chair and hustled back to the arbor.

The camp was bustling as everyone headed to the arbor. The singers at the big drum started pounding as the lead singer called the first song. Leroy just made it back to give Hal his chair. The sun dancers started moving around the Sacred Circle. They were ready to go in. All the supporters stood as the singers began to sing.

"Listen here, little buddy," Hal started as he put cedar on the fresh coals in an old coffee can. He shook the battered can by a makeshift handle made out of bailing wire. The cedar crackled and popped, sending the smoke over the arbor. "Wait here until the dancers walk through the east gate, before you go back to your post. Ben can open the gate up for them. Sit tight with me for a few minutes."

"Okay," said Leroy watching the beginning of the dance with anticipation. Inside the arbor, near the west gate, stood an empty chair. It was covered with a Pendleton blanket and had a picture on the seat. It caught Leroy's eye and raised his curiosity. "Hal, what's with the empty chair?" Leroy asked.

"Oh," Hal started. "One of the sun dancers didn't make it back this year. He crossed over the west gate and went home. So they honor him up that way."

"What happened?"

"I don't like to gossip, but he's not here to tell it himself. He had a hard time staying sober. I think his liver gave out. Those spirits in the bottle claimed another one," Hal explained. "It's a darn shame. He was a good man."

The sound of the big drum echoed through the land. Voices were raised in song as the dancers lined up single file for the Going In Ceremony. They walked around the Sacred Circle starting south of the west gate. As they reached the west gate, the dancers stopped for a brief second and raised their hands in the air. They honored the ancestors of the west, the Thunder Beings, the Wakinyan Oyate.

A shrill piping sound of the eagle wing bone whistles kept time with the drum as the dancers moved north around the Sacred Circle. Dressed in their sun dance skirts, the men dancers were painted red from the waist up. Their faces were painted red too. Red represented all that was sacred, including the Earth. When our spirits pass on to the Spirit World, our bodies return to the Earth.

Upon their heads, the sun dancers wore a holy, soft green sage wreath and eagle plumes. Circled around their wrists and ankles were wreaths of sage. The women dancers wore eagle feathers in their hair and followed behind the men. As they arrived at the north gate, they raised their arms to greet the ancestors of the north.

At the front of the procession, an elder sun dancer carried the buffalo skull. In the arbor, it would be placed on the sacred altar and facing east. This honored the holy sacrifice the buffalo made to sustain the people for centuries.

As the dancers approached, Ben opened the east gate, allowing them to pass. While he held the rope, old powerful feelings stirred inside him. Ben watched as old Rod walked passed by him carrying the buffalo skull. Rod's eyes were straight ahead and his step was full of purpose.

One by one, the dancers filed into the Sacred Circle. The main helpers directed them into a formation of rows, facing the morning sun. As the big drum pounded, the sun dancers raised their arms to greet the dawn of a new day. In the heavens, Tunkashila and the Higher Powers heard the sacred songs of the people and took notice as the first round of the dance progressed.

The call of the people resounded throughout eternity as the dancers moved through the arbor in a sunwise direction. Throughout the day, they honored the four directions. As a portal of the divine, the rays of the sun blessed all life on Earth.

After a small break, came the round where the eagle dancers pierced. The eagle dancers were experienced sun dancers who pledged to pierce to the Tree of Life for the entire four days. Before they pierced, they were guided to the Tree of Life to pray.

Leroy had his eye on the first eagle dancer who was ready to pierce. His name was Little Buffalo. Two red circles were painted on his chest where he'd be pierced. The main helpers guided Little Buffalo by his sage wristlet to the Tree of Life. For a while, he knelt and prayed while the helpers fanned him with their eagle fans. Little Buffalo lay down on the buffalo robe under the Tree of Life. A medicine man pierced his skin and placed a wooden dowel through the skin on his chest.

With his eyes fixed on Little Buffalo, Leroy didn't hear so much as a yelp coming from him when the medicine man pierced his chest. The flesh of his body was the only thing Little Buffalo could sacrifice, that he could call his own.

After the piercing, the helpers got Little Buffalo to his feet. Next, he spent a few moments at the tree, then went to his place in the arbor. He'd stay there, the rest of the dance. As soon as he put his rawhide tether on the dowels through his chest, Little Buffalo started dancing. When he leaned back on the rope that tied him to the Tree of Life, tree started to shake.

"Psst," said Hal to Leroy as he noticed him staring. "Keep your eyes on the tree! Focus on your prayers."

Leroy averted his eyes, but he couldn't help watching how the tree shook and shook. By this time, Larry was walking around the shade arbor in his white tennis shoes. He had a cedar can in one hand and his eagle feather fan in the other. Walking around the Sacred Circle, he smudged off the supporters. When he got to Hal, Hal stood up and let Larry give him the full treatment.

A few feet away under the shade arbor, stood a young woman clutching her shawl. She was standing a couple feet from Ben. When he took notice, she smiled at him and whispered "Hello."

452

"Morning," said Ben as his gaze met her eyes. She was nervous about something, he could tell.

"This is my first dance," she whispered. "My friend invited me a few years ago and I finally took the time to come."

"Umm," said Ben. "Where's your friend now?"

"In the moon lodge. I thought I'd end up there too, but not yet." She paused as she bit her lip. Then, she whispered to herself, "I just hope I'm not pregnant."

Ben couldn't help but overhear her whispered prayer. There was no wedding ring on her finger. He gave her a gentle look.

"Is it alright if I stand here with you?" she asked after a few minutes.

"Oh sure," said Ben. "I'm Ben."

"I'm Robin."

"Well Robin, it's good to meet you," said Ben.

It wasn't long into the morning, when the sacred clowns started walking backwards around the arbor. Dressed in goofy costumes, the clowns pranced around like bumbling idiots. They challenged all the rules of the dance. Their goofiness made the people laugh, especially when things got too serious.

Across from Leroy, one of the clowns walked right down the east gate. This was taboo for all the other people. Leroy almost said something. On his face were Groucho Marx sunglasses, with a thick, fluffy mustache and a big nose. For his outfit, he wore red and white striped stockings with goofy oversized shoes. His funky plaid shorts were held up by red suspenders. The whole outfit was covered by a top coat with tails and a top hat. Hal took one look at him and said "Morning Kevin!"

For a moment, the clown chuckled. "A likely story... and probably true," he winked as he waved his unlit cigar through the air. Removing his hat, Kevin bowed before Hal. Then, he flipped his tuxedo tails up and swept his oversized top hat through the air like royalty.

The big drum pounded with voices raised in song as the summer sun climbed through sky. As he watched the dancers, Leroy felt an kinship towards Little Buffalo. His dedication to this prayer was genuine. Before the first long break, the eagle dancers were all pierced to the tree.

When evening came and the last round ended, the dancers filed out of the arbor through the east gate. The eagle dancers gathered their sleeping bags and set up camp under the Tree of Life. This was a warrior training Leroy had never witnessed. After an evening sweat lodge, the other sun dancers disappeared into their sequestered village to have a night of rest.

That evening as the men walked back to camp, Hal looked at Leroy. "I don't know if you know this, Leroy, but Ol' Custer got defeated at the Little Big Horn during Sun Dance."

"I think I read something about that," Leroy recalled.

"From what I understand," started Hal. "There were some 3000 Lakota and Cheyenne camped along Rosebud Creek. They had their Sun Dance here in Montana. Before the Custer attacked, another 3000 Arapaho, Cheyenne and Lakota came off the rez to join up with Sitting Bull. Ol' Custer had himself a big surprise when Crazy Horse and Sitting Bull got the upper hand."

"You mean when they got slaughtered," said Leroy. "I heard the women took their awls and pushed then into Custer's ears, so he'd hear better in the next life."

Walking quietly beside them, Ben spoke up. "Sitting Bull had a vision. Great Spirit showed him how when the soldiers attacked his people, there were as many as grasshoppers. But this time, those blue coats were upside down and fell into the river with their horses hooves in the air. Their hats fell off their heads and tumbled to the ground."

"Yeah, Sitting Bull had great vision. But, those white soldiers were plum outnumbered. Ol' Custer only had himself about 350 men," Hal said.

"But that wasn't all Sitting Bull's vision said," continued Ben. "His vision gave a warning."

"What was that?" asked Leroy.

"Don't take the spoils from the fallen soldiers bodies or great misery will befall the people," Ben said in a faraway voice. "But the people didn't listen and took everything they could from those dead blue coats."

"But that's normal," said Leroy. "Those are the trophies of war."

"What you don't understand is," Ben cautioned. "Those 'trophies' are tethered to the angry spirits of soldiers who were slaughtered."

"What does that mean?" Leroy asked perplexed.

"Damn Skippy, Ben. You're right," said Hal as a light went on. "The spoils of war carry the energy of the dead. Great Spirit had a condition when He gave our people that victory, but they didn't heed it."

"What? You're saying, if a man falls on the battlefield and I take his gun, his spirit will follow me around?" asked Leroy disbelieving.

"That's exactly what Ben's saying," Hal concurred. "That's what Sitting Bull's vision warned. And since they didn't listen, all that misery boomeranged right back to our people and we've been miserable ever since."

"I don't know if I believe that," Leroy asserted.

"It don't matter if you believe it or not," said Hal. "Living in the world of duality, every force has a counterforce. The more radical the change, the more powerful the counterforce. When Custer and his men got slaughtered, that was a big humbling for the US military. To save face, they had to avenge Custer's death by chasing our people to the ends of the Earth and putting us in a corral."

"You mean reservation," Leroy said.

"Call it whatever you want. It's still a prison. A couple years ago, I read the President signed an apology to the Native American people for all the harm the federal government did to our people," Hal commented. "Congress called it the 'Native American Apology Resolution. The fella who wrote it, admitted all the destruction the US government did: the Trail of Tears, the boarding schools, the broken treaties and the bloodbath of wars. He called for an official apology to the Indian tribes to start a reconciliation."

"That wound's been festering for many lifetimes. You can't wash it away with a few words. Saying I'm sorry isn't a remedy for what they've done," Ben replied, having lived in the federal government's communist prison camp. "It don't matter what people say, it's what they DO that counts. Amends means change."

"What do you want from forked tongued people? They don't want to clean up their mess. Those Christians just want to be forgiven!" Hal exclaimed.

"Those people are nothing like Christ!" Ben shook his head. "When Christ healed that cripple, he told him 'Stop sinning or something worse may happen to you.' Nowhere in that holy book, did I read where Christ said to go out and slaughter everyone who didn't believe in Him. I didn't read that anywhere! But, those Christians think they got the right to murder in His name. And then they want to say 'I'm sorry!' I don't think those Christians ever read their holy book."

"Probably not, but they finally admitted their wrongdoing and that's a start," said Hal. "Don't worry Ben, what goes around comes around. What goes around comes around." Hal let out a big yawn. It'd been a long day. "Don't take this personal, but I'm turning in."

"Night, Hal. See you in the morning," said Leroy as he

456

sat down to work on his pipe stone carvings. Grandma Moon was almost full as she crept over the eastern horizon. Her silvery light cast shadows over the land. Leroy settled in by the lantern with his carving tools. There was just enough light to see.

Morning came early, as the second day of Sun Dance began. After a dust off Inipi, the men made it down to the arbor. The smell of frying bacon made Hal's mouth water as they walked by the main kitchen.

"You know what," Hal started. "I think I'm gonna get some of that bacon and a couple hotcakes. When I sun danced, the smell of bacon made my stomach growl."

"I know what you mean," agreed Ben as they headed into the main kitchen.

Feeding more than a hundred people, the main kitchen ran like a well oiled machine. To run properly, it needed harmony. One elder women believed that a cook in a bad mood called on black magic. When cooks were angry, bad energy went into the food and made people sick. So while they were cooking, no grumbling was allowed. In fact, if a cook showed up cranky, they chased her out of the kitchen.

The arbor was quiet before the dance started. As Leroy walked passed the sun dancer's Inipi, one of the fire keepers caught his eye. Issac was there the morning before, when Leroy took his first shift at the east gate. Isaac was still keeping fire after the last round of the dance last night. Called to the fire, Leroy stopped to say hello and get some fresh coals for his morning shift.

"Hey," said Leroy. "Weren't you here yesterday morning and last night?"

"Yeah," laughed Issac. "Two women fire keepers mooned out yesterday and went to the moon lodge. We were short handed last night." Isaac scooped some hot coals in an old coffee can and handed them to Leroy.

"Do you need some help?" Leroy asked.

"Yeah, do you keep fire? We need some chopped wood and someone to keep fire for the lodge later," Isaac said.

"Yeah, no problem. I keep fire for Hal back home," Leroy said.

"I know Hal," said Isaac as he wiped the sweat off his brow.

"Yeah, he brought me here. It's my first dance," said Leroy. "Look, I got my shift over at the east gate, but I'll come back and find you, okay."

"Yeah, I'll be here," laughed Isaac.

From the Inipi, Leroy heard the sun dancers inside yell, "AHO MITAKUYE OYASIN!" Isaac opened the door and the steam billow out. Soon, the dance would start. After he relieved the night shift, Leroy spent a while cleaning off the fresh cedar. The morning was quiet as the sun started traversing the endless blue sky.

Hal and Ben arrived shortly before the lead singer pounded on the big drum to get the community down to the arbor. As they settled in for another day of prayer, it did Hal's heart good to see Leroy cleaning the cedar.

"You got down here fast," Hal remarked to Leroy.

"Yeah, I stopped by the fire place and talked to Isaac. Turns out they need some help. Two of the women fire keepers went on their moon," explained Leroy.

"Yeah, that happens a lot," laughed Hal. "The Sun Dance ceremony itself actually creates the moon lodge."

"Oh yeah, how's that?" asked Leroy.

"Well, an elder woman explained it this way," Hal started. "See, women on their moon are in their own purification ceremony. A woman's cycle follows the moon's cycle. Traditionally, we don't mix ceremonies. In the Sun Dance arbor, the energy spirals up clockwise to the sky. The

458

current of energy is so strong, that women just start their moon. Sometimes they'll even start two weeks early. See, mooning energy spirals down into Mother Earth, counter clockwise. Mooning women actually anchor down the sun dancers in the arbor. Sometimes, by the second day, even women sun dancers get called to the moon lodge."

"So the mooning women act like a ground wire," Leroy thought out loud, going back to his electrical training.

"Exactly," said Hal. "Ground wires carry the current to the Earth. They keep people from being electrocuted when working with powerful currents. They also give a return path for the energy. So, while the Sun Dance energy is spiraling up to Creator, the mooning woman's energy is spiraling down to Mother Earth. What you got to understand is, they're both in a separate ceremony. That's why mooning women are sequestered in the moon lodge and the sun dancers are sequestered from the community."

"So, in a way, the mooning women keep the sun dancers from getting short circuited by grounding the energy into the Earth," Leroy said after he cogitated on this for a while.

"You got it. The Earth knocks out the static electricity," said Hal pleased that Leroy understood how the power of ceremony worked. "That's why mooning women don't come to sweat lodges. Not because they aren't clean, like the old testament said. But, because their energy is going the other way. One energy spirals up, while the other down, which makes them uncomfortable."

"This is starting to make sense," said Leroy. "Mooning women have an important job here."

"You bet they do," said Hal. "They anchor the prayer down. It's a powerful time because a woman's prayers are especially strong. So you gonna step up and help out at the fire?"

"I was thinking about it," said Leroy.

"That'd be a good place for you to start," suggested Hal.

Later that afternoon, Leroy found Isaac resting under a shade tree. Leroy brought Isaac a sandwich and some water to drink. Most of the time, fire keepers don't have time to run to the main kitchen to eat.

"Thanks," said Isaac as he bit into the sandwich and took a swig of water. "The main kitchen is good about sending food. But, I'm burning a lot of energy."

"No doubt," said Leroy. "When I keep fire back home for the guys at the VA, it's a lot of work."

"How's that?" Isaac asked.

"Well, Hal runs a warrior Inipi for the guys coming home from the war. It washes off the war madness that they bring back from there," Leroy said with knowing.

"That's a good thing," said Isaac. "Listen, why don't you come back after the last round and help out then. The dancers have their Inipi and we keep the fire going all night."

"All right, sounds good," said Leroy.

"Hey, tonight's the full moon. The sun dancers do a round about midnight to honor Grandma Moon," offered Isaac. "You might want to hang around for that."

"Sure thing," said Leroy taking it all in.

After a good day in the arbor, Leroy found his way to the fire place. With his experience keeping fire for Hal at the VA, it was second nature for Leroy to dust off the Stone People and carry them into the lodge. He felt useful chopping wood and carrying water. Working behind the scenes, Leroy got to see for himself all the work it took to carry out this dance.

That night just before Grandma Moon reached her zenith, Leroy heard the singers gathering around the big drum. Her silvery light cast shadows across the Sacred Circle, illuminating the leaves on the Tree of Life. Dressed in white skirts, the dancers lined up south of the west gate.

Breaking the midnight silence, the head singer pounded on the big drum. Supporters gathered around the arbor as the singers began the Going In round. Twinkling stars filled the endless midnight blue sky, while the wind gently swayed through the leaves on the sacred tree. This was the Moon, Hanhepi Wi, when the chokecherries are black. It began the harvest, when the corn was ripe.

Standing by the fire, Leroy peered across the arbor and saw Ben and Hal near the east gate. Next to the wood pile was a battered coffee can used for smudging. Leroy filled it with fresh coals and brought it over to the man guarding the east gate. On her wings, Tah-tay carried the cedar smoke across the Sacred Circle.

In the shadows of the moonlight, the big drum pounded, while voices carried medicine songs to the four directions. The sun dancers walked into the Sacred Circle through the east gate. Their white skirts were illuminated by the shimmering moonlight.

While Hanhepi Wi, Grandma Moon, traversed the heavens, the sun dancers and singers honored her with songs and prayer. Standing outside the arbor, Leroy felt gratitude to witness to this moon dance. His last bit of hard-heartedness broke away when he realized how blessed he was to be there.

By the third morning of the sun dance, a powerful energy had built up in the arbor. The tremendous Love and Light of Great Spirit cascaded down from on High. It flooded through the Sacred Circle and was anchored to the heart of Mother Earth.

After praying and fasting for three days and nights, the sun dancers were bathed in a continual flow of sacred love. This gave way for powerful healing energy to come through. Elders in wheel chairs and people with illnesses were brought to the Tree of Life for healing. The Power of Great Spirit was channeled by the medicine man who performed a doctoring.

By the break, the heat of the noon day sun was

461

scorching. The eagle dancers sought shade under the Tree of Life, while the other dancers went out of the arbor. The sun dancers were definitely tied to the Spirit World. Their sacrifice and prayers reached the Powers of the Wakan. Fiercely thirsty, Leroy drank water all day long. He could only imagine how thirsty the dancers must be.

After the break, the sacred clowns had their own round. The Thunder Dreamers had the power to heal emotional pain and reverse the spirit of despair through the power of laughter. Their crazy antics tested the dancer's weak spots, showing them what they were made of.

One sacred clown walked around the arbor eating juicy watermelon. With every bite, the watermelon juice ran down his chin. In total defiance, he stood in front of the dancers and tempted them. The dancers hadn't eaten in three days. At one point, the sacred clown tore some of the juicy watermelon meat out and dripped it on a dancer's face. But the dancer never flinched or reacted in anyway. Instead, the dancer stared straight ahead. His feet kept time with the drum and he remained focused on his prayer.

The sacred clowns tried to distract the supporters from their prayers. Little children shied away and hid behind their mother's skirts. Another clown heckled the singers. He took a drum stick and pounded on the drum out of time. People couldn't help but laugh at their goofiness.

In the first piercing round of the day, Hal decided he' drag buffalo skulls around the arbor. Dressed in his sun dance skirt, there were two red circles painted on his back where the wooden dowels would go. While Hal lay face down on the buffalo hide in at the base of the tree, Leroy focused his prayers intently for his mentor and friend. Hal wasn't afraid of pain. In fact, sometimes he welcomed it, because then he knew he was still alive.

A trickle of blood ran down Hal's back as the medicine man pierced and placed the dowels through the skin. Afterward, the helpers walked Hal over to the Tree of Life where he offered his body to Great Spirit. Then he walked over to the west gate, where the buffalo skulls were waiting.

Like a steam locomotive, Hal started jogging around the arbor, dragging the buffalo skulls behind him. As soon as he passed Leroy and Ben, Ben jumped out behind Hal and followed him.

"Come on, Leroy!" Ben shouted as Leroy jumped in close behind. More and more supporters followed behind Hal, as he powered around the arbor. Hal's tough old skin wouldn't break easy. So he gave it one more round.

By the second round, Hal was huffing and puffing. He slowed down some, but still couldn't break free. The main helpers found some children and sat them on the first 3 skulls. Hal pulled and pulled, but his tough old skin still wouldn't let go. Finally, Gene, a main helpers, linked arms with Hal on one side, while another helper linked with Hal on the other. Together, they'd bring extra force.

"Come on, my brother," Gene said as he linked arms with Hal. The children anchored down the skulls, while Hal pulled with all his might. On the fourth tug, Hal finally broke free. The supporters cheered, while Hal jogged his victory lap around the arbor again.

While Leroy followed Hal on his victory run, he watched Hal's long salt and pepper hair fly through the wind. Leroy felt grateful for his second chance at life. This old warrior brought it all to the table. By his example, Hal taught Leroy that the true battle isn't out in the world. But within the self. Many times, Hal thumped on Leroy, saying "Half measures don't get you shit!" Now, Leroy knew what he meant. A true warrior masters his greatest enemy, the demons within himself.

At the end of the round, several sun dancers lined up at the south gate, holding their sacred pipes. A main helper sought out people from the community. Packed with prayers, the Cannupa's were offered to the community to smoke. Searching the crowd, the main helper pointed his eagle fan at

Leroy. He walked over to the south gate where others lined up.

Standing across from the sun dancers, Leroy remembered not to meet their eyes. Their spirit eyes looked up, while their hands were extended holding the Cannupa. The sacred pipe was offered four times and accepted by the supporters on the fourth pass.

As the Cannupa was passed to Leroy, he felt deeply moved. Quickly, he looked for Hal and Ben in the shade arbor. He felt extremely honored to be chosen to smoke this Cannupa with his friends and the people in the community.

As Leroy sat down, a small group of people formed a circle. They sat on the Earth under the shade arbor. Hal found a lighter and passed it to Leroy. Leroy lit the sacred pipe. The first few puffs he blew on the pipe bowl. Then, he blew the sacred smoke on pipe stem and himself. Leroy blew one puff at Hal, Ben and around the circle of people. The Cannupa was passed around the circle sunwise. Each person took a few puffs.

A peaceful silence fell on the arbor as they smoked the Cannupa in small circles. When the holy smoke was finished, Leroy shook everyone's hand. Then, he brought the pipe back to the south gate, where others had lined up. The sun dancers were called and the sacred pipe was offered four times. It was accepted on the fourth pass by the dancer. Standing across from this warrior, Leroy had such appreciation for his sacrifice. The round ended and then came a long break.

After a good lunch, Leroy went back to sit in the shade arbor. Only the eagle dancers were in the Sacred Circle. Tethered to the tree, Little Buffalo and the other eagle dancers found a patch of shade under the Tree of Life and rested there.

The night before, Leroy helped out at the fire place, chopping wood and keeping fire. During the Sun Dance, the fire never went out. With a few other fire keepers, Leroy spent the better part of the night keeping the fire going.

Finding a shady spot, Leroy put his blanket down on the

ground. With a few birds chirping in trees nearby, it was peaceful. Smokey cedar drifted through the air as Leroy leaned up against a post. His heavy eyes felt like sand paper as his body longed for sleep. Within moments, he fell into deep slumber.

Drifting into dream time, Leroy found himself walking through a large meadow. Off in the distance, along a babbling creek, was a circle of teepees. Something drew him there. Near the creek-side, deer grazed while puffy clouds passed overhead. Momentarily, they stopped chewing as Leroy walked by. Their deep brown eyes looked up at him. In the vast blue sky overhead, a hawk cried as it circled high above. Several crows cawed in the trees surrounding the camp. As if they foretold of Leroy's arrival. A young boy came running when he spotted Leroy.

"Grandpa's waiting for you," the young child said. "Come with me. I'll show you where he is."

Leroy followed the child into the center tipi. As he opened the door flap, several elders sat around a fire. In the middle stood an old man. Leroy recognized his face from a photograph his mother had sitting in the living room. The old man looked up at Leroy and smiled. "Here, my son, this is for you," he said as he handed Leroy a Cannupa. Leroy held the Cannupa in his hand and looked up at the old man. The old man smiled deeply. It was good.

Full of excitement, Hal bounded down the small knoll, looking for Leroy. When Hal spotted him, Leroy was dead asleep, holding his hands out in front of him.

"Hey little buddy," said Hal in a whisper. He didn't want to disturb the eagle dancers rest. "Look, I got something for you."

With a start, Leroy's eyes popped open. In front of his face, all he could see was Hal's outstretched hands. He was holding something wrapped in cloth. "What is it?" asked Leroy groggily as he stretched his arms out and yawned.

"It's a gift, Leroy. And a commitment, if you take it," said Hal gently.

Yawning, Leroy sat up and straightened himself out. He slowly came out his nap. Hal handed Leroy the gift wrapped in cloth and Leroy opened it up. In his hands, lay a large piece of red pipe stone.

"It's for your own Cannupa, Leroy," said Hal. "One of the elders came up to me and Ben. He'd heard your story and saw how hard you were working. He wanted you to have this. I can show you how to make your own sacred pipe."

"That's too strange," said Leroy remembering his dream.

"What kind of answer is that?" Hal shook his head.

"I don't know what, but I just had this dream that my great grandpa handed me a Cannupa. Then you woke me up," said Leroy feeling kind of dizzy.

"Boy, that wasn't a dream. You had yourself a vision," said Hal shaking his head. "You must have some powerful medicine behind you. Maybe there's a good reason Kyle and I found you that day." Then Hal thought to himself, '*Maybe I'm not such a hero after all.*"

"So what does this make me?" asked Leroy feeling a little sleepy.

"Well.... first, you start out as a pipe carrier," said Hal. "That sacred pipe is a powerful way to communicate with Creator. It's not that you need a piece of wood and stone to pray, Leroy. True prayers come from the heart. But the Cannupa will help you focus your prayers. That sacred pipe came to us from White Buffalo Calf Woman, Pte San Win."

"Ben talked about Pte San Win in my first Inipi," Leroy recalled. "I meant to find out more about her."

"Well, Creator's sent powerful helpers to teach us for a long time. Ohiya told me a story about White Buffalo Calf Woman. It's a little different from the others I've heard," Hal started.

"Yeah, how's that?" asked Leroy.

"Well this is how Ohiya told it to me," Hal started. "Before White Buffalo Calf Woman came to Earth, there were many Spirits that made up the Great Mystery. They governed all of Creation. When the Star Nation struggled and was close to extinction, they prayed for assistance. The Great Mystery answered and offered Medicine directly to the Star Nation. Then, the Eagle Nation had similar struggles and prayed for assistance. The Great Mystery answered and instructed the Star Nation to pass the Medicine onto the Eagle Nation. So our ancestors from the Star Nation carried the Medicine to the Eagle Nation and they accepted it. Now, through the teachings, ritual and ceremony, that sacred medicine healed the Eagle Nation. How long the medicine was with the Eagle Nation is unknown. But then the Buffalo Nation was in trouble and asked Great Spirit what to do. The Great Mystery answered and asked the Eagle Nation to pass the Medicine to the Buffalo Nation. And this is where White Buffalo Calf Woman comes in."

"Oh, so this is what 'Mitakuye Oyasin means,'" Leroy nodded.

"All my relations," said Hal. "Everyone of us is related to the Great Mystery. Now, when the people were in trouble, they prayed and asked for help. The Great Mystery sent White Buffalo Calf Woman. Ohiya said she carried two bundles. One for the external medicine ways and one for the internal. But the people weren't ready for the internal. So that bundle was returned to the Great Mystery."

Leroy chewed on that for a while. "So, the external was the ceremony?"

"Well, Pte San Win gave seven sacred rites to the people," Hal said.

"So what do you think the internal is?" asked Leroy after a time.

"Well, personally, I think it's the prayer," answered Hal.

467

"Ceremony is the vehicle for prayer."

"I can see that," said Leroy.

"That ain't all," started Hal. "For me, it took the Twelve Steps to clear out my internal junk. That opened the way for Spirit to guide me. I was pretty useless when I was drunk."

"Yeah, I can relate," said Leroy remembering his last drunk.

"Now, if you accept this commitment, Leroy, we'll go down to the river and find a young cottonwood. I'll show you how to make the pipe stem out of the top of a sapling. Back home, I got the tools to drill out the pipe stone. I'll show you how to do that too, if you want to take on this commitment."

"What's the commitment?" asked Leroy wanting to know what Hal was getting him into.

"Hmm...," Hal started. "The commitment is to walk in a sacred manner and to be of service to Creator and the people. It's not a small deal, Leroy. You'll get tested right and left, when you carry a Cannupa. Creator tests you where you're weakest, just to see what you're made out of."

"Yeah, I know the drill," Leroy laughed quietly.

"Look, when I started on the Red Road, some things I liked and other stuff, I couldn't stand to be around. I met every kind of person on the Red Road. They come because they need healing. That's why they're called. Now that being said, I didn't like everyone I met at ceremony. Sometimes, they'd mistake my kindness for weakness. Many times, I stepped back and looked things over before I decided one way or another. That way, I saw the good and bad in every thing. Sometimes you got to move slow and study the terrain before you wander down into it. Walking in a sacred manner takes a lot of patience and focus. Maybe you should think about it."

"Well, it's not much different than what we've been doing at the VA with all the veterans," said Leroy. "It takes a lot of walking your talk to just stay sober."

"Well, you're right there, little buddy" said Hal. "Staying sober is being of service to Creator and the people, because most drunks are only of service to themselves. The hardest lesson I ever learned was that insanity was doing the same thing over and over and expecting different results. To get sane, I had to walk my talk and learn from my mistakes. Most people don't, you know. There's a bunch of carrot-danglers out there. They promise all kinds of things but never deliver."

"Isn't that what you've been teaching me all along?" asked Leroy. "To walk my talk and be of service to Creator. Isn't that the purpose of the Twelve Steps?"

In that moment, Hal realized the boy had been listening all along. One of the rarest finds in all the world was a man of integrity who kept his word. Leroy was becoming one of those men. Someone who knew the difference between vice and virtue and chose the harder, but higher road.

"You know what Leroy, I've been in AA and sun dancing so long, that the lines between the two, bleed into one another. But you're right, the whole deal is to come to know yourself and Creator and be of service. It don't matter whether you're a sun dancer or working the Twelve Steps. And from the looks of things, you've been doing a good job. You make me proud, Leroy." Hal got choked up a moment.

While Leroy studied the piece of pipe stone in his hand, he considered all the things Hal had shown him. A year ago, none of this way of life would have made sense. But he watched how Hal kept his word and lived sober on the Red Road. Leroy knew he'd been given a second chance and he didn't want to pass it by.

"Yeah, I'm in," said Leroy as he held the piece of pipe stone in his hand. "Thanks Hal for bringing me here."

"You're welcome, little buddy," said Hal as he patted Leroy on the back.

Near the south gate, the lead singer and others started milling around the drum. The shadow of the Tree of Life, where the eagle dancers rested, pointed north-east. The long break was just about over.

Next, there'd be a healing round. Here, the entire community was invited into the Sacred Circle. Everyone could touch the Tree of Life and be blessed off by the sun dancers. As the big drum began pounding, the sun dancers lined up south of the west gate.

For three days, the sun dancers sacrificed their hunger and thirst while they prayed for the people. All the dancing and praying called to the Powers from on High. Within the Sacred Circle, the Power of Great Love was tangible.

The Going In Round began as the dancers filed through the east gate. Inside the arbor, they lined up in two rows, starting at the west gate and going to the Tree of Life. Another two rows lined up from the Tree of Life to the south gate. The two rows of sun dancers created an L-shaped walkway for the supporters to go through.

Entering the Sacred Circle at the west gate, the supporters walked between two rows of sun dancers to the Tree of Life. With radiant faces, the dancers blessed them off with their eagle feather fans. Then, the supporters touched the Tree of Life. Some were compelled to stay a few minutes at the tree to pray. Afterward, they walked between two rows of dancers and exited out the south gate by the drum.

For the last three days, Robin stood with Ben in the shade arbor. Her moon time never started. A large crowd waited in line as Robin's big brown eyes turned towards Ben. "Can I go in with you?" she asked him.

"Sure," said Ben as he stepped ahead of her. Then, like a father, Ben reached back and took Robin by the hand. As he did, a strong Voice spoke to him in his mind. "My name is Dylan," the Voice said. "I'm glad my mom found these ways."

Looking behind him, Ben caught Robin's eye. "Don't get mad," Ben started. "But your boy's name is Dylan and he's glad you found these ways."

"How do you know that?" Robin asked astounded.

"Well, he just told me," said Ben. "You're not going to the moon lodge any time soon."

Holding hands, Ben and Robin walked through the west gate. The Love of Great Spirit radiated through the smiling eyes of the sun dancers as they fanned off Robin and Ben. The power of Great Spirit enfolded them in His brilliant love. It surged through Ben's body. He was overcome with joy. The feather tips of the eagle fans brushed across his shoulders and back as they walked to the Tree of Life.

As he came to the Tree of Life, Ben knelt down with his forehead against the trunk. He embraced the tree like a dear old friend. Tears of joy streamed down his face. Then, in his mind's eye, he saw himself pierced to the tree. Elsie stood beside him. At that moment, he knew he needed to pierce up before the end of the dance.

For eons of time, mystics have searched for communion with the Divine. Yet here in the space of a few days, the Divine cascaded down to Mother Earth. It's powerful, healing Love flooded through the Sacred Circle and anchored down to heart of Mother Earth. Everyone was blessed.

Tears streamed down Ben's face as he felt the Power of Tunkashila. This tremendous Power flowed around him everywhere. It bathed him in love. In that moment, he realized that each of us, being children of Creator, were connected. We are all One. We all have the same parents. As he stood up, he walked towards the south gate. He was one with all life. In his heart, Ben knew he came to Earth to make a difference, for his people and himself. The sorrow washed away, as the sun dancers blessed him with their eagle fans.

The morning of the fourth day, Ben was down at the arbor early. He made himself ready to pierce up to the tree. All the memories of dances past came flooding into his mind as he dressed in his Sun Dance skirt. Since he last danced, his body may have aged some. But his heart was as strong as ever. As promised, Hal and Leroy were there to support him.

During the piercing round, Ben knelt before the Tree of Life and prayed hard. He thought about all the funerals he'd attended. Days before they'd left the reservation, he got word that the firewater spirits took two more of his kin. A brother and sister both died of cirrhosis of the liver within days of each other. The brother was 43 and the sister was 38. Their funerals would be going on right now.

In his mind's eye, he saw the faces of his grandsons. He remembered the times he'd stood by helplessly while those tempters in a bottle called to his people. Those firewater spirits only did this to torment them and lay their bodies to waste. The burden of all that pain, welled up deep inside him. It made him feel old and threadbare. From this pain, Ben needed to break free.

This was the day of the Going Home rounds. Before it was over, the eagle dancers would break free. They'd been tied to the Tree of Life for four days and nights.

As Ben lay down on the buffalo hide, he looked deeply into the wizened eyes of the medicine man. Within the deep of his brown eyes, lay the wisdom of the ages. No words were needed. Gene, a main helper, got Ben to his feet after the medicine man pierced and put the wood dowels through Ben's chest skin.

After Ben spent a few moments at the Tree of Life, Gene guided Ben to a place in the arbor and helped him put the rope tether on his dowels. A small trickle of blood ran down his chest as Ben closed his eyes. In gratitude, Ben lifted his hands to the heavens. Tah-tay rustled through the cottonwood branches as his feet danced with the beat of the drum. Then, Ben walked backwards, pulling the rope taut. At that moment, Elsie stood right beside him. "ELSIE!" Ben cried out. "YOU'RE HERE!"

Elsie simply smiled. A brilliant light radiated from her Spirit as she took his hand. "But Elsie, you're not allowed in the arbor," Ben said in a moment of confusion.

"I AM NOW," Elsie said to her man. A powerful surge of energy jolted through Ben as he leaned back, pulling the rope taut with his chest. The tree shook fiercely while he pulled and pulled and pulled.

Snap! Ben's tethers broke free as the ropes flung back towards the tree. Hal, Leroy and the supporters cheered. War whoops echoed through the arbor from his fellow sun dancers. Standing directly behind Ben, Hal was ready to catch his best buddy, in case he fell backwards.

Not long ago, Leroy would have scoffed at all this spiritual mumbo jumbo. But, now he stayed to pray. He was thunderstruck when he heard Ben call out Elsie's name. From his face, Ben looked happy and relieved. A great weight had been lifted off his shoulders.

Afterward, Ben took off on his victory run around the Sacred Circle. Running close behind were Hal, Elsie, Leroy, Robin and other supporters who followed him around the arbor. Throughout the Star Nation, the ancestors watching the dance cheered for their brothers.

On the last round of the day, the Tree of Life shook and shook and shook. When the eagle dancer's leathered skin broke free from their tethers, the ropes snapped off the dowels and flew back at the tree. Cheers and war whoops echoed through the prairie. Every step was a victory. A new year had begun.

After all was said and done, the sun dancers lined up single file. In gratitude, the big drum pounded as singers sang everyone home. Holding the buffalo skull carefully in his hands, the elder dancer headed up the procession. As the dancers took their last walk around the Sacred Circle, Ben stood with Robin, Leroy and Hal near the east gate. Here, the dancers would finally exit the arbor for the last time.

"Okay, Leroy," said Hal. "You got a good chance to get that yellow flag from the east gate, if you play your cards right."

"What do you mean?" asked Leroy not sure what Hal was implying.

"Well, once the dance is over, this whole arbor gets taken down. You can take those prayer ties and flags home if you want," Hal. "I got a few of the prayer ties on my dashboard for protection. After the last dancer passes through the gate, those prayer flags and ties are up for grabs."

With a keen eye, Leroy assessed the situation. It was just like Hal to bate him with a challenge moments before it was time.

"Did I ever tell you the first word Ohiya, my Heyoka buddy, said to me?" Hal asked as the sun dancers started to make their way around the arbor.

"No," said Leroy.

"Well, I was a helper at my third dance. I'd been guarding the east gate all four days. Me and my buddy Robert had the afternoon shift. So, it's the end of the dance and the last sun dancer walks past me. Behind me, there's another guy waiting to grab the prayer flag, too. So I got some competition. Just as I'm getting ready to lunge for the flag, I hear this voice say "NO!!!" I stop dead in my tracks and look up. And there's Ohiya, the feared Heyoka in the silver skirt, bringing up the rear of the dance. So, I stepped back and let him pass. Then, I grabbed the yellow flag."

Swift like the wind, Leroy moved in towards the east gate. Like a cougar, he inched up coyly to the flag. Leroy watched as the last sun dancer passed out of the Sacred Circle. A few people had their eyes on the yellow flag, before Leroy swept in and claimed it as his own.

The big drum pounded as the singers sang their last sun dance song for the year. Sure enough, as the dancers left the arbor, children and people claimed the prayer ties for themselves. This way they all had a piece of the Sun Dance to carry with them, wherever they went.

Late that afternoon, there was a great feast. The whole community turned out. They sat in the shade of a few trees, eating and talking. Walking through camp, Leroy ran into Little Buffalo in his street clothes. Their eyes met and they smiled. "Hey," said Leroy. "Thanks for dancing."

"Thanks for watching the east gate," he paused. "Say, how do you know Hal?"

"You know, it's a long story. But he kinda saved my life," said Leroy. "Then he brought me here, so I could get a new one."

"He's a good man," said Little Buffalo. "Tell him I'll stop by later before he goes."

"Will do," said Leroy.

Building a Tiospaye, an extended family, starts with making relations. It's how new families are formed. Leroy met so many good people in the last few days. Living in this Sun Dance camp, everyone worked together. It made him think about how life was for the First Nations People before the white man came to Turtle Island. Every night, Leroy fell into a deep sleep. He was exhausted after keeping fire and guarding the east gate. He'd made some new friends. It felt good to be here.

For the next couple days, they helped take down the arbor, until only the sacred cottonwood tree was left. After the dance, people visited the tree and prayed there. Trees were the part of Creation which had its roots in the Earth and its head in the sky. Much of camp had cleared out, when Hal's truck was packed and they were ready to go.

"So what happens to the tree, after the dance?" asked Leroy.

"Well, when they take it down, they use the wood to start the fire for next year's dance. All the tobacco prayers are given to the fire and sometimes the fabric is donated to make star quilts," said Hal as he walked through their camp site. He gave it a good once over to make sure that he left camp in better

475

condition than when he found it.

Back at home, Kyle was busy working the Twelve Steps. He and his dad, Jed, took the vow "DON'T DRINK, NO MATTER WHAT." After a time, he found his life began to change in a good way. Ever since the sweat lodge, he didn't hate his brother anymore. The ceremony brought a healing between them. Now, his family joined Ben and Hal at the Inipi once a week.

One afternoon, Kyle searched the internet for Inipi songs. He wanted to learn the songs his mom was forbidden to sing when she was at the Indian boarding school. To be a Keeper of the Songs was an important part of the ceremony. Every word uttered was a prayer.

Vera and Kyle stared at the computer screen watching videos of singers around a big drum. Hearing the songs her grandmother used to sing, woke up the buried language deep inside Vera. Down in the basement, Vera found an old suitcase from her parents. Inside was an old hand drum. The smile on Kyle's face couldn't have been bigger, when his mom handed it to him. Together, they learned many Inipi songs.

Not looking to escape from boredom anymore, Kyle began doing well in his studies. At one point, he even stopped feeling sorry for himself. Going through the Twelve Steps, self-hatred no longer plagued him. By the time he finished making his amends, his mind was clear. After that, Kyle found his passion. His mind loved to chew on the history of his people. Around the fire place, Kyle talked to Hal about the Indian wars. It was obvious, after Custer's Last Stand, the U.S. government retaliated by ignoring the treaties and taking the Black Hills away from their people.

At the community college, Kyle enrolled in a tribal law class. His mind loved chewing on the history of his people and the law of the land. In his studies, he did so well that he received scholarships to great universities.

With an open road in front of him, Kyle took advantage

of the monies afforded Native Americans for education. Knowing the trials that faced his people, he wanted to give back. In his dreaming, when he finished his law degree, Kyle wanted to intern in Washington DC at the Office of Tribal Affairs. Then, he'd have an overview on how to help his people.

On the way home from the dance, Ben knew in his gut, he had to pass these medicine ways on to someone. While Hal drove the long stretch through the prairie, Ben stared out the window. The feeling gnawed at him. But who'd be willing to learn what Ben knew to be true? Most people lived in a sinkhole of indifference when it came to learning spiritual truths. Living sober on the Red Road was hard. But it was better than being dead. It was the only way Ben knew, that made sense to him.

When they rolled into town, the rez dogs barked up a storm as they chased Hal's old truck down the street. The men had been gone a good two weeks and looked forward to coming home. It didn't take long before Frank and Ernie showed up and helped unload the truck. They stayed long into the afternoon to hear all about their adventure. Within seconds, the whole town knew they were home.

Sam's mom, Tess was on the phone with Lynn when Hal's truck rolled by. "Oh, dad just got home," said Tess. "I bet they're pretty beat from the trip."

"We should make dinner. I want to hear how their trip went," said Lynn.

"I'll send Sam down to tell them. What time are you thinking?" asked Tess.

"Well, I got a roast I can put in the oven. I'd say around six," said Lynn.

"Sounds good. I'll call you later," said Tess as she hung up the phone.

"SAM!" shouted Tess.

"What mom?"

"Your grandpa's home. Go run down there and tell him to invite Hal and Leroy over for dinner. Tell them around six, okay!" Tess heard the screen door slam as Sam flew to his grandpa's house. Tah-tay swept up behind him and they raced the whole way there. When Sam came flying up the street, Hal was unloading the camping gear. "Hey there, little buddy," said Hal as he set his stuff down.

Sam stopped running when he got to the porch, completely out of breath. "Mom..." breath in and breath out, "wants ..you ..to ..come," breath in and breath out.

"Well, take a minute and catch your breath, Sam," said Hal as he sat down on the porch. Just then Ben walked out of the front door, holding a cup of coffee.

"Sam!" said Ben affectionately as he tussled the boys hair.

"He's catching his breath," said Hal. "He started to say something about us coming somewhere. But that's all I got."

Sam took a deep breath and then spit it out. "Mom wants you to come for dinner at six," said Sam.

"Well, that sounds good. We've been eating road food the last couple days," said Ben sitting on the other side of Sam.

"How was your trip grandpa?" Sam wanted to be the first to hear his grandpa's stories.

"Well, Sam, it was good. I saw your grandma Elsie there. She was in the arbor," the old man said.

"Sam, your grandpa's a true warrior and don't you forget it. He pierced up to the tree and broke free in nothing flat. You should have seen that tree shake!" said Hal.

"Really grandpa?" asked Sam.

"Well, you can see where he pierced up," said Hal.

"Can I see grandpa?" asked Sam.

The old man unbuttoned his shirt. On his chest were

two red wounds where the skin pulled free. Alongside, there were some old scars from when he sun danced as a much younger man.

"Did it hurt grandpa?" Sam's voice was full of concern.

"Well, let me explain it to you this way," started the old man. "It's not about the pain, so much, as the understanding. When a man pierces to the Tree of Life, it's the only way he'll understand the pain women go through birthing children."

"How's that, grandpa?" Sam asked.

"Well, when a woman carries a child in her womb, she's tied to it by a cord for 9 months. When that baby comes into the world, there's a lot of blood, screaming and tearing of flesh. A man will never understand what that feels like, until he's tied to the Tree of Life and has to break free. Even then, it's only for a short while. But it gives us men some knowing about what women go through."

"Yeah buddy, the womenfolk have it much tougher than us men," Hal agreed. Tah-tay rustled through the buffalo grass as the men were silent for a time. It took a while for Sam to cogitate on this whole Sun Dance business. He wondered what it was about.

"What do you have to do to be a sun dancer?" asked Sam breaking the silence.

"Well, little buddy, it's a long road," Hal started. "But it's a good one. How old are you?"

"I'm going to be twelve next month," said Sam.

"TWELVE!" Ben shook his head. "Where'd the time go?"

"Well," Hal started. "From what I was taught, that'd be the time, you'd go up on your first vision quest."

"Hmm," said Ben in agreement. "That'd be a good ceremony to bring you into manhood."

"Yeah buddy, it's time to cut those apron strings," Hal agreed. "After you do a vision quest, you start by helping out

479

around the arbor for four years. When you know your way around the Sun Dance, the arbor might call to you. If it does, you can make a Sun Dance pledge for four years. Now, this is a way of life, Sam. Every year, sun dancers do a vision quest. That way, they get rid of the monkey mind."

Sam laughed. "What's a monkey mind?"

"It's plum craziness," said Hal. "That's why a sun dancer goes up on the hill for four days. It's how he gets wisdom from beyond his own mind. When he sits in quiet with his sacred pipe, away from everything, he can hear the Voice of Creator."

Sam thought about this for a minute. He was intrigued by what Hal and his grandpa were saying.

"Now, just so you know, you don't pierce up the first four years of your Sun Dance pledge," Hal started. "After you get a feel for the dance, then you can pierce on the second four year pledge."

Sam started counting the years in his head. "That's 12 years. Four years of helping, four years of dancing without piercing and four years of piercing."

"Well, little buddy, it's a way of life for some," Hal began. "After you finish your second four year pledge, you can sign up for four more and be an eagle dancer. That's where you're pierced to the Tree of Life all four days."

"But why do you do it?" Sam asked after a while.

"Because it called to me," Hal started. "When I listened to the drum, I heard the heartbeat of Mother Earth. I felt the Power of Creator in the Sun Dance arbor. When I was of service to the Creator, everything came together. When I was in service to myself, everything fell apart. The first time I went on the hill, I found peace and wanted more of it. It taught me how to live in the moment. When I went with Wyatt to the Sun Dance, it called my name. I've lived that way ever since."

"Do you want to learn these ways?" asked Ben as he looked at his grandson.

"Would you teach me, grandpa?"

For years Ben waited for one of his children to ask him that question. But they were too busy chasing the white man's dreams. Looking into Sam's eyes, he knew why he'd lived one more year, even amidst the heartache and loneliness.

"Well, what do you think, Hal?" Ben queried.

"Hmm..." said Hal standing up. "Let me take a look. I'll do a little inspection." Hal walked around Sam. "Looks like all the parts are working," said Hal as he picked up Sam's arm. "I'd say we give it a go."

"Grandson, you make my heart smile," Ben started. "I'm going to ask you to come to four Inipi ceremonies and see what it's like. I know you've never been in one. If you still want to learn these ways after the Inipi, then we'll talk some more."

"You know what Ben," Hal started out. "I'm going to teach Leroy how to make his own Cannupa. He got that pipe stone from the elder at Sun Dance. How's about I teach Sam how to make one too. That way, he'll be ready for his first vision quest, after he turns twelve."

"Well, Sam, if you learn how to make a sacred pipe with Hal, I'll teach you how to do a pipe ceremony. You can come pray with me in the mornings, when the sun rises," Ben said.

"Okay, grandpa. I'll be here in the morning," said Sam with a big smile. "Will you teach me the songs too?"

"You bet," said Ben with a big smile.

"Sam, come with me a minute, would ya," said Hal as he stood up. They walked over to the truck. The old door creaked as Hal opened it and rummaged around in the glove box. Then, he found what he was looking for.

"Now, Sam, I'm going to teach you the Old Way of asking someone to do something for you," said Hal as he held out a pouch of tobacco.

"After you come to the Inipi four times, like your

grandpa asked, then you can make a good decision. That way, you'll know if these Old Ways are for you. It's good to give it a try, before you decide. Now, some things, you'll know they aren't right for you, from the get go. But with the lodge, it's good to come four times."

"Then, what do I do?" asked Sam.

"Well, that's what I'm going to show you," said Hal. "Take this tobacco home and put it some place you won't forget it."

"I'll put it in my pillow," said Sam. "That way no one will mess with it."

"Well, that's a good a place as any," Hal started. "Now, after you sweat four times and you want to learn more, offer the tobacco to your grandpa and ask him to teach you again. If he takes the tobacco, that means he'll do it. If he don't take it, you may not be ready. But, either way, you'll know for sure. I got to warn you, these Old Ways aren't easy. It's the hard road. But, on the hard road, you'll build muscle and faith in Creator to handle anything that comes your way."

Down in his bones, Hal knew the underlying Power of Creator was infinitely greater than human force. But, there was no way to teach this. It had to be experienced. Ceremony gave him the place to witness Creator in action. In ceremony, he had a sense of awe, a sense of reverence and a sense of the Great Mystery.

"Thanks Hal," said Sam as he put the tobacco in his pocket.

The next morning, just before sun up, Sam was out the door bright and early. The morning air was brisk as Tah-tay chased him down the River Road. Roosters crowed in first light when he flew by the farms on the reservation.

The coffee maker was brewing, when Ben got out his pipe bag. He'd give the boy a few more minutes, before he headed up the hill. His morning pipe ceremony had been a solitary practice for many years. It was the way he greeted the day. A true student was a hard find. Not many wanted to live a sober and holy way of life. The dark side of the white life was more enticing. Most paid a hard price for that choice. Ben never forced ceremony on anyone. Often, that put a sour taste in their mouth. But Sam showed some promise.

The first rays of sunlight crept behind the eastern hillsides, when Sam met his grandpa at the door. With a simple nod the old man greeted him. In silence, they walked up the hill where Ben did a pipe ceremony most mornings. Tah-tay came to blow his iron gray braids from his back as Ben laid down his blanket.

"Good morning Tah-tay," he whispered as he sat facing the rising sun. Sam settled down beside him, waiting for his grandpa to talk.

"Now Sam, I don't claim to know the only way to do a pipe ceremony," Ben started. "I'm just going to show you the way I was taught. After you make your Cannupa, you'll become a pipe carrier. Remember, your prayers are between you and Creator. As a pipe carrier, you'll pray for the people. True prayers are from the heart. And just so you know, a strong heart isn't selfish. Even your enemies are your brothers. So, if a man strikes you down or hurts someone you love, it's better to search your heart and find forgiveness."

In the silence of the morning, Sam watched as his grandpa smudged everything off. Ben got quiet for a moment as he gathered his thoughts. In this world of duality, for every good action, there was an equal but opposite force or reaction. The dance of opposites kept things in balance. When there was too much darkness, Mother Earth had a way of balancing things out. Many times, She'd call upon the Wind, Water and Fire spirits to wipe things clean off the planet.

"Now Sam, some people pray for bad things. Their hearts are pained because their mind is weak. That isn't what the Cannupa is for. Do you understand?"

"You mean like the man who lives down in the hollows?" Sam asked.

"Well, that old sorcerer has been around a long time, Sam. He just went down a different path," Ben started. "He serves Creator by opposing the good."

"What does that mean?" Sam asked not sure if he wanted to know.

"Well, on Earth, we've got duality, the good and the not so good. It's the two teams, the Light and the dark. Now, both sides work for Creator. One creates and the other destroys. What you got to know is, our adversaries make us stronger."

"But why are people afraid of him?" Sam asked.

"Well, some people are weak. That old conjurer wakes up their hatred and evil passions to destroy them. Weak people only learn lessons the hard way. They pay Creator no mind when He taps on their shoulder or whispers in their ear."

"What do you mean, grandpa?"

"It's pretty simple, Sam," Ben started. "When a man uses sorcery, he goes after the evil in men's own hearts. He finds their hidden faults and makes them worse. His power gets that hateful fire burning so hot, that they destroy each other."

"How does he do that grandpa?"

"Well, he uses his power to control the minds of the weak. After he finds a way in, he'll call on dark spirits, like the spirit of jealousy or anger and gets them on the warpath. When those unfriendlies spread their madness all over, people get so riled up, they kill each other," Ben started to explain. "Let's say your weakness is anger. If the man down in the hollows wanted to start a war, he'd fan that angry flame inside you until you exploded and hurt somebody. Then, he'll send spirits to whisper angry thoughts in your head and get you all confused."

"But how do you stop him, grandpa?"

"Get rid of your weaknesses," Ben said staring this young boy down. Sam went silent as he thought this over.

"What you got to know Sam is, the Light of Creator is stronger than any dark medicine that old conjurer can send. If your heart is strong and pure, his medicine won't work against you. To win that battle, I had to master my weaknesses. Otherwise, he'd have an open door and I didn't want to let him get in."

"Did he try to hurt you grandpa?"

"Oh sure he did," Ben said thinking about how far he wanted to go with this conversation. "But when that old sorcerer sent me demons, I sent him Angels. The Oglegla are much more powerful, you know. When he put me to the test, I learned real quick whose side I was on. I was grateful to be sober and that I had a Higher Power to call on when the storm clouds started brewing."

Sam always knew there was something different about his grandpa. He knew things other people didn't know. The world of Angels, the Oglegla and dark spirits was something Sam read about in story books, but his grandpa knew it to be true.

"Now, I met a medicine man who carried a Cannupa Sapa, a black pipe. He followed Heyoka medicine teachings. Some people are afraid of the Heyoka," Ben said.

"Why is that grandpa?"

"Because the Thunder Dreamers are lesson givers in another way. A Heyoka draws the poison out of a man's heart so it can be healed by the Love of Creator. But, a Heyoka is different from a sorcerer, grandson," Ben explained.

"How's that grandpa?"

"Well, they got different reasons for being," Ben started. "A sorcerer uses the evil in men's hearts to destroy them. Now, if that old conjurer can't tempt you through your hidden faults, he'll find a way to use your love against you."

485

"What do you mean grandpa, he'll use my love against me?"

"Well, that old Tempter is mighty crafty when it comes to knocking down good-hearted people, especially those who are aware of their faults and are trying to get rid of them. He'll find out what they love or good passions, their loyalties and use it against them. He'll use your love against you."

Sam cogitated on this for a moment. He couldn't grasp how someone could do this kind of work. "But how does he do it grandpa?"

"The devil is a great flatterer," the old man said. "But his honeyed words don't mean anything. He's just laying a trap to get what he wants. When he lays it on thick, you got to look closer to see the truth of his intentions. He's got a lot of tricks up his sleeve for unknowing people. Keep this in mind, he's trying to get you on his side. If he can't snare you through your hatred, he'll tempt you with what you love. Just remember, there's more than one way to skin a cat."

Sam's young mind whirled, trying to make sense of all this information. "But what about the Heyoka?"

"Ah, I knew I was leaving something out," Ben admitted. "Now, the Thunder Dreamer uses his medicine ways for healing. He'll draw the poison out of your heart and expose it. Sometimes so the whole world can see."

"That sounds embarrassing, grandpa," Sam said thoughtfully.

"Well, sometimes it's the only way to get a hard head's attention. But, once that ugliness is out in the Light, it can be healed through ceremony. Does that make sense? Can you see how different their purpose is?"

"Well, the sorcerer wants to destroy and the Heyoka does healing work," Sam said thoughtfully. "So, I see how that's different."

"Good," said Ben. "Just know, we all have our place on

the medicine wheel, son. We're all children of Great Spirit. Together, we're all one. Do you understand?"

"I think so," said Sam.

"When I started on the Red Road, I met people who were bent up like a run over tin can. They were unwanted, unloved and alone. The goodness was squeezed out of them or so it seemed. Most were called to the Red Road for healing. When you smoke this Cannupa, just remember the power of love is much stronger than hate. You'll never go wrong if you pray good blessings for everyone."

Ben understood that there was unity in opposites. The Great Mystery created both. The endless dance of creation and destruction were two rivers flowing in opposite directions. This way, Creator revealed the hidden and deep understandings of the Universe. Through these two paths, the Great Mystery came to know Itself, the good and the not so good. This was the journey. When the dance became imbalanced and destruction dominated, eventually everything would be in ruins. Then, the sacred hoop of Creation would begin again.

"Mom always says, 'what goes around, comes around,'" said Sam. "So if you pray good things for people, that good will come back to you."

"Well, that's as close to the truth as I know it," said Ben. "I find it's better not to pray when I'm angry."

"Why not grandpa?" asked Sam curiously. His grandpa knew things.

"Well, when my anger goes out into the Universe, it comes back to smack me upside the head. You know, angry spirits answer angry prayers." Ben laughed. "One time, I got mad at this old jalopy I was driving. I hated that car. I yelled at Creator and told Him the car was a heap of junk! I wanted it smashed to smithereens."

"Then, what happened grandpa?" asked Sam with big eyes.

"Well, a month goes by and I forgot what I yelled at Creator. Then, one snowy afternoon, I'm driving down the road, when I hit a patch of black ice. That piece of junk spun around and around. It flipped upside down and went flying into a ditch. I was stuck hanging upside down from my seat belt." Ben started laughing.

"What's so funny, grandpa?"

"Well, when I got to the hospital, I remembered my angry prayer. Sure enough, it got answered pretty quick," smiled Ben.

A moment of silence enveloped them as Sam cogitated on his grandpa's stories. After a while, Ben took his Cannupa from the pipe bag. The wooden pipe stem and his eagle bone whistle were wrapped in an altar cloth. The pipe stone bowl was in a separate pouch. Ben unwrapped the pipe stem and placed the altar cloth on the blanket in front of him. After that, he removed the pipe stone bowl and placed it on the altar cloth.

In another small pouch, Ben had his pipe smoke. It was a red willow bark tobacco called Chan-shasha. Ben's Chan-shasha was a mix of different herbs, like red willow bark, bear berry and a few other herbs. He didn't use tobacco in his pipe or any herbs that were mind altering.

"Now, have I told you the story about White Buffalo Calf Woman, Pte San Win?" asked Ben.

"I don't know," answered Sam. "Maybe."

"Well, a few centuries ago, Creator answered a prayer by sending our people Pte San Win. Our people were in trouble. They were hungry and couldn't find anything to eat. When she came, she brought a holy medicine bundle, the sacred pipe. The Cannupa is a powerful way for us to communicate with Creator. That medicine bundle was passed down from Creator to our ancestors, the Star Nation. Then the Star Nation passed them to the Eagle Nation, who passed them to the Buffalo Nation, who passed them on to us."

"Is this the story about the two hunters who met a beautiful woman?" asked Sam.

"That's the one. Good, so I did tell you the story," smiled Ben, realizing Sam paid attention.

"Well, now," said Ben as he picked up the pipe stone bowl in his left hand and the stem in his right. "The bowl is the feminine. She receives the pipe smoke. The wood stem is the masculine." He passed the bowl and stem over the smoldering sage and gently put them together. "When you connect them, Creation happens."

"After you put them together, you add the pipe smoke. With every pinch of the Chan-shasha you make your prayers. After that, you light the fire and pull on the smoke. That holy smoke carries your prayers to Creator."

"Before I forget, hold the bowl in your left hand. It's closest to your heart and don't let the bowl fall off, because that ends the ceremony. Every morning, when you smoke the Cannupa with me, I'll teach you more about the pipe ceremony. It was the first ceremony given to us by Pte San Win," said Ben. "Did I teach you the pipe loading song yet?

Sam wasn't sure. "I don't know, grandpa."

"Well, I'll sing it with you now," said the old man as he held his Cannupa in his left hand. Standing on his knees, Ben picked up his eagle bone whistle and blew into it. First to the east, then the south, the west and then the north. The Spirits of the Four Winds heard him calling.

"Kola lecel lecun wo.... Kola lecel lecun wo... Kola lecel lecun wo, hey...." Ben's voice was carried across the prairie by the four winds. Sam stood on his knees next to his grandpa and sang along. At one point Ben glanced in his grandson's direction. His heart smiled hearing the boy's young voice blend with his.

"Now Sam, I'm going to load the Cannupa with 7 prayers made with a pinch of Chan-shasha. The first prayer is to

489

Creator, the Great Mystery. Then, a prayer to the ancestors of the east, the south, the west and the north. One prayer to Mother Earth and the last prayer is to the sacred fire within our heart, the Wakan. With each pinch, I'll thank Creator and my ancestors for my life and pray for the people."

Sam watched while his grandpa took a pinch of Chan-shasha and smudged it over the smoldering sage. Then, he raised it above his head. Sam heard his grandpa whisper "Wakan Tanka, Tunkashila, Great Spirit, Grandfather, ...thank you for my life...." the rest of the prayer was whispered so quietly, Sam could barely make it out. Then Ben placed the Chan-shasha into the pipe stone bowl.

With the next pinch of pipe smoke, his grandpa smudged it off and offered to the east. Sam only heard the first words of the prayer, "Wakan Tanka, Tunkashila, Great Spirit, Grandfather and all my ancestors of the east, thank you for my life..." Then, the prayer went quiet. The sun rises in the east. It's light blesses Mother Earth and all her relations.

Then his grandpa offered the next pinch of Chan-shasha to the south. "Wakan Tanka, Tunkashila, Great Spirit, Grandfather, and all my ancestors of the south... thank you for my life..."

When his grandpa prayed to the west, Sam heard him mention the Thunder Beings, the Wakinyan Oyate. The west is where the sun goes down and the day comes to an end. Sam understood that prayers were private. He felt honored to sit with his grandpa and do this ceremony.

Next his grandpa prayed to the north, the place of knowledge and wisdom. Every pinch of Chan-shasha was smudged and prayed with. Afterward, it was placed in the pipe stone bowl.

When his grandpa prayed for Mother Earth, he put his hand, holding the Chan-shasha, onto the Earth. Mother Earth provided equally for all the children of Creator. All our relations, every leaf, plant, rock and creature, were made by the same Great Spirit. We are all related and equal under the One.

The last prayer, his grandpa held the Chan-shasha to his heart, Within is where the Great Mystery placed His sacred fire. Once the sacred pipe was loaded, Ben offered it to the seven directions. Then he passed the Cannupa to Sam.

"Now, go ahead and make your prayers. Hold the bowl in your left hand and the stem in your right. When your done, pass it to me and we'll smoke it. I'll smoke the first part and you'll smoke the last. Only pull the smoke into your mouth."

As he passed the sacred pipe to his grandson, Ben was mindful to hold onto the bowl, lest it slip out and the prayer be brought to an immediate stop. When the boy received the Cannupa, he held the bowl in his left hand. When Sam closed his eyes, a moving picture flooded into his mind.

In his mind's eye, Sam saw the Missouri lined with teepees. The chiefs and old medicine men sat around a council fire, while young children played along the river bank. From far and wide, warriors rode in on horseback across the Great Plains. Some women were busy skinning the buffalo which the men brought back to feed their families. Other women watched the children or gathered berries and wild turnips for their food.

Tears flowed down Sam's face as he sat on the lap of Mother Earth. An eagle's cry pierced the silence of the morning, as it swept across the Missouri. In his mind's eye, he witnessed his ancestors living in harmony with Mother Earth and all their relations. He felt the sacredness of life in all things, great and small. The power of the Wakan flowcd through the sacred pipe as Sam made his prayers. When Sam opened his eyes, his grandpa was smiling.

Afterward, Sam handed his grandpa the Cannupa. Ben struck a match and lit the Chan-shasha. After he pulled the holy smoke up the stem, Ben blessed the bowl with the holy smoke. Then, he blessed the stem. He blew some holy smoke at his grandson and some at the Earth. With each pull, the glowing cherry in the bowl got brighter and brighter. Sam took it all in. Peace settled over the land.

The first rays of sunlight flooded across the prairie as Ben passed the Cannupa to Sam. "Just pull the smoke into your mouth, grandson," Ben instructed.

The pipe stone bowl in Sam's left hand felt warm from the fire inside. He pulled hard on the holy smoke. As it filled his mouth, he looked into his grandpa's smiling eyes. Sitting on the hilltop, where his ancestors had lived for generations, became a moment filled with awe. A boy began his transition into manhood.

When Sam finished the pipe smoke, he passed the Cannupa back to his grandpa. Ben raised the Cannupa over his head and thanked the Great Mystery for his life and all the answered prayers. After that, Ben removed the pipe bowl from the stem and placed them on the altar cloth. Next, he sang a familiar gratitude song, one that Sam had heard since he was a baby.

Together, their voices carried across the prairie by the wind as they welcomed in the morning. "Wakan Tanka, Tunkashila... Pila maya yelo hey... pila maya yelo hey... wiconzoni wan myacuelo...pila maya ye... pila maya yelo hey... Cannupa wankaca myacuelo hey... pila maya ya yelo hey... wiconzoni wan myacuelo pila maya ye...pila maya yelo hey..."

When the ceremony was finished, Ben blew into his eagle bone whistle, sending the Spirits off to go do their perfect work. It was in this way that man and Spirit worked together in harmony. For a while, Ben sat with his grandson in the quiet of the morning. That is until Ben heard Hal bellowing at Leroy.

"COME ON LEROY! WE'RE BURNING DAYLIGHT!" Hal's voice boomed across the prairie. His heavy boots stomped across the front porch as he carried his coffee cup back to the tipi. Back at the ranch, Roy was getting some new horses delivered early that morning. Hal and Leroy needed to get back to work.

"Well Sam, it looks like the day's starting," said Ben as

he tussled his grandson's hair. "How about we go over to Kelly's and get some hotcakes?"

"Okay, grandpa," said Sam as they got everything together and walked down the hill.

Days later, Sam went to his first Inipi. Inside the lodge, he sat next to his grandpa and put cedar on the stones. Listening to songs of the ancient ancestors, the stories his grandpa shared, all came together. In the drum, he felt the heart beat of Mother Earth. Knowing most of the Inipi songs, Sam sang along. It touched Ben's heart hearing his grandson sing. It was a prayer answered from long ago.

After Sam's forth lodge, the fire keeper cooled off some coals from the sacred fire. He put them into a bandana and gave them to Sam. That way, Sam would have a little bit of the sacred fire with him, wherever he was.

Later that afternoon, when Sam got home, he knew he wanted to learn more about ceremony. He liked being around the fire place. It felt like home. The next morning, Sam offered his grandpa tobacco to teach him these Old Ways. When Sam passed Ben the tobacco, his heart lit up. He'd have a student after all.

It wasn't long after that Hal taught Leroy and Sam how to make a Cannupa. Early one morning, they walked the Missouri. Sam and Leroy each found a young cottonwood sapling. They offered it tobacco and made a prayer of gratitude. Hal showed them where to cut off the top of it. This part of the cottonwood would become the pipe stem. By then, Leroy had made many pipe stone carvings. When it came time to make his own sacred pipe, he carved a buffalo on the pipe stone bowl.

Becoming a pipe carrier was a life long commitment, in service to Creator and the people. To walk the Red Road took courage and compassion, along with a generous, yet humble and forgiving heart. Hours of labor and sweat went into making a sacred pipe.

By itself, a pipe is just a piece of wood and a rock. For it to become Sacred, the person carrying the Cannupa needed to serve the original purpose and instructions given by White Buffalo Calf Woman. Giving your life to serve Creator was a hard road. It meant respecting Mother Earth and all life, as sacred.

After Sam and Leroy made their Cannupa, they met with Hal and Ben. The four men conducted a pipe ceremony to bless and awaken their new Cannupa. Having lived these ways for many years, Hal and Ben were in continual service to Creator. It was a great responsibility to pass these Old Ways onto a new generation.

Early one morning, they gathered on top of the hill by Ben's house. While Leroy sang the pipe loading song, Ben and Hal loaded their sacred pipes with Chan-shasha. The newly made sacred pipes lay on the altar cloth, waiting to be blessed and awakened. After Hal and Ben finished loading their Cannupa, Leroy and Sam smudged the pipe stone bowl and stem of the new Cannupa with sage.

The two young men held the pipe stone bowls in their left hand and the stem in the right. The older warriors blew the holy smoke from their Cannupa onto the new ones. Spirits were called to awaken and bless the new Cannupa. Once it was blessed, Leroy and Sam loaded the Cannupa with Chan-shasha and had a smoke.

All these medicine teachings prepared Leroy and Sam to go on the hill to do a Hanblecha and cry for a vision. Going on the hill would be Sam's ceremony into manhood. Afterward, the men would begin teaching him things he needed to know to live in harmony. Sam and Leroy embraced the Old Ways and learned all life was sacred and deserved their respect.

The following summer, the big drum beckoned the men back to Sun Dance. This time Sam traveled along. While Leroy was busy tending the sacred fire, Ben and Sam kept watch over the east gate. Every morning, after the singers came through camp, the men made it down to the dust off sweat.

During the dance, Hal and Ben pierced and dragged buffalo skulls around the arbor. Running behind his grandpa in support, Sam saw him with whole new eyes. When Hal was ready to break free, the head dancer called Sam and a couple more children from the shade arbor to sit on a buffalo skulls.

Being a tough old bull, Hal's leathered skin wouldn't let go. Like a steam locomotive, he mustered all his strength. Finally, his tough skin gave way. SNAP! Went the rope when the Hal broke free. Sam let out a war whoop and quickly got to his feet, running behind Hal for his victory lap.

Over time, Sam proved to be a dedicated student on the Red Road. He found himself welcomed into the small band of Sun Dance brothers in this reservation town. With a pitchfork in his hand, around the fire place, Sam felt right at home. Under his grandpa's knowing eye, he learned the movements of ceremony. Before he turned seventeen, Sam made a four year sun dance pledge. Leroy made his sun dance pledge the year before.

As Ben stood under the shade arbor, the next year at Sun Dance, he witnessed something he thought he'd never see. But there stood Vera and Jed, behind Leroy in full support of his Sun Dance pledge. At the east gate, Kyle kept watch with Hal. Standing beside him, was his daughter, Tess supporting Sam in the arbor. Ben prayed to the Tree of Life, thanking Creator for letting him live long enough to witness this miracle.

That morning, the Sun Dance Chief invited parents to bring their children into the arbor for a blessing. Facing the morning sun with her wiggle worm, Robin's little son, Dylan, broke away and started dancing around the Sacred Circle. This long-haired, little chubby boy moved his moccasin-ed feet in time with the big drum. His happy little body showed the dancers how to move. Smiles erupted on everyone's faces. After the round was done, the Sun Dance Chief thanked Tunkashila for sending a short dancing messenger to bring love to the people.

With a forgiving heart, Ben apologized to the Spirits for

his grouchiness after Elsie passed away. Back then, Ben had no idea that Creator would bring life back to the Inipi on his land. And now, he was with his children at Sun Dance. The big drum pounded in rhythm to the heartbeat of Mother Earth. Ben found his joy.

After Leroy finished his four year sun dance pledge, Hal passed him the dipper and the bucket. Now, Leroy would pour water for the warriors at the VA hospital. Hal moved over and let Leroy give it a go.

Before the Inipi, Leroy loaded his Cannupa as Hal sang the pipe loading song. With a bandana wrapped around his forehead, Sam kept fire. The glowing flames reflected in Ben's glasses as he thought back to when Hal snatched Leroy from the jaws of death. Ben was grateful his doubts about Leroy were never realized. As mule-headed as Leroy was, his hard heart softened after years of sobriety and ceremony.

The end of the pitchfork held glowing stones just inside the door of the Inipi. Leroy sat behind the bucket, while Hal sat at the door and placed the stones in their cradle. Smoke curled up as Ben put the cedar on the ancient grandfathers. Leroy walked plenty of miles in the moccasins of his fellow warriors. He knew the trail well. Now, he could show other soldiers how to break free from their spiritual bondage. This was no small task. It took great courage, compassion and a humble heart.

A year later, Sam finished his four year Sun Dance pledge. He was twenty one years old. Under his grandpa's tutelage, he'd never had a drink of alcohol or taken any drugs. He grew up with respect for his elders, a broadening respect for Mother Earth and the Great Mystery. Even though he'd witnessed tragedy amongst his people, his heart was not hard. More than anything, Sam had a healthy respect for a spirit called alcohol.

Kyle and Leroy were living examples of men who got sober in the nick of time, before the spirits in the bottle laid claim to their lives. Sam was witness to what a Higher Power could do, when asked in a deep, respectful way.

One morning Ben waited on the porch for Sam. The steam from his warm coffee mug billowed slightly in a breeze coming from the river. His pipe bag lay by his side. Ben's mind was quiet this morning. Inside him was an unexplained laughter, a bubbling joy, a feeling of mission accomplished. While he sipped on his coffee, he pondered over how much his life had changed since Hal's rumpy old truck pulled into the parking lot of the AA meeting all those years ago.

In the wee hours of the morning, through the mist from the river, Ben heard his grandson's footfalls coming down the River Road. Chasing the wind, Sam sprinted the last quarter mile to his grandpa's doorstep. Like most mornings, he was slightly out of breath when he got to the front porch.

"Morning Sam," smiled Ben as Sam came to a running stop. He hunched over trying to catch his breath. "You running with the wind again this morning?"

"Yeah.... But I think she beat me this time," Sam smiled, giving his grandpa a wink.

"Well, get used to it. Tah-tay's got an unfair advantage. She's got no legs," Ben chuckled. When Sam caught his breath, the old man beckoned him to come sit down on the porch. Something was different. Usually, they'd walk in silence up the hill and have their ceremony. This morning, Ben had something to say.

Sam sat down in the quiet of the morning on his grandpa's porch. As he looked out on the prairie, he realized he'd spent most of his life here, listening to his grandpa's stories. He never grew tired of them. The old man's iron silver braid hung halfway down his back again. There was a twinkle in his eye.

"You know Sam, I lived a long life thanks to my sobriety. Most of the drunks I've known are long gone. I know you've been to enough funerals in your young life. What I wanted to know is why you never took a drink, like the other boys I see running around here?" asked the old man.

"Heck grandpa, I don't know. Maybe cuz you been keeping me so busy with ceremony, it just never crossed my mind. Hal don't drink, Leroy quit and so did Kyle. I don't hang out with many other people," Sam replied.

"Well, that's true. When you got good spirits around you, the bad ones tend to stay away. But that don't mean you won't get challenged now and then," said the old man.

"No, I guess you're right there," said Sam. "Hal just says 'Indians can't drink' and people leave him alone."

"Well, that's true too," said the old man. "Now, I've been thinking about this a long while and I want you to hear me out, before you say no."

"Okay," said Sam wondering what all this was leading up to.

"When I was a young man and Hal found me drunk in that Army nuthouse, I never thought I'd live to see thirty years old. Then, he drug me around to ceremony, just like he's doing with Leroy now. We sat down with Wyatt and we made our Cannupa, the same way Hal showed you and Leroy. I've been carrying this sacred pipe for most of my life. It's been my way of life, through the good and not so good times. I trust it to carry me through. I want to give it to you," Ben said.

Sam didn't know what to say, he started to protest, when Ben put up his hand. "I'm not finished yet."

"Sam, my braid's gone white. Now, that don't mean I'm dead. But I know it's my time to pass these medicine ways to someone or I'll be taking them home with me. You're a good student, Sam. When it's my time, I want to leave here with no regrets." Ben went silent. The importance of what he was saying seeped into the ground water of his mind.

"But what about our pipe ceremony?" Sam asked after a moment of quiet.

"Oh, you'll still come fetch me in the morning and we'll

take care of the pipe. Only this way, you'll be the one who loads the Cannupa. Like an old goat, I've been walking up that hill every morning, leading the way. It's time for you to lead, Sam." The old man got up from his chair and went in the house. "Come with me," he said.

Ben went over to his cedar box where he kept all his Sacreds. Since Sam was a child, he wondered what was in there. Ben opened the lid of the cedar box and the smell of the cedar filled the room. Wrapped in an old pillow case were the moccasins Elsie made all those years ago. As Ben held them in his hand, he got misty-eyed.

"What do you got, grandpa?" Sam asked as Ben held the moccasins in his hand.

Ben unwrapped the beaded moccasins and held them out. "Your grandma made these for me, many years ago. Any time, I'd even get a tear in them, she'd rework them. Her love and her prayers are in these moccasins, grandson."

When Sam walked over, Ben handed them to his grandson. "Here, I want you to try them on."

"Are you sure, grandpa?"

Ben just held them out in front of him. No words could come. There was a chicken bone of strong feelings stuck in his throat.

Sam sat down on the edge of the bed and pulled off his tennis shoes. The leather on the beaded moccasins was soft. He slipped them on his feet and tied the leather cord that pulled them together at the top. They fit.

Ben studied his grandson. This moment had finally come. For years, he doubted anyone would step up to carry this calling. When he was a young man, in his early years of sobriety, Hal took him to ceremony. Now it had come full circle.

"The last time I wore those in the arbor, your grandma came to me," Ben sighed as tears welled up in his eyes. Sam

499

stood up. He took the corner of the pillowcase and wiped away the tears rolling down his grandpa's cheeks.

"She wouldn't want you to cry anymore, grandpa," said Sam as he dried the old man's tears.

"No, she wouldn't," said Ben. "I kept her spirit close to me a long time, grandson."

"All these years grandpa?" asked Sam knowing a little about how a soul is kept after a loved one passes away.

"Well, after she passed, your grandma was around me all the time. Most nights, she'd come to me in my dream time. Sometimes, I'd go looking for her. I'd usually find her sitting on our favorite log, down by the river. That woman had a lot of spunk. Even in the spirit world, she caught me off guard. One night, she turned the lights on and off, just to let me know she was there. But, I never wanted her to be stuck here," Ben admitted as he lit some sweet grass from his cedar box.

Sam listened intently. He remember his grandma's hands, holding him close when he was a little boy.

"So late one night after she passed, I burned all her clothes. Then, after a year went by, I told her to go Home, so many times. It tore at my heart to tell her to leave. But I didn't want to be selfish. My heart was so lonely," Ben's heart was overcome with emotion.

"I'm sorry grandpa," Sam said compassionately.

"Well, your grandma had a mind of her own, you know. Even spirits have free will. Then, when we fired up the lodge for Leroy, I felt her spirit sit down right next to me. Up at Sun Dance, when I was pierced up to the tree, she was in the arbor, standing there... next to me."

"That's strong love, grandpa," Sam remarked.

"Your grandma was a strong woman. Through the worst of it, she held our family together. I still got a lock of her hair in that red cloth," Ben pointed to a small dresser next to the bed. There was a bundle of red cloth next to a picture of Elsie.

500

Within the next few moments, Sam found out what was in his grandpa's cedar chest. In a piece of folded cardboard was his eagle fan, along with some eagle feathers and a few hawk feathers. Folded up in the corner of the box was all Ben's Sun Dance regalia. There was a leather pouch of red willow bark, along with some other herbs that Ben used in his pipe smoke. He'd kept a bag of beads that Elsie used in her bead work. Next to that, was his hand drum, his cedar bag and a few pieces of soft leather Elsie used to mend his moccasins.

"Now, I'm not going to need any of this medicine where I'm going, Sam. I wanted to give it to someone who would use it in the right way. In my heart, I believe that someone is you," smiled the old man.

"I'm honored grandpa," Sam said.

"Well, there's a few other things I want to talk over with you," Ben started. "Ever since Hal passed the VA lodge to Leroy last year, I've been thinking. I know it's a lot of work, but I think you're ready to pour a lodge yourself. I'll ride shotgun for a while and show you how it works. Frank and Ernie are good fire keepers. They've never let me down. But so you know, keeping the lodge going, and making sure everyone is safe, is the first priority in my book."

"Grandpa...." said Sam completely overcome.

"Now, I said it was a lot. But, I've got faith in you son. We'll go smoke on it and Creator will guide you with what to do," said Ben as he closed the lid of the box. "Let's go take care of that pipe."

Sam started to pull off the moccasins, when Ben stopped him. "Go ahead and keep those on, son. There's some good medicine in those moccasins." When they got to the bottom of the knoll in front of his house, Ben stepped aside. "Come on son, it's time for you to lead."

Feeling a little uncomfortable, Sam stepped in front of his grandpa. As he lead the way, he was mindful of his grandpa's steps behind him. There was a time, when he was young, he would have raced up the hill, especially if he was in front. But now, he paced himself, so he wouldn't get too far ahead.

As they reached the top, Ben laid down his old Indian blanket, like he did every morning. The dew was heavy on the buffalo grass this morning. The wind swept up from the west, bringing cool air from the Missouri. Ben stood facing his grandson. He held his Cannupa out in front of him.

"Now, we'll pass this Cannupa four times back and forth, just like they do at Sun Dance. If, on the fourth pass, you decide to carry this sacred pipe and make it your own, you'll take it then," said Ben. "Understood."

"Yes," said Sam. All time stood still as Ben passed the Cannupa to Sam four times, back and forth. Tah-tay, the wind, held her breath as she watched this holy instant. Deep in his bones, Sam knew this was an important moment. So many thoughts went racing through his mind as the Cannupa passed through the air. He couldn't imagine walking this Red Road without his grandpa, but someday it would happen. On the fourth pass, Sam accepted the Cannupa. Ben felt a sense of relief. He knew he'd made the right choice.

Twirling in circles, Tah-tay and the spirits of the land danced across the prairie, knowing the Old Medicine Ways would stay alive another generation. For centuries, the Elementals, the spirits of Fire, Water, Earth and Air depended on the few gifted medicine people who honored Mother Earth. Without their kind and generous prayers, the Elementals would have left man and his ignorance to starve a long time ago. The Elementals were the first Beings to live on Mother Earth. Each one carried parts of the others within them. Without the fire from the sun, air or water, physical life would not exist.

Ben looked up to see Tah-tay swirling the dust around in mini cyclones across the hillside. "Look at that Sam, the old girl's dancing for you."

In the quiet recesses of his heart, Sam's spirit smiled

within. To begin his pipe ceremony, he called to the four directions with his eagle bone whistle. As he looked across the endless prairie, Sam lifted up the Cannupa to the heavens. "Great Spirit, Grandfather... thank you for my life," Sam whispered.

That morning, Ben sang the pipe loading song while Sam loaded the Cannupa with Chan-shasha and prayers. Sam thought a lot about his grandma Elsie. Wearing the beaded moccasins, she'd made by hand, he wanted to honor her with every pinch of Chan-shasha. "Grandpa, do you think I should make a prayer so that grandma Elsie goes Home?"

"Well, as long as you know, she's got a mind of her own," Ben smiled as a deep silence enveloped them.

"Are you ready to let go?" Sam asked knowing he was going into deep waters.

"Well, that's the tougher question, isn't it?" Ben fell silent for a long moment. Small tendrils of grief still bound Elsie to him. It was time to let go. He'd never stop loving her. But it was time to mend his heart.

"Yeah," Ben sighed as he motioned Sam to make the prayer. Once the Cannupa was loaded, Sam offered it to the seven directions. Then, he handed it to his grandpa, to make his own prayers. Holding the Cannupa in his hands, tears rolled down Ben's face. It was a powerful moment of letting go.

Riding on the wind, Elsie's spirit stood before him. She smiled as she saw her hand made moccasin's on Sam's feet. With all her heart, she blessed her grandson. She was grateful that in the winter of his life, Ben could finally pass on all the Medicine Ways he carried.

"Ah, woman," Ben sighed as he felt her spirit around him. He called on the Higher Powers to cut the cords of grief that bound them together. The love would always be there. Once he was done with his prayer, Ben passed the Cannupa to Sam.

With a strike of a match, Sam lit the Cannupa and blessed off the sacred pipe with the holy smoke. In his mind's eye, Ben could see the Spirit-helpers come and cut the cords of grief. Ben pulled the tendrils from his heart and gave them to Mother Earth. When the grief was dissolved, Elsie's spirit was free.

After they smoked the Cannupa, a peace filled the land. Sam ended the ceremony by blowing his eagle bone whistle and sent the Spirit-helpers to do their perfect work. The two men sat in quiet and watched as first rays of sunlight crept over the hillsides of the east.

"I'll do it, grandpa. I'll run the lodge," Sam spoke after a long while. "I knew I was meant to do this when we took those long walks after Johnny died."

"You remember all the talks we had, son?" asked Ben.

"All of them. In my mind's eye, I can still see the spirits in Kelly's bar, when we had breakfast that morning," Sam smiled.

"Well, just don't go talking to spirits in front of people," Ben warned. "They'll think you're crazy. And the white coats will give you all kinds of pills that will block you from Creator."

"Oh, I won't grandpa. Trust me, I won't."

"You just need to know how to weed out the good from the bad," Ben instructed. "The unfriendlies like to steer you in the wrong direction, so they get a good laugh out of it."

"But how do you know?" asked Sam.

"Well, I just ask them if they're filled with the pure love of Creator. If they're not, they won't say yes. If they're pure, they'll say so."

"Hmm," Sam said as he mulled it over. "There were a lot of spirits at Sun Dance. It was a good thing they kept the cedar can going."

"Well, the fire calls them to ceremony and the cedar

weeds them out. So does the sweet grass and the sage," Ben started. "But listen, if you really want to help those earthbound spirits out, just remind them to go Home. There's some lonely spirits who've been stuck here for hundreds of years. They're tied to Earth because of fear or jealousy. That muck keeps them stuck. Either they didn't get what they wanted or someone done them wrong."

Sam thought about what his grandpa said. The ceremonies for the deceased were an important part of their culture. The Old Ones knew it was necessary to wipe away the tears, so the spirit of their loved ones could go home. Often, unhealed grief bound spirits to their loved ones. The heartache was felt across the ethers.

Down the hill, Ben heard Hal's boots stomping across the front porch and the front door slam. "Well, it looks like the morning's starting," said Ben as he stood up.

Sam packed the Cannupa in the pipe bag as Ben picked up the blanket and shook it off. They shook hands in thanks before they headed down the hill.

It turned out that Sam was a natural in the Inipi. At the next lodge, Sam sat behind the water bucket and poured water on the stones. He watched as the breath of the Stone People blessed everyone. Feeling right at home, Sam had an inner knowing, like his grandpa, when it came to these Old Ways.

This time, Ben put cedar on the stones. Occasionally he whispered what to do in Sam's ear. Frank and Ernie worked the fire and Leroy sat at the door. With the antlers, Leroy set the glowing grandfathers in the stone pit. For the first time in years, Hal just took care of his prayers. Inside the lodge, the drum passed from one sun dancer to another. Each sang a favorite Inipi or Sun Dance song.

It was good to give the younger generation a chance to grow into positions of responsibility around the fire place. Even Kyle came around more often and found his place around the Inipi. The fire spirits whispered to him as he learned to keep fire with Frank and Ernie. Sun Dance proved to be a powerful, life changing experience. When the big drum beats in your heart, it's only natural to sing along.

A quiet freedom took hold of him as Ben watched Leroy and Sam assume the responsibilities of ceremony. His shoulders finally relaxed and he felt himself become one with all life around him.

Sometimes Leroy struggled with his sobriety. In town, when he passed by the bar, he'd hear Hal's voice in his head. "BOOZERS AND LOSERS!" It wasn't that Hal wasn't compassionate, he just didn't have any use for that life style anymore.

After pages of inventory, Leroy saw what was bothering him. Over and over, he found the same thing to be true. Anytime he was in the pit of despair, he easily climbed out of his trouble, if he reached up to Creator and helped someone else. Riddled with the residue of war madness, many veterans came home with countless struggles.

If working with others didn't clear Leroy's head, Hal had watchwords for him. "GET YOUR HEAD OUT OF YOUR ASS AND WIPE THE SHIT OUT OF YOUR EYES, THEN YOU'LL HAVE A BETTER VIEW!"

Around the sacred fire, these harsh life lessons began to make sense. Staring into the flames of the purifying fire of the Inipi, it often revealed a hard-bitten truth. Inside the lodge, Leroy's mind wandered through wormholes in the Veil and entered into the Infinite Mystery. It was in the stillness that all peace existed.

Hal explained that for an alcoholic, it was important to keep their side of the street clean. Otherwise, every five years or so, they'd trip over a mess they'd made in the past, which still cluttered their way. Most people never stopped to wonder how their behavior affected others. Some just didn't care. But for an alcoholic, these emotional slips could become nasty bottoms. Unresolved issues mixed with character flaws often lead to fatal train wrecks.

In Hal's mind, he saw no benefit in having a 'slip and slide' sobriety. The Twelve Steps were meant to be worked over and over again. The benefit of this work was a quiet mind and a peaceful heart.

The secrets of the Great Mystery were profound, yet simple. Only the heart knows its divine contract with Creator. The heart's desire revealed what each of us are destined here to do. Yet, how many truly follow the dictates of their heart?

Late one night, a full moon rose in the east as Ben lay down on his bed. Its silvery light shone into the small kitchen window. All in all, it'd been a good day.

Earlier that morning, Sam sat behind the bucket inside the Inipi and Ben didn't whisper one suggestion. The Inipi had become his own. In the arbor, Sam was coming along as a sun dancer. He pledged to dance another four years. Watching these Old Ways come alive in his hometown, gave Ben peace of mind. More and more people came. Between Sam and Leroy, they poured two lodges a week.

As he closed his eyes, Ben settled into his bed and fell into a tranquil slumber. In his dream time, Ben walked north along the Missouri. The sun was setting in the west across the river. His gait was light. The soft sand along the river bank molded to his moccasin-ed feet. Up ahead, an eagle cried as it soared over the water and landed in a cottonwood tree.

In his single, long dark brown braid, Ben wore an eagle feather. When he got closer to the cottonwood tree, the eagle flapped its large wings and flew a short ways ahead to another tree. There, the eagle waited for Ben to catch up. Off in the distance, Ben saw the glow of a council fire. Again, the eagle waited until Ben got close. Then, he flapped his wings and flew in the direction of the fire.

Many people stood around a bright fire which illuminated everything in all directions. When Ben got closer, he recognized the old chief of his village standing near the fire in the east. As the eagle lit down on the tall branches of a cottonwood tree, alongside the fire, it showed Ben where he needed to go.

When Ben approached the fire, the council of elders turned around. In the circle, was Ben's grandfather. With a bright smile, his grandfather welcomed him into the circle.

"You've done well, my son," his grandfather said. "Your mission is complete." The elders of the council nodded in agreement. "You committed your life to the Cannupa and serving Creator and the people. Because of your willingness to guide the next generation in the Old Ways, ceremony will continue to live amongst our people."

The flames danced as Ben stared into the sacred council fire. In his mind's eye, he had a remembering. Before he was born into this life, he stood before the council of elders. He vowed to carry the Old Ways into the future, to guide the next generation in the ways of the Cannupa. He wasn't alone in making that vow. He stood in the midst of chiefs and warriors from different clans.

Many souls of First Nations people stood with him. Some had stood by helplessly, during the times of the Gatling gun when their people were slaughtered. Others danced the Ghost Dance which instilled fear into the white soldiers. This fear forced the U.S. government to make their sacred ceremonies illegal. Others perished in Indian boarding schools when the wasicu mindset tried to bleach the red out of the Indian and make him white.

In the Spirit World, it mattered not what tribe they originated from. The Apache stood with the Sioux. The Algonquin embraced the Seminole. The Crow, the Black Foot, the Navajo, the Chumash, the Taino, the Comanche, the Aleut, the Quechua and other nations came from across the globe, to gather together. The mission at hand was greater than their individual differences. The survival of the future generations of the First Nations people depended upon unity among them. When they stopped warring amongst themselves, they began making relations. Enemies were turned into allies. Realizing that Spirit was greater, their differences were minor.

Troubles began for the First Nations People in the fifteenth century. Guided by their holy book, under the order of the pope and king and queen of Spain, the Spanish Conquistadors set out with double-edged swords to take possession of any land not ruled by the Catholic Church. Aided by cannons and guns, the Spanish priests sailed their galleons across the big waters to the New World. As they sang praises to their God, the wealthy, ruling elite set out to enslave, divide and conquer the First Nations People. Through brutality and fear, these tyrants kept the indigenous people powerless and dependent on reservations throughout the land.

But in the Spirit World, these diverse clans united under a common cause. Together, they found that their spirituality was a powerful tool. With drum in hand, they sought to anchor the Old Ways back onto Mother Earth.

Ben's grandfather looked at him in earnest. "The others who stood with you, when you made your vow, their souls were born into the colors of the four directions. There are Red Indians, White Indians, Black Indians and Yellow Indians. Their blood was mixed and they created a rainbow nation. That is why you see so many nations of people represented in the Sacred Circle. They're drawn to the Inipi and the Sun Dance. The circle will grow ever wider. Those with pure hearts are being called to the big drum, to the Old Ways of our people. You will know your ancestors by their eagle eyes, their high cheek bones and their love of freedom."

"In my heart, I've always known this grandfather," Ben said with respect. As Ben looked across the river, a fish flew through the air. Its fins were stretched out and cut through the air streams like sharp razors. Then he saw another fish fly though the air. Ben thought of the eagle nearby. As he did, the eagle flew down and landed on his shoulder.

Joy swept though Ben's being as this holy raptor enfolded his shoulders in its outstretched wings. The eagle was a old friend, a familiar. An old woman across the circle looked hard at Ben. Her mind captured the image of this sacred moment.

Following the path of Spirit, the First Nations People would survive. In his lifetime, Ben witnessed how many races of people were instrumental in preserving these sacred ways. Because the people joined together, the 39th President of the United States signed acts into law to preserve their sacred burial grounds and allow them the religious freedoms afforded white men in the United States Constitution.

But the journey wasn't over. Many of the First Nations People were still lost in the darkness of the white man's ways. They needed to be welcomed back. The laws designed to protect the spiritual practices of the First Nations People were controlled by a foreign government and defined by bloodlines. There was still much work to do, so the sacred ways could be practiced freely by all called home to the big drum, regardless of their tribal affiliation.

"You must prepare, my son. The Wise Ones will be calling you Home soon. Your spirit will journey farther up the path of Light into the Great Mystery. Soon, They will be calling you home." As his grandfather said these words, the eagle flew off to the north, into the ways of wisdom.

Bright as a lantern, the silvery moon rays shone through the kitchen window. Ben woke up with a start. His heart was beating through his chest. The old floor boards creaked as Ben bounded out of bed and paced the floor. The last time he'd seen his grandfather around a council fire was before he got sober. Back then, his grandfather told him Great Spirit couldn't protect him if he continued to dance with the firewater spirits.

It all started to make sense now. The whole mission of his life was to carry the Cannupa in a sacred manner and bring these teachings to the next generation. By teaching Sam and Leroy, the Old Ways wouldn't die out. Adrenaline pumped through his veins when he realized he was done! How long had he waited for this day?

"I HAVE TO PREPARE!" Ben said out loud. But, then came the burning question. "What do they want me to prepare?"

The moonlight burst through the front door as Ben went outside and stood on the front porch. Tonight, the wind was quiet. She waited with Ben on the porch for the answers to come from on High. As Ben looked towards the twinkling stars, the quiet overtook him.

"Aho Mitakuye Oyasin," Ben started. "What do you want me to prepare?"

While the stars twinkled brightly against a midnight blue sky, the heavens remained silent. The Higher Powers wanted Ben to search his own heart for the answer. Then, a simple thought entered Ben's mind. "What have you left undone?"

EPILOGUE: OHIYA'S STORIES

WRITTEN WORDS BY OHIYA WAGU

Honoring male and female in us all...
Respect for the Thunder Beings:

Some of the medicine ways of the Thunder Beings involve work with many Spirit-helpers of the West. As I understand it, these are some very brief descriptions of some aspects of the Thunder Beings:

There are "Clowns" who make fun where there is none. "Winktas" bring female energy, which helps to balance out masculine energy. "Spider Beings" play tricks with people's faith. "Fools" try to get in the way and distract knowingly. "Backwards Ones" are inexperienced and mischievous; they play, mock others and disrespect all things around them. The "Mindless" have to blindly follow instructions to hurt, maim and kill the innocent.

However, of all of the many aspects of the Spirit-helpers of the West, the internal Medicine Way of the Thunder Beings are the most difficult to work with. For example, there are those to whom the Spirit shows the "Reversal" of growing things, such as how cancer, AIDS and other sicknesses that eat away the body can be reversed.

This is some of my experience with the Heyoka medicine:

In the summer of 1993, I was praying with my pipe, sitting on the bank of the Cannonball River. I was asking how I could be of service to the Creator. An eagle landed on one of the standing dead cottonwood trees nearby. I asked again, "How can I be of service to you, Creator?" Then a white-tailed deer came out of its hiding place and looked up at the eagle.

I asked again, "How can I be of service to you Creator?" The eagle, in a powerful voice, said, "Look up here. All I fly over is sacred. All I see is holy. I'm a holy eagle that's bringing you a medicine; take this and follow me."

I received the medicine and followed this Spirit. I felt a flow of energy. I felt the presence of many relatives who passed on into the Spirit World, saw the river starting to flow backwards and felt the wind on my face. These things that I experienced helped me to see that I was going somewhere that I had never been before.

While I was flowing with that energy, the eagle said, "My people's leader took the Medicine Ways to the Buffalo Nation, to help them to survive through their hard times. As they healed their nation, the medicine brought understanding and balance to their people. In honoring the holy flow of the medicine that brought them back into balance with internal peace, they passed the medicine on to your people, human beings. They passed the medicine to your people by way of a sacred woman. She taught the people ways of connecting with the holy Creation, so that they may find their way home to the internal fire."

Suddenly, all the energy flow stopped and I felt a powerful presence of peace and the warmth of love. I felt these words: "Honor and respect your mother and father to know the way home. To bring balance inside your home, you must honor and respect the holy life force that is in all beings."

With a strong rush of energy, I started to feel the importance of us as a people. We all, as individual holy children of the Creator, need to share so much love with one another to help us through the coming changing times.

I know that there is a lot of powerful medicine in our Native Ways of connecting with the Creator. When we trust and honor our own medicine walk on this Mother Earth, we will only see other humans walking that same road of life. Most of the time we never get to learn how to work with the internal medicine that we all were born with. People are too busy trying to make ends meet or trying to out-do one another.

Over all, I feel that this system that we live in is at war with nature. For hundreds of years, this wasicu mind-set systematically got us addicted to this greedy, capitalistic, consumer-oriented society that we live in today. The children are broken away from their connection to natural law by this society. When a child first enters this world, they are often taken away from their mothers and given "formula", with sugar and milk from cows.

The first thing that helps us to learn about the holy hoop of life is natural mother's milk. Connecting with the natural elements, talking to and listening to the Wind, Water, Fire, Earth and all the spirits around us, are all natural to people who live connected to nature from birth. When we accept that we are made by a man and a woman and that both energies are in us, then we can learn about our own holy medicine that can help to heal us.

I believe that if love, honor and respect are given equally and whole-heartedly to our parents and if they feel that from us, then that will help us with the process of healing the sacred hoop of life. Honoring our parents helps us to feel secure and whole inside of the connection between ourselves and our parents and therefore, between ourselves and the Creator. That is the internal pipe ceremony.

The physical stone and wood used in a pipe are symbols of the male and female aspects of ourselves being put together and made whole. We pray with the pipe so that we can learn more about our holy walk of life. By connecting to and nurturing the feminine and masculine aspects of the holy power of life, that's in each of us, we get healthier and stronger. By staying clear-minded and working towards living in a healthy body, we can keep our fire of life burning. These are some of the ideas that I think about, that I wanted to share.

With respect, Ohiya

My grandfathers and uncles have passed to me these

ceremonies to pray with all people. I will always welcome all people into any ceremony I'm conducting. The Spirit that helps me in the ceremonies, teaches me I must keep this open altar for all people.

OHIYA'S SECOND WRITING: IN FRONT OF GOD AND EVERY BODY

Returning to my sleeping area to get ready for the day, I saw this eagle feather on my bedroll. I picked it up and saw that it was a center tail feather. The medicine that it represented was very old and healing. I placed the feather back on my skirt and made my self ready for whatever was coming to share with us some powerful teaching. I mixed together some pipe stone powder with bear grease and some of the other medicines that I was given for this ceremony, so that I could help if I was asked.

Everything was quiet and still. I could feel the heavy footsteps of the buffalo spirit that was out in the arbor. All around us, I could see the eyes of the old people, looking at the tree with such a strong intent and focus. I had to tell the others, who were not aware of what was happening in the arbor, to stop what they were doing and help the people to pray.

All the people that were getting ready to dance that day gathered in the rest area. All started to focus towards the tree. In the early light of dawn, I could see an old pickup drive up to the camp and park on the south end of the camp. I got my skirt on and put on my anklet and wristlet of sage, and I started to put some of the medicine that I made on my face, hands and feet.

Feeling the shift in the energy, I turned and looked towards the west to see the white rolling clouds coming towards us. Behind them were huge black clouds. We could see lightning flashing and hear thunder rumbling off in the distance.

In the matter of minutes, the strong wind hit our Sun dance camp with such force that teepees were picked up and thrown down and smaller tents were all blown down. There was total chaos. People were running everywhere. All the sun dancers and singers were looking for a place to hide.

In the wind, I heard a song being sung. The words were going through my whole body, giving me energy and helping me to stand and make a prayer. I could hear the wind say, "They run from their place of worship; they must not need it." I could see the wind pick up a small tent and throw it at the arbor. The tent got stuck in the rest area and the wind started to shake the arbor. The Sun dance fire was blown out.

I could hear the soft beat of a drum through the wind's talking. Looking towards the south, I could see the old gray pickup. The passenger got out with the drum that he was using in his hands. I could feel the magic of the moment. I felt the heartbeat of our Mother Earth as he walked towards the smoldering Sun dance fire place, singing and drumming.

He walked to the west side of the pit and turned towards the Sun dance tree. He stopped drumming and started to say a prayer in his language. I felt inside my heart that I should get my medicine and go to the tree to help. As I entered into the west gate, I could hear the words of my elder brother from behind me, talking to Creator. He asked how he could be of service and gave thanks for the blessing of that moment in time (to be alive).

Reaching the Tree of Life, I made a prayer on the west, then on the north, than on the east side. I walked out to the east gate and turned around to face the Sun dance tree, the west gate, the Sun dance fire pit and my older brother. I could hear my brother talking to the center of this circle, the internal fireplace of Creation. I could hear some voices hollering in the background asking people to stop running and to pray.

My brother finished his prayer and turned towards the

516

south. He started singing and drumming. Then he turned towards the west, stopped drumming and started to talk to the Thunder Beings. As he talked, the Sun dance leader and all his helpers walked to the east side of the fire pit and knelt down to pray with their pipes. The center tail feather in my right hand started to feel warm and I could hear a low hum from the feather.

I started to dance to the beating of Creation, as I looked toward the west. I could see the Thunder Beings; some danced south and some danced north. They moved, all in a respectful way, from being asked in an honorable old way to dance this way and that way. As the Thunder Beings danced, my brother sang this song to honor them.

"In a sacred manner, they have sent voices. Half the Universe has sent voices. In a sacred manner, they have sent voices to you."

Over and over he sang, as the storm parted and went around us. When he finished singing, the storm was to the east of us. He walked around to where the Sun dance leader was kneeling and told him to stand and take care of his fireplace. The leader started getting people to get the fire started and giving orders again. My brother stopped him and said, "Come with me to the tree."

As they entered the west gate, I started to walk to the tree from the east. We met at the Tree of Life, my brother, the leader of the dance and myself. I stood on the east side of the tree, while my brother was on the west side. The leader was told by my brother to kneel on the south side of the tree. My brother walked around on the north side and touched the tree. He turned to me and smiled and he said, "Thanks for helping and can I have my feather back?"

I reached out to hand him his feather and he reached out with his left hand. We touched the feather at the same time. As soon as we both touched the feather, it melted into nothing. My elder brother smiled and walked past me, out the east gate, to his old gray pickup. When he got in, the driver flashed his headlights and drove back down the dirt road, the way they came.

I turned to the leader, who was still kneeling at the tree. I asked him to take care of the fireplace and I walked out of the arbor through the west gate, into the rest area. The leader and his helpers came over to me and asked if I could help them with their Sun dance. I was honored to be asked, so I asked the leader, "What about my brother who helped to honor the Thunder Beings? Is he from around these parts? Do you know him?"

The leader looked at me with shock in his eyes and said in a shaky voice, "There was nobody else; it was only you and your medicine way that helped us."

I said, "What about the gray pickup and the drum, the songs and my (elder) brother?"

The leader gave me a puzzled look and with tears in his eyes, he said again, "Uncle, there was no one else out there but you and me."

In front of God and everybody, my brother touched me again from the other side.

Ohiya

OHIYA'S THIRD WRITING: UNFORGETTABLE MEMORIES OF THE RED ROAD

From my perspective, the Red Road was started by our ancestors in 1492 when the Nina, the Pinta and the Santa Maria first came over the horizon from the east. When the boats landed, the indigenous people walked towards the west carrying their sacred instruments, looking for a safe place to honor the gifts that the Creator blessed them with.

When the Mayflower came into view of our Turtle Island, the ancestors who carried the vision for this Red Road,

518

were at the western gate, where the Chumash people lived, by the rainbow bridge on the West Coast.

In 1805, when Lewis and Clark traveled to the Pacific Ocean, the sickness of greed reached our ancestors on the West Coast. Again, they moved to a safer place to honor the gifts that the Creator blessed them with.

Today, in the ceremonies, when I look inside, I see the safe place that our ancestors found to honor the gifts that the Creator blessed them with.

When you stop for a little while on that Red Road that you are walking on and turn around and take a good hard look at what you are walking on, you'll see the reason why the old people call it the Red Road.

For hundreds of years, people walked, ran and even crawled on their hands and knees when they had to. They continued to walk on this path, carrying the medicine ways for the future generations that are walking behind us.

The bleeding, the physical pain, the mental suffering, the spiritual battles that our relatives went through to keep these ceremonies alive is what you'll see and feel when you take the time to look back on this Red Road that you are walking on.

Spirit remembers and knows what it took for our ancestors to lay the foundation that this Red Road is built on.

For me, with each step I take on this Red Road, I remember how so many people have died to keep this way of connecting to Creator alive, how so many nations were wiped away without a trace of their existence. Their Medicine Ways can still be felt in the Wind, Water, Earth and Fire.

I remember the invasion and the early resistance to this melting pot, from the Taino people on the eastern islands to the Iroquois confederacy, the eastern woodland peoples, the plains and the prairie peoples, all the way to the fishing peoples of the Pacific Northwest.

I remember the murdering and the suffering that was

done to our people in the name of GOD. These memories have been kept alive from all the way back, from when the eastern people who survived, fled towards the west. Even when they could no longer walk or run, they crawled on their hands and knees, keeping their gifts and memories to pass on down to us.

Remember: The Trail of Tears, the Sand Creek Massacre, the Wounded Knee Massacre, and all the countless times when our people were thrown to the ground and beaten, killed and butchered, just because they were free to walk on this road of life that the Creator gifted us with.

I remember the suffering, the pain and all the blood that was spilled onto our Mother Earth from the systematic killing of our people and the resulting destruction of our nations, by the European people infected with the conquering wasicu mindset.

With each step I take on this Red Road, I remember what it took for our ancestors to lay this foundation, so that today we can talk about this good Red Road.

Ohiya

OHIYA'S FOURTH WRITING: GRANDMA'S HANDS

I was always looked at differently, from way back when until now. Sometimes, I feel and move in the world in the same open way that I did when I was born. I remember that time as if it were happening right now:

I feel the warmth of Grandma's hands welcoming me into the world. In her hands, I feel the safety of Creation. In the warmth of the fluids that are covering me, I feel the protective hands of Creation and I feel whole, powerful and connected.

Dancing in the flow of the magic river of life, You reach your hands out to me. Sparks and flashes of lightning light the dark sky, as the snow lightly falls to the ground.

Feeling the wind, and the snow from inside my protective coating, I couldn't talk to You.

In Grandma's hands, I was taken out into the dark night to talk to You. I feel her hands washing me clean with snow and making me ready to meet the day; feeling the snow being rubbed all over my body, my coating being taken away by the snow; feeling cold wind, and the snow fall softly on my body.

Hearing You dancing this way, I feel the love of Creation. I hear Your words:

> "Look at the tree, look at the stones, see the fire burning inside. Look at the fire that's in the center of all Creation; the cool clean water of life fuels the internal fire, which brings light into the darkness."

I feel the words of the stories being told to me by the wind and snow. I hear the loud presence of the darkness. I see You dance all around me and Grandma. I feel the magic of Your steps that leave no prints behind. I see You, I hear You, I feel Your words of wisdom.

In the dark of the night, I can still see You, off in my peripheral vision. I see You dancing; I hear the heart beat pounding. I hear songs of old people who passed into the Spirit World long ago; I hear their songs echoing through the night.

Being lifted into the air, high above my Grandma's head, I feel the warm safety of her hands holding me with love. In a soft, gentle voice, Grandma says to the dark night and to the Spirit that dances around us, "Mother and father of this child, I give you thanks this day for my grandson. I will call him Anpeyoka, First Light of Day, the Power that awakens the people."

As she finishes speaking, the first light of dawn flares out from the east. In a flash of bright light, a spirit reveals its name as "Chebrom;" it holds a flaming sword in its right hand. Then it sings in a powerful voice, "This way to the Tree of Life."

My Grandma finishes her prayer and takes me back into the little log house, where my mother and father are waiting. From the softness of my Grandmother's arms, I am placed into my mother's loving hands. I am given this holy drink of life, my mother's milk, which helps me to know about the history of our people. With every swallow, I feel my mother's milk flowing through my veins and all through my body. With that essence, she passes to me my family's history from all the way back; from before the coming of the wasicu mind set, when we were free.

Today, with every drink of water, I remember and feel the wrongs done to the Old Ways by my brothers and sisters, infected by this wasicu mind set. However, I will never forget the beauty and peace that runs through my veins from the time of my birth. Never.

Ohiya a.k.a. Anpeyoka

AUTHOR'S NOTE

Writing this book was risky. Deep lines of prejudice and hate were carved across Turtle Island over the sands of time. There is a fear that these Old Ways will be exploited, tainted, spoiled or fall into the wrong hands. This fear keeps the color lines firmly intact. It was a dream of Ohiya to bring back ceremony and sobriety to the reservation village where he was born. When we met, he told me he wanted to write a book about these sacred Old Ways. We spent months traveling from one ceremony to another. I had a teacher and he had a student. I took copious notes and volunteered to help write his book. By that time, I'd gone to several Sun Dances, done a vision quest for four days and attended Inipi ceremonies for years. This does not make me an expert. It only demonstrates that I have some experience.

In an email Ohiya wrote to me, he told me this:

"My grandfathers and uncles have passed to me these ceremonies to pray with all people. I will always welcome all people into any ceremony I'm conducting. The Spirit that helps me in the ceremonies, teaches me I must keep this open altar for all people."

No disrespect for anyone's beliefs around these ceremonies was intended in the writing of this book. I am reminded of a dilemma that was posed to me in a psychology class. A man's wife was near death. The pharmacist had the cure, but the man could not afford it. He was an honorable man. The dilemma was this: Should the man break the law and steal the remedy to save his wife or obey the man made laws about stealing and let his wife die? Which would you chose?

Many of our soldiers are coming home from this war in the desert. They need healing. Ceremony and AA can offer that healing. Should we break tradition and share these sacred ways with them or let them die? Can we really afford to be selfish with each other, regardless of our color?

I'm just the messenger. Take what you like and leave the rest. Blessings on your walk.

ABOUT THE AUTHOR

When I walked into my first Twelve Step meeting in 1980, I was a suicidal bulimic with a tequila affliction. Whether I over ate or drank too much, I knew I'd be puking it all up. I was tortured that way for years. Since I was five years old, the spirit of suicide had me convinced that I was not for this world. I tried to get out of my divine contract by ending my life. But Creator had other plans. The moment I decided to end it all, the phone rang. It was my sponsor, who I hadn't talked to in days. She asked me how I was. For the first time I was honest. My life changed.

I grew up in a violent, alcoholic home. It seemed I always had a gun to my head. "Do this, or you'll get beat! Hurry up! Do it now!" There was no mercy at the wrong end of my father's belt, the wooden spoon, the fly swatter or the shoe. To a child, those instruments are weapons of mass destruction. When I grew up, there was no mandated reporter at school. No one reported violence to the authorities. To this day, a certain tone of a man's voice will freeze my heart between beats.

My parents were immigrants from a country which lost the war. They moved here after World War Two. Being from the wrong country, we were the enemy. I dealt with that shame most of my life. Even though I didn't kill anyone, I was crucified because of my heritage. There was much pain in our home growing up. The war never ended. The demons in the bottle wielded a doubled edged sword which drew a lot of blood. Needless to say, I was one of the walking wounded.

But then something happened. I found myself sitting in a smoke filled room, full of laughing people who were sober. I didn't want to be there. But every time I went, I felt better. After a while, they remembered my name. What a powerful thing.

I had to get sober before I could let go of binging and purging. That's how it worked for me. I was dually addicted.

To recover, I had to treat alcoholism and compulsive overeating in different 12 Step programs. Underneath those afflictions, was a gaping wound, oozing with hurt. I used food, drugs, alcohol, men, shopping, television, Harley rides, did I say shopping...to anesthetize the pain. Anything which distracted me from the ache, I abused until it didn't work anymore. I was a mess.

I am forever grateful to the founders of Alcoholics Anonymous for their sacrifice and willingness to share freely what they found. I truly believe the 12 Steps are a powerful vehicle for change, if used correctly. There are countless people in the hallowed halls of AA, OA, Al-anon and other programs, who use the 12 Steps as a medium for change. I'm grateful to all who freely give their time and experience so I may walk free. For myself, nothing is more gratifying, than witnessing how the 12 Steps work wonders in the lives of others. In that way, giving is receiving.

Interestingly enough, there is now a program called Criminals and Gangsters Anonymous. It's damn near impossible to reform an addict through the force of will. But they can be transformed through the Power of Love found in the 12 Steps.

About 10 years after I got sober and abstinent, I happened upon a Native American book store. There was a woman there, Marie, who I'll never forget. She invited me to my first ceremony. The combination of prayer, fire, cedar, sage and song stirred an ancient knowing in my heart. I found my way home. My soul remembered these ancient ways, as the piping hot breath of the Stone People sang their songs in the Inipi. I'd searched for a long time for a place to pray. And though I was raised in a church, I never felt fed there. It wasn't until I prayed in the dirt, that I knew I was home.

Some of the characters in this book are a compilation of my dearest mentors. At some point in our relationship, each of them gave me permission to write their stories. I never got around to it, until the last one passed away. But maybe I had to have all this experience, for it to become a book in the first place. Many of the events in this story are true. But the names, places and faces have been changed to preserve their anonymity.

Ohiya and I met at Sun dance. Dressed in a silver skirt, he was the feared Heyoka who walked backwards in the Sun dance Arbor. On the last day of the dance, he spoke his first word to me. That afternoon, I was guarding the east gate. The last round of the dance was ending. The procession of Sun Dancers were leaving the arbor. I had my eye on the yellow flag pole. I wanted to take it home. After the last sun dancer walked through the gate, I lunged forward to grab the pole. This stern voice said "NO!!!" As I stepped back, Ohiya walked past me in his silver skirt. He was the last sun dancer out of the Arbor.

Years later, Ohiya invited me to attend his Heyoka Sun Dance. Through his teachings, I learned the mysteries of the Old Ways. He'd been looking for a dedicated student to teach ceremony to. I took notes, recording these Old Ways as he spoke. Before he passed, he wanted to write a book to preserve these teachings.

After a while, the blankets of our lives wove themselves together. In November of 2009, we found ourselves driving across the prairie in a rented U-haul. It was filled with winter clothes for the people in his hometown on the reservation.

This adventure all came together when Spirit touched ground in a town in the Pacific Northwest. My friend Marie and her friends gathered winter clothes and things for this mission. As we got on the road, I saw four bald eagles that day. It was a blessed trip.

Snow had already fallen as we coursed through the Rocky Mountains in Montana. Crossing the Rocky Mountains in a U-Haul was a little nerve-racking. I heard many stories about black ice and spinning cars.

When he was a young man, Ohiya enlisted in the

military. It turns out that more Native Americans have served in our military than any other ethnic group in America. When he got out, his dad had a naming ceremony for him to honor his years of service. His new name was Ohiya Wagu, "Return's Victoriously (or Coming Back Winning)." His father was a minister. Both parents came from a long line of hereditary chiefs. That distinction would have passed to Ohiya's older brothers, but they died in their own battle with the spirits in the bottle. Ohiya was the last son left.

Though he came from a long line of tribal chiefs, he had no desire to get caught up in tribal politics. He'd traveled the world and wanted to bring solutions back to the reservation to end the alcoholism, poverty and dependence on white man's energy. As we traveled back to his home town, we planned to start an AA meeting and he would run a sweat lodge and a Sun dance.

While driving across Montana, we stopped in a small town. Ohiya found a book by Eduardo Duran, titled "Healing the Soul Wound." I read the book with zeal. It discussed the idea of historical trauma and how it affected the First Nations People.

In Chapter Five, Dr. Eduardo Duran had a conversation with his mentor Tarrence. His mentor summed up the spiritual malady of alcoholism. Alcohol was a medicine. It was a spirit with a dual nature. It could be used for good or not good. When the spirit of alcohol was invoked in its lower nature, the price contracted for having a good time was high. Most people paid with their lives.

In writing this book, "A Spirit Called Alcohol," it had several inspirations, along with life experiences that cannot be discounted. Eduardo Duran along with Bill Wilson, the Big Book of Alcoholics Anonymous and the founders of AA described alcoholism as a spiritual malady. But, Tarrence, Dr. Duran's mentor revealed the spiritual malady and brought it to life.

Another inspiration was a trilogy of books titled, "Letters

from a Living Dead Man" written by Elsa Barker in the early 1900's. This body of work was done through automatic writing. Here, a judge who passed away, writes through the hand of Elsa Barker. He describes how earthbound spirits whisper temptations to drinkers, so they can inhale the aroma of alcohol again.

I also credit the "I AM Discourses" for their description of discarnate entities and their influence on the living. In the I AM Discourses, discarnate entities are credited with causing most long term mental illness.

More than a year after Ohiya was killed, the characters in this book began talking to me. In the wee hours of the morning, they'd sit on the edge of my bed. I'd listen in while they talked. At one point, they asked, "Are you going to write this down?" What started out as a simple blog, suddenly became an incessant flurry of movies in my mind's eye. Their voices followed me everywhere, urging me to write down everything they showed me.

They waited centuries to tell their story about how the demons in the bottle and the spirits of the seven deadly sins wreaked havoc on their lives. But, more than that, they wanted to share a solution. I am humbled to be of service in this way. My prayer is only that you find your way, as I have found mine. May the Creator bless you on your walk, with clean hands and a peaceful heart. Aho Mitakuye Oyasin.

OHIYA'S DREAMS

You won't find him in a piece of wood
You won't find him in a stone
You won't find him in a feather
Or an eagle bone
For he took his altar home

He carried that altar in his heart
Given by Spirit from the start
A Sun Dancer for 35 years
Living through his blood, sweat and tears

You'll see his smile in the rays of the Sun
Because he went home to be with the One
His voice will whisper in the wind
Asking, "Are you ready to begin?"

Find your altar, make your way
Don't wait long, begin today
He looked for a student here and there
One who could carry what he used to wear

In an earnest voice to me he'd say
Sweetheart, with the medicine most only play
But who could walk long in his shoes
Listening, while they emptied their hearts, sharing their blues

The task was heavy, ceremony was his way
To heal tattered hearts made of clay
His eyes melded with the fire
Watching, as spirits soared higher and higher

Drums beating long through the night
Faces lit up by fire light
Round the tipi moves the drum
Until morning water comes along

Tunkashila, Wakan Tanka, we call you
Hear us, heal us, so our hearts are true

On the morning of December ninth
Something came and seized his life
Fanatical cries of anguish arise
Who is responsible for his demise?

The karmic wheel of Justice will turn
The dark hearts responsible
Will continue to burn
Until the truth is told and amends are made
Peace is restored and Justice prevails

"Returns Victoriously" is his name
Now only his Spirit remains...

In our walk on Mother Earth, we live many days. The most salient are the powerful ones which change our very lives. They compel us to reflect on what's important and ask life rendering questions as to what our true purpose for being here on Earth really is.

Spending the last few months with Ohiya before he passed, proved to be a powerful, life changing experience for me. As the anniversary of his death draws near, my mind replays everything we did together in his last days. On the morning of December 7, 2009, we woke up on the train going north through Klamath Falls headed for Portland. The tall pine trees, lining the rail, were heavily laden with snow. The spirit of winter was purifying everything with its white, glittery sequins.

By the time I'd met Ohiya, he'd traveled around the world, walking to the beat of a different drum. Being a full blood Native American, a veteran, a father, a Sun dance Chief and Native American Church ceremonial road-man, he had insight most people rarely considered. His phone rang incessantly with people who were troubled and wanted prayers. It was heavy work. He was well known in ceremonial circles. Ohiya was sometimes loved, sometimes hated. His Heyoka medicine dealt excruciating blows when it targeted the weakness in people.

It was September 2009, when we came home from a summer of Sun dance. All distraught, he looked at me and said "We don't have much time. You don't know what they're telling me. There are people trying to kill me."

What do you say to something like that? At the time, he was hard pressed to tell me all he could about ceremony. He'd been looking for a student for a while, someone who'd follow him to every ceremony and learn these ancient ways.

I wanted to help. So I volunteered to take notes and help

him write his book. Over the next few months, he'd talk and I'd write. "Don't interrupt the teacher" he'd often say when I hurled questions at him. Questions interrupt the flow, changing the direction of the conversation.

Story after story unfolded. Living on the reservation was tough. Life expectancy for a man was 42 years old. One of Ohiya's brothers was murdered, two others were killed by a drunk driver and another died of complications from alcoholism. Alcohol played a part in all their deaths. With Ohiya being the only one left, I could only imagine how deep his pain went.

After doing ceremony on the West Coast for years, Ohiya longed to do something for his people back home. There was so much knowledge out West. He looked for something to alleviate the suffering on the reservation. I agreed this would be a good mission. That's how our journey began, dreaming of a better life for his people back home.

Confiding Ohiya's dreams to my good friend, Marie, she revealed how she always wanted to bring clothes to people on the reservation. But didn't want to look like some 'white do-gooder chick.' No sooner did she say those words, Ohiya confided, "Winter is coming and there are many of people on the reservation who don't have winter clothes."

What happened next, I can only say, were stars aligning and the Heavens conspiring to bring miracles. I put Ohiya on the phone with Marie. They talked. After a few conversations, Ohiya and I boarded a train, leaving the sunshine of the West Coast behind.

As we headed for the wintry Pacific Northwest, Marie's town gathered a garage full of winter clothes, school supplies, books, shoes and other things. Everything came together. We loaded a U-Haul truck and across the back country of the Midwest we went. That first day, crossing the Rocky Mountains, I saw four bald Eagles. It was a glorious beginning.

Before we left on this winter clothes mission, Ohiya

confided that the greatest spiritual quest is to leave everything behind. With only a back pack, we'd trust Great Spirit will fulfill our every need. He'd been living that way for years. One morning, he looked at me intently. "I love you, sweetheart and I want you to be my wife." I cried. After he asked me to be his wife, I quit my job. I packed a couple suitcases, left my family and we set out. Over the next few weeks, everything we needed to fulfill this winter clothes mission was provided. The Spirit of the Universe smiled.

Notes to myself: Day One, November 5, 2009 Thursday, Amtrak

Trains. Their sleepy, rolling motion driven through carved out hillsides. Glancing into backyards and country sides. Unnoticed. Cows graze on oceanfront property, unaware of dropping property values. Trees, streams, hillsides, marshes, a blue heron standing on the ocean's shore.

I knocked on Heaven's door this morning in my sanctuary of warm standing water. "I'm on a journey," I announced.

"Yes, we know," They replied. "Don't you remember, we sent you there when you volunteered to help."

"I did?" I questioned. "But I really don't remember..." my voice trailed off.

"To 'RE-MEMBER' is the journey, the mission at hand," They continued.

"But how?" I asked.

"Light the fire, be the spark and know that each flame will recognize itself," They whispered.

"Light the fire? Be the spark? Is that a metaphor? What fire?" my mind whirled.

Silence followed. After a while, a picture came into my

mind. I saw a huge fire. A bonfire, in my mind, in the middle of a desolate land, flat with no trees, with dry grasses growing everywhere. I started to dance around the fire in the movie in my mind. As I danced around the fire, a song came to me and I gave it voice. The longer I danced around this blaze, I saw others gather around the fire, as if to get warm. And then one by one, they danced.

"Light the fire, be the spark and know that each flame will recognize itself."

"NEXT STOP, PASO ROBLES," the conductor bellowed.

Cows grazed outside my cabin window, littering the hillside. 'Cows recognize their own,' I thought. You don't see them pulling out guns and trying to steal the meadow. How did humans get so confused?

Now, I sat staring out the window. I realized this was no small mission, which was trying to be accomplished. But how to light the fire? Where? Would others share the same vision? Am I up to the mission? Am I capable? Can I overcome the obstacles that are within myself? The judgment, sadness, hurt, mistrust? Does it matter, as long as the fire gets lit?

So many questions, sometimes I wondered if I could be part of something so great. I remembered more of the vision, more of the fire, the people around it. I realized yes, they did recognize the sacred flame which burned within them. It was simply my job to light the fire and those, whose hearts recognized it, would come.

So many failed to recognize who they are. So many don't remember their Source. We came from something so Powerful, so Great. Yet we choose poverty, destitution, despair. We imprison each other, our hearts, our beings and then set limitations on each other. Maybe we don't exactly put out the flame. But we throw a wet blanket on top, smoldering the flame and making each other small.

The river runs to the sea
No matter how many boulders there be
The water flows, destination in mind
Around every boulder that it finds

The ocean awaits the return of every raindrop
It knows the water will not stop
The river, it flows, knowing its home
An endless journey of cycling return

Outside my window, silver whiskered road warriors roared down the interstate on their thunder steeds, amidst the caravans of trucks and RV's.

****

And that's how our journey began. The two of us in a sleeper car, bound for the Pacific Northwest. Our hearts were high. Two weeks prior, Ohiya said, "I love you, sweetheart. I want you to be my wife." I accepted the challenge. A road-man's life isn't an easy one, as I guess this story shows.

After 20 plus hours of driving, we pulled up to his sister's house on the reservation. There was a small cluster of houses. There were no trees the lined the streets or rose gardens with manicured lawns. Just houses, government issue, plopped on top of the tall buffalo grasses. Some of the houses were boarded up. The rez dogs prowled the streets, chasing down cars. No one had a garage.

Before I agreed to go on this mission, Ohiya warned me that no one on the rez would talk to me. In fact, they might just hate me. He had married outside of his culture before. His wife and children were not well accepted. His mother fought hard for him to marry within the clan. But he traveled in the military and came home with a girl from Europe.

The next morning, I watched as the matriarchs of the village came over to the house. We stood knee high in piles of clothes that overwhelmed the front room and front porch. The mothers of the village spent two days sorting through all the clothes. There was much laughter, talking and sharing stories. I was grateful to have witnessed it.

When all the sorting was done, we took the rest of the clothes to the thrift store, in another small town 15 miles away. This town had mostly dirt roads, only the main street was paved. There, the local shopkeeper invited us to an Inipi ceremony at his house. I was humbled to pray in the dirt, with full bloods only.

Being born on the reservation and growing up there, all Ohiya's dreams stemmed from necessity. The goal was for his people to become self-sufficient. Something they hadn't known in over a century. Though the dreams were simple, pulling them off would take a miracle.

INIPI AND SUN DANCE CEREMONY

Native American ceremony was outlawed for almost a century. Christianity was forced in its place. Ohiya's first goal was to bring the Inipi and the Sun Dance back to his home town. Walking the prairie along the Missouri River, Ohiya showed me where the Inipi and Sun Dance would be. In this small village, there were maybe a hundred houses, several bars and over a dozen churches of every denomination, but no Inipi.

In October 2009, three wealthy people died in a sweat lodge, conducted by a non-Native man in Sedona, Arizona. These people paid close to $10,000 to become spiritual warriors in the matter of five days. Their leader, a white

537

preacher's son, was never initiated by anyone knowledgeable in these sacred ways. Ohiya showed me an article written by Tim Giago from the Native Sun News called "Can the ceremonies save a people?"

We talked about the genocide, the alcoholism, the diabetes and the rest of the challenges Native people faced. Growing up in the city on the West Coast, I saw those challenges everyday.

Out West, there are war zones in the city. If you hang the wrong color bandana from your pocket, it could get you killed. For myself, I had to face my own demons: alcoholism, domestic violence, eating disorders, suicide. To overcome these, I had to align my will with the Creative Power of the Universe. Not the other way around. Creator doesn't bend to my whim. I had to align my will with His. All the Bo-jangles of the outer world never sated my unquenchable thirst. The Twelve Steps and Ceremony fulfilled an internal need. But I had to relinquish the instant gratifications of the outer world in order to have inner peace.

In the article written by Tim Giago, he states how he sees his Native people attending ceremony, then heading to the bar or smoking a joint and bragging about the sacrifice they made. He called them hypocrites. My humble opinion is they are probably addicted and seeking relief. Yet, addiction is genocide. Every time we put a drink to our lips, we invite in a deadly spirit which leads us to our destruction. To win this fight, we must step away. Step away from the bar. Step away from the slot machine. Step away from the buffet. Get off the couch. Walk it off.

Ohiya sought to teach these Old Ways, so they wouldn't be forgotten. "Everyone is a pipe carrier," he told me one day. "Just because we're human. But most don't heed the call."

Walking in a sacred manner and relinquishing the clamoring demands of the ego are not easy. There are many distractions to pull you off your prayer, as any Sun Dancer knows. But it's worth it. The Cannupa is powerful. Prayer is powerful. Especially when we align ourselves with a Higher Power and come with clean hands and a peaceful heart.

There are many factors contributing to poverty and unemployment on the reservation, which begins with its desolate location. There is no industry or shopping malls close by. In Ohiya's small town, there was no grocery store. The closest grocery store was 20 minutes away by car. The only gas station was near the casino.

Off the reservation, the city with a shopping mall is over an hour away. Without employment opportunities, these forgotten people are crippled by government handouts as their only means for survival. There is an inbred sense of hopelessness. In their zeal for land acquisition and control at any cost, the White government took away their native buffalo and their land, shoved them on reservations and left them without.

Because of the systemic prejudice and hatred experienced by Native Americans, leaving the reservation is like going into hostile territory. Coming from the West Coast, where all races live, I rarely experienced such blatant prejudice.

One night, we were out at dinner at a buffet restaurant. Ohiya and I sat down at a table. Me, being non-Native and Ohiya being full blood, this elderly woman stared at me. As her eyes bore into my soul, her mouth gaped wide open for a long time. Her jaw must have ached! Growing up in the city, I barely noticed if a famous person sat down at the next table, let alone someone of a different color.

With those evil eyes fixed on me, I felt uncomfortable. I said to Ohiya, "She's staring at me." He replied "Get used to it." Being rather a jokester myself, I fought the urge to go shake her hand and say "I'm not Paris Hilton! You can quit staring."

SOUP KITCHEN

Homelessness was another urgent situation on the reservation. Drunkenness and gambling were attributed to its cause. Ohiya's sister made extra food and fed the homeless people in town. Ohiya's second goal was to help his sister set up a soup kitchen, along with a homeless shelter and sober living facility.

There was an abandoned building Ohiya showed me which could serve this purpose. Having watched the show, "Extreme Makeover" on television, I wanted to ask them what it would take to renovate this abandoned building. And turn it into a soup kitchen, with an adjoining room for Alcoholics Anonymous meetings, which was the third goal on our list.

ALCOHOLICS ANONYMOUS

Since we were given free will, Spirit never intrudes when we're making a big mistake or lead down the wrong path. There's always a good lesson to be learned. The Spirit of Sobriety waits patiently in the clouds for a moment of willingness and a prayer for help. All the while, the demons in the bottle continually wreak havoc on the Indian Nation.

Spirit always waits until it is invited. They only come if you call. I've met other sober Native Americans. There is a Native American Indian Alcoholics Anonymous. They can be reached on the web at naigso-aa.org. We hoped to start an AA meeting in Ohiya's home town and invite the Spirit of Sobriety to return.

SELF SUFFICIENCY THROUGH ENERGY TECHNOLOGY

Since Ohiya lived out west, he saw the advances of energy technology. This could greatly assist his people in becoming self-sufficient. In winter, many elders on the

540

reservation often ran out of money. In subzero temperatures, they had no heat to warm their government issue homes. Grandmothers froze to death in this tragically forgotten land.

Here, many new energy technologies would come in handy. The wind and sun turned into usable energy, would allow his people to heat their homes during the long winter months. It would break the dependence on the current energy companies and create self sufficiency. This was another goal.

GREEN HOUSES

Since the Indian Removal Act of 1830, when Native Americans were forced from their ancestral lands by gunpoint and placed onto reservations, one unforeseeable effect was starvation. By the 1890s, the goal of the US government was to get rid of the Indian, one way or another.

What they didn't expect was how resilient the American Indian would be. White hunters almost annihilated the buffalo, which provided Natives with a lean protein and supplied most of their basic needs. Once the numbers of the buffalo nation dwindled, the US government supplied Native people with substandard food. One hundred and thirty years later, obesity, heart disease and diabetes have destroyed the health of Native Americans. But without their traditional hunting grounds, they relied on the government issued commodities. Otherwise, many would have starved to death.

In Ohiya's own family, poor nutrition took a toll. His sister went to dialysis three times a week. Her husband suffered a stroke due to hypertension, obesity and a poor diet. These afflictions did not exist in Indian Country a hundred years ago.

To address the poor nutrition, Ohiya wanted to build green houses. This way, they could grow the fruits and vegetables which are expensive for Native Americans to buy.

With acres of unused reservation land, there is ample space for green houses. Future horticulturists at the local college might find income that way. Ohiya also had a place, a small ravine, by the river where he wanted to plant fruit trees. Asparagus grows well along riverbanks and is a great source of nutrition.

TRIBAL COUNCIL V. HEREDITARY CHIEFS

Without personal knowledge of tribal government, I only know the corruption in the American government is systemic. One of Ohiya's missions was to address Tribal Council versus Hereditary Chiefs. What is their mission statement? What is their purpose? What are the responsibilities of a public servant? How can people best be educated into public service? Where does a person's personal agenda fit in, when it comes to public service?

A higher purpose in tribal government is paramount. Ohiya sought to address the greed, selfishness and ego based agendas which harmed his relatives when it came to government. What is the roll of the casino and how are those profits distributed to the people so everyone is taken care of? Can the profits of the casino be used to build a sober living facility or green houses to grow good food?

NATIVE AMERICAN CULTURE, LANGUAGE AND HISTORY

One of the last goals we discussed at length was the resurrection of the Native American culture, its languages, art and history. In the days before reservations, there were tribal societies, like the warrior society and others. Today, they've been replaced by gangs, drugs and destruction. Seeking a solution, Ohiya wanted to bring the artwork of his people out West and western remedies to combat drug and alcohol addiction, back to his people. In this way, we'd develop an exchange, which served everyone.

On the West Coast, many souls are hungry for the straightforward teachings of the Ancient Ways. The problem is, there are few teachers of Native American ways on the West Coast.

These were the goals we discussed as we headed east into the wintry Great Plains. We were in great spirits as our train ambled through the Rocky Mountains. For Christmas, the town where Marie lived, collected more winter clothes for Ohiya's reservation. The collection started out as a small truckload for the elementary school's Secret Santa. But then, they took an ad out in the local newspaper. The whole town emptied their closets and filled a third of a semi truck. Ohiya didn't want his sister to unload this on her own, so we headed back.

It was the morning of December 8, 2009. Ohiya wouldn't be alive another 24 hours. That frosty morning, going through the Rocky Mountains, the railroad tracks broke. The train stood idle for a few hours while they repaired them. Ohiya dressed all in black, even black socks and black shoes. When I saw him dressed in black, my first thought was, *"Are you going to a funeral?"*

Hours later, our train was delayed in Shelby, Montana for another hour and a half. It was a beautiful sunny afternoon as the train stood idle. Wanting some fresh air, I went outside and made snow balls. I threw them at the window while Ohiya talked on the phone. That evening, around 9:30 pm, in the most calm voice Ohiya said, "There are people trying to kill me." I didn't know what to say. He was all dressed in black.

When our train pulled into the train station in the early morning hours, (2:30 am on December 9, 2009) there were three men waiting. A chill went through me as they called out our names. After the plain clothes Narcotics officers searched through our things, Ohiya was arrested. Several times, Ohiya told the officers I had nothing to do with the medicines he carried. Handcuffed, he stood in the doorway of the train station. I hugged and kissed him one last time. The last thing he said to me was, "Go to Sissy's house. I'll be out in 3 weeks."

In California, Ohiya's doctors prescription was legal. He had bone on bone knees and was in constant pain. But the medicine wasn't valid in North Dakota. Before sunrise that morning, Ohiya was dead. He was in custody a mere three hours. He hadn't seen a judge. There was no arraignment or a sentence.

That morning at 9 am, there was a knock on my hotel room door. The county sheriff and chaplain came to tell me Ohiya committed suicide. I knew they were lying. Ohiya would never do that. He was a strong man, a Sun Dancer, who came from a long line of hereditary chiefs.

Christmas decorations were everywhere when Ohiya's death was announced. All over the country, Ohiya's community members got readings from channelers, clairvoyants and Yuwipi men. Each reading came back the same. Ohiya did NOT kill himself. He was murdered by two men in the county jail. They covered it up and made it look like suicide. Hearts cried out for justice. Across the country, in Sun Dance arbors and Inipi ceremonies, many people prayed for the truth to come out.

The day before his funeral, the semi truck rolled into that small reservation town. It carried all the winter clothes collected from Marie's town. This act of generosity became Ohiya's giveaway. The entire gymnasium was overwhelmed with clothes, books, shoes, bicycles, toys, jackets, socks, you name it. Sitting on the bleachers, I watched the people show up for his funeral. Afterward, they stayed to fill up boxes with things they could use. Even in death, he provided for his people.

The winter following Ohiya's death in 2010 was brutal for the Midwest, with record cold temperatures and snowfall. On some days, it was minus 53 degrees. The cold weather made the news on the West Coast.

In the spring of May 2011, came another news flash. The North Dakota town, where Ohiya was killed, was under 15 to 20 feet of water. As the winter snows melted, the raging rivers overflowed their banks. Endlessly, the water kept rising. The national guard was called. Cars were swept away. Houses were underwater. Working with the Thunder Beings, Ohiya's Heyoka medicine provided a cleansing for this hardhearted North Dakota town. Just by melting the snow.

Earth is an amazing classroom. It's filled with tyrants to distract you from your path and Angels to light the way, when you're ready to pick up where you left off. Lessons will be repeated until learned, of that, you can be sure. For healing to happen, purification is necessary first. Pray hard relatives, pray hard.

Ohiya and me before his last Heyoka Sun Dance. This would be the arbor. July 2009

www.ingramcontent.com/pod-product-compliance
Lightning Source LLC
Chambersburg PA
CBHW070539030726
47505CB00001B/88